A DRAGON
OF
BLACK GLASS

TOR BOOKS BY JAMES ROLLINS

The Starless Crown
The Cradle of Ice
A Dragon of Black Glass

A DRAGON
OF
BLACK
GLASS

BOOK THREE OF THE MOONFALL SAGA

JAMES ROLLINS

TOR PUBLISHING GROUP
NEW YORK

A DRAGON OF BLACK GLASS

Copyright © 2025 by James Czajkowski

Map provided and drawn by Soraya Corcoran
Creature drawings provided and drawn by Danea Fidler

A Tor Book
Published by Tom Doherty Associates / Tor Publishing Group
120 Broadway
New York, NY 10271

www.torpublishinggroup.com

Tor® is a registered trademark of Macmillan Publishing Group, LLC.

The Library of Congress Cataloging-in-Publication Data
is available upon request.

ISBN 978-1-250-76817-9 (hardcover)
ISBN 978-1-250-39362-3 (international, sold outside the U.S.,
subject to rights availability)
ISBN 978-1-250-76816-2 (ebook)

Our books may be purchased in bulk for promotional, educational, or business use.
Please contact your local bookseller or the Macmillan Corporate and Premium
Sales Department at 1-800-221-7945, extension 5442, or by email at
MacmillanSpecialMarkets@macmillan.com.

First Edition: 2025

Printed in the United States of America

0 9 8 7 6 5 4 3 2 1

TO JENNIE AND ROY BLOMQUIST,

*for their friendship, for sharing their growing family,
and, of course, for all the warm cookies.*

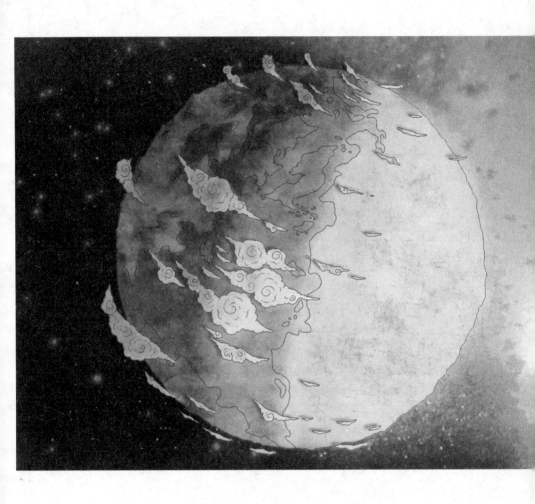

When the world stopped turning,
new lands were born.

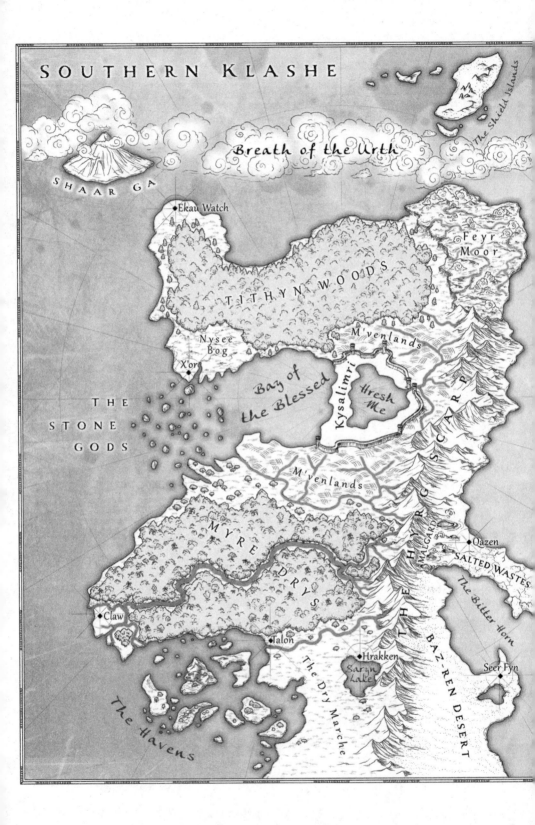

SOUTHERN KLASHE

The Shield Islands

Breath of the Urth

SHAAR GA

• Ekau Watch

Feyr Moor

TITHYN WOODS

Nysee Bog

M'venlands

THE STONE GODS

X'or

Bay of the Blessed

Kysalimri

Hresh Me

M'venlands

MYRE DRYS

THE HYRG SCARP

MALGARD

• Qazen

SALTED WASTES

The Bitter Horn

• Claw

• Talon

• Hrakken

Saryn Lake

The Dry Marche

BAZ-REN DESERT

• Seer Fyn

The Havens

EASTERN CROWN

Far Freesland

Islands of Tau

T A B L E L A N D S

WHITE DESERT

The Hinters

Fhal
Kaer'nkal

Wyldweald

AMON
TOR

Joalian Wall

Domain
of Gjoa

Ward
Isle

Riven

Road

Teassl

Ayrs
Gorge

Ironcopse

Kettle

E B R O   M O U N T A I N S

Spindryft

Wysdom

Archipelago
of Rhys

Quizlan

Wystrel Wood

Strent

Fortuud

Tarn

Farlan

Toltok

Kingdom of
Bhestya

D O L M A N   P E A K S

THE BARRENS

1000 LEAGUES WEST
OF THE TABLELANDS

KHAGARSAN

SAMSKRAG CLIFFS

Els Dalia

Shil'nurr Plains

Örgös Forest

Köös Nuur

Tosgon

EVDERSYN
HEEP

Ghödlökh

CAST OF CHARACTERS

RELATED TO EVENTS INVOLVING THE *FYREDRAGON*

Aamon: a vargr, brother of Kalder; died during the battle atop the Shrouds

Ablen hy Polder: one of Nyx's two brothers, now deceased

Abresh: Chanrë huntress

Arik: raash'ke rider under Daal

Arryn Sahn: brother to Esme

Asha Sahn: daughter of Arryn

Barrat: raash'ke rider under Daal

Bashaliia: a Mýr bat, raised alongside Nyx as an infant, currently shifted into the body of Kalyx

Bastan hy Polder: one of Nyx's two brothers, now deceased

Brayl hy Tarn: one of Darant's two daughters, now deceased

Crikit: a juvenile molag

Cynth hy Albar: Rhaif's mother; native of the Kethra'kai in Cloudreach and granddaughter of Xan of the Kethra'kai; died of Firepester when Rhaif was eleven

Daal: formerly of the Crèche, of mixed Noorish/Panthean blood

Darant hy Tarn: pirate-captain of the *Fyredragon*

Dräshra: legendary Breaker of Dragons

Drys ry Acker: philosopher-king of Bhestya

Esme Sahn: Chanaryn native of the Barrens

Faryn: a raash'ke mount

Fenn hy Pashkin: navigator of the *Fyredragon,* hails from the nation-state of Bhestya

Floraan: Daal's mother

Freya hy Pashkin: sister of Fenn

Frysh: a raash'ke mount

Geryd hy Pashkin: brother of Fenn, hanged for failing to denounce his father

Glace hy Tarn: one of Darant's two daughters and a member of the *Fyredragon's* crew

Gramblebuck: a century-old bullock owned by Trademan Polder, and Nyx's companion while growing up in the swamps of Mýr

Graylin sy Moor: Nyx's father, also known as the Forsworn Knight, named for breaking an oath to the Hálendiian king

Hakyn Sahn: son of Arryn

Hasant: Chanaryn overseer in Seekh

Heffik: Tamryn's raash'ke mount

Henna: Daal's sister

Hyck: former alchymist, now serves as the *Fyredragon*'s engineer

Hylia hy Pashkin: wife of Orren

Irquan: huntmaster of Tosgon

Jace hy Shanan: former journeyman of the Cloistery of Brayk; longtime friend of Nyx

Kalder: a vargr bonded to Graylin; brother to the deceased Aamon

Kalyx: a Mýr bat, corrupted and poisoned by Iflelen alchymies, whose body was possessed by Bashaliia

Krysh hy Eljen: alchymist aboard the *Fyredragon;* hails from the rugged ranchlands of Aglerolarpok

Lachan: underling of Rahl hy Pek

Marayn: Nyx's mother, former royal pleasure serf, lover of Graylin; died in the swamps of Mýr

Meryk: Daal's father, a purebred Panthean

Mirash: village leader of Tosgon

Nyx hy Polder: daughter of Marayn and Graylin; raised from infancy by a Mýr bat, then adopted by Trademan Polder in the swamps of Mýr

Orren hy Pashkin: uncle to Fenn

Perde: *Fyredragon* crewmember; hails from the Hegemony of Harpe; his twin brother, Herl, was murdered by Hálendiian attackers in the Crèche

Pyllar: Daal's raash'ke mount

Rahl hy Peck: brutal leader of a cabal of cutthroats and oppressors in Seekh

Randa hy Lenk: hieromonk scholar at the school in Toltok

Rega sy Noor: explorer knight from centuries earlier, former captain of the *Fyredragon*

Regina, Nys: eldest of the *Nyssian* sisters, who recognized the blood-heritage shared by Graylin and Nyx

Rhaif hy Albar: Guld'guhlian thief who rescued Shiya from the depths of the mines of Chalk

Shiya: a former Sleeper, ranked as an Axis—a *ta'wyn* of high status, second only to the Kryst caste

Spider, the: a *ta'wyn* Root of the Brackenlands who enslaved the raash'ke for centuries with his corrupted bridle-song

Tamryn: a Panthean, second saddle in the raash'ke crew

Tann: religious elder, teacher of Arryn

Vikas gy Wren: quartermaster of the *Fyredragon,* born a mute, with Gynish blood in her lineage

Yazmyn Sahn: Arryn's heart-bound

RELATED TO EVENTS IN THE WESTERN CROWN

Aalia ka Haeshan: empress of the Southern Klashe, daughter of the deceased Emperor Makar, sister to Jubayr, Paktan, Mareesh, and Rami; she is wedded to Prince Kanthe

Althea: second-in-command of the *Shayn'ra*

Angelon: former leader of the Shield (the Klashean imperial ground forces), fourth cousin to Jubayr; died during the attempted insurrection of Aalia's rule

Augury of Qazen: see "Tykhan"

Bkarrin: Iflelen working with Wryth

Brija: elderly woman chaaen-bound to Kanthe; an aide in matters of Klashean language and customs

Cassta: Rhysian assassin, the youngest of Saekl's crew

Draer: former leader of the Wing (the Klashean imperial air fleet); died during the attempted insurrection of Aalia's rule

Eligor: a *ta'wyn* leader, a Kryst; his ancient Klashean name means "Morning Star" or "Betrayer"

Fay hy Persha: former Hálendiian royal midwife of the Massifs (delivered Kanthe and Mikaen), now called Sister Amis, serving as a nonne under the supervision of Abbess Shayr in X'or

Frell hy Mhlaghifor: alchymist and formerly Prince Kanthe's mentor at Kepenhill

Garryn: commander of the Sail (the Klashean imperial naval fleet)

Gheel: grand cross of the Klashean Shield

Hessen: Eye of the Hidden, the Klashean spymaster

Hesst: grand treasurer of Hálendii

Hrash: a Chaaen; adviser to Aalia ka Haeshan

Illias: young member of the *Shayn'ra*

Jester: Guld'guhlian thief, brother to Mead; missing the lower half of his left leg

Jojan: commander of the Shield (the Klashean ground forces)

Jubayr: Rami's eldest brother; died during the attempted insurrection of Aalia's rule

Kanthe ry Massif: son of the former highking of Azantiia; Mikaen's twin brother, wedded to Empress Aalia ka Haeshan—and now titled Kanthe im Haeshan

Lassan, Sister: nonne under the supervision of Abbess Shayr in X'or

Laugyn: Chaaen alchymist

Liss: novitiate under the supervision of Abbess Shayr in X'or

Llyra hy March: Guld'guhlian guildmaster of thieves in Anvil

Loryn: a Chaaen and adviser to Rami

Magritte: Chaaen hieromonk

Makar ka Haeshan: former god-emperor of the Southern Klashe, father of Aalia and Rami; died during the insurrection against Aalia's rule

Mareesh im Haeshan: traitorous second son of Emperor Makar, brother to Rami and Aalia, who sought to usurp Aalia's rule

Mead: Guld'guhlian thief, brother to Jester

Mikaen ry Massif: highking of Hálendii, twin brother to Kanthe

Millik hy Pence: envoy from Qaar Saur

Myella: Mikaen's wife, of the House of Carcassa in the Brauðlands

Odyn: son of Mikaen

Olia: daughter of Mikaen, twin to Othan

Orkan: a royal healer

Othan: son of Mikaen, twin to Olia

Paktan: third son of Emperor Makar, brother to Rami and Aalia; beheaded by Mikaen

Perash: commander of the Wing (the Klashean air forces)

Phenic: young Iflelen acolyte

Pratik: chaaen-bound to Kanthe; bears the iron collar of one who has earned the Highcryst of alchymy; named after Prya, the Klashean god of fate

Pyke: a Chaaen, bound to Rami

Rami im Haeshan: fourth son of Emperor Makar, brother to Aalia

Regar: an imperial Paladin

Saekl: Rhysian captain of the *Quisl;* hails from the Archipelago of Rhys in the Eastern Crown

Shayr, Abbess: governess of the gardens and pools of X'or; one of the most esteemed healers of the Klashe

Skerren il Reesh: former Shrive of the Iflelen cabal; a true alchymical genius; killed by Nyx in the Frozen Wastes

Syke: Hálendiian liege general

Symon hy Ralls: former alchymist at Kepenhill, now a member of the Razen Rose

Tazar hy Maar: leader of the *Shayn'ra,* and Aalia's lover

Thoryn vy Brenn: captain of the Silvergard, a Vyrllian knight

Toranth ry Massif: former highking of Hálendii; head of the House of Massif; father of Mikaen and Kanthe

Tykhan: aka the Augury of Qazen, a role he filled for over four millennia; in reality, a Root (the lower caste) of the *ta'wyn*

Venga: captain of the *Sharpened Spur*

Wryth il Faash: Iflelen leader of Hálendii, born as a slave in the Dominion of Gjoa

Zeng ri Perrin: former head inquisitor of the Dresh'ri; slain by Pratik during the attempted insurrection of Aalia's rule

A DRAGON
OF
BLACK GLASS

After returning from the cartographer—a mapmaker who swore in blood to keep my secrets—I find myself adrift once again. It is an ailment of age and bereavement. I sit listlessly in my chair and struggle for the verve to continue to tell her story. The sun shines brightly through my attic window. The light prisms through leaded glass and casts shimmering spectrums across the walls, revealing the breadth of color hidden inside a single beam of light.

Perhaps this is a harbinger of what comes next in this tale I must tell.

For she is much like that sunbeam.

While outwardly she may appear to shine with a simple light, within that glow, she contains ineffable shades of complexity and depth that only take the right lens to reveal—and soon she will crash headlong into that very prism, in the shadowless furnace lands, where sand is blasted by time and heat into hard glass. What that fire will forge, what will be revealed, is not a simple girl of the swamplands, but something both darker and brighter. This is the story that I must write next—of the death of innocence and a resurrection born in blood and flames.

I dread the telling of this tale.

Even seated in my attic croft, I hear the continual scour of grains across windblown dunes and the ringing of chimes of black crystal. But most of all, I cannot escape the strident bellow of the Dragon.

I clamp my hands over my ears, trying to squeeze it away. I close my eyes against an avalanche of memories that try to rise. It's all too much to bear in its entirety. I can endure the retelling only by letting each moment trickle out, one after the other, like a single grain of sand tumbling down a dune.

But before we can continue on, I must glance over my shoulder, to use the past to center myself.

Where last I left her tale, she and her allies were escaping the eternal ice of the sunless Urth and rushing headlong toward the eastern half of the Crown. Behind her, the western side was embroiled in battle, as kingdom fought empire. Yet even that conflict was but a spark of the greater war to come—for there remain forces buried deep, entombed in granite, who wait to wreak havoc upon this world.

As I ponder this, a rain-heavy cloud passes over the sun and snuffs the dappling of light across my croft. I release a breath I hadn't known I was holding. This gloom feels more fitting, as if she had turned her back on me in this moment—as she did in the past.

So be it.

Like the skies outside my attic, storm clouds are growing for her, too. I can already hear the thunder—which sounds like the drums of war.

ONE

CLOUDBURST

Whilst a gale bends the tronke of a tree, its roots digg ev'r deeper.

—Adage attributed to Scyk pa Renn,
eyeless mystic who wandered the
Wystrel Woods of Bhestya

1

BOWED LOW IN her saddle, Nyx rode out the tempest atop Bashaliia. Her mount's leathery wings were swept wide, their tips vanishing into the dark clouds to either side. It was as if Nyx were part of the storm, birthed from its fury, heralded by thunder, framed by lightning.

She leaned closer to the furry warmth of her winged brother. But their truer communion was in the shared thrum of bridle-song. She sang to Bashaliia, a tuneless chorus of reassurance, while he keened back at her, twining his golden melody to hers.

Her message was a simple one.

Return to the ship.

Within the storm's grip, Nyx peered through goggles that protected her eyes. The world around her was reduced to swirling mists and lashing rain. Hail pelted her leather-clad body. Above, black clouds cloaked the sun. Below, the land and sea had vanished.

She shivered in the cold and clung tight to Bashaliia. It was as if they had never escaped the Frozen Wastes and were still trapped in its perpetually icy darkness.

But that's not so.

Last midwinter, she and the others had fled from the Crèche aboard their wyndship. Even with the *Fyredragon*'s huge forge-engines, it had taken them until the tail end of spring to reach the broken scarp of the Ebyn Mountains that bordered the Eastern Crown. Unfortunately, it was just in time to run into the teeth of the monsoon season, where storm after storm swept the region. The ship's navigator, Fenn—who had lived most of his life in this half of the world—had warned them of this danger.

Still, with the threat of moonfall drawing ever closer, they had dared not wait. Plus, Graylin and Darant had believed the *Fyredragon* could use the cover of the storms to cross this arc of the Crown, to avoid the eyes of their enemies.

But such was not the will of the gods.

As they entered the Eastern Crown, the storms had proven far worse than expected. Four days in, lightning struck the ship. The blast ripped away the stern cables that secured the ship's balloon and destroyed one of its flank forges. The damage forced them to land on the island of Spindryft in the middle of the seas of the Eastern Crown.

Repairs proved tedious. Two months slipped away, and now midsummer would soon be upon them. They all sensed the press of time, especially with the looming threat weighing on them.

Moonfall . . .

A full year ago, Nyx had her poisonous vision of the moon crashing into the Urth and destroying all life, a prophecy further supported by the alchymies of Frell and Krysh. Through their farseeing lenses, the moon's full face had been growing incrementally larger, drawing inevitably closer to the world. Back then, they had all heard Shiya's own assessment, gleaned from *ta'wyn* knowledge reaching back to the Forsaken Ages. The bronze woman had placed a date upon this doom.

In five years' time. Maybe as short as three.

And now a year of that span was gone.

Urgency sharpened Nyx's bridle-song to a demanding note.

Bashaliia responded and dove steeply through the lashing rain. Even this storm—unusual for midsummer—was a reminder that all was not right with the world. The ship's alchymist, Krysh hy Eljen, had expressed concern that the savagery of the season's storms was likely fueled by the moon's approach. Tides had become more extreme. Quakes continued to rock the globe. It was as if the Urth itself trembled at the inevitable doom to come.

As Bashaliia dove lower, the dark clouds broke around rider and mount. The seas appeared below, lit by flashes of lightning. White-capped waves lined the dark waters, sweeping toward the forested island of Spindryft. The atoll was ringed by reefs and protected by spires of black rock that stuck out of the sea. The route to its small port was treacherous, even in calm waters. Still, ships—bearing sigils from many lands—crowded the docks below. Spindryft was part of no kingdom or empire. It served as a neutral trading post for most of the Eastern Crown. Even long-haulers out of the Western Crown circled the Urth's seas to come to this side of the world to barter for spices, silks, and rare ores.

Bashaliia sped toward the island without any guidance. By now, the Mýr bat knew his way back to their ship. The *Fyredragon* occupied a berth in Spindryft's mooring field, positioned in the highlands above the port. Scores of wyndships filled other slots, their balloons jostling in the storm winds.

Nyx easily spotted the *Fyredragon* among them. Not only was it the largest, but its sculpted draft-iron figurehead had been carved into a wyrm with its head rearing high, its wings outstretched, hugging the bow's flanks. Firepots across the open upper deck blazed in the rainy gloom, setting the dragon afire.

Their ship's berth lay off to one side, separate from its neighbors. None dared approach too closely, especially given the *Fyredragon*'s dangerous cargo.

Nyx guided Bashaliia toward their encampment.

As they neared the fiery ship, Bashaliia swung in a smooth arc toward the stern, keeping the bulk of the gaseous balloon between them and the other vessels. Nyx had been warned by Graylin to keep her flights hidden from sight. The cover of the storm had offered her this rare opportunity to venture forth with her winged brother.

But now it was over.

Bashaliia raced the last of the distance. He cupped his wings and landed deftly in the meadow behind the moored ship.

Raised voices drew Nyx's attention to the side. Graylin and the pirate Darant hy Tarn crowded with a group of men near a tent. It served as a makeshift smithy for their repair work. The damaged forge-engine had already been restored and was being dragged on sledges, ready to be remounted onto the ship. Darant and his daughter, Glace, had also used the time to inspect the remaining forges, resecure the ripped cables, and fill the balloon's gasses.

The hope was to be underway in the next few days.

But there remained one critical refurbishment of the ship that was beyond the scope of Darant's crew. Before they traveled into the sunblasted Barrens, it would have to be completed.

Nyx stared through the storm toward the west. She pictured where they must travel next and felt a hopeless despair.

For untold millennia, the Urth had circled the sun with one side always facing the burning glare of the Father Above, while its far side remained forever frozen in icy darkness. The Crown lay between those extremes—a circlet of land trapped between ice and fire.

Last winter, Nyx and the others had crossed the Urth's frozen darkness, traveling from their homelands in the Western Crown to this eastern side of the world. In those icy lands, they had discovered the Crèche and its people— the Pantheans—who made their home deep under the ice. There, they had also encountered the distant brethren of Bashaliia—the raash'ke—deadly ice bats who shared those dark and frigid lands. The colony had been tainted and enslaved by a half-crazed *ta'wyn*, an immortal bronze sentinel named the Spider, one of the traitorous *Revn-kree* who sought dominion over the planet. The Spider had been tasked to guard one of the massive world-moving machines, the *turubya*, hidden in the Frozen Wastes. Nyx and the others had defeated that deadly guardian, freeing both the raash'ke and the Pantheans. In doing so, they had also activated the *turubya*, readying the great engine to do the impossible: to set the world to spinning again—as their planet had done untold millennia ago.

Such was the only hope of stopping moonfall, of driving the moon back into its proper orbit. But to achieve that required activating a second *turubya,* one buried far in the Barrens, the sunblasted half of the Urth. By all accounts, the journey there would be even more treacherous than the one taken this past winter, especially given the threat that awaited them. The *turubya* in the Barrens was guarded over not just by a single *Reven-kree,* but by a small army, one led by a *ta'wyn* far more powerful than that bronze Spider.

Nyx searched to the west, recognizing a hard truth.

How can we hope to defeat such a force?

Still, her fingers tightened on her reins, accepting what was equally certain.

Because we must.

A shout rose behind her. "Nyx!"

Startled, she swung in her saddle and spotted Jace hy Shanan, her friend and former tutor, rushing toward her from a gangway into the *Fyredragon.* He lifted an arm and smiled broadly, his cheeks flushing above his ruddy beard.

The ship's alchymist, Krysh, accompanied Jace. The lanky older man hailed from the rugged ranchlands of Aglerolarpok and kept an easy pace with his long-legged strides.

"You're both back!" Nyx called over as she slid out of her saddle and landed in the wet grass. Still, she kept one palm on Bashaliia's flank.

The two men were dressed in traveler's cloaks fitted with hoods. They must have come directly from the port. The two had left a fortnight ago, sailing south to the Kingdom of Bhestya. Their goal was to scour ancient texts related to the Barrens. The librarie complex at the kingdom's capital was said to have the most extensive collection pertaining to those sunblasted lands.

Jace closed the distance toward her. "You must hear what we have to tell you! And see what we found! Not just a crate of books, but also a crude *map* of the Barrens. I can't wait to show it to Fenn."

Nyx had no doubt the ship's navigator would find such a chart immensely useful, as little was known of the lands beyond the sandy necropolises that bordered the edge of the Crown.

When Jace reached her, Bashaliia twisted his neck with a low hiss of warning. Still attuned to her winged brother, Nyx felt the frazzle of emerald fire behind the golden glow of his bridle-song.

Jace backed a step. "Sorry. I should know better than to rush at him."

"At least he didn't snap at you this time," Krysh added, keeping a wary distance himself.

Heat rose to Nyx's cheeks. "Between the storm and being cooped up inside the ship for so long, he's in poor spirits."

She ran a palm over the crown of the bat's head, knowing neither explanation was the truth. After defeating the Spider, Bashaliia remained plagued by bouts of fury, which was so unlike his typical calm manner. She pictured the corrupting bridle-song that had trapped not only the raash'ke, but also Bashaliia for a spell. Nyx had broken him free, but some damage remained.

She pictured her winged brother when she had first encountered him a year ago. He had been no bigger than a winter goose. Poisoned shortly thereafter, Bashaliia had died, but not before his spirit and memory were preserved by the immense horde-mind of the Mýr bat colony and moved into another body—one larger and older. Then last winter, Nyx had been forced to slit his throat, to free him yet again. With the help of the raash'ke, she had moved Bashaliia's essence into the abused body of Kalyx, a Mýr bat who had been enslaved by Iflelen forces and tortured into a monster.

Nyx's fingers felt the old scars across Bashaliia's scalp, hidden now under his regrown pelt. They marked where copper needles had been drilled into Kalyx's brain. The enslaving needles had been removed, but some damage remained—wounds that went far deeper than flesh and bone. It fueled a fiery madness, an ailment that might never fully heal.

As bound as she was with Bashaliia, she herself was not unscathed. It was a burden she accepted and shared, knowing she owed Bashaliia: for his love, for his brotherhood, for his sacrifice. Even the bat's wary reaction to Jace might not be solely born of madness, but possibly incited by Nyx's own deep-seated misgivings about Jace.

She stared over at her friend, studying him circumspectly.

Like all of them, Jace had not escaped the Frozen Wastes untouched. He had nearly died—and maybe had for a spell—after being blasted by the energies of the *turubya* when it had been activated. Before he had been revived, Nyx had probed him with strands of her bridle-song. She discovered a vast emptiness inside him, one far larger than could be contained within his small skull. Even now, that memory iced through her. After Jace had recovered, that emptiness had vanished. He seemed like her same old friend.

Still . . .

She hid a wince. Guilt ate at her for her continuing wariness of him, especially for a friend who had always been loyal. She stared up at Bashaliia.

Have you been sensing my unease? Is that why you reacted so poorly?

To soothe her own heart as much as Bashaliia's, she sang chords of reassurance to him and shook off her angst.

She stared up at the bulk of the wyndship. "I'd like to see that old map, but first I must get Bashaliia settled into the hold. I'll meet you both at the *Fyredragon*'s wheelhouse. I saw Fenn up there before I headed out."

Krysh's eyes narrowed. "I'll leave that task to you and Jace. I must secure the crates in my cabin and begin cataloging the books. In the meantime, hopefully the map will offer some guidance for Fenn and the ship's captain to determine the best route across the Barrens. We must be underway as soon as possible. We're already drawing too much attention."

The alchymist glanced over to Bashaliia.

"What do you mean?" Nyx asked.

Jace's next words grew doleful. "Over in Bhestya, word of a dragon-helmed ship, one carrying a hold full of winged beasts, has spread to those shores."

"And rumors will continue to fly farther afield the longer we sit idle," Krysh added. "Until word reaches the wrong ears."

Nyx understood. They may have escaped the Hálendiian forces in the Frozen Wastes, but surely the enemy was still hunting them. She had no doubt that both the king's legions and the Iflelen dogs led by Wryth il Faash were scouring the Crown for any sign of them. So far, it seemed their group had not been discovered. But every day they tarried in Spindryft, the risk grew.

Nyx pointed to where Graylin and Darant wrestled the repaired ship's forge-engine toward the *Fyredragon*. "Jace, alert Graylin and Darant about what you heard."

"I'll let them know." Jace swung away but glanced over a shoulder. "Then I'll meet you at the wheelhouse."

Nyx nodded her acknowledgment and set off with Bashaliia toward the *Fyredragon*'s stern ramp.

Krysh followed her, but he kept a buffer between him and the massive Mýr bat. The alchymist suddenly stopped midstride. He stared up at the layer of dark clouds, which hugged close to the top of the firelit balloon of the *Fyredragon*.

Nyx followed his gaze.

Dark shapes scythed out of the storm—one, then another, then three more.

Nyx's heart clenched into a knot, but it wasn't out of fear. She recognized those who swept down toward the ship. Before leaving the Crèche, the Pantheans had gifted their group with *five* of the raash'ke to accompany them on this journey, to serve as formidable mounts for the task ahead of them. The hulking ice bats carried riders—all trainees—saddled on their backs. Like her and Bashaliia, the group must have decided to use the cover of the storm to hone their skills.

The five shapes spiraled down, sweeping in a tight formation.

Though the storm cloaked them all, Nyx had no trouble identifying their leader. She sensed the well of power held at his core. To her bridle-blessed eyes, he was a falling star, blazing through the gloom.

She whispered his name, half prayer, half sorrow. "Daal . . ."

Krysh must have heard the pain behind that syllable. "He will learn to forgive you."

Nyx lowered her face. "Better he should not."

2

DAAL GUIDED HIS mount with gentle pressure from his knees. By now, his efforts were instinctual—more so than any of the other riders. Then again, he had helped refine the saddle they all used, tweaking its cinches from the Panthean tack and gear used to ride the orksos, the horned beasts that swam through the seas of the Crèche. Back home, he had been proud of his skill at hunting those waters from the backs of such magnificent creatures.

Only after Nyx and the others had crashed into their world beneath the ice had Daal come to understand his unique bond to the orksos. He had always known he carried Noorish blood, from a lineage that traced back to a group of Hálendiian explorers who had arrived centuries earlier and been stranded in the Crèche. The crew had traveled there by the very wyndship moored below. Over time, the Pantheans and Noorish people had learned to live in an uneasy alliance, resulting in mixed-blooded individuals like Daal.

But unlike most mixed-blooded descendants, Daal had inherited a special gift: his Noorish blood contained traces of bridle-song. That innate talent had allowed him to bond and control the orksos better than most. But the same blood-gift also drew the attention of others: the tentacled *Oshkapeers,* the god-like Dreamers of the Deep. Those ancient creatures had probed Daal, nearly drowning him, and honed his bridle-song into a great weapon, a font of raw energy, meant to serve as a wellspring of strength for another.

As Daal stared below, he felt that draw upon him even now. It tugged at his blood and quickened his heart. He had no trouble spotting the lodestone that called to him from below. He watched Nyx hurry toward the open stern door into the *Fyredragon.* He remembered how she had once described their unique bond.

You be my flashburn, I'll be your forge.

Daal easily recalled what that felt like back at the Crèche, when the two melted into one, palms pressed, fingers clenched together. With each breath, his blood-borne font of power flowed into Nyx, allowing her access to that well of energy, to refine that force into purpose. In those moments, both were bare to each other, unable to keep any secrets, each knowing the other's thoughts, wearing the other's skin, feeling everything together. It was both unnerving and intoxicating.

Such intimacy had drawn them closer. How could it not? But months ago, just as they had reached the Eastern Crown, it had all abruptly ended. The arduous journey had taken its toll on everyone: the stress, the terror, the tension, had strained them all.

But that was not the true reason for their falling-out.

He watched Nyx vanish with Bashaliia into the ship. Only then did he lift an arm and whistle sharply into the wind, mimicking the cry of a kree-hawk, the hunting birds that nested in the ice cliffs at the Crèche. The other Panthean riders recognized that note from their homelands. So, too, did their raash'ke mounts, who had shared that cold world.

In such small ways did Daal keep his homelands alive in his heart. He refused to completely forsake the Crèche. He had already given up so much. To make this sojourn—to serve as a source of fuel to Nyx's forge—he had abandoned his mother and father, along with his young sister. His parents had understood the necessity. Still, it did little to assuage his guilt, especially knowing his family's fate should Nyx's group succeed in setting the Urth to spinning again.

According to Shiya—based on ancient *ta'wyn* knowledge—the only way to cast the moon back into its proper place was to set the world to turning. This would prevent the planet's destruction, but it would also lead to its own cataclysm, resulting in deaths beyond measure. Millions would die. With the world set to spinning, the Frozen Wastes would melt. The sunblasted Barrens would flood. The Crown would be torn apart by quakes, storms, and tides.

No corner of the Urth would be untouched.

Even my home.

His mother had faced this tragic fate with a resoluteness that still escaped Daal. Her words stayed with him: *No one knows their end. The future remains a mystery until it's written. We'll live as if we have endless days ahead of us—and none. What else can any of us do?*

His parents also recognized that if the moon crashed into the world, not only would the Crèche be destroyed, but all life on Urth would end.

Better some should live than none, his father had said, gripping Daal's arm as they said their good-byes.

Daal closed his eyes for a single breath.

I must not fail them.

With this determination, he opened his eyes and guided the other riders toward the towering wyndship. Winds, lashed with hard rain, battered them. Lightning lanced in jagged arcs across the belly of the clouds. He smelled the power in the air, felt the energy dance across the small hairs of his bare arms. It was as if the storm were drawn to the well of strength hidden inside him.

He gritted his teeth and dove steeply, fleeing the storm's reach—as much as Nyx now fled from him. He pictured the fall of her hair, so dark a hue that it could be misconstrued as black, but within its shadows hid golden strands, as if bridle-song had been braided into those tresses. Her skin was the color of warm honey, her eyes as blue as polished ice, with flecks of silver shining there, too.

Anger flamed through him, both at her abrupt rejection of him and at his continuing ache to rekindle what had been lost. He fought against reliving that moment from months ago when passion had turned to heartbreak.

Still, the memory burned brightly, fueled by the pain in his heart—and his forearms.

For Nyx had shattered more than just his heart.

Unable to stop himself, he fell back into that past.

As the Fyredragon *crested high over the Ebyn Mountains, Daal ignored the crystalline glare off those icy peaks and gaped at the fiery orb sitting on the horizon. For the past half-moon, as the wyndship neared the edge of the Crown, leaving the Frozen Wastes behind, they had been traveling through a perpetual twilight. Each day, the pyre at the horizon had grown brighter and brighter, until the full breadth of the sun rose into view.*

"It's more wondrous than I'd ever imagined," Daal whispered to Nyx.

She kept next to him, an arm around his waist, and smiled at the awe in his voice. "Welcome to your first true dawn," she said, then added with a tired sigh, "We in the Crown take such a sight for granted. The sun never sets during our lives. It only makes a slow, small circle in the sky, one revolution per year."

Fenn stood on his other side. "I wager you'll get sick of the sight of the Father Above, especially after we head into the Barrens, where the sun will rise higher and higher until it's hammering us with its unforgiving heat."

Daal noted the sour turn to the navigator's voice. Fenn had shown a clear and growing reluctance to cross this eastern half of the Crown. As the navigator kept vigil with them, the young man's lips were drawn into bloodless lines. The emerald of his eyes was shadowed by heavy lids. His snowy-blond locks, though, reflected the sunlight, as if he were born out of mountain glaciers below, but Daal knew Fenn was actually from the Kingdom of Bhestya, one of the many lands on this side of the Crown.

Still, the navigator's mood had darkened with every league closer to his homelands. According to Jace, Fenn had made sure their ship's course stayed well north of Bhestya. Any inquiries about his past were met with a stern silence, a dismissive wave, or a muttered curse. He was clearly reluctant to talk about how he had come to leave his homelands and ended up as a navigator for a brigand like Darant.

"We should head below," Nyx said. "You don't want to stare too long at the sun."

Daal disagreed. "I could look at it forever."

But Fenn bolstered Nyx's warning. "Once we crest over these mountains, the crosswinds will have us shaking wildly."

As if reinforcing this, a strong gust struck the massive gasbag overhead and sent the ship into a hard roll. Daal clutched the rail to stay upright. Fenn simply balanced on both legs.

Nyx's arm tightened on Daal's waist. Even through the wool of her sleeve, he felt the cold burn of her skin as it sought to pull the heat from his body, reminding him of the bottomless hunger inside her. But he had hungers of his own and freed an arm to pull her closer.

"Maybe we should return to your cabin," Daal suggested.

Nyx stared up at him. The silver glints in her eyes shone brighter with a mischievous gleam. "Then let us be quick about it—before we get tossed overboard."

They waited until the ship's rocking eased enough for them to cross the deck to the forecastle's door. They clambered down to the middeck, where cabins lined a long passageway that ran from bow to stern.

Nyx had a room to herself nearest the wheelhouse at the front.

As they reached her door, another strong wind buffeted the ship. A hard roll of the deck tossed them across the cabin's threshold. They stumbled together into her room, clutched together, both laughing.

Once the ship smoothed its flight, Nyx closed the door, her cheeks flushed.

Daal was still breathless from seeing the sun for the first time. Amazement kept his heart pounding. The blue skies, the shades of pink spanning the horizon, had seemed from another world, one foreign to all he understood. Even the stars—which had blazed continually in the skies of the Wastes—had vanished into obscurity, wiped away by the sunlight.

"What wonders you've shown me," he whispered to Nyx. "How I wish Henna were here to see this, too."

A pang of homesickness struck him as he pictured his exuberant younger sister, with her bright eyes and bottomless sense of wonder.

Nyx lowered her gaze, trying to hide a wince.

He inwardly kicked himself for his words. He knew Nyx carried a measure of guilt for dragging him from his home, from all he knew, from all he loved. He reached to her shoulders and drew her into an embrace.

"I will show her the sun one day," he promised.

"I hope that's true."

Daal used a fingertip to raise her chin. "We'll make it so."

Despite his words, Nyx's eyes remained haunted. It was her prophecy that set *them on this course, a path that, even if successful, would lead to so many deaths, so much destruction.*

He tilted his head to catch her gaze. "You're not alone in this."

To convince her of this, he leaned down and brushed his lips across hers. A now familiar fire ignited at that touch. She sighed into his kiss, sinking into him, blurring the line between them. As this happened, he sensed that dark well inside her. He allowed the heat of his bones' marrow to flow and temper that hunger, which further drew them together, binding them even closer.

He again felt that dizzying fall into her. The softness of her lips stirred him, while simultaneously he felt the rough brush of his own stubble. After a time, his tongue probed deeper and became hers. Their breaths mingled, growing harsher. He hardened and pressed himself against her, but he knew she was already aware of his firming ardor, for he felt her own rising passion: the warming of her loins, the tender piquing of her nipples.

His hand rose to gently brush a thumb across that tenderness. The fire of that touch ran through him as much as her. Her gasp rose from his own lips. Her fingers reached to his swollen urgency and rubbed that fire into a pyre that burned through them both. Lost in each other, they fell to her bed. There, they explored each other, discovering the familiar balance of their shared senses.

Her desires, too, whisked through him, guiding him to where she wanted to be touched. Fingers fumbled with buttons until skin found skin. With each movement, he was rewarded in turn, as he experienced that exquisite tension himself. His tongue took the place of his thumb. With each teasing lick, fire flamed through his body, reflecting what she experienced.

Each gasp was the bellow of a forge, whetting their flames hotter.

They remained balanced on that fiery edge until the room vanished and time grew meaningless. Daal wanted more, knew she did, too, as they could hide nothing from one another, but they had also decided at the outset of this journey to temper their passion, to carry on no farther than this.

Fear, as much as restraint, firmed this line.

He drew his mouth from her breast and returned to her lips. It took all his strength to do so. He lifted his face to stare down at her. Her eyes remained closed, her body arched under him.

He whispered into that fire. "Nyx, we must stop—"

"No," she moaned, that single word rife with bridle-song, full of command, along with a hint of a dark edge. "Don't."

She reached under his belt, cupping his length. Trapped by their combined lust, along with the bridling that linked him, he shuddered under her touch.

Unable to stop himself, he let his weight fall upon her, upon what she clutched, but he continued to fall, sinking ever deeper into the dark well inside her. Its hunger now stoked to a feverish ravening. With each stroke of her hand, with each unstoppable thrust of his hips, power flowed out of him.

He fought to hold it, to dam that tide.

Then came one stroke too far.

He cried out with the explosion. It emptied everything inside him, spilling forth between them, while bursting that dam within. He flailed down her well, carried by his torrent of energy, unable to escape.

Still, even then, he felt everything she did. She gasped as much as he had, experiencing the same explosion as if it were her own. Through her senses, he felt the power swelling into her.

He fought against losing himself, knowing that he risked death if too much was stolen from him. As he struggled, his hands found Nyx's shoulders. He tried to push away from her, using all the strength in his arms.

As his energies flowed into her, a star appeared down deep in that well, fed by his power. He rushed headlong toward it. As it grew, the star formed a fiery sigil.

Nyx recognized it. So, of course, he did, too. In such moments, there were no secrets between them. Fleeting memories from Nyx shredded through him.

This sigil was a gift, one granted to Nyx by the raash'ke horde-mind before it was destroyed. It was a map to turn intent into purpose, to give bridle-song the strength of physical force.

Unable to help himself—perhaps fueled by Nyx's own darkest desires—he reached to that star as he fell past it, like a drowning man grasping for anything to keep afloat. With the briefest touch, that sigil exploded into a sun, infinitely brighter than what shone in the skies.

The blast shattered the darkness, while shoving him away, too.

He flew back into his own body, into his own skin, but there was no escaping the backlash of power. It exploded out of Nyx as he hovered over her, holding her at arm's length.

With his fingers still clutched to her shoulders, his forearms caught the brunt of that blast. Bones shattered under the force. He got thrown from the bed and crashed onto the hard floorboards. His head cracked, sending the world into a twirling confusion.

Nyx tumbled after him, landing on her hands and knees. "Daal . . ."

He tried to reach her, to console her, but his arms were bent at useless angles. Agony flared and shrank his world to pinpoints.

"I'll get help," Nyx called as he fell farther away.

She fled from his side, from him, maybe from herself. Her last words, guilt-ridden and tearful, followed him into oblivion.

"I'm sorry . . ."

*   *   *

DAAL'S MOUNT LANDED in the meadow with a hard jolt, shaking him back to the present. To either side, the other four riders alighted with buffeting sweeps of leathery wings. He leaned forward and rubbed the damp pelt of his bat's neck.

"Thank you, Pyllar," he intoned gratefully.

His mount tilted a large black eye toward him. The velvety ruffles surrounding Pyllar's nostrils vibrated, accompanied by a soft keening. The contentment and pride could be felt as much as heard. The gift in Daal's blood was strong enough to perceive all of this. He even spotted the slight glow in those dark eyes, shining with bridle-song.

Pyllar leaned back, offering an ear to be scratched.

Daal could not refuse. His fingers found those tender spots and dug nails until Pyllar rumbled with pleasure. As he did, Daal's forearm ached. The splints had only come off a fortnight ago. This morning was the first time he had been deemed fit enough to take Pyllar aloft.

Daal regretted having to neglect his mount these past months, but he dared not risk his life by flying while impaired. It was with the same fearful reluctance that Nyx had withdrawn from him. The two of them had been careless, playing with a fire neither truly understood—not just the physical act, of stumbling over a threshold neither had been prepared for, but also the incendiary flow of powers between them.

Afterward, the anguish in Nyx's words still wounded him: *If I had broken more than just your arms . . .*

Daal knew his death would have destroyed her. It was a guilt she could not have survived. Plus, his loss would be a blow to their cause. Nyx needed Daal for more than just his companionship. She needed the power welded into him by the Dreamers. He was a tool forged for her. And in the throes of passion, they had come close to shattering it.

Such an act could not be risked again.

Nyx had firmed this while he recovered: *Our wishes are of no importance, not when balanced against all the lives of the world.*

Daal had no way to argue against it, even if he had wanted to try. So, he had stayed silent, his tongue tied by fear as much as grief. He could still remember tumbling headlong into that darkness inside her. He could still feel the blast of fury that ignited from that blazing sigil. It had been branded into him, become calloused into his bones.

He knew his silence in that moment had hurt Nyx. She likely mistook his reticence as anger, but it was not that.

Daal stared toward the hold where Nyx had vanished.

She scares me.

Yet it was not the force of her power, or the depth of her passion, that he feared. He knew Nyx was not solely to blame for what had happened. It had not been bridling that drove him onward, to cross over that threshold with her.

I had wanted it as much as she did.

His gaze lingered on the door into the ship's hold. He pictured Nyx's eyes glowing in the dark, the warmth of her lips, giving himself fully to her.

It had taken him these past months to accept a harder truth.

I would do it all again.

And that terrified him most of all.

3

Nyx PACED THE length of the *Fyredragon*'s cavernous wheelhouse. She watched the storm through the arc of bow windows. Winds continued to batter and shake the moored wyndship. It felt as if the large craft were struggling to break loose and fly away.

It matched her own tense mood.

"We've been grounded here too long," she muttered to herself.

The complaint was heard by Hyck, a defrocked alchymist who served as the *Fyredragon*'s engineer. "Not long enough, by my reckoning, lass. I would happily take another full swing around the sun to get this old bird in shape before venturing off into the burning Barrens."

The bony older man lay on his back, half buried under the ship's maesterwheel, working on adjusting the controls. His occasional sharp curse reminded Nyx of his presence—and of the patchwork condition of the *Fyredragon*.

The wreckage of the centuries-old wyndship had been discovered in an ice cavern back at the Crèche. It had taken the skill of Darant's crew, along with the help of the Pantheans, to resurrect the large ship from its frozen grave. To patch and repair the *Fyredragon* had required scavenging the blasted remains of their own smaller craft, the *Sparrowhawk*. Even the maesterwheel that confounded Hyck at the moment had come from their former swyft-ship.

Other cranks and control levers, original to the *Fyredragon*, flanked to either side. Yet these also needed constant adjustments and modifications. During the long journey here, Hyck had continued to repair the wyndship as it flew across the Wastes, and the work was still ongoing.

"It's those infernal forges," Hyck sighed out. "While they got us here, their new fuel is far more powerful than ordinary flashburn. This old bird wasn't built to fly so fast. Such speeds keep shaking feathers loose, and I keep having to hammer them back into place. Can't have that continuing."

Nyx understood. An alchymical mix of flashburn and *whelyn flitch*—a flammable oil harvested from the great sea beasts of the Crèche—fueled the *Fyredragon*'s modified forges. The unique concoction was fivefold more powerful than the regular flashburn used in the Crown's forges.

"A problem or not," Nyx warned, "we may soon need that speed."

"Aye," Hyck conceded. "That be true enough."

They all knew their only hope lay in staying ahead of their enemy.

And if word has truly reached the wrong ears . . .

Nyx resumed her pacing. She had crossed the breadth of the wheelhouse twice more when muffled shrieks—panicked and distraught—echoed up from the lower hold of the ship.

She froze in place.

The raash'ke.

Something had riled the beasts up. She also discerned the shrill keening of Bashaliia among the frightened chorus. She took a step toward the wheelhouse door, determined to go to their aid.

But another had already discerned the source of their distress.

Hyck, still on his back under the maesterwheel, shouted to her. "Hold fast, lass! We're gonna get shook hard!"

Only then did Nyx note the trembling of the planks underfoot. Before she could take a breath, the ship jolted, bucking her off her feet. As she crashed down to a knee and a hand, a loud *twang* drew her eye to the starboard-most arc of windows. Outside, a mooring line lashed wildly in the rain, ripped loose by the quake.

A glint of metal flashed at the rope's end, marking the steel screw that had secured its hold. The line whipped back at the ship. The screw struck the window and shattered through it.

Nyx lunged to the side. Steel speared past her in a shower of glass. The screw cracked into the planks and impaled itself. A shard of glass drew a line of fire across her upper arm.

She gasped and rolled farther away.

The ship shook through another few small tremors, then settled again. The writhing mooring line went slack, leaving its screw still impaled.

Hyck ducked out from under the maesterwheel, but he kept to his knees. He scowled at the new damage. "Are you all right?"

Nyx wasn't sure if he was inquiring about her welfare or his ship's. She checked her arm. The glass had sliced through her sleeve and grazed her skin, but nothing worse.

"Just a scratch," she assured him.

Hyck sighed. "That's the worst rumbler so far," he said. "It's like this sardin' island wants to toss us off of its shoulders."

Nyx nodded. She also wanted to be free of this island. The escalating number and severity of these quakes reflected the slow approach of the moon and warned of the doom to come.

Knowing this, she came to one firm conclusion.

We must leave now.

* * *

BY THE TIME the next bell clanged throughout the ship, Hyck and a team of crewmen had cleared the wheelhouse and set about boarding up the broken window to keep the rain out.

Still, another storm blew into the wheelhouse.

Nyx turned as the door banged open behind her.

Jace shoved through, his face even redder than before. He tugged at his beard, a sign of his consternation. The source of his aggravation followed him.

Graylin sy Moor growled a complaint as he stomped inside. "You're certain no one in Bhestya knew you came from *this* ship? That none of your inquiries could be construed as suspicious, to draw eyes this way?"

Jace frowned back at Graylin. "Do you take Krysh and me to be fools, to speak out of turn? During our investigations, we were as guarded as necessary, without seeming to hide anything. We walked a knife's edge. We couldn't seek knowledge of the Barrens without asking pointed questions. Otherwise, we would've learned nothing. We certainly would not have recovered the old map."

Graylin frowned with consternation. Still, his expression softened as he spotted Nyx amidst the chaos of repairs. The deep creases around the flint of his ice-blue eyes eased.

Nyx looked upon him stoically. The man's clothes were soaked to the skin, his dark hair wet, making the aged silver strands shine all the brighter. He limped on his left leg, likely from the dampness plaguing his old injuries. Decades ago, he had been beaten and tortured after he betrayed his oath to the Hálendiian king. Graylin had broken his vow for the love of a woman, Marayn, a pleasure serf of the same king. Graylin's attempt to escape with her had led to his capture and the eventual death of his beloved. Only the *result* of their forbidden union had survived, birthed and abandoned in the Mýr swamps.

Nyx searched the knight's face for the thousandth time. She sought for any resemblance to this man who was her father. Scars mapped the hard planes of his cheeks, but that chart remained unreadable, speaking only to the pain he endured for daring to love someone bound to another. After his failed escape, Graylin had believed his child with Marayn had died in the swamps—until fourteen years later, he discovered how wrong that assumption was.

Nyx had survived. She still had hazy dreams of that time. When she was a babe, abandoned and mewling in the swamp, she had been taken in and nurtured by a massive she-bat, but that succor had come at a cost.

She touched her eyes, remembering when her sight was only a blur of light and shadows. The suckling milk of her foster mother had inadvertently poisoned her, clouding her eyes, all but blinding her. Still, in return, she had been granted another gift, another sense. During that most tender time, enfolded within the constant chorus of bridle-song that bound the winged colony together, her own innate talent was melded and molded into something uniquely powerful.

Yet such a fostering could not be sustained. The milk-poisoning had risked her young life. Perhaps recognizing this danger, the she-bat had left Nyx in the path of a swamper, a kind man who adopted her, loved her as much as he did his own sons. They were all dead now, sacrificed to keep her alive after another near-fatal poisoning returned her sight and instilled a feverish dream of the moon crashing into the Urth.

That memory, that loss, still wounded her, leaving her breathless at times.

Still, in the ensuing horror and chaos, she and Graylin had been reunited. At first, neither was sure if the knight was truly her father. Then, back at the Crèche, an elderly *Nyssian* seer had recognized the blood-heritage shared by the two, confirming Nyx's parentage. And while Nyx had no reason to doubt such a reading, knowing the powerful gifts of such blessed women, in her heart she still found it unfathomable.

She knew who her true father was. She pictured the kind eyes and swamp-worn features of her dah. She felt no such warmth or connection with this flinty, hard man who now stalked into the wheelhouse. In fact, any affection toward him felt like a betrayal of her dah.

The only real family she had left was Bashaliia. While Nyx had lost her two brothers, she had been reunited with another—for when she was a babe, another had nestled alongside Nyx in the care of the she-bat. A dozen years later, that winged brother came to her aid, filling a void she had not known was there until he swept back into her life, thrumming with bridle-song, awakening a connection buried deep in her blood and bones.

That's my true family.

Graylin seemed to read her coldness and turned away, merely offering her a nod.

Another greeting was more exuberant.

From behind Graylin, Kalder came trotting forward, tail held high, shaking the dampness from his thick fur. The massive vargr, whose haunches reached Graylin's waist, hailed from the cold twilight forests of Rimewood. His dark coat, stippled with shades of tawny gold, was made to hunt such a shadowy glade. Amber eyes glowed warmly toward her, while his tufted ears swiveled, ever alert, taking in every tick and groan of the storm-swept ship.

Kalder brushed his muzzle across her thigh, while she let a hand drift down and ruffle his mane. At the same time, her throat hummed with notes beyond hearing, casting out golden strands that touched the wildness of the vargr's savage heart. While Kalder shadowed Graylin, seemingly tamed to the man, Nyx knew the beast was no hunting dog. The two were more brothers, bound not by command and subservience, but by hardship and tragedy. For the *two* had once been *three*.

Aamon—Kalder's brother—had died protecting Nyx.

Even now, she could hear the echoing howl of that kinship, the ghost they carried with them. She read how it bound the hearts of beast and man. She sang to acknowledge that sacrifice, to burnish that memory. She felt the warmth of a shared bed, the thrill of a hunt, and the blood-tang of a fresh kill on the tongue.

Kalder rumbled his contentment, bumping her again before returning to Graylin's side. The traceries of Nyx's bridle-song wisped away, but not before she caught the vargr's sense of the knight next to him, the kinship the two shared. Through Kalder, she read the beast's respect and hard affection for his two-legged brother.

She eyed Graylin in this light, struggling to feel that same kinship—but again she failed. While she accepted that she and Graylin shared blood, her heart remained untouched. It was too full of grief for all she had lost, leaving room for little else. And if she were honest with herself, it wasn't just sadness, but also a measure of resentment—unfair or not—that he had abandoned her, that he had never sought to confirm what he could only suspect.

Many nights, her thoughts drifted to a different fate.

What if he had found me back then? What might my life be like?

She shook away this reverie, accepting the path before her, before them all.

Graylin's eyes narrowed upon her, finally noting the rip in her sleeve, edged by drying blood. He stepped abruptly toward her. "You're hurt."

It wasn't a question, but a statement, one that he thought required his immediate attention. She backed from him. "It's nothing."

"Are you sure? Let me check."

He reached for her, but she pushed his arms away, ignoring his wounded look. She did not need him doting on her, not when they had far greater measures to address.

Her gaze slid to the door. "Where are Darant and Glace?" she asked, having expected the *Fyredragon*'s captain and his daughter to accompany these two to the wheelhouse. "We must discuss leaving here."

"They're installing the repaired forge," Graylin said, and glanced over to Jace. "If we're truly exposed, we must make haste in departing."

Nyx heard her own worry expressed by the man. She nodded in rare agreement with him.

Jace searched the vast wheelhouse. "If we're going to set off, we need to show Fenn the map we found. I thought he was already up here?"

Hyck answered with a hammer in hand from repairing the window. "The lad's taken to his bed. Upon my orders. He's barely slept since arriving here. Got circles under his eyes so dark that he looks like a masked bandit."

"We need him back up here," Graylin said.

"I was waiting until everyone had gathered before rousing him," Nyx explained. "No need to wake him any earlier."

Graylin nodded, but he turned to Jace, bringing up another concern. "You and Krysh, were you able to glean anything else in Bhestya? Any word about the fighting spreading across the Western Crown?"

Jace winced. "Skirmishes continue between Hálendii and the Southern Klashe. But after last winter's battle, both sides are hunkered down, seeking alliances from other regions to bolster their resources. They're forcing neighbors to pick sides. In doing so, the war is slowly circumscribing the breadth of the Crown. In fact, emissaries from both Hálendii and the Klashe arrived in Bhestya a few days ago, petitioning the king for support."

Graylin growled under his breath. "Has King Acker been swayed either way?"

"Rumor is that he plays one against the other, with no firm commitment as of yet."

"That's good—at least for now. But if emissaries have landed here, then spies must have, too."

"No doubt," Jace agreed, tugging on his beard again. "And if they heard the same rumors we did—about a dragon-helmed ship carrying winged beasts—it won't be long before they'll be looking this way."

"If they aren't already," Graylin intoned dolefully, then added with a sigh, "I had hoped we'd have more time."

Threat or not, Nyx was done waiting. "I'll go and stir Fenn."

Jace stepped to follow. "I'll join you." But he offered Graylin one last warning. "The fear out there is that tensions are reaching a fevered pitch. And when war does erupt, it will likely burn across the Crown."

"Then we must not be here when that happens." Graylin waved them toward the door, while trailing with Kalder. "Fetch Fenn. I'm going to check on Rhaif and Shiya. See how their work on the *ta'wyn* coolers is going. We can't cross into the Barrens without them."

Nyx understood. Back in the Frozen Wastes, at the citadel of the Spider,

Shiya had recovered massive cooling units from that *ta'wyn* stronghold. She and Rhaif had been struggling to get them fitted and running—but so far, their efforts had failed. Without those coolers functioning, their group dared not travel into those sunblasted lands, where the heat would blister skin and sear lungs.

Until those units were fixed, they all knew the truth.

We're trapped here.

4

RHAIF CIRCLED THE massive *ta'wyn* device installed at the center of a storage room. Its spherical shape—all bronze and dark crystal—rose to twice his height. Another unit had been fitted on the portside. Ductwork burrowed throughout the ship, extending outward from each device. It had taken the bulk of the journey to the Eastern Crown to complete this installation.

But that was not the hardest task.

"Maybe try kicking it," Rhaif offered. "Like urging an ox to move."

Down on a knee, Shiya cocked her head to one side, as if trying to listen to the heartbeat of the device. She held a palm against its lower flank. Her bronze figure looked like a statue sculpted to hold up the metal-and-crystal sun.

Then again, the two were forged from the same furnace, creations of the ancients, those who walked the world while it still turned.

Rhaif scratched the stubble over his chin, remembering all that Shiya had shared, about her past, about her creators. Those godlike beings had feared the catastrophe that the Urth now faced, of the moon crashing into the planet. Those elder gods had left guardians that could survive the Forsaken Ages, the turbulent millennia that followed the Urth's sudden stoppage.

Rhaif stared at Shiya as she worked. She was one such guardian—part of a collective known as the *ta'wyn*. The ancient word meant *defender* in the Elder tongue, but in the Klashean texts, they were deemed *undying gods*—which was closer to the truth. The *ta'wyn* were creations, sculpted of bronze, fueled by ancient alchymies, and imbued with near-eternal life, along with an intelligence that surpassed those whom they had been crafted to defend.

Rhaif studied the flowing metal that made up Shiya's form, constructed by the ancients to survive the passing millennia.

But those Elders had crafted with more than just *bronze*.

Other guardians had been forged of flesh and blood.

Like Bashaliia.

Colonies of great bats, attuned to the moon, had been imbued with bridlesong, enhancing their natural abilities into a potent weapon. It was a gift powerful enough to merge the colony into a great horde-mind, an undying intelligence that could carry memories across thousands of years. Their duty was a simple one: to monitor and watch for the possible doom to come—and if that should happen, to awaken the buried Sleepers with their bridle-song, stirring them to save the world.

Shiya was one of those Sleepers.

Rhaif remembered discovering Shiya deep in the mines of Chalk, of her violent birth from a copper egg. She had come out damaged. Even worse, her memories—preserved in a vast crystal archive—had been shattered by the enemy. It had left her with only shreds of instinct and a fleeting understanding of her true role.

That *enemy* had also been *ta'wyn*.

Rhaif shook his head.

Maybe those Elder gods shouldn't have made the ta'wyn *so blasted intelligent, so self-aware.*

It had proven to be a costly mistake.

Lost in the mists of the Forsaken Ages, a great war had broken out among that bronze collective. Originally, the *ta'wyn* had been tasked to cross into the inhospitable halves of the world—the frozen dark and the burning brightness—and build the massive *turubya*, world-turning engines, to ready those enormous forges to get the Urth to spinning if the worst should happen.

Alas, during the turbulent times of the Forsaken Ages, the *ta'wyn* had fractured. A large group broke away from their creator's path, coming to believe the Urth belonged to them, not to those whom they were meant to protect. They called themselves the *Revn-kree* and were led by a *ta'wyn* named Eligor. They were eventually thwarted and their leader shattered into pieces. Unfortunately, the enemy had succeeded in securing the two *turubya*.

Even after the war, agents of the enemy proved to be insidious. Over the passing millennia, they hunted and destroyed Sleepers—those *ta'wyn* who had been buried away, seeds planted against the possible apocalypse to come.

Though compromised, Shiya had survived. With their group's help, she had recovered enough of her memories to reveal the world's hidden past, along with the locations of the two *turubya*.

But so much remained lost.

Like how to accomplish the task before them now.

Rhaif frowned at the towering sphere of bronze and crystal. It remained dark and inert. Shiya was confident she had successfully installed it. Yet she seemed incapable of stirring it to life.

Still on a knee, Shiya hummed quietly, her emanations warming her fingers to a meager glow. Her bridle-song—or *synmeld,* as the *ta'wyn* called it—was potent, yet it still failed to wake the hearts of the two devices.

"It can't hurt to try kicking it," Rhaif offered again.

He had no sounder advice. His former life had been as a thief in the city of Anvil, where he had been part of a guild before being handed over to the authorities by the guildmaster herself, Llyra hy March. Thus, he had ended up imprisoned in the Guld'guhlian mine, where he had eventually escaped with Shiya.

"Physical force will do no good," Shiya whispered, her voice still melodic from her efforts to divine an answer to this puzzle box.

The pounding of boots drew Rhaif's attention to the door. Graylin stalked into the room, trailed by Darant, who looked like a bedraggled cur at the moment. The pirate-captain had shed his blue half-cloak, exposing a roughspun shirt stained in oil. Dark stubble shadowed his cheeks, and his eyes were two black diamonds. He looked both exhausted and furious.

The two men were followed by the knight's vargr, who pushed inside and curled a lip, as if in distaste at the lack of progress.

Darant seemed no happier, especially with the news he brought. "Enough with this puttering," he blustered. "Word of our ship has spread as far as Bhestya. Worse yet, Hálendiian emissaries are swarming into this half of the Crown. We move now, or we may never get a chance."

Graylin crossed closer and circled the room's bronze sun, pulled into its orbit by trepidation. "How are you faring? Darant's crew has already test-fired the repaired forge. And Jace and Krysh have secured a rough map of the Barrens. Beyond a few minor repairs, we're set to go."

"Except for one glaring problem," Rhaif said.

Darant joined Shiya. "Mayhap we should set sail, continue to work on these damnable devices while in the air."

Graylin scowled at this idea. "And if we still fail? We won't make it more than fifty leagues past the sandy necropolises that mark the Barrens' border before the heat forces us back."

Darant challenged Shiya. "Is there any hope you can stir this to life? Or are you simply wasting our time?"

Rhaif stomped over, coming protectively between the captain and Shiya. "Back off, Darant. She's doing all she can. Without her knowledge, we wouldn't even have these cooling units."

"Fat lot of good they're doing us now," Darant groused.

Shiya stood up, only now seeming to acknowledge the others' presence. She rose to her full height, a head taller than Rhaif's bowlegged stature. She was draped in a simple shift that reached her knees, but the grandeur of her form could not be so easily hidden. Her bronze face was a handsome oval, her hair a plait of the same, so finely wrought that the strands shifted with her motion.

Even her skin swirled in soft hues, flowing as easily as any flesh, all warmed by the power at the heart of her figure.

She turned her gaze upon Darant, then Graylin. Her eyes, an azure blue, shone in the dimness. Her lips, a rosy metallic hue, parted with a sigh of resignation. "I believe I've done all I can."

"What about consulting with Tykhan again," Graylin offered. "Perhaps he could offer further counsel."

Rhaif grimaced. Shiya had not been the only Sleeper to awaken. Many centuries ago, Tykhan had been attacked where he had been buried in his copper egg, but he managed to survive, defeat his assassin, and escape. Woken far too early, he went out into the world and took on the role of the prophetic Augury of Qazen. He hid his *ta'wyn* heritage behind artifice and paint. Still, he remained loyal to the original imperative given to the *ta'wyn*—to defend the Urth. To that end, he now aided their allies in the Western Crown, where the others faced their own daunting task: to secure a relic from the defeated *Revnkree* leader and use it to hunt for a lost key needed to control the two *turubya* once they were activated.

For any hope for the world, both sides had to work in tandem.

To help with this, Tykhan had taught Shiya a means of communication through the air, but it came with a risk. The Iflelen dogs who aided the Hálendiian king seemed to have a means to track such messages. Fearing this, both groups knew every outreach had to be brief and sporadic. They also guarded how much knowledge to share, wary that it might fall into the wrong hands.

To reach out again now, to simply gnaw over this same difficulty, risked too much.

Shiya reinforced this. "I've already employed all of Tykhan's recommendations, but to no avail." She shrugged. "Maybe if he were here. Instead of at Kysalimri."

Graylin persisted. "Still, it might be worth contacting him once more and—"

Rhaif cut this off with a growl. He suspected that even if Tykhan were aboard the ship, the result would be the same. "We dare not reach too often into that well," he reminded Graylin. "We all know who might be listening."

Graylin nodded, conceding this point. "Then what do we do? Do we tarry here and hope for a breakthrough? Or set off and pray we can get this to work before we reach the Barrens?"

All eyes turned to Shiya.

She stood tall before their combined gazes. "I have reached a firm conclusion from my inspection of the cooling units."

"Which is what?" Darant asked.

She turned to the captain. "I cannot activate them."

Rhaif coughed to cover his shock.

"No one can," Shiya added.

"Then we've failed before we've begun," Graylin moaned. "We'll never be able to cross the Barrens."

Shiya simply cocked her head. "That is not true. I've surmised that the units are self-activating. The devices are already emanating vibrations. It's taken me until now to discern their function. They appear to be monitoring the very particles in the air surrounding the ship. I've concluded that the units will only stir to life once they detect excessive heat."

"So, when the air gets hot enough outside," Rhaif said, "they'll come to life?"

"I believe so."

Darant looked even more dour. "You *believe* so? We'll be staking all our lives on that belief."

"And the lives of everyone on the Urth," Graylin added.

Shiya's silence answered them both.

Rhaif swallowed hard. "Is there any way to test it? Like heating the air around the ship with the firepots atop the deck."

Shiya shook her head. "The devices will not be fooled. The emanations reach farther out than any pot or forge can warm."

Graylin shook his head. "Then we must fly blindly into the Barrens and hope the devices ignite on their own . . . is that what you're saying?"

"That is my assessment."

Graylin and Darant cast uneasy glances at one another.

Rhaif reached over and took Shiya's hand. Her fingers folded over his. He felt the warmth of her body, the pliant nature of her skin.

In this moment, he felt like a mudtoad next to a goddess. Rhaif had inherited his squat form and rocky countenance from his Guld'guhlian father. Luckily, the blood from his mother—a huntress who hailed from the forests of Cloudreach—had softened those rough edges, while adding a few fingers of height and an unruly mop of fiery hair. He had also gained her natural agility, speed, and balance, all of which had served him well as a thief.

Still, Rhaif knew he was no prince of the realm—not in appearance, certainly not in manner. Yet he and Shiya had grown closer during the long journey here. While they could not share the intimacy of flesh, they found other ways to be tender, to show affection, though it was still more one-sided than he would have preferred.

But that didn't lessen his conviction.

He put it into words.

"I trust her fully," Rhaif declared. "So, the answer is clear. We trek onward."

Her soft fingers firmed on his, expressing her thanks.

Darant blew out a long sigh, finishing with, "Not like we have much choice." He headed toward the door. "Let's go plot a course."

Graylin followed, but he looked back at the dark bronze sun. "And pray we're not doomed already."

5

NYX KNOCKED ON Fenn's door. Jace shadowed her.

The ship's navigator had a cabin to himself, one level below the wheelhouse. Back aboard the *Sparrowhawk,* the quarters had been tight, requiring the crew to double or triple up in a room. The salvaged *Fyredragon* was far larger, with a cavernous hold vast enough to house the five raash'ke and Bashaliia, while also leaving plenty of room for gear and dry goods, which were stocked to the rafters for the coming voyage into the Barrens.

Sadly, the loss of so many crewmen during the battle at the Crèche also contributed to the plentiful accommodations. Even Darant's other daughter, Brayl, had died after a betrayal that had stung them all.

Still, a score of Pantheans had agreed to join them, refilling their depleted crew. Those newcomers were quartered a deck below, where they kept to themselves. While the language barrier had mostly broken down—due to Daal's tutelage—the two crews continued to maintain their distance, sticking to their own traditions and customs.

Nyx knew this must not continue. The crew needed to be united if they hoped to face the challenges ahead. But the divisions persisted. Even she and Daal had fallen away from one another.

That must change—for all our sakes.

Nyx stared at her toes, picturing those Pantheans. A few were pure-blooded, with silvery green hair and emerald eyes, along with a green cast to their smooth skin. More striking were their pointed ears and webbed fingers. They looked born from the steaming green waters of their inland sea. Others, like Daal, shared blood with the descendants of the original Noorish explorers who crashed the *Fyredragon* into the Crèche. That mixed heritage darkened their hair and blunted those points. Several had eyes of blue.

Daal's eyes were especially striking.

She swallowed, remembering how their color would change with his moods. Icy when he was angry. Watery when he thought of home. A deep indigo when passion fired through him. Regret and guilt panged through her.

Jace drew her back, reminding her of the task at hand. "Why isn't Fenn answering?"

Nyx collected herself and faced the door. "He must truly be exhausted. Like Hyck said."

"Tired or not, we need him."

"We do."

Nyx knocked again, harder this time.

Finally, a tired croak called through the door, "Hold on already."

A shuffling of feet, a clatter of wood, and a muttered curse followed. The door swung open. Fenn leaned on the frame. He still wore the same breeches and loose shirt as before. The only ease to his dress were a few undone buttons and a lack of boots.

It appeared whatever sleep he had managed had been fitful. His white-blond hair, normally oiled and smooth, had been mussed into peaks. His moss-green eyes were bloodshot, the lids heavy and shadowed. He was the youngest of Darant's crew, only seven years older than Nyx, but at the moment, he looked aged and weathered.

His homecoming to the Eastern Crown had clearly taken its toll.

Still, he managed to notice Jace's presence. "Ah, you're back. How did you and Krysh fare out there?"

"Well enough," Jace admitted. "We could've accomplished more if you had joined us."

"I would've been more hindrance than help. Trust me on that."

"They did secure a crude map of the Barrens," Nyx said.

"Truly?" Fenn's eyes glinted with a measure of his usual avid interest. "What is the provenance of this chart? Do you have it on any authority that it's more than just some fanciful creation, one with no bearing on what's really out there?"

"Krysh gained the confidence of a hieromonk over at the school in Toltok, a man whose studies concentrated on the histories of the Barrens."

"What was his name?"

Jace scrunched up his nose, as if trying to sniff out that answer. "Randa hy . . . I can't remember exact—"

"Randa hy Lenk?"

Jace straightened with his brows riding high. "That's right. He was an old man, but in his youth, he had spent a decade scouring the necropolises that border the Barrens. He uncovered a cache of texts in an old crypt, sealed in a copper chest. Even the scrolls were sheets of copper."

Fenn's look went pensive. "Lenk was always a good scholar."

Nyx frowned. "You knew him?"

Fenn shrugged. "In another life."

Nyx wanted to press him. She knew that as skilled as Fenn was, he must have studied navigation.

Had he been a student at that school?

"Let's get upstairs and take a look at your map," Fenn said.

Before leaving, Fenn returned to his room and grabbed his boots. In his haste, he simply carried them. Nyx suspected this renewed vigor was less from Fenn's academic interest in the map and more about the possibility that it would send them sailing from these lands.

Fenn hurried out into the passageway and led the way toward the stairs to the wheelhouse. "Do you have the original copper scroll?"

"We were only allowed to make a copy," Jace admitted. "Which we did. Not just of the map, but also of several other copper scrolls. Those that pertained to the map."

"Very good. We should also—"

Fenn stopped, so abruptly that Nyx bumped into him. Fenn lifted an arm and pushed her farther behind.

"What's wrong?" Jace asked.

"Stay back."

Nyx stared past Fenn's shoulder. She struggled to understand what had alarmed him. The long hallway appeared empty, mostly in shadow, lit by a few draft-iron wall sconces. Their oiled wicks flickered the view.

Nyx squinted. "I don't see what—"

Then she did, though its true nature was difficult to discern. Something flowed across the shadows at shoulder height. When it hovered, its shape would vanish, fading into the woodwork, camouflaging into invisibility. Only in motion could its shape be seen—and even then, it appeared more phantom than substance.

The creature's body was thin and snakelike, striped in black to blend into shadows. It carried its length—easily as long as Nyx's arm—on translucent wings. Its tongue flickered from scaled lips, tasting the air.

"A *kezmek*," Fenn whispered, speaking its name like a curse. "A Bhestyan assassin-wing."

Fenn did not sound surprised. Instead, his timbre was resigned, maybe a touch relieved—as if he had been expecting such an arrival.

"A single drop of its poison could kill a score of men," he warned.

As if to prove this threat, the kezmek hissed softly, baring fangs that unfolded into view.

"It's bridle-bound to its master," Fenn explained, warding Nyx back. "Don't dare hum a single note to try to wrest control of it. A kezmek is lightning fast, trained to strike any threat to its master's hold. Whether that be by song or knife. It will kill anything that approaches it until it reaches its target."

Jace drew Nyx farther away. "Why's it here?"

"It's a scent hunter, insidious and inescapable, fixed to a target's blood." Fenn never turned his eyes from the threat, his voice certain. "My blood."

Nyx fought her pounding heart out of her throat. "Who . . . Who sent it?"

"My uncle," Fenn said. "He must know I'm back."

6

WITH A TIRED sigh, Daal climbed from the ship's lower decks to its mid-level.

He had shed his wet riding leathers and changed into a dry pair of breeches and a loose shirt. While warmer, he found the clothing uncomfortable; the fabric was far rougher than the smooth sealskin he wore at the Crèche. Worst of all were the stiff leather boots. The pair were well fitted, but they still chafed with every step. Back home, he went barefoot, only occasionally wearing sandals. The bulky boots weighted down each leg, making every stride leaden.

Still, what truly burdened him was his heart. He could not shake the sight of Nyx dashing into the ship's hold with Bashaliia. She must have spotted his descent atop Pyllar. Even this small rejection stabbed at him.

"What do you think this summons is about?" Tamryn asked, scaling a step behind Daal on the stairs.

Daal glanced back. "I spotted Jace and Krysh when we were descending through the storm. They likely come with news from Bhestya."

Tamryn simply shrugged. She was two years older than Daal and had quickly risen to be his team's second rider, straddling atop a raash'ke named Heffik. Her mount was a smaller doe, but the bat made up for her size with a speed and agility that confounded the other bucks. As such, Tamryn had quickly earned her position, a ranking she took great pride in.

And not just that.

Tamryn hailed from a pure Panthean bloodline. Even now, she walked stiff-backed with a fixed look of disdain. Her green hair was shorn short, making her pointed ears stand tall. In the shadowy well of the stairs, her eyes shone a hard emerald, reflecting the scant lamplight.

"Maybe this summoning means we'll be leaving soon," she said.

"We can only hope so."

Half a bell ago, Captain Darant had dispatched a crewman down to the lower deck, ordering Daal to come up for a meeting. Upon hearing this, Tamryn had insisted on accompanying him: *More than one Panthean should attend such a gathering.*

At the time, Daal had scowled, noting the insinuation behind her words.

Especially not someone of only Noorish blood.

It seemed some prejudices had survived both the battle at the Crèche and the long journey here. For ages, those of Noorish descent had always been looked down upon, their mixed blood considered tainted. Daal had no doubt Tamryn vied for more than just the second saddle. She surely wanted his position. He had not discouraged this aspiration. It had lit a fire under her to train harder, driving her to hone her skills to a finer edge.

So be it.

Such talent would no doubt be tested before long.

Upon reaching the level of the middeck, they heard voices echoing out to them. Daal could not make out the words, but he recognized Nyx's tone. Though she was not casting out any strands of bridle-song, his blood still stirred. His breath caught in his throat. His heart thudded harder as his body responded to the fear tracing through her voice.

He froze at the threshold to the middeck.

"Why have you stopped?" Tamryn scolded.

He held up a clenched fist, a signal among riders to hold fast. He pushed off the stairs and stared toward the trio gathered halfway down the passageway. He recognized Jace and Fenn, both guarding Nyx, but he spotted no threat in the shadowy hall.

"What's wrong?" he called over.

Fenn backed a step and warned hotly, "Don't get any closer!"

Only then did Daal spot a shift in those shadows. Something glided toward the others, carried on thin wings, fading in and out of view. It spun a wary circle at his sudden arrival.

He had no idea what it was, but from the trio's reactions, it was a threat.

His gaze caught on Nyx's.

She shook her head, her eyes huge, warning him back. But he refused to shy from her, not any longer, not with her in danger.

He took a step forward—which proved a mistake.

The winged beast cartwheeled, then lunged toward him, vanishing as it did.

He stumbled back, colliding into Tamryn, who blocked his retreat.

NYX SHOVED PAST Fenn.

No . . .

Her throat clenched, then burst forth with a chorus of bridle-song. Golden strands shot through the darkness, cast forth from her lips and her upraised fingers. They wove into a net, one meant to capture the beast—or, failing that, to draw its attention her way.

"You fool," Fenn groaned, shouldering Nyx aside.

He stepped forward, and a knife appeared at his fingertips. He slashed his palm. Blood flowed in a wash, running down his wrist.

Nyx understood. Fenn intended to sacrifice himself, to use the scent of his blood to attract the kezmek.

Still, Nyx refused to relent. She wove her song into a wall between them, ready to capture the creature when it raced back this direction, drawn by her bridling and his blood.

During the journey here, she had practiced her craft, training with Shiya. Taking a deep breath, Nyx lowered her chin. She girded herself to stop the attack, but her target had vanished into the shadows again, camouflaging itself fully.

Where are—

Then the kezmek struck her shielding. It burst back into sight, emblazoned by golden fire, thrashing in her net. She tightened her palate, finessing her control of the song's weave.

I've got you.

In that moment, she also caught a glimpse of its master, the one who wielded the reins of this beast. She followed those enslaving strands to a hooded figure, hidden among the moored ships, maybe a league away. The man shared the senses of his kezmek, not perfectly, but enough to guide it.

The assassin must have sensed her, too, in that moment. There was no panic, no fear, not even surprise, only a pall of amused satisfaction—and with good reason.

In the hallway, the kezmek faded from view, going ghostly again, shedding her fire as it did. It appeared the beast's talent at camouflaging extended to an ability to avoid any touch of bridle-song. She fleetingly wondered how such a slippery creature had ever been bound to a master.

Still, the damage was done.

The kezmek escaped her net and sped toward them. Nyx struggled to recapture it. She retracted her golden strands, but she knew it would be of no avail.

Fenn must have recognized this, too. He stepped forward and lifted his bloody hand higher. "To me, you bastard," he muttered.

Then another figure appeared ahead of them, emerging out of nothingness as readily as the kezmek had. Jace moved with a swiftness that belied understanding. His arm lunged out. Fingers clamped at the air—and captured the kezmek by its neck.

The beast writhed in Jace's strangling grip.

Fenn gasped out, stumbling back, "How . . . ?"

By now, Nyx's net had reached Jace and the kezmek, draping over them both. Her bridled senses took in everything at once. The beast's heart fluttered in a panic—then froze cold. She felt the life drawn from it in one beat—not by her bridle-song, but by another power. It ripped away not only the creature's life, but all tracery of the bridling that had snared the beast ages ago.

Still, that hunger didn't stop with the kezmek. It trailed down the reins of control to the creature's wielder. The man hidden out in the moorings collapsed to his knees. He clutched a hand to his throat, as if trying to throttle the song being stolen from him. But the hunger was too great. It snuffed away his breath, his bridling, his life.

The assassin fell dead into the wet grass.

With the threat ended, Nyx turned her attention to the source of this ravening hunger. Her strands delved deeper into Jace, drifting past cloth and skin—where again she found nothing, only an endless cold void that craved all fire.

Even her own.

She gasped as that emptiness sucked at her power. She tried to escape, letting her golden strands waft to nothingness. Her feet scrabbled backward, but there was no escape. Her fire spilled out of her, feeding that insatiable void.

Jace dropped the limp kezmek and faced her. His eyes appeared as empty as his expression.

"Jace, no," she moaned.

He ignored her. As more of her golden song was ripped from her, ice raced toward her heart. Though panicked, she understood what was happening. It was not unlike when she drew on Daal's well of strength.

As the cold spread toward her core, she fell to her knees, too weak to stand.

But another sensed the danger.

Daal appeared behind Jace with a dagger raised.

"Don't . . ." Nyx croaked out.

Again, she was ignored. Daal's arm slashed down—but at the last moment, he turned the blade and struck the hilt into the back of Jace's skull with a loud crack. Jace stumbled forward. His eyes rolled back, then with a confused expression, he toppled toward the deck.

Daal caught Jace as he fell and cradled him to the floor. Daal looked across at Nyx. He extended his arm, offering what he could: his warmth to refill what had been stolen from her.

She took a stuttering breath, then shook her head. Her fires would restoke on their own. She could not do to Daal what had been done to her, not to simply speed her recovery.

She meant this gesture as a kindness, but given Daal's wounded expression, he did not take it as such.

Fenn interrupted, a bloody fist at his chest, fingers clenched to stanch the flow. He looked from Jace and Daal over to Nyx.

"By all the gods below, what just happened?"

7

GRAYLIN CLUTCHED THE pommel of his sheathed sword, a blade that had
been in his family for eighteen generations. It was called Heartsthorn, and it
bore sharp silvery thorns across its guard, which dug into his palm as his hand
clenched the top of the weapon.

He stared down at Jace, who knelt groggily on the planks of the wheelhouse. The young man fingered the knot at the back of his head, wincing at
the tenderness—or maybe it was from guilt.

Nyx had explained all that happened below. By now, everyone had gathered in the wheelhouse, trying to assess what this all meant.

Darant leaned next to the maesterwheel and absently filled a pipe. Shiya
and Rhaif stood near the door with their arms crossed. Krysh had come with
a healer's bag and had helped revive Jace. After a brief examination, the alchymist had deemed the young man to be unharmed.

Graylin wondered if that last should be corrected. His fingers tightened on
his sword. Considering what had happened, Jace posed a danger—not just to
Nyx, but to their cause.

Maybe it would be better to dispatch this threat now.

Nyx glared across at Graylin, as if sensing his intention. She knelt protectively at Jace's side. She waved to Fenn, then to Daal and Tamryn, who both
stood off to the side.

"No matter the danger," she said, "Jace did save us all."

Graylin had to concede this point, but only begrudgingly.

Jace grimaced, his face pale. "I truly don't know what happened. I have no
recollection beyond the moment when Nyx confronted the kezmek. I took a
step forward, trying to go to her aid—then I was gone. The next thing I remember was my head exploding with fire and my body falling toward the floor."

Graylin turned to Nyx. "And *you* . . . why didn't you tell us that you had
sensed something strange about Jace, back when the *turubya* had ignited and
he had nearly died?"

Nyx shook her head. "It was a fleeting moment in all the chaos. After that,
Jace appeared totally normal. I thought little of it afterward."

Graylin noted her eyes narrow on what was clearly a lie.

Krysh must have suspected as much. "Bashaliia also seemed to be wary of
your friend."

Nyx simply looked at her knees.

Darant spoke up, puffing as he lit his pipe. "Something clearly lurks in the boy. Something that can sap away bridling. Maybe it's a boon, maybe a curse. But in all my travels, I've never heard of such a thing."

Krysh glanced over from where he had been putting his healer's bag back in order. "Your travels have never been into the Wastes, to an ancient *ta'wyn* stronghold. The strange alchymies of the *turubya* are beyond all our understanding."

Darant raised a brow. "Maybe not to *all* of us."

Several gazes swung toward Shiya.

Graylin pointed to the bronze woman. "Have you experienced anything like this? Do you have any knowledge of it?"

Shiya stirred slowly, as if warming from within. "Much of my memory is lost to me," she reminded them. "Even if that were not true, the conflux of energies held within the *turubya* is beyond most comprehension, except perhaps for the Kryst of the *ta'wyn*."

Graylin frowned. "But we have no access to a Kryst."

He knew the *ta'wyn* were divided into three castes, each with its own tasks and abilities. Lowest were the Roots, the worker drones with malleable bodies. Then came the powerful Axises, like Shiya, who were granted potent gifts of bridle-song. But above all were the Krysts, the true leaders and overseers, creations of cunning intelligence and wisdom. The latter had long vanished from the world.

Fenn turned to the bronze woman. "But, Shiya, you were able to activate the *turubya* in the Wastes. Surely you must know something."

Her azure gaze fell upon the navigator. "I was only a key. No more. It takes a source rich in *synmeld*—what you call bridle-song—one like me, to trigger the *turubya*. It drains all in that moment, burns it away."

Graylin remembered Shiya collapsing out of the crystal cocoon after activating the great world-engine. She had nearly expired in that moment.

Nyx's brow furrowed. "I felt something similar . . . with Jace. A void that sought to strip everything from me, possibly my life with it."

Jace closed his eyes, clearly wounded by her words.

Nyx missed it, still focused on Shiya. "You said the *turubya* drained you and burned that energy away."

The *ta'wyn* bowed her head in acknowledgment.

Nyx turned to Daal. "At first, I thought what had happened below was like with the two of us. Where your power would flow into me, stoking my reserves as a font for me to be cast forth."

"I'm your flashburn . . . you're my forge," he muttered, his voice forlorn, maybe with an undercurrent of wounded anger.

Nyx faced the others, seemingly as oblivious to Daal's distress as she had been to Jace's pain. "But down below, helpless before the enormity of the void, my bridle-song was not *stored* away. It immediately *burned* up, consumed on the spot. It felt as if my song ceased to exist as soon as it rushed into that emptiness."

Graylin noted a pinching of Shiya's eyes and challenged the woman. "Does this have any meaning to you?"

Shiya remained quiet for a spell, then spoke softly. "A faint memory. It's barely there."

"Of what?" Nyx asked.

"I mentioned *synmeld*—a talent the ancients imbued into their creations, both the *ta'wyn* and creatures of flesh and blood, like the world's great bats."

"And the *Oshkapeers,*" Daal reminded them. "The tentacled Dreamers of the Deep."

Shiya nodded. "But there was something related to that gift. Related but *opposite,* created in tandem with *synmeld.* Twin in power, but the antithesis of the other. It was called *dysmeld.* I know little more, only that the two must be kept apart."

"Why?" Graylin asked.

"Once joined, they consume each other, destroy one another. Possibly explosively so."

Jace's face went even more pale. "Are you saying something like that might be inside me?"

"I do not know. It is beyond my comprehension. Only a Kryst might know more."

"Like Eligor," Graylin said.

"Before he was destroyed," Darant said.

"Not completely," Nyx reminded them.

Silence settled over the chamber. They all knew that the Iflelen had secured the decapitated head of Eligor, the leader of the *Revn-kree* hordes. For untold ages, the cabal had been performing arcane experiments upon it. It was that relic that their allies in the Western Crown needed to secure. Tykhan believed the bronze bust held the secret to discovering a lost key to controlling the two *turubya*—which was critical. Even after the two ancient devices were activated and seated deep into the Urth's crust, they could only be controlled with this hidden key.

Krysh finally spoke up. "This pairing of *synmeld* and *dysmeld* makes a certain sense. The gods, the natural world, all require a balance of extremes, a symmetry of opposites. Winter and summer. Night and day. Fire and ice. Even predators require prey." He nodded to Shiya. "Perhaps *dysmeld* and *synmeld* are a similar pairing of extremes. Maybe it's *dysmeld* that powers the *turubya,* but it requires *synmeld* to be consumed as a means of jolting it to life."

Shiya remained silent, unable to offer any further counsel.

Jace twisted toward the alchymist. "But if you're right, *how* is it in me?"

Rather than Krysh, Rhaif offered a possibility. "We know *synmeld*—or bridle-song—could be cast into bronze or flesh." He motioned to Shiya, then to Nyx. He then placed his palm over his own heart. "And that it can be passed inadvertently. My mother's people, the Kethra'kai of Cloudreach, are steeped in this gift. They believe it came from the great bats, that the talent seeped into their tribes, somehow flowing into them during their long worship and interaction with the neighboring colonies."

Graylin understood Rhaif's line of conjecture. "You're thinking the same might be true for *dysmeld.* That Jace's exposure to the blast of energy from the *turubya* somehow imbued him with this gift—flowing from bronze to flesh."

"But is it a gift?" Darant added, casting out a pall of smoke. "Or a curse?"

Rhaif shrugged. "Does it matter? The lad clearly has no control of it. Like a new bridle-singer coming into their power."

"Yet, he has no one to guide him, to instruct him," Graylin noted. "Which could prove a danger to us all."

"That may be true," Darant said. "But there's a greater and more immediate threat. One that we know as little about."

Graylin frowned, then noted the pirate scowling at his ship's navigator.

Fenn closed his eyes, fingering the bandage over his sliced palm.

"Someone sent an assassin aboard my ship." Darant straightened from where he leaned by the maesterwheel. "And I mean to find out who."

NYX AGREED WITH Darant. She was also happy to see those accusatory gazes sweep from Jace to Fenn. She knew the navigator was stout enough to weather such a storm. Jace—her friend for ages—was more fragile, terrified and unmoored by all that had transpired.

She reached over and placed a hand on Jace's thigh.

He shivered, then his hand found hers, covering it fully. He glanced to her, his voice tremulous. "I'm sorry . . ."

"No. I shouldn't have stayed silent. You shouldn't have been forced to discover this in such a dangerous moment."

He swallowed. Terror shone in his eyes. "But what am I?"

She turned her hand, joining their palms, then fingers. "We'll find out together."

He nodded and let out a long breath. Still, his fear never faded.

Without any way to help further, she turned her attention as Darant confronted Fenn.

"I took you into my crew three years ago," the pirate said. "As with most aboard, I've never questioned or judged one's past. Only that you swear allegiance and loyalty to me and mine."

Fenn nodded. "I cannot express what it meant to find my place here. Hopefully, I've earned it, too."

"Aye, you have. But now your past threatens us, so it is time to bare what you've kept hidden."

Nyx stood up. "You said you believed it was your *uncle* who sent the assassin."

"Not a belief, but a fact." Fenn stared around at the others. "My father served King Acker of Bhestya as his high minister, one of his most trusted advisers. Then three years ago, my father was accused of treason, of plotting the king's death with a cabal of others in the court."

Fenn's face darkened with an anger likely long suppressed. "He was hanged, as was my mother."

Nyx winced, knowing the particular agony of such a loss.

"My brother—older by a year—was also dragged to court. He had been serving as a cadet in the kingdom's sea brigade. They wanted him to denounce our father. He refused and was beheaded."

"And you?" Darant asked. "Were you put to the same question?"

"No." Guilt etched Fenn's voice. "During all the tumult, with the king's men yanking the accused from their beds, my sister arrived in the dead of night to my school. She came with her maid, both cloaked. She warned me to flee, gave me a heavy purse to do so. She told a tale of my uncle's betrayal of my father, an accusation made in secret. While the plot was real, my father had nothing to do with such foul treachery. But forged letters and seals suggested otherwise."

Graylin looked skeptical. "How can you be sure what your sister claimed was true?"

"Is she still alive?" Nyx interjected.

"As far as I know, Freya still breathes. She is married to my uncle's cousin, who loves her dearly, more so after she gave him a son. He would not let any harm come to her."

Graylin pressed him. "This ploy by your uncle . . . how did she learn of it?"

"The two houses—my uncle's and his cousin's—have servants with familial ties going back generations, split between their estates."

Darant nodded, wafting out a spiral of smoke. "No one knows better what truly goes on within a household than those with their backs bent in chores or in servility."

"Freya is loved by more than just the man sharing her bed," Fenn said in a pained voice. "She has a heart for all, a trait once shared by my father. Someone must've taken pity upon her and carried a stolen skrycrow missive to her, from one house to the other. The letter laid out and exposed my uncle's treachery. He intended to destroy my father and climb his gallows to rise to greater glory— which he did. He now serves as high minister, taking my father's place."

"Couldn't your sister have taken that stolen letter to the king?" Nyx asked. "And shown proof of your uncle's treachery?"

All eyes turned Nyx's way, their gazes pitying.

"If it were only that easy," Fenn mumbled.

Darant explained, "It would not be believed, especially when delivered by the accused's daughter. Any such attempt would likely only get her killed, and maybe the rest of her family."

"Freya is no fool. Her heart might be huge, but it does not blind her."

Nyx frowned. "What about the servant who dispatched the letter as a warning? Could they not add support?"

"Even if they dared risk it," Graylin explained, "there is no weight behind the breaths of such lowbred."

Fenn nodded. "The generosity of this warning to my sister was only meant to expose the truth, to let a daughter keep her pride in her father—and per- haps to let a son escape in the night."

"Which you did," Darant said.

"By the narrowest of margins. I barely had time to stuff a bag. Still, I nearly ran afoul of a trio of assassins, one bearing a crated kezmek. Maybe the same one that attacked us below."

Graylin looked dour. "If so, if your uncle has discovered you're aboard the *Fyredragon,* this will not be his only attempt."

"But why does your uncle continue to pursue you?" Nyx asked. "It's been three years. Already seated as high minister, what does he gain by your death?"

"My flight from Bhestya was taken as further proof of my father's duplicity. While I escaped, as I said, my brother did not. My sister did not have a way of warning him, not when he was aboard a ship at sea." Fenn's lips drew to bloodless lines. "Yet, by fleeing, I pointed the executioner's ax at my brother's head. Geryd would never denounce our father."

Darant clapped a hand onto Fenn's shoulder. "Do not take that burden upon yourself. Your sister risked much to get you running. And I wager your brother would gladly have given his head to let you live."

"Also, by surviving," Graylin added, glancing toward Nyx, "one day you may be able to right a grievous wrong."

"Your uncle must fear the same," Rhaif said. "That's why he continues this hunt. But take some comfort in knowing this."

Fenn scowled. "Comfort? How?"

Rhaif's eyes glinted. "Because your uncle has been harboring a deep-seated fear—of a son's vengeance, maybe even of exposure. It's likely formed a knot in his gut, one that's grown more embittered over these three years."

Darant barked a smoke-filled laugh. "No doubt that's true."

Fenn, his face still dark, looked little swayed. "Regardless, my uncle will not stop. Not until one of us is dead."

"Yet, that's not the greatest threat he poses." Graylin turned to the bow windows, searching the stormy skies to the south. "King Acker entertains emissaries from both the Klashe and Hálendii. While he teeters at the moment, if his high minister learns that this ship—one harboring Fenn—is the same one being hunted by Hálendiian forces, then that bastard will surely tilt that scale against us."

Darant straightened. "Then we must be gone before that happens."

Jace stirred, glancing over to Krysh. "The map we secured. We need Fenn to study it."

Graylin waved this away. "That can wait. We must cast off immediately. We'll make for the necropolises that border the Barrens. We can use that map to chart a course from there."

Nyx let out a breath she hadn't known she had been holding. She followed Graylin's gaze out the windows, but she stared to the west, to the dangers that lay ahead. Back in the Wastes, they had defeated the Spider—a lowly Root of the *ta'wyn,* one driven nearly insane. But the Spider had also given them a warning about what they would face out in the Barrens. A powerful Axis—the same caste as Shiya—guarded the second *turubya,* along with a small *Revnkree* army.

Nyx felt no terror at this daunting challenge, only relief. The long journey, the waiting, had weighed upon her, kept her sleepless many nights. While much still remained unknown, one certainty had firmed.

Even if it takes all our lives, we must not fail.

Still, she knew the burden of the world did not solely rest on her shoulders. She turned her gaze to the east. Another carried the same responsibility—and was hopefully as resolute in his duty. She didn't know who faced the greater challenge. But she took some solace in one burden that was not her own.

At least I don't have to kill my own brother.

Arkival limne of a Kezmek (native to Bhestya)

TWO

BREAKWATERS

Oh, the unlukky exile who finds a path bakk hom, for hom is ne'er the same, nor the banish'd. Both ere changed bi time & circumstaunce. Bett'r still, bett'r for all, to seek a neu path.

—The wisdom found in *The Dialogues*
of Neffron the Lesser

8

KANTHE RY MASSIF—the high prince of Hálendii and consort to the empress of the Southern Klashe—heaved his belly's contents over the edge of the ship's rail. In all his eighteen years, he had never developed a stomach for sea travel. Or maybe his queasiness rose from the tension at this homecoming.

He wiped his lips and scowled at the approaching shoreline.

Though midday, a heavy fog masked Azantiia's dockyards. Lanterns and fire-pots glowed through the gloom. Beyond the port, the city climbed a series of hills, leading to the Crown of Highmount, the palacio and citadel of its new king—Kanthe's twin brother, Mikaen. The towering walls pierced the fogbank and shone brightly. Kanthe pictured the breadth of its encircling parapets. They formed a six-pointed sun, part of the Massif royal sigil.

My family's crest.

Kanthe swallowed down bile as he gazed at his former home. He took deep breaths of the salty air to clear his head. His brother was not in residence at the moment, having retreated to his wife's ranchhold in the rolling plains of the Brauðlands to the northeast. Lady Myella—*Queen* Myella—was rumored to be with child again. Her third. Kanthe could only imagine Mikaen's joy. The king already doted upon his firstborn twins, a boy and a girl: Othan and Olia.

My niece and nephew . . .

The children were nine months old, but Kanthe had never set eyes upon them. A pang of regret ached through him. He prayed Mikaen did not pit one sibling against the other, as their father—King Toranth—had done with them, creating a painful chasm between the two brothers.

With Mikaen's first breath, he had been declared the firstborn of the twins and destined for the throne. He certainly fit that illustrious mold. Though a twin to Kanthe, Mikaen looked as if sculpted from chalkstone, matching their father's countenance, including his curled blond locks and sea-blue eyes.

Kanthe, on the other hand, took after their dead mother. His skin was burnished ebonwood, his hair as black as coal, his eyes a stormy gray. He was forever a shadow to his brother's brightness. As such, tradition mandated that Kanthe be a "Prince in the Cupboard," a spare should his older twin die. His lot was to sit on a shelf in case he was ever needed. Still, in order to serve a useful role, he had trained at the school of Kepenhill, in preparation as a future adviser to his brother.

But that will never be . . .

Kanthe looked down at the remains of his left arm, severed below the elbow. It had been fitted with a bronze replacement, sculpted by Tykhan using
ta'wyn alchymy. It took a keen eye to discern the new limb from the real thing.
With some attention and concentration, Kanthe could even open and close
those fingers by working his arm muscles.

Many nights, he still woke to the pain and shock of Mikaen's sword slicing
through his arm. They had battled last winter, but it felt like yesterday. Mikaen had not intended the mutilation to be a mortal wound. Instead, he had
meant to deny what had adorned Kanthe's hand. During the fight, Kanthe's
finger had borne a ring belonging to their mother, who had died shortly after
giving birth. The heraldic ring had come with a story—from the midwife who
had witnessed their birth. While still in her bed, their mother had hurried
the midwife off with the ring, along with the tale of the *true* firstborn of
King Toranth. According to their mother, it had not been the bright son
who had shouldered out of her womb first, but the darker twin.

During last winter's fight, with brother pitted against brother, the ring had
shone with the truth: Kanthe was the actual heir to the Hálendiian throne.
Not Mikaen.

Kanthe knew this very fear had long plagued his brother. Rumors had
abounded throughout their young lives. The aspersions, mostly bandied in jest,
had nonetheless found fertile soil in Mikaen's heart.

To deny that ring, Mikaen had hacked off Kanthe's forearm. But his brother
had not stopped there. For another certainly knew the same truth: their father, King Toranth. With friction already growing between the father and
son, Mikaen had taken a sword to the king, usurping the throne in one blow
and silencing any threat to Mikaen's birthright—and that of his children.

Kanthe reached down and rotated the cuff to seat it better over his stump.

"Does it need an adjustment?" a voice asked from behind, startling him.

Kanthe turned to find the limb's sculptor standing there. Tykhan had approached with nary a creak of the ship's planks, which was unnerving considering the sheer tonnage of this bronze figure—not that anyone would suspect
such an unnatural physique by looking at him.

Tykhan had disguised his metal face and hands with paint and artifice.
Dressed in a dark gray cloak, belted at the waist and sashed in crimson, he
could pass as a pale-skinned merchant out of Delft—which was the story their
group shrouded themselves in. To add to this conceit, Tykhan had leaned
upon a talent unique to a Root.

Kanthe studied Tykhan's features, appreciating the new hawkish hook to his nose, the slight pinch to his eyes, all features of someone from the lands of Delft, at the twilight edge of the sunlit Crown.

As the lowest of the *ta'wyn* caste—creations designed for construction and scut work—Roots had been gifted with a fluidity of form, an ability to mold their bronze at will, to change bodily shape to match the varying needs of their work.

If only I could change my face and destiny with such ease . . .

Tykhan reached over and lifted Kanthe's artificial limb to examine it. The bronze forearm had been painted to match the same pale complexion as Tykhan's—as had all of Kanthe's skin. His dark hair had also been cut short and dyed a rich auburn, all to further mask his countenance as a prince of this realm.

Tykhan squinted at his creation. "Is the limb causing you pain?"

Kanthe pulled the arm back and mumbled, "Not physically."

Tykhan lifted a brow, plainly understanding. "Then it is best we shall make landfall while your brother is gone. At least for another fortnight. By drawing a portion of his legion with him, he's left less of a force at Highmount."

Kanthe scoffed at this. "Less is not *none*. From what Llyra's spies reported, Mikaen took his Silvergard—his personal Vyrllian attendants—along with fifty knights. Highmount still bristles with plenty of swords, pikes, and spears."

Tykhan shrugged. "Still, less *is* less. And we have no choice but to attempt this gambit."

Kanthe frowned. "Nyx and the others could've given us more warning, more time to prepare."

"We've already had half a year. We know what we must do."

Kanthe cursed under his breath.

A fool's course, if ever there was one.

Three days ago, Shiya had spoken through Tykhan's lips—utilizing the strange means of *ta'wyn* messaging. She informed them that the *Fyredragon* had set off for the Barrens. Apparently, Nyx and her allies had drawn unwanted attention and had to depart quickly, ahead of their original plans. They had kept murky the reason behind such a rushed departure out of fear of who might be listening.

Still, this was the signal for Kanthe's group to act.

A loud laugh cut through his melancholy. From the forecastle, two figures crossed out onto the deck. The bark of amusement had come from Rami im Haeshan, the fourth son of the former emperor of the Southern Klashe and brother to Aalia, the land's current empress.

Rami's dark hair hung loose to his shoulders. His complexion—the color of bitterroot steeped in honey—remained unblemished by paint or disguise. The only change from his usual countenance was that his cropped beard had been grown out bushy. In addition, Rami came garbed in a drab black robe belted in leather. A silver pendant hung from his neck. Its ornament depicted a man's face with the lips sewn shut by a golden thread.

As the pair approached, Rami lifted an arm in greeting.

Kanthe barely acknowledged it. Instead, he focused his attention on Cassta, the lithe young woman who accompanied Rami. Kanthe swallowed hard at the sight of the youngest of the Rhysian assassins. Black leathers accentuated her comely shape and long legs. Her snowy skin needed no disguise of paint—not that anything could hide her nature. She hailed from the far-off Archipelago of Rhys, near the southernmost turn of the Crown. It was a matriarchal society renowned for its deadly skills. Like her sisters, Cassta carried silver bells braided into a tail of dark hair. It was said that the last sound many a victim heard was the single tinkle of a bell, marking the time of their death.

Such was not the case now. Cassta strode so smoothly across the deck that not a bell chimed. She wore five of them—one more than when they had first met—marking her rise from an acolyte to a position of full sisterhood.

She turned to whisper something in Rami's ear, triggering another bright laugh from the man—and a pang of jealousy in Kanthe's chest. Those two had grown closer over the past half year, while Kanthe had been sequestered in endless meetings and debates of strategy, allowing him to catch only rare glimpses of her.

I'm also married, he reminded himself.

Cassta's gaze caught his as they reached Kanthe's side. As if she could read his thoughts, the shadow of a smile ghosted across her lips, then vanished.

Rami stepped to the ship's rail as Tykhan headed off again. Rami frowned at the fog. "It seems the weather is as gloomy as your mood, my brother."

"Brother by marriage," Kanthe reminded him. "Not that Aalia has ever considered such a union as anything more than a contract." He glanced toward Cassta, making sure this was understood.

She ignored him, staring at the approaching coastline.

Rami shrugged. "It's best my sister never bedded you, or you would've found yourself equally poked—only by Tazar's dagger in your back."

Kanthe knew this to be true. While Aalia and Kanthe had been married, uniting a bloodline between the empire of the Southern Klashe and the Kingdom of Hálendii, her heart belonged to Tazar hy Maar, the head of the *Shayn'ra,* a clan of militant rebels who now fought alongside the Klashean armies.

Kanthe sighed. "A dagger in the back might be better than what awaits me ashore if our ruse fails to work."

"Delft has signed a pact with Hálendii," Cassta reminded them. "They've agreed to supply iron to the kingdom, sailing in shiploads to smelt into weapons of war. If we're careful, none should cast us more than a glancing eye."

Rami nodded. "Commandeering one of their freighters, flying their flag, should get us to shore safely. Still, we'd best not tarry. Our disguises will not likely survive more than that glancing eye."

"Especially if you insist on talking," Kanthe warned. "Your Klashean accent will ruin us all. Best you stay as quiet as the man on your pendant." He pointed to the sewn lips on the embossed face. "You're supposed to be a Gjoan scribe, someone hired by us Delftans to be a *silent* witness to transactions and negotiations."

Rami scowled in disdain at this role. The Dominion of Gjoa notoriously cut out the tongues of scribes—as they did to disciples of their mystic orders. It seemed knowledge needed as much safeguarding from errant tongues as matters of coin.

Luckily for their group, additional protection came in a shape far more appealing.

Kanthe eyed Cassta. Her duty was to play a Rhysian bodyguard, one hired to guard their Delftan leader—a role best suited to Tykhan. The *ta'wyn* had stridden the Crown for millennia and had grown fluent in every language. Tykhan's Delftan accent was indeed flawless.

As the winds off the Bay of Promise pushed their vessel toward a fog-shrouded shore, a heavy silence settled over the trio. The ship aimed for a darker section of coastline, where eyes would be less likely to spy upon them. As the fog slowly parted, the view opened onto a patchwork of ragged docks, sucking siltfields, and crumbling buildings. Birds swept in languid circles, looking as listless as the setting. The smell of algal rot and spoiled sewage carried to them.

"No wonder you fled from here," Rami whispered. "Not exactly a welcoming expanse. Especially for a homecoming."

"This is the Nethers," Kanthe explained. "Not the main city."

He took a deep breath, not shying from the stink. A pang of wistfulness swept through him as he inhaled the breath of this region. He had spent many a debauched night in this section of the city, back when he had lived in his brother's shadow.

Kanthe pointed to a towering bulwark farther from shore. "That's Stormwall, a furlong-thick fortification. It encloses the city proper and has never been breached." He nodded closer at hand. "Everything below the wall forms the Nethers."

While a student at Kepenhill, Kanthe had been taught the city's history. As centuries passed and the populace grew, Azantiia could no longer be constrained by the Stormwall. It spread in all directions, even out into the bay where silt-fields were dredged and packed, requiring the dockworks to be extended farther and farther out, forming the Nethers.

Outside the protection of the Stormwall, this region was prone to sudden floods, with large swaths often drowned or blown away. It was said the Nethers were as variable as the weather. Maps of the place were drawn more with hope than on any reading of a sexton—and certainly never with the permanency of ink.

"Here is the perfect place to lose oneself," Kanthe assured them.

As I did so often in the past.

He stared at the approaching coastline.

Let's hope the same holds true today.

AS THE FIRST bell of Eventoll rang through the misty air, the Delftan ship reached the shore. The hull ground against a storm-broken stone quay, its rocks coated thickly with black barnacles and slippery with dark green algae. Crewmen tossed ropes and fought to hold the craft steady. They would not be tying off. The ship would depart as soon as Kanthe's group departed.

Overhead, a squadron of gulls screamed and shat in complaint at their arrival, likely not accustomed to trespassers to this lonely corner of the Nethers' docks.

Kanthe ducked from the assault and headed for the gangway. Rami and Cassta followed.

"Where's Tykhan?" Rami asked, searching the deck. "We don't want to tarry too long, even cloaked in fog."

The sweep of a forecastle door answered him. The *ta'wyn* strode out, leading the final member of their small party—one critical to this endeavor.

Frell hy Mhlaghifor crossed to join them. The lanky alchymist had shed his usual belted black robe and came outfitted in Delftan clothing. He adjusted the matching cap over his ruddy hair, tied into a tail at the back. His pale features needed no paint to complete his disguise—though at the moment, anger darkened his features. His eyes, always wrinkled at the corners from squinting at faded ink, narrowed as his gaze fell upon Kanthe.

Frell blocked the way to the gangway and pointed a finger at Kanthe. "You should not have come. I urge you to leave with this ship when it departs. You risk much by returning here so soon."

Kanthe faced the man, not shirking from his hard gaze. "So soon? I've been gone a full year."

He meant to keep his tone light, but it came out bitter. This matter had already been settled back in Kysalimri. Kanthe did not wish to rehash his decision to accompany the party. But clearly Frell intended one last attempt to persuade him to retreat.

"I refuse to sit idle any longer," Kanthe argued. "As consort to the empress, my role is no more than that of a puppet, dangled on strings both political and practical."

Frell opened his mouth to protest, but Kanthe lifted a palm—something he would've never risked when the alchymist had been his tutor at Kepenhill.

"When I left these shores, I was a *falsely* accused traitor. Now I return as a *true* turncoat. We don't know what difficulties will lie ahead, but having a prince—even one from a cupboard—may prove useful."

Rami added his support. "Before we departed from the Southern Klashe, our spymaster—the Eye of the Hidden—reported that a small but determined faction of the city rankles under the fist of their new king. Not only against his ever-stricter dictates and taxes, but also against the drums of war."

"Why is this the first I'm hearing of this?" Frell asked, the flush receding from his cheeks.

"You missed the last meeting. You were down with Pratik in the Abyssal Codex, overseeing the repairs to our librarie."

Kanthe knew Frell and the Klashean scholar had taken upon themselves to overhaul the fiery ruins of that great archive, to try to salvage what had been lost.

"What you also failed to hear," Rami continued, "is that Kanthe's name has been whispered in dark corners of the city, as a possible remedy to the harsh new king. Maybe not in great numbers or enthusiasm—but perhaps that sentiment could be stoked higher and spread wider."

"And we'll have a better chance of doing that if I'm here in the city," Kanthe added, "not atop a throne in Kysalimri."

"Or you'll end up dead," Frell said sourly. "With your head on a pike."

"That must not happen," Tykhan said.

Kanthe nodded. "I'm in full agreement with that."

Tykhan rubbed his chin, a casual mannerism so human that it was unnerving. "If we hope to avoid moonfall, the Hálendiian kingdom and Klashean empire *must* be united. It's why I took such pains to bring Kanthe and Aalia together. If we fail in this effort, all will be lost."

Kanthe frowned at the *ta'wyn,* knowing how much their group leaned on Tykhan's predictions of the future. Even stranger, his oracular statements were based not on mystical guidance, but on knowledge gained over millennia of experience.

Kanthe studied Tykhan, trying to fathom the ancientness of this figure.

The *ta'wyn* had been prematurely woken from his slumber as a Sleeper and had been forced to wander the Crown for millennia, watching kingdoms rise and fall. He had observed the lives of untold millions and retained it all. Over such a span, he had come to recognize the threads—the trends and variables—that formed history. He had also learned to pull and weave those strings. He had become so skilled at reading those paths that he took on the role of the Augury of Qazen, becoming a revered oracle of the Klashean people.

Kanthe remembered Tykhan's explanation for this skill: *While I might not be able to predict the outcome of the fall of a single coin, I know after thousands of tosses that the two sides must eventually fall an equal number of times. Time is like that on a grander scale. There are tides that flow, where the accumulation of past trends points to future events.*

Those words still haunted him. Kanthe had considered himself a puppet in Kysalimri, but Tykhan was far more adept at pulling his strings—and those of countless others over the centuries—all in an attempt to bolster the chances of avoiding moonfall.

Frell also seemed to bristle at Tykhan's control. "Whether what you say is true or not, we did not come to these shores to install Kanthe on the throne of Hálendii. Our goal is to verify another of your claims. That the Iflelen possess the decapitated head of the *Revn-kree* leader, Kryst Eligor. Nothing more."

"That's not nothing," Rami said. "That alone will be challenging enough."

Frell pointed at Tykhan. "You've tasked us with acquiring this relic. But first we must know if it truly *exists* and *where* it might be hidden. Only then can we conspire to secure it."

Tykhan bowed his head in acknowledgment.

"I can accomplish such a task as readily on my own," Frell said. "I still have allies in Kepenhill, even in the Shrivenkeep below it, where the Iflelen maintain their abhorrent lair. With discreet inquiries, I can get the answers we need."

"Perhaps." Tykhan shrugged. "But fate weaves an ever-changing tapestry. I've learned never to trust a lone thread. What you claim you can do alone is not certainty. You've been gone a year from these shores, just like Kanthe. You assume that all is as you left it. But with a king slain and a son raised to the throne, nothing can be certain."

"Still, I believe—"

"Belief is no more than a frayed thread," Tykhan interrupted, shaking his head. "Only a fool hangs his fate upon such a feeble support." Frell's face darkened at this insult.

"There are many strings—other unknowns—that must be considered." Tykhan ticked them off on his fingers. "Friends could be dead. Allies turned into traitors. Doors sealed that were once open."

Frell sighed, clearly finding no argument against this.

Tykhan waved an arm to encompass their group. "Over time, I've found it best to have many threads at hand, so when the warp and weft of fate unfolds, I have plenty of material to weave into it."

Kanthe appreciated the support from the Augury of Qazen, but those words unsettled him. Tykhan was correct.

So much could go wrong.

The pounding of boots on rock drew their attention to the quay. A trio of shadowy figures rushed down its length toward the ship.

A thin blade flashed into Cassta's fingers.

Rami dropped a hand to a short sword sheathed under a fold of his robe.

Frell pushed Kanthe behind him.

A shout rose, scolding and rushed. "Get your arses off that damned boat!"

Out of the fog, the speaker appeared. The woman's short stature and biting tongue left no doubt as to her identity. Llyra hy March scowled up at those lined along the rail. She was dressed in linens and leathers, corseted so tight that her leggings looked painted on.

She swept a fall of blond hair from her eyes. "Move!"

Confused and concerned, Kanthe hurried to the gangway with the others. He struggled to understand Llyra's alarm. The woman was the guildmaster of a den of thieves out of the city of Anvil in the Guld'guhl territories. She had been aiding their cause, rousing as many of her ilk as possible to forge a secret army in case they were needed, one that was spread across whorehouses, thieveries, low taverns, and dark dens.

Llyra's two companions finally caught up with her, having neither her speed nor her litheness. Kanthe recognized Jester and Mead. The two Guld'guhlian thieves huffed and panted. The pair had the same squat height as Llyra, only with stockier builds and more brutish exteriors—forged of gristle and scars. Additionally, Jester had suffered a blow much like Kanthe's. The thief had lost half a leg to an ax, with the stump now pegged with wood.

Kanthe lifted an arm in greeting as he reached the quay.

Jester returned the gesture in an obscene manner.

Llyra stepped to meet the group, her eyes glinting a hard copper. "I've just heard word. Unfortunately, it's come later than I would've wished."

"What word?" Frell asked.

Llyra levied her gaze on Kanthe. "This one's brother. He's headed back to Azantiia."

"Wh . . . Why?" Kanthe stammered in dismay. "I thought he was staying away for a full fortnight."

"It seems there was a problem with his unborn child. Rumors hint at a possible poisoning. The king rushes in a fury to bring his queen to the city's physiks. They'll be here by the morning. His legions are already locking down Highmount."

"Then we must hurry," Frell said. "We must finish our task before Mikaen returns."

Llyra swung around. "Come with me. I've gathered everything you asked for."

They set off down the quay.

Once onto sand—stepping upon Hálendiian soil for the first time in a year—Kanthe cast a glance back. The Delftan ship was already sailing away, fading into the fog.

Maybe I should've heeded Frell's warning . . .

As he turned around, he found Tykhan staring at him. In the gloom, his eyes glowed with the inner fire of the *ta'wyn.*

Still, it wasn't only fire that blazed there.

But also *certainty.*

Just as Tykhan had warned moments ago, fate often wove a fickle tapestry.

Kanthe stared up at the breadth of the city.

And now I'm trapped in it.

9

MIKAEN RY MASSIF cradled his queen across his lap. He kept her feverish body wrapped in velvet and held her close as brutal gusts buffeted the royal barge. The wyndship's outer armor rattled under the assault, setting his teeth to aching. The noise cut through the roar of the craft's forge-engines, all stoked to a full blaze, as the ship raced across the rolling hills of the Brauðlands.

Trying his best to ignore it all, he placed his hand upon the damp brow of his beloved. He felt the fiery heat burning within, a deadly pyre slowly consuming her.

She moaned at his touch. Her eyelids fluttered open, looking upon him beseechingly. His heart ached at the misery he read there. She reached toward his face.

He pulled back, shying from her palm lest her finger brush aside the silver mask that shielded half his countenance. Already suffering, she did not need to look upon the scarred ruins of his face beneath. Even after a year, he could barely stomach his own visage.

"Myella, rest." He caught her hand and folded it back under the velvet blanket. "We'll be back in Highmount by Eventoll's last bell."

"Olia . . . Othan . . ." she whispered.

"With the maids. The children are safe."

She stared at him, silently asking what she feared to put into words.

"They show no illness. No fever," Mikaen assured her. "They appear unharmed."

With a weak sigh, Myella sagged in his embrace, her lids slipping closed again.

Mikaen took solace in offering her this small comfort.

He brushed a lock of damp hair from her brow and kissed her gently. He felt the burn of her skin under his lips. "Rest, my love."

A light rap on the cabin door drew his attention. A pang of irritation spiked through him. He slipped from the bed, careful not to disturb Myella. He pulled a fold of velvet over her swollen belly, protecting the child inside.

Seven months along . . .

He knew what this meant. This illness risked more than the life of his queen. He prayed for mercy, resting a palm over the growing babe.

I cannot lose you, too.

Unable to do more, he tightened a fist and headed to the door. With each step, fury narrowed his vision and squeezed his chest. He yanked open the door to find the only man who would dare disturb him during this painful time.

Thoryn vy Brenn—captain of his Silvergard—bowed his head. Even in such a posture, the knight towered over Mikaen. He came in full armor, its silvery polish reflecting the lamplight. He carried a plumed helmet under one arm.

"I'm sorry to intrude," Thoryn stated stiffly.

As the captain straightened, anger darkened his crimson features. Like that of all Vyrllian knights, his skin had been tattooed a ruddy hue, meant to mark their full-blooded status and to terrorize enemies. In addition, black ink etched half his face, forming the sun and crown of the Massif family crest. All nine members of the king's elite Silvergard wore this inked emblem, mimicking the sigil sculpted into Mikaen's silver mask, honoring their wounded king.

"What is it, Thoryn?"

"Your Majesty, we've just received a skrycrow from the Carcassa ranchhold." The captain lifted a curled scroll. "They've discovered the poisoner."

Mikaen pushed Thoryn out into the hallway, then followed and closed the door behind them. Myella did not need to hear this.

"So it is indeed a poisoning?" Mikaen said.

Thoryn acknowledged this with a nod. "Surely meant for your lips, not the queen's."

Mikaen's anger could not be constrained by the walls of the narrow passageway. He shoved past Thoryn and stalked toward the doors to the open middeck, drawing the captain with him.

Mikaen pushed out into the winds. He took in deep draughts of the cold air. The gasbag overhead shook and strained against its draft-iron cables. The rumbling roar of the forges matched his mood.

He crossed to a rail and gripped it hard to anchor him against the storms within and without. He turned to Thoryn as the knight joined him. Mikaen trusted Thoryn above all others. The vy-knight had briefly served as his liege general, but Mikaen had requested Thoryn return to his side, tolerating no others to be so close.

"Tell me, Thoryn. Who would dare attack in such a cowardly manner?"

"The true villain remains unknown. But in tossing the kitchens—where last night's repast was prepared—a vial of rykin was discovered buried among the spices and salts."

Mikaen turned to Thoryn. "Rykin?"

"A toxin derived from a fungus that only grows in the forests of the Myre Drysh."

Mikaen's knuckles turned white as he gripped the rail hard. "A forest that lies within the Southern Klashe . . ."

Thoryn nodded at the implication. "A kitchen whelp had been instructed to add the poison to the spiced wine served after dinner. He had been told it was merely a drab of pennyroyal and honey, a mulling preferred by the royal family."

Mikaen closed his eyes. He had never developed a taste for spiced wines, a brew unique to the Brauðlands. He remembered leaving his glass untouched, but to Myella, it had been a taste of home.

"Who tricked this whelp into such a murderous act?"

Thoryn grimaced. "We cannot know. The boy had barely begun to speak when he started to thrash and convulse, his face going blue. He died without another word."

Mikaen understood. "Someone poisoned the poisoner."

"So it would seem. All in attendance are being put to the question. But many had been in contact with the boy, both before and during the interrogation. It was all chaotic. We may never know who in that household is a traitor to the crown."

"Still, we know *who* ultimately wielded that hand." Mikaen fixed Thoryn with a hard look. "It must be spies of the Southern Klashe. Likely guided by the empress herself . . . or by my brother."

"We will continue to root out the truth," Thoryn promised.

"And what of Myella? Is there a cure for what afflicts her?"

Thoryn stared down at his boots. "There are remedies that can stave off death, but only for a time. Perhaps days, maybe weeks. Ultimately it will kill. There is no cure. I've already dispatched skrycrows to Highmount. To rally physiks and alchemists. We'll do all we can, but doom is certain."

Mikaen remained silent. His next words were nearly lost to the wind. "If we attempt to stave off death, will Myella suffer?"

Thoryn swallowed hard, which was answer enough.

Mikaen asked the more difficult question. "The child she carries . . . can the queen be made to live long enough for the babe to grow further, to afford us the time to cut the child from her womb before she expires?"

"It will take a physik to best answer that," Thoryn admitted with a wounded look. "But there is hope that a child in the womb might resist this poison."

Mikaen straightened, drawing hope where he could. Clearly, Thoryn had already taken this detail into consideration.

"Rykin is said to attack the lungs, to slowly destroy the lining and tissues." Thoryn glanced toward the forecastle. "An infant in the womb, with lungs barely formed, might be spared. But know this, it will be torturous for the queen to endure such a path to the child's salvation."

Mikaen remembered the agony in Myella's eyes when she had inquired about Olia and Othan. "The queen would do anything to save the child she carries."

I know this with certainty.

Thoryn lowered his gaze, plainly recognizing this truth, too. The knight slid a hand down the rail, as if to console Mikaen. But he pulled away. At this moment, any attempt at solace sickened him. He needed to be steadfast and resolute.

The child must live.

Thoryn withdrew his hand. "With your leave, I'll dispatch another crow to express this intent, to ready Highmount."

Mikaen dismissed him with a wave. As Thoryn headed off, Mikaen remained at the rail, needing a moment to himself. He trembled at what lay ahead. He reached to the pocket inside his royal doublet and slipped out the stoppered ampoule of poison.

The Iflelen Shrive who had secured the rykin had promised the babe would be safe. The poisoning would cost only the life of his queen. Such a tragedy would rally the people of Hálendii, who had been growing more vocal in their protests to his reign. Worst of all, the tides had been steadily turning against the growing threat of war. Even Kanthe's name had been rumored to be whispered among the discontented.

Mikaen tightened his grip on the vial.

That must end.

None would deny a grieving king, one fiery in his heartache and fury. With the Southern Klashe—and especially his brother—accused of murdering the queen in such a cowardly manner, the drums of war would beat harder.

Mikaen pictured Myella's sweet countenance. He loved her with all his heart, as she did him. But her martyrdom would serve the kingdom far better than her life.

For the sake of Hálendii, for the sake of her king, for the sake of their children . . .

Myella must be sacrificed.

He opened his fingers and let the poisonous vial roll from his palm and fall into the mists below.

Still, fury throttled him. He pictured the Iflelen Shrive who had secured the poison, who promised only *one* would die.

Not two, not his unborn child.

He stared south, toward Highmount. He imagined the one-eyed necromancer hidden deep in his Shrivenkeep lair, buried amidst his foul *arkana*. Of late, the bastard seldom showed his face to the sun. With Mikaen's attention turned to war, the Shrive had receded deep into the shadows, lost in his own machinations, pursuing black alchymies known only to the Iflelen, those who worshipped the viperous god, Lord Đreyk.

Even when Mikaen had summoned the Shrive to his private chambers and set him upon this poisonous task, the man had scarcely paid him any heed, his gaze a thousand leagues off. Yet, in the end, the venomous ampoules had been delivered, along with the assurance that the king's unborn child would survive.

This had better prove true, Wryth.

Mikaen cast a scowl south, plagued by a nagging concern. He pictured that thousand-league stare from the one-eyed bastard.

What has you so preoccupied, Wryth? What holds your attention more than a kingdom at war?

Suddenly suspicious, Mikaen pushed from the rail and headed toward the forecastle door.

By all the gods, I will find out.

10

WRYTH BOWED HIS way through a tangled forest of copper and glass. He took care not to snag his gray robe on the metal thorns of the vast machine surrounding him. The ancient device—the great instrument of the Iflelen— filled the domed chamber of the order's inner sanctum, its shine reflecting off the polished obsidian.

As Wryth aimed for the instrument's center, he ran fingers along a branch of copper piping. The oldest sections had tarnished long ago. Only the newest additions at the edges of the device shone with unblemished metal. He cast his gaze toward one spot, where the latest bloodbaerne bed had been constructed.

The thirteenth—*nine* more than half a year ago.

He noted a shadow bent over the new site. Phenic, a gangly-limbed acolyte, had been tasked to watch over the bloodbaernes. The latest, a girl of four or five, lay atop the bed. Yesterday, Wryth had installed her himself, wanting no mishaps. He had administered the soporific elixir, cleaved her chest open, exposing a quivering heart, and wired her vessels into the bed. Even now, her pink gossamer lungs billowed up and down, pumped by bellows through a tube down her throat.

But for how much longer?

He imagined the girl would burn out within the next four days, her life sacrificed to the machine. Of late, most lasted no more than a week. The machine's hunger had grown insatiable, steadily rising with every turn of the moon. Fortunately, with tensions high and war looming, filling those thirteen beds had become easier. The disappearance of an urchin, beggar, or waif raised few questions.

But even that could end—especially if this hunger continues to escalate at this pace.

Nagged by this worry, Wryth turned away. He knew there was no other course but to continue along this path. As he forged onward, he listened to the burble and pulse of the instrument's fluids, steaming through crystal pipes, glowing in hues of amber and emerald. It all served one purpose: to feed the life of the bloodbaernes to the mystery hidden at this forest's heart.

From ahead, Wryth heard the whispers of his fellow Iflelen, those Shriven who had been hand-selected to assist him in this grand endeavor. Few knew what transpired here, including the bulk of Wryth's order. Only the most trusted had been given knowledge of the miracle that had woken in the bowels of the Shrivenkeep six months ago.

From that moment onward, the doors to the sanctum had been placed under heavy guard. Rumors spread and expanded, but only a handful knew the truth. Complaints persisted, fueled by bruised spirits and malign curiosity.

And with good reason.

Prior to this, the sanctum—the order's most holy and revered space—had been open to all Iflelen. In this chamber, each member knelt and swore an oath to Lord Ðreyk, the dark god of forbidden knowledge.

Wryth had done the same.

Sixty-four years ago . . .

Of late, Wryth felt his age. Even the potions he consumed to extend vitality no longer spared him such discomforts. He touched the leather bandolier—his Shriven cryst—strapped across his chest. Its length was studded with iron and lined by square pouches, each etched with symbols. His fingers inspected the sealed pockets. Most of his brethren's crysts held nothing but mawkish charms, each intended to memorialize one's long path to the holy status of Shriven.

Not so his own cryst.

His fingertips read the symbols burned into the leather. Each of his bless'd pockets hid dark talismans and tokens of black alchymies: powdered bones from ancient beasts, phials of elixirs leached from the dread creatures, ampoules of poisons sapped from venomous fiends. But the most treasured of all were the scraps of ancient texts scrolled into pouches, their faded ink indecipherable but hinting at the lost alchymies of the ancients, of the darkest arts hidden before this world's histories had been written.

In truth, Wryth cared little for the here and now, except where it served his ends. This world, he sensed, was but a shadow of another, a place of immeasurable power, and he intended to gain access there. To that end, no knowledge would be forbidden to him. And no brutality too harsh to acquire it.

For this reason, he had bent a knee to Lord Ðreyk, joining the Iflelen order—first as an acolyte and now as its master. Though, in many respects, he had lost that position to another six months ago.

Even Wryth's arrival this evening had come upon the orders of another: a new god who had woken in this chamber, a being who would make Lord Ðreyk quail.

Wryth finally reached the heart of the machine. Six others in gray robes labored around a stout iron table, serving now as an altar. Typical of all Shriven, their long hair had been braided and tied in nooses around their necks. Their eyes were banded by a stripe of black tattoo, meant to imitate a blindfold, representing such men's abilities to see what all others could not.

The leader of the six, Shrive Bkarrin, noted Wryth's arrival by straightening and offering a deferential bow of his head. "It's good you've come. Since the ringing of the last bell, his ire had grown heated. Two bloodbaernes burned out under the fire of his fury."

Wryth glanced toward where he had spotted Phenic. *No wonder the young man had been so diligently inspecting the latest addition.*

Facing back around, Wryth shooed the others from the iron altar. "What has so roused him?"

"I do not know." Plainly distraught, Bkarrin gripped the braid of stone-gray hair under his chin, as if fearing it would strangle him. "He just stirred to life, boomed your name, and demanded your presence."

Grimacing, Wryth approached the altar and the bronze figure sprawled atop it. His gaze settled on the glowing countenance of this mystery. The face was that of a curly-bearded man in slumber. The finest strands of hair waved, as if stirred by invisible winds. Across cheeks and brow, an aura of energy roiled in a storm, fueled by the glowing tanks that surrounded the altar, fed by the life of the bloodbaernes.

Wryth noted the closed eyes, frilled by bronze lashes. "He sleeps again?"

"When the two bloodbaernes burned away, the remaining eleven were not enough to sustain him." Bkarrin waved an arm. "I've already ordered new bloodbaernes to be interred."

"Very good," Wryth said, knowing the younger Shrive needed this reassurance.

Bkarrin released his hold on his braid with a sigh of relief. "The two should be settled shortly."

Wryth nodded and used this time to study the slumbering enigma. The bronze bust of the figure had been discovered two millennia ago, buried deep under the roots of an ancient tree. Afterward, the bodiless head had passed through countless hands. It had been studied, dismissed, and come to adorn many kings' halls, until it finally made its way to Azantiia.

Over time, following the guidance in ancient tomes, the Iflelen had learned how to fuel the artifact and stir it back to life. Still, it had taken centuries to wake the talisman from its slumber and glean what little they could. The head had spoken only four times, each utterance cryptic, whispered in a language no one understood.

Until six months ago . . .

The memory came with a stab of pain in the hollow socket of Wryth's right eye. While a leather patch covered the ruins, it could not smother the terror of that moment—when the bust had burst to furious life. He pictured those bronze eyelids snapping open, shining forth with an azure fire, like two brilliant suns blazing with infernal energies.

The intensity had driven Wryth to his knees, as had the demand in the ringing voice. It had commanded him to action, tasking him to a duty he could not refuse.

Two fateful words forever changed the course of his life, an imperative spoken through bronze lips.

Rebuild me.

Wryth stared across the breadth of the iron altar. What once had only been a bust had grown and stretched into the skeletal form of a towering figure. Guided by the arcane knowledge shared by this bronze god, Wryth and his ilk had slowly been constructing a new body. The wisdom gained had been as unfathomable as it was terrifying, yet undeniably thrilling. Still, Wryth recognized he and his group were mere blacksmiths, doing crude work, supplying raw material, some so rare it cost a king's ransom to obtain.

Instead, much of the growth came from the bronze figure himself. With enough fuel, burning through hundreds of bloodbaernes, bronze melted on its own, taking shape before their eyes. Matrixes of crystals grew throughout, spreading like hoarfrost across the hollow interior. Likewise, wires wended and divided, over and over again, until fading from sight.

Early on, Wryth had tried to compel the secret behind such miracles, but azure eyes had looked upon him with disdain. The only answer had been cryptic. As best as Wryth could understand, the bronze bust had acted like a seedpod, one rife with engines a thousandfold more powerful than the Iflelen's towering instrument, yet so small that millions could fit atop a pinhead. With enough resources, those tiny engines could fabricate order out of chaos, build form out of nothingness.

Wryth gaped at the sprawl of the bronze god on the altar. Such a claim seemed impossible. Yet here was proof of those assertions.

Frustration clenched his fingers. Though he had gained much knowledge, it only served to highlight his ignorance. He sensed the towering wall that still remained, standing between him and the hidden world beyond.

Anxious to learn more, he studied the bronze figure—still half-formed—trying to read it like a tome written in a lost language. The body looked not unlike that of the bloodbaernes who sustained it. The chest lay bared and open, shining with crystals and a mosslike spread of metallic tendrils. Energies flowed throughout the matrix, scintillating and fiery. Outward from there, limbs had taken shape. Most remained more outline than substance, but one arm looked nearly complete. It extended from the shoulder in a muscular form, ending in a large hand with vaguely contoured fingers, like raw dough that had not fully risen to its proper shape.

Over this half year, Wryth had witnessed this progression with eager trepidation. Given the number of bloodbaernes burned upon this pyre, it would not take long before the transformation was complete. Rubbing his chin, he stared at the glowing tanks, bubbling with lifeforce. Crystalline tubes and copper channels flowed into the gestating figure, all of which served to chain this god in place, to keep him tethered to this altar—which gave Wryth some sense of control.

But after that, what then?

Worry itched through him.

After being given this task, Wryth had pursued it with a frantic fervor, driven by his lust for lost knowledge. But of late, anxiety had grown in equal measures. When the bust had first woken, Wryth had learned two additional details.

The first was this god's name.

Kryst Eligor.

The second was the *cause* behind this creature's sudden wakening. A name had stirred it awake, spoken in the Elder tongue: *Vyk dyre Rha.* It referred to a prophetic daemon—the Shadow Queen—a malignant force carried on wings of flames, who would destroy the world.

Wryth had come to suspect—as did many of his fellow Iflelen—that the *Vyk dyre Rha* had been born anew, taking the form of a swamp girl with strange powers, a strength potent enough to send a warship to its ruins in the Frozen Wastes.

Wryth's hand rose and touched the patch over his right eye. He had suffered this wound during that attack, which served as a constant reminder of this threat.

If only I hadn't pursued her . . .

For nearly a year, he had hunted the girl and her allies—not on the basis of this dark prophecy, but because they carried with them another bronze figure, a woman, one whom Wryth had unearthed in a Guld'guhl mine, only to have it stolen from him, a loss that still stung.

He stared at the slumbering form.

But now I have my own.

While this treasure should have satisfied him, a growing unease tempered his enthusiasm. Wryth had become suspicious—especially in regard to this figure's true intent.

Eligor had expressed a passion to stop the *Vyk dyre Rha,* claiming it was her rebirth that had stirred him to life after millennia of slumber. But Wryth suspected there was much about Eligor's intent that remained unspoken. He feared this god's rebirth could prove as dangerous and threatening as that of the Shadow Queen.

But what else can I do?

Once started down this path, he dared not turn back.

To reach even this point, he had forsaken his duties to the kingdom, which risked his standing in the court. He had spent decades worming his way into one king's ear, then another. His powerful position within the regency had served him well in his pursuit of forbidden knowledge. But after Eligor's wakening, Wryth had cast off his responsibilities to the court, handing them to lesser members of the Iflelen. He only interceded when absolutely necessary— like to deal with the practicality of poisoning a queen.

Wryth could trust no other with such a delicate matter.

Let's hope that wins me some favor in the king's eye.

"Look!" Bkarrin blurted out, drawing Wryth's attention. He pointed beyond the altar. "The installation of the new bloodbaernes must be complete."

Wryth quickly noted what had roused Bkarrin. Two of the surrounding tanks, dark when Wryth had first arrived, now glowed brighter. The radiance waxed and waned, as if mirroring the beating hearts of the new bloodbaernes. The amber shine steadily rose until the tanks grew flushed with replenished lifeforce.

Wary, Wryth retreated from the altar. He had only managed a single step when those bronze eyelids flashed open. An eruption of fiery azure burst forth.

Wryth gasped as the head swung toward him and fixed him with a terrifying gaze. Never before had the bust been able to turn from its eternal stare upward.

Bronze lips parted, then pulled back into a sneer. "Wryth . . ."

Around the altar, the other Shriven dropped to their knees. Wryth lowered to only one, dipping his chin. "Kryst Eligor, you summoned me."

"I should not need to *summon*." The tone sharpened further. "A dog serves its master best by never leaving his side."

Wryth rankled at the aspersion, but he kept his head bowed. "What is the urgency, my lord?"

"I sense another *ta'wyn*."

Wryth lifted his gaze, his brow pinching. He had learned these bronze entities went by that ancient name—*ta'wyn*. "Another? Do you mean the one stolen from Guld'guhl?"

Just this past day, rumors had reached Highmount. Nyx and the others had been spotted in the Eastern Crown. Did Eligor's statement confirm that the bronze woman was still traveling with them?

"No!" Eligor boomed. "Someone closer. It tries to hide itself, but as my strength rises, I catch glimpses of its emanations. Whispers. Shadows. It approaches even now, fading in and out of view."

Shocked, Wryth stood up. "What comes? Is it an ally or an enemy?"

A long pause followed. The fire in those eyes smothered. The next words came as a whisper. "I do not know."

Wryth squinted, taking this new facet into account. He weighed how to turn it to his own advantage.

Eligor must have been calculating the same. "Still, whether ally or enemy, it matters not. The *ta'wyn* will do what I most desire. Something I cannot do on my own."

"Which is what?"

For the first time, the bronze arm lifted from the iron altar, bending at the elbow. Embryonic fingers formed a fist. The next words cast ice into Wryth's veins, as if this half-formed god could read his innermost thoughts.

"Break these chains that bind me."

11

Kanthe hurried with his small group down the torchlit tunnel. The cavernous passageway, as wide as it was tall, stretched a furlong in length, boring through the breadth of the Stormwall, the towering rampart that encircled the city proper.

Hundreds of citizens and scores of carts, drawn by oxen or mules, bustled within the tunnel, impeding their group's progress. The scent of dung, sweat, and piss ripened the air, trapped by the bulk of stone overhead.

Kanthe glanced upward with a wince—not at the weight pressing down upon him, but at what lay hidden up there. Long ago, the mountainous Stormwall had been burrowed through with armories and barracks, its outer face peppered with arrowslits. Untold numbers of armies had shattered against its ramparts.

And now we sneak through it like rats along a sewer.

Frell nudged Kanthe with an elbow. "Keep your face down."

Acknowledging this warning, Kanthe dropped his gaze and tugged his Delftan cap lower over his brow. He did not need someone recognizing him through his disguise.

"Almost out of here," Rami whispered, pointing toward the glow of daylight ahead.

This observation earned an exasperated scowl from Frell. The alchymist wagged a finger toward the medallion on Rami's chest, at the sewn lips of a Gjoan scribe, reminding the Klashean that he was supposed to be mute.

Rami's shoulders rose sheepishly.

Ahead of them, Tykhan led the group, striding alongside Llyra. The guildmaster rushed their group toward the tunnel's exit. Cassta kept to Tykhan's other side, maintaining her role as bodyguard.

Behind them, Jester and Mead followed. The two thieves muttered to each other, mostly complaints mixed with curses. Though barks of laughter burst out, too. The pair seemed unruffled by this risky endeavor.

"Looks like someone just paid their tunnel toll," Mead groused.

Kanthe looked over his shoulder. A coin purse rested in Mead's palm. Then with a flick of a wrist, the pilfered satchel vanished as if it were never there. Though Kanthe appreciated the thief's deft-fingered skill, their group did not need to draw the attention of a city's guardsman.

Jester noted Kanthe's attention and waved him onward. "Mind your own toes."

As if reinforcing this, the ground shook underfoot—first a tremble, then a hard shake. Shouts and cries echoed off the walls. The quake worsened into bucking jolts. A pair of oxen bawled in panic and trampled toward the exit, dragging a cart with them. Overhead, bricks cracked with thunderous claps. Dust billowed down.

"Follow the beasts," Tykhan warned, and hurried in the wake of the oxen.

Their group rushed toward the tunnel's end.

Stones fell and clattered around them.

Even with the path cleared by the battering cart, the shuddering and shaking underfoot turned their flight into a drunken rout. Then a massive quake threw Kanthe into the air. The others fared no better. Only Cassta and Tykhan kept their feet.

"Hurry," Tykhan bellowed as he scooped Llyra up.

The guildmaster shook off his help and waved them forward. "Keep going. Stay close."

With the ground still tremoring, they rushed toward the exit. A storm had blown in while they were crossing through the Stormwall. Rain pelted them as they made their way out.

Once in the open, Kanthe defied Frell's earlier admonishment and raised his face to the downpour, letting the cold rain temper his feverish skin. His feet slowed, and his heart lowered from his throat.

Then a blow struck him from behind. Hands grabbed him and lifted him to his toes.

"Don't stop, you fool!" Jester hissed in his ear.

Mead clutched Kanthe's other side as the thieves rushed him forward.

The reason for their alarm exploded with a deafening boom. A massive slab of the Stormwall's facade broke free and cleaved like an ax toward the tunnel mouth.

Kanthe found his feet and fled with the thieves. The others pounded with the rush of the crowd, a chaotic stream of panicked citizens and animals. When the wedge of ancient stone struck, it shattered like a bomb. Rocks and boulders flew and smashed all around them. A wagon got crushed into splinters. People screamed. Shards of granite knocked others down.

Dust choked through the rain, chasing them, plastering clothes and skin.

Kanthe coughed and spat until the air finally cleared. He stumbled onward, letting the rain wash over him.

Llyra pointed to the right, to a side street. "This way!"

They shambled in a daze after her.

Kanthe glanced back to the Stormwall. Through the pall, the tunnel mouth had vanished, obliterated by debris. He gaped at the sight. For millennia, the rampart had survived countless assaults and withstood them all. And while it still stood, it had taken great damage.

In all his years, he had never experienced a quake of such ferocity in Azantiia. As he turned around, he spotted Frell staring up at the likely reason. Overhead, the moon glowed through a break in the rain clouds.

As Kanthe followed his gaze, he strained to judge if that silvery face had grown any larger, but the clouds closed again, smothering the brightness.

"Time's bleeding out," Tykhan warned. "With every passing day, the moon's forces tug more savagely at this world."

"That's not the only urgency," Llyra reminded them, and got them moving at a faster clip. "I've secured a house. But we'll only stop long enough to grab what we need."

WITH ALARM BELLS still ringing across the beleaguered city, Kanthe headed with the others across a section of the city called the Midlins.

Most of Azantiia's wealth flowed through this area, spreading outward from the fly-bit butcheries near the Stormwall, through hostelries, dressmakers, and cobblers, to the silversmiths, jewelers, and bankers that hugged the edges of Highmount.

As they climbed higher into the city, it grew clear that these heights had escaped the worst of the quakes. Little looked damaged. Larger homes appeared on either side, adorned with flowering window boxes. Many villas kept tiny, perfumed gardens hidden behind walls or closed off by spiked gates. Even the rain seemed to fall more gently across the Midlins, dappling the leaves and petals, tapping against the marble facades. At these heights, the air—salted from a continuous blow off the bay—washed away the reek and filth of the Nethers.

Still, Kanthe recognized changes that had nothing to do with the quake. Several villas had their windows boarded over. One had been put to the torch, leaving a charred hulk. Smaller details revealed themselves, too: weeds strangling window boxes, gardens overgrown and unkempt.

Frell noted all of this, too. "It seems your brother's taxes are taking their toll."

Kanthe motioned to the burned-out home behind them. "Someone must've protested a bit too loudly."

The mood of the Midlins had certainly changed. The few people they passed kept their heads bowed, as if fearful of catching the wrong eye.

Ahead, a spate of laughter drew Kanthe's attention. The joy was like sunlight amidst all this gloom. An older woman, perhaps a governess from her simple garb, led a pair of handsomely dressed boys in hand. Unperturbed by the quake, or maybe excited by it, the youngsters chattered brightly and splashed through puddles.

Kanthe smiled at their antics, remembering a time when he and Mikaen had been just as joyful in each other's company. He pictured their feigned jousts, their endless games, their raucous flights through Highmount, even their daring escapades to steal honey pies from the kitchen.

Kanthe stared up toward the towering walls of Highmount.

How have we come to these straits?

One of the passing children trampled past their group, collided into Kanthe, then bounced away without a care or apology.

The governess drew her charge closer. "Sorry, sir."

"No harm done," Kanthe assured her, finding his smile again.

The woman nodded gratefully, but as she turned away, she looked sharply back with a wrinkled brow. Caught staring, she just as quickly swung around and hurried the boys at a faster clip.

Frell cursed at this and reached to Kanthe's chin. As he lowered his hand, he showed the smear of paint on his fingers. "The rain. It's starting to wear away your disguise."

Kanthe touched his face, then glanced toward the retreating trio. *Had there been a glint of recognition in the governess's eyes?*

Frell must have feared the same. "We must get off these streets."

Luckily, their destination lay only a few turns away.

Llyra led them to a dressmaker's shop, evident from the carved thimble on the shingle hanging above its door. No lights shone from the windows at the lower level, but up higher, lamps glowed through wispy curtains.

Llyra knocked a rhythm on the door that had to be a code. A moment later, the way opened. A pair of shadowy figures blocked the threshold. Kanthe noted the reflected flash off a sword.

Llyra waved their group inside. "Let's get you all ready."

Kanthe hesitated as the others entered. He stared back the way they had come, still worried about the governess, whether she had recognized the prince behind the paint.

Tykhan gathered Kanthe up and pushed him inside. His next words only served to stoke Kanthe's unease.

"Now comes the treacherous part of our journey."

12

FRELL CROSSED HIS arms and inspected Tykhan's body and face, both transformed again into a new configuration. The resculpting of his bronze form had been both disturbing and fascinating to watch, like a candle melting of its own volition.

Frell squinted as he circled the *ta'wyn*. He intended to make sure every detail looked correct. There could be no mistakes from here.

Without turning away, he pressed Llyra again. "And you're certain nothing in the abbot's features has changed since I left a year ago. No grown beard? No new scar or scab? No change to the style of his hair?"

"Nothing," Llyra confirmed. "That haughty bastard strikes me as a man who does not stray from the expected."

That was certainly true.

Frell had known Abbot Naff for two decades. For the entire length of Frell's study at Kepenhill, the abbot had served as the speaker of the Council of Eight, the four alchymists and four hieromonks who oversaw the school. From his lofty position, Naff had guided Kepenhill with a steady hand and an unyielding commitment to protocol, rules, and tradition. The only detail that changed in the man was the expanding circumference of his belly.

Frell circled Tykhan one last time and pointed to the ponderous midriff. "Naff's girth is a touch wider, I believe."

Llyra nodded. "When last I spied him, he looked more toadstool than man."

Tykhan rested a palm on his belly. "Alas, I can do no better. I only have so much bronze to work and shape."

Frell cocked his head. To achieve even this girth, Tykhan had shrunk a full head in height, which matched Naff's squat form. "It'll have to do. Hopefully, the looseness of your robe will disguise the difference."

Llyra had supplied them with hieromonk's white robes and crafted the crimson sash that marked Naff's position in the council. Tykhan had donned it and allowed Frell to make final adjustments.

Frell lifted the robe's hood and drew it atop Tykhan's head, which with paint and a wig looked remarkably like the abbot's. "As a precaution, keep the hood up. You look enough like Abbot Naff that none should question you, especially if we do our best to stick to the shadows."

"A recommendation that applies to all of us." Tykhan turned to a door that led into the neighboring room, where the others had been outfitted with guises of menials who often accompanied the abbot, a mix of scribes and servants.

Frell had another role to fill. He had changed out of his alchymist's black robes and donned the gray attire of a Shrive, one of the rarefied few who had achieved the Highcryst in both alchymy and religious scholarship. He had also been supplied with a wig, speckled with gray, and braids that tied under his chin. The final touches required a swath of black paint across his eyes.

His role was to play a visiting Shrive from Ironclasp, a cloistered school in the stone forest of Dödwood in the Guld'guhl territories. Tykhan, in his disguise as Abbot Naff, would act as the local guide for this newly arrived scholar.

Frell tugged at the leather cryst hung across his chest. A part of him chafed at this ruse. He had not earned the honor to wear such attire.

Maybe in some ways, I'm as trapped by tradition as Abbot Naff.

Llyra grunted her impatience. "Enough tinkering. We've wasted a full bell, far longer than we should've. The king and his forces will soon return to Highmount. Afterward, with his queen poisoned, they'll quickly lock everything down. We best be in and out before that happens."

Tykhan headed toward the door. "Let's hope this gambit proves fruitful. If the head of Eligor is truly hidden in the depths of the Shrivenkeep, we must discover *where* and *how* it's guarded. Only then can we determine a method to secure it."

"Getting those answers will be challenging," Frell said. "The Iflelen guard their secrets well."

"Fear not. I have ways to loosen a tongue."

Frell eyed Tykhan as he followed the *ta'wyn* out.

I pray you're right.

Their goal seemed simple enough: travel as deep into the Shrivenkeep as possible and reach the fringes of the Iflelen lair, where the sect of Shriven who worshipped Lord Ðreyk hid their most loathsome studies. The group intended to grab an Iflelen and, away from prying eyes, interrogate him. Depending upon what they learned, the group would then either retreat and plan a method to steal that bronze bust—or, if opportunity and circumstance afforded, nab it this night.

The latter seemed unlikely, but Frell had no wish to cross into that lair more than once. Still, the most critical element to this mission could prove the most difficult of all.

Our trespass must not be discovered.

If they triggered an alarm, they'd never have another opportunity to breach the Shrivenkeep. Knowing this, Frell studied the others as he and Tykhan joined them. Rami still wore the garb and medallion of a Gjoan scribe. Kanthe and Cassta wore the modest shifts, leather sandals, and demure headscarves of school servants. They carried with them flasks of wine and baskets of fare to satisfy any cravings of their charges.

Llyra, along with Jester and Mead, had changed into the blue-and-gold livery of Guld'guhlian guards. They would pose as escorts to the scholar from their lands. To complete this look—and to help in their efforts ahead—the trio carried short swords in scabbards at their hips.

"I have a wagon and horses waiting in the rear court," Llyra said. "It's a short ride to Kepenhill from here."

They followed the guildmaster down the stairs to the back of the dressmaker's shop. In short order, the group ducked through the drizzling rain and piled into the sealed wagon. With a crack of the drover's whip, they were off.

Frell took a seat by a window. As the wagon climbed a series of switchbacks, he got a view of the towering heights of Highmount. But his gaze settled on the school outside its walls. Kepenhill rose in nine massive tiers. Its topmost level flickered with twin pyres that were always lit, one representing the discipline of alchymy, the other the scholarship of gods and histories. The smoky glow shone through the veils of rain, beckoning him home.

Frell wondered if his private scholarium was as he had left it a year ago, full of books and lensed instruments to study the movement of the stars and moon. A melancholy longing ached through him. A part of him wished he'd never noted the growing face of the moon, a discovery that had warned him of the doom to come and set him on this dangerous path.

In this moment, he recognized a lesson he wished he had learned sooner.

Ignorance can be its own blessing.

Still, knowing he could not turn aside, he lowered his gaze from the school. Their goal this night would be found not among those nine tiers, but far beneath them. The Shrivenkeep lay buried under Kepenhill's foundations, delving as deep as the school rose high—possibly even deeper.

Frell swallowed hard.

He had only ventured down there a few times, to visit the Black Librarie of the Anathema, the great archive hidden in the Shrivenkeep. Among its stacks, he had recovered ancient records of the moon, accounts from other scholars that showed the slow and incremental changes to its silvery countenance.

And now I must delve deeper into the Shrivenkeep.

To where a secret was locked in bronze.

A secret perhaps as dangerous as moonfall itself.

13

DEEP UNDER THE foundation of Kepenhill's nine tiers, Kanthe stood inside a chamber carved from a massive vein of obsidian. The glassy walls and domed roof had been polished into large facets, reflecting their group a hundredfold. Sealed doors, twenty in number, led off into passageways that wormed throughout the school overhead, even into the neighboring castle of Highmount.

It seems all roads lead to this insidious cellar.

But only one door, carved of ebonwood, held Kanthe's attention.

He shivered at the sight of the emblem etched into its lintel: a book clutched in the fangs of a viper. The symbol warned of the poisonous knowledge found within the Shrivenkeep.

When he was a student here, rumors had abounded of this place: of arcane rituals, of chained monsters, of witchcraft and warlockry. Kepenhill's teachers had sought to allay such stories. They insisted the Shrivenkeep was merely a monastic hermitage of deep study and scholarly pursuits. It was here that the Shriven pursued dangerous inquiries, delving into cabalistic experiments, seeking paths beyond all boundaries of horizon and history. To ensure their secrecy, and for the safety of all, their labors had to be buried away. Even the school's alchymists and hieromonks rarely ventured down into its levels.

Kanthe appreciated that caution now. Whether any of the stories of the Shrivenkeep were true, he did not have any particular desire to find out.

But there's no retreating now . . .

Frell passed a surreptitious glance around the domed chamber. "We must not tarry," he warned. "With the earlier quake, most gazes look outward, but that won't last. Especially with Mikaen rushing back to Highmount."

So far, their party had made good progress, raising no suspicions. Luckily, Abbot Naff had been summoned to Highmount due to the queen's distress, to offer counsel and to bring in scholars fluent in poisons and venoms.

It left their path to these cellars unobstructed.

After arriving at the school in the wagon, their group had quickly made their way down. They kept to a tight knot. The few students and teachers who crossed their path cleared out of the way with bows and downturned gazes—not just due to the respect for the rotund form of Abbot Naff, but also out of a wariness at the sight of a Shrive passing among them. Such esteemed scholars—considered holy by many—rarely showed themselves, sticking to their subterranean keep or moving through passages and hidden doors known only to them.

From here, their group would need to be even more circumspect.

Tykhan eyed each team member, as if weighing their resolve. Finally, he drew forth a large key—one secured by Llyra—and stepped to the door. He quickly unlocked the way, exposing a torchlit tunnel beyond, and led them inside.

"Everyone keep close," the ta'wyn warned.

Frell followed, while Tykhan retrieved a glowing lantern from a hook on the wall. Rami headed in with Cassta and Llyra.

Kanthe balked at entering—until Jester and Mead all but shoved him across the threshold. He stumbled inside and stared down the throat of the passageway. He had never set foot in here and had hoped never to do so. Its halls were said to be shivered by screams, both from the throats of men and those of daemons.

Kanthe listened for those howls.

Rami looked equally discomfited. He whispered through his beard, "Does this warren hide any vile creatures . . . like the Venin who haunted the Abyssal Codex of the Dresh'ri?"

Cassta winced at his words.

Kanthe pictured the mutilated faces of the Venin, guardians of that buried archive. In his nightmares, he still heard their insidious bridle-song, a chorus strong enough to ensnare and bend victims to their will.

Frell overheard this worrisome query, but rather than scolding Rami for speaking, he tried to assure them—and maybe himself. "I've heard no such stories."

But Frell did not sound particularly sure on this matter. The alchymist had run afoul of the Venin, and from the sour set to his lips, he did not care to repeat that experience.

Tykhan held up his lantern and motioned Frell onward. "In the past, how deep have you traveled into this keep?"

"Only to its librarie. No further."

"Then get us that far. From there, we'll make inquiries and try not to rouse suspicions."

Tykhan set off with Frell, who guided them through a growing labyrinth of crisscrossing passageways, each tunnel more crooked than the next. They also traveled deeper, traversing narrow stairs worn at the edges by centuries of sandals.

Care had to be taken as they swept past gray-robed Shriven, who ducked out of their way, clutching dusty texts to their chests, likely forbidden tomes from the Black Librarie of the Anathema. Most barely gave them a glance. The few who acknowledged them did so with a nod to the abbot or a curious squint toward Frell in his Shriven attire.

Cassta watched the latest passerby retreat down the tunnel. A flick of her fingers and a black knife vanished into a wrist sheath. "So far, our disguises continue to hold."

But for how much longer?

As they continued, Kanthe's ears strained for any sound of alarm, but all he heard were muffled voices, disembodied by distance, echoing eerily as if from the throats of the dead. The smoky air also grew tainted, stinging his nostrils with the reek of bitter alchymies from the Shrivenkeep's countless laboratories or scholariums.

Worst of all, the flaming torches set into wall sconces grew ever scarcer. The darkness and dancing shadows set Kanthe's heart to pounding harder. It reminded him how far they had descended from the shine of the sun, of the endless glory of the Father Above.

Finally, Frell stopped at the mouth to yet another stairwell that spiraled down. He pointed to a side passageway. "The librarie lies that way."

Kanthe stared down the dark hall. The ghostly voices sounded more fervent in that direction. Many of the Shriven must be gathered at the archive, pursuing their dark studies.

Cassta stepped to the stairs. "The air rising from below smells of brimstan."

Kanthe shifted over and confirmed the same, noting the sulfurous stench.

"What do you think?" Tykhan asked Frell. "Do we continue down on our own or seek a willing guide from the librarie?"

Frell studied the winding stairwell. "Over my years at Kepenhill, I've heard how the Iflelen often reek of burning brimstan, the stench clinging to their robes. And Lord Ðreyk—their dark god—is said to travel the world through rivers of the same."

Llyra offered her own input. "Mind you, if we must make inquiries of these gray-robed brothers, best we do it when we're down as deep as we can manage on our own."

Jester added, "And far from prying eyes."

Rami supported this. "When it comes to trespassing, we should heed the wisdom of thieves."

While everyone looked worried, nods followed.

"Then it's decided." Tykhan mounted the steps and headed down. "We continue on our own."

14

By the time Kanthe reached the bottom of the steps, his eyes wept from the sulfurous burn in the air. His stomach churned queasily. His throat had tightened, as if trying to keep the stench out of his lungs.

The stairs finally emptied into a dark, serpentine tunnel. With no other direction open to them, the group followed along it.

Rami covered his mouth and nose with the drape of his scribe's robe. "We may suffocate before we ever find this damnable lair."

On Kanthe's other side, Cassta moved with an easy grace, unperturbed, as if strolling through a dark garden. The trio followed behind Tykhan, Frell, and Llyra, while Jester and Mead guarded their backs.

"Look here." Cassta pointed to an emerald vein that cut through the black stone. It glowed faintly with a venomous gleam. "What do you make of this?"

Frell dropped back, clearly drawn by the question. "The hill that Highmount sits upon is riddled with such veins. Many believe it to be a corruption that traces back to the Forsaken Ages, when the world sank into millennia of chaos."

Tykhan lifted a palm toward one of the shining seams, as if warming his hand before a hearth. "Despoiled ranium from ancient works. Tainted by alchymies lost to time. It still exudes a weak but poisonous spirit."

Frell waved them onward. "I've heard the Shriven consume a salted elixir derived from gynkin seeds to shield them from the debilitation found down here."

"What about us?" Kanthe asked.

Frell shrugged. "Best we not linger. Especially this deep."

Kanthe swallowed as he followed, keeping away from the walls.

The group continued in silence, coughing occasionally against the sulfurous reek. After a short trek, the source of the stench appeared. Ahead, a steep-sided ravine cut across the passageway, as if the subterranean god Nethyn had cleaved it with his obsidian blade. A narrow stone bridge spanned the steamy gap.

Warded off by the stifling heat and the wretched smell rising from below, their group slowed as they approached it.

"Look at the pillars flanking the bridge," Llyra noted.

Kanthe wiped his eyes free of stinging tears. Ahead, a pair of columns rose on either side of the span. They had been sculpted into towering snakes, reared high, with necks flared into cowls, their heads topped by thorny crowns.

A faint and steady hissing rose from them.

"What are they?" Rami whispered, plainly not as well-versed in the pantheon of Hálendiian gods.

Kanthe answered, *"Horn'd snaken.* Sigil of the dark lord, Ðreyk."

Tykhan drew them all closer. "Then this must mark the entrance to the Iflelen den."

No one doubted this.

"Keep going," Frell urged them.

The group mounted the bridge and headed across, moving more swiftly again.

Unable to stop himself, Kanthe peered over the edge. The hissing had come not from the sculpted snakes, but from the sulfurous steam rising from below. The chasm stank so heavily of brimstan that it choked his throat. Through weeping eyes, he spotted a baleful shine far below—the same sickly emerald of the glowing seams that ran through the black stones.

He shuddered, remembering Tykhan's warning, and rushed the last of the way across the bridge. He joined the others as they gathered under an archway that fronted a large tunnel. The stone above had been scribed with arcane symbols, all glowing that abhorrent green, as if the very veins of the rock had been bent to the will of the Iflelen.

"We must take even greater care from here," Frell warned them.

Kanthe balked at this threshold, as he had at the doorway into the Shrivenkeep, only this time Jester and Mead failed to push him forward.

In fact, no one moved.

Only concerned looks were exchanged.

Away from the hissing chasm, they all heard an echo of faint screams, agonizing and full of blood. A deep thudding reached them, too, felt through the soles of their feet, as if the black heart of Lord Ðreyk beat beneath them.

Tykhan finally shifted forward, taking one step, then another, into the tunnel. His next words, rather than encouraging, came out unsure, a rarity from the mouth of the Augury of Qazen. "Something is amiss . . ."

Rami followed with a cringe. "No need to tell us that."

Tykhan continued onward. Ahead, not a single torch lit the way. The *ta'wyn* led with his lantern raised high, trying to push back the darkness.

No one spoke, stifled by the threat. Especially as the distant screaming abruptly cut off. The silence unnerved Kanthe, accentuating the drumming underfoot. The tremoring shook up his leg bones, rattling through his body.

It sent a clear message to his heart.
We should not be here.

As ANOTHER CLANG of a bell chimed the passage of time, Kanthe and the others continued ever deeper. By now, iron doors appeared to either side, closing off rooms or the entrances to other passageways. One door had been welded shut by bars across it, as if whatever lurked inside must never be released into the world.

Rami finally whispered what they all must have been wondering. "Where is everyone?"

As if summoned by his question, a door opened ahead of them, its hinges grating and loud. Lights flared into the passageway, illuminating two shapes who stepped into the hall. One stood taller than the other. The pair froze, apparently startled to find a lamplit group only paces away.

The taller of the two, bony-limbed and gaunt, wore the gray robe of a Shrive. Only this one's hair had not grown long enough to braid under his chin. Kanthe guessed he was an acolyte, someone new to the Iflelen order. He held a pale girl by the hand, a child of six or seven. She stood naked, with strange scrawls inked across her thin chest.

Kanthe remembered rumors from his time at Kepenhill. Whispers of secret passages, hidden doors, and students whisked off to bloody sacrifices.

Frell stepped forward, revealing the length of his gray robe. "I am Shrive Greysh," he extolled haughtily. "Newly arrived from Ironclasp. I come with Abbot Naff to seek the counsel of the Iflelen."

The acolyte remained silent, as if unsure how to respond. Then without a word, he turned and fled away, abandoning the child, who continued to stand in a dazed manner.

Rami stepped forward to give chase, drawing Kanthe with him.

But there was no need.

Ahead of them, the acolyte's panicked flight ended abruptly—with the tinkle of a single bell.

The young Shrive's body swung around to face them again. Behind him, Cassta stood at his shoulder, clutching a fistful of robe.

Kanthe glanced to his side, where Cassta had stood a moment ago, as if expecting to find her still standing there.

How had she moved so quickly, without drawing an eye?

His respect for her Rhysian training spiked higher, along with a trickle of fear. He swallowed down his shock.

Cassta pushed the acolyte toward them, resting the tip of a dagger under his chin. "A *quisl*," she whispered in her captive's ear.

She plainly trusted that this scholar—even one so new to his robe—would recognize the name for the poisoned blade often employed by Rhysian assassins.

From the hike to the man's chin, he did indeed.

As Cassta drove her charge back to the group, Llyra checked on the child. The girl remained in a stupor, with eyes glazed over and limbs leaden. Likely either spyllcast or drugged.

Llyra scowled at the young Shrive. "What foulness had you planned for this girl?"

The man seemed reluctant to talk, but Cassta dug her blade and freed his tongue.

"To . . . To be a bloodbaerne . . ." he finally gasped out, now on the tips of his toes to keep clear of the dagger.

Kanthe did not know what this meant, but Frell stumbled back a step. His face went pale, visible even through his painted features. Llyra scooped the child up, looking equally aghast.

"Such black alchymies are long forbidden," Frell stated, biting off each word. Fury returned to flush his cheeks. "What is your name?"

"Ph . . . Phenic," the man stammered. "Acolyte to Shrive Wryth."

Frell cast a glance toward Kanthe, then back to their captive. "If you wish to live, you'll tell us what you know of an ancient artifact, the bust of a man done in bronze."

Phenic's eyes darted around in a panic, showing plenty of white, but also recognition. "It is *you*. He . . . He said you would come. But we did not know when. You remain wispy shadows to him."

"Who are you talking about?" Frell asked. "Your master? Wryth?"

Kanthe cringed at that name, fearing they had walked into a trap set by that Iflelen fiend.

"From bronze lips," Phenic continued, his tone now exultant, "he foretold your arrival."

Frell frowned. "What do you mean by—"

Tykhan groaned behind them, drawing everyone's attention. His lantern fell from his fingers and crashed to the floor. The glass shattered, but the flame held.

"No . . ." the *ta'wyn* moaned, retreating a step, then another. "He wakes . . ."

Kanthe followed. "Tykhan?"

The *ta'wyn* stopped, shivering in place. He looked frozen, yet he clearly strained against it. His lips forced out words. "He . . . has hold of me."

Confusion spread through the group.

"What's happening?" Cassta called over.

Rami grabbed Tykhan's arm, still half raised, as if in defense. It would not budge. "Something has him trapped."

Kanthe joined Rami and added his strength, trying to unroot the statue.

"Do we flee?" Rami asked. "Try to carry him with us?"

Kanthe knew that was impossible. They did not have enough hands to haul that weight of bronze. To make matters worse, bells suddenly clanged deeper down the dark tunnel.

"We've been discovered," Frell warned. "We can't stay here."

"And leave Tykhan behind?" Kanthe scoffed. "To hand him to the Iflelen? Are you mad? He's our only means to communicate with Nyx and the others."

"No matter." Frell pointed a finger at Kanthe. "You must not be captured, not with your brother returning home."

Kanthe kept hold of Tykhan's arm. Through that grip, he felt the trembling war being waged within. "He's still fighting."

Down the passageway, shouts—angry and determined—joined the klaxon of bells.

"We must flee," Frell demanded. "Better Tykhan be captured than all of us."

Kanthe recognized this, but he remained at Tykhan's side. He had come to consider the *ta'wyn* not only an invaluable resource, but also a friend, a loyal ally who deserved their support.

Though Tykhan could not turn his head, his gaze shifted to Kanthe. From the fury shining there, the *ta'wyn* agreed with Frell. Lips parted with exaggerated effort. "Go . . ."

Rami drew alongside Kanthe. "We must."

Kanthe refused, even as torchlight flared down the tunnel. "Tykhan, you've walked the Urth for millennia. Longer than any *ta'wyn*. There must be a way to melt yourself free."

Tykhan tremored, still trapped in place by an unknown force, but the panicked defeat in his eyes dimmed. His gaze appeared to turn inward.

"Think . . ." Kanthe urged him.

Tykhan's body shook. Kanthe tried to tighten his grip on the *ta'wyn*, but the bronze turned soft. His fingers sank into the warmed metal. Disturbed by this strangeness, Kanthe let go and drew back.

Rami pulled him another step away. "What is he doing?"

Kanthe had no answer.

Slowly, Tykhan's efforts melted free one arm. Even this must have taken all his strength. The azure glow of his eyes flared, bursting around the lenses that covered his crystal orbs. His features ran under the strain, streaming through the paint.

"Keep fighting," Kanthe urged him.

Tykhan lowered his molten arm, his fingers now melded together. Still, he managed to rip open his robe. His palm lowered to his navel. With a loud groan and another burst of fire from his eyes, he lifted his hand away.

As he did, a glowing cube melted into view, flowing through his bronze.

Rami gasped at the sight of the crystalline object, veined in copper and pulsing with a golden mass at its core. "What is that?"

Kanthe recognized it. A year ago, Shiya had recovered a similar cube from a *ta'wyn* archive beneath the Shrouds of Dalalæða. Once seated inside her, it had served as a boundless forge that fueled her. Prior to that, she'd had to bask her bronze skin in the fiery heat of the sun to sustain herself.

Tykhan tossed the cube to the floor, then stumbled back, weak and unsteady. It was as if the pulsing box had been the anchor holding him trapped. Still, his body continued to roil, as if trying to right itself, like a ship broken loose during a storm.

Rami retreated from the glowing object, as did Cassta, as if both feared it was a bomb.

Tykhan gasped out a warning, adding to this fear. "Destroy it . . ."

No one moved, still too shocked, too unsure how to accomplish this task.

Another proved not to be so leery.

Phenic used this moment of confusion to wrest free of Cassta's grip and knock her aside. He lunged forward, snatched the glowing cube from the floor, then leaped away. He fled toward the ringing bells, the shouts, the pounding boots.

By now, robed figures carrying torches appeared down the passageway.

Phenic raced toward them, but he had not escaped unscathed. He held a hand pressed to his neck as he fled. Blood flowed through his fingers. The *quisl* had bitten deep.

Cassta set off after him, but Phenic reached the torchlight.

"Stop!" Rami warned her. "It's too late."

This proved true for Phenic, too. His panicked flight turned into a drunken stumble. Unbalanced, he struck the wall and rebounded toward his brethren. In a handful of steps, driven more by momentum than muscle, he fell dead into the clutches of the Iflelen in the lead.

Kanthe recognized the grim countenance of Wryth, now adorned with an eye patch. Their gazes momentarily met across the distance. The bastard's face shone with both anger and satisfaction, especially as he lifted that golden cube from his dead acolyte's grip.

Then hands grabbed Kanthe and tore him around, pushing him toward the exit. Rami kept hold of his upper arm. "We must run!"

With no other choice, knowing a noose or worse awaited him if caught, Kanthe fled with the others. Tykhan kept pace, at first faltering, then more surefooted as he gathered the residual energy available to him. But there was no telling when those reserves would bottom out, turning Tykhan into a bronze sculpture again.

They needed to reach sunlight.

They hit the bridge, pounded across it, and passed between the two carved snakes. A glance behind showed their pursuit had ebbed. Torches glowed on the far side of the bridge, but they approached no farther.

Fearing that might change, they did not slow. They followed the tunnel, returned to the stairs, and clambered up toward the main keep.

Rami huffed heavily, staring behind him. "Why . . . Why have they given up the chase?"

"They must have secured what they wanted." Frell's brow crinkled with concern. He stared toward Tykhan, looking for an explanation.

The *ta'wyn* remained sullen and silent.

At the top of the stairs, the group resecured their hoods and robes, doing their best to resume their roles. But Tykhan remained too weak to melt his bronze into the rotund form of Abbot Naff. All he could manage was a weak approximation. To help hide his crude features, he drew the robe's cowl over his head, shadowing his brow and keeping his gaze bowed down.

Still, it proved enough.

The group escaped the Shrivenkeep and soon headed through the school, which thankfully appeared empty. The reason became clear as they exited into Kepenhill's stable yard, where their wagon still waited.

Students, alchymists, and hieromonks lined balconies and crowded the tiers. Faces stared upward. High above Highmount, a trio of armored wynd-ships blazed in the sky, framed by the fire of their overheated forges. They circled and lowered toward the royal mooring field within the castle walls.

Frell shoved Kanthe into the wagon. "It seems your brother has returned."

Llyra followed them. She still carried the girl they had recovered, wrapped in the blue-and-gold cloak of the guildmaster's disguise. "From the gathering out there, word of the queen's poisoning must've spread, too."

Once the group had piled inside, the drover got the wagon moving.

As the carriage rocked and jolted, Frell never took his eyes off Tykhan. "What happened back there?"

Tykhan remained grim, but he finally spoke. "Among the orders of *ta'wyn*, I'm a Root. Shiya is an Axis. We each have our own talents. But above all stand the Krysts. They have the ability to bend a *ta'wyn* to their will. They can emanate a force that enslaves both Root and Axis."

Kanthe remembered how the Venin had been able to combine their bridle-song into a chorus that broke the will of men. The Krysts must share a talent like that, an ability to control another *ta'wyn* by commandeering a victim's gold-pulsing forge. By shedding his cube, Tykhan must have wrested himself free.

But at what cost?

This seemed to worry Tykhan, too. "I never suspected Eligor could have woken already. Not in his decapitated state. Especially to stir forth with such strength."

Frell nodded to the girl clutched by Llyra. "Wryth and his ilk must be using bloodbaernes to somehow fuel their efforts."

Tykhan rested a palm on his belly, where the cube had melted out of him. "With what was stolen from me, bloodbaernes will no longer be necessary. Eligor can now set himself free."

"What does that mean for us?" Kanthe pressed him.

Tykhan fixed Kanthe with his glowing gaze, dimmer now but with a glimmer of gratitude. "He surely wanted *all* of me, not just the *schysm* I carried. If he had secured my body, too, he could have scavenged its resources. His rebirth would have been shortened to weeks, if not days."

Rami patted Kanthe's knee. "It seems your steadfast devotion saved us all."

"And it is appreciated," Tykhan said. "I would not have attempted such an effort without your encouragement. But know this, such an act has only bought an extra measure of time. Nothing more."

"Then what?" Frell asked. "If the Iflelen have that cube—your *schysm*—what does it portend?"

Tykhan lowered his gaze. When he answered, it came with the finality of a prophecy. "It means we've lost already."

A stunned silence followed.

"That can't be," Kanthe muttered.

Tykhan lifted his face, displaying his conviction. "It took a vast *ta'wyn* army to defeat Eligor before. An army we don't have and can never raise."

Kanthe's heart sank at these words. He pictured the others who were striving to reach the *turubya* in the Barrens. He sat straighter, refusing to accept this judgement, especially knowing who was out there.

"You've never met Nyx," Kanthe argued. "While she lives, there is hope."

Tykhan looked sadly upon them all. "I've read all paths forward. Every weft and weave. With Eligor risen to full power, doom is inevitable."

Those glowing eyes firmed with certainty.

"Even for her."

15

WRYTH'S HEAD POUNDED, the pain heightened by the ringing of the last bell of the day. He sat in his private scholarium, where a lone incense burner curled redolent smoke, striving to push back the persistent reek of sulfurous brimstan that pervaded these depths of the Shrivenkeep.

Around him, shelves lined the four walls, filled with cryptic texts, some indecipherable, waiting for their secrets to be unlocked. Interspersed among them, tall cabinets held drawers pocketed with ancient bones, unidentifiable crystals, dried specimens from across the Urth, and petrified images of the past trapped in stone. Elsewhere, artifacts collected over decades filled empty niches. Some were so strange that they defied understanding.

But none more so than what rested on his desk.

Wryth stared at the crystal cube, veined through with copper. He cocked his head to study its core, where a golden fluid pulsed and undulated in a mesmerizing fashion. He had positioned a large lens to magnify its mysteries. He had sketched its every surface into his journal.

Another book lay open next to it. It was one written not by his own hand, but by an alchymical genius who died out in the Frozen Wastes. Skerren il Reesh—an ancient Shrive and Iflelen colleague—had meticulously drawn a similar object, accompanied by voluminous notes, scribblings, and conjectures. He had obtained the glowing artifact while excavating the blasted ruins of a copper egg from which the stolen *ta'wyn* woman had been birthed.

Skerren had speculated the cube functioned like a tiny flashburn forge, but one of limitless power. With it, Skerren had engineered a listening device capable of detecting emanations from the stolen bronze woman over a great distance. They had used it to track her, but during a fierce battle, both Skerren and the artifact had been lost.

Now, here is the same strangeness once again.

He hated to part with it, but he knew who demanded it. After Kryst Eligor had ensnared the other *ta'wyn*—whose existence still enthralled Wryth—their gestating bronze god had fallen into a deep slumber. The effort had clearly sapped his strength, burning out another bloodbaerne in the process.

Wryth used the spare time to study what had been ripped from the other, delivered into his hands by Phenic before he died. In the dark passageway, Wryth had caught a glimpse of the other trespassers, which included Prince

Kanthe. For the invaders to travel so deeply, to risk coming down here, they must have some hint of what the Iflelen possessed.

Wryth had already alerted Highmount about the return of the traitorous prince, leaving it to King Mikaen and his legions to address. Afterward, Wryth had given it no further attention, though he was still mystified as to the origin of this new *ta'wyn*.

Still, at the moment, he had a far more important task to attend.

He stared between his sketch and Skerren's. He had noted subtle distinctions between the two. The copper veining of each mapped out a different pattern. Also, Wryth's cube had slightly rounder corners. But most striking of all was the disparity in sizes.

Wryth again lifted a measuring stick and used his lens to recheck those dimensions. He frowned, comparing his result to the crisp notations in Skerren's journal. They did not match, and knowing his dead colleague's exacting nature, Wryth did not doubt Skerren's accuracy. The conclusion was clear.

This artifact is smaller than the one obtained before.

Before he could ponder it further, a sharp rapping drew his attention to the door. "What is it?" he called over harshly.

"Shrive Wryth, we need you. Right away!"

Wryth recognized the urgency in the Iflelen's voice. He stood with a groan, crossed to the door, and unlatched it.

At the threshold, Bkarrin shifted nervously, as if about to bolt. His gaze darted into the room and away again. "Kryst Eligor has awoken. He rages wildly, demanding you bring the artifact to him. I fear in his furious throes he could do significant damage to the great instrument that sustains him."

Wryth took a deep breath, wishing he had more time to study the crystal cube, but he dared not refuse this bronze god. He turned and collected the artifact from his table and waved Bkarrin ahead.

"Let's see what other miracles this stolen treasure can perform."

WRYTH STOOD WITH the six Iflelen whom he had handpicked to oversee the restoration of Kryst Eligor. The group ringed the iron altar of their new god, but they kept a wary distance. Around them, the burbling, ticking, and wheezing of the order's great instrument had taken on a more furious timbre, reflecting the temper of the creature at its heart.

Eligor's arm—the only one capable of movement—beckoned Wryth. Azure eyes fixed to him, to the object that Wryth carried on a silver tray. The blaze in that lustful gaze grew into two blinding suns.

"Bring me the *schysm*," Eligor demanded.

Reflecting that raw desire, the entire instrument vibrated with anticipation. The nearby tanks, glowing with the lifeforce of the bloodbaernes, boiled and bubbled.

Bkarrin had not understated the danger.

Still, Wryth hesitated and stared down at his tray. In this one moment, he had already learned a new detail: the name of this artifact. In the *ta'wyn* tongue, it was called a *schysm*.

Wryth also did not doubt its purpose. He had witnessed the cube being ripped loose from the belly of the other *ta'wyn*, who seemed to abandon it in an effort to break free from Eligor's commanding control.

Wryth also recalled Skerren's assessment of the artifact, how his colleague theorized the *schysm* acted as a flashburn forge of near-infinite power.

Wryth lifted his gaze to Eligor.

The cube must fuel these ta'wyn—*far better than our feeble instrument and its bloodbaernes.*

As he stared over to the altar, he remembered Eligor's last words to him, what the bronze god hoped to gain.

Break these chains that bind me.

Eligor's gaze narrowed upon Wryth, squeezing that azure blaze to a blinding urgency. "Do as I say. Grant me what I've delivered to you. And you will partake of knowledge beyond your ken, beyond anything you could imagine. This I promise."

Those words drew Wryth closer, quashing his misgivings. It was everything he had dreamed of for decades. Yet he moved slowly, a part of him still fearful of unleashing this being into the world.

With Eligor bound to the instrument, Wryth had a measure of control. He hated to sever those reins. Even now, his mind struggled for ways to achieve the same, but by the time his legs drew him to the iron altar, he had failed to come up with a resolution.

Before him, azure eyes stabbed angrily, demanding he act.

Behind him, his fellow Iflelen murmured, their tone a reverent mix of awe and fear. Wryth knew if he refused this order that he would risk his standing among the Iflelen. The bronze bust had been the truest heart of the order for millennia, the mystery upon which it had been built. To stumble at this last step would surely bring great wrath upon him.

Still, none of this—not the demand in those eyes, not the murmuring urgency of his brethren—motivated Wryth to lift the *schysm* off its tray. What drove him to obey was far simpler, a desire that had fired his ambition throughout his life.

Raw curiosity.

At heart, Wryth remained a scholar. Mistake or not, he wanted to witness whatever transpired next, to see for himself the result of this action, to be the force behind it.

How could I not?

Wryth lifted the cube over the gaping chasm of the bronze chest. Within, the encrusting crystals glowed hungrily. Energies leaped and danced across the hollow space in glowing spasms and sparkling coruscations of power, all fed by the great instrument surrounding them.

As he lowered the *schysm,* sparks snapped up to the cube. Fiery arcs followed, striking like lightning. Energy danced and scintillated across its surface.

Wryth gasped—not in pain, but awe.

Despite this, his hands hesitated, hovering the artifact over that glowing chasm. Something deep inside him rose up in warning. The small hairs over his skin pebbled up with terror. His breath choked with certainty.

I must not do this.

Then any choice was stripped from him.

Before he could withdraw his hands, bronze and glassine tendrils shot up from the depths of the open chest. They tangled over the cube's surface, fusing to the copper veins, snaking over the crystal.

Horrified, Wryth let go.

The golden glow within the *schysm* burst into a bright sun, one strangled by those tendrils. In another breath, more swarmed over it, finally smothering and eclipsing the sun. As it did, the cube was drawn into the depths and vanished away.

Wryth stumbled back—and not a moment too soon.

The bronze body convulsed, arching off its back. A blinding brilliance burst forth from the chest, from those eyes, from a mouth torn open by a silent scream. The tanks behind the altar shattered. Glass exploded with a wash of steaming amber fluid.

Wryth ducked and shielded his one good eye, remembering another cascade of broken shards that had stolen his other one. He stumbled away, colliding into Bkarrin.

"What's happening?" the younger Shrive wailed.

"Backlash . . ." Wryth hissed out, staying low.

The entire chamber quaked underfoot. The great instrument rattled. Energies spat down its pipes. Jagged bolts leaped throughout, striking with crackling booms. Copper ripped apart. Crystal shattered. Fluids sprayed high.

Wryth pictured the *schysm*'s power flooding throughout the instrument, overwhelming it—then that surge reached the end.

Bloodbaerne beds jolted high.

Bodies exploded in bursts of blood and flying gobbets of flesh.

As those beds crashed back to the stone floor, the wild energies subsided, fading into irritable spasms and prickly arcs. Then even those died away.

Wryth straightened and gaped at the ruins of the great instrument. It continued to fall apart with coppery bangs and tinkling glass. The other Iflelen picked themselves up off the floor; a couple stayed on their knees. They all shared expressions of dismay and horror.

Wryth ignored them and turned to the source of it all.

Like the great instrument, the bronze figure had settled. His body had gone slack on the altar. While his chest and eyes still blazed, the fire within also dimmed.

Wryth noted Eligor's lips moving.

He shoved near enough to hear faint words.

"I see her . . ."

Wryth leaned closer. "Who?"

"The *Vyk dyre Rha* . . ."

Wryth stiffened at the name of the Shadow Queen. He wanted to know more, but the fiery glow in Eligor continued to fade. Wryth sensed it wasn't dissipating, but drawing within, gathering the remaining strength after discharging so explosively. He suspected it would take time for the body to recuperate after shattering those chains.

Wryth glanced to the ruins of the great instrument.

To the side, the glowing died across the iron altar. Still, a faint whisper sighed out of those bronze lips.

"The *Vyk dyre Rha* . . ."

The last words came with a dreadful firmness.

"She flies toward her own destruction."

THREE

WHISPERS OF
THE DEAD

Whilst histori can be record'd by ink on parchment, to truli know the past, I embold'n one to ræde the scatter of bones leff behind by the ancients, those grave markers to a lost age. I beseech ye to wandr the Necropolises of Seekh, to walk amongst the wonders pummel'd under the grind-stone of time. Onli by breathing that dust, can ye hope to understand the most importante lesson of alle:
    That one day we alle retourne to the sand.

        —Prologue to *A Testament to a Forgotten Age,*
            by Malton hy Dent, a hieromonk
           who vanished into the White Desert

16

FROM ATOP BASHALIIA, Nyx watched the *Fyredragon* descend toward a spread of sandy ruins at the westernmost edge of the Eastern Crown. It had taken their ship four days to reach this border.

As Nyx swept high, she gaped at the vast expanse of the ruins below. The crumbling structures stretched a hundred leagues to the north and south and half that again to the west. They formed a shattered maze that framed where the glistening White Desert ended at the towering cliffs of the Tablelands.

Back at school, she had read about the Necropolises of Seekh, but words on a page failed to capture the breadth of these ancient ruins. She had never imagined she would set eyes upon this haunted relic from the Forsaken Ages.

Some sections had tumbled into the sand long ago, falling off those rocky escarpments into the desert, where shifting dunes sought to bury them. The rest sat both atop and *within* those cliff faces, turning the edges of the Tablelands into a treacherous labyrinth of cavernous ruins that burrowed deep into the rock. Across the top, sections of the necropolises poked higher, protruding out of the depths. But centuries of blowing sand had scoured it all to a macabre smoothness, making those sections look like the weathered bones of a half-buried god.

Even now, scavengers continued to pick at those bones.

From her saddle, Nyx spotted a scatter of ramshackle villages, both in the desert and atop the heights. She spied hundreds of small figures scurrying about, decked in white to reflect the sun's heat. Larger armored shapes—massive black sandcrabs—labored and scrabbled throughout. Elsewhere, smoke rose in curls, marking deeper mineworks hidden in the ruins.

Over untold centuries, the Necropolises of Seekh were slowly being stripped of their resources: ores and metals, bricks kilned by ancient ovens, glass said to be as hard as steel, but the most desirous of all were the arcane artifacts from the Forsaken Ages, objects that could fetch a fortune. Despite the treacherous risk of such foraging, the ruins drew treasure hunters from across the Crown, along with alchymists and hieromonks who wished to unlock the mysteries of the past.

Nyx swung a final pass over the necropolises, then followed the *Fyredragon* as it descended toward one of the villages burrowed into the ruins atop the Tablelands.

With tension knotting between her shoulders, she glanced behind her. The sun reflected off the crystalline surface of the White Desert, setting the sand on fire. To spare her eyes, she wore goggles secured in Spindryft. Their amber lenses blunted the glare, but only enough to save the shine from blinding her.

Ignoring the sands below, she searched the skies.

The sun shone higher than she had ever seen it. Its heat already sweltered, but Nyx found some relief at these heights, where cooler air flowed in a continual current from the Crown. Even higher up, a hotter river returned from the furnace of the Barrens. It was those two streams—forever flowing in two directions—that blessed the lands of the Crown with a livable clime. Hieromonks believed it was due to the twin gods, the fiery Hadyss and the icy giant Madyss, who blew those rivers across the skies, while alchymists insisted it was due to some natural bellows created between the two extremes of the Urth.

She didn't know which to believe. All she knew was that the *Fyredragon* intended to ride that cooler river for as long as possible. But such relief—as little as it was—would be short-lived. The scorch of the Barrens would eventually burn all away, leaving only a lung-searing heat.

It was this fear that drove the *Fyredragon* toward the village. They needed to discover all they could about the terrain ahead, especially as the *ta'wyn* coolers remained stubbornly inoperable.

Jace and Krysh also wanted to confirm the details of the map secured from the librarie in Bhestya, and perhaps to expand upon it. Besides being a site of excavation and study, the Necropolises of Seekh served as a way station for nomads of the Barrens, ancient tribesmen who made a hardscrabble living in that harsh land. Surely such folk had greater knowledge of what lay ahead, information that could prove vital.

Still, the stop here would have to be brief.

Though *how* brief remained unknown.

Nyx continued to scan the horizon behind her, searching for that answer. *Where are you?*

Her fear escaped in a trickle of bridle-song, a whispery twinge of anxiety. It reached Bashaliia, causing him to swing yet another circle above the *Fyredragon*. Earlier, Nyx had taken flight from the ship, to stretch her brother's wings but also to search for any sign of Daal's return.

At the first dawn bell, Daal and his raash'ke team had piled out the rear of the *Fyredragon*. While the massive wyndship had forged westward, he and the others had hung back in its wake. They were to scout for any evidence of pursuit. After the attack by the kezmek, they dared not be caught off guard again. No one knew if Fenn's traitorous uncle would continue his hunt—or worse yet, if he had succeeded in convincing the Bhestyan king to join forces with Hálendii.

Nyx squinted against the reflected glare.

She pictured Daal crouched low in his saddle, whisking over the dunes. She tried to sense that wellspring inside him. Bridle-song escaped the clutch of her throat, giving substance to that desire, a prayer from her heart.

Return to me.

As if drawn by this summons, a black mote appeared in the distance. Nyx squeezed her eyes, trying to discern mirage from substance. She whistled for Bashaliia to head toward it.

Her brother dove to catch air, then shot higher, sweeping faster.

Moments later, the dot grew into a frantic flutter of wings. They beat wildly and sped across the desert. It became clear this was not a lone raash'ke struggling for home, but something far smaller.

The black arrow formed the outline of a skrycrow, whose passage could outpace any bat—Mýr or raash'ke. While it could be any messenger sent aloft, Nyx knew this was not so.

She winced with trepidation.

The crow sped toward her, already angling toward the retreating wyndship.

Daal's crew had been sent off with a caged bird, a way of casting forth a warning if danger approached. The skrycrow dove and passed under Bashaliia, ignoring those massive wings, focused on its duty.

Nyx stared back along its trail, searching for any other wings racing home.

The skies remained achingly bright and clear.

Apprehension grew with every beat of her heart.

Where are you all? What is happening out there?

She ached to head there on her own, to discover those answers. Bashaliia responded to this unspoken desire and dug his wings, scooping air, sailing eastward. But Nyx reined him in with golden strands of bridle-song. She swung her brother and headed toward the *Fyredragon,* chasing after the skrycrow.

She recognized a hard truth, one she chafed against but accepted.

If the others are in danger, I can never reach them in time.

To learn what that threat might be, she sped after the crow.

Still, she repeated a prayer, casting it eastward to Daal.

Return to me.

17

DAAL SAT TALL in his saddle, balancing on his knees atop Pyllar, as his mount glided a smooth path through the air.

From his perch, Daal clutched a farscope in hand, extended to its farthest reach. Through its lenses, he spied upon the trio of wyndships sailing toward them. The fires of their forges blazed against the blue skies. He focused upon the two largest vessels, clearly warships from the battery of cannons stationed across their decks, set amidst rows of ballistas armed with huge arrows. To Daal, the latter looked like the harpoons used by hunters at the Crèche.

He had already confirmed that one ship waved a green flag bearing a crest of a rearing crimson beast with daggered claws and a fanged mouth. It was the sigil of the Kingdom of Bhestya, representing a monstrous panther, the symbolic defender of its shores and forest.

Fenn had warned him to watch for that flag.

What of the other ships?

He swung his scope. The angle and the breeze kept him from confirming the second warship hailed from the same land. Before he could learn more, a massive shadow swept across his view.

He cursed and lowered his farscope. Tamryn angled back around, tilting Heffik up on a wing. The Panthean rider drew abreast of Daal.

She called over to him. "Why do we tarry? It will take most of the day to return to the others."

Even with her shouting, Daal heard the disdain in her admonishment. He bristled against it. "To return with only a warning is not enough," he bellowed back. "It's just yelling into the wind. We must discern the true extent of this threat."

She scowled at him from beneath her goggles.

He ignored her and cast his gaze toward the team's other three mounts: two bucks and another doe. They spun a slow circle under them. The riders stared up, waiting for orders. He recognized their exhaustion and sun-weariness, both in their expressions and in the flared nostrils of the raash'ke as the beasts sought to shed the heat.

He let out a long breath, recognizing that Tamryn's concern was not unwarranted. She irritated him, like the crust of sand at the edges of his lips and goggles, but he knew he should heed her in this regard. There was a reason he had chosen her as second saddle.

She is arrogant, but not to the point of blindness.

He stared westward toward the distant line that marked the cliffs of the Tablelands. It stretched twenty leagues away, which made for a long flight to reach the *Fyredragon*.

He nodded and fixed his gaze on Tamryn. "Lead them back!"

He reinforced this by signaling those below. He raised his free hand, formed a fist with his thumb and smallest finger extended. He swung his arm to the west, his message easy to interpret.

Fly home.

Tamryn frowned in puzzlement. "If I'm to lead," she shouted, "what of you?"

Daal swung to face the enemy, still three leagues off. The wyndships had barely entered the White Desert, having sailed out of the mists that covered the sultry jungle of Wyldweald.

"I'm going to get closer," he answered, and pointed his farscope. "Try to assess what manner of danger they pose. We need as much knowledge as possible if we're forced to confront them."

Tamryn shook her head. "I'll go with you. Barrat can take the others west."

"No. One set of wings will be easier to miss. Any more risks discovery."

Tamryn stared at him, with Heffik teetering under her as if the doe were silently expressing her rider's waffling.

Daal didn't know if this hesitation was born of concern for his safety or irritation that she wouldn't share in any glory gained by spying upon the enemy.

Finally, Tamryn huffed, tilted Heffik, and dove to the waiting crew. Signals spread among them, faces glanced up at him, then Tamryn led them away.

Daal watched the four depart for several breaths, then returned his attention eastward. The trio of vessels continued their blazing flight across the blue skies.

What are we about to face?

Daal shifted his weight forward, guiding Pyllar into a low glide. He aimed for the ridges of rolling dunes, interspersed with the blinding glare of salt flats. He intended to use the latter to help blind his approach, to hide in the reflected glare.

As he descended, the air grew hotter. It seemed the desert reflected the sun's heat as much as its shine. He reached a hand forward and rubbed his fingers through the ruff that ridged Pyllar's neck.

Thank you, my friend, for taking on this burden.

Under his palm, he felt the thunder of his mount's heart, along with the rumble of contentment, acknowledging Daal's words. Daal lowered closer, letting the wind ride over him. His lids closed against the glare below, allowing his eyes rest. For a moment, the darkness shimmered away, replaced with a sweeping sight of the passing landscape below. He shook his head and the view vanished, like the mirages that haunted these sands.

Daal sat straighter. Over the past half year, he had experienced such glimpses before, but only in flashes, brief and fleeting. It was as if he were seeing through Pyllar's eyes. As infrequent as they were, he had wanted to dismiss them as fantasies, but lately they had been occurring more often.

"Pyllar . . ." he whispered.

The bat's ears pricked at his name, forming wide bells. Dark eyes swung toward him, then away again. In that moment, Daal had recognized the golden glow of bridle-song shining behind those pupils. Such a gift was potent within the blood of the raash'ke.

And in my blood . . .

While Daal's gift of bridle-song had been forged long ago into a wellspring of power, he wondered if his time spent with Pyllar had begun to merge them.

Am I beginning to sink into Pyllar's heart as I did with Nyx? Is that why my control over him has grown so acute?

He stared down at his saddle. He had designed the gear based on the harnesses and tack used for riding the sea-dwelling orksos back at the Crèche. He had modified them with a strap over the lap to secure a rider to his or her seat. Plus, he had added reins that led forward and were tied to tufts of fur behind a bat's ears. While raash'ke could be guided by shifts in weight and pressure, the reins allowed for quicker communication between rider and mount.

Daal noted the laxness of his own lap strap. He and Pyllar rode with such coordination that he had never felt the need to cinch it any tighter. Likewise, his reins hung loose over his saddle's pommel. He had yet to use them, finding no need.

Is it our shared gift that forged this bond between us?

Before he could ponder it further, Pyllar rumbled beneath him. Again, for a breath, there was an unsettling doubling of his vision: one dimmed by amber goggles, the other burning brightly. He blinked away the confusion, until his sight settled to just the view through his own eyes.

By now, the trio of ships had swept closer, flying only a league away.

Daal lifted his farscope again and studied the vessels. He fixed on the second warship and searched its flag. Once more, he spotted the reared crimson panther of Bhestya.

Clearly, Fenn's uncle was not sparing resources in pursuit of his nephew.

As Pyllar continued to sweep closer, he noted the trajectory of the ships. The trio was not aiming toward where the *Fyredragon* was set to land among the ruins of Seekh.

These hunters must not know the exact position of their prey.

Still, the ships headed toward the only prominent feature of the White Desert: an oasis that surrounded the lake of Kaer'nhal. It sheltered a village of white stones on its shores. The town of Fhal served as a trading post, a place of respite and commerce in this unforgiving landscape.

But Daal feared it also suited the enemy for another reason.

He adjusted his farscope and spotted a flurry of black specks winging between the town and the approaching ships.

Skrycrows . . .

Daal gripped his scope. The commander of those forces must be seeking information from the villagers, inquiring about a wyrm-helmed ship traveling over the desert. Daal frowned at this. The *Fyredragon* had indeed skirted not far from that lake, passing it to the south.

Eyes surely spotted its passage.

Worried, Daal continued forward. He aimed for the lake, the only watering hole across much of the desert. Birds of all sizes stalked across the shallows or flocked throughout the sky in swirling dark clouds. Daal trusted that the constant motion through the air, the blinding sheen off the lake, and the focus of the ship on the village would help mask his approach.

As he raced low, he finally got an angle on the third, smaller ship: a sleek corsair with a tapered balloon. Fascinated by such wyndships, Daal had learned all their various shapes and sizes from Jace. Corsairs had been designed for speed and nimbleness. Daal searched its decks. With the exception of a pair of cannons at the bow, it was not as heavily armed as the Bhestyan warships.

He lifted his gaze to its flag and flinched at the sight of a white flag, emblazoned with a black crown set against a six-pointed gold sun.

The Hálendiian crest . . .

Clearly, Bhestya had chosen sides in this growing war, which only made his group's circumstances more dire.

Daal reached the oasis that fringed the lake and glided over the grove's dense canopy. Heavy fronds stirred under his passage. He kept bowed in his saddle, but his gaze remained high. Once he reached the lake, he ducked Pyllar into the stir of flocking birds, trying to mask his mount's wingspan, doing his best to hide in the blinding glare off the water.

On the far side of the lake, the streaming of skrycrows flowed toward one of the Bhestyan warships. Wanting a better look at who led this force, Daal

angled Pyllar up, but he dared get no closer. He lifted his farscope and focused on the bow of the lead ship, where the skrycrows spiraled.

He twisted the lenses and searched the forecastle. Figures clustered there.
He watched an armored knight strip a message from a crow and pass it to a tall,
older man. This one wore a dark blue half-cloak, trimmed in gray fur, over a
snowy waistcoat. His white hair had been oiled to a steely-flat sheen.

Daal felt no shock at the sight of this regal-looking figure. Fenn had described the man in great detail, even down to the trim beard that etched his
chin and lips.

Thus, Daal had no difficulty identifying him.

Fenn's traitorous uncle.

Satisfied, Daal urged Pyllar to swing away, to start the journey back to
the others. But as his mount tilted on a wing, Daal caught sight of a woman
standing at the forecastle rail. An armored knight clutched her upper arm, as if
fearing she might throw herself overboard. Abject despair shone in her face. A
bruise shadowed an eye. Still, defiance stiffened her back. Her hands gripped
the rail, where chains linked her wrists.

A prisoner . . .

Daal had no trouble recognizing her, too. Not from any description given
to him, but due to a clear resemblance. She had the same ice-white hair, the
same slim nose and generous mouth, as the *Fyredragon*'s navigator. She could
be his twin, but Daal knew she was not.

There stood Fenn's older sister.

Daal remembered the navigator's story of an uncle's betrayal and a warning
by a sister in the night. It seemed that tale had not come to an end. The passage of the *Fyredragon* across the Eastern Crown had stirred it all into motion
again.

Momentarily shocked, Daal spun Pyllar a full circle—then a fiery pain sliced
through his shoulder. The agony came close to tossing him off his mount. He
crumpled tight against the pain, dropping his farscope. One hand clutched his
lap strap, helping to hold him in his saddle. The other grabbed for his burning
arm, as if his palm could smother that fire. He needed to stanch the flow of
blood.

But his fingers only found intact leather.

No blood.

At least, not his own.

His gaze—already turned in the direction of the pain—noted a crimson
stream flowing from the edge of Pyllar's wing. His mount swung sharply. Daal
only kept his seat due to his grip on the saddle strap.

A shadow speared past them, glinting with steel at the tip.

Pyllar had dodged this new threat, but more of the harpoon-like arrows flew across the sky. Daal traced them to their source. Focused on the lead vessel, he had failed to note the second Bhestyan warship drifting closer. Searchers there must have spotted him.

Fighting down panic, Daal shoved his weight forward and sent Pyllar into a steep dive, but his partner was already in motion—whether out of self-preservation or innately responding to Daal's unspoken desire to escape.

The lake rushed up toward them. Birds burst out of the way with raucous screams and explosions of panicked feathers. Steel-tipped shafts peppered the water.

As Pyllar swept the lake, his wingtips grazed the surface, casting up sprays. Daal urged him away from the ships, but he knew Pyllar needed no further guidance. The fiery ache continued to burn Daal's unscathed shoulder, reflecting his mount's wound.

Together, united in purpose and heart, the two fled across the lake.

A glance back showed the trio of ships turning toward him. Their forges flashed brighter as the enemy set off in pursuit.

Daal ducked lower, while picturing what was needed of his partner. Pyllar again responded. Out of range of the deadly ballistas, the raash'ke slowed his flight. His steady glide wobbled. Wings slapped the lake, splashing water to either side.

Keep going . . .

Daal held the image in his head, knowing that Pyllar must see it, too.

He pictured a sight from the Crèche, of a frost-sparrow fleeing a kree-hawk. Such small prey often feigned injury, bobbling and spinning, to lure the threat away from a nest in the cliffs.

Pyllar imitated that now, dipping and rising, quavering with great shudders. His angle of flight turned erratic. Still, as they escaped the lake and fled for the sands, their general path led north—away from where the *Fyredragon* had been headed.

Like the frost-sparrow, Daal hoped to lure the hunters astray. But unlike the sparrow, he was not feigning.

He stared to his left.

Blood streamed from Pyllar's wing, spattering into the wind, leaving a clear trail across the sand. With the two already exhausted, their flight could not last much longer.

Daal recognized this grim reality and knew what it meant.

Eventually the hawk will catch the sparrow.

18

ESME SAHN CLIMBED the rope ladder, aiming for the next crumbling tier of the ruins. Sand and sweat slicked her palms, but the pounding of her heart urged her to greater speed. She paused for two breaths, while staring up.

The blue sky looked a league away, blindingly bright in the shadows that cloaked these depths. Overhead, the broken levels of Seekh formed a maze of shattered walls, tilted slabs, and brick rockslides, all squeezed together by the Tablelands' sandstone bluffs. Across it all and strung throughout were a tangle of ladders, planked bridges, and twisted cables. The latter were hung with rusted ore barrows for hauling scavenged treasures from the deep diggings.

She watched a cart grind up, overloaded with stacked bricks and twisted metal recovered from the depths. She considered leaping the gap and riding that barrow skyward, but it moved too slowly.

Goading her onward, angry voices echoed up from below.

She took one extra breath before continuing. She leaned her forehead against a rung and whispered a prayer to the god Messik, who blessed the intrepid if they won his favor. She wished she had a sandraat to sacrifice to the blind god, to burn an offering to reach his nose, but she had little stomach and no time for such an act.

A scrabbling noise drew her gaze down.

It rose from her companion.

"Hurry up, Crikit," she scolded the young molag.

Below her, Crikit's jointed legs—eight in number—dug into cracks in the crumbling mortar, broken bricks, and creviced sandstone. A black chitinous plate armored its back, toothed like a saw at its edges and ridged the same along its back. A heavy leather pack hung there, carrying Esme's shovels, picks, brushes, and axes.

Large foreclaws snapped and waved, as if urging her onward. Six stalked black eyes reinforced this, glinting in the wan light reaching these depths.

"I know, Crikit," Esme whispered.

She set off up the ladder. She could not risk being caught, not with the treasure strapped across her back. She dared not even let Crikit carry it, though she fully trusted the young molag. She had raised him from when he was little bigger than a melon, newly hatched from an egg.

That had been four years ago.

He had since bulked up into the size of a foundling ox. His back now reached higher than her hips. Still, he was only a juvenile molag. Older sandcrabs crested to thrice her height. And in the deepest reaches of the Barrens, where her tribes roamed, ancient crabs were said to grow to the size of craggy hills.

Not that she had ever seen such a creature.

But, by all the Chanaryn gods, I will one day.

Holding this desire to her heart, she clambered more swiftly, moving nimbly, barely shaking the ladder. Crikit paced alongside her, occasionally chittering at her.

A sharp shout echoed up to her. "I see her!"

She grimaced and rolled off the ladder onto a sandstone tier. A planked bridge led off from here. She crossed and pounded across it, chased by Crikit. As she did, her recovered treasure clattered and clanked across her back. This lone artifact could buy her enough resources to head back into the Barrens.

I cannot lose it to those ravagers.

She cursed herself for being so careless, for failing to note another scavenger spying from the shadows. But the discovery had been too astounding. It had held her full attention. All else had faded around her as she freed the treasure from its sandy grave. Afterward, she had spent too long gently brushing its bronze surface free of grit and age.

I should've known better.

Over the past four years, she had lost other prizes to ravagers and reavers, those who scavenged upon scavengers. In the depths of Seekh, carelessness got you killed—or worse. Too often, she had stumbled across the mutilated corpses of those who fought back, or who tried to hold their tongues, to keep from revealing the location of a stakehold that had suddenly proved fruitful.

I can't let that happen to me—not when I'm this close.

She reached the end of the bridge and clambered up the next ladder. A glance back showed a scurry of shadows on the dusty tier below. Her pursuers continued to close on her.

As she faced up, out of the corner of her eye she caught the dull sheen of bronze over her shoulder. It protruded from the roughspun blanket she had wrapped the treasure in. Her scrambling flight must have shaken it loose, as if the artifact refused to be hidden again.

From the blanket, metal fingers stuck out into view.

She did not have time to resecure it. She pictured what else the blanket covered. It was a disembodied arm, sculpted of bronze, so perfectly wrought that small fibers formed fine hairs across its length. A peek inside its severed shoulder revealed a shine of crystals, like amethysts lining the broken shell of a rock.

She had no idea *what* she had dug out of the sand, only that it was ancient, likely from the Great Tything, what those of the Crown called the Forsaken Ages. Such a treasure would surely fetch a princely sum from the Guilders who oversaw the necropolises.

Enough coin to find my brother.

That's all that mattered.

She reached the last rung of the ladder and leaped to a slab of rock that formed a sandy ramp upward. She searched higher, her eyes stinging with sweat. Above, the gap of sky had widened, grown all the more blinding.

Still, she had far to go.

Swallowing back despair, she scrambled up the slab. She aimed for the next ladder. Shouts and curses rose behind her. She swore she could smell the stink of those hunters, carried on the breeze flowing upward. It reeked of shite and piss and fury.

Crikit scrabbled in her wake, but the slab's sandy surface, worn smooth by the passage of centuries of leather sandals, betrayed those spikes. The young molag slid backward.

"No . . ." Esme moaned.

Over her eighteen years, she had lost too much and refused to forsake more. She skidded back down the stone and grabbed one of Crikit's pincers.

She pulled him closer. "Grab hold."

Crikit's eyes waved in panic, then fixed into a steady determination. He thrust out a claw and snatched onto her belt.

Esme knew the molagi—whom many considered to be simple beasts of burden—were far sharper, hiding an astuteness behind their armor. She pitied those larger crabs, broken by time, often bridle-bound into servitude. Outfitters and wagoners typically severed those claws, both to protect themselves and to cripple the crabs from ever being able to return to the sands.

She could never abide such cruelty.

Esme set off up the slab. She did not have the strength to drag Crickit on her own, but she served as enough of an anchor that her friend could gain his balance and keep up with her.

Together, they reached the top, then separated again. Esme leaped to the next ladder, while Cricket mounted the neighboring wall and scrambled along it.

Behind them, the hunters shouted—now ringing with a note of triumph.

Esme stared up, refusing to succumb to defeat.

Not again—never again.

* * *

AMIDST THE ASHES of the Chanaryn wagons, Esme knelt in despair. A few carriages still showed their blackened ribs. Debris lay scattered across the sands. A pall of smoke clung close to all, as if trying to hide this anguish from the gods.

Those who had survived the slavers' raid—only a dozen or so—had begun the slow repacking of their remaining molagi. Other crabs lay about, killed by spears and axes.

Esme refused to move.

Before her knees rose a cairn of stones, marking the graves of her father and mother. Esme tried to shut out the memory.

The attack had been sudden, the slavers bursting out of a ravine, riding atop horses. Her father had forced Esme and her brother under their family wagon. Then a slaver had trampled past, cast out a rope, and snared their mother by the neck. With a cry, her father sought to save her, chasing her across the sand, only to take a spear to his gut. But even that effort proved for naught. Their mother, struggling for freedom, broke her neck, strangling in that noose.

Then as quickly as the attack had begun, it ended.

Another band of Chanaryn rushed in and chased the marauders off, but not before twenty of her clan were stripped away, taken by the slavers.

A shadow passed over Esme as she blessed their graves with her blood. She barely felt the sting of the stone blade across her palms.

"We must go," Arryn urged her.

She did not have the will or strength to resist as her brother pulled her to her feet. She hung in his arms, clinging to him, refusing to let him go.

"Come with us," she moaned.

He hugged her closer. "My path lies elsewhere. To where the gods call me."

She stared up at him, her eyes pleading.

Arryn was two years older—passing his sixteenth summer, marking his rise to manhood. He had survived his trials of sand, water, and rock. Marked with the scars of his success, he had chosen the path of a shaman, falling under the stern tutelage of an aeldryn who had gone sunblind but was still hale of limb.

She studied her brother's face, fixing each contour, etching them behind her eyes. They were not unalike, standing tall among the Chanaryn, a head higher than most. Her black curls, oiled and braided, hung a handspan longer than his. They shared eyes of cobalt blue. Their matching skin shone like the black glass of the blasted sands.

The only striking difference was the pattern of pale facial scars that heralded Arryn's passage to manhood—whereas her skin remained unblemished, as she was still too young for her trials.

Though in this moment of parting, she did not feel youthful.

Despair weighed upon her, aging her.

"Must you go?" she begged him. "Please stay with me."

He looked down upon her mournfully.

Once packed, she and the others would set trail for the Necropolises of Seekh, to join other displaced Chanaryn. Their clan, too small now, could not survive the sands on their own, especially with the loss of most of their wagons. Other clans would shun them, deeming this attack to be providence of the gods. They would be branded as gyan-ra, *or godforsaken. The only path open to them was to eke out a living in Seekh, to hopefully marry into another clan, allowing a few to return to the sands.*

But that was not the road Arryn would take.

"Aeldryn Tann cannot make the journey into the deep desert on his own," Arryn said. "To seek guidance from the gods, I must join him."

"Then I should go with you. I can tend the fire. Prepare your meals."

"No, Esme. You know that is not our way. Only those god-bound can make this trek."

She recognized this and knew there was no convincing him otherwise.

"I will find my way back to you," he said solemnly, swearing this with three fingers pressed to his heart.

She stared at that hand. Scars marked the flesh between his thumb and forefinger. He had not earned those from any trials. Long before, the markings had been burned into his skin by needles soaked in akcid oil. Those pale lines formed the jagged rays of the sun—or rather half of a sun.

She lifted her own hand, placing it next to his. The other half of that pale sun glowed between her thumb and forefinger.

Forever joining brother to sister.

"I must go," he whispered.

She accepted this defeat, but not without her own demand. "If you don't return, Arryn, I will seek you out. Even if it means my bones join yours in the sand."

She gripped his hand in hers, squeezing hard, binding her words to him, intent never to break this promise.

As Esme climbed, that oath still burned inside her. Over the past four years, the promise had driven her deep into the ruins. It made her spurn anyone who showed an interest in sharing her bed, especially those who sought more from her. When she returned to the sands, it would not be pledge-bound to another.

For any hope of finding Arryn . . .

I must be free.

To that end, she fled faster. The oath to her brother spurred her upward. It fueled her heart, fired her limbs, and quickened her breath.

Crikit followed in her wake.

As she scaled ladder after ladder, the sun grew ever brighter. Its heat invigorated, rather than sapping her strength. The hunters continued their pursuit but gained no further ground. Their doggedness worried her. They were creatures of the shadowy depths. She had hoped the glare of the sun and risk of exposure would drive them back down.

Shouts belied this, as they continued to chase her.

While this kept her panicked, it also spoke to the value of what she carried. Such determination by these thieves only stoked her hopes.

Finally, she reached the last ladder and flew up its length. It ended at a plateau where a wide arcade of stone steps led out of the ruins.

"Stay close," Esme warned Crikit.

Together, they rushed up the stairs into the trading post that served this corner of Seekh. The village lay amidst a spread of ruins that poked higher all around, as if the dead were trying to push out of their graves only to be scoured back down by sand and storms.

To Esme, the village was a sunken pox on a corpse. It smoked and stank and flowed with open troughs of sewage that streamed into the depths of the ruins. It screamed and shouted and cursed.

Esme pushed into the chaos. People crowded its narrow streets and alleys. Hawkers barked their wares. Braziers flamed with grease fires. Mongers leaned in doorways, baring a breast or a mottled thigh.

Esme rushed through it all, but only after folding her treasure back into its blanket. She kept her head down, drawing her hood up. Crikit followed, clacking loudly in warning. Still, shoulders jostled her. A hand tried to relieve her purse from her belt, but she batted it away. A leering man with no teeth eyed her as if she were something fallen from one of the grills.

She gritted her teeth and forged on. She aimed for the corner of the village that served as home to the Chanaryn, those like her who had washed out of the desert and ended up here. It lay near the outskirts of the village, farthest from the gateway into the ruins.

Esme kept close watch behind her. If the hunters continued their pursuit, she could no longer spot them.

I pray the same holds true for me.

She forded through the crush, the smoke, the noise, until finally the crowds thinned. Away from the ruins' entrance, the shops eventually dwindled into rickety structures of rust and crumble.

Esme found her breath easing. Soon, her nose took in the spice and incense

from countless Chanaryn devotions. Lamps and candles burned in the shadowy depths of windowless shacks. Most lacked doors, too. Her people could
not abide confinement. For the clans of the Chanaryn, where the open spaces
of the Barrens spread to all horizons, these homes felt like slavers' cages. Out in
the desert, even their beds were dug into the cooler sand, over which a lizard-
hide tarp was rolled, whose outer scales reflected the endless sun and its heat.

As she headed through this corner of the village, she noted clusters of
Chanaryn gathered in doorways or out in the alleyways.

Crikit suddenly bustled in front of her, his eye-stalks waving, clearly agitated.

"What's wrong?" she whispered.

His pincers waved at the sky, drawing her attention upward. While crossing the village, she had barely lifted her face. Concerned, she craned her neck
and pushed back her hood—then fell back a step.

Beyond the village outskirts, a small mooring field had been dug out of the
surface ruins. Wyndships came and went, but even such sightings were rare.
Most of the wealth dug out of Seekh ended up on the backs of molagi, or
shipped out on long trains that crisscrossed the necropolises, drawn by teams
of larger crabs.

Only what rose before her, moored in the neighboring field, towered over
this corner of the village. A wyndship—easily twice the size of the largest that
Esme had ever seen—formed a mountain of wood, iron, and balloon. But
what strangled her breath was the sight of the iron beast that formed its prow.
A huge, sculpted dragon loomed down at the village. Its wings were spread
wide to either side, sheltering and protecting the bow of the ship. As if alive,
the dragon rocked gently in place, stirred by the winds.

Under its steely gaze, Esme felt trapped, like a dustrab frozen before a sway-
ing cobra. She finally shuddered herself free and took another step back. She
swallowed hard as dread trickled through her. Stories of winged monsters
filled many of the Chanaryn's most ancient stories, tales of angry gods and
fiery destruction.

From the fearful whispers and gestures of warding, others in the street were
equally dismayed. For her people, such a sighting was a portent of doom.

Unfortunately, this proved true as a hand grabbed Esme's arm and spun
her around.

A hulking, shaven-headed man scowled down at her. His craggy brows
shaded pinched eyes, as black as the deepest pit. She had no trouble recognizing him. All knew this rogue, the scourge of the village.

Esme cringed at the sight of Rahl hy Peck, the brutal leader of a cabal of cutthroats and oppressors. While the village had its headman and serjeants, no one dared cross Peck and his ilk.

Hard fingers dug into Esme's arm.

Peck leaned closer, his breath ripe with sour ale. "You have something of mine, lass. Can't have anyone stealing from me, especially not a sand grub."

Esme tried to pull free, but Peck tightened his fist on her. No one came to her aid—at least, none of the Chanaryn.

Only Crikit, sensing the animus and threat, came to her defense, but Esme waved the young molag back.

Especially as Peck had not come alone. Five men, winded and grimed, stood past the rogue's shoulder. Their faces streamed with sweat.

Esme knew these must be the ravagers who had been hunting her. Word must have been dispatched upward. Perhaps by skrycrow. Or through the foul strands that spread across the village, linking such scum, until it had eventually stirred the spider who had spun that web.

Still, Esme refused to back down. "I stole nothing. I dug this artifact out on my own. By right of the scavenge, it is mine."

"Grubbing liar," spat one of the men behind Peck. A ragged scar split his face from hairline to chin, gnarling his upper lip into a perpetual sneer. "She pilfered it while I weren't looking."

"Lachan is right," another blurted. "I saw her take it."

Esme's cheeks heated up. Among the Chanaryn, theft was considered as wretched a deed as murder. "I am no thief."

Peck's eyes narrowed. "I don't think you understand. It fekking doesn't matter. *Everything* in this village is mine until I say it ain't." He pulled her closer. "Show me what you lifted from the ruins."

She stiffened her back, refusing.

Peck motioned two of his men forward. The pair carried daggers in hand. The other three drew short swords, warding away any of the Chanaryn from interfering, not that anyone tried.

Unable to stop them, she was forced to submit while the thieves cut loose her harness and freed the wrapped treasure. They carried it around to Peck, who still kept hold of her.

"Show me," Peck demanded, spittle flying from his lips, all but salivating.

The pair unrolled the blanket across the sandstone. The bronze arm clattered free. Though it was spottled and blackened with age, some metal remained untarnished and shone dully in the sunlight.

Gasps rose from those gathered. Even from Lachan, the snarl-lipped bastard—which gave proof to his lie of discovering it.

Peck pushed her away and examined it more closely. "Ock, as grand as this appears, I may not even kill you. You've handed me a great boon, lass."

"What is it?" another of the thieves asked, his eyes bright with greed.

The answer came from behind Esme.

"It is a piece of a *ta'wyn*."

She turned around, but she refused to retreat from the treasure at her feet. Three men approached, accompanied by Aelder Hasant, who served as the overseer for their stranded clans.

The tallest of the three strangers—outfitted in the black robe of an alchymist— had spoken.

Esme squinted suspiciously at him. She had run into her share of scholars, those who sought to study the mysteries of these ruins.

A younger man with a fiery red beard whispered to the alchymist, as if consulting him. From his traveler's cloak, Esme guessed he was an aide to the scholar.

Peck cleared his throat. "A *tarwren,* you say? How much you willing to pay for it? I suggest a steep price, enough to convince me not to take it to the Guilder's office."

Esme stepped between them all. "It is not *his* to barter. It is *my* find."

The scar-lipped Lachan closed on her with his dagger, intending to silence her claim.

She ignored him and focused on the trio of strangers. The final member of the group had his head bowed with Hasant. Both men's eyes settled on her, with the overseer giving a small nod as if in acknowledgment of something.

She studied this last stranger. He had skin the color of rain-darkened sand, with hair of oiled shadows. He wore a dark blue half-cloak, matching his breeches and tunic. His lips hinted at a smile, but she read the danger in the glint of those black eyes.

The alchymist turned to this man. "Darant, what do you think?"

"I think . . ." Darant said, stepping forward. "I'd rather negotiate my own terms."

The man flared his cloak wide and swept out two swords, one gripped in each hand. The blades were so thin that they vanished as the swordsman swept a flourish through the air.

Esme had seen such weapons only once before, wielded with far less finesse. *Whipswords . . .*

Peck reared back to his feet and waved to his men. "Kill them. And the grub."

The five men spread wide.

From the shadows, another four thieves appeared, shedding into view. Peck had come prepared. To survive this long, he surely knew not to underestimate an enemy.

The alchymist backed away, drawing Hasant with him.

The red-bearded aide stepped forward. He shrugged aside his traveler's cloak and swung a large blue-hued ax into view. He swept it in a vicious arc, scribing a pattern of threat.

"Get behind me," the young man ordered Esme.

She refused. She wasn't about to leave her treasure unguarded. By now, Lachan had reached her. He leered, holding his dagger low. With no snide word, only deadly intent, he lunged and stabbed at her chest—but Esme was no longer there.

Years ago, knowing she would eventually travel into the Barrens, likely alone, she had trained with a *hesharyn*, a Chanaryn sand-dancer, an expert in blades and balance.

Esme twisted sideways, escaping the thrust of the dagger. A bone blade already rested in her palm. She continued her spin. Caught off guard and a slave to momentum, Lachan fell past her.

He caught himself from a tumble by bracing a leg. He turned to her—only to meet the point of her dagger. She jammed it under his chin, yanked the blade out, and stabbed it in again.

Snakes have two fangs, her teacher had instructed her.

Lachan fell off her knife, tripping backward, spewing blood. He toppled to the stone, where he gurgled away his life.

Esme knew not to savor this victory, but to ready herself.

She crouched low, one leg swept to the side, her toe firm to rock.

From this position, she gaped at the slaughter of Peck's other men. The caped man swirled through the skirmish, a sand devil come to life. Screams and blood followed in his wake. The bearded youth cleared the rest, cleaving a path with his ax, wielding it with determined intent.

Still, Peck had not survived this long by being cowed.

Instead, he acted while his men died.

He grabbed the bronze arm from the blanket and retreated with it. His narrowed eyes gleamed with the stolen wealth.

No . . .

Esme set off after him, but the fighting rolled in front of her, cutting her off. She could only watch as Peck escaped with her treasure, taking with him all hope of her ever finding her brother.

But her anguish reached another.

Crickit leaped from the side, where Esme had sent him. The molag struck Peck. Pincers cleaved through the bastard's wrist in one snap. Peck bellowed in horror. A hand of flesh and an arm of bronze struck the stone.

Peck stumbled away, at first slowly, then in a rout of panic. His remaining hand clutched his wrist, trying to stem the pulsing arc of blood.

Esme called Crikit to her, while rushing to the abandoned treasure.

By now, the fighting had ended. One survivor fled after Peck, leaving his own trail of blood.

Esme collected the bronze arm and turned to the strangers. She held up her bone dagger. "This treasure is mine. I will not give it up."

Darant shrugged. "Keep it. It's not the artifact we want."

She frowned at him.

Hasant hobbled forward, leaning on his staff, accompanied by the alchymist.

"*Ree plya nishka,*" the overseer said formally in the Chanaryn tongue. He pointed his staff toward the towering dragon looming over the village. "*Trys shishen wyn.*"

The red-bearded young man nodded, though he was surely ignorant of the Chanaryn language. "We need a guide. To join us aboard the *Fyredragon.*"

Esme kept frowning. "A guide to where?"

The alchymist answered, but he sidestepped her question. "We've been rebuffed by your clansmen. All seem fearful of traveling with us."

Esme understood this, which Hasant confirmed with his next words, spoken with conviction.

"*Neey auguran.*"

"What does that mean?" Darant asked.

"It means *bad omen,*" Esme explained. "No Chanaryn would risk riding a ship with such a beast at its prow."

The alchymist stared back at the huge ship. "Why does—"

"Where are you all going?" Esme continued, ignoring him. "Why do you need a Chanaryn guide?"

"We intend to travel deep into the Barrens," the red-bearded man answered. "Likely farther than any of your people have ever gone."

Esme pictured Arryn's face as last she saw him.

Maybe not all of us . . .

"Will you come with us?" Darant said.

She stared across the trio, keeping her face stoic, trying to hide the hope bursting inside her heart. For the past four years, she had sought a path deep into the desert, far out into the Barrens.

Could this be my best chance?

Still, she could also not discount an icy thread of fear—not from any worry born of bad omens, but in concern about the fate of her brother. All these years, she had prayed that Arryn still lived, refused to accept otherwise. It had kept her going, driving her from day to day.

Now I have a chance to discover the truth.

But she also knew such knowledge—if the worst proved true—would destroy her.

Still, there was another concern.

She glanced to the trail of blood leading away, knowing Peck's retribution would be brutal if she was discovered here. And no doubt his wrath would also fall upon the Chanaryn villagers here.

For that reason, too, I must be gone.

She faced the strangers. "When do we leave?"

Darant shaded his eyes and searched the skies. "We're still waiting for stragglers to return to the ship."

She nodded. "Then I will gather what I need. And for Crikit, too."

"Crikit?" the alchymist asked.

Esme signaled her friend. The young molag scurried to her side, lowered to his belly, and clicked softly with worry.

She reached down and scratched behind his eye-stalks. "Don't worry. I'm not leaving you behind."

She stared defiantly at the others, daring them to refuse her.

Darant shrugged and glanced with consternation at the alchymist. "What is it about all these young women . . . and their affinity for strange beasts?"

19

NYX STOOD VIGIL with Bashaliia. The pair watched from the stern of the ship's cavernous hold. With the *Fyredragon* still moored, its rear hatch had been left open to the sky. Hot winds blew a dusting of sand inside. Overhead, the sun blazed, baking the wind-scoured ruins.

She kept her gaze fixed to the east, searching for any sign of Daal and his crew. A farscope hung loose in her hand. She had raised it repeatedly, but its lenses had offered no remedy to her distress.

Where are you all?

Her other hand rested on the saddle atop Bashaliia's back. She had never removed his tack after her last ride, when she and Bashaliia had followed a skrycrow back to the *Fyredragon*. The bird had carried word of an approach of a trio of ships, with one bearing the Bhestyan flag.

That had been an entire bell ago. If Daal and the others had retreated after dispatching the crow, following in the bird's wake, they should've returned by now.

Nyx lifted her farscope yet again and searched the horizons. Her heart pounded, demanding that she leap atop Bashaliia and set off to the east. She fought against that urge. Such a flight would only serve to foreshorten this vigil, to allow her to spot the returning raash'ke a bit sooner than merely waiting in place.

Little else would be gained.

Still, Bashaliia sensed her desire. Warm breath caressed her cheek. Velvet nostrils brushed under her chin. A soft pining filled her ear, echoing her need, in harmony with her heart. In his song, Nyx recognized his notes of long- ing . . . and loneliness.

This, too, resonated inside her.

She shifted her hand from the saddle and rubbed the tender spot behind Bashaliia's ear, trying to soothe him as much as herself. He ruffled content- ment, but that melancholy undercurrent still remained.

While she missed Daal, Bashaliia pined a similar loss. He had spent all his life within the bosom of the Mýr colony back home. There, he had been both himself and part of a greater whole, communing within the vast and ancient horde-mind that made up the past and present of his brethren.

To join Nyx, he had forsaken so much, but with the five raash'ke aboard the *Fyredragon*, Bashaliia had found some semblance of a family again. She often came down into the hold and discovered him nestled with the others, sharing the warmth of their bodies, the quiet chorus of their song.

Now he's alone again.

"They'll return," she whispered to him, doing her best to reassure him—and herself.

A treading of boots rose behind her, amplified by the breadth of the hold. She knew who approached—both from the stolidness of his pace and from the patter of paws that accompanied him.

She turned as Graylin strode toward her, his face stern. Kalder trailed him, his tail swishing in agitation, likely a reflection of his partner's tension.

She hardened herself at the graveness of Graylin's manner, fearing the worst.

Has another skrycrow arrived? Did I miss its passage?

"What's wrong?" she pressed him as the pair joined her.

Graylin stared out the hatch, his gaze extending to the horizon. "Krysh just returned," he finally said. "They were able to secure a guide, a young woman from the nomadic tribes that travel the Barrens."

This could not be the reason behind the knight's dour countenance.

We need that guide.

He continued, "Darant and Jace stayed behind with her, while she gathers her belongings for this trek. But there was trouble. A skirmish with a rabble of rough men. It could lead to problems if we stay."

Nyx noted Graylin's eyes narrow, just a pinch. He clearly knew how she'd react to such a suggestion. She didn't disappoint him. "We can't leave," she insisted forcefully. "Not before the others return."

"They can still follow us."

She shook her head. "Daal and the others will be exhausted and hard-pressed to fly even this far. To expect them to carry on . . ."

Graylin lifted a palm against her objection. "We do not have to go far or quickly. Just enough to put some distance between us and the fire that was lit below."

She opened her mouth, then closed it, recognizing the sense of such a plan.

Graylin reinforced it. "With a Bhestyan warship already en route, we cannot be caught tied down, especially if trouble arises on the ground."

Despite her misgivings, Nyx slowly nodded.

Graylin looked relieved, which irritated her. Plainly, he still viewed her as a stubborn child, one blind and deaf to reasonable caution.

Does he think so little of his own daughter?

Nyx knew this thought was ungenerous. Since embarking on this journey, she had slowly found her voice, one steeled by the weight of her responsibility, by the tragedies endured, by the blood spilled. She had also noted how Graylin had grown to accept this, to listen to her—not as a daughter, but as a part of this crew.

But not always.

Too often, her newfound voice still rankled him—as if he could not see the woman she had become and only viewed her as the child he had lost.

Graylin continued, "I've ordered Darant's men to free our mooring lines. We must be aloft as soon as Jace and the captain board with our guide."

Before she could respond, a low rumble rose from Kalder. The hulking vargr had shifted closer to the open door. As he stared out, he chuffed heavily with his hackles shivering tall.

Next to him, Bashaliia also cast out a sharp note of alarm, shaking his wings wider. Both beasts' eyes were fixed to the horizon.

Nyx crossed between them.

Graylin followed. "What's riled them?"

Nyx squinted. Through the glare, she spotted black specks.

As she lifted her farscope, relief and trepidation warred within her. She prayed it was Daal's crew rushing home. She twisted the scope's lenses to focus on those specks. At such a distance, the view wavered in and out.

"Is it them?" Graylin asked.

She took a breath, held it, and steadied her hands. Through the glare, she finally discerned dark wings, beating rapidly, racing with the winds. She blew out a breath, thanking all the gods, and answered Graylin.

"Yes, it's—"

Then she stiffened.

It cannot be.

Choking down her terror, she focused again and confirmed her fear.

With a gasp, she shoved the farscope into her riding vest, turned to Bashaliia, and leaped for his saddle. Already sensing her intent, her brother lowered and caught her in the leather seat.

"Nyx!" Graylin shouted to her.

"It's the raash'ke," Nyx called back to him. "Just not *all* of them."

In her heart, in her bones, she knew who was missing.

Graylin must have guessed her intent. "Nyx, don't—"

Without word or song, Bashaliia bounded out of the open hold. Her brother needed no encouragement beyond the will of his rider. His wings snapped wide, cupped air, and set off eastward.

Graylin called after them, but the rush of winds scoured away his words, leaving behind only the angry tones of his judgement.

Nyx ducked low, accepting this.

Maybe I am the stubborn daughter you know after all.

She sang to Bashaliia, urging him faster.

So be it.

20

DAAL FLED ACROSS the salt flats of the White Desert. Sand scoured his skin raw. His eyes, even shielded by his amber-lensed goggles, ached from the constant glare. Winds tore past his ears—but failed to mute the growing roar of the forge-engines behind him.

He twisted his neck.

The three ships rode high above the desert, drawing ever closer. The lead ship fired a single ballista. A massive steel-tipped arrow arced through the air, but it fell short of Daal's position, spearing into the sand.

But that will soon change.

Pyllar's wing continued to stain the salt flats with blood. His mount's flight wobbled as one wing beat stronger than the other.

Still, Daal felt the determined thrum of his partner's heart through his thighs. He reached a hand and dug nails through Pyllar's ruff, casting his appreciation and love deep into that stout heart. He drew in his mount's musk, salted with sweat, steaming from his overheated body.

"You've done well, Pyllar," he mouthed into the wind, trusting his partner to understand.

Daal stared forward. The broken edge of the Tablelands rose as a dark line ten leagues off. Under him, the salt flats had begun to churn up into rolling dunes—at first mere ripples, then growing into ever higher ridges. The landscape of blowing sands looked like waves washing toward those distant cliffs.

Cliffs we will never reach.

Daal recognized this, taking solace that he and Pyllar had led the hunters off course, well to the north of where the *Fyredragon* had been headed.

A whisk of movement drew his eye to the right. A giant spear sped through the air before its heavy steel tip pulled it down. The arrow slammed into the face of a dune, burying itself deep.

They're upon us . . .

He knew he could ask for no more speed out of his failing partner. This wounded sparrow could never outrace those hawks. Still, Pyllar fought, seeking the strongest winds blowing westward to help buffet them along.

Unfortunately, his mount's path slowly edged southward, too.

"No, Pyllar," Daal urged. "North . . . keep going *north*."

Daal reinforced this by shifting his weight to the right, away from the

Fyredragon's path. But Pyllar ignored him and continued southward, as if trying to reach home before he died.

Daal recognized the heart-worn exhaustion of his mount. He reached for his reins for the first time, to try to direct Pyllar to the north. With a sigh, he let his hands drop. He refused to bend that stolid heart to his will, to scold him in this manner.

Instead, he simply let Pyllar fly.

"M' bevvan raash'ke," Daal intoned in Panthean, praising his mount's bravery and steadfastness. *"M' laya brenna."*

Both were true.

I will be proud to die with you, my brother.

Knowing they had done all they could, Daal looked past his shoulder. As expected, the ships had drawn closer. But to his dismay, one of the warships had rolled away from the others. It had set off toward the south, already crossing a league in that direction.

No . . .

Daal remembered the flock of skrycrows racing between the lead ship and the town of Fhal. Maybe a late-arriving message had alerted the hunters about a huge dragon-helmed wyndship flying south. Either that, or someone aboard the retreating ship had figured out Daal's flight across the desert could be a ruse.

If so, he could guess *who* that was.

Fenn's uncle.

Another arrow shot through the air, spearing closer but still driving into the sand. A cannon also boomed. From the closing warship, fire flashed and thunder echoed. A dune shattered on Daal's left.

Rather than shying from the fountain of blasted sand, Pyllar dove through it, still angling south. Daal knew he could do nothing more about it. He had bought Nyx and the others as much time as he could manage. He prayed their sacrifice—his and Pyllar's—would not be wasted.

He swung forward, determined to lure the remaining two ships with him. *At least for as long as we still draw breath.*

He leaned closer to Pyllar, determined to stretch out this chase.

Then, directly ahead, a spat of sand rushed high, spiraling into a whirlwind. Dark shadows fluttered there, looking more mirage than real. Daal blinked against the sight, trying to make sense of it.

Pyllar simply strove toward it, as if he had been aiming there all along.

Deep in his ears, Daal felt his mount's desperate keening. It rose and trembled out of Pyllar's chest. Then Daal heard an *answer*—though it was likely perceived through Pyllar's ears rather than his own, blurring their senses together in this moment of hardship.

As the whirl of dust cleared, Daal made out a pair of raash'ke. The two spiraled into view for a breath—then dove into the sand.

Daal struggled with his confusion.

As Pyllar closed the distance, the landscape revealed the answer. Past the next mountainous ridge of dunes, the ground had been split by a ragged crack, a deep ravine that cut across the desert.

The two raash'ke had vanished into it.

Pyllar tipped steeply and followed. As they entered the ravine, the dunes vanished on either side, replaced by walls of rock. The dark sandstone looked raw and sharp-edged, as if this crack had only broken open a short time ago. Wind and rain had yet to polish the rock to a desert smoothness.

One of the raash'ke sped onward, heading south. The other hovered back, allowing Pyllar to draw abreast.

Daal recognized the doe Heffik—and her rider.

"Tamryn!" he called over. "I told you to head to the *Fyredragon*!"

"And I told you that Barrat could take them home as well as I." She lifted a farscope in hand. "We all witnessed the attack. Saw your flight north. Then we came upon this rift in the Urth."

Daal understood. She must have split off with this other rider, sending the remaining two to the *Fyredragon*. Then she used the ravine to traverse the desert, staying out of sight until she and the other rider could reach here. He also recognized why Pyllar had swung to the south. His mount must have heard the near-silent cries of the approaching pair and angled to meet them.

Still worried, Daal glanced toward the strip of blue sky overhead, then back behind him. He did not know what the hunters would make of his sudden disappearance. He imagined that they, like Daal, would quickly recognize the ravine as the reason behind it. But they could not know if he had fled south or north. He wagered the two vessels would split off from one another and hunt the ravine in both directions.

Still, the momentary confusion should give Daal and the other two riders a greater chance to escape. To help that happen, Daal concentrated on his flight. As rock walls rushed past, he again noted the stone's rough contours. He could guess why. With moonfall approaching, the world had been plagued by storms and quakes.

This must've cracked open during one such shake.

Daal thanked the gods for this boon. While moonfall risked ending the world, in this instance, it had saved him and Pyllar.

"Can your mount make it back?" Tamryn called over, pointing at the blood weeping from Pyllar's wing.

Daal gritted his teeth, troubled by the same fear. As they sped along the rift, Heffik whistled and pined her own distress for Pyllar. The doe tried to use the edge of her wing to support Pyllar's injured one. Out of the direct sun, the cooler air seemed to revive his mount.

Or maybe it was this reunion.

Pyllar and Heffik had bonded over the months of confinement aboard the *Fyredragon*. The two—ignoring the friction of their respective riders—had grown closer, nearly inseparable.

Tamryn stared across the gulf between them. Even with her head hooded and her eyes goggled, Daal recognized the worried set to her lips, the hard grip on her reins.

He pointed below. "The deeper we go. Farther from the sun's heat. It may help Pyllar."

Tamryn nodded and led them down into the depths. After the glare of the desert, the thickening shadows clouded his vision. Still, Daal trusted Pyllar and the other raash'ke to traverse the ravine. He heard their shrill cries echoing off the walls, offering them guidance.

Daal occasionally caught flashes from Pyllar, of broken walls and massive boulders, all stripped of color, just outlines and reliefs.

Amazement wore through his anxiety.

But not completely.

Through his thighs, he felt the thudding of his mount's heart. He read the strain in each beat. Daal's whole body grew slowly heavier—again mirroring Pyllar's own weakening state.

"How much farther?" Daal gasped out.

Tamryn answered, her voice ringing with a lie. "Not far. We'll make it."

Daal twisted with great effort and searched behind them.

Far above, the thin strip of the sky carved a ragged line across the darkness. As Daal stared, a shadow rode along it, eating away the brightness, traveling along its course.

One of the hunters had not given up.

But is it the Hálendiian corsair or the Bhestyan warship?

Daal could not know, so he clutched to one certainty, willing it to Pyllar.

We must keep going.

But *will* alone proved not enough.

Pyllar's wings shuddered one last time, then folded in exhaustion.

Mount and rider plummeted into the depths of the ravine.

21

Nyx circled above the dark scar that split the crystalline sands. She tried not to picture herself as a marsh vulture spiraling above a ripe corpse.

Let them still be alive.

She cursed herself for not having joined Daal and the others when they had abandoned the *Fyredragon* and set off on this patrol. Across the ravine, another rider—a skilled Panthean named Barrat—matched her pace around the ragged cut.

She had sent the other rider winging back to the ruins, to alert the *Fyredragon* of all that had transpired. She would not return until she discovered the fate of the others.

But she knew that might not be possible.

She eyed the large ship flying toward them. It must be the warship that Daal had warned them about, the one bearing the Bhestyan flag. Farther to the south, a smaller ship sailed above the rift, following its course in this direction, too.

While this boded badly, Nyx took a measure of comfort in this other's path. If those aboard were tracking the ravine, hunting its depths, then maybe Daal and the others were already on their way back.

Earlier, Barrat had explained how a pair of riders—Tamryn and Arik—had rushed off to intercept Daal and lead him home. He had also shared what had goaded those two riders to act: Daal's mount had been wounded in an attack.

Fear laced through her.

Such an injury would surely slow them all down.

She lifted a farscope and focused on the small ship. It appeared to be a corsair from its sleek shape. She tried to make out its flag, but the whipping wind and distance confounded her. All she could do was pray it was not heavily armed.

As she lowered the scope, a flash of fire caught her eye. It rose from the corsair's deck, from its forecastle. A muffled boom reached her.

Cannon fire.

The hunters must have spotted their targets or were attempting to flush them out.

Nyx gauged the distance from here.

Two leagues.

She lowered the scope and cast her gaze toward the approach of the Bhestyan warship. She swallowed, recognizing how tight this gambit would be.

But it didn't matter.

She called to Barrat, "Head back to the *Fyredragon!*"

"But—"

She shoved an arm to the west. "Go!"

Without looking to see if her order was obeyed, Nyx cast her desire to Bashaliia. Her winged brother broke away, diving steeply. Winds tried to rip her from her saddle, but her lap strap kept her seated.

As they ducked into the ravine, walls swallowed them. Another blast echoed up the canyon. She cringed against it, but she did not slow.

Bashaliia swept into the shadows, then snapped his wings wider, catching the cooler air. Nyx sank into the saddle as the bat turned his dive into a swift glide. Nyx sang her encouragement, binding her to his heart.

As they flew, Bashaliia's keening shed the darkness ahead of them, piercing the gloom.

She shared his sight and cast her song farther out, sending forth a promise. *I'm coming.*

DAAL DUCKED AS a cannonball shattered the rock wall on his right. Cursing, he clung to Pyllar and fought to keep clear of the ravine's bottom. His mount's wings trembled and beat with the last of his ebbing strength.

A short time ago, the pair had come close to crashing into the depths— only to have Heffik dive beneath them and push Pyllar's chest up. The smaller doe could do little more. Even Tamryn tried using her arms to keep Pyllar aloft. The pair could only hold that weight for a handful of breaths, but it was enough for Pyllar to get his foundering wings back under him.

From there, they managed to glide into the deepest shadows, through cooler air. The raash'ke were creatures of ice and cold. The chill helped Pyllar tap into the last dregs of his strength.

Still, their pace inevitably slowed, allowing the corsair to close upon them. Another cannon boomed overhead. Sandstone exploded, filling the air with rubble.

Arik took a stone to his head. It sliced through his leather and bounced off his mount's wing. He barely kept his saddle, but he held tight. As he straightened, blood ran from under his hood, darkening half his face.

Tamryn rushed over, but he waved her off. She fell back to Daal's position. Her face was as dark as Arik's, but not from any wash of blood.

Daal understood.

"Go!" he ordered her. "Get Arik to the ship. I'll follow on my own!"

He stared up at the corsair's shadow. From his earlier spying, he knew the ship had only two cannons. It would take time to reload them. Hopefully, the delay would offer Tamryn and Arik a moment to escape.

Tamryn scowled at this, but she spun Heffik forward again. Gestures were exchanged, and Arik headed off, faster now. It did not take long for the shadows to swallow rider and mount.

Tamryn fell back again to Pyllar's side.

Daal started to object, but Tamryn thrust out an arm, as if rudely gesturing to him. Instead, a curl of rope unraveled from her hand. She must have retrieved it from her saddle pack. The rope's length—tossed with the expertise of a skilled Panthean casting a net—struck Daal in the chest.

He snagged it one-handed but failed to understand its significance.

Tamryn tilted back, revealing her end tied to her saddle horn. She motioned for him to do the same at his end. He recovered quickly and wrapped a fletch-knot around Pyllar's pommel, leaning on the memory buried in his bones from all his years plying the sea with his father.

With the line secured, Tamryn urged Heffik forward. The doe, looking equally determined to help her buck, pulled the rope taut between them. Tamryn and her mount towed Pyllar, sharing their strength.

Slowly, their pace increased, but not by much.

The raash'ke—raised in the harsh ice—had bulky, smaller bodies. It took most of their strength to carry a rider. Even with Heffik's imparted vigor, they had not gained much speed.

Another cannon blast warned of the continuing threat. A huge boulder cracked free, dislodged by the impact of an iron ball. It plummeted toward them. They barely escaped its impact, diving clear at the last breath. Rock shattered behind them. Shards chased after them, clattering all around.

Daal ducked from the worst of it, recognizing a hard truth.

We'll not survive another blast.

He freed his knife and lowered the blade to the rope. The tautness of the line had snugged the knot too tight to undo on its own.

Tamryn shouted at him, clearly noting his dagger—but her cry had nothing to do with his attempt to free himself.

Ahead, a huge shadow swelled into view.

Black wings stretched wide, nearly filling the ravine.

He struggled to comprehend this visage—until bridle-song washed over him, filling the squeeze of the canyon. It struck him like a wave, carrying with it no words, only intent.

I'm here.

* * *

NYX HAD HEARD the boom of the cannon, the explosion of sandstone. Fearing the worst, she had urged Bashaliia to greater speeds. She trusted his senses, his echoing cries that stripped away shadows.

Moments ago, she had swept past Arik. Blood streamed down the rider's face. She had barely slowed, especially as he waved and shouted a single word that set fire to her heart.

"Hurry!"

She obeyed that command.

A final turn of the canyon, and she spotted a pair of raash'ke. The darkness made it hard to discern one from the other. But even before sighting them, she had felt the font of power welling ahead of her. It called to the empty hunger inside her.

She immediately knew it was Daal lagging behind the other.

She rushed toward him, spurring Bashaliia onward. Her eyes kept fixed upon Daal's hunched form. Off to the side and gliding higher, the other rider—Tamryn—motioned frantically, as if urging her to come faster.

But that was not the message.

Bashaliia suddenly jerked into a roll, swinging vertically on a wingtip. Nyx got thrown sideways, hanging only by her lap strap. The Mýr bat sped past the two raash'ke. Only then did Nyx notice the rope joining the two mounts together.

She had failed to spot it. Bashaliia's original path would have swept into that rope, sending all three crashing in a tangle.

Clear of the threat, Bashaliia angled sharply around once he was past Daal and Tamryn. Nyx regained her seat as their flight evened out. She stared ahead at the rope and understood its purpose.

Tamryn is towing Daal's wounded mount.

As Bashaliia chased after the tethered pair, the shadow of the corsair loomed overhead. At these lagging speeds, they'd never escape that hunter.

Knowing this, Nyx tightened her chest and sang her desire into Bashaliia's heart. Golden strands formed a design of intent. It blazed across both their eyes.

Bashaliia understood and whisked forward. He dove beneath Pyllar and slowed into a steady glide, riding a bit ahead of the other.

Nyx craned her neck and shouted up to Daal, "Jump! Join me on Bashaliia. He can carry us!"

But that was not the only reason.

Nyx stared past Daal to the corsair's shadow.

I will need us both.

* * *

As Nyx yelled again, Daal winced. He did not fear such a leap, but he
hated to abandon Pyllar. He reached to his mount's ruff, felt each struggled
breath and each hard thump of his heart.

Nyx called up, her face flushed with panic and frustration. "Unburdened
by your weight, your mount can fly faster with Heffik and Tamryn."

Daal cursed himself for not recognizing this. Exhaustion—both his own
and Pyllar's—had dulled his thinking. He quickly tossed aside his lap strap,
slipped a leg from its stirrup, and shifted the limb under him.

Below, Nyx stared up at him. While her goggles hid her eyes, her intensity
still burned to him. Daal noted the golden aura glowing about her. She had
stoked her bridle-song into a bonfire, a blaze too strong for her body to hold.

As he balanced atop the saddle, her power called to the wellspring inside
him. It stirred deep in his chest, quickening his heart, tightening his ribs. His
skin flushed, as if already warmed by the blaze below.

A part of him wanted to leap *away* from that bonfire, but he knew he could
not. It called to him—and he had no choice but to answer.

Daal leaped from the saddle, flew through the air, and fell into those flames.

22

As Daal landed behind the saddle, Nyx held tight. His impact shoved them all deeper into the ravine. Rocks and boulders swept beneath Bashaliia's belly, brushing the downy fur below. A few sliced deeply, reaching skin.

Nyx winced from the shared pain.

Above, without the anchor of Daal's weight, Pyllar rose higher, as if buoyed by the lift-gasses of a wyndship's balloon. Heffik towed him on ahead, clearing past where Bashaliia glided.

With the way free, Nyx urged Bashaliia away from the sharp rocks. She glanced back to check on Daal. His legs, bent at the knees, straddled to either side. His hands clutched the bases of her lap strap. She wished those arms had wrapped her waist, but she knew she had to stay focused.

Ahead, Heffik flew onward, her wings skimming and beating. Pyllar kept pace. He showed enough renewed vigor to allow the tethered rope to go slack at times, but not always.

Despite this boon, Nyx knew this reprieve would be short-lived. Pyllar would eventually need the crutch of his tether. And that was not her only concern.

Daal voiced it. "We're still moving too slowly."

Nyx stared up at the corsair's looming shadow. She had hoped for more speed after unburdening Pyllar, but that was not the main reason she had asked Daal to make that leap.

She sang a rising storm of notes, driving Bashaliia upward, climbing out of the shadows.

As they headed toward the bright sky, Nyx shouted down to Tamryn, "Keep going! Get everyone to the ship."

Tamryn acknowledged this with a raised fist before vanishing into the shadows.

Bashaliia continued upward.

Daal understood her goal. "You mean to confront the corsair."

"We must stop it, or at least delay it. It's our only hope to escape."

Punctuating this, twin bursts of cannon fire erupted above. The fiery flashes limned the ship's shadow. Thunder shook dust from the walls. Iron balls shattered cliff faces and sent cascades of flying rock into the ravine.

Nyx looked below, searching.

As best she could tell, Tamryn and the two raash'ke had escaped.

If they had been any slower . . .

Daal leaned closer. "The corsair will need to reload their cannons."

"Then we dare not waste this moment."

She urged Bashaliia into a steep, spiraling climb out of the ravine. Daal clutched her lap strap. His breath gasped at her ear. Above, the desert glare blinded. She squinted against it, but they dared not slow to allow their eyes to adjust.

With every beat of Bashaliia's wings, the heat grew more intense.

Finally, they swept clear of the ravine and out into the open, rising like a whirlwind. She could only imagine what this sight must look like. They had exited a short distance from the corsair's bow.

She sang Bashaliia higher until he crested above the ship's sleek gasbag. Below, she caught glimpses of figures scurrying across the deck. Most of the bustling centered on the ship's two cannons. Yet even those men fled back from the sight of a monstrous bat sweeping past their bow.

As Bashaliia circled to face the corsair, Nyx scowled at the flag waving atop the balloon. The sigil of a dark crown and gold sun stoked a fury inside her. That symbol—of the Massif royal family of Hálendii—had plagued her for most of her young life. It had slaughtered her mother, crippled her father, orphaned her as a babe. It had pursued her across half the world.

And here it is again.

She steadied Bashaliia before that threat. Half a year ago, under the frozen stars of the Wastes, she had faced another Hálendiian ship—a battle barge—and had shattered it to pieces. She could not hope to do the same here. Back then, she had been rife with power, raw and untamed, her body overflowing with wild energies after absorbing a firestorm that had raged inside a copper-and-crystal *ta'wyn* dome. She had carried the maelstrom out into the endless night, driven to the edge of madness, unable to contain such a force. She had unleashed it all with such fury that it had cracked the barge in half, sending its fiery ruins crashing into the ice.

Nyx trembled at that memory, fearful of ever having to contain and wield such power again. She knew with certainty it would destroy her—if not in body, then certainly in mind.

She had barely survived the first time. It took Daal to draw her back from a dark precipice of madness. In doing so, she had come to realize the true gift given to her by the *Oshkapeers,* those Dreamers of the Crèche. They had forged Daal to be not only a wellspring of power for her, but also an anchor, one she would need to steady herself.

As Nyx faced the corsair, she appreciated the heat of Daal's body at her back, his breath on her neck, his simple presence. Without touching his wellspring, she drew strength from him.

Be my anchor once more.

Still, part of her balked at what she must attempt. Over the past half year, she had trained with Shiya, worked with Daal, all to hone her skill with bridle-song. But she had never again touched the sigil burned into her mind by the raash'ke horde back in the Wastes.

At least, not purposefully.

In her ears, she heard the shattering of Daal's bones, his cry of agony.

Dread tempered her anger at the sight of the Hálendiian flag.

"Nyx . . ." Daal whispered at her ear, sounding equally worried.

Without turning, she answered that fear. "Do it."

We have no choice.

Daal hesitated for another breath. Then he unlatched his hands from her saddle belt. Iron-muscled arms reached and wrapped around her chest.

The song Nyx had been holding at bay, a tempest bridled to her will, responded to his touch.

Fire ignited between them, melding two into one.

With a gasp, she fell into Daal's embrace—and kept falling. Into him. Into herself. Lines blurred between them. She felt his heart thundering in her own chest. Each beat pounded more energy into her, feeding the bottomless abyss within.

He is flashburn, and I'm the forge.

Fueled by his wellspring, her bridle-song burned brighter.

She remembered the last time this had happened, entwined in Daal's arms, lost in each other's bodies. She fought to hold control as more power flowed into her, drawn from the marrow of Daal's bones, from the iron in his blood, from every fiber of his muscles.

Still, the demand inside her grew greater.

She loosened a hand and grabbed his arm.

Nails sought to dig through leather, to reach skin.

Daal pushed her away—but not in rejection.

He slipped his fingers, then his whole hand under her riding vest. He searched and clawed until his palm discovered bare flesh, just under her bosom. He placed his hand over her sternum. Her back arched at the burning ember of his touch.

Still, she breathed deeply and drew heat from that fire.

The darkness inside her cried a single word.

More . . .

Daal responded. His lips found her neck, a searing kiss offering all of himself, casting everything atop her burning altar.

"Daal . . ."

She could not say who spoke it.

It was both name and warning.

Lost in each other, she sensed the inescapable pull between them. He was a fiery sun. She was a black hole from which nothing could escape, an abyss that could never be sated. She drew upon his power and his life, sucking all from him, leaving him cold.

She let the power build and build until it filled every corner of her, spilling from her skin, out each breath. She could hold it no more—not without risking all.

Fear grew—both hers and Daal's.

Trapped by the tides flowing between them, Nyx fought to tame that maelstrom. She used the echo of breaking bones to help her focus. She refused to be a slave to her dark desires, to the raging power inside her.

Never again.

Fixing this determination, possibly drawing the same from Daal, she reached a golden strand of bridle-song toward the sigil that burned like a fiery sun inside her. She hesitated, still terrified of the untapped power in that branded symbol.

A warning rose at her ear.

"The corsair," Daal gasped out. "The cannons . . ."

Through the fire across her mind's eye, she focused back on the Hálendiian ship. At the bow, two cannons had been cranked upward, their black muzzles aiming toward the sky, toward them. A pair of crewmen held flaming tapers and lowered them toward oiled wicks.

Nyx had no more time.

Like those crewmen, she brought her fiery strand of bridle-song to the wick inside her, the sigil branded into her by the horde-mind of the raash'ke.

The symbol exploded at her touch—at the same time the cannons blasted.

From the sigil, arcane encodings beyond her comprehension burst forth. Ancient words, written in fire, spilled from her lips. She swung her arms high and clapped her hands—the first note of a dreadful chorus.

She opened herself, releasing a song of fury, encompassing all she had to endure until this moment. As she did, the sigil turned power into *purpose.*

She cast out her energy, all that Daal had given to her. As before, her spirit was carried with the tide of her unleashed power.

From the corsair, twin blasts responded. Iron balls exploded toward her. She shrugged them aside as she passed, sending them arcing away. Still, this effort sapped a measure of her strength, more than she had expected. It reminded her that Daal was not a bottomless well of energies. He could offer nothing close to what she had absorbed in the Wastes. She carried only a fraction of that raging power.

Still, she concentrated, tempering the strength inside her. While she could not forge it into an icy sledgehammer like before, she pictured Heartsthorn instead—Graylin's family sword. In her mind's eye, she bound all her golden song, all its potent fire, imagining a single length of sharpened steel.

She rode that blade to the corsair, striking it at its weakest point. She sliced through the thick fabric of its balloon, severing cables and inner supports. She swept past the ship, leaving a ragged rip in her wake.

Horrified screams followed her passage.

With her energies spent, her golden fire snuffed out. The sword faded from her. In the darkness that followed, her spirit fell back into her own body, into Daal's arms. Still, the darkness stayed with her. As before, gutted and hollowed, she had no strength left. Even her eyesight returned to the gloom of her childhood, reducing the world to shadows once again.

She teetered in her saddle.

Daal kept his arms around her. "I've got you."

But with his wellspring drained dry, they no longer shared the intimacy of their merged bodies. This loss pained her—more so than the shadows that stole her vision.

Still, she took solace in knowing both would return with time.

She prayed for that to be true.

Below, a splintering crash reached her ears, silencing the chorus of screams from the corsair's crew. She did not know the extent of the damage, or loss of life. In this small manner, her blindness was a blessing.

"It's done," Daal whispered.

She nodded and sagged into his arms. He was no longer a font of flashburn. She was no raging forge.

Only a man and a woman.

Tears rose as she wished it could always be so.

Weary, she called to Daal and Bashaliia.

"Take me home."

23

Esme clutched the deck rail of the massive wyndship. She tried not to stare below as the Necropolises of Seekh retreated under her. She had never imagined she would fly aboard such a vessel—nor had she ever wanted to.

She preferred the sand under her feet.

Like all Chanaryn.

Behind her, men and women hurried about, shouting to each other, as the *Fyredragon* set off from the mooring field. She sought to keep clear of the trampling crew. Rather than looking down, she craned up at the massive balloon overhead. She struggled to understand how they could be rising so effortlessly. She distrusted such alchymies.

Especially with my life.

Another must have read her skepticism.

Jace stared up along with her. "Back in Spindryft, we modified the *Fyredragon*'s balloon. Sealing it up and filling it with lift-gasses. Before that, to escape the Frozen Wastes, Krysh and I had devised a method of using heated air to raise the ship."

Esme looked at him askance, letting her skepticism show. While packing her few belongings, she had heard a sketch of this group's story. Much remained unsaid. Still, what was told strained credulity. Of the moon crashing into the Urth. Of strange mekanicals that could stir the world into turning. Of an ancient war that had started again, between people and undying gods.

Jace had promised he would supply proof of the latter, but the ship was in such a tumult to depart after they had arrived that any further explanations had to wait. She did not press the matter, not wanting to discourage their haste.

She pictured the anger in Rahl hy Peck's pestilent face.

Best we be gone as quickly as possible.

Upon boarding, she had been shown to a cabin, planked in aged ironwood, all polished to an amber hue. Inside, she had her own bed, even a small porthole. She had never experienced such wealth. Still, she had balked at entering. All she had managed, with Jace's help, was to toss her packs into the room, then she had set off for the open deck.

While the *Fyredragon* was more spacious than she could ever imagine, she still felt trapped inside it, confined by walls that pressed toward her. She wanted to blame it on a Chanaryn's innate distaste for tight spaces, but she knew her difficulty breathing had more to do with her growing trepidation. She feared her decision to act as a guide had been a foolhardy one.

She should have been more patient, especially after securing her bronze treasure—which now rested on her bed in her cabin. Her decision to come aboard had been a rash act. She was abandoning everything and everyone she knew.

She glanced down.

That isn't entirely true.

Drawn by her attention, Jace studied Crikit, too. His eyes grew pinched, shining with curiosity. It looked like he wanted to pin the young molag to the deck and dissect the crab.

Esme trusted he would never do that. She sensed a deep-seated kindness in the man—in his eyes, in his manner—a gentleness that defied his ax wielding in the street. She imagined he must have once been a softer man, until adversity had tempered him into something harder.

She had also learned he was journeyman to the alchymist, a man named Krysh. Jace certainly demonstrated that, expressing a keen interest in her, peppering her with questions about the desert, the ruins below, about the Chanaryn people. She finally had to ask him to stop, to give her more time to settle herself.

He had obliged, his face flushing with embarrassment.

Still, there was no escaping that intellect. He returned his gaze to the balloon, continuing where he left off, explaining what she had not bothered asking about.

"We had to switch to lift-gasses due to our trek into the Barrens. We feared the heated air inside the balloon would be challenged by the scorch of the deep desert. In the Frozen Wastes, that was not a problem."

She nodded, barely hearing him. Instead, she tried to imagine the other half of the world, covered in ice, forever turned from the sun. To the Chanaryn, the sun was a constant. It was their god Pecche'kan, a fiery molag who scrabbled a tiny circle in the sky over the course of a year, forever shining down upon her people.

Even this part of the group's story—of crossing the eternally dark Wastes aboard an ancient ship salvaged from an icy tomb—defied belief.

Maybe these people were all mad, addled and deluded.

If so, I'm even madder to be with them.

Still, she pictured her brother's face: Arryn's crooked smile, the twinkle in his eye, his hiccuping laughter that sounded like a braying mule. As grief welled up, she rubbed at the tattoo of a half sun between her thumb and forefinger. More than anything, she wanted to make it whole again.

On the journey ahead, this ship would undoubtedly cross paths with other groups of Chanaryn nomads, those making sojourns into the deep Barrens. The ship would surely stop and seek knowledge of the lands ahead by asking questions of those deep-desert nomads.

But I will have my own queries for them, too, about any sightings of a god-bound group on a pilgrimage.

Knowing this, she felt more resolute, settled in her decision to board this ship.

To discover Arryn's fate, I will tolerate any madness.

A horn blared from the ship's stern, drawing Esme's eyes. Jace hurried in that direction. Esme hesitated, then followed, letting go of her grip on the rail. Crikit skittered after her, his armored legs tapping loudly.

All three climbed the steep stairs to the top of the aft-castle. This rear section of the ship stood higher than its middeck, rising even taller than the forecastle on the other side.

Once atop the raised castle, Jace rushed to the rail at the stern. Esme kept at his heels, trailed by Crikit. A few crewmen danced out of the way of the scrabbling molag.

The horn blew again, clearly a warning.

But of what?

Off in the distance, a large ship darkened the horizon.

"It's the Bhestyan warship," Jace mumbled.

Esme didn't know what this meant or why Jace's face had gone paler. Then the man stiffened and let out a sigh of clear relief.

"Thank all the gods, there they are." Jace pointed, whether for her benefit or simply out of excitement. "They made it."

She followed his arm and spotted a scalloped shadow racing a league or so ahead of the other ship. She could not make any sense of it.

Jace leaned over the rail and stared down, drawing her eye, too.

Below, a wide door hung open, forming a huge ledge leading into a dark hold below. Another matching door was closed above it, likely marking another storage space.

This ship is massive.

The horn blew again, sounding less like a warning and more like a clarion call summoning a straggler home.

She remembered how the caped swordsman, Darant, had mentioned the ship had been waiting on latecomers. While boarding herself, she had caught a brief glimpse of shadows shredding out of the sky and diving into that dark hold. But with the bulk of the ship and its balloon blocking her, she could not discern who had arrived.

Clearly, though, one more straggler had remained unaccounted.

Esme watched with Jace as the racing shadow grew into a giant bird—or some other winged beast. She squinted into the glare. She made out two figures riding atop the creature. As they approached, the wings grew ever wider, leathery but translucent at their edges. Tall ears stood high atop a head with a crushed muzzle.

Fear drove her back, forgoing her hold on the ship's rail.

No . . .

A strange whistling filled her ears and itched across her scalp. Even this fit the old stories. She covered her ears and retreated farther.

It can't be . . .

Jace glanced back, clearly noting her distress.

She backed again as the beast swept high, exposing a furred belly and trailing a pair of legs ending in massive claws. Then the creature tilted and dove down, sweeping past the cliff of the ship's stern and vanishing out of sight.

She pictured it disappearing into the hold below and remembered those other shredding shadows.

How many of them are there?

Jace joined her, his eyes concerned. "Esme, what's wrong?"

She had to swallow twice to answer. "What was that?"

"I told you we still had much to explain."

This answered nothing. He tried to reach for her arm, but she pulled away.

"I should not be here," she moaned out. "None of us should."

Jace tried to console her again. "Bashaliia may look frightful, but there's not a kinder spirit aboard this ship. His story is a long one. Let me share it with you, then you'll understand."

She took deep breaths, trying to slow her heart. She cast her gaze to the bow, to where the head of a draft-iron dragon stood high, leading them toward the Barrens.

"You sought me as a guide," she whispered. "So heed this. The oldest tales of the Chanaryn people speak of winged daemons of the deep desert. We call them *mankrae.*"

"Sand wraiths," Jace said, using the common tongue.

She nodded. He clearly had been studying their language, which despite her terror endeared him to her.

"The aeldryn of our people, the god-blessed of the Chanaryn, recite ancient stories, carried on the tongue from the deepest past. They speak of the mankrae as enemies of the gods." She stared up at the sun, at the fiery form of Pecche'kan. "They're always harbingers of doom."

Jace frowned and turned to the east.

A roaring rose all around, accompanied by a fiery glow along the ship's flanks and rear. The *Fyredragon* slowly edged away, heading west, driven by its massive forges.

Another horn blared, bleating loudly, again sounding like an alarm.

From a nearby copper tube, a hollow voice full of command echoed out. "Gather in the wheelhouse!"

Jace stared another breath at the warship sweeping toward them—then turned and motioned for her to follow. "Let's hope that doom isn't already upon us."

24

GRAYLIN LEANED NEXT to Fenn at the ship's navigation station. Others continued to gather behind them, summoned by Darant to the wheelhouse.

The captain now manned the large maesterwheel, guiding the *Fyredragon* across the spread of ruins. He shouted orders to the crew operating the vessel's secondary controls that flanked his position. Levers were pulled and screwlike subwheels were spun. The massive ship slowly gained speed and height.

Graylin glanced past the tall arc of windows. The Necropolises of Seekh rolled under their keel. Off in the distance, some thirty leagues away, the ruins ended. Beyond its borders stretched a broken landscape of sand, salt, and scoured rock.

It marked the true edge of the Barrens.

The journey ahead would be difficult enough.

Even without hunters at our back.

Fenn straightened from the ship's array of scopes. The navigator shook his head, his face flushed with fury. "They're still in pursuit—and continue to draw closer."

Graylin expected no different. The Bhestyan warship had surely spotted the *Fyredragon*. With the target in sight, they had no doubt stoked their forges to their fullest. Already in motion, the enemy had the advantage. The *Fyredragon*'s massive bulk took time to get a head of wind behind her, for the forges to push her faster.

We should've left sooner.

He turned to the reason for their delayed departure. Nyx entered with Daal. She hung on his arm. Both looked drawn and hollowed out. Even from across the wheelhouse, Graylin noted the bluish clouding over Nyx's eyes, marking the toll it had taken for her to rescue Daal and his remaining crew.

He wanted to rush over to help her, but he resisted, knowing he would be rebuffed. He had come to accept such attempts at drawing closer to her were selfish on his part. He had only come into her life a year ago—a year of strife, hardship, and loss. He had no right to add to her burden by trespassing where he was not wanted, where he had no role in her life beyond a shared bloodline. Instead, Nyx had found solace in another, in the arms of the young man at her side now.

Graylin had already heard their story, of what had transpired out in the desert. The second rider of the raash'ke team, Tamryn, had rushed up with her report, while Daal and Nyx had settled Bashaliia in the hold and seen to Daal's mount, who had been injured. He had also learned how a Hálendiian corsair had been left broken and stranded in the desert.

One less threat.

He glanced over to Nyx. Despite his anger at the risk she had taken, she had accomplished something remarkable in ripping the enemy from the skies. But there remained another danger out there.

Graylin turned back to Fenn. "Any sign of the *second* Bhestyan warship?"

"None. Daal's diversion must've sent them well off course to the north. They cannot recover in time to be any danger."

Graylin nodded.

"But what are we to do with the bastards behind us?" Fenn pressed him.

Graylin understood the anger that stiffened the navigator's every movement— also the fear shining in his eyes. According to Daal, Fenn's uncle had been spotted aboard the warship, along with the navigator's sister, who appeared to have been abused and was found in shackles.

The young man looked ready to cast off in one of the *Fyredragon*'s sailrafts and go after his sister. This passion clearly trembled through him. Even now, Fenn's hands clenched into fists.

Graylin hated to quash that desire, but he had to be clear. He had already discussed this with Darant and Krysh.

"We can't risk a direct confrontation," Graylin explained. "The warship has us outgunned. Twice the cannons, four times the ballistas. And what we have atop our decks is centuries old. Most of which is crusted by rust and weakened by age. Even if we survived a battle with the Bhestyan ship, the damage sustained could cripple us."

Graylin sighed at his own words. He had hoped to be able to upgrade the *Fyredragon*'s aged weaponry while in Spindryft, or even out here. But harried at every turn, they'd had no time.

Graylin ended with a blunt truth. "We dare not engage the enemy—not even to save your sister. The world's fate depends on us reaching the *turubya* out in the Barrens."

Fenn closed his eyes, as if trying to shut out these words.

"I'm sorry, Fenn."

The navigator's shoulders slumped, but when he opened his eyes, he stared toward Nyx. "But we have *another* weapon at hand. One strong enough to down a corsair."

Graylin followed his gaze. "It will take days for Nyx to recover. Same with

Daal's reserves. And we cannot put them in harm's way again. You must know that."

Even if Nyx did not.

Irritation flashed through him at her rash action. She had risked not only her life, but the fate of the world, too.

"Then what do we do?" Fenn asked, his voice sharpened by pain.

"We fly on. With every league gained, the heat will grow. They cannot pursue us very deep into the Barrens. Not without cooling units. The scorch alone may shake them loose from our path."

Darant approached, after turning the maesterwheel over to his daughter, Glace. The pirate had heard this plan. "Mind you, we may also hit that same fiery wall if we can't get those coolers humming," he warned. "If that happens, we'll be trapped between the scorch and a warship."

"In such a case, nothing will matter from there," Graylin said. "If the cooling units fail to churn, then *all* is lost. Moonfall will become inevitable."

Darant scowled. "So we just run."

"And pray those coolers engage," Graylin finished.

He knew Rhaif and Shiya remained below, monitoring for any change, struggling for any other solutions.

A commotion drew their attention to the door. Graylin straightened, praying for some hopeful news from below. Instead, Jace and Krysh hurried inside. A young woman in white desert garb followed, leading in a calf-sized black crab.

To the side, Kalder burst to his legs at the sight of these newcomers, especially the strangeness of the eight-legged creature. The vargr rushed forward with a deep-throated growl, a ridge of hackles raised across his back.

Graylin stepped forward to scold Kalder away, but before he could utter a word, the crab scuttled to face the challenge, clacking and snapping a pair of foreclaws in clear warning.

Kalder skidded to a stop, then retreated from the noisy display. The vargr's home in the Rimewood had no such beasts, and clearly Kalder did not know what to make of it. From a distance, Kalder skirted a wary circle, sniffing and chuffing, taking in the strange scent, doing his best to judge this threat.

The woman, in turn, stared wide-eyed at the massive vargr. She mumbled angrily in the Chanaryn tongue.

Graylin interceded before matters escalated. He gestured Kalder back, reinforcing it with a firm order. Kalder took several steps away but kept on his legs with his hackles raised.

Satisfied, Graylin faced the others. "What has you rushing in here?"

Jace lifted a hand, holding the map he had secured in Bhestya, while Krysh raised a folded parchment. "Esme may have already helped us. Come see."

Krysh headed toward the open door into the neighboring chart room. "I want to check my calculations to be sure. If I'm right, we may have a problem."

Graylin scowled.

As if we don't have enough already.

GRAYLIN GATHERED EVERYONE inside the *Fyredragon*'s chart room. Even Nyx hobbled into the cramped space with Daal. Not that she could see much with her clouded eyes.

Inside, a single lamp hung from a chain overhead, illuminating walls covered in hundreds of round cubbies, all crammed with curled scrolls of countless maps. Atop a center table, a drawing had been splayed and tacked down. A sextant rested there, along with a sheaf of papers with scrawled calculations in charcoal, marking the labors of the navigator and Krysh.

Graylin had studied this chart countless times. One side had been sketched with the border of the Eastern Crown. The rest showed an expanse of the Barrens, with several known landmarks embellished on it. Most of the additions clustered near the Crown's border. Deeper into the Barrens, those numbers dwindled away to blank paper, waiting to be filled as the *Fyredragon* crossed those lands.

A few flagged pins had been stuck into that empty expanse. Tiny writing marked features that had been copied from the Bhestyan map onto this chart. They hadn't been inked onto the page, as Jace, Krysh, and Fenn were still struggling to assign distances and exact locations.

Looking at the bare chart only highlighted the daunting task ahead.

Jace circled to one side of the table and spread out the copy of the old Bhestyan map. He waved a hand across those pinned flags. "Over the past days, we've been able to correlate a rough approximation of this ancient map to the breadth of the Barrens. Then I ran into Krysh while headed to the wheelhouse with Esme . . ."

The alchymist nodded. "As the ship was already underway, I asked Esme to stop and look at the map we secured, to see if any of what's drawn on it matches what she knows of the deep desert of the Barrens. While she couldn't verify every detail, she did confirm enough."

Graylin glanced to Esme, who looked overwhelmed, her eyes wide and unblinking.

Jace nodded. "I asked her if she knew anything *past* where this map ends."

Krysh unfolded the parchment in his hand and laid it across the chart, to the east of all those flags. "She was able to add a few more details. Nothing she witnessed personally, but the Chanaryn have a rich oral history. She had heard stories of strange sights in the deep desert."

Krysh tapped at places he had crudely sketched onto his parchment. "An ancient lake bed, dried and crusted in bright emerald crystals. Pools of pearlescent black oil that bubble and cast forth poisonous gasses. Deep caves with cold springs."

More spots were marked, but Jace cut him off, plainly too excited for this litany to go on. "But there were even *older* stories she knew. Of sections of the desert even beyond the edge of Krysh's parchment."

"That's right." The alchymist nodded to Esme. "Tell them what you told us, about the gods of the deepest desert, where sand turns to glass."

All eyes turned to the Chanaryn woman. She looked strangled by their attention.

Jace touched her shoulder, not to spur her to talk, but in support.

She sighed out her tension. "I know little more. The Chanaryn have great odes, ancient sagas. The telling of which can take days. But one of the oldest speaks of a strange forest of living crystals. Of vast sands blasted into black glass—and a great beast sleeping beneath it."

"A beast?" Nyx asked, squinting, clearly struggling to pierce the veil over her vision.

Esme stared out the door toward the front of the ship. "A giant *draakki*."

"In the common tongue," Jace translated, "a *dragon*."

"According to our sagas, the creature goes by many names. Most often it's simply called the *Draakki nee Baersh*. Or the *Dragon of Black Glass*. Sometimes it's described as a god, other times as a daemon. But all those stories agree on the *threat* it poses."

"Which is what?" Daal asked.

Esme stared around the table. "According to legend, when the *Draakki nee Baersh* wakes—the world will shatter."

Graylin winced. This apocalyptic warning sounded eerily prophetic of moonfall. Others must have thought so, too, as silence settled around the room. Still, they also knew that if the *turubya* lay in that direction, they dared not turn aside.

Only Krysh seemed oblivious to all of this. As Esme shared her account, the alchymist had collected a scatter of navigational tools and had set about laboring at the far end of the tacked-down chart, opposite the sketch of the Eastern Crown. He had been meticulously measuring with a scissored compass, marking lines in charcoal.

Graylin suddenly guessed where this was all leading. "Esme, according to your stories, how *far* out into the desert does this dragon sleep?"

The young woman reached and touched the sketch that Krysh had drawn on the parchment. It showed the deep cave with a freshwater spring—which surely had to be an important landmark to the Chanaryn nomads. "From here, it takes *yegga menna twil yegga* to reach the Dragon. Or so most sagas claim."

Graylin frowned.

Jace tried to explain. "The Chanaryn measure time by the cycles of the moon. That passage means *five moons times five.*"

"Or roughly two years." Krysh straightened. "But that's across the sand on foot. Aboard the *Fyredragon,* we can cross that distance in less than a tenth of that time."

So, about two months.

Krysh pointed the tip of his measuring compass toward the lone emerald flag staked on that side of the map. Shiya had marked that location long ago. It was their destination in the Barrens, where the second *turubya* was hidden.

"As I feared," Krysh warned, "here is where the Dragon of Black Glass sleeps."

Graylin scowled. "And where we must go."

"And where we dare not *disturb* its slumber," Jace added.

Before anyone could respond to this revelation, a door crashed open out in the wheelhouse. The noise drew them out of the chart room.

Graylin led the way. He discovered the ship's quartermaster searching the wheelhouse with great distress etched on her face.

Vikas gy Wren stood a head taller than Graylin and massed twice his size. She was all muscle and grimness encased in leather armor. She carried a broadsword, one so lengthy it had to be sheathed across her back.

"What's wrong?" Darant asked.

The quartermaster lifted an arm, formed a fist, and stuck out her thumb and smallest finger. She waggled it under her other palm, then turned that hand over to reveal a small scroll sealed in crimson wax.

The gesture was easy to interpret: *A skrycrow reached the ship, carrying a message.*

Darant nodded and took the scroll from her.

Vikas had been born mute—due to her mixed Gynish blood, which also accounted for her sheer size. The craggy giants of the northern steppes—the Gyns—had lost the ability to speak in the distant past, possibly due to the perpetual howl of winds across their cold lands, which deafened all. To compensate, the Gyns spoke in a language of gestures and expressions. Vikas had taught this same to the raash'ke riders, to aid in coordination through the air.

"Who sent the message?" Nyx asked.

Graylin could guess.

Darant confirmed it by turning the scroll and revealing a symbol stamped into the wax. It showed a rearing Bhestyan panther. "I'd say this came from Fenn's uncle."

The navigator rushed over, reaching for the scroll.

Darant rebuffed him. "My ship, my message."

"Read it," Graylin urged.

Darant broke the seal and unrolled the missive. He scanned it silently, his expression darkening as he did.

"What?" Fenn pressed. "Tell us."

"It's an offer. Signed by Orren hy Pashkin." Darant glanced to Fenn. "Your uncle, I presume."

Fenn's angry glare acknowledged this.

Darant lifted the scroll and read it aloud. "'Hand over Fenn hy Pashkin, traitor to the realm, and we guarantee free passage from here. Refuse and we will hang his sister in his stead, from the prow of the *Sharpened Spur* at the first dawn bell. Thenceforth, we will hunt your vessel down with great haste, without mercy. None will be spared.'"

Fenn retreated, as if to flee the horror of those words.

Darant crumbled the scroll. "Sod that. Anyone who uses the word *thenceforth* is not worth the last drip of piss from my cock."

Graylin rubbed his chin, eyes down, weighing their options. If handing over Fenn would end the threat of the warship, it had to be considered. They didn't need an enemy at their back. But he also knew this enemy could not be trusted.

He cleared his throat, sweeping his gaze over those gathered in the wheelhouse. "We must all harden ourselves if we hope to stop moonfall," he stated firmly. "Sacrifices were made in the past and will be made again. In this decision, in this moment, we must weigh *one* life against all the world."

"No!" Nyx stumbled free of Daal's support. Though near blind, she came at him unerringly. "We can't hand over Fenn. If it means a battle, so be it."

Graylin sighed. "We'll do *neither*, Nyx." He could not keep a scolding tone from his words. "Orren's offer of free passage is as worthless as Darant so eloquently attested. The Bhestyans came with a Hálendiian corsair. No doubt promises were made. Fenn's traitorous uncle surely knows what could be gained—both for the kingdom and for himself—by securing us. He will not let such a prize sail off."

"Then what do we do?" Nyx asked.

"We stay the course as planned. We continue forward and pray the desert burns these bastards from our trail."

"But my sister . . ." Fenn moaned.

Graylin turned to him. "Like I said, we must weigh *one* life against all the world."

Fenn looked aghast, knowing who would pay that price.

Graylin offered the only solace he could. "I'm sorry."

A heavy silence followed. They all knew he spoke the truth. Even Nyx stumbled back into Daal's arms.

An objection finally broke through, coming from an unlikely source, stated with absolute certainty.

"We cannot go forward."

All eyes turned to Esme. The Chanaryn woman had drifted to the windows fronting the ship.

She pointed toward the horizon. "Ishuka sweeps toward us. We cannot escape her wrath."

Graylin frowned, spotting no threat, only a glaring haziness.

Jace joined her. "In the Chanaryn tongue, *ishuka* is both the name of a deity and their word for *sandstorm*. I've read of these monstrous squalls. How the two air rivers—flowing east and west—tangle into a snarl that pulls the desert far into the sky."

Graylin squinted. As he watched, the haziness at the horizon darkened, climbing higher and higher, erasing the line between sky and land. Soon, the true breadth of the Chanaryn god revealed itself. The desert rose up into a wall of churning sand, stretching north and south, towering ever taller, certainly beyond their ship's ability to sweep above it.

"She will rip you from Her skies," Esme promised with a dread solemnity.

"What can we do?" Jace pressed her.

"To survive Her wrath, you must bury yourself deep in the sand, while burning offerings to the god above."

"In other words, we must go to ground." Darant shook his head and scowled at Graylin. "So much for your plan to let the desert rid us of our problems."

Graylin ignored the gibe. He knew the storm wasn't the only threat. If they were forced to land, there would be no escaping the Bhestyan warship, no flying from this confrontation.

The faces around him reflected that grim reality.

Except for Fenn.

He looked relieved.

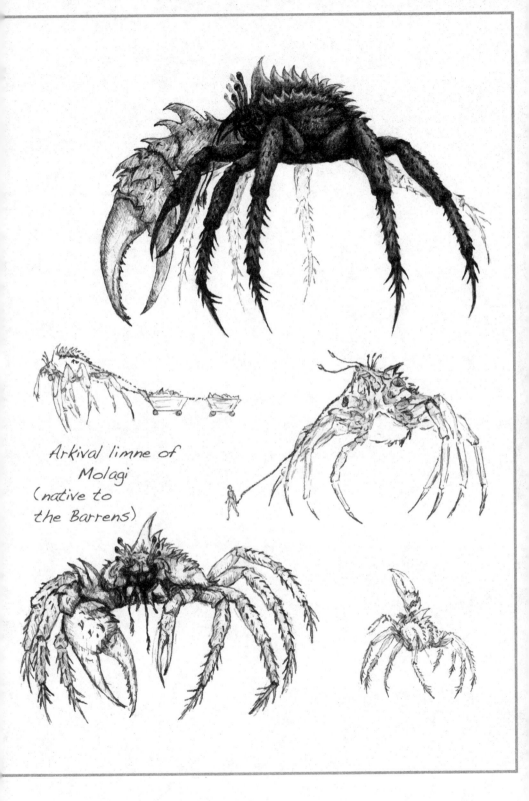

Arkival limne of
Molagi
(native to
the Barrens)

FOUR

A TARNISH
OF BRONZE

Feer not decay. It is meerly a reflection of the time's passyng. Doth not the worm ete the corpse? The tarnish fade the metal? The mold rott the apple? Onli one form of decay should be dread'd by alle: the corruption of the spiryt that wastes a godli man into a feend.

—From the sermon by Gresh im Dellaphon,
royal hieromonk during the Xendorian dynasty
of the Southern Klashe

25

KANTHE SULKED HIS way up the steps of the Blood'd Tower of Kragyn, named after the Klashean god of war. It was the second-highest spire in Kysalimri, second only to the royal residence. The Blood'd Tower housed the empire's map rooms, war libraries, and all manner of chambers devoted to tactics, strategies, and weaponry.

All dedicated to the god Kragyn.

A sculpture of the warmongering deity, chiseled out of granite, rose high out of the Bay of the Blessed. It was one of the thirty-three Stone Gods that graced the harbor into Kysalimri. Kragyn's statue depicted him with four muscular arms, bearing aloft a shield in one, a sword in another, and an ax and spiked mace in the others.

The monument to this fierce god had not been a welcoming sight when Kanthe and the others had returned from Hálendii two days ago. They had arrived sullen in defeat, certain their sojourn had only worsened their circumstances.

With Eligor risen, what hope do we have?

Tykhan's warning had cast a dark cloud over their return to the shores of the Southern Klashe. They had come here to regroup. They had little choice. With Mikaen's return to the city, bearing his poisoned queen, Azantiia had become too dangerous, especially with Wryth having spotted them in the depths of the Shrivenkeep.

By the time they had set sail, the king's legions were already rousting the city, turning over every rock, searching for them. To make matters worse, rumors flew more swiftly than the fastest skrycrow. The reported presence of the traitorous Prince Kanthe in the city bolstered a growing belief that the Southern Klashe had poisoned Queen Myella, risking also her unborn child.

In this way, too, their failed mission had only exacerbated the situation.

How can we hope to ever discover the key to controlling the turubya*?*

A complaint rose behind him. "If you climb any slower, we'll soon be treading backward."

Kanthe grunted back at Rami, "You try dragging this heavy cape up these stairs."

"Ah, but you strike such a handsome figure in it. Most regal, indeed."

"Not that it did any good."

Kanthe tugged the garment higher over his shoulders. He had been abruptly summoned to the strategy room by Empress Aalia, the Illuminated Rose of the Southern Klashe. Prior to that, he had been attending a midday meal with emissaries from Qaar Saur, whom the empire was trying to woo into supplying more draft-iron for the Klashean forces. Such alchymical metal—light but strong—was essential to expanding their fleet of wyndships. Unfortunately, the negotiations had not gone well. The Qaar envoy had not been impressed to break bread with the king consort of the realm, instead of the empress herself.

Even when I came all primped, coiffed, and oiled.

He scowled at the exuberance of his royal attire. He wore a traditional *imri* cap and a splay-sleeved robe that reached his knees—which was all tolerable and matched what Rami wore. But from Kanthe's shoulders, a heavy cape hung. Its gold-and-silver embroidery formed the Haeshan family crest of a mountain hawk in flight, where its eyes were thumb-sized diamonds and its claws were solid gold, all of which weighed as much as a suit of armor.

Rami smiled, finding only amusement in Kanthe's exasperation. "There's a Klashean saying. *The heavier the cloak, the thinner the man.*"

"Which means what?"

"That only the insecure seek to deck themselves so resplendently, to hide what they lack."

Kanthe sighed. "Our Qaaren guests must have believed as much."

"If so, they would be sorely mistaken. I've shared many a steam bath with you. And there is nothing *thin* about you. Especially what hangs between your legs."

Kanthe tripped a step, taken aback at such blunt talk. Even after a year spent on these shores, he still found such rawness discomfiting.

The Klashean culture had a notoriously rigid structure, divided into a dizzying array of castes, but the main division was between the ruling *imri*, which meant *godly* in their tongue, and the baseborn, those who had to remain covered from crown to toe when outside their homes. The Klasheans even had an adage for this strict caste system: *Each to his own place, each to his own honor.*

Still, despite this rigidity, Klashean relationships remained weirdly fluid, both inside and out of wedlock. It was why Kanthe could wear a kingly cloak, sit on a throne next to an empress, yet never hold her heart or share her bed. All knew that honor belonged to another. Still, no one expressed any disdain or ridicule regarding this situation.

At least, not to my face.

Kanthe remembered Frell's earlier explanation for all this. The alchymist had theorized that this fluidity might have something to do with the Klasheans' rigid caste system.

When one screw tightens, another must loosen, Frell had offered.

Which certainly proved true.

Especially with Rami.

The prince shuffled both men and women through his bed, sometimes at the same time. Upon first arriving here, Kanthe had been offered the same accommodation by Rami, who expressed an interest in him that his sister never did. Kanthe had rebuffed him at the time, unable to be that loose. But Rami had taken it in stride, showing no offense, accepting it with his usual cavalier blitheness.

Still—like now—all of this sometimes caught Kanthe off guard. He knew Rami's statement was not a veiled attempt to lure him into bed, but simply a statement of fact.

Kanthe returned it with the same blunt honesty. "I may not be *thin,* but you, Prince Rami, are blessed by the gods."

Rami drew alongside him and clapped him on the shoulder with good-natured appreciation. "It's why I share my bed so freely—to pass that blessing on to as many as possible."

"All must admire your generosity of spirit."

Rami cast him a sidelong look. "And some don't know what they're missing."

Kanthe didn't trip a step this time, knowing Rami was only trying to get a rise out of him. He didn't fall for it. "I suppose some must suffer such a loss. For me, I've got my eye on another."

"Ah, I imagine you do." Rami cast him another amused look. "But are you man enough to shake those bells to ringing?"

Kanthe blushed, picturing Cassta, wondering what effort it would take to do just that. He suspected he might not survive such a challenge.

Rami's voice turned more serious. "My brother, you should truly speak to her. Pining from a corner will get you nowhere."

Before he could answer, the top of the steps appeared. Kanthe rushed the last of the way, leaving the question unanswered. He had no time to ponder dalliances, especially after the disaster in Azantiia.

He climbed into a curved antechamber at the top of the tower. The only level above this housed a battery of nests, where bridle-singers trained and dispatched hundreds of skrycrows each day. Overhead, muffled cries and squawks echoed down.

Kanthe turned his back on the closed doors into the strategy room and crossed to a window that had been cranked open. He stopped to cool his heated brow after the long climb in the heavy cloak. The breeze carried the salt of the sea—and the sharp bite of crow shite.

Still, he lingered there, knowing Aalia had summoned him to discuss what to do next. He girded himself for that hard talk, recognizing there was little they could do.

Past the window, the breadth of Kysalimri—the Eternal City of the Southern Klashe—still stole his breath. Even after a year, his mind struggled with its vast expanse. The city could be a country in and of itself.

Off in the distance, the blue waters of the Bay of the Blessed glinted under the bright sun. Closer at hand, the imperial citadel rose like a marble mountain from the banks of Hresh Me, a central freshwater lake. The palace's walled grounds occupied a landhold as vast as most cities, rising in a hundred spires, so expansive that it took a multivolume series of atlases to map its countless rooms and passages.

But even this fortress paled in scope to Kysalimri itself. The Eternal City spread from the sea in a concentric series of blazing white tiers, climbing in stacks of walls, each more ancient than the last. Thousands upon thousands of white towers pointed at the sky, all crafted of the same white marble, set ablaze by the sunlight. The stone had been mined from the neighboring mountains of the Hyrg Scarp, an enterprise that had worn those peaks down to nubs.

Kanthe finally had to turn away, too daunted by the immensity, by the responsibility it represented. Last winter, a fierce battle had been waged, resulting in great destruction, with thousands of lives lost. The city was still rebuilding those damaged sections.

But if we fail to stop moonfall, none of this will matter.

Tykhan's defeated words still haunted him.

With Eligor risen to full power, doom is inevitable.

Kanthe took a shuddering breath, then shoved down his despair. He refused to accept that judgement. He intended to fight to the very end. He had no choice.

None of us do.

One person certainly agreed with this assessment. A sharp voice cut through the sealed doors into the strategy room. It rang with fury, with frustration, and with the weight of an empire behind it.

Rami stood before the doors and looked back at Kanthe. "It seems our Illuminated Rose is baring her thorns."

26

AALIA IGNORED THE ornate seat, tall-backed and carved with scenes of ancient battles. It towered over a massive ironwood table. The storm inside of her wanted to break out of this confined space.

The walls of the strategy room spread in a circle, built to mimic the shield carried by the war god, Kragyn. The design was to reflect the importance of this room in protecting the realm. Around its walls, hundreds of maps hung in a ring, forming the entire circlet of the Crown's lands.

She swept her gaze across the full range of it. Her efforts were meant to protect *all* these lands—including Hálendii and those regions aligned to it.

For moonfall threatened everyone.

She railed against the shortsightedness of those who had failed to recognize the doom to come, whether out of spite, ambition, or simple denial. It wasn't just Highking Mikaen and his Iflelen dog, Wryth. It was every sovereign, potentate, lapdog, who cast their lot with Hálendii.

She wiped a palm across her brow, as if she could erase her frustration. In fact, it wasn't only those who swore allegiance to Mikaen that drew her ire. She knew many of her own supporters did so out of greed or to abide by century-old pacts—not to thwart the threat of moonfall.

How could they not acknowledge the worsening storms, the tidal surges, the fiercer quakes? The signs are all around.

She wished she could rip the scales from their eyes. Or bludgeon them into submission.

But not even I have that strength.

With a sigh, she returned her attention to the table. Its ironwood surface had been inscribed with a map of the Southern Klashe—the only bastion to stand against moonfall.

She knew it was a fortress she must hold. It was all she could do. The others had their own tasks: to stir the second *turubya,* to secure the location of a key to those ancient devices, and to set the world to turning.

She struck a fist atop the table.

Until then, this is my duty.

She stared around the table to the men and women gathered here. Leaders of her imperial forces—the commanders of the Sail, Wing, and Shield—flanked her seat, joined by their most trusted subordinates. The Eye of the Hidden was also in rare attendance, bringing word from his spies in Azantiia.

In this room, when it came to strategy, no one was above another. She heeded all counsel, though ultimately any final decisions were her own. It was a responsibility as heavy as the cloak she had tossed over the back of her chair.

One pair of eyes recognized this burden and its strain on her.

Tazar hy Maar sat at the far end of the table, opposite her seat. Though he attended as the representative of the *Shayn'ra* rebels, the man had also won her heart long ago. He stared at her, but he did not rise to comfort her, to console her. He only offered her the barest nod, trusting her to make these decisions and to support her how he could.

She drew strength from the firmness of his resolve. That was all she needed from him—at least until later, when they were alone together. For now, she took in his strong features: his hard jaw, wide cheekbones, his bright violet eyes. The curls of his ebony hair matched the sheen of his dark skin. The only blemish was a scar that ran from brow to cheek, crossing through the white paint over his left eye, that marked him as *Shayn'ra*.

While Tazar had not been born *imri*, due to his elevated status here, he could have worn the *gerygoud* habiliment of the ruling caste, which consisted of a short tunic and a white robe with splayed sleeves. Same as Aalia wore now. Instead, he came dressed in the *byor-ga* garb of a baseborn. It was a robe of drab gray brown, belted at the waist. Only he shunned the usual leather cap and veil that hid a baseborn's features—as did all the *Shayn'ra* who rebelled against the caste system, boldly showing their white-striped faces.

Aalia supported the *Shayn'ra* philosophy. Even now, with war brewing and doom threatening, she strove to break down those barriers and create a more open society. But she dared not pull too hard on that thread, lest all order come apart. Chaos would not serve the realm during this time of strife.

It was yet another burden placed upon her shoulders.

She searched the room. She had just finished lambasting everyone due to the lack of progress across multiple fronts. She knew much of her scolding had been ungenerous. Still, sometimes her frustration grew too much.

Is there not someone willing to share a fraction of this weight?

The doors into the chamber swung open.

Rami led the way inside. Behind him, Prince Kanthe—now king consort of the realm—hauled himself in, dragging the heavy cape of his station.

She called over, needing some good tidings. "How did you fare with the Qaaren envoy? Did you get them to increase their draft-iron shipments?"

Their dejected looks answered her query.

Kanthe elaborated. "It seems they will not settle the matter until they have an audience with the empress herself." He tugged at his cloak. "Apparently this was not impressive enough."

She frowned.

Or was it the man beneath?

Again, she found this fleeting thought to be ungenerous. The Qaarens were a people of meticulous decorum. They would take her absence as a slight and respond accordingly.

"I did tell the envoy that there might be a chance you'd meet him," Kanthe said. "That hope has kept him rooted for now. I wager even some acknowledgment by your presence will sway them."

She nodded, appreciating this compromise. "I've already scheduled an Eventoll audience in the throne room. The Qaarens aren't the only ones who need similar assurances. I will add them to the list. We *need* that draft-iron, especially for Tykhan's secret project."

Rami crossed and swept into an empty seat, while Kanthe remained standing. "How is that faring?" her brother asked.

Wing Perash cleared his throat. He seemed hesitant to answer, maybe unsure how much to say aloud. The young commander of the imperial air forces was the son of the former Wing, who had died during last winter's battle. Newly positioned, he plainly struggled to find his footing, though he had already shown himself to be brilliant. Even Tykhan had expressed as much while working with both Perash and Sail Garryn, the commander of their sea forces.

Tykhan's project required both men's involvement.

Aalia nodded for Perash to respond to Rami.

"All is going well," the commander reported. "We're still working through some difficulties. But without a generous supply of draft-iron, we will be challenged in our efforts."

Shield Jojan frowned. He was also new to his command, replacing the bravery of Angelon, who fell defending the throne with his knights. "When will we learn the extent of this project? My men guard its edges, but all are kept in the dark."

It was a fair question. Tykhan's work had been kept hidden behind a walled series of canals trenched from the Bay of the Blessed. The area had since been sealed off and kept heavily guarded.

Aalia weighed whether to reveal more, but motion drew her attention to the weathered form of Eye Hessen, spymaster of the realm. He touched a crooked finger to a corner of his lip, warning her this was not the time. Hessen had crossed his eightieth year. His frail form and rheumy eyes hid a mind sharper and more calculating than any scholar, sometimes frightfully so.

Aalia heeded this silent counsel and addressed Shield Jojan. "Any explanation must also wait for a renewed supply of draft-iron. Otherwise, there will be nothing to reveal."

Hessen lowered his finger to his chin, acknowledging the wisdom of her words.

Shield Jojan looked ready to press the matter, then settled back into his seat. Even he must know that caution had to be taken. Not just in fear of the wrong word flying to Hálendii. The empire had its own enemies within.

Aalia's only other surviving brother—Prince Mareesh—had attempted to use the winter attack on the city to wage a coup against her. In the end, he had been thwarted and driven off, burned and half-blinded, but he was still out there. According to Hessen, many still remained loyal to Mareesh, deeming a woman unfit for the throne.

Wing Perash spoke up again, apparently finding his footing in these procedures. "Beyond the issue with a draft-iron supply, we must consider how much narrower our time has become to complete this task."

Hessen responded, his voice raspy and dry but easily reaching all. "Every skrycrow carries the worsening stakes in Hálendii. The queen's poisoning is blamed upon us, which is no surprise."

Rami stirred. "Did we actually *do* that? Was it a failed attempt by our spies to assassinate their king?"

Hessen frowned harshly, which was expressed by the tiniest tick of his lips. But his irritation was directed not at such a dastardly scheme, but at its result. "We would not have failed."

Aalia interjected, "How far has this accusation spread? How deeply has it been seeded?"

"With both princes—Kanthe and Rami—spotted in the Shrivenkeep, it has taken little effort to convince the populace of our guilt. Especially with the queen just poisoned. The timing was . . . well, not opportune."

Kanthe, who still stood behind Rami, cast his gaze down.

Hessen continued, "And Wing Perash is right to be concerned. Any hope of stoking those early rumblings of dissension among the Hálendiian people has now been dashed. The kingdom rallies anew to their grieving king, which only pushes the advent of war closer."

Kanthe raised his eyes to Aalia. "Which means Tykhan's plan to unite kingdom and empire is now ruined. Remember, Tykhan served for centuries as the prophetic Augury of Qazen. It was his millennia-long evaluations of the tides of history that made him believe such a union was a necessary step to stop moonfall. If Tykhan is right about this, we may have already lost."

Aalia's frustration spiked. With her gaze fixed on Kanthe, her voice grew heated. "Going to Hálendii was a foolhardy risk. I stated as much. More caution should have been taken."

She expected Kanthe, already guilt-ridden, to wilt under her tirade.

Instead, he rode it out, not breaking her gaze. "Aalia, I'm sorry we've reached this impasse, but I'm *not* sorry we attempted what we did." He waved a hand to encompass the encircling map of the Crown. "All will come to ruin if we don't stop moonfall, which requires securing the key. If anything, in retrospect, we should have attempted this gambit long before now, before Eligor gained enough strength to thwart us. It was *caution* as much as foolhardiness that brought us to this brink."

Kanthe glowered across the table. Rami lifted an arm to try to calm him, but he pushed it away.

Aalia recognized that Kanthe was not entirely wrong. Perhaps they had been too judicious, too prudent, in their efforts and plans. When it came to facing the threats ahead, perhaps a measure of recklessness would serve them better.

Still, a stubbornness kept her from acknowledging his words. Instead, she challenged him. "Then what do you propose we do next?"

Kanthe sighed, letting some of his anger go. "Anything we can. First, we must hope Frell, Pratik, and Tykhan can discover something in the Abyssal Codex about Eligor that might offer a direction forward." His gaze hardened to flint. "And then we must strike immediately. Whether we're ready or not. And bring this fight to Hálendii."

Aalia stared at the former prince, now her consort, gaining a new measure of respect for him. Still, she kept her features stoic. "If so, we'll need more than *knowledge*."

Kanthe frowned—then smiled with understanding. "We'll need more draft-iron."

Aalia swept her cloak from her chair and headed for the door. "Come. Let's get that done." As she passed him, she tossed him the smallest compliment. "Maybe it's wise that I did marry you."

Rami followed. "If you ever took him into your bed, you might discover another reason."

She ignored her brother.

Behind her, Kanthe groused to Rami, "Don't get me killed."

Rami sighed with exasperation. "By all the gods, I'm only trying to slide you into *someone's* bed."

27

DEEP IN THE Abyssal Codex beneath the imperial citadel, Frell fought down the daemons inside him. He hated entering the ruins of this ancient librarie. Even after half a year, the reek of smoke persisted from the firestorm that had swept through it. The flames had destroyed most of the multilevel archive— once the domain of the Dresh'ri, the scholars and protectors of the librarie.

The inferno had killed many and had come close to killing him, too.

Frell's heart pounded in his chest, as if he were still outracing the war dogs and foul Venin who had haunted these stacks. His hands clutched hard to one another, as if in prayer.

Still, Pratik had insisted that he and Tykhan join him. The Chaaen scholar had discovered a half-burned book, one cryptic but possibly pertaining to the *ta'wyn*.

Frell respected Pratik's judgement in this matter. The Klashean had an iron collar welded around his neck, marking his status as an alchymist from Kysalimri's lone school, a brutal place called the *Bad'i Chaa*, or the House of Wisdom, where failure meant death.

Besides the collar, Pratik's body bore other evidence of the school's harsh tutelage. Beneath his robe, scars crisscrossed his dark skin, but the foulest cruelty of all came early on. The House of Wisdom demanded purity from its students and enforced it by clipping their firstyears, castrating the boys and doing worse to the girls. In the end, those few who survived were rewarded by being collared and indentured to the *imri* class, to forever serve as chaaen-bound advisers.

Pratik had eventually been unbound, but he still kept the collar—whether out of some misplaced nod to tradition or out of pride—with the iron serving as a symbol of his accomplishment.

"How much farther?" Frell called forward as he followed Pratik down a spiral staircase.

"We're close."

As they continued, each of the archive's levels was smaller in circumference than the one above it, forming an inverted pyramid pointing deep into the Urth. Frell noted bright motes of lanterns held by students and scholars shining in the darkness of the fire-gutted tiers. They marked regions of ongoing renovation. Hammering, pounding, and shouts also reached the central staircase.

Tykhan's heavy footfalls trailed Frell, sounding like drumbeats on the stone steps. "You've made great progress on the repairs, Pratik."

"The work is both gratifying and heartbreaking. So much was lost."

"Yet, something was recovered," Frell pressed him. "Why did you not simply bring it to us? Why must we come down here?"

"You'll understand," Pratik said. "It's on the next level."

As they wound down to it, Pratik led them off the steps and onto the second-to-last tier. A single lantern glowed out in the darkness, like a lone star in the Frozen Wastes. Pratik retrieved another oil lamp that had been abandoned by the steps. With a flash of flint on iron, he sparked a tiny flame to life.

"This way."

He set off across a floor whose rock remained scorched and black. Refuse had been shoveled to the sides, waiting to be hauled away. Frell noted charred bones amidst the wreckage. Many of the Dresh'ri had died during the fire.

"I discovered this site after you all left for Hálendii," Pratik explained as he headed toward the shining star in the darkness. "I feared disturbing it, lest I damage the artifact."

Frell's curiosity dampened his terror. "Artifact? You claimed it was a half-burned book."

"Yes and no. It's the best way I could describe what I found." Pratik glanced back, the lamplight reflecting off his collar. "And I could be wrong. It might be nothing, but I found the artifact in the section of the Codex that pertained to the legends of the *Vyk dyre Rha,* the Shadow Queen. It's why I had to take you to nearly the bottom of the librarie."

Frell understood.

The Dresh'ri buried their greatest secret as deeply as they could.

For ages, the Dresh'ri had slaughtered anyone who learned of this legend, reserving all knowledge for themselves. They both worshipped and feared the *Vyk dyre Rha.*

Pratik hurried forward, as if his discovery were a lodestone drawing his iron collar. "Most everything was consumed by the flames, but in doing so, it revealed what had been hidden even deeper."

Frell and Tykhan followed. Ahead, the lantern's light slowly illuminated a mountain of charred lumber, piled across the far wall.

Pratik guided them toward it with his lamp held high. "For months, I've been sifting through this debris, preserving every scrap or page that survived the fiery purge. Then three days ago, my excavation finally reached the wall behind it. I thought my search was over. But then a glint caught my eye. It reflected the lantern light, shining past where a few fire-cracked bricks had fallen away. So, I set about carefully chipping at mortar and removing more bricks."

"What lay behind the wall?"

"At first, it looked like a panel of ancient glass. I thought it might be a bricked-over window, something carried down here as decoration, then covered up later."

After reaching the pile of debris, Pratik led a crooked path through it. The smell of charred resin and woodsmoke choked the throat.

"This morning," Pratik continued, "I cleared enough to uncover the edge of the hidden glass. Rather than a thin window, the chunk of crystal appeared to be over a handspan thick. I didn't know what to make of it—until I remembered your story, Frell."

"My story?"

"Of another librarie. Composed of tomes carved from crystal."

Frell stiffened, nearly tripping. "You mean the *ta'wyn* archive we discovered beneath the Shrouds of Dalalæða?"

Frell pictured the vandalized remains of that librarie, of shelves filled with crystal volumes, of others cracked and ruined. He glanced to Tykhan, remembering his explanation, how such places were incorruptible storehouses of *ta'wyn* memories. The one under the Shrouds had been meant to preserve Shiya's knowledge, but most of it had been destroyed, crippling her past— enough that Tykhan had come to question her loyalty, fearing she might actually be an agent of the *Revn-kree,* that perhaps her memory of a traitorous past had been shattered away. He feared she might one day remember her true loyalty.

Frell refused to believe that, but caution was warranted.

"Show us," Frell said.

Pratik crossed the last of the distance, climbing past a stack of bricks to reach a gap in the far wall. Through an opening in the middle, a waist-high chunk of crystal sat atop a stone slab. The bench itself looked familiar. It matched another slab that Frell had seen down here, one used as an altar in the past.

A chill passed through him.

Tykhan, though, had a far greater reaction. He rushed forward, bumping both Pratik and Frell to the side. "You were correct, Pratik. It truly is an *arkada!*"

Frell knew *arkada* was the *ta'wyn* word for their crystalline books. According to Tykhan, knowledge could be preserved in that form until the universe went cold.

"Who put it there?" Frell asked.

Pratik shrugged. "I can't say. I asked one of the Dresh'ri, a wrinkled prune of a hieromonk. He knew the history of the Abyssal Codex, having studied it all his life. He claimed the wall had been in place for three thousand years. So, whoever hid it did so a long time ago."

"But why? To protect it?"

"Maybe, but I don't think so. To me, it appeared the Dresh'ri fully trusted their safeguards."

Frell nodded his agreement, picturing the bridle-singing Venin.

Pratik rotated the collar about his neck, an absent-minded gesture that Frell had come to recognize as contemplation. "It's almost as if they grew to fear the artifact and walled it away—not for its safety, but for their own."

Frell sensed he was right. "Maybe they couldn't bring themselves to destroy it. The Dresh'ri were scholars and archivists. Despite their fear, they might have wanted to preserve it."

"So they hid it in the dark."

Until now.

Ahead of them, Tykhan ran his palms over the glass, noting its thickness. He traced a finger along a spiderweb of old cracks. He then used the hem of his shirt to try to rub away some of the scorch from the bricks.

The artifact did indeed look like a giant half-burned book.

Pratik stepped toward Tykhan. "What do you make of it? Considering where it was hidden, it must relate to the legends of the *Vyk dyre Rha*. It's almost like this is the seed planted that grew into this section of the librarie dedicated to the Shadow Queen."

"Could there be anything valuable still retained in there?" Frell pressed him. "Something we can use? Did you not say these *arkada* can store knowledge over a great span of time?"

"Yes, but this one is damaged." Tykhan passed a finger again along those cracks. "It may be useless. Still, I will try. But I must concentrate."

He waved the two men off.

As the first bell of Eventoll echoed through the hollow librarie, Frell attempted to pace away his anxiety. Tykhan continued to remain a statue fixed before that crystal window, a possible link into the past.

What is taking so long?

Pratik stiffened, raising an arm. "Look!"

Frell spun around to face Tykhan. Nothing appeared to have changed, but Pratik stepped closer, drawing Frell with him.

Tykhan still held his palms pressed atop the glass. Only now a glow had appeared beneath them, as if warming those hands. It was hard to discern if the shining came from his bronze fingers or from the crystal beneath his palms.

"Something's happening," Pratik whispered.

Frell hushed him, fearful of disturbing Tykhan's concentration.

Slowly, the glow spread across the crystal, clouding its clarity, turning it milky white. The shine reached the edges, then grew ever brighter, slightly pulsing, as if something were trying to break through.

Tykhan finally gasped, while keeping his palms on the crystal. "I can make out something." His voice was a hoarse whisper. "Most . . . Most of it's chaos. Just pieces. Glimpses. From thousands of eyes."

"Of what?" Pratik asked.

"War."

Tykhan leaned forward, nearly resting his forehead against the glass, his back bent by his efforts. The glow grew brighter. The crystal vibrated, casting out a ringing chime that ate into Frell's skull.

Tykhan continued, his voice drawn and pained. "It's . . . It's an account of the ancient battle among my kind. But seen through the gazes of the *Revn-kree.*"

Frell swallowed, fearing this question. "What of Kryst Eligor? Do you see him?"

"Yes . . ." That one word strained out of Tykhan. "Only from a distance. Atop a mountain. He's limned by fire . . . but his shape at the core is pure darkness, more abyss than body, as if his form is drawing all sunlight into it."

Frell knew the *ta'wyn* could draw verve from the sun.

Is that what Tykhan is describing? Or is it something more?

Frell longed to commune with Tykhan, to share this vision—though he suspected his mind would be destroyed in the process.

"Such power," Tykhan moaned, his form trembling in awe and terror. Then the *ta'wyn* stiffened, as if in sudden realization. "*Too* much power . . ."

Pratik must have noted the change in Tykhan's timbre—from horrified defeat to an inkling of something else. He shared a worried look with Frell.

Before they could raise a question, Tykhan's body jolted with a cry of horror.

"No . . . it cannot be . . ." Raw terror entered his voice, fierce enough to drive Frell a step back.

"What?" Frell pressed him. "What do you see? Something about Eligor?"

"No," he gasped out in despair, in denial. "I see *another.*"

Pratik stepped forward. "Who?"

Tykhan bellowed in pain, crashing to his knees. As he did, the crystal flared with a blinding brilliance—then exploded in a shatter of glass.

Tykhan got buffeted back, his bronze ringing under the assault.

Frell swung away, but shards pierced his robe, sliced his skin. A piece severed off the tip of his right ear with a lash of fire. To the side, Pratik had balled himself up. Luckily, he had been close enough to Tykhan that the *ta'wyn's* bulk acted as a shield.

Then it was over.

Crystal tinkled off into the darkness before going silent.

Frell covered his injured ear, but he barely felt the pain. He stumbled forward and confronted Tykhan. "At the end? What did you see?"

Tykhan climbed to his feet, which appeared to take great effort. The life looked drained out of him. His face had stiffened, like hardened wax. The azure shine of his eyes had faded to a dull glow.

Pratik noticed this, too. "He expended too much of himself. We need to get him back into the sunlight."

"No." Frell blocked the way. "What did you see, Tykhan? Who else, if not Eligor?"

Tykhan struggled to free his leaden lips, to get words to spill forth. "A threat . . . a weapon . . . brandished by the *Revn-kree* . . . glimpsed through a thousand eyes. It rose from behind Eligor, cresting above the black sun of his body."

"What threat?" Frell grabbed Tykhan's arm, finding the bronze unyielding and cold. "What did you see?"

The waning glow in Tykhan's eyes fixed on him, still showing a sheen of terror. "It was the *Vyk dyre Rha*."

Pratik gasped, "What? How?"

"I saw a woman raging atop wings of fire . . . descending from the mountaintop, ripping through us . . ." Bronze fingers clamped onto Frell's wrist. "Eligor . . . was wielding her like a sword."

Frell fought to free his wrist, but Tykhan's fingers could barely move. Still, Frell tugged himself loose and stumbled away—both from the stiffening bronze and from those words.

Frell swallowed and pointed up. "Pratik, get Tykhan back to the sun."

"What are you—"

"I need a moment."

Frell grabbed the lantern from the floor and set off. He fled through the darkness to reach the stairs. Rather than climbing free of this foul den, he headed toward its bottommost level. He hurried down, sweeping along the last curve of the stairs. It ended at a set of tall doors, one half of which stood open. As his feet slowed, his ears strained for the dreaded singing of the Venin, who once nested within.

They're gone now, he had to assure himself.

He forced himself over the threshold. The room beyond was small, carved of bare rock, the innermost sanctum of the Dresh'ri. With a shudder, Frell crossed to a waist-high slab of stone at the back. It looked very much like the bench upon which the crystal *arkada* had been perched.

It made him wonder.

Had the Dresh'ri known of the story buried in glass? Had some ancient ta'wyn *told them, maybe accessed it for them? Is that what terrified them?*

Frell raised his lantern, casting its light above the slab. Across the back wall, glowing emerald veins traced throughout the stone, all appearing to radiate from a drawing in the center. It had been sketched in soot and black oil.

It depicted a giant full moon rising from behind the altar. Silhouetted against it was a black beast with outstretched wings, edged by fire. Atop it rode a dark rider, as hunched as the beast itself. The rider's eyes were stabs of that same vile emerald, glowing with menace.

Frell named this rider. "The Shadow Queen."

By now, all suspected the prophesied *Vyk dyre Rha* referred to Nyx. Frell had attested as much in this room, revealing her identity to the vile leader of the Dresh'ri. But in his ears, as if etched here, Frell again heard the dread chanting of the Venin in this sanctum.

Vyk dyre Rha se shan benya! Vyk dyre Rha se shan benya!

Frell knew what those words in the Elder tongue portended. He whispered them aloud. "She is the Shadow Queen reborn . . ."

The last word stuck in his throat.

Reborn.

But for someone to be reborn . . .

There had to have once been *another.*

He turned to the door, picturing the shattered *arkada* and the secret it had hidden for millennia. According to Tykhan, the past incarnation of the *Vyk dyre Rha* had been enslaved to Eligor's will.

Frell struggled to understand what this meant—both in the past and now.

He returned his attention to the malignant sketch on the wall. He pictured Nyx, replacing her with the emerald-eyed daemon atop those wings of fire. Their group had always feared that any remaining *Revn-kree* would fight to destroy Nyx, to keep her from stopping moonfall, an apocalypse that would destroy all life and leave the empty world in control of the *ta'wyn.*

But what if we're wrong? He closed his eyes, hearing again Tykhan's testament as to who controlled the Shadow Queen. *What if the enemy, rather than seeking to destroy Nyx, wants to retrieve the fiery sword they had dropped long ago?*

Frell kept his head bowed, weighing the steps forward. Nyx was on the opposite side of the world. Whether she proved to be an ally or enemy in the end, it was beyond their control. Only one path lay open to Frell and his allies.

A goal that had been theirs all along.

Only now it was more important than ever.

Frell opened his eyes, picturing a towering bronze figure atop a mountain. If Nyx ever became that creature's fiery sword, there remained only one hope for the world.

We must wrest that key from Eligor's fingers—or die trying.

28

KANTHE STIRRED WITH the ringing of the third bell of Eventoll. He had drifted off into a drowsy slumber while seated on his throne. He raised his chin from his chest and gazed blearily across the cavernous expanse of the grand audience chamber.

The space could have accommodated a wyndship floating under its arched rafters. Massive pillars—so wide that it would take ten men's linked arms to circle one—held up the roof. Between them and off to the sides, tiered galleries of polished wood climbed the walls. They could seat thousands, but this late in the day, only a handful dotted those levels. Same held true for the rows of benches lining either side of the floor. The aisle between, shining in white marble, led from a spread of huge doors on the far side and arrowed straight toward the two gold thrones.

To work loose a crick in his neck, Kanthe stretched his shoulders and swung his chin from side to side. He almost dislodged the thin silver circlet that crowned his head. He craned up at the golden sheen of his seat. It stood notably shorter than its neighbor, where Aalia sat with a stiff back, nodding as a courtier bowed and scraped. The latter was clearly overwhelmed to be in the presence of the Illuminated Rose.

Kanthe had to admire Aalia's fortitude. Over the past two bells, she had sat with the same pasted smile, maintained a quiet tone and demeanor, no matter if the petitioner sought a great boon or simply a nod of her head.

But at least the end's in sight.

The last supplicant waited to greet Aalia. It was the envoy from Qaar Saur, whose demeanor certainly matched his land's name. The *sour* set to his lips spoke of the man's impatience. The white-bearded envoy had changed out of his midday garb. He stood now in a stiff green cloak that looked freshly ironed. Its fox-fur trim had been neatly brushed. Beneath the cloak, shimmering silver scales covered his satin surcoat, reflecting the room's thousands of lanterns.

The envoy whispered to his entourage, who were also finely attired, just not as grandly as the man himself—no doubt upon his orders.

Finally, Aalia lifted a hand adorned with rings, including the one that bound Kanthe to her. She motioned the last group forward. "Ah, Millik hy Pence, I'm glad you could lengthen your stay. I had hoped to meet you, to welcome you properly to Kysalimri."

He swept forward, each step more grandiose than the other, requiring much sweeping of his cape. He looked like an aging rooster trying to impress a young hen. As Millik approached, he ignored Kanthe, his eyes only on Aalia—which Kanthe could understand.

Aalia wore a silver gown laced with the faintest image in gold of the Hae-shan Hawk. Above her brow, she carried a circlet of meteoric black iron imbedded with sapphire gems. But the most magnificent sight hung from her shoulders. Her matching cape had been spread wide across her seat, sweeping out like wings, revealing the rubies sewn across the inner silk, forming the petals of a rose.

The same image glowed above her as the sun shone through a rosette of stained glass. It was Aalia's namesake: the Illuminated Rose of the Imperium. But the ethereal sight was flanked by two outswept golden wings and grounded by two massive obsidian swords in front of them. The latter represented the land's symbol, the crossed blades of the Klashean Arms. Though, after Aalia had been crowned empress, many referred to the swords as the Black Thorns of the Rose.

Millik approached with a sweeping bow, then dropped to a knee. "It is an honor, Your Majesty."

She bowed her head in acknowledgment.

As the pleasantries continued, Kanthe could not keep his chin from drifting lower. The droning lulled him.

Then a sharpness of tone drew his attention back up. He had clearly missed a significant portion of the conversation.

"Hy Pence," Aalia said sternly, using the envoy's last name, "our two lands have a long history of shared cooperation. Going back centuries. Was it not our Wing and Sail forces that shut down the piracy that plagued the seas around your archipelago? Yet, you begrudge us some additional tonnage of draft-iron from your forges."

The envoy's eyes flicked above, likely noting those Black Thorns. "We would be happy to oblige, but in this war footing, there has been a vigorous demand for our resources, with iron fetching much higher margins. You must appreciate our situation."

"I appreciate that, in this time of great need, Qaar Saur turns its back upon its staunchest ally."

"That . . . That is not our intent, Your Grace. We merely seek adequate compensation, especially with the shortness of delivery. It will be quite taxing to meet your schedule."

Aalia leaned forward. Kanthe swore it was the first time over the last two bells that she had shifted in her seat. Her features darkened from honeyed bitterroot to shadowy storm clouds. By now, he knew Aalia could only be pushed so far. From the deeper lines edging her eyes, she was clearly exhausted, which always shortened her temper.

Kanthe had also learned much about the Qaar Saur envoy during their midday repast. He knew wounding this man's pride would only serve to compromise these negotiations. Before the situation worsened, Kanthe cleared his throat.

Gazes flicked toward him, as if surprised to find him sitting there.

Kanthe lifted a hand. As the second-born son of a king, he had learned to study those around him. It had served him well in the past. While Mikaen shone brightly, Kanthe found the shadows offered him better opportunities. With a keen enough set of eyes, one could discern details that others missed.

Millik had already shown himself to be a coxcomb, full of pride, and no doubt seeking ways to enhance his standing—both at home and perhaps here.

Kanthe decided to test the man's mettle.

"Millik hy Pence," he stated formally, "I was delighted to see you included your daughter and son in your entourage."

Kanthe nodded to the pair, who stood below the dais, shadowed by their father. The daughter looked to be a year or so younger than her brother, a touch mousy, but not without some beauty. The son, maybe a year older, was about the same age as someone Kanthe knew well.

"It seems Prince Rami has found himself forlorn of boon companions. He spends too much time locked away by himself. I can't think of a better pair suited to draw him out, to perhaps become great friends—if not more."

Millik glanced to his daughter, then to his son. When he faced back around, his eyes shone brighter, his back straighter. "Is that so?"

"It is indeed." He turned to Aalia. "Would you not agree?"

Aalia leaned back, the storm fading from her face. "It is sadly true. My brother is sorely in need of true confidants. With the empire upon my shoulders, I'm afraid I've sorely neglected him. Especially considering he's second to the throne."

Millik licked his lips. "I must say I'd be honored to have my children spend time in Kysalimri. To learn what they can, to get to know your dear brother much better. As you said, our two lands share a long history of cooperation."

"To that end," Kanthe said, "I'm sure we can work out this other matter to everyone's satisfaction, could we not? It is nothing compared to the bonds forged between families."

Millik nodded, bowed, then bowed again more deeply. "I will make it happen. You have my word."

Kanthe nodded, tried to stand, but he got pulled down by the weight of his cloak. The scabbard of his ceremonial sword clanked loudly against the edge of the gold throne. He settled back to his seat, lest he embarrass himself further.

Besides, I've done enough for one day.

KANTHE WAITED IMPATIENTLY for his freedom. With the royal audience coming to an end, he let the final pleasantries and promises wash over him. Eventually those in attendance filtered away.

Finally . . .

Aalia lifted a hand and a cadre of Paladins crossed to her side. The royal knights—decked in light armor and chain mail—served as attendants and bodyguards. They dropped to their knees before her.

Aalia waved them up. "I believe we're finished here, Regar. We're ready to return to our residences."

The Fist of the Paladins rose to his feet. "Of course, Empress."

As Aalia stood, she abandoned her massive ceremonial cloak atop the throne. A trio of her chaaen-bound rushed forward to collect it.

Her other thirty Chaaen—a mix of men and women, all harshly educated at the *Bad'i Chaa*—had taken seats in the front rows of the hall. Though indentured into servitude, they acted as aides, advisers, counselors, and teachers. As was tradition, the head of the imperium had thirty-three Chaaen, one for each god of the Klashean pantheon.

Kanthe had twelve assigned to him, too, but he could not even remember all their names. In fact, he seldom saw them.

After assuming the throne, Aalia had loosened the demands upon the Chaaen. Normally, in public, the Chaaen were bound by silver chains that ran from their collars to their charge's legs. Aalia seldom required this, reserving such a display for only the most ceremonial of occasions. Still, she had not cast aside the custom entirely.

It was a balancing act that Kanthe respected—especially as he had never learned to walk while dragging twelve Chaaen behind him by his ankles.

Sometimes he found the Klasheans to be a bewildering people.

But at least, they're on the right side of this battle.

Kanthe hauled to his feet, drawing his cloak with him. He refused to ask any of his Chaaen to carry this burden.

Aalia joined him. She took his hand in a rare show of support as they set off with their cadre of Paladins. "You did well back there. Though I'm not sure Rami will think so. He will not be happy with you foisting those two Qaarens on him."

"That's what he gets for retiring early and leaving us to the wolves."

"True. And whether he appreciates your effort or not, I did. Though I could do with a bit less of your snoring."

He glanced at her, looking frightfully offended. "I don't snore."

"I think the entourage from Hrakken would disagree. I could barely hear what they wanted."

She squeezed his hand with a ghost of a smile, then let him go. As they exited the throne room, Tazar swept up to take his place. None of the Paladins cast the *Shayn'ra* leader a second glance.

As Aalia took the rebel's hand, she hung heavily on his arm, plainly exhausted, like a rose near to wilting. Tazar leaned down and kissed the crown of her head. They murmured to one another as they continued down the maze of hallways, aiming for the guarded residence tower.

Kanthe noted this quiet affection, wishing he had someone to share his burden—or at least this damned cape.

As he forged on, his feet began to drag.

But he was not the first to stumble.

A Paladin on his left tripped, tried to catch himself, then fell headlong with a rattle of armor. Kanthe frowned. He had never seen a knight take a misstep.

Then another fell.

And another.

Tazar swung Aalia under him, shielding her with his body. "We're under attack."

Kanthe could not fathom from where. Then he felt taps on his cloak. He stared down at the little feathered darts peppering the thick fabric. He recognized them—from when he had been ambushed last winter while lounging in a bath in X'or.

Assassins . . .

Tazar grunted, then slumped to the floor, plainly struck. His gaze swept to Kanthe, pleading, desperate—not at his own predicament, but in concern for Aalia.

The first Paladin who had fallen had begun to convulse on the floor. His armor chimed like an alarm bell against the marble tiles.

Poisoned . . .

Back in X'or, Kanthe had only been knocked out, drugged into oblivion.

That's not the case here.

Kanthe spun and whipped off his cape. He threw it over Aalia, covering her fully. "Stay down!"

By now, Tazar had gone limp.

More knights fell, attacked by darts from unseen assailants.

The last—the Fist of the Paladins—managed to free a horn. He had wisely crouched low, balling up tight. The posture bunched his armor into a shield, while offering less of a target to the darts.

Regar blew his distress, a deafening blare that echoed away. Hopefully it reached the tower residence, whose entrance was heavily guarded.

Kanthe understood the choice of the location for this ambush. In these hallways between the throne room and the tower, their defense dropped to its weakest point.

Taking advantage of this, four shadows dashed into view. Three came from ahead, one from behind. With the horn sounded and time running out, the assassins had abandoned their blowguns, especially as Aalia remained shielded by the cloak.

To remedy that, the four rushed at them, carrying swords.

The three in front swarmed Regar, pinning the Fist down. Steel clashed amidst low grunts. There were no harried shouts. The determined silence spoke to the assassins' skill.

Kanthe moved to block the fourth man, who sprinted up from behind, racing for Aalia. Kanthe yanked out his ceremonial sword. The curved blade was his only weapon, but steel was steel, and its point was sharp.

Kanthe recognized the dark garb of the assassin. The clothing was belted at hip, knees, and elbows, leaving little loose cloth to snag. A scarf covered head and face, revealing only eyes. He had seen such gear before and knew who attacked him now.

The Brotherhood of Asgia.

It was the same mercenary group who had kidnapped and delivered Kanthe to Mikaen last winter. The Brotherhood's talent was notoriously daunting, but that did not stop Kanthe from defending Aalia.

He lifted his sword.

Clearly unimpressed, the attacker did not slow. He swept close and leaped at the last moment. Kanthe tried to feint to the left, but the assassin was not fooled. The assassin's sword pierced Kanthe's guard and stabbed for his throat.

Reacting on instinct, Kanthe took the only action he could. He jammed out his hand and grabbed the sword. As the blade struck, it found no flesh. Its steel clanged against the bronze palm of Kanthe's replacement hand.

Shock narrowed his assailant's eyes.

Kanthe used the moment to drive his blade into the assassin's belly. The curved blade arced deep and high, passing under the rib cage to the heart. Fueled by panic, Kanthe's thrust lifted the man off his toes. The assailant hung on the sword for a long breath. Blood poured through the scarf over his mouth. Then his body toppled away, tearing the impaled sword from Kanthe's fingers.

No . . .

Kanthe lunged after it, especially as he heard the soft pad of an assassin's sandals rushing this direction. He clutched the sword's handle and tugged, while twisting around.

A black-garbed figure raced toward Aalia. Past him, Regar was down on both knees, one arm hanging limp, his sword on the marble. Two bodies lay sprawled in spreading pools of blood.

The third assailant hadn't bothered to dispatch the wounded Fist.

Not with the true target vulnerable and defenseless.

Kanthe yanked his sword free, but he was already too late.

The assassin ripped away the heavy cloak.

As he did, Aalia sprang out of hiding, leading with her ceremonial sword— her true Black Thorn. She stabbed the blade under his chin, twisting as she did so. He fell backward, off the sword, his neck torn to the spine—then collapsed dead.

Kanthe hurried to Aalia, holding aloft his blade.

Regar stumbled to join them, leaving a trail of blood.

Then shouts reached them.

Knights and guardsmen rushed in from all directions.

Aalia ignored them, pushing free of Kanthe and Regar's protection. She fell to her knees before Tazar's form. Two Paladins continued to rattle in convulsions. The others lay still, already dead.

"Tazar . . ."

She tried to grab his hand—but a savage convulsion ripped it away.

29

AALIA HELD DOWN Tazar's shoulder, leaning all her weight atop him.

Still, he thrashed and bucked under her. Froth poured from his lips. His eyes had rolled so far back that they only showed white. She wanted to sob, to throw herself across him and weep, but she held him down harder, refusing to let him go.

Kanthe sat on Tazar's legs, his face gaunt with distress, especially as his gaze swept over the dead Paladins. Aalia dared not look that way or despair would overwhelm her.

A sharp shout drew her attention up. Two women shoved through the crush of knights and guardsmen.

The taller of the two elbowed her way forward, scolding those around her. "Get back! All of you!"

Aalia searched her face. "Saekl, is there anything you can do?"

The long-legged woman was the leader of the Rhysians. She wore Klashean black leather, but her features were snowy, nearly silvery, with ice-blue eyes. Her braids reached midback, lined by silver bells, the length of which reflected the extent of her skill.

Saekl dropped to a knee next to Aalia. She quickly lifted Tazar's eyelid and placed a hand over his heart. She called to the other woman without looking up.

"Cassta, any luck?"

Aalia turned. The younger Rhysian had descended upon the black-garbed bodies like a furious hawk. She ripped through their wrapped cloaks, tore their belts loose. She yanked out a black pipe and shook loose a feathered dart. She rubbed its sharp tip between her fingers and sniffed at it.

"Almendra," Cassta assessed. "Threefold potency."

Saekl grimaced.

Cassta cast the dart aside and continued her search of the bodies.

Kanthe watched her efforts. "What are you looking for?"

"The Asgians," Saekl said, nearly spitting out the word, "they won't carry a poison without a counter, a warding agent. In case a misstep requires intervention."

By now, Tazar's convulsions had quieted to tremors.

Aalia looked to Saekl, searching her face, trying to judge what this meant.

Saekl swung to Cassta, her voice sharper, scolding. "Anything?"

Cassta rolled and leaped from the body as if it were a foul daemon. As she joined them, she held forth a fistful of tiny crystal ampoules, tipped by needles. "I found four. How many—"

"All of them." Saekl grabbed two for herself. "Hurry. Before his heart stops." The Rhysian shifted to Tazar's head, her gaze on Aalia. "Pull his chin back."

Aalia did so, exposing Tazar's neck.

Cassta crossed lower, shouldered Kanthe aside, and spread Tazar's legs. Her fingers probed high along his inner thighs. "Ready?"

Saekl leaned closer. "Now!"

Both women stabbed their needles into Tazar. Saekl struck both sides of his neck; Cassta used two fists to jab the inner thighs. They held the impaled ampoules in place.

"With his heart beating," Saekl explained, "his flow of blood should draw out the elixir."

Everyone remained fixed, afraid to move.

After several tense breaths, Tazar's tremoring body relaxed, going slack. A bubbling sigh escaped his lips, along with a flow of froth.

Again, Aalia studied Saekl's face. The woman sat back, looking worried but resigned. She removed the impaled ampoules and tossed them away. Cassta did the same.

Kanthe looked between the two Rhysians. "Will he be all right?"

"We've done all we can," Saekl said. "He'll either survive or not. Best he be taken to the healer's ward."

Aalia finally stood, her legs shaking. Kanthe supported her with a hand on her arm. "Get him there," she ordered those gathered.

Aalia stumbled out of the way as they obeyed. She wanted to follow them up, but she remained in the bloody hall.

As Tazar was hauled off, another replaced him. Rami came rushing in, wearing only a loose robe. As he joined them, his eyes grew huge at the blood, the bodies. He cast questioning looks at Kanthe and Aalia.

"We're all right," Kanthe said.

Aalia was not sure that was true. She could not keep her limbs from trembling. Still, she challenged those still here. "Who sent these bastards?"

Aalia knew the Brotherhood of Asgia were the dark mirror to the Rhysian sisterhood. Both assassin groups rose out of the Archipelago of Rhys, near the southernmost turn of the Crown. Both sold their talents, but the Rhysians tempered their choices with consideration and a sense of justice. The Brotherhood operated under no such restraint. They were purely mercenary, brutal and cruel.

"Someone had to hire them," Aalia insisted.

Rami offered the most obvious culprit. "It had to be King Mikaen. He already has a history with the Brotherhood, using them to kidnap Kanthe last winter. And with Queen Myella poisoned, his revenge was inevitable."

Kanthe shook his head. "As much as I'd like to cast this at his feet, I'm not convinced. It doesn't fit my brother's temperament." He cradled his bronze forearm to his chest. "When it comes to revenge, he would want it delivered by his own hand, not from afar."

"Then who?" Rami asked.

Kanthe looked between Rami and Aalia. "There is *another* brother who is as bitter as Mikaen and looking to empty a throne and take its seat. And one more likely to know a way to sneak assassins into the citadel."

"Mareesh," Aalia said.

She pictured her traitorous brother fleeing the throne room last winter, his body on fire.

Kanthe shrugged. "Though, in truth, it could be either of them." He waved to the bodies in the hall, where Saekl and Cassta continued to strip them down. "And they're certainly not going to tell us."

Cassta rolled to face them. "The dead always have tales to tell."

Aalia frowned. "What do you mean?"

Cassta lifted a torn scrap of parchment. It looked like it might have come from a skrycrow. "It's incomplete, but easy enough to interpret."

"What does it say?" Kanthe asked, shifting closer.

Aalia did the same.

Cassta read it solemnly: "'—reesh, do what you must. You will be rewarded in kind.'" She looked up. "It's signed *Highking Mikaen ry Massif.*"

Kanthe stumbled away. "So, it wasn't one brother . . . or the other."

Aalia struggled to believe Mareesh would debase himself enough to work with the empire's long-standing enemy. But she had to accept the harsh truth and admitted it aloud.

"It was *both.*"

30

MIKAEN PACED THE marble floor outside the queen's bedchamber—same as he had done when Myella had birthed the twins. Back then, joy and trepidation had fired his blood. Now, there was only miserable despair.

After he had returned a fortnight ago, physiks and alchymists had flocked in and out of Myella's room. From the start, no cure could be hoped for. The goal was to keep Myella alive long enough to allow the baby inside to grow strong enough to be wrested free, to be torn from that poisonous womb.

To that end, ice baths fought fevers. Tonics kept her faltering heart beating. Water and gruel were forced into her belly through a snaking tube. Twice, she had come close to dying, requiring pounding on her chest and elixirs to pull her back from the brink. All the while, she grew more frail. Her body wasting, burning away to bones and jaundiced skin.

Still, he had spent every night in her bed or at her bedside. He kept a vigil, barely sleeping, refusing to look away from the agonized aftermath of his actions. He knelt beside her, casting up prayers. He begged her for forgiveness until his voice grew hoarse.

He loved her deeply. She had been the only one to hold his heart, to accept all of him: his stormy moods, his petty outbursts, his miserly spirit, even his cruelties that sometimes lashed in her direction. In her arms, he found his only haven. She had recognized that he only wanted the best for their family, for their lineage, for the future of Hálendii. She appreciated how brutal choices had to be made to preserve all.

He stared toward the sealed bedchamber doors.

Like now.

Despite his misery, this sacrifice had accomplished much. Word of the queen's suffering, of her brave struggle, had spread far—not only throughout Azantiia, but across all of Hálendii's territories, from the cold frontiers of Aglerolarpok to the dusty forges of Guld'guhl. All now rallied to their grieving king. Any dissension withered to naught.

You've done well, my love. Your pain has forged our future—mine, your children, all the peoples of these lands.

He had already commissioned a great tomb to be built in her honor. It would forever be draped by lilies from her home in the Brauðlands. Incense would continually burn her sacrifice up to the gods themselves.

This, I promise.

The doors to the bedchamber crashed open. A young healer rushed out, her face ashen. Horror etched her every feature. Blood soaked her garment, splattered her face. She dashed away, covering her mouth, clearly struggling to hold down the contents of her stomach.

Mikaen stepped toward the door, but it slammed shut in front of him. He caught the brush of a gray robe inside.

Iflelen . . .

He motioned to one of the Silvergard, one of the six Vyrllian knights manning the queen's antechamber. Mikaen nodded toward the fleeing healer. The knight's crimson-stained face remained stoic. He settled a hand on his sword and set off after the woman.

Mikaen resumed his pacing.

None must know what transpired within. The cadres of healers in attendance would be slain, silencing their tongues. A short, sharp cry from the hall outside confirmed this command.

From an opposite doorway, another of his Silvergard entered. Captain Thoryn strode toward him. Mikaen knew him well enough to recognize the slight narrowing of the man's eyes and what it meant. He came with a problem.

Relieved for this momentary distraction, Mikaen turned to face the man. "What is it, Thoryn?"

The knight tilted his head, indicating he wished to talk more privately, even away from his fellow Silvergard. Mikan nodded and followed Thoryn to the side.

Once at a safe distance, Thoryn held out the curled missive of a skrycrow. "This just arrived. Dispatched to the royal nest."

Mikaen took it. "Who sent it?"

"It's from the Brotherhood."

Mikaen took a deep breath and unrolled the message. He read it, but he knew from Thoryn's attitude that matters had not worked out as Prince Mareesh had planned.

"Your brother still lives," Thoryn said.

"As I had asked," Mikaen muttered. "At least, in this regard, my gold did not go to waste."

Mikaen had financed this assassination attempt. He had learned through intermediaries that Prince Mareesh sought his help in usurping the Klashean throne, with the promise of a halt to hostilities. It would've been a small cost to end this pending war.

So, he had agreed, lending Mareesh the services of the Brotherhood. Though, in truth, Mikaen cared little if this act succeeded. He welcomed war. In battle, he shone his brightest.

And peace is a paltry prize.

Mikaen had greater ambitions.

He pictured the full breadth of the Crown.

The Massif family had ruled Hálendii for centuries; eighteen generations had claimed its throne before Mikaen. His son, Othan, would be the twentieth. Mikaen would brook no end to their dynasty. To ensure and firm that lineage, he intended to extend his reach across the Crown.

And the Southern Klashe must be the first to fall.

"I see Mareesh's efforts failed to kill his sister, too." Mikaen crumbled the scroll in his fist. "But he did spare my brother as I requested. Kanthe will not die in the dark, upon a poisoned blade."

"Perhaps, but I've heard through other channels that Kanthe was attacked as savagely as the others. His survival might have nothing to do with Mareesh honoring your request."

Mikaen considered this. He knew the Klashean prince could never be trusted, and this confirmed as much.

Thoryn straightened. "How do you wish to respond to Mareesh's failure?"

Mikaen glanced to the bedchamber doors. He had much to dwell on already. He finally shook his head and faced the captain. "We'll do nothing."

Thoryn's eyes widened.

Mikaen explained, "The survival of Mareesh's sister—thwarting him from the throne—will be punishment enough for now. Plus, he did manage to get the Brotherhood deep within the imperial citadel. Such insight may prove useful in the war to come. So, for now, let the bastard lick his wounds. We can use this failure as a wedge later, to force Mareesh to abide our orders with a greater commitment."

Thoryn bowed his head. "Wise indeed, Your Grace."

Mikaen pictured Mareesh's snide face, so full of Klashean disdain.

That must end.

He remembered a lesson that had been drilled into him during his harsh tutelage at the Legionary, reinforced by whippings and blows to his body.

It is a beaten dog who learns to obey his master.

Mikaen clenched a fist, looking forward to teaching that same lesson to Mareesh.

AS THE RINGING of the second Eventoll bell echoed away, the door to the queen's bedchamber swung open with a heavy sigh of its thick hinges.

Finally . . .

Mikaen swung toward it, turning his back on Thoryn. The two had been

talking strategy, mostly how to address the aftermath of the attempted assassination. They had no concern about the imperium casting blame in this
direction. It was the *failure* that had to be considered. Such a botched attempt
could cast doubt on Hálendii's adeptness and competence, which could harm
the alliances that still needed to be hammered down.

But all that can wait.

As the door opened, the tall form of Shrive Wryth stood at the threshold,
blocking the view within. "It is done, Your Majesty," the Iflelen intoned dolefully.

Despite the long wait, Mikaen hesitated, suddenly fearful of crossing into the
room. Still, he took strength from the weight of Thoryn at his back. He headed
across the tiles. He had planned on entering alone, but instead he waved to the
Silvergard captain.

"With me, Thoryn."

Mikaen continued, hearing the heavy footfalls of the knight behind him.
As he reached Wryth, the Iflelen stepped aside to allow them to enter. Wryth
eyed Thoryn, clearly surprised at this addition, but he remained silent as he
closed the door behind them.

"How did you fare with the queen?" Mikaen asked, bitterness frosting his
query.

"Come see."

Mikaen noted Myella's empty bed, the blankets in disarray. On a table, an
incense burner cast a lonely curl of smoke. He had lit it this morning, casting
a prayer to the Mother Below to intercede.

Off to the side, a corner of the chamber had been draped off with dark
curtains. Voices murmured within, accompanied by a hushed rhythmic
wheezing.

Mikaen balked at crossing there.

Wryth added to his trepidation. "Brace yourself, Your Grace."

Mikaen scowled at the man. "If this ends badly . . ."

He let the threat hang in the air, but it came out muted. He didn't have the
breath to add any true force to it.

Still, Wryth bowed his head, accepting responsibility.

As well he should.

While Mikaen's hand had poisoned Myella, it was Wryth who had supplied the rykin elixir. The Iflelen had promised that, while the queen must die,
the child would be spared.

That proved not to be the case.

This morning, Physik Orkan had roused Mikaen from his bed, urgently
warning him that Myella had to be drawn again from the brink of death and

that she would not last the day. The healer had urged him to come share his last words, to summon the clerics who would seal her fate with balms to help guide her to the gods.

Instead, Mikaen had stalked deep beneath Highmount, bringing with him his entire Silvergard. He had raged through the lair of the Iflelen, demanding Wryth's presence. His rampage ended at a pair of tall ebonwood doors, sealed with the *horn'd snaken* of Lord Ðreyk. It closed off the innermost sanctum of the Iflelen.

Even the Silvergard balked at breaking that seal.

In the end, the violation proved unnecessary. Wryth stepped out to face Mikaen's wrath. Upon learning of Myella's danger, the Iflelen had demanded to be taken to her. Wryth had set off immediately, such was his haste.

Mikaen hurried after, but not without a final glance back at those sealed ebonwood doors. He suspected the man was hiding something. Whatever foul alchymy that had kept Wryth distracted from his duties lay behind those doors. Mikaen intended to find out, but first Myella had to be attended to.

Upon examining the queen, Wryth had demanded privacy. His words had driven out everyone, all but a few of his fellow Iflelen and a handful of healers. Wryth had then clutched Mikaen's arm with a dire warning: *If you wish Queen Myella to live long enough for her child to thrive, you must do as I ask. It is her only chance, the only hope for your child.*

Mikaen had heeded those words.

Not only did he fear losing the child, but such a tragedy might sour the sentiment at large. While such a death could be blamed on the Southern Klashe, others would take it as a punishment from the gods, some portent that Mikaen had fallen out of their favor. Dissension could rise again.

That cannot happen—not after the sacrifice I took.

Wryth led the way to the curtains and reached a hand to part them. "Hold firm, Your Majesty. This will be difficult."

Wryth pulled the drape aside and motioned everyone inside to retreat, opening the way for the king to greet his queen.

Mikaen stepped forward—then halted abruptly at the threshold. He struggled to comprehend the sight before him.

Myella now rested in a new bed, one of copper and iron. She lay naked on her back, half-reclined, a small blanket over her waist offering privacy. But the true violation lay bared above.

Thoryn stumbled back, horror driving him to a knee.

Mikaen remained where he was, knowing this must be faced.

Myella's head had been craned back. A tube snaked past her pale lips.

Smaller ones defiled her nostrils. Blind eyes stared up at the frescoed ceiling. Someone had shaved her head, leaving a landscape of stubble.

Still, Mikaen recognized her. A hand rose to his mouth, not in revulsion, but in remembrance of those lips upon his, those dead eyes looking upon him with love, his fingers stroking her hair as her head rested in his lap.

The memory drew him forward, one leaden step at a time. He stared unblinking ahead at what Wryth had revealed to him, a view of his beloved that he had never seen, could never see.

Myella's chest had been cleaved open, cutting a window into her, framed by her sawed rib cage. The ends of the bones shone white, tipped by red marrow, still weeping blood. Past that window, lungs billowed up and down. A fist of a heart clenched and relaxed, over and over again.

Mikaen continued forward, drawn by the sight.

Beyond the bed, large tanks burbled with amber fluid. More tubes ran to areas where Myella's skin had been flayed open. Another mekanical box wheezed and pumped, in harmony with the rise and fall of her gossamer lungs.

"What have you done?" The question came not from Mikaen's lips, but from Thoryn's.

"We call it a bloodbaerne," Wryth answered. "It will sustain her. Long enough to harvest the child when the time is ripe."

Mikaen finally reached the bed.

Wryth repeated what he had stated before. "It was the only way."

Mikaen slowly nodded. He shifted closer and gently lifted Myella's hand, grasping it in his own. He squeezed his love into her, his appreciation of her sacrifice. He willed her one last message.

Be strong, my queen, for a little while longer.

Before he could lower Myella's hand, her frail fingers shivered and closed over his.

He didn't know if this was a reflex or if Myella was aware somewhere in that ravaged body, struggling to communicate with him. He was too afraid to ask Wryth, too fearful of the answer.

Instead, he bowed down and kissed the swollen belly rising above the blanket. As he did, he whispered a promise to the child within.

"I will save you."

31

AALIA KNELT NEXT to Tazar's bed in the imperial ward of the residence tower. A row of cots ran under tall windows, currently covered in drapes to shadow the sun, as it was deep into Eventoll. Each bed had additional canopies and curtains surrounding them, both for privacy and to help the sick and injured to sleep.

Only Aalia wished her beloved's slumber would come to an end.

She held Tazar's hand, feeling the slight tremors in his fingers as the poison still had hold of him. Froth flecked his lips with each breath.

"Come back to me," she whispered.

Across the bed, another woman sat with her head bowed. She quietly intoned prayers to X'or, the Klashean goddess of healing. A white marble sculpture of the deity, robed and holding aloft a bowl, stood in the center of the ward. Water spilled from her basin into a pool at her feet, creating a peaceful sound of rain in a quiet grove. Small candles floated there, amidst drifting crimson leaves from the sacred Talniss trees.

"I appreciate your prayers, Althea," Aalia said. "May X'or bless us both."

The tall woman was Tazar's second-in-command, though of late she had taken on much of the burden of managing the *Shayn'ra* rebels in Tazar's stead.

Though her role may grow far larger if he does not survive.

Althea nodded back. Her dark eyes stared from under a sweep of black hair and through the white stripe of her *Shayn'ra* marking.

A commotion rose from a canopy a few beds down, a mix of pleading and growled threats. Aalia stood, her body going tense. Her fortitude remained strained after the attack two bells ago.

A small-framed maidenhest—an apprentice to a physik—burst out of the canopy, searching frantically up and down. She spotted Aalia and rushed over. Once close enough, the woman dropped to her knees. Her momentum slid her closer to the empress of the realm.

The maidenhest bowed her forehead to the floor, her words to the marble. "Your Grace, we must beg your guidance."

A bellow echoed from the other canopy, making clear *where* that guidance was needed. Aalia also recognized the voice behind that fury. She waved the maidenhest up and strode quickly. With each step, her anger grew. Her patience was even more strained than her fortitude.

She reached the canopy and tore open the drape. Inside, two physiks held down a bare-chested man, his bandaged arm in a sling. He thrashed in their grip and likely only failed to break free due to his injured limb and his recent loss of blood.

It was the Fist of the Paladins.

Regar's eyes fell upon Aalia. She read the agony in his face, the shame and humiliation.

"He demanded his sword," one of the healers said, straightening and nodding to a stack of light armor and weapons.

"He intended harm to himself," the other stated, his voice ringing with annoyance. "A clear insult to our efforts."

Regar's gaze swept down. "I failed you, Empress. Disgraced myself. There is only one path to penance."

"Upon the point of your blade."

Regar slumped deeper, his back bent by guilt.

Aalia stepped to his bed and sat near the foot. "My Paladin, I do not give you permission to seek penance. I will not give the Brotherhood the satisfaction of taking another life from my side. If it's penance you seek, then live long enough to mete out my justice. Such is my will."

Regar remained bent. "Yes, Your Grace."

Aalia leaned down to catch his eye, lowering her voice. "I would not feel safe without my Fist at my shoulder. Is that understood?"

He swallowed hard, then nodded.

Aalia stood. "And quit fighting those who seek to put you back on your feet, to return you to my side."

"Yes, Your Grace."

The two physiks bowed their appreciation as she left. She crossed and returned to Tazar's bed. Two more women had joined the vigil.

Saekl leaned over Tazar, testing an eyelid, then his breath, while Cassta hung back.

Aalia stared on with concern. "You know this poison better than any physik. What do you surmise his chances to be?"

Saekl's answer was blunt. "Slim but not none."

Aalia could not hide her anguish as tears welled. "Is there nothing else we can do?"

"Only time will reveal his fate. His body must rid the poison on its own, clearing what the tonic could not reach. Each day he keeps breathing, his odds will rise."

Cassta shifted closer. "Tazar is strong," she said firmly, perhaps seeking to soften the other's frankness. "And he has a good reason to fight. When the heart has a goal, the body often follows."

Aalia nodded, praying for that to be so. She shifted and took Tazar's hand. She brought its back to her lips. To her, it felt like his tremoring had diminished, but it might only be a reflection of her own heart's desire.

Across the bed, Althea confronted Saekl. "What of the Brotherhood? Were you and your sisters able to determine how they reached the heart of the citadel?"

Saekl shrugged. "We uncovered a trail of bodies, hidden from sight, exposing the point of entry—a spot that only someone with intimate knowledge of the citadel could've known about."

Aalia grimaced.

Mareesh . . .

"No other members of the Brotherhood have been discovered," Cassta added. "They would've fled. Such is their way. Still, our sisters are out hunting."

Saekl nodded. "In addition, your Eye of the Hidden has dispatched his crows along their path—both those with wings and those who traverse the shadows."

"Still, we must take care," Cassta warned.

A voice called from down the ward, accompanied by a rush of footfalls. Rami closed the distance, breathless. His gaze swept those gathered around the bed, then settled on the fever-sheened figure under the blanket.

"How is Tazar faring?"

Aalia stood, having no desire to rehash the grim assessment. "What do you want, Rami? Why have you flown down from your room?"

"To bring you up there." He pointed above. "Frell, Pratik, and Tykhan just returned—though it took some convincing for them to get through the cordon of knights bristling at the base of this tower."

"Did they discover anything in the Codex?"

"Something, but I don't know what. They were very guarded."

"Why meet in your room?"

"Besides the fact that I have the best reserve of wine and tabakroot, it's clear no one's crossing over to the Blood'd Tower anytime soon."

That is certainly true.

"Yet, that's not the main reason," Rami explained. "What the others have to say is meant only for a few ears."

Aalia glanced to the bed, hating to leave Tazar's side.

Althea must have noted her distress. "I will watch over him. If there's any change, I'll dispatch a messenger."

"Thank you."

Saekl stepped away, too. "I must attend to my sisters. Cassta can go in my stead, if that's agreeable?"

Rami grinned. "Actually, I know one person who would be quite *disagreeable* if she didn't come."

KANTHE GATHERED WITH everyone around the long table in Rami's suite of rooms. An Eventoll repast lay spread across the top: platters of braised duck, bowls of spiced beans, steaming loaves of dense brown breads, rounds of cheese, and herb-infused oils.

Most of the fare remained untouched.

The lack of interest had nothing to do with the Klashean tradition of avoiding topics of import while breaking bread. Kanthe had learned of this custom from Brija, a brittle-backed Chaaen hieromonk who had been bound to him early on. She insisted that mealtime conversations must always be light, as a means to aid digestion. Her admonition stuck with him.

Sour talk leads to a sour stomach.

This evening, the group had ignored the spread, all struggling to digest their respective stories: of assassins in the dark, of a strange crystal *arkada*, of glimpses of a war lost in the mists of time.

From their expressions, sour stomachs plagued them all.

Still, each found their own balm.

Kanthe swirled a crystal glass of Aailish wine, staring deep into its dark red mysteries. Aalia tore pieces of bread in her fingertips, likely picturing a certain traitorous brother. Pratik slowly turned the iron collar about his neck, seemingly unaware he was doing it. Frell remained deep in thought as he rolled a legion of peas back and forth across his plate, as if scribing a battle strategy.

Two of the group had already abandoned the spread.

Rami stood to the side by a cold hearth with a long pipe at his lips, wafting twin streams of smoke from his nostrils. Cassta had spread blades across a table and was meticulously sharpening them.

One of their party had never come to the table.

Tykhan stood by the window, its heavy drapes parted, bathing his bronze body in the Eventoll sunlight. He still struggled to soften his form, to regain his strength after being drained in the darkness.

Tired and heavy of heart, Kanthe finally broke this moment of contemplation. "What does it truly matter if there was another *Vyk dyre Rha* in the past?"

Attentions swung his way.

"We know nothing about who she was, how she came to be, or the manner in which Eligor turned her into a weapon." Kanthe swung his gaze around. "What we *do* know is that she's not Nyx."

Frell abandoned his peas in the battlefield. "That may be so, but to ignore the lessons of the past is a fool's path."

"Then what do you propose?" Aalia asked. "Send word to the others? Have them kill this woman on the oft chance she becomes enthralled by the enemy in the future?"

Frell frowned. "Certainly not. Without Nyx, I doubt the others will ever get the second *turubya* stirring. But we must look steps ahead. Once both *turubya* are spinning, there is only one means of controlling them."

"The key that Eligor hid," Pratik answered.

Frell nodded. "We must waste no time in obtaining it. Once that second *turubya* is running, whoever possesses the key controls the world. Tykhan has warned us of this. Nothing else matters after that."

Kanthe set down his wine. "How can we hope to gain this key? Where could it be?"

"I don't know. At the moment, I doubt Eligor is in possession of it. Which means at some point he will need to secure it himself. But with him now awake, possibly able to break loose, that risk rises with every passing day. And if Nyx returns and somehow becomes enthralled like in the past, then we've lost before we've begun."

Rami shifted from his post by the hearth. "You're clearly leading somewhere, alchymist. Spit it out."

Frell gained his feet, staring around the room. "We must secure the key—or at the very least learn its location—*before* the second *turubya* is activated, *before* Nyx returns with the others. We can't risk Eligor obtaining the key first, and we can't risk him turning Nyx against us."

Rami sighed. "If so, then we have no time to spare. As I understand it, barring any mishap, the others will reach the region in the Barrens with the *turubya* in a little over two months."

Aalia looked grim. "How? How could we possibly wage a war in such a time line?"

"If we hope to somehow lock down Eligor, to strip the location of the key from him, we can no longer wait for war to come to these shores." Frell turned to the empress. "We must attack Hálendii first."

Aalia shoved up. "You expect us to win a war, one that has been brewing over centuries between our two realms, in . . . what? In two months' time?" She shook her head, sputtering through her shock. "It's rash, irrational, certain to fail."

Kanthe offered his own viewpoint. "No, Aalia, it's simply *reckless*."

He emphasized the last word, reminding her how their first attempt to secure Eligor had failed due to an overabundance of caution. At the council meeting, he had warned her that they all needed to be far bolder if they hoped to stop moonfall.

"Frell is right," Kanthe said. "We have no choice. The attempt must be made. With doom drawing ever closer, we must act. If we lose this war, the world ends. But if we don't try at all, then we've lost already."

Rami blew out a stream of smoke. "So, the only hope for the world is a reckless gambit, to start a war we'll surely lose."

Aalia's features darkened with her usual storm clouds. Kanthe readied himself to face her fury. Instead, she swung to Tykhan. "How long will it take to finish your project?"

Tykhan stirred, going from statue to man. "Were you able to secure the draft-iron that I requested?"

Aalia shared a look with Kanthe. "We did."

"That is good. But still, two months is tight. And that's assuming Qaar Saur delivers as promised." Tykhan's expression turned dour. "With so little time, we will be hard-pressed to take over an entire kingdom."

Aalia dismissed this concern with a wave. "We don't need to seize and hold a kingdom. Not even the city of Azantiia. We merely must commandeer Highmount. To hold it and the throne long enough to deal with Eligor. Even if it's only for a day or two."

Rami lifted a brow toward Kanthe. "In such a case, my brother, you will have the briefest reign of any monarch in Hálendiian history."

"I've already got one throne that fits me poorly. I don't need another."

Pratik stirred. "We're all forgetting one important detail."

All eyes swung to the Chaaen.

"With Eligor powered by a *schysm,* we have little chance to defeat him." Pratik nodded toward the sunlit window. "And according to our bronze friend, *no* chance."

Kanthe closed his eyes, fighting against despair, but Tykhan's words burned inside him and refused to be ignored.

With Eligor risen to full power, doom is inevitable.

Kanthe had railed against that portent, refusing to accept it, but he struggled to maintain that unflinching footing. They had all heard Tykhan's description of Eligor blazing atop a mountain, wielding some version of a *Vyk dyre Rha.* Kanthe rubbed a knuckle under his rib cage, where guilt had poured acid into his gut, knowing he had delivered the *schysm* into the enemy's hand, all but dooming the world.

How can we hope for victory when facing such a bronze god?

Tykhan stepped from the window. His features had softened enough to show a strain of guilt, too. Only his next words revealed the source of his shame.

"In communing with the past, I realized an error, something I had not considered after my shock of losing my core." One hand settled to where he had extracted his *schysm*. "In that crystal-preserved vision, I witnessed the sheer strength and fiery power wielded by Eligor—which only underscored the impossibility of our small group's ability to ever challenge such a being."

"Then what error are you referring to?" Frell asked, sharing a look with Pratik, as if this had significance to the two alchymists. "What do you mean?"

Tykhan stared down at the hand on his belly. "I could never wield such strength as Eligor showed in the vision." He lifted his gaze to the group. "It requires far more power than can be produced by the *schysm* of a mere Root. Each of our forms—Root, Axis, and Kryst—have cores suited to our tasks. The most powerful and largest, of course, belongs to a Kryst."

"Like Eligor," Kanthe said, feeling a slight brightening of his despair. "If he only has your *schysm,* that of a Root, then he might be compromised, constrained by its limitations."

Tykhan bowed his head in acknowledgment, but when he lifted his face, a hopelessness sagged his demeanor. "But do not be mistaken, he will still remain extremely strong. And with time, his body may adjust and compensate, reaching its full potential. In many ways—more important ways—a Kryst's form is more malleable than even my flowing bronze body. They must not be underestimated."

Kanthe sat back down. The momentary lightening of his gloom dimmed again. "How long will it take Eligor to achieve this?"

Tykhan shrugged with a sad shake of his head. "I cannot say. But I agree with Alchymist Frell, we dare not wait any longer than necessary."

Aalia challenged him. "Do we even have two months?"

Tykhan's grim silence spoke loudly.

Frell cleared his throat. "No matter. We forge ahead and pray for the best. We can do no more."

Kanthe sighed and cast his gaze to the north, peering through walls and distance to Hálendii, one question foremost in mind.

What will we face when we get there?

32

EXHAUSTED AND WORRIED, Wryth paused before the towering doors of the Iflelen's inner sanctum. With the passageway empty, he allowed his forehead to rest against the cold ebonwood. He needed a moment to center himself before entering the sacred chamber.

The cavernous room had been his sanctuary over all these decades. He had come here often to meditate, to ruminate, to ponder the deepest mysteries of the universe. To him, it represented the barest peek into a hidden world of arcane knowledge. It also held the promise of piercing the veil of the *Pantha re Gaas*—the Forsaken Ages—of opening a gateway to a time before history itself.

That desire still glowed behind his eyes.

Fueled by all that he had endured.

For most of his life, Wryth had been powerless, a victim to circumstance, a shivering prey to those stronger. Memories of that time had been branded into him, but he had buried them deep.

Yet there was no escaping one's past, not fully.

Born a slave in the Dominion of Gjoa, hunted across kingdoms and empires, finally schooled on the Island of Tau, Wryth had endured a youth marked by cruelty, abuse, and humiliation. He had been whored, beaten, raped. After having traveled most of the Crown, he felt no fealty to any kingdom, nor any god—not even Lord Đreyk.

Even now, after achieving so much, he could still waken that old pain. It stoked the cold fire inside him, to never again be under another's thumb. To ensure that, he intended to let nothing and no one stop him from becoming a formidable force, one more potent than any king.

Especially one king.

Wryth pictured Mikaen, broken before his queen.

The misery on display there gave Wryth the strength to lift a key and unlock the door, breaking the seal of the *horn'd snaken*. He pushed the heavy door with his shoulder and entered the inner sanctum.

A shiver swept through him as he relocked the door.

Throughout his decades here, the Iflelen's great instrument had thrummed and beat, marking the mekanical heart of their order. Alongside it, the outer ring of bloodbaernes had wheezed a hushed chorus, one that had spanned centuries.

Only now, the very heart of their order had been snuffed out.

As Wryth turned, the only movement out there was the shuffling of a single Iflelen, Shrive Bkarrin. Fluids no longer bubbled. Joints in the copper no longer steamed. The entire machine had gone dark and quiet, adding to the solemnity of this grave.

Wryth headed toward Bkarrin. He threaded his way through the maze of cold piping and dull crystal, a forest poisoned by what had taken root at its core. He found himself walking more carefully, trying not to disturb this tomb.

Still, shattered glass crunched underfoot. Bits of copper tinkled away, bumped by his toes. His robe snagged and tore on the jagged end of a broken pipe.

As Wryth traversed the ruins of the machine, he flashed to a fortnight ago, when he had lowered the cube of pulsing gold into the chest of the bronze figure. He remembered the devastation it had wrought.

He stared through the tangle of pipes to the ring of empty bloodbaerne beds.

At least I had one to spare, to be turned into the queen's new throne.

Wryth had personally overseen the installation of Myella. The procedure, already a delicate process, had required subtle changes. Without the need to feed her life into the great instrument, the bed should sustain the woman for a month, maybe two. Enough for her child to continue to grow in her womb and be harvested later.

Still, Wryth had some misgivings that he had not voiced to Mikaen. He saw no reason to further anger the volatile king. He would deal with any repercussions if they should arise.

For now, he had a greater challenge.

He reached Bkarrin and posed the question that had been plaguing him for days. It had kept Wryth locked in this chamber, sleeping atop blankets piled on one of the bloodbaerne beds. He had not left here until a raging king had forced him out, demanding he save his queen.

"Has he woken yet?" Wryth asked. "Or even stirred?"

Since the events from a fortnight ago, Kryst Eligor had remained in a locked slumber, some strange hibernation. A slight glow swam over his bronze, rhythmic and steady, suggesting something was still brewing, still gestating inside there.

"He has not moved," Bkarrin confirmed. "But his transformation continues at an astounding pace."

Wryth circled the iron altar and the sleeping god atop it. The body's gaping chest had nearly sealed over, forming a muscled abdomen, a strong chest. A fine frill of curled hair had sprouted, matching the bust's beard. Down the center, a remaining fissure offered a glimpse into the bed of shining crystals and twining bronze fibers.

Wryth leaned over and tried to peer deeper, to spot the pulsing crystal cube of the *schysm,* but it had buried itself too deep.

As he straightened, he took in the rest of the body. If standing, Eligor would tower over most men, maybe even taller than the Gyns of the steppes. By now, his limbs had fully formed, with fingers and toes deftly sculpted, down to fine-lined nails and wrinkled knuckles. Already Eligor could easily be mistaken for a man in slumber. Adding to that illusion, a set of genitals hung heavy and limp between his legs.

Wryth shook his head, wondering at the latter's necessity.

Certainly, this god would never need to piss.

Bkarrin shifted closer, dropping his voice to a whisper. "You mentioned that Eligor spoke of the Shadow Queen before falling silent."

Wryth turned to Bkarrin. "Yes, the *Vyk dyre Rha.* Along with a grim pronouncement."

Bkarrin winced, falling back a step.

Wryth failed to understand his reaction.

The Shrive pointed past Wryth's shoulder. "His hand . . ."

Wryth jerked around. He caught Eligor's fingers clenching into a fist. Worried, but suddenly hopeful after the long vigil, Wryth struggled for a breath. He suspected *what* had stirred the sleeping figure. He remembered last winter when the bust had burst to life, blazing with azure fury.

I had spoken the same name back then, too.

Wryth attempted it again. He leaned closer, near to Eligor's perfectly sculpted ear. *"Vyk dyre Rha."*

Wryth held his breath, but there was no reaction.

Bkarrin shifted closer. "Maybe louder—"

Bronze eyelids slit open before them, casting out narrow beams.

Bkarrin stumbled away. "He's waking."

A groan escaped those metal lips.

Wryth withdrew with Bkarrin, unsure what to expect. Still, some distance was warranted after what had transpired before.

Their heels crunched through glass.

As they retreated, Wryth's ears sensed a change in pressure, as if he had been thrust deep underwater. Sounds muffled away. He winced as the pressure grew rapidly, squeezing his head in a vise.

Bkarrin suffered the same, covering his ears.

Then it all released, so suddenly something tore in Wryth's skull. He felt lifted off his feet, rising to his toes, as if sucked forward.

Ahead, a booming cry burst forth.

The bronze body flared in a blaze of blinding light. The sight burned into the back of Wryth's remaining eye. Still, he could not look away.

Deep in that sun, a shadow stirred.

Eligor's black form sat up, his head hanging. Then heavy legs swung to the floor. Heels struck rock, cracking the obsidian. Hands clasped to the altar's edge, ripping iron beneath their grip.

Bkarrin dropped to his knees.

Wryth remained standing, staring into that blinding sun, at the god being born from it. Eligor shoved to his feet, baring all his glory, limned against the brilliance. As he strode forward, the rock under his feet smoked, burning under his fiery majesty.

Wryth shivered in terror, one thought foremost.

What have I wrought?

He fell back a step, despairing.

What have I done?

Eligor suddenly weaved drunkenly on his feet, then stumbled back to the altar. He struck it hard enough to sink into the iron, melting it to bright sludge beneath him. The fiery sun dimmed around him, revealing a bronze god seated in a fiery throne of iron.

Across Eligor's chest, the remaining fissure shone brightly, marking a jagged lightning bolt across his chest. Wryth's gaze fixed on it, recognizing this god had not fully risen to power.

Not yet.

As Wryth took a step forward, a darker thought now filled him.

How can I wield this weapon? What must I do?

FIVE

BLOOD IN THE DUST

Ruel 16: Kill with a Borrow'd Daggere
   En battle, do not ignore the opportuniti to stele the stryngth of another, ev'n from an alli at your side. Dishonor comes with its own rawarde—& vikoriti its own forgivenesse.

—From *The Ruels of Conflict* by Erif sy Karn,
master-commander of the Legionary

33

GRAYLIN STOOD NEXT to Darant at the *Fyredragon*'s maesterwheel. He watched as the captain sweated the massive ship toward a treacherous berth. Darant had discarded his half-cloak and leaned off to the side of the wheel, which he clutched in a white-knuckled grip. The man's nose hovered near the bow window.

Beyond the glass, crumbling walls of ruins and sheer cliffs of sandstone rose on all sides. Dust swirled into a gritty fog, blown by the ship's forges, lit by their flames. Higher up, the front edge of the storm had reached them. The rumbling howl of the desert god's approach drowned out the roaring of their forge-engines.

It had taken them too long to find this berth for the ship, a dubious haven to ride out the *ishuka* to come. Esme had warned them they had to find shelter, to bury themselves away from the worst of the sandstorm. Even landing and tying the *Fyredragon* down with mooring lines would not be enough. The *ishuka*'s rage would rip them loose, tear the balloon from its cables. Their Chanaryn guide had suggested one possible shelter, a rocky anchorage where they might weather the storm.

Graylin cringed as the *Fyredragon* continued its descent into a craggy pocket of the Seekh ruins. With jagged rock all around, they had little room to spare.

The Tablelands offered their only refuge. Cracks and deep ravines split the sandstone massif, exposing the depths of the buried necropolises. After a desperate search, they had chanced upon this wider, deeper pocket, one barely large enough to hold their massive ship. But they had no time to search for a better one.

The dark tempest, raging with the fury of an angry god, had risen into a towering black wave of churning sand, sweeping across the desert. It threatened to crash atop them at any moment.

"How's the starboard look!" Darant bellowed.

"Clear!" Fenn shouted back from his station, where he skipped between the eyepieces of various scopes, whose mirrored lenses let the navigator view all sides of the ship. "Draw us forward by four cubits! Need more space for the stern."

Darant pressed closer to the bow window. "Don't have that much room ahead of us."

"My scopes say you do."

"My fekkin' eyes say we don't!"

"Then give me three cubits. We can just squeak by with that."

Darant cursed and called orders to the crew flanking him at the substations' wheels and levers. The ship drifted forward as the forges brightened the dusty gloom. Ahead, a facade of shattered bricks loomed closer. Ancient chambers pocketed its surface, looking like a broken honeycomb that had petrified millennia ago.

The ship's sculpted prow skimmed nearer. The jutting dragon kissed the wall, jarring the ship. Bricks trenched loose as the draft-iron figurehead dragged its nose down the surface as they descended.

"Back 'er a nudge!" Darant called out.

Bow engines flared, pushing the prow away.

Fenn hollered from his side, "Hold! What did I just say about—"

From the stern of the ship, a loud scraping tremored throughout the vessel.

Darant winced and growled out final orders, doing his best to deepen their descent. Scraping rose from all sides. Cables shook. The gasbag overhead rattled between walls.

Finally, the captain bellowed to his crew, "All stop!" Darant leaned over to the mouth of the highhorn and called through to the open deck. "Secure our mooring lines!"

Graylin stepped closer to the window and stared up, past the front edge of the balloon. Sand gusted and whipped across the top of the cliffs, not far from the crown of the gasbag.

"Are we deep enough?" he asked.

Darant followed his gaze. "If you want this dragon to still have its wings, this is as far as we go. We'll be patching holes as it is. Still, we must pray the storm doesn't pop this cork out of its bottle."

Graylin glanced behind him, as if his gaze could pierce ship and rock. "What about the Bhestyan warship, the *Sharpened Spur*? Did they make it to a shelter, too?"

Fenn answered. "I kept an eye on them. Saw them descending shortly before we found this berth. Though they outman and outgun us, their ship's smaller. Gave them plenty more options to choose from."

"How far away?"

"Half a league to the northeast."

"Did you chart their position?"

"As roughly as I could on our map of the Tablelands."

Graylin didn't doubt the navigator's accuracy. He knew Fenn had a vested interest in knowing exactly *where* the warship had docked. His sister remained

a prisoner aboard the *Spur*. The navigator was surely also tracking the passage
of time. His uncle had given them until the first dawn bell to hand Fenn over
or they would hang his sister.

It made for a tight schedule.

According to Esme, the *ishuka* would blow itself out by then.

*Which means we have until dawn to decide what to do about this Bhestyan
threat.*

Darant shoved away from the maesterwheel, grabbed his half-cloak, and
whipped it over his shoulders. "I'm heading topside. To check on our moorings. If we want this cork to stay put, we'd best snug ourselves tight."

"I'll go with you."

Graylin drew alongside the captain and crossed the empty wheelhouse.
Darant had chased everyone else out earlier, to eliminate any distractions
during this descent. His crew needed to stay focused.

Graylin had also urged Nyx to go with Daal down to the lower hold, to try
to keep their winged crewmates calm. It had taken no convincing. With her
eyes still clouded, there was little she could see up here. Still, Graylin knew
she had agreed mostly out of concern for Bashaliia. Daal had seemed similarly
worried about his own charges.

At least this put her out of harm's way, with someone trusted at her side.
Plus, surrounded by those beasts, she had plenty of additional protection. Still,
Graylin had sent Kalder down with her, too, especially with Nyx so compro-
mised.

He prayed she stayed put.

For once.

To HOLD HERSELF steady, Nyx gripped a column in the ship's hold. The
tremoring of the planks underfoot had stopped, as had the cringing scrapes
of rock on wood.

We must have come to a halt.

Though far from recovered, Nyx cast out faint wisps of bridle-song. To her
shrouded eyes, they glowed like soft embers through the gloom. They brightened upon reaching Bashaliia, ensuring her brother remained calm. She sang
faint chords of reassurance to him. They were echoed back, both in confirmation and to check on her.

I'm well, too.

As she withdrew those strands, they brushed across the stout heart of the
vargr. Kalder still guarded over her, seated nearby, maintaining his post. She
quietly thanked him, which drew a rumble—one of slight warning.

She cast her gaze around. Through the veil of her vision, fiery pools of brightness marked lanterns deeper in the hold. A shadow swept over one, eclipsing its glow.

She didn't need her eyes to tell who approached. She recognized the salty musk of his scent, as if he carried the sea of his home with him. She knew the rhythm of his breaths, which ended each exhalation with the barest wheeze, like a soft sigh.

"How is Pyllar?" she asked Daal.

"Doing well." Relief softened that sigh even more. "Some seepage through his wrap. But nothing concerning. Heffik is also keeping a close watch on him."

"That's good. We can't afford to lose any of the raash'ke, and I know how close you two have become."

A silence followed, stretching into awkwardness. She heard the scuff of a foot, the slight strain to his breathing.

"What's wrong?" she asked, sensing something was amiss.

Did bringing up the deeper bond between rider and mount remind him of what we have lost?

She longed for that closeness again, especially after just communing so intimately. It had wakened all that she had forsaken. In her head, the decision months ago had made cautionary sense, but now her heart fought against such restraint, wanting so much more—which of itself was a warning.

I can lose myself so easily in him.

"It's Pyllar," Daal explained. "There's something I've wanted to talk to you about."

Pyllar . . . ?

Nyx hid her disappointment. Daal's silence had nothing to do with her or what they had shared in the air.

"What . . . What about Pyllar?"

"There are times I feel I can touch his senses, see through his eyes, hear through his ears." His voice gained a timbre of embarrassment, as if disbelieving his own words. "It only comes in snatches, brief and fleeting. If I give it too much attention, it wisps away. I feared talking with the other riders, lest they think I'm mad."

"No, Daal, it's not madness. Bashaliia and I often share the same. Sometimes felt more strongly, other times only faintly. It depends on how powerfully I'm singing."

"But I can't sing like you."

She shook her head. "I doubt it matters. Clearly it doesn't. I wager the innate strands of your bridle-song are weaving you two together. You're finding a harmony with Pyllar that's been growing over time. It's nothing to fear, but to rejoice in."

She reached to him. Though he remained in the shadows, she easily found his hand. Upon his touch, her fingers warmed as they closed. While it was nothing like the fire ignited in the past, the connection was there. The burgeoning wisps of their bridle-song—both his and hers—drew them together.

Daal's breathing deepened.

She expected him to let go, but his fingers firmed on hers. She stepped closer, while at the same time he pulled her gently, tentatively, nearer. She found herself on her toes, balancing there at the edge.

All her senses sharpened in that moment, heightened both by her lack of sight and by her desire. The air—already warmed by the stern forge under the hold's planks—grew hotter. Her nose picked up the oily note of flashburn from the engines, but also the tang of guano and the malt of dry hay from the nests nearby.

But all that faded away until the world became the hearth of Daal's body, now only a finger's breadth from hers. The warmth carried his scent to her, off his skin, from the fall of his hair. She smelled the sea, the musk of raash'ke pelt, even the iron of blood from a wound tended with love.

She leaned until her lips found his, as unerringly as ever.

There was no explosion of fire, no falling into each other. Most importantly, no danger. The faint strands of bridle-song echoed in the background, but they were mere whispers, nothing to fear. They only served as a distant chorus, a melancholy reminder of what they had been forced to set aside.

For now, though, this was more than enough.

Here they were safe with one another.

Still, Daal drew back. "Nyx . . ."

She heard the caution in his voice. She flashed to the last time he had pulled away, her name a warning on his lips. She had ignored it before to disastrous results.

Can't I have at least this?

Before anything more could be said, a shout rose behind them from deeper in the hold.

"Daal! Come shut down this squabble!" It was Tamryn. "Before someone crosses a line . . . one they can't come back from."

Overhead, muffled bangs and shouts echoed down from the Pantheans' cabins.

Daal retreated farther. "I should go," he mumbled. "See what's stirred them up."

Nyx took a step back, bumping into the column behind her. Kalder came around and brushed across her legs. She reached down and drew the vargr closer. Off to the side, Bashaliia whistled a pining note.

It took her a moment to collect herself.

"I'm well," she finally whispered to her brother, repeating her earlier assurance.

But am I truly?

She listened as Daal retreated with Tamryn. The woman's words stayed with Nyx. She wondered if their sentiment mirrored Daal's intent when he had pulled away. Had he been trying to warn her, maybe both of them, that they needed to stop?

And for the same reason that Tamryn had stated.

Before someone crosses a line . . . one they can't come back from.

ATOP THE DECK of the *Fyredragon*, Graylin cringed at the sharp *twang* as another ballista erupted. The massive crossbow, hewn of age-hardened ash, unleashed a steel spear dragging a thick rope, its length reinforced with draft-iron fibers. The shaft flew through the air and struck the wall with enough force to bury its tip deep into the sandstone.

"Haul in the line!" the chief boatswain bellowed.

Burly men drew the rope taut and snugged the ends to stanchions along the deck.

A blast on the portside signaled another line being secured. A half dozen ballistas towered on both sides of the ship, while between them stood the same number of cannons. Around the ship, ropes strung out in all directions.

The *Fyredragon* looked like a fly trapped in a draft-iron web.

Darant nodded at his men's handiwork. "That's the last of our lines. Pray it's enough."

Graylin leaned over the rail, staring up, trying to spy past the rattling balloon. Its fabric quaked, and its thigh-thick cables groaned with the stress. Higher up, the blue skies had gone dark, obliterated by blasting sand. The sun remained a wan glow through the gloom. The roar of the desert god steadily rose.

And this is only the storm's front edge.

"We'll be in the teeth of it shortly." Graylin turned and faced the captain. "You'll need to do your best, Darant, to keep the ship safe."

And all those aboard her.

"It's a mad ruse you're planning," Darant warned.

Graylin shook his head. "The Bhestyan warship must be dealt with. We can't have the *Spur* continuing to pursue us once the storm breaks. The bastards are only a half league off. With their smaller, more agile ship, they could be upon us before the *Fyredragon* can reach open air."

Darant knew this danger, too. Still, he looked hard at Graylin. "I heard you're taking Fenn. You're not planning on handing over my navigator, are you?"

Graylin offered the truth. "Only if necessary."

"What if you took more men, more of my crew—"

"No." Graylin shut this down. "We'll manage with those I picked or not at all. If I fail, you'll need every cannon, ballista, and free hand to fight your way free." He gave the captain a stern look. "When the storm breaks, you run. Whether we're back or not. Is that understood?"

Darant stared him down for a long breath, but the former pirate had enough sense to finally nod. The captain knew the stakes as well as anyone.

"Does Nyx know you're taking Jace?" Darant asked.

"He volunteered. I left it up to him whether to inform Nyx or not. And he's proven himself no slouch with his ax."

"Aye, he has. Considering the potbellied scholar he once was, he's turning into a fine pirate."

Graylin nodded, but that wasn't the true reason he had accepted Jace's offer. He didn't want to leave Jace behind with Nyx, not after what had happened back in Spindryft. Graylin feared the stress of the next half day might trigger the daemon inside Jace to rise again.

I can't take that chance.

Graylin had also handpicked a few others for this gambit, but one detail remained paramount. He squinted at Darant. "Have you heard from Hyck? Has he finished what I asked for?"

"I'll check. But I've heard no loud booms, so I assume my engineer has not blown himself up." Darant turned to face the broken cliffs and bricked escarpments. "Do you think she can lead you to the other ship?"

Before Graylin could answer, the storm erupted with a savage wail, quaking the balloon, shaking the ship. Sand spun and whipped down into the trough. The sun vanished into darkness. One of the mooring lines tore out of the wall. The boatswain and two crewmen ran toward its stanchion.

Graylin looked up, studying the sweeping black skirt of the desert god, Ishuka. "We'll never reach the Bhestyan warship by crossing overland, not through the storm." He lowered his gaze to the spread of dark ruins before him. "Only one path offers any hope."

And only one woman can lead us along it.

34

Esme should have heeded the wisdom of her Chanaryn elders. As she waited in an upper hold of the huge ship, she eyed those gathering with her. She had not expected to be struck so soon by the doom predicted by the *neey auguran,* the *bad omens* that this dragon-helmed ship portended.

Worse, if I had known what lay in the larger hold beneath this one, I would never have boarded this accursed vessel.

Earlier, Jace had allowed her to peek at what nested there. He had tried to get her to enter that hold, promising she would be safe. But she had balked at getting any nearer to those winged beasts. Five had been smaller, shaggier, but the true monster shadowed deeper in the hold. It was the same brute she had spotted carrying two riders. She wanted nothing to do with such beasts, especially knowing the Chanaryn sagas about winged daemons.

To Esme, only one creature aboard this ship made any sense. Crikit tapped back and forth behind her, expressing his nervousness. He chirped quietly, clearly anxious to escape this ship, too.

She understood his dismay. She stared over at the line of five sailrafts at the rear of the hold, all stanchioned in launch brackets positioned before the stern door. The vessels were used to evacuate a crippled wyndship. Esme wished she could flee aboard one of them. But at the moment, that was an impossibility. The stern door abutted tight against the sandstone, making it impossible to open.

Resigned to her fate, Esme studied the others in the group. She fixed on the gruff-faced knight, whose demeanor was as hard as his scarred face. Graylin had asked her to lead this excursion across the ruins to reach the Bhestyan warship. She didn't know if she could scout such a path, but she would do her best.

But that wasn't the main reason I agreed.

She watched Graylin nod, while another member of their party gestured with hands and expressions. "We'll be underway shortly, Vikas," he assured her.

Esme tried not to gawk at this mountain of a woman, one incapable of speech. Out in the desert, such a child would've been abandoned as a babe, left to the sands to scour away such a taint. Such was considered mercy, not cruelty.

Esme had come to doubt that, having witnessed others far more afflicted in

Seekh who fared well, who thrived amidst the sandy ruins. It was one of many lessons she had gained from her years foraging the necropolises.

Another was how to properly outfit oneself while traversing the ruins.

She had shared the knowledge with the others. Upon her recommendation, the group had outfitted themselves in desert whites, which consisted of a belted tunic over loose breeches. Hard boots had been exchanged for leather-soled sandals, flexible enough for surefooted climbing. She had taught them how to wrap a scarf about their heads, leaving a scrap hanging to pull over mouth and nose when the sand blew hard.

Which it certainly was now.

The hollow roar of the *ishuka* penetrated down into the hold. The entire ship shook and jolted. Muffled shouts marked the crew's fight to keep them in place.

A rushed trampling of feet drew her attention to the stairs behind her. A thin, squat figure burst off the last step and hurried over, breathless and red-faced. She didn't recognize the man, but from the gear he wore, he was the last member of the group.

"About time, Rhaif," Graylin scolded him. "Grab a pack. We need to be off. We've delayed long enough."

The newcomer patted a satchel belted at his hip. "Got everything I need. Lockpicks and files, oils for hinges, mirrors for spying. All a thief needs to sneak aboard a warship and bring her down. Who needs cannons and ballistas?"

Jace approached, shifting his shoulders to balance the broad-ax across his back. "I'd take both if we could carry them."

"We'll have enough to haul as it is." Graylin herded everyone to a stack of packs. The bags held ropes, climbing gear, hand picks, and shovels. "Everyone load up."

As they obeyed, Jace caught Esme staring quizzically at the last of the group. "That's Rhaif hy Albar, a thief out of Anvil in the Guld'guhl territories. His skills may prove as vital as yours."

"If we can get there," Graylin muttered to the side, having overheard them.

The ship's navigator, Fenn, hauled a pack over his shoulders. His skin had drawn tight over the bones of his face, his complexion pale to the point of translucency.

Esme recognized that familiar hollowed-out look of fear and worry. She had seen the same expression on many boys headed into the desert to start their manhood trials. Except her brother, Arryn, who had simply looked excited as he set off to prove himself amidst sand, water, and rock.

As Esme watched Fenn, she understood what terrorized the navigator. She had heard his story from Jace, a tale of betrayal and murder, and now a sister imprisoned, threatened by death.

For Fenn, this trek was more about rescue than sabotage. Still, he seemed to accept which was more important, having expressed as much earlier. The warship had to be crippled. But from his countenance, she wondered how truthful he had been. Still, they needed him. Someone with the face of a Bhestyan might prove critical when invading one of the kingdom's warships.

Esme shook off such speculations.

None of it matters.

She hauled up one of the packs and carried it to Crikit. She quickly and expertly harnessed it to his back. Another bag already burdened her friend, snugged down on the far side of his carapace's central ridge. As a scout, Esme needed her arms and legs free to quickly explore and scramble a path forward, leading the others through the ruins.

Jace joined her. "Do you need any help?"

"Crikit will manage." She checked the straps one final time. "He can easily keep up with me."

Or so I hope.

She tried not to stare at the pack on the far side. Jace smiled at her, his manner so genuine, so good-natured, so unlike those who dwelled in Seekh. Guilt panged through her, knowing her plan.

She had to remind herself.

This is not my battle.

While readying for this trip, Jace had fleshed out the others' stories: of a girl awakened by poison in the swamp, of prophecies of pending doom, of wars being fought on the far side of the Crown, and of a far more ancient battle among undying gods. It was all madness. After her years in Seekh, she had her fill with the deluded and the foolish. Plus, the words of Aelder Hasant still haunted her, of the dark portent of such a ship.

Earlier in the day, she had not heeded his warning.

But now I will.

While this ship had promised a chance to cross into the deep desert, to aid in her search for Arryn, she recognized now that it came with too much risk. She should have stuck to her original plan.

Knowing this, she could not stop herself from eyeing the first pack she had tied to Crikit's back. Inside, she had hidden the treasure she had recovered from the ruins, an artifact worth a king's ransom, enough to buy her passage out to the Barrens.

I do not need to shoulder this group's burdens.

Boarding the ship had been a rash act. She intended to correct that mistake. Once out in the ruins, she would take off with Crikit, abandoning the others to their own mischief. From there, she would make her way to another village, one not overrun by Peck and his ilk, and sell this treasure to the Guilders, funding her own trek into the Barrens.

Still, her stomach churned at this choice. She knew she had to be as harsh as the desert. While she didn't *like* this betrayal, she would learn to *live* with it. Shame could be dealt with. The sun would eventually bake it out of her.

Graylin waved everyone toward the starboard side of the hold. "Let's be off."

Before they could step away, loud footfalls drew their attention back to the stairs. Wood groaned under a heavy tread. From the sound, Esme expected someone even more massive than Vikas to appear.

Instead, a tall, lissome woman swept elegantly into the room. A long robe brushed her calves. She entered with such easy grace, Esme wondered if she was from some noble line, a lost lineage of ancient queens.

Rhaif hurried toward her.

Jace shifted closer to Esme, his brow crinkled with worry. "I'm sorry. I should've warned you sooner . . ."

The thief reached the stately woman. "Shiya, what are you doing here? Did you get the coolers running?"

"No," she intoned, turning the one word into the first note of a song.

Esme found herself mesmerized.

The woman—Shiya—continued, "As a precaution, I've sealed each chamber, to keep sand and dust away. We dare not risk any damage."

Rhaif took her hand. "Then why . . . ?"

She smiled at the thief. Her expression was so warm and appreciative that Esme found herself mirroring the same affection for this thin man. "I came to see you all off."

Shiya drew the man into a brief embrace.

Jace took Esme's hand, his palm slick with the same worry as before. "I had hoped to brace you first. Give you more time to acclimate, especially after your reaction to Bashaliia and the raash'ke. I didn't want to overwhelm you."

"Why?" she whispered, unable to turn her gaze from the woman. "Who is she?"

Shiya stepped closer, nodding in greeting to Graylin.

"She is a *ta'wyn*," Jace said.

Esme frowned, struggling for a breath to understand—then she did. She had heard that word before, when trapped between Peck and the strangers. It was a term used to describe the treasure she had pulled from the sand.

By now, Crikit had crossed over and danced around the woman with plain curiosity, his eye-stalks high. Upon his back, he carried a limb from the same being.

A *ta'wyn* . . .

Esme stumbled away, supported still by Jace, but no strength of limb could anchor her. She finally recognized that the woman's skin was not richly sun-kissed but was made of bronze—only this metal appeared warm and malleable as any flesh.

How could this be?

Even the curls of the figure's hair shimmered a darker sheen, as if tarnished, composed of filaments so fine that they begged to be brushed aside. The cheeks blushed through hues of pink and darker red. The lips gathered the latter colors, creating a rosy aspect that accentuated the bow of her mouth.

Esme touched her forehead. "I must be going mad."

But as she stared into the figure's eyes, their brightness burned away any doubt.

Esme tore her gaze from the impossible figure and faced Jace. "Your stories . . . all of them . . . they were true."

"As best I can attest," he said softly, clearly wounded for causing her this pain.

Esme let all those wild tales flow through her. She wanted to dismiss them again, especially the apocalypse at the center of it all. But she could not.

The truth shone in bronze before her.

Graylin stepped before Esme. "I'm sorry. But we must be going. Are you all right to continue?"

I'll never be all right.

"Can you guide us to the other ship?" he pressed her.

Off to the side, Fenn cranked open a hatch, lowering the door to form a bridge out to the ruins. He was plainly anxious to be underway, to reach his sister.

Behind Graylin, the *ta'wyn* woman gave the thief a brief hug, then headed away, with her own duties to attend.

But what of my own?

The grizzled knight stared at her, waiting for an answer.

Esme's neck had stiffened, harder than any bronze. She forced her head to nod. "I will . . . I will try my best."

"Thank you." Graylin headed toward Fenn.

Esme turned to Jace, who still held her hand. She gave his fingers one squeeze, then freed herself. "We should go."

As they headed toward the hatch, trailed by Crikit, Esme glanced to the shadowy doorway where the miracle had departed. Facing forward, she pictured the tarnished limb hidden inside the crab's pack, a treasure that could buy her freedom.

She considered her plan, once certain, now less so.

This is not my battle, she reminded herself.

Upon reaching the bridge that led off into the ruins, she stared into the familiar shadows. They offered more comfort than the strangeness of this ship. As she headed out, her promise to Graylin echoed in her head.

I will try my best.

She had spoken the truth, but what had she meant? To do her best to escape with Crikit . . . or to help these others? She still didn't know.

She headed toward the ruins.

I will only discover my answer out there.

35

ORREN HY PASHKIN scowled at his niece through the bars of her cell.

Freya shifted in the straw, her wrists chained to iron rings. She sat on her legs, curled to one side, her manner unconcerned, almost regal. Her long silvery white hair hung over one shoulder. She seemed to find no distress in her blackened eye or her swollen lip, which still seeped blood after he had cuffed her hard.

She looked upon him with raw disdain.

He eyed her in turn, tapping a thumb against his forehead, considering how best to deal with her continuing insolence.

He failed to see what his cousin ever saw in such a gaunt waif of a woman. He preferred a shape heavier of bosom and hip, like his wife, Hylia. Though of late she had gained so much girth, feasting on the spoils of his position as the king's high minister, that it had grown impossible to separate bosom from hip.

As such, Orren often sought pleasures in the perfumed alleys of the Meershen district, where whores were shapelier and willing to perform acts his wife would not do—and if she did, he would scorn her for them. He also sought release in Meershen for a more practical reason, one pursuant to his endowment, or lack thereof. Due to Hylia's size, he could no longer reach that which had been afforded him in the past, though it had already been a struggle prior to Hylia's new girth.

A part of him wondered if his wife had gained that weight on purpose, to keep him off her. She certainly refused him in all other ways.

Orren stared over at his niece, wondering if he should adjust his tastes to suit his circumstance. Maybe a thinner woman had its appeal. He would test this notion upon Freya when the time was opportune, before she was hung from the prow of the *Sharpened Spur*. Orren already despised her husband. If he couldn't bugger the bastard, he would find satisfaction here in this cell.

Back in Bhestya, his cousin continued to pronounce Freya's innocence on his knees before King Acker, likely willing to suck the royal cock if it would earn his wife any clemency.

Not that she will ever return to Bhestya.

Orren needed to burn this thorn from his side once and for all. He had rid the world of one of his brother's sons—Geryd—and he intended to end the rest of the line before leaving this damnable desert. He only kept Freya alive as bait for her remaining brother and to entertain the hope of torturing and killing Fenn in front of her. Though in truth, he remained undecided who should die first.

Both had appeal.

"What do you want, Orren?" Freya spat at him. "There's only so much gloating I can stomach."

He straightened, his cheeks flushing hotly at her rudeness. To make matters worse, the ship's quartermaster stood at the door to the brig, bearing witness.

Orren sneered, while fingering the silver medallion hanging from his neck. It rested over his white waistcoat, framed by the wolf-trimmed edges of his cloak. Stamped into the silver was a stylized eye, marking him as Acker's high minister.

"I'm not here to gloat," Orren said coldly. "Only to share knowledge."

"Concerning what?"

"The hunt for your brother is over. They're trapped by the storm." Orren looked up, cocking his head to the howl of the sands, a bit of providence that perhaps heralded his righteous efforts in this desert. "They are buried only half a league off. Once the storm lifts, there will be no escape. Not in that lumbering, aged ship. We will be atop them like a mouser on a cornered rat."

Freya sighed, her eyes casting down, perhaps in resignation. Then she shook her head and lifted her gaze. There was no defeat in that hard shine, only certainty. "Your treachery will be exposed, Orren. Nothing stays buried forever. Look at these ruins we're hiding in. Eventually the past always pushes out of the dust."

His shoulders stiffened, knowing he had to be careful with his next words. Only the *Spur*'s captain, who was complicit in the betrayal, knew the truth. Venga's continuing silence had earned him this ship. Orren had also promised the man a position in the king's council if this venture ended well.

Which is now guaranteed.

With the quartermaster at the door, Orren feigned great umbrage. He puffed out his chest. "Even such vile accusations only prove your duplicity— and that of your brother. Until now, you've been spared by my cousin's love and blindness. But at long last, your father's traitorous actions will be brought to their just ends."

Laughter, bright and mocking, burst from Freya.

Orren's face heated. His hands clenched into fists. "Quiet!"

Freya refused, her body trembling with mirth. "Have you learned nothing, Orren? Do not forget even a cornered rat sometimes kills the cat."

Orren growled, ready to be done with this matter. He knew words that would silence her. "Mind you, dear niece. Sometimes the cat doesn't wait for a rat to get cornered."

She frowned, turning to stare at him with her unblemished eye, one sharp with suspicion.

Orren took this moment to quash any hope. "As the *Spur* was lowering into the sands, Captain Venga dispatched thirty ra-knights from the ship, the elite of the king's legions. He cast them off into the desert, under the edge of the storm. With ropes and sand spikes. They're already crawling beneath the whipping dust to drop atop the other ship. They will be upon them before the next bell rings."

He enjoyed the look of dismay on her face. All in Bhestya knew the skill, resolve, and ruthlessness of the king's ra-knights. To a man, each was an armored daemon.

"Unlike the past," Orren promised, "there will be no escape."

He turned and strode away, content with the misery he had wrought. Still, he paused, tapping his thumb upon his brow, wondering if this was punishment enough. He decided it was not, especially with her mocking laughter, especially in front of a witness. To reassert himself, he stopped next to the quartermaster and cocked his head toward the cell.

"Go in there and break her arm."

36

DAAL PUSHED OUT onto the open middeck of the *Fyredragon*. He wiped the blood dripping from one nostril. Despite the searing heat, the lash of gritty sand, he needed to be free of the confines of the ship.

As he strode across the deck, he noted the world had grown far darker, the sun now shadowed by the storm. Lanterns had been lit. A few firepots danced with flames. He headed through the bustle of the crew. He barely noted their efforts to work the mooring cables, which thrummed under the strain of holding the massive ship.

Tamryn rushed out behind him, giving chase. She had to yell to be heard over the roar of the storm. "They'll be at each other again before long!"

He whipped around to face her. "And whose fault is that?"

Tamryn skidded to a stop, her eyes widening, flashing with anger.

As he scowled at her, he took in the paleness of her skin, the emerald cast to her shorn hair, the peak of her tipped ears.

By all Panthean ideals, she was beautiful. Even Daal, with his Noorish half blood, appreciated it. It was a standard that had been instilled into him. All his life, he had been shamed by the blue of his eyes, the ebon streaks in his hair, the curled fur that sprouted and coarsened his chest and limbs—so unlike the smoothness of a pure-blooded Panthean.

He had suffered for all of it, humiliated and scorned due to his Noorish heritage. Even here, that same taint continued to divide the sixteen who had left the Crèche and joined the crew. Rather than be united, they remained divided, stirred by slurs and slights, by bickering and shouts, until eventually these flared into fights.

Daal managed to quell the latest, but not without injury. He swiped again at the blood. He knew the tension of the past day had likely stoked this fire, but there would be worse dangers ahead.

"We need to come together," he shouted at Tamryn. He waved toward the scurrying men and women. "We're already outsiders here. The crew's numbers are twice ours. How can you expect them to treat us as peers, when we can't treat each other as such?"

"Then what would you have us do?"

He stabbed a finger at her. "For one, you can show me some respect. Your disdain steams from you as hotly as the boiling seas of our home. All see it.

Same with your condescension and contempt. Why should any of your fellow full-bloods act any differently? As second saddle, you're respected among them. You know that, Tamryn."

Her anger died into something that looked like consternation. "It's not . . . I don't mean to be so . . ." She huffed heavily, clearly struggling to explain. "Daal, I can't help how I feel."

She reached for his arm.

He pulled away, turning his shoulder to her. "Try harder."

He strode toward the portside rail, needing a moment to shed his anger and frustration. Tamryn followed, but she kept a distance. Daal ducked through the bustle, nearly getting bowled over by a burly-limbed crewman. Still, he reached the rail and grabbed hard. Blood dribbled to his upper lip.

He stared across the vibrating mooring lines. The planks underfoot shook the same. Overhead, the balloon rattled, while its cables moaned with deep-throated notes of strain.

It all echoed his own agitation.

Tamryn reached the rail, her head hanging, studying the array of mooring lines. This precarious hold upon their berth worried them all. But she clearly had other concerns.

"Daal, you were right in some regard, but not about—"

He lifted a hand, clenching a fist, not in anger but in warning.

Movement caught his eye. While the crew continued to focus on the mooring lines, Daal had been looking up. Shadows dropped along the sandstone cliffs, bounding off brick walls, dislodging a few. Thick ropes unfurled beneath them. Their passage was barely discernible in the murky stormlight.

Daal swung around and grabbed the nearest crewman, the same massive man who had almost knocked him over, a brigand named Perde. The man had stripped to his chest, baring a splay of tattoos depicting scenes of carnage, likely preserving the histories of past exploits.

We may need that same savagery now.

Before Perde could rip loose, Daal hollered to him and pointed to the glint of armor flashing down the rock. "We're under attack!"

The momentary flash of confusion on the pirate's face hardened into fury. Perde cursed, then shoved back with a bellow and boomed across the deck, "Rouse out! Ready to propel boarders!"

Already on edge, the crew responded quickly, even the few Pantheans sharing the deck.

Past Perde's shoulders, Daal spotted ropes dropping and snaking past the starboard side, too. Large shapes vanished along them, plummeting below. He struggled to understand—then recognized the danger.

No . . .

He burst past Perde and fled across the deck.

Tamryn chased after. "Where are you going?"

Behind him, Perde continued rallying the crew. "Flog your arses!"

Daal reached and slammed his stomach into the starboard rail, hard enough to nearly get tossed overboard. To his right, past a cannon, a dark shape in blue-hued armor swung off another line and crashed to the deck. To Daal's left, another pair struck farther away.

Daal ignored them and stared below. A bulky shadow swung and landed on a bridge that spanned from the flank of the ship to the ruins, marking the open hatch used by Graylin and the others when they had departed. As Daal feared, it had been left open, awaiting their eventual return.

The invaders must have spotted it, too, recognizing a way deeper into the ship.

Below, a half dozen shadows barreled inside, swords flashing in their grips.

Daal rolled away and fled for the door to the lower decks. As he ran, shouts and bellows chased him, punctuated by clashes of steel. With every step, the battle raged more fiercely. He did not stop, one fear foremost, picturing who hid in darkness below, all but blind.

Hold fast, Nyx.

THE MUFFLED CLAMOR of fighting reached the lowest hold. The screams and distant ringing of steel stirred the raash'ke flock. Though Nyx's vision remained clouded, she recognized their growing unease. Leathery wings ruffled nervously. Claws dug at the planking. Keening cries echoed off the walls, accompanied by sharper pipes of distress.

Nyx did her best to calm them, while her own heart pounded. She cast out golden strands of bridle-song, but she remained too weak to rein in their growing alarm. Even to her own eyes, her efforts appeared as feeble glows through her shrouded sight. The pools of lantern light shone far brighter.

Must get closer to them.

She set off across the hold with her arms out. She extended one foot, then the other. She wished she still had her cane from her years in Brayk. The thin length of wood had acted as an extension of her senses.

But even here, she was not without resources.

Kalder growled up beside her, bumping her leg. She grabbed his scruff in one hand.

"Get me to Bashaliia," she urged him.

She reinforced this with a nudge of bridle-song.

Ahead, she had no difficulty discerning her winged brother's location. She heard his fretful whistles of concern. As Kalder guided her closer, a rich golden glow emerged out of the gloom, marking the font of Bashaliia's rich song.

"I'm coming," she whispered.

Harsh, furtive voices suddenly rose from the far side of the hold, echoing down the steps that led here. They spoke in a pidgin of Bhestyan, a smattering of which Fenn had taught her during the long voyage.

"Eeshyn, cripple the sailrafts. You four with me."

While Nyx had already suspected the attack had come from the warship, this confirmed her fear.

Boots pounded down toward her, growing louder.

The raash'ke grew more agitated at the approaching noise, either perceiving the threat or perhaps sensing Nyx's rising panic. Wings beat harder. Cries sharpened.

She hurried toward Bashaliia, pushing Kalder ahead of her. She reached deep inside herself, down to her diaphragm, trying to dredge up as much strength as she could muster. She needed to ready herself and those in her charge. Terror— amplified by the dark, by her lack of sight—bolstered her golden strands to a brighter shine. She cast them toward Bashaliia.

I need you.

Distracted by the panic in the raash'ke, Nyx had failed to note the emerald fire smoldering at the core of Bashaliia's glow. It marked the residual madness that her winged brother carried with him, born of the brutality that had been inflicted on Kalyx, the body Bashaliia now wore. That scar persisted, indelible, grained deep, calloused by fury and agony. The current fear in Bashaliia inflamed that madness, loosening its reins.

Nyx recognized this too late.

Before she could stop herself, before she could recall the golden chords from reaching out, they struck Bashaliia. Her own alarm, carried by her song, swelled into her winged brother. She had meant those chords to rouse him, to ready him to defend the hold and those within it.

Instead, emerald fire burst brighter, flaring through her shroud.

Bashaliia screamed in fury.

"No . . ."

Nyx let go of Kalder and ran blindly toward her brother, seeking to tamp that fire—but again she was too late.

Bashaliia burst high, carrying that emerald fire with him. The edge of a wing, maybe a claw, struck Nyx across the chest. She flew back, both the wind and song knocked from her chest as she crashed down. Her head rang against iron-hard planks.

What little sight she had dimmed to blackness.

Bellows of surprise rose across the hold. The invaders must have finally spotted what nested here. No doubt appalled, struggling to understand. But these attackers were clearly battle-hardened, inured to any shock that could immobilize them.

A command confirmed this. "Ready yourselves, men!"

Raash'ke scurried back with a scrape of claws and keening calls, plainly unsure, confused. But behind them, a greater danger screamed madly, ready to lash out at anything that drew too near.

Nyx reached for any strength left to her but found nothing.

Another shout rose from the marauder's leader.

"Slay them . . . slay them all!"

37

GRAYLIN SCALED SIDEWAYS down a narrow crack in the sandstone. To squeeze along, he had to carry his pack in hand. He panted through his dust-scarf. Sweat glued cloth to skin, while grit covered every surface of him. Still, he hurried after Esme, fearful of losing her in the dark.

Overhead, the storm still raged, howling its fury. Occasional gusts swept deep, scouring stone, ripping past them, forcing them low. Still, Graylin appreciated those moments. It allowed glimpses of the sky, and the pitch-darkness of the tunnels brightened to a murky gloom.

Otherwise, the group crept through dark passageways, their traverse lit by a lone lantern carried by Esme. They were often forced to crawl on their bellies over crumbling bricks and plaster. Broken spears of pipes and jagged pikes of curled iron threatened to impale the unwary. Many times, their trek involved moving backward as much as forward, as if Esme's scouting expressed some hesitation on her part.

Though at the moment, the young woman hurried onward. Her dexterous form moved swiftly. Above her head, her crab matched her pace, his chitinous legs outstretched between the walls, their sharp tips balancing atop pebbles of rock or spiking into crevices. The beast moved as easily as a horse fording a shallow stream.

The thought of water dried Graylin's mouth.

Behind him, Jace followed with Fenn, trailed by Rhaif and Vikas. The group had begun to drape out, separating from one another as the strain of this traverse challenged them. Only Fenn kept close, looking ready to leap past Graylin, fear for his sister clearly stemming any exhaustion or thirst.

Still, the others dragged farther behind.

"Slow down!" Graylin yelled to Esme. "Let's close our ranks."

"A way opens ahead," she called back. "Not much farther."

She rushed on, vanishing around a bend with Crikit.

Graylin grumbled under his breath. He slid and scooted, but her words proved true. The gloom lessened, and the winds picked up. After a final tight squeeze, he fell out of the crack and into another corner of the ruins. The storm howled overhead. The sky remained black with blowing sand.

Fenn followed and dumped next to him onto a wide ledge.

Ahead, a deep chasm blocked their way.

So far, the group had managed to avoid having to break out their ropes. Esme had found other ways around, often using ledges and outcroppings to skirt past such obstacles.

Again, luck favored them.

As Graylin waited for the others to exit the ravine, he studied this lonely corner of the necropolises. Across the chasm, the entire facade showed an eroded surface of bricks, twisted metal, pocked by chambers and tunnels built by the ancients. Rockfalls scarred vast swaths. The rest had been worn by the grindstone of ages into a dusty sculptural smoothness, creating a haunted skeletal feel to this place. But more than that, the air hung with a melancholiness that weighed on the heart. The wail of the storm overhead and its shrouded gloom added to this impression.

These ruins had been deserted long ago, well before the Forsaken Ages— only to be abandoned again more recently. Ropes and ladders were strung throughout its tiers, draping down into the dark depths. Ore carts lay topped or crushed. Anything of value had been mined out long ago. All that was left were these moldering trappings and useless tools, discarded by laborers who had moved on to richer veins.

Still, a thick rope remained, strung across the deep canyon, creating a ready bridge for them to cross.

Fenn reached up to test its merits as Jace and Rhaif joined them, panting heavily, sweating even more.

"It won't hold," Esme warned without looking up, rummaging through Crikit's pack.

Graylin frowned. The rope looked stout, as thick around as his wrist.

Fenn must have doubted her, too—or maybe anxiety goaded him to avoid any unnecessary delays. The navigator leaped to the cord and hung there, swinging slightly. "Looks plenty—"

The rope did not snap. Instead, a section in the middle simply dissolved to dust, as if it had been an illusion, a mirage of the desert. Fenn crashed to the ledge, corrected by the mercilessness of time and decay.

Esme had another lesson for him, too. She stood and tapped to a sign tacked under the iron hook holding this end of the rope. The board was covered with cryptic scrawls, symbols, and arrows.

"If you can't recognize a bad rope—something anyone who survives Seekh quickly learns—there's a warning written right here, telling no one to cross." She stood and tapped a crude skull. "This is the fate of anyone who dares try."

Rhaif helped Fenn up.

Jace leaned closer to inspect the old sign. "What do all these other scrawls tell you?"

"Directions mostly. From miners in the past. To various regions of the ru-ins. It's easy to get turned around down here."

"What about this one?" Jace asked. "Does it indicate a path that might take us toward the Bhestyan warship? According to Fenn's chart, we must be close to it by now."

Esme stared to the northeast, where they had spotted the *Sharpened Spur*. "The sign does mark an old dig site, one in that direction. If it's a well-traveled route, it should be reinforced. If so, we'll make good time."

Jace nodded, turning away.

As he did, Graylin caught Esme's gaze swinging to the west, with a contem-plative cast to her eyes.

Fenn scowled and dusted off the seat of his breeches. "We still must get across here."

Graylin nodded. "Can we find another path around?" He looked to either side, searching for ledges, outcroppings, any way to skirt around it. "Or must we backtrack again?"

By now, Vikas had squirmed her large form out of the ravine, her skin raw, her clothing torn in places. It had been an extraordinarily tight fit for her. She heard Graylin's inquiry and let out an exaggerated sigh. She tossed her pack down and thrust her hand up and flicked her thumb—the Gynish equivalent of *Sod that*.

"We don't have to backtrack," Esme declared. She had returned to her pack and withdrew a thin rope. Its length glinted in the gloom. "A climbing line, threaded through with draft-iron fibers. Much like your ship's mooring cables."

"And what do you plan to do with it?" Rhaif scoffed. "Leap over there and tie it down?"

"Not me."

Esme bent and held out the length toward Crikit. The crab grabbed an end with the larger of his two pincers. Esme then pointed to the ruins across from them.

"Can you make it?" she asked, as if the crab could possibly understand.

Crikit's eye-stalks waggled. Some tilted toward the chasm, others toward Esme. Finally, the crab scuttled to the edge of the drop.

Esme straightened. "He can make it."

Before Graylin could question this, Crikit lowered to his belly, cocking his jointed legs under him— then sprang away, shooting impossibly high. The crab flew across the chasm, dragging the thin line. Crikit landed on the far side and skidded into a chamber's shadows. He jarred back into view, skittered over to a spar of torn metal, and danced around it, anchoring the cable.

The crab had clearly done this many times.

Upon witnessing this, Graylin had a greater appreciation for such a companion among these ruins.

Esme acknowledged Crikit's feat with a wave of her arm, then tied her end of the rope to the old hook in the wall. She then took a nub of charcoal and crossed out the skull, marking the crossing now safe.

"I'll leave the line hung," she said as she yanked it tight. "In case we have to retreat this way."

Graylin hoped that wouldn't prove necessary.

In short order, they readied to cross the bridge. Vikas went first. If the rope could hold the quartermaster's bulk, it should hold all of them. Once she was safely across, Jace, Rhaif, and Fenn followed.

Graylin waved Esme to go ahead of him. "I'll bring up the rear."

The woman didn't object, which Graylin appreciated. Esme grabbed the line, hooked her legs, and scooted swiftly, going headfirst. Her lantern hung from her belt, swinging wildly.

As he waited, Graylin secured his pack over his shoulder and cinched its straps. His bag was the heaviest, and he dared not lose it. He stepped back to the cliff's edge. Esme was already halfway across.

Movement below drew his eye, from a lower section of the ruins. At first, he thought it was a trick of the light from Esme's bobbling lantern. Then something clearly crept out of one of the shadowed chambers and crawled up the wall. He could barely make it out. Then it stopped, nearly disappearing against the bricks, looking more boulder than life now.

"Esme!" Graylin called over. "Below you! There's something—"

As his eyes adjusted, he realized it wasn't just *one* boulder, but dozens protruding from the rock face, already perched there, waiting. Some as large as a full-grown ox. Then, upon some silent signal, they all began to lurch upward with a faint scrape of claws.

He remembered the skull drawn on the sign behind him.

It hadn't been a warning about the rope.

"Esme! Hurry!"

ESME FROZE AT the first shout by the gruff knight. Hanging by hands and legs, she twisted her neck to explore beneath the sway of her rope. Shadows filled the depths, all the darker due to the *ishuka*. The jiggling lantern at her belt made it difficult to judge movement.

She squinted, searching for any threat.

Then a darker patch surged upward, leaping from a lower tier of the ruins to a closer one. Then it went still again. She quickly realized the shifting shadows below had nothing to do with her swinging lantern.

Danger stalked upward.

She could guess what. She freed a hand and opened her lantern's shutters to their widest. The flare of light stung but confirmed her worst fear.

Yinkan . . .

She had only heard of this scourge. They were a rare threat found in the loneliest corners of the ruins. They were said to hunt by ambushing prey.

Like now.

A swing of her lantern stripped shadows from the closest one.

A squat shape bulged from the wall, its skin pebbled like a rock to keep it camouflaged. Even the shine of its globular eyes was dulled by an inner lid. Its wide mouth, stony lipped, looked like a fissure across a boulder. To either side, legs ended in splayed footpads with hooked claws. The hind pair were far larger than the front, to aid in leaping.

Caught by her light, those inner lids blinked open—then the beast bounded upward. At the same time, that fissure in the boulder cracked open. A black tongue spat out, faster than a striking viper.

Esme let go of her hands and swung down, hanging by her crossed legs. The tip of the tongue hit the rope, striking where she had been, and stuck there. The slimy surface shone with oil, a paralytic meant to stun its prey.

Below her, the beast swung by its long tongue. As it retracted the appendage, the yinkan's bulk shot up toward her. Such creatures normally feasted on crabs, giant cave spiders, birds, even the orange-tinged crakadyls that swam through the poisonous lakes in the deepest depths of the ruins.

Only this nest had trapped new prey.

As the yinkan rushed upward, Esme struggled to grab the line again with her hands. Before she could manage it, a sweep of silver passed beneath the curve of her back. A sword severed the tongue just as the beast was nearly upon her. She caught a glimpse into its fanged maw, lined by row upon row of sharp teeth that ran deep into its gullet.

Then the creature fell away, tumbling into the dark with a sharp screech.

"Go!" Graylin shouted.

Esme got one hand back on the rope, but they'd never make it across. A dozen more yinkan perched below, ready to ambush. They looked momentarily frozen by the death cry of the dispatched beast.

That would not last.

Already another shifted forward, leaping to a higher tier.

Esme grabbed for her only weapon. With her free hand, she unhooked the lantern from her belt and swung it hard. She tossed it toward the wall. Its flame blew brighter as the lantern spun. Then it smashed into the bricks, exploding into a wash of fire.

The crash struck close to a yinkan, spattering flaming oil across its eyes. The beast hissed, tried to retreat, but in a panic it dislodged from the wall.

It fell, flailing away.

Without waiting, Esme sped down the rope, scurrying along its length. Below, the fire drove several beasts back. A few held firm. The brightness likely blinded them, too, but the flames had begun to burn out.

As Graylin jostled the rope behind her, she rushed on, expecting to be struck at any moment, yanked from the rope. But she finally reached the end. With a gasp, she swung off the rope and rolled into the others.

As Vikas helped her up, Esme choked out a warning and pointed to a crumbling passageway. "Into the ruins. Away from this chasm."

Graylin landed behind her with a grunt. "Do as she says."

The yinkan, being ambush hunters, would likely not pursue them.

At least, I hope that's true.

The group rushed off—but one was too slow, too distressed.

Crikit bleated out a sharp note.

Esme swung around. Crikit got yanked away, struck by the tip of a black tongue. It had glued to one of his packs. His eight legs scrabbled and dug for purchase, but it was to no avail as he skidded backward.

No . . .

Then a dark shape leaped from the side, shoulder-rolling to Crikit. Jace deftly swung his ax off his back and slammed its blade across the tongue. Blood spattered far, and Crikit was released.

The molag rushed toward her, chittering in panic. His pack had been ripped open during the struggle. From inside, something clattered free. It bounced and rattled across the stone, flashing tarnished bronze.

Jace scooped up the broken *ta'wyn* limb as he followed behind Crikit. He knew how much she treasured it. Once he reached her, he passed the cargo into Esme's embrace and herded her forward.

As she hurried with him, she glanced down at the bronze arm, then up to him and over to Graylin. The Chanaryn believed in blood debts, often spanning generations. But she knew that wasn't what motivated her next action.

She gripped the *ta'wyn* limb and flung it away. It flew far behind her, out across the chasm, and fell away into oblivion—where another hunter might eventually stumble upon such a rich find.

Let them.

Jace stared at her with a puzzled expression, clearly wondering why she had discarded what she had held so precious.

She looked across the group ahead, at those who had saved her, at those who had rescued Crikit. She silently answered Jace's query.

Because this is treasure enough right here.

38

NYX SHOVED OFF the planks, her head still ringing after being knocked flat by Bashaliia's outburst. Dizziness still churned her stomach. Her darkened vision swirled with brighter patches—from the lanterns, from the fonts of the raash'ke bridle-song. She fought to focus on the golden glow ahead of her, where a fiery emerald storm raged.

Bashaliia . . .

She had to get her winged brother under control, lest he blindly rip through everyone. But he was not the only threat. Boots pounded deeper into the hold, marking the trespass by Bhestyan raiders. Five, as best she could count. They closed upon the frightened raash'ke, who retreated in confusion, unaccustomed to strangers, unable to tell friend from foe.

Not without guidance.

That arrived with raucous shouts of fury and the pounding of many feet. One voice rose above the tumult. "Protect the mounts!"

Daal must have roused the entire Panthean contingent, a dozen or more. They fell upon the marauders with ringing steel.

"Close tight!" the Bhestyan leader bellowed, even now sounding unintimidated by the assault. "Pick them off!"

Daal shouted again, *"Yee wah nayl!"*

Though spoken in his native tongue, these words were meant not for his fellow Pantheans—but for those he had trained. His command reached the raash'ke.

Attack the enemy!

The bats needed no further instruction. Already nervous and suspicious, the raash'ke struck at the nearest threat, those whose scent was surely different from that of anyone aboard the ship. Wings beat the air and claws shoved against planks. The pack lunged at the strangers with screeches of pent-up fury.

Moments later, men screamed, their voices full of blood.

Bashaliia responded to the clashes of steel, to the moans of the dying. Emerald fire spread, consuming his golden glow. His wings thrashed the air, readying to attack.

Nyx knew she did not have the strength to rein in that wildness.

But another might.

She turned to the battle, searching the gloom. She faintly made out a swirl of golden light rising from a familiar well, weak but present.

Would it be enough?

She cupped her mouth and called over, "Daal! I need you!"

But the fighting drowned out her words.

She required a louder voice. With a last wisp of bridle-song, she nudged her wish into Kalder. The vargr responded and howled across the hold.

She followed it with a desperate hope.

Hear me.

THROUGH THE DIN of battle, Daal cringed at a familiar wail.

Kalder . . .

Earlier, when Daal had left to settle the squabble among the Pantheans, the vargr had remained with Nyx. Kalder must still be guarding over her. Daal also spotted the battering of Bashaliia's wings.

Something was wrong.

With a sword in hand, he sought a way past the fighting. Two of the five Bhestyan knights had fallen. Three Pantheans also lay on the ground. But Daal's people no longer had to attack. They formed a defensive wall with their hammers, axes, and pikes, pinning down the three remaining marauders.

The raash'ke closed behind the enemy. One buck lashed out and sank venomous fangs into a knight's throat, lifting the man off his feet. A strong shake, and his neck snapped, killing the man before the poison could reach his heart.

Knowing the battle was over, Daal shoved through the cordon of Pantheans. He shouted back to Tamryn, "Finish them off!"

As he ran, he heard the clash of a fiercer battle being waged above, as the larger contingent of Bhestyan raiders fought the *Fyredragon*'s crew.

Daal ignored it and focused on his greater concern.

He spotted Nyx standing next to Kalder. She must have heard or sensed his approach. Relief softened the strain of her lips—but just barely.

As he rushed toward her, he searched for the source of her distress. Kalder guarded one side of her. Bashaliia hovered on the other, his huge wings thrashing, struggling to keep aloft within the confines of the hold, clearly responding to Nyx's distress.

Daal hurried to close on her, confused and panicked.

Nyx stepped toward him. "Watch out!"

Daal noted a flash of emerald fire and instinctively dodged from it, remembering when last he had witnessed that vile tinge. Back at the *ta'wyn* stronghold in the Frozen Wastes. He leaped away as Bashaliia lunged and snapped at him. Even the barest graze of a fang could kill him.

Though his heart pounded, Daal recognized the danger now—what afflicted Bashaliia. He had experienced this savage raving before. He continued his roll and reached Nyx, crashing into her.

He hugged his arms around her.

"Take what you need," he gasped out.

NYX DID NOT hesitate. The abyss inside her already demanded it, but at this moment, they were of one mind, one need.

She pulled Daal to her, drawing his feverish cheek to hers. She again felt the familiar fire as two melded into one. But it was weak, reflecting the shallowness of his wellspring. Still, she took everything from Daal, knowing it was the only hope. She dragged every erg of strength from him, not only from that well, but also from his life.

She felt his heart tremble.

His body went cold in her embrace.

Their communion faded, pushing them apart.

I'm sorry . . .

Still, his arms tightened on her, urging her to draw more.

But she dared not.

Instead, she gathered his warmth, his fire. She stoked it inside her lungs, her heart, her throat. All the while, she watched Bashaliia. After attacking Daal, he spun a circle, trailing a mix of emerald and golden fire through the air. He appeared momentarily dismayed at failing to strike his target, perhaps baffled by the refuge Daal had sought.

At the same time, Kalder paced around Nyx, matching the bat's path with a low growl of warning.

This impasse would not last much longer.

Knowing this, Nyx lifted her cheek from Daal's and cast forth a twining trail of golden song toward her winged brother. She folded in chords of reassurance, memories of the two nestled together in a wagon, when Bashaliia was no larger than a winter goose. She added in the smell of silage from the swamplands, the whisper of wind through the rushes, the sonnet of frogs under a dark canopy.

Remember . . .

She cast this chorus up into that raging storm of emerald and gold fire. She forged her song into a beacon, an anchor to help draw Bashaliia out of the madness. She had done something similar back when she had wrested the raash'ke from the enslavement of the *ta'wyn* Root out in the Wastes.

Remember who you are . . .

Bashaliia struggled to respond. A soft pining flowed through the madness. But still, the storm inside him raged too strongly. It battered and ripped at her song. The anchor it represented threatened to be torn away.

I'm still not strong enough.

She felt Daal's cold arms around her, knowing the offer they represented. But she could take no more. As if sensing this, the madness inside Bashaliia flared brighter, stoked by her defeat—or maybe it was due to a new threat winging toward them.

Past Daal's shoulder, a golden glow bloomed. Another had recognized the danger and rushed over to help, drawn by a shared bond.

Nyx stiffened.

No, Pyllar, stay back.

Daal echoed the same, his head lolling to Nyx's shoulder. "No . . ."

Both were ignored.

As Pyllar approached, Bashaliia reared up. The Mýr bat was twice the size of the smaller raash'ke. A scream of rage burst from Bashaliia's throat.

Still, Pyllar clawed closer, one wing beating weakly.

Daal's grip tightened on Nyx. "Save him," he begged hoarsely. "Save them both. Even if it means my life."

Nyx recognized the bond the two shared. Daal had expressed as much only moments ago. She saw it now, too. Blinded from all else, she could finally tease out those wisps that wound rider to mount, a joy that Daal had only begun to experience.

Still, she refused to take more from him, to risk his life.

Not even to spare Pyllar.

With great regret, she returned her focus to the golden anchor in the emerald storm. She did her best to bolster its hold, but she could not get that glow to shine any brighter, to withstand that storm.

Bashaliia lifted higher, his wings battering against the rafters. He was about to dive upon Pyllar, to destroy that tender new bond.

Nyx stiffened.

That bond . . .

She cast her shrouded gaze lower, noting again the twining connection between Pyllar and Daal—not just to the man, but also to what he represented.

She again reached deep into Daal's cold and empty wellspring, praying she was right. She remembered Jace extinguishing the life of the kezmek, then following the cords that bound the creature to its master, where life was sucked from the assassin.

Could the same hold true here?

She searched inside Daal.

Please . . .

Then she found it, where this new bond tied rider and mount together. With Daal as a conduit, she drew upon that link. She sang to Pyllar's heart, begging for his grace, reminding the raash'ke that Daal needed him.

Pyllar heard.

Through that bond, golden fire flooded into her.

As it did, a cascade of memories and sensations rushed through her: sweeping over ice as a young bat, tasting torn flesh. She felt the weight of a saddle, at first cumbersome, then joyous in its promise. It all blurred into one, a lifetime in the passage of a heartbeat.

Daal gasped, sharing the same.

Nyx had no more time. She gathered all that love and life and sang its golden beauty up to Bashaliia. The Mýr bat loomed high, limned in emerald fire. The fading anchor flared brighter, becoming a sun. The radiance outshone the emerald flames, driving them down, tamping that madness.

She continued her song, focusing on one memory now.

Their earliest together.

She softened her chords, burnishing a past nearly forgotten. She sang of the safety of a shared nest, of warm wings enfolding them both, of sweet milk, and of a mother's heartbeat through thick fur.

She lifted her chorus, along with a beckoning arm toward her brother.

Come back to me.

And finally, he did.

Bashaliia's frantic struggles died along with that emerald fire. As he settled back to the planks, he sagged into himself, trembling, frightened by what had happened.

She rushed over to console him, while Daal pushed heavily to his feet. He stumbled over to Pyllar to do the same.

Overhead, furious shouts and the clang of steel echoed down to them.

While this battle in the hold had ended, a larger one still raged.

Daal met Nyx's eyes, looking to her for guidance.

She gripped a fistful of Bashaliia's fur. While she had doused that emerald fire from her brother's heart, some of that fury had touched hers.

And maybe some of the madness.

So be it.

She swung her gaze up to the fighting.

"Let's show those bastards the true heart of this dragon."

39

FROM THE SHADOWS of a tunnel, Graylin studied the towering bulwark of the *Sharpened Spur*. The curve of the warship's hull rose in a great wave in front of him. Higher up, lanterns glowed. Echoes of patrols reached him. Above, the sleek gasbag shuddered and quaked, buffeted by storm winds.

To help anchor the *Spur*, scores of mooring lines had been cast out—from the deck to the walls, but also down to the shelf of sandstone beneath the keel. The warship, being smaller in size than the *Fyredragon*, had dropped almost to the bottom of the pocket. Its captain had clearly wanted as much distance as possible between his ship and the storm.

Still, despite its smaller bulk, the *Spur* remained formidable.

Graylin frowned at its rows of armaments, recognizing the threat they represented. Countless times while trekking here, he had questioned this mission, especially after the attack by the creatures in the chasm. But upon seeing all of this, he knew this attempt had to be made.

Overhead, iron cannons bristled across the open decks. Giant cauldrons lined bow and stern, likely already sloshing with oil. Once set aflame, those pots could spill fiery ruin on a ship below. Everywhere else, where space afforded, scores of giant ballistas held steel arrows at the ready, waiting for those massive bows to be cranked taut.

Graylin shook his head, trying not to be intimidated, especially when viewing their own weapon of assault, one not unlike a ballista.

Vikas held a small crossbow at her shoulder, one she had unfolded from her pack. She aimed it toward the lower curve of the hull.

Crouched by her side, Rhaif pointed. "That should be the hatch into the mizzen hold." He turned to Fenn. "Is that right?"

The navigator tore his gaze down. He looked ready to leap that distance and scale up the side of the ship, but he nodded. "That's the one."

Rhaif patted Vikas and pointed higher. "Aim two spans above it."

Without any acknowledgment, the quartermaster pulled the trigger on the bow, timing the shot to a loud wail of the storm. The bolt struck where Rhaif had wanted. It also dragged a scaling rope behind it. The line's length was looped with footholds.

"Well done," Rhaif said. "Of course, you've left me the hardest part."

Vikas sat back and repeated an earlier Gynish gesture: *Sod that.*

The thief shrugged, then lifted the trailing end of the line. He hooked his toe into a loop and glanced to those gathered behind him. "See you aboard."

Rhaif cast himself out of the tunnel and swung in a sweeping drop over to the hull. He struck it deftly, raising no more than a quiet thump. From there, he used the loops to climb to the hatch.

As Rhaif undid the satchel as his belt, Graylin turned to the group, his gaze falling on Esme. "You've gotten us this far as promised. You and Crikit retreat into the tunnel. In case anything goes wrong."

"I can fight," she argued. "I've trained years with a *hesharyn*, a Chanaryn sand-dancer."

As if proving this, she flicked a wrist and a dagger appeared in her hand.

Graylin reached over and pushed her wrist down. "If it comes to a fight, we'll lose. We're outmatched. Stealth is our only hope. If trouble arises, someone needs to make their way back to the *Fyredragon,* to let them know of our failure, to ready our ship for a battle."

Graylin frowned up at the bristling line of weapons.

With the *Fyredragon* so badly outmatched, their group had no choice but to risk this foolhardy attempt.

He turned to face Rhaif.

But to do that, we must first get inside.

RHAIF BALANCED ON his line and slowly turned a crank, drilling a thumb-sized hole through the outer hatch with a steel awl. Shavings drifted out, but he caught them in his lap. While it was unlikely anyone would spot a rain of curls falling below, he couldn't shake his old habits.

His training within the guild had been severe, exacting, and pitiless.

Especially under Llyra's strict tutelage, where those same three dictates applied whenever she took him into her bed.

He sighed, feeling wistful, wishing he had never left. Of course, it was Llyra who had eventually betrayed him, selling him out to gain leverage with the archsheriff of Anvil.

Still, he missed those years with the guild.

Even her.

He shoved this down and continued working.

Nostalgia did not serve a thief.

Finally, the tip of his awl broke through to the other side. Rhaif paused, leaning his ear to the hatch, making sure no alarm was raised. He glanced up, too, but the curve of the hull kept him out of view of any patrols.

He withdrew the awl, dropped it into his satchel, and replaced it with a narrow tube tipped by a fish-eye lens. He passed the tool through the hole and spied upon the hold on the far side. The space appeared empty. Long shelves lined both sides. They held bolts of thick fabric, for crafting patches to repair any tears in the gasbag. Thick dust covered the rolls. The *Spur* likely hadn't seen a battle in ages—if ever. It was why this point of entry had been picked. With the ship docked down here, there would be little reason for anyone to be inside the room.

Satisfied, Rhaif slipped out the lens and inserted tiny tools with small blades. He set about blindly cutting the interior guide rope, to free the door from the latch inside. It did not take long. As he felt the tension snap, he hopped to the side and caught the drop of the door on his shoulder. He lowered the hatch until it lay flat, forming a bridge not unlike the one they had used to exit the *Fyredragon*. Only this one didn't extend all the way to the wall. A short hop would be necessary to mount it.

To encourage this, Rhaif stepped off his rope and onto the open hatch door. He bowed with a sweep of an arm, inviting the others to join him.

He expected Graylin to leap first, but before the knight could move, Fenn jumped across and shouldered past Rhaif, nearly knocking him off his perch.

Rhaif scowled at his rudeness.

Clearly someone's spent too much time aboard a pirate ship.

Still, he kept this to himself and offered more gracious words.

"Welcome home, Fenn," Rhaif said as he followed the navigator inside. "But let's not overstay our visit."

GRAYLIN LED THE way out of the mizzen hold.

Next to him, Fenn had changed into a habiliment of Bhestyan finery: silken breeches, calf-high boots, and a waistcoat lined by silver hooks. The navigator had retained this old clothing after joining Darant's crew. Some wear and moth-bitten holes marred the grandeur, but Fenn's new appearance should suffice if they needed a moment of confusion or distraction.

If nothing else, Fenn did strike a regal figure, looking very much like the son of a high minister. The clothing also fit the task given to Fenn and Jace.

When Graylin reached a set of steep stairs heading down, he called a halt to the group. From here, they would split up. Fenn had sketched out a schematic of the warship. Trained as a navigator in Bhestya, intending to serve as honorably as his dead brother in the kingdom's brigade, Fenn knew all the ships of the royal fleet.

As such, both groups knew where they had to go from here.

Graylin shifted his pack higher on his shoulders and stared around the group. "Mind the time," he warned them all. "After Vikas and I plant Hyck's bomb under the flashburn tanks, we must be quick. Hyck trimmed a quarter-bell fuse. We have only that much time to get clear. Is that understood?"

After everyone confirmed this, Graylin pointed to Fenn. "Go to the brig. Seek out your sister. If she's not there, you head straight back to the mizzen hold." He swung his finger to encompass Jace and Rhaif. "Drag him back if you must."

Graylin had allowed this much latitude in this mission. He owed it to Fenn, for all the lad had done in the past, for what would be needed in the future. But Graylin refused any more leniency than that.

He got nods from the others—firm from Jace and Rhaif, reluctant from Fenn.

Satisfied, Graylin set off with Vikas. He wondered if he should have taken up Darant's offer of more men. Their two groups looked far too small considering the size of this warship. He knew from past experience that *stealth* often only got you so far.

Still, Graylin had staked out this path and had no choice but to walk it.

He prayed it ended well.

RHAIF USED A small mirror to spy around the corner. A door, flanked by two hanging lanterns, stood closed with a heavy bar across its frame. A guard leaned on its jamb, his chin resting on his collarbone, looking near to drowsing off.

So far, they had made it to the brig without raising an alarm. Though it was less from any skilled slyness and more about the lax nature of the crew. It seemed the cover of the storm had created a warm, sandy blanket for the crew to nuzzle into. Aboard such an armed warship, what did anyone need to fear?

Let's find out.

Rhaif turned to Jace and Fenn, his words a breathless whisper lest he disturb the sentry's slumber. "One guard." His eyes settled on Fenn. "Better be quick about it."

The navigator needed no such motivation.

Fenn straightened his back, strode around the corner, and marched toward the door. Rhaif bent down and spied again with his small mirror. He watched Fenn close upon the guard, a stout-limbed Bhestyan with a purple birthmark marring one cheek.

The guard stiffened at the sudden intrusion, casting a pinched gaze up
and down Fenn's finery. He clearly struggled to understand the arrival of
this finely attired nobleman. The man shifted nervously, as if wondering if he
should bow or question this intrusion.

He finally settled on the latter, but as a matter of caution, he decided to be
civil about it.

"Sir, are you lost?"

Fenn's response was far less courteous. He whipped the dagger from behind his thigh and thrust it through the guard's throat. The blade severed any
ability to shout. As the man slumped, gurgling, to the floor, Fenn grabbed his
arm and hauled him aside.

Rhaif and Jace hurried forward to help.

Fenn passed the man over and crossed to the door. He grabbed the bar
and heaved it off. He looked ready to toss it aside, but Rhaif hissed at him,
reminding him that the clang of an iron bar across the planks might wake
this sleepy ship.

Fenn obeyed and quietly set it aside.

Rhaif understood the navigator's haste and fear. If his sister wasn't here,
then there was nothing more to be done. Rhaif left the guard, who bubbled
his last breath, with Jace and ducked over to Fenn.

He lifted his mirror. "Let me crack the door and check inside first."

Fenn ignored him and yanked the way open. He rushed across the threshold, drawing Rhaif with him. Inside, no lanterns glowed, but enough light
filtered from the hallway to illuminate a row of five cells.

Fenn swept along them—then stopped, grabbed the bars, and sagged with
relief. "Freya . . ."

A scuffle of hay sounded, along with a clink of chains. A hoarse, exhausted
voice responded, "Who . . . Who are you?"

"Freya, it's me, Fenn."

A long silence followed, which only served to sharpen the woman's voice.
"It . . . It can't be. What new cruelty is this?"

Rhaif understood her confusion. He imagined Fenn looked more shadow
than substance in the gloom. Jace rectified this when he dragged the dead
man inside, then fetched one of the lanterns from the wall outside.

The flare of brightness revealed all.

Fenn slumped down the bars. "Sister, what have they done to you?"

With his face lowered, she recognized him in turn. "Fenn, by all the gods . . ."
Words rushed out of her. "How . . . How did you get here? Were you turned
over? Our uncle will never adhere to any promises. You must know that."

Rhaif turned to Jace, who was patting down the guard's body after closing the door. "Any keys?"

Jace looked up with a wince. "No. Not a one."

Rhaif nodded, accepting this. Thieving was never that easy. When it was, it usually meant trouble. He hurried over to Fenn, already reaching into his satchel. "Move aside. This tender reunion can wait another moment."

Fenn shifted over, making room. "Hurry."

"I wasn't planning on pausing for a sip of wine."

Rhaif dropped to a knee and fished out his pick and tools.

As he set to work, he did his best to ignore the sorry state of the prisoner. Fenn's shock was well warranted. His sister, bloodied and bruised, knelt in filth. A chain secured one wrist to the wall. Next to it, another iron cuff hung loose. The reason was plain. Freya cradled a crooked arm to her chest. It was slung in a wrap made of her own ripped bodice.

Despite the pallor of agony, her eyes shone hard. "You must leave, Fenn. Escape while you can."

"Not without you."

Fenn turned and glared at Rhaif, urging him to hurry.

"I've almost got—" Then the stubborn lock finally released. "Done."

Rhaif hauled the door open. Fenn rushed in first. He skidded on his knees and embraced his sister, mindful of her arm.

"Freya, how I've missed you."

Rhaif hated to tear them apart, but he waved Fenn off. "She's not going anywhere unless I can free that cuff from her wrist."

Fenn nodded and scooted on his knees to the side.

Rhaif set to work again.

Jace brought the lantern closer. "We must be quick," he warned, reminding them that a quarter-bell was never as long as one wished it to be.

Rhaif licked his lips and worked at a lock that was more rust than iron. The corrosion confounded his efforts.

Or maybe I'm the one who's gone rusty.

He labored on. A trickle of sweat ran into one eye. He didn't bother wiping it. Such delicate work required tender fingers, not sharp sight. Still, every beat of his heart marked their shrinking time.

Fenn's breathing grew heavier and heavier.

Jace paced, crossing frequently to peek out the door, fearing discovery.

Freya simply hung her head, as if already accepting defeat.

"I have an ax," Jace offered.

"The chains are too thick," Fenn noted. "And the noise will be heard."

Jace clarified his suggestion. "Better to lose a hand than a life."

Rhaif cringed at this—but the small movement proved just enough to tweak his pick and break the lock. The cuff fell loose.

Fenn hauled his sister up, supporting her under her good arm.

Jace rushed to the door and swung it open—only to be knocked back as a bolt struck his shoulder. He spun around and crashed into the cell behind him.

Barked orders followed. "Show yourselves!"

Rhaif cursed his slowness. Llyra would've taken a finger after such a sloppy effort. And deservedly so. It had ruined them all.

He lifted his hands and stepped into view.

Jace groaned, voicing that he yet lived.

Outside, an armored figure towered in the passageway, his shoulder emblazoned with a quartermaster's wings. He was flanked by a man on a knee with a crossbow. On his other side, a ra-knight guarded over a robed physik—who carried a tray crowded with splinting material and a glass bottle flushed white with poppy's milk.

They must have come to attend to Freya's injuries. Rhaif suspected this small act of kindness had not been ordered by her torturer but was a secretive act of mercy behind the man's back. Still, upon arrival, the group had spotted the blood on the planks outside, heard the hushed voices inside, and closed off any escape.

Realizing this, Rhaif decided to forgive himself.

It wasn't my slowness that ruined us.

It was mercy.

Either way, the result was the same.

Warning bells rang throughout the ship, rising louder and louder.

Rhaif hoped their other two companions were faring far better.

WITH FLAMING TAPER in hand, Graylin froze as countless bells clanged with danger. At his knees, Hyck's bomb had been shoved deep under the curve of a steel flashburn tank. Only its fuse protruded, a length of dusted cord.

Vikas loomed over him, staring across the hold. When they first got here, the space had been patrolled by four men, but he and Vikas had quickly dispatched them.

Now a stampede of boots rushed in from all directions. With no more time, Graylin lit the fuse and kicked its length under the tank. If he'd had more warning, he would've trimmed the fuse shorter.

"Let's go," Graylin ordered.

He set off with Vikas. If they couldn't escape, he prayed their flight could lead the hunters astray, to distract them from the bomb. The weapon contained a potent alchymical mix that Hyck had concocted using flashburn, Panthean *flitch,* and black powder. The result produced a powerful blast.

As he and Vikas reached the door, shouts rose overhead, rising from gangways that circled the top of the storage hold. Not knowing if they'd been spotted, Graylin rolled out into the hallway and raced for the stairs.

But as he neared them, armored figures piled down, filling the hallway.

"Back," Graylin urged, turning and colliding into Vikas.

More Bhestyan warriors crowded behind her. Graylin grabbed his sword's hilt, but a huge figure broke into view. Graylin recognized a battle commander of the ra-knights.

"Enough!" the man barked. "We have your allies. Submit and mercy may be granted."

Graylin noted the firm steel in the commander's eyes, shining through the crossbars of his helm. Recognizing a lost cause, Graylin lifted his palm from his hilt. "I so submit."

He tried not to flick a gaze toward the open door to the storage hold, but even this proved for naught. A crewman covered in oil, clearly a pumpman, appeared, escorted by another knight. The pumper carried Hyck's bomb, its fuse severed in half.

"Found this hidden away," the crewman said.

Graylin swallowed down his resignation, but he was not surprised. Any good captain knew saboteurs would strike for those tanks. The security of these massive barrels was a priority—whether in battle or not. To aid in their protection, an armed garrison was manned nearby.

It accounted for the swift response.

"Take them topside," the battle commander ordered. "To join the others."

Hands stripped him of his weapons. Vikas suffered the same. They were then marched at the point of a sword—several swords—up the stairs.

As they ascended, Graylin recognized it was his softheartedness that had led to this fate. The others must have been discovered, triggering the premature alarm. If not for their attempt to rescue Fenn's sister, the mission might have succeeded.

Still, he could not blame them.

I agreed to it.

Finally, they reached a set of double doors that opened out onto the *Spur's* middeck. Sand whipped and scoured across the planks. Lanterns lit the gloom. A single firepot danced with flames.

The fiery light showed four figures on their knees, ringed by armed men.

The ra-knight commander marched Graylin and Vikas over to join them. The group looked sullen, suffering each in their own way. Jace leaned on Rhaif, his shoulder and upper arm drenched in blood. Fenn looked stricken and pale. The reason for his distress knelt next to him. The family resemblance left no doubt that the battered woman was his sister. Her arm lay broken in a sling of torn cloth.

As Graylin reached the others, a tall figure greeted their arrival. This one also needed no introduction. The rich attire, the wolf-trimmed cloak, but more importantly, the silver-eyed medallion of a Bhestyan high minister, all left no doubt this was Fenn's traitorous uncle—Orren hy Pashkin.

The man smiled, but there was no amusement, only dark satisfaction.

"Commander Trask," he intoned, "thank you for bringing these last strays to the fold. Now we can put an end to many matters."

Trask gave the smallest nod, clearly unimpressed with the man.

"Foremost, of course . . ." Orren turned to Fenn and Freya. "What glad tidings to unite brother and sister at long last. Though, I suspect I'll find more pleasure in this reunion."

Graylin tried to salvage what he could. "You have your nephew, High Minister Pashkin. We bear the Kingdom of Bhestya no ill will. All we ask is to be allowed to leave." He nodded to Trask. "There was word of mercy if we submitted."

Orren turned to Graylin with one brow raised. "Mercy comes in many forms, does it not? To forgive a slight. To tend a wound. To comfort the sick. Even the mercy of a swift death."

Graylin frowned.

"I will honor the commander's word," Orren said. "Granting one of the greatest mercies of all. The gift of life."

Graylin suspected a trap.

Orren revealed it with a wave toward Rhaif and Jace. "Pick the one who will live. The other will be put to the sword immediately. Granted the mercy of a swift death. I'm only offering this boon because I'm feeling exceptionally generous with the return of my brother's son. Choose now or both will suffer."

More to delay this than from any hope of relief, Graylin pressed Fenn's uncle. "And what of the rest of us? And our ship?"

"Your ship?"

"When the storm breaks will you allow it to leave unmolested?"

Orren exaggerated great sadness. "I'm afraid such a request comes too late. Thirty of Commander Trask's fellow knights, his handpicked best, were sent out before the storm truly struck. They should've reached your vessel some time ago."

Graylin turned to Trask, who acknowledged this with another nod, one more sorrowfully deep.

Orren drew his attention back. "But I will grant you one last mercy."

Graylin faced the bastard. "What is that?"

"To bury your dead."

40

Nyx crossed through the slaughter that spanned the *Fyredragon*'s deck. She rode bareback atop Bashaliia. Daal paced alongside her, mounted on Pyllar, but she needed no escort, no protection, even with her vision dimmed to plays of shadow and light.

No one dared approach the massive Mýr bat.

Or the hulking vargr who stalked her other flank.

Spots of brightness marked pools of flames from shattered lanterns. Firepots burned everywhere. The winds stung with scouring sand, heavy with the coppery scent of blood. Her ears pricked to the dying screams of the last of the Bhestyan marauders.

One cry rose sharper on the portside, then faded quickly, falling away into the distance. She pictured an attacker plummeting into the depths below the moored ship—though she could not tell if the man had been tossed overboard or if he had flung himself off in terror after seeing what had risen to the deck from the bowels of the ship.

If she cared, she could have discovered which was the truth.

Daal carried with him a font of bridle-song, not from his cold wellspring but under him, beating strongly along with Pyllar's heart.

Over the past bell, she had leaned upon that source, shared through Daal, as she and the others led the raash'ke horde through the ship. The beasts had tucked wings and scrambled down passageways seemingly too small, but they managed. Even Bashaliia forced his larger bulk with them.

All the while, Nyx had sung a chorus, shared among four hearts: hers, Daal's, Bashaliia's, and Pyllar's. With focus, she caught peeks of the fray viewed through other eyes, both bat and man.

—a corner of a battle that broke into the lower decks

—an enemy's look of horror at the sight of the slathering beasts clambering out of the shadows

—the snap of fangs, the rip of limbs

Still, Nyx had limited such sights to brief glimpses. It was not due to a soft heart or weak stomach. Instead, she reserved most of their shared harmony to hold Bashaliia steady, to stoke the golden shine in his heart, to keep at bay any trickle of emerald fire.

A shout rose ahead of her. "Nyx! Daal! Rein in your beasts."

She recognized Darant's voice. She allowed herself to catch a brief snatch of the pirate through Pyllar's eyes. The sight strangled any attempt to respond. The captain strode through the carnage, soaked in blood, with a cut exposing the bone of his cheek. Across the deck, bodies shifted amidst crimson pools, some stirred by the ship's rocking, others crawling, broken and maimed.

While most of the dead wore blue-tinted steel, too many did not.

The pounding of victory in Nyx's heart, the satisfaction of ridding the *Fyredragon* of its trespassers, quickly died away, tempered by the misery, the loss of so many. One raash'ke dragged a wing that scribed a crimson path across the planks.

She choked down a sob and let the song die in her chest.

Her weave of golden strands had no place here.

Daal shifted next to her and shouted in Panthean, calling to the raash'ke, gathering them out of the way, to allow the wounded to be tended, the dead to be mourned.

As Darant approached, the tread of his boots sounded firm but weary, a single drumbeat marking the finality of this battle.

"My men are sweeping the decks," he announced. "Making sure there are no others. We have two captured Bhestyans on their knees, too maimed to offer any threat. But the point of my blade freed their tongues. If they spoke truthfully, these marauders are but a fraction of those aboard their warship."

Daal stirred. "How many?"

"Fivefold the number that attacked us."

Nyx pictured such a legion—along with the heavy armaments the warship carried.

Darant rattled out a sigh that matched Nyx's fear.

Not for the threat expressed.

But for those who had been headed toward it.

Though blind, she turned to the east. "Someone must help them."

She turned to Darant.

But who?

41

ESME READIED HERSELF to make the leap. She stared across the gap to the open hatch of the mizzen hold. Earlier, she had heard the bells clanging in alarm throughout the massive ship. The frightful noise had driven her down the tunnel. She had intended to obey the grizzled knight's instruction, to carry word of defeat to the *Fyredragon*.

Still, as she had fled, she could not escape the ringing, even as shadows closed over her. In her gut, she knew such a trek was pointless. The captain of the *Fyredragon* had shown himself to be practical and farsighted. He didn't need her rushing in and warning him to ready his ship for battle. If the others never showed, he would take those measures anyway.

So, her feet had slowed to a stop in the tunnel.

In the dark, each sharp ring of the bell had struck her heart, spiked her guilt. It also stirred memories, of hiding under a wagon as her clan was slaughtered, of a mother strangled and a father gutted. All the while, she had remained buried.

She refused to hide any longer.

Even her time in Seekh was just another form of burial. While she had sworn an oath to return to the desert, to hunt for Arryn, she could have trekked out there on her own at any time. She had used the excuse of gold, of needing enough provisions, of honing her skills, but down deep she had simply remained buried, as surely as the dead who haunted these necropolises.

But no more.

Esme studied the towering ship. Though the bells had gone silent, her heart had taken over, pounding with warning. Upon returning here, she had raided the others' abandoned packs. She stood with a coil of rope hung over one shoulder and a heavy bag that clinked softly at her hip.

Ready, she stepped to the ledge, needing only one last bit of outfitting.

"With me, Crikit."

She craned her neck. Harsh voices echoed down to her from the open deck. While the storm winds ripped away any words, she recognized the familiar rub of sandstone that marked the grizzled knight.

He was up there, angry, denying some demand.

Hopefully the others were there, too.

Before she could glance down to the open hatch, a flash of brightness sparked across the black sky. From her long years in the desert, she knew Ishuka's dark cloak often danced with lightning, as jagged and fierce as the goddess's heart.

Esme clenched a fist, praying this was a small blessing from Ishuka, an omen cast across Esme's path. Gathering this hope to her hammering heart, she crouched and leaped out of the tunnel.

She landed deftly atop the open door, but rather than ducking inside the mizzen hold, she reached high and grabbed the scaling rope that the thief had left behind. She hooked a toe into the line's loop and pushed herself up with one hand. At the same time, she fished a climbing peg from her bag and placed the spiked steel between her lips. Reaching higher, she searched with her experienced fingertips for a split board or a crack between planks. Once she found it, she slammed the spike home, anchoring it deep, then cinched her rope over its hook.

Over her years in Seekh, she had scaled countless sandy cliffs and crumbling walls. This was no different. Slowly, spike by spike, she worked her way up the ship's hull.

Another wondered at her dusty pace.

Crikit stuck to the planks above her, as if glued in place. One jointed leg tapped against the wood, the meaning clear.

Hurry up.

As if to encourage her, the molag skittered upward.

Esme gave chase, all the while searching the sky, looking for another sign from Ishuka, another bright flash to inspire her, but the goddess's mood must have darkened.

And not just Hers.

Above, angry words flared with furious fire.

Cut through by a scream of pain.

42

GRAYLIN HOLLERED AT the Bhestyan high minister, "Leave him alone! If you wish to exact punishment, inflict it upon me."

Orren stood, contemplatively tapping a thumb against his forehead as he stared down at Jace. One of the crew had cut away the young man's tunic, stripping it to his waist. The rough handling had jarred the crossbow bolt impaled in Jace's shoulder, wrenching a cry from his lips.

Blood flowed more heavily now, flooding down Jace's chest and arm. He gasped and gulped, as if trying to swallow down the pain.

Graylin had endured months of torture in the Hálendiian dungeons, leaving him calloused and broken. In many ways, he had earned that punishment—for breaking an oath, for failing to save Marayn, for never considering his daughter might be alive.

Jace did not deserve this suffering.

"Torture me, if you must," Graylin demanded.

Orren turned with a shrug to face Graylin. "I believe I already am. Especially as you continue to refuse my generous gift of life. Salvation requires only a simple choice." He flicked a hand between Rhaif and Jace. "One or the other?"

Rhaif pleaded with his eyes and with his words. "I've lived a long life, Graylin. Certainly longer than Jace. Not that I wouldn't take another decade or two more."

Orren flipped that wrist toward the Guld'guhlian thief. "See. It does not have to be difficult. But I do need to hear it from your lips."

By now, Graylin had tried everything he could think of to delay, to wheedle some compromise, but this bastard's patience had worn thin.

Fenn tried to intervene. "Spare them," he pleaded. "I . . . I'll return to Bhestya. Upon my knees before the king, I'll confess my involvement. This I swear."

Orren scoffed. "I have enough signed declarations of your guilt. One more, even from the lips of the traitor himself, serves no one."

Graylin knew such an offer would be refused. The high minister could never risk Fenn returning to the king. The only part of the young man that would arrive in Bhestya would be his head, preserved and ready for a pike.

Orren flushed, plainly irritated by Fenn's words. The high minister swung away, no longer enjoying his play. He stalked to Jace, clearly recognizing how to inflict the worst pain—to strike at the most innocent, the one who had garnered so much sympathy.

Leaning down, Orren grabbed the impaled bolt and twisted it savagely. Jace's back arched, his lips peeling back. Agony trapped a scream in his throat. When it finally burst out, blood sprayed from his nostrils, such was the pain. His cry echoed to the sky, seeming to rattle the gasbag overhead.

Jace slumped backward, going limp, mercifully dragged into oblivion.

Still, Graylin continued staring up, as if in prayer.

But it was actually in relief.

Finally . . .

Only he caught the flash of fire, bright enough to light the top of the balloon—but all heard the deafening blast. Fabric shredded into flaming ribbons, then the volatile lift-gasses ignited.

Graylin leaped and covered Jace. Vikas did the same with Rhaif. Fenn—oblivious of this countermeasure—instinctively pulled his sister under him.

As a large section of the balloon exploded, the concussion slammed them flat, paining ears, crushing chests, squeezing hearts. Searing heat flashed over them. The air burned lungs and set fire to the fringes of clothing.

Graylin moved quickly, still deafened. Fiery sections of fabric rained all around. More got blasted against the walls, draping flaming ribbons across the sandstone. Overhead, the tattered remains of the gasbag flailed, on fire, smoking thickly.

Then, through the smoldering inferno, its source plummeted down.

Graylin had been watching for this.

A shining shape—a falling star of burning bronze—crashed through the flaming debris and struck the deck. Planks cracked under the impact. Shiya dropped to a knee in the crater, her body still shrouded in flame and smoke.

Men, already knocked flat or patting out fiery clothing, bellowed in shock and stumbled away in all directions—as if a god had dropped from the sky to punish them.

Overhead, a large aft section of the balloon still billowed. Warships had compartmentalized gasbags, divided by fire baffles and thicker blast shields. Still, what remained intact was not enough to hold the ship.

The *Spur* lurched downward with a heavy groan. Mooring cables ripped loose. Then its keel crashed to the bottom, which luckily was not far. The entire deck canted sideways as the ship rolled.

Struggling to stay upright, Graylin got everyone moving toward that smoking crater. Vikas dragged Jace's limp body. Fenn helped his sister.

Rhaif rushed to the new fiery bronze god. "Shiya . . . how . . . why . . . ?"

The thief held back from embracing her as her body still shone with the heat absorbed by the blast. She rose to her feet, naked, her clothing burned away or perhaps scoured off by blowing sand.

Graylin had no time to explain. He had enlisted Shiya's help in secret, keeping this plot even from Rhaif, who surely would have objected. Only Vikas and Darant knew of this secondary plan. Hyck had built *two* bombs. While Graylin's group had carried one, he had dispatched the other strapped to Shiya's back. He had sent her overland, through the storm. Only her bronze shielding and massive weight had any chance of passing through the claws of the storm. Still, Graylin did not know—and Shiya expressed the same concern—whether such a trek was possible, even for her. She could get buried in the sand, or mired down to the point of immobility, or damaged by the intensity of the *ishuka*'s fury.

Knowing that, Graylin had sent the bombs on two different courses and prayed one would reach its target.

Graylin stared up at the flaming ruins of the gasbag. Fires burned everywhere. One of the bronze cauldrons had tipped over, spilling oil that had caught fire, creating a flaming waterfall running over the tilted deck.

Men scrambled to put out the fires. Others helped the injured. A few simply leaped overboard, fearing a flaming shroud drifting down and smothering the deck—which was a likely risk.

But this was a warship, manned by the Bhestyan elite.

Out of the smoke, blue-armored knights closed upon them. Fury masked their faces. Even the presence of Shiya left them undaunted, though she was someone they should rightly fear. She had the strength of ten men and nigh their speed. But clearly the task given to her had taken its toll. She weaved slightly, limping on one leg, likely damaged by the crash to the deck. While strong, she was not without her limits.

Plus, Graylin's group had been stripped of weapons and remained vastly outnumbered.

Still, he held out one hope, a way to break this impasse before more blood was spilled. He stepped to the edge of the crater. By now, he judged the battle commander to have a core of nobility, a righteous spirit—though at the moment, a cold fire burned in those steely eyes. The blast had knocked away his helm, revealing a hard countenance and an iron-sculpted jaw.

Graylin faced the man's fury, knowing a warrior's pain for lives lost. "Commander Trask! You've brought this ruin upon yourself. I sought a modest concession. A simple request. To have you collect what you were charged to secure"—he waved to Fenn—"and let us go in peace. But this was denied."

Trask stepped closer, sword in hand. "Your request was not mine to refuse or accept. I serve the ship's captain and swore an oath to a king—which extends to his minister during such times."

"Then know this. You've been deceived. You protect the true traitor to the crown. You do his bidding. Does your sworn oath extend to one who betrays his own brother to gain a silver-eyed medallion?"

Fenn voiced his same rage. "My uncle's lying tongue killed my father, hanged my mother, and beheaded my brother. You raise your shield and lift a sword to defend such a one?" He pointed to his sister, to her broken arm. "Does this look like the act of an honorable man?"

A scoffing bark answered him—but it didn't come from the commander.

Orren stepped around Trask's shoulder. The bastard appeared unharmed, only shaken, likely shielded by the ra-knights.

"Is it any wonder the king ordered him killed?" Orren spat out. "The last of a line who can twist lies into truths with such a deft tongue. Before your end, Fenn hy Pashkin, that very tongue will be cut out and nailed to the burning mast of the *Spur*. This I swear."

"Then you'd better hurry," Rhaif commented, "while you still have a perch for such a prize."

Even during this brief discourse, the flames had spread. Smoke flowed heavier. Men continued to fight those flames.

Orren turned to Trask. "King Acker showed you what was signed, what was sworn, what your countrymen have admitted in ink and oath."

Trask slowly nodded, swayed enough to firm his grip on his sword.

"Lies!" Freya called over. "All lies. Bought with gold or threat of torture."

Orren shrugged. "What other words would you expect from a traitress?"

Another stirred among their group, as if ready to argue. But it was only Jace, waking again. He sat, rocking slightly, with his head lolling. Then, as if pulled up by strings, he gained his feet. He lifted a face devoid of pain, devoid of anything.

Rhaif went to help him, but Vikas drew him back.

Jace took a step—then his form blurred a breath, as if shaken by the hand of a god. In a blink, he stood several steps outside the crater. His head cocked one way, then another. He pressed a palm over his heart, then lifted it away. From that spot, a shape wafted out of his chest, snaking through the air, carried on thin wings.

"The kezmek," Fenn gasped.

It appeared ethereal, fading in and out of view, a phantasm of the real creature, perhaps some essence of what the void had consumed before.

Orren stumbled back and ran into Trask. The high minister bounced off the commander's armor and tried to escape. By now, a wall of knights surrounded them, holding everyone in place, trapping Orren as thoroughly as Graylin's group.

All the while, the phantom kezmek tracked its only prey.

Graylin remembered Jace had fallen under such a sway when defending Nyx. Clearly whatever possessed him also valued Jace's life, rising to his defense. It clearly knew *who* had threatened him, *who* had harmed him, and perhaps *who* had sent this very beast aboard the *Fyredragon*.

Orren made one last futile effort to escape—then the kezmek attacked, as swiftly as its real counterpart. Jaws opened, fangs unfolded, and the beast struck Orren in the chest, mirroring where it had been born out of Jace.

Orren screamed, fell to his knees, and batted at it.

His hand passed through the creature as if it were smoke, revealing the mirage. Relief shone in Orren's face, which quickly soured to scorn.

"Ha, what trickery is—"

Jace cocked his head again.

Orren spasmed, back arching. The ghostly kezmek materialized more fully, seeming to gain substance as it fed off something vital inside the man. Orren's skin bled of color, while agony stretched his lips into a rictus.

"Stop," he gasped out.

All eyes turned to Jace, who looked on dispassionately.

Fenn stepped forward, clearly ready to take advantage of this moment, of the man's terror. "Tell us the truth, Uncle. And be set free."

Orren's eyes went wide, the whites purpling at the edges. His cheeks sank in as if inhaling a deep breath, but the one drawing strength was Jace.

"Tell us," Fenn demanded, moving closer.

The high minister trembled, trapped by the bite of the kezmek.

"Confess!"

Orren finally broke—whether out of panic, pain, or hope of release.

But Graylin suspected it had more to do with a weakening of spirit, a dulling of control, as Orren's essence was stripped away, exposing the vileness beneath. This grew plainer as his sordid history unfolded, told with an increasing leadenness, reflecting a lack of will.

Graylin watched Commander Trask's face during this litany of crimes, treacheries, and betrayals. The fury faded from his eyes, replaced with shame and horror as he came to realize whom he had been serving.

Another had a stronger reaction. "What foulness is this?"

A rotund figure shoved through the knights, breaking a gap in the wall of armor. The man's face purpled with rage. Blood ran from a split brow. Upon his shoulders sat the mountain eagles of a captainship.

"Explain! The *Spur* burns and you all—"

Orren cut him off, raising a trembling arm. "Venga conspired. Planted letters. In Geryd hy Pashkin's locker aboard his royal frigate. To cast the son as conspirator with the father."

Trask turned to the ship's captain. "Is this true?"

Venga shook his head, backed a step, then snatched a crossbow from a crewman. He aimed it at Orren, then—proving he had been eavesdropping for some time—swung the weapon to the true source behind this confession.

Toward Jace.

Before he could pull the trigger, a thin-limbed figure rushed up from behind on the quietest desert sandals, as if to share a secret with the captain—which in this case was his death.

A dagger stabbed into his neck, then out again, as swift as a lightning strike, nearly too fast to perceive. As blood shot from the wound, pumped from a panicked heart, the dagger kissed the other side just as deftly.

Stunned, still not recognizing his end, Captain Venga stumbled away—from a snake as deadly as any kezmek. He crashed to the planks, thrashed once, then slumped flat.

The assassin fled past the wall of knights and hurried to Graylin.

"I thought I told you to return to the *Fyredragon*," he scolded Esme.

She waved over to a scrabbling black form. "Crikit wanted to stay. Besides, I never climbed a wall that tried to roll on top of me—while my rope was burning." Her explanation was rapid, breathless. She stared unblinking at Shiya, then pantomimed, passing a hand overhead. "Think I saw her before . . . thought it was lightning."

Rhaif shouted behind them, "Fenn, don't!"

Graylin swung around. It seemed another had found a knife, likely discarded during the chaos. Fenn pressed the edge against Orren's throat. By now, the high minister had shrunk to a skeletal thinness. The blade raised a crimson line across the gaunt throat.

"He killed most of my family. Upon his confession—witnessed by all—I demand retribution."

Freya stumbled over to him. "Fenn, no. It's over."

This proved true.

Orren gasped one last breath, his eyes wrinkling back into their sockets, his tongue withering into black leather. The kezmek vanished, and Orren slumped to the ground, away from Fenn's knife.

With this release, Jace stumbled back, landing hard on his backside. He gasped in agony from the impact. He leaned heavily onto his good arm, confusion shining through the pain.

Vikas moved over and helped the young man return to his world.

Rhaif finally circled an arm around Shiya, who had cooled enough to touch. "Next time you feel like running off," he scolded her, "tell me first."

Closer at hand, Fenn sank to his knees.

Freya dropped next to him.

Both were now far freer, no longer burdened by the stigma of betrayal. Their damaged pasts could be made whole again.

Still, one remained unsatisfied.

"He deserved a worse death," Fenn muttered.

Freya sighed. "Death is death."

Graylin wondered if this was true. He remembered Nyx's description of her encounter with the void inside Jason, how it had not only drawn her bridle-song, but utterly destroyed it, as if it never existed.

Was the same true here?

Had the essence of this traitorous bastard been burned away, leaving no hope for rebirth or ascension?

Just nothingness.

If so, then perhaps this death had a certain balance of justice to it after all.

Graylin looked over to Trask, wondering if the two of them could achieve the same balance. The commander strode over, looking dazed as his ship burned around him.

"How does this end?" Graylin asked him.

"It seems I must reconsider your request." Trask turned, lifted a scabbard from the hands of another knight, and returned Heartsthorn to Graylin's palms. "Once the storm breaks, you all are free to go."

Graylin bowed his head in thanks.

"Please take no offense . . ." Trask stared over at Jace, then to the towering bronze of Shiya. "But I pray I never see any of you again."

43

FIVE DAYS AFTER flying free of the ruins, Nyx climbed up into the wheel-house of the *Fyredragon*. She wiped sweat from her brow. Her clothing clung to every crevice of her body. Her mouth remained as dry as the desert beyond the window. Each breath scorched her lungs.

Jace noticed her arrival from where he was bent with Fenn at the navigation station. He straightened and turned to her. His injured arm hung in a sling, but otherwise he looked recovered. Whatever lurked inside him, some dark mirror to her bridle-song, continued to remain locked away.

"How are the raash'ke and Bashaliia faring in the heat?" he asked, his gaze sweeping over the drench of her body.

"Even in the shadows, it's like an oven down there. We need more water for their troughs. They're going through barrels by the bell."

"Take what you need. I checked our cisterns. We'll easily make it to the caverns that Esme marked on our map—the watering hole for her nomadic people. Sounds like those caves break into a deep aquifer."

Fenn stretched a kink from his back. "Hopefully our hoses will reach down that far, so we can use our hand pumps. Otherwise, we'll be hauling up bucket after bucket."

Nyx noted that the navigator's eyes had regained their usual sparkle. Fenn also moved with greater ease, a lightness of being that reflected his lifted burden. Nyx was glad he had decided to continue with them. He had tried to get his sister to come, too, but she had a husband, two children, and traitorous slanders to challenge in Bhestya. With the support of the *Spur*'s battle commander, the latter should not be hard. So Fenn had departed, leaving his sister to await rescue by the other Bhestyan vessel.

When their two groups had parted, it had not been without some bitterness and rancor. Too many had died on both sides. Even with the blame cast at the high minister's feet, those losses, still fresh and raw, were hard to forgive. The *Fyredragon* had lost five Pantheans and eight of Darant's men. Not counting the injured and wounded, some who might not live. One of the raash'ke—a buck named Faryn—still nursed a damaged wing. It remained unknown if he would ever fly again, which crushed his rider, Arik.

Still, Faryn had become a flag around which the Pantheans had rallied. The raash'ke represented everything they had endured or lost. Daal had noted this change, too—a union forged by blood and suffering. He did not know if it would last, but for now it was enough.

Contrary to this closeness, Nyx and Daal had returned to keeping a cautious distance from one another. His wellspring had replenished—along with the danger it represented.

Not that the two had much time to discuss it.

Before they departed Seekh, their dead had to be buried. The Pantheans had inked final messages onto the skin of their fallen, as was their custom. But here, there was no watery grave for the bodies.

Just sand and rock.

Still, their tomb was honorable enough. With great solemnity, they had interred their dead into the vastness of the Necropolises of Seekh, to add their spirits to a pantheon tracing back to the lost mists of time.

Yet Nyx knew this was not enough. No words or burial shrouds could truly cover the amount of innocent blood spilled into that ancient dust.

Before a heavier melancholy could weigh her down, Jace offered some better tidings. "I heard Esme and Krysh were successful in collecting water from the air. A method of tarping used by the Chanaryn people. With so much unknown ahead, every drop will be important."

Nyx pushed back her shoulders, grateful for even this small measure of success. "That's wonderful."

Jace nodded, thoughtfully tapping a thumb against his forehead. "Of course, there's still the matter of the growing heat."

Nyx heard Graylin and Darant murmuring the same concern. It had been on all their minds. Still, she shared a glance with Fenn, who was staring at Jace's tapping thumb. The navigator had raised a private concern with her. She had already been told about the strange apparition of the kezmek, returning in some phantom form after their encounter back in Spindryft.

And now this . . .

Nyx had known Jace for ages, knew his every mannerism, but she had never noted this tic of a tapping thumb. But Fenn had. *Orren did that all the time,* he had explained. They both wondered if some bit of what had been drawn into the void persisted, some echo that remained. There was no way of knowing. It could be meaningless, some quirk to all of this.

With her bridle-song replenished, Nyx had considered probing Jace with some tentative strands and exploring deeper. But she feared disturbing what slept inside him.

In the end, without any obvious harm or danger to all of this, she and Fenn had decided to keep this worry to themselves. At the moment, far more troublesome and immediate concerns needed to be addressed.

Darant raised another. "Even if we could withstand the heat, this blasted scorch is starting to challenge our forge-engines. Hyck says they can't take much more. At best, he believes we can travel another four days, maybe five, before we'll be forced to turn back or risk getting stranded when they fail."

Nyx drew closer. This was the first time she had heard of this danger. "We can't head back," she warned as she joined them. "In that direction lies certain doom. Moonfall will become inevitable. We must reach the *turubya*."

Graylin nodded. "She's not wrong. We have no choice but to forge ahead, even if it means abandoning the *Fyredragon* and crossing the Barrens on foot."

"I'd rather not see that happen." Darant ran a palm over the maesterwheel. "Much blood has been spilled to raise this dragon from its grave and bring it this far."

"You're also not wrong," Graylin admitted, staring out at the sunburned desert.

Nyx kept vigil with them. Dunes rolled into the distance, vanishing into a harsh glare. Dotted throughout, wind-sculpted black rock scarred the red sands, looking like stranded ships, a reminder of the danger they faced. Across it all, faint dust trails rose across the dunes, marking Chanaryn caravans. Elsewhere, whirling wisps spun into the air—the *breaths* of the goddess Ishuka, according to Esme.

Nyx prayed for that desert goddess to continue her slumber.

Unable to face the challenge any longer, Nyx turned away. As she did, hushed whispers rose around the wheelhouse, as if the ghosts of the Elders had swept into the ship, rising from the ruins, bringing with them the cold touch of the tomb.

Nyx lifted a hand to her cheek, feeling the brush of cool air. She turned to the source of the whispering. It flowed out the ends of the small copper tubes, which snaked down to the giant bronze spheres below.

"The coolers . . ." Graylin murmured, lifting a palm to the chill.

Darant struck his fist atop the wheel. "The bastards are working!"

Jace rushed over. "Shiya must've been right. About them igniting on their own when the air grew too hot."

They were not the only ones to note the change. Muffled cheers rose throughout the ship.

With her palm still on her cheek, Nyx faced the desert again and the challenge it represented. For the past year, they had been chased and hunted, pursued from behind, harried at every turn.

But no one can follow us past this point.

Still, Nyx found little relief. She knew what lay ahead, beyond the sun's glare.

An army led by a *ta'wyn*—an Axis—one as powerful as Shiya.

And a Dragon.

Whom they dared not wake.

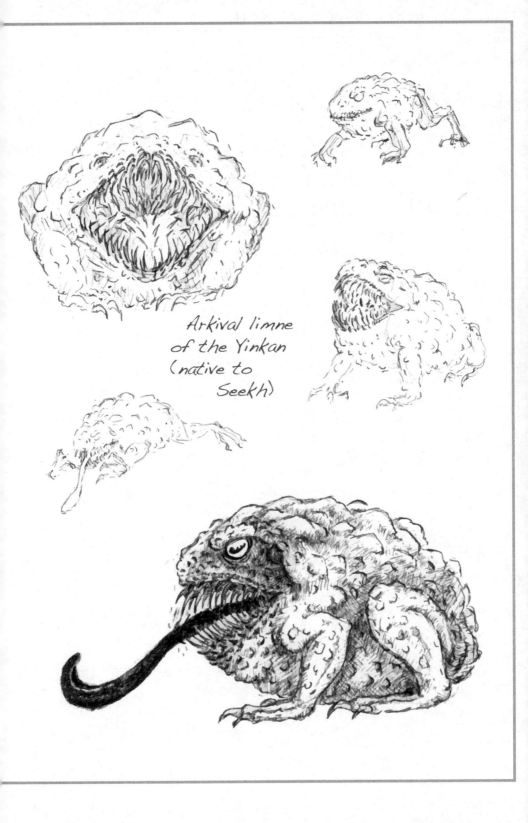

Arkival limne
of the Yinkan
(native to
Seekh)

SIX

POISON'D TONGUES

NEMIDES: *How is truthe dyfferent from a lie?*

STUDIENT: *The truth marketh certinty. A lie onli falss-hood.*

NEMIDES: *Ah, but does not the lyere make a falsshood sound as the truthe? And turn truthe's certinty into a lie?*

STUDIENT: *If so, it marketh a villein, doth it not?*

NEMIDES: *Or a hero. Or a surviver. Or one who simpli hopes a lie is the truthe. But hold this to haart: best not to slander a lyere, as they mae spake the truthe without knowing it.*

—From *The Logik of Morals*
by Nemides hy Pah

44

ATOP A STALLION draped in chain mail, Kanthe rode through the flooded ruins of lower Kysalimri. Two rows of armed horsemen, a cadre of the royal guard, followed behind. Drapes of silver mail veiled their lower faces, allowing only their hard eyes to show.

In addition, a pair of Paladins on armored warhorses flanked Kanthe. Ahead, a lone standard-bearer carried aloft a black flag bearing the crossed gold swords of the Klashean Arms.

Rami also trotted beside Kanthe. The Klashean prince's usual mirth had been smothered by the surrounding devastation.

"What a ridiculous spectacle we must look," Kanthe muttered, casting a glance at his companion.

Rami wore a rich *gerygoud* habiliment, threaded in gold and silver, which sparkled in the few beams of sunlight piercing the froth of high clouds. Kanthe was similarly decked out, only his head was crowned by a silver circlet. He wanted to throw a cloak over them both, finding their richness loathsome in these grim surroundings.

"Such are our roles," Rami stated with a tired sigh. "To be a shining promise during bleak times."

Bleak hardly described this circumstance.

As their entourage continued, their mounts' hooves splashed through the pools of water left behind by a sea surge that had swept into the lower city two days prior. Their passage stirred up a miasma of salt, algal rot, and the bloated reek of the dead. While spectacularly high tides had already challenged this region, another huge quake two days ago had sent a massive wave pummeling deep into the dockyards, ripping away pylons, shredding piers, and slamming through homes and parks.

Hundreds had died, and many times more were injured.

Throughout the wreckage, people moved sullenly, sifting amidst the piles of debris that had washed into tangled heaps. Most wore the *byor-ga* robes of the baseborn castes, keeping their features hidden, as if to dull the view of the destruction. Still, there were many barefaced *imri* among them, their distress and grief visible to all.

When passing an alley, Kanthe spotted a row of covered bodies, with mourners kneeling nearby, their candles flickering in the shadows. His jaw muscles ached with despair, knowing this was but a small harbinger of worse yet to come as moonfall approached.

He searched the skies and scowled at the source of all this destruction.

Around him, voices called out in various Klashean dialects. Most of the patois was too thick-tongued for him to understand. But the meaning was clear enough, especially when accompanied by the kissing of thumbs that were then cast skyward. The sufferers were pleading for a blessing from the gods, which many of the baseborn believed flowed through those who sat atop the imperial thrones.

Rami lifted an arm in acknowledgment. Kanthe could not bring himself to do so, even when Rami cast him a hard look.

If only I had such power, I would grant all their blessings.

Instead, Kanthe intended to do what he could.

This journey outside the imperial palace was meant to serve many purposes: to inspect the damage, to bolster morale, to let those afflicted know they were not forgotten. Behind their group, wagons followed, laden with supplies, with food, with balms and alchymies for the hurt and wounded.

Kanthe also hoped, time permitting, to visit Tykhan's project at the edge of the bay. Huge sea gates fronting the worksite's canals had protected the area.

If only the same were true for the rest of Kysalimri.

Still, he accepted that perhaps the gods had blessed them in this regard. They dared not lose ground on Tykhan's labors.

As they continued, Kanthe noted the wash of dried petals and wilted blossoms floating in the pools and gutters. They were left over from the midsummer celebrations ten days prior, when all of the Eternal City had been adorned with bright bouquets and strewn with blooming garlands. Giant icons of the Klasheans' thirty-three gods, sculpted entirely of flowers, had been paraded throughout the city.

Now those petals only served to consecrate the dead.

Those floating blossoms, wilted and dried, also reminded Kanthe of the relentless march of time. A month had already passed since the decision was made to strike at Hálendii, to attempt to secure Eligor and unlock the secret held by the Kryst.

And we still have so much work left to do.

Across the expanse of the massive city, Sail, Wing, and Shield all readied their forces, while striving to hide their true intent, to make such efforts appear to be routine exercises. They dared not alert Hálendii, though no doubt suspicions were already being raised in the northern kingdom.

"We're here," Rami stated, sitting taller in his saddle.

Kanthe searched past the flapping banner.

A large cobblestone square opened ahead, one of the largest in this drowned corner of Kysalimri, big enough to hold thousands. Kanthe girded himself against what was to come. He had counseled against it but was ignored.

He glanced behind to the train of horsemen and wagons. He focused on an enclosed carriage near the front, drawn by two draft horses. It looked like many of the others. Only that particular carriage hid a surprise, one watched over by Frell, Pratik, and the hulking Paladin Regar, whose injuries from the attempted assassination last month had mended.

The carriage marked the *other* reason behind this sojourn into the flood's aftermath, one meant as a secret. Still, word must have filtered out.

As Kanthe headed toward the square, he overheard reverent whispers of *"E Y'llan Ras"*—naming the one person onlookers hoped would appear and shine her blessings upon them all.

The Illuminated Rose.

Rami hissed, "Quit staring, my brother. Lest you ruin it all."

Kanthe swung forward as the entourage swept into the square. The train of horses, men, and carts rode out and around the open space with a loud stamp of hooves and a rattle of wheels over cobbles. The parade circled, eventually surrounding the lead wagons, especially a certain carriage. It stopped before a raised stone platform, an ancient stand that had survived the flood, anchoring the square.

Rami and Kanthe trotted their horses closer.

The standard-bearer passed up his banner to a pair of knights standing atop the platform. The taller of the two planted the pole into a drilled hole, then stepped back. The flag whipped in a breeze off the bay, which shone a shimmering blue through a row of shops and homes lining that side.

Finally, the carriage door opened. Regar exited first, bowing his large frame out. He then lifted a hand to the door. A slim figure stepped free. Her clothing outshone Rami's and Kanthe's habiliments. Though at the moment, the finery was clouded beneath a thin veil of grayish-silver cloth, the color of mourning, which draped her from head to toe. Still, glimmers of gold and silver twinkled in muted glints, holding the promise of joy to come.

Voices rose from those gathering in the square, growing in number and fervency: *"E Y'llan Ras . . ." "E Y'llan Ras . . ." "E Y'llan Ras . . ."*

Regar guided his charge up the steps to stand before the banner.

Kanthe remained mounted, not wanting to upstage the proceedings—not that he could have. He swept his gaze over the crowd as it swelled. People pushed in from side streets and alleys, coming from every direction as word spread. Hundreds soon grew into thousands. The call for Aalia grew louder, punctuated by sharper pleas, with much kissing of thumbs and outthrust arms.

This only encouraged others to do the same—especially as, atop the stone platform, a draped arm lifted in acknowledgment.

The cries of expectation and hope spread.

Kissed thumbs were raised all around.

Then, from the fringes of the square, a flash of flames shot high.

Rami must have noted the same and swung his horse around to face the
threat.

Kanthe stated the obvious, unsurprised and all the more miserable for it.
"We're under attack."

FRELL CRINGED AS screams rose outside the carriage. He pushed to a small
window and peered outside. A storm of fiery arrows swept high across the
sky, rising from every side of the square.

Beyond the ring of imperial horses and guardsmen, the crowd fled in a panicked rout, trying to escape the square. Many others simply ducked low, staying in place, reading the trajectory enough to know they were not the target.

The barrage rained down upon the platform. Steel tips sparked off stone.
Hafts shattered to fiery splinters.

Pratik shoved next to him. "Aalia?"

"Unharmed," Frell reported. "At least for now."

Shields had been raised at the first sign of threat. Paladin Regar held the
largest, lifted high as he protected his charge under him. Arrows struck the
steel and ricocheted away.

"I warned everyone this was a foolish venture," Frell said. "We've put Aalia
at needless risk."

"The empress insisted. To instill hope, she believed the—"

Pratik ducked as the carriage caught the edge of the attack. Arrows pum-
meled the top, but none penetrated the steel that lined the interior of the
carriage. The outer wood hid the armored surface beneath.

"We need Aalia back inside," Frell hissed.

This became clearer as a ululating roar rose from every side. A huge mass
of armed men, three hundred or more, surged into the square from the surrounding streets. They shoved through the cowering baseborn crowd, ignoring those who knelt low in submission, and drove for the platform. The
attackers came cloaked, their faces wrapped. Some wore mail or armor, others
simply leather or roughspun. All, though, wore armbands bearing a pair of
black swords crossed over gold wings.

The sigil of the traitorous Prince Mareesh.

The raiders slammed into the circle of horses and guardsmen, attacking with swords, hammers, spears, and axes. The battle raged with the ring of steel, the clatter of hooves, the screams of fury, and the pained cries of the wounded. The din deafened but proved short-lived. Vastly outnumbered, the guardsmen were quickly subdued, either slain, wounded into submission, or driven to their knees. Riderless horses cantered through the carnage.

Around the platform, a sea of swords and pikes threatened those remaining atop the stone island. At the first volley of arrows, Rami and Kanthe had leaped with their Paladins to defend that bastion. Now all were trapped.

A thunderous command boomed to the side. "Hold!"

A tall figure rode into the square atop a black stallion. He came in full royal armor, polished to a mirrored sheen. With a sword in one hand and the reins of his warhorse in the other, he trotted through the throngs of those who cowered below. His path was cleared by a phalanx of armored knights, all wearing the same armband as their leader.

"Prince Mareesh," Pratik muttered with clear disdain.

Frell clenched a fist. "The bastard finally shows his face."

Mareesh drew his charger to a stop within a sword thrust of the platform. He tossed his reins to one of his escorts, then drew off his helm, revealing a savage smile. A black silk scarf wrapped the crown of his head, likely hiding what fire had burned away last winter. Still, several puckered wheals, scars from severe blistering, marred a complexion that matched his siblings' countenances.

Mareesh's eyes fixed upon those stuck atop the platform, his gaze focused on the draped figure, guarded full around. "Dearest sister, you've sat upon your stolen throne long enough. Perhaps you should not have abandoned it this day."

Before she could respond, Kanthe stepped forward, holding his sword high. "It's not just *one* throne you need to concern yourself with, Prince Mareesh. I challenge you, blade to blade, to prove your worth."

Frell groaned.

The Klashean outweighed Kanthe by a third, stood a head taller, and had decades of training in the armed forces.

Frell cursed his former pupil.

What are you doing?

45

KANTHE GRITTED HIS teeth as laughter, harsh and full of ridicule, burst from Mareesh. The Klashean prince eyed his opponent up and down.

"I would not dishonor my sword with such traitorous Hálendiian blood. Especially for such a mouse of a man, one who doesn't have enough of a sword between his legs to even bed his false queen."

Kanthe sneered at the slight and lifted his blade higher. "Then test my mettle. Or are you too much of a coward?"

Mareesh ignored him and turned to his true adversary. "Aalia, let us put an end to this. Submit and I'll spare those who are still on their feet or down on their knees. Even our dear brother, Rami, will find a place in my imperium. This I swear."

Kanthe shifted to block Mareesh's view. He refused to let this bastard anywhere near her. If he had to lay down his life, so be it.

"Enough!" The command rang sharply across the square.

A gloved hand touched Kanthe's shoulder and, with gentle but firm pressure, shifted him aside. Regar tried to stop her from leaving the shadow of his protection, but the Paladin was shirked aside just as readily. She stood straight-backed, her veiled gaze sweeping the dead and moaning.

Then she sank to one knee.

Kanthe reached to pull her back up.

But her words, pained and defeated, spilled out first. "I so submit."

A stunned silence followed, only interrupted by the distant screech of a gull.

Mareesh's smile widened, delighted and righteous. "I accept your abdication."

The Klashean prince slid from his saddle, landing amidst his escort of knights. Ensconced within them, he climbed the steps to the top of the platform. His knights swept up, pushing all back, allowing sister and brother to be reunited.

Kanthe stood his ground, but Rami drew him back, fury inflaming his words.

"Aalia has submitted. Once spoken, by Klashean law, a submission cannot be revoked."

"But—"

"Do not dishonor her."

With no other choice, Kanthe allowed himself to be forced from her side, from a woman who had captured his respect as much as his heart.

Mareesh closed upon his prize, guarded over by his men. "Let all of Kysalimri bear witness to the end of one reign and the start of a new one."

He ripped the veil from the kneeling woman.

Before shock could drive him back, his victim rose smoothly, as if newly betrothed and about to greet her husband. In her gloved fingers, a thin blade came to rest under the prince's chin. Mareesh was warrior enough to recognize the reveal of black hair, the braid of silver bells—and the poisoned nature of the knife at his throat.

Cassta reinforced this. "Do not move, lest this *quisl* kiss you deeply."

Upon this signal, the hundreds of baseborn, still cowering on their knees, burst to their feet. They ripped away headpieces and cowls, revealing the white-striped faces of the *Shayn'ra*. With harrowing screams, the horde descended upon Mareesh's men, attacking with curved swords and daggers. More of the enemy fell under a barrage fired by bowmen hidden in attics of the surrounding buildings.

A knight to Kanthe's left toppled backward, a crossbow bolt through the eye.

Another clattered to the stone, wounded or dead.

Regar dispatched a third.

The remaining two Paladins guarded over Kanthe and Rami.

To Kanthe's right, one of their own knights—the one who had been waiting here for them and planted the Klashean banner—tossed his helm aside, likely happier to fight with his sight unencumbered. Another white stripe was revealed, lining the face of the *Shayn'ra* leader.

Tazar bellowed, his violet eyes sparking with fury, ready to unleash his anger upon those who had instigated his poisoning. Freshly recovered, he made short work of another pair of Mareesh's men.

Still, more danger remained.

Cassta had driven Mareesh to his knees, balanced upon the delicate point of her poisoned blade. She circled her captive as two of Mareesh's knights closed on her. Distracted, she failed to note Mareesh's hand slipping a dagger from his boot.

Kanthe shoved past his Paladin and ran at the prince. He fought to free the warning trapped in his throat as Mareesh yanked out his dagger. The prince plunged the blade toward Cassta's blind side.

Before the dagger struck, Kanthe swept his sword down and cleaved through the back of the prince's hand. Fingers and blade fell to the stone.

Cassta darted a look, offered the barest nod to him, then swung around. As Mareesh screamed in pain and horror, she turned her *quisl* on the two knights. The poisoned blade darted into cracks between plates of armor, finding flesh for its deadly kiss. Within breaths, strength died in their limbs, stolen by the poison, which then took their lives.

All the while, Kanthe guarded over Mareesh, who moaned and rocked, cradling his ruined hand to his chest.

Cassta joined Kanthe. *"Kreshna,"* she whispered in a rare moment of appreciation.

The Rhysian word was both thanks and acknowledgment of a debt owed.

He nodded, trying to force his heart out of his throat. Upon reaching the platform, he had hated to abandon Cassta's side, fearing this very danger. Earlier, her words and actions had been meant to lure Mareesh atop the platform. Their group could not risk the bastard slipping away again, escaping under the protection of his main force.

To prevent that, they had needed to lure Mareesh *close.*

Still, Kanthe had hoped to usurp Cassta's role, to keep her from danger, by urging Mareesh up with a challenge. Unfortunately, the Klashean prince had heeded Kanthe no better than the Qaaren envoy had a month ago, both choosing to ignore the king consort.

It seems everyone only wanted Aalia.

With a grimace, Kanthe stared across the square. As quickly as the counter-assault had started, it ended. Overwhelmed, caught with their backs turned, Mareesh's small army had been decimated, with those still breathing down on their bellies or knees. A few stragglers escaped, but they no longer mattered.

Not with Mareesh captured, wounded, and humiliated.

But this pageant had not reached its conclusion yet.

Another on the platform stepped forward. It was the second knight who had been waiting with Tazar. As the figure approached, Tazar reached to a series of clasps behind the knight's back. Armor fell away from the form beneath.

Like a butterfly from a steel chrysalis, Aalia stepped free.

She was dressed in silken finery, embroidered with gold. From her arms, the snowy wings of her loose sleeves caught the sea breeze, wafting wide. But there was nothing fragile or soft in the fire in her eyes. She also carried a sword in one hand, still ensconced in a steel gauntlet.

With the tip of her blade, she lifted Mareesh's chin and stared down for a long breath. By now, others had started to regather. Their group did not need many in attendance, just enough to spread the word, to let the story grow grander in its retellings.

"Submit, dear brother," Aalia said firmly, her words carried across the square. "Or die like a dog upon this stone."

Mareesh inhaled hard breaths. While a bastard, he was still a seasoned knight and knew defeat. He inclined his chin slightly. "I so submit."

Rami shifted closer. "And so it is witnessed."

A few cheers rose from the fringes of the battlefield.

Kanthe felt little joy, only relief, and not a small measure of grief. He stared across the many dead, heard the moans of the wounded, watched crimson streams flowing into the stagnant floodwaters.

So much blood had been spilled to end Mareesh's villainous insurrection.

Kanthe knew the prince had to be stopped, his rebellion quashed completely, even at the cost of all these lives. If dissension had been left to fester and grow, the price could have been much worse later.

Rami stepped closer, his gaze not on the battlefield, but on his brother. Since last winter's attack, Rami had hoped Mareesh might redeem himself and eventually be brought back to the family's fold.

Kanthe saw that hope die in his friend's eyes.

Still, Kanthe offered as much reassurance as he could muster. "Mareesh had to be crushed. Especially as we start a war with Hálendii. We could not leave a viper at our back, nestled and spreading its venom throughout the city, especially with that poison already leaching all the way to my brother in Azantiia."

Rami sighed with a slow nod. "No doubt Mareesh would have used the cover of that war to attack Aalia's rule again, to strike while the empire was at its most fragile."

"Like he did last winter."

"And again this day, following the tragedy of the flooding."

Kanthe nodded.

Aalia had counted on her brother's unscrupulous tactics to continue. Following the tidal surge, she had devised this hurried plan, to take advantage of this devastation to lure Mareesh out of his viper's nest. She had spread word surreptitiously that she would be heading into the besieged corner of the city, to stage a rally for the people, and to sustain such a surprise, she would travel with a limited guard.

No one knew if casting out such bait would draw Mareesh from hiding. If not, no harm would have been done. Aalia could have held this very rally to instill confidence in her reign—a necessity in a city beset repeatedly by the ravages of the approaching moon. She had to fight any whispers of her reign being cursed by the gods, to shine as brightly as possible amidst the gloom.

In the end, Aalia's risky strategy had proven shrewd. Her brother had been lured out.

How could he not?

Mareesh was surely frustrated with his lack of success following the poisonous ambush last month. And now, with the imperial citadel locked tight, the bastard must have feared this could be his last chance. Plus, with the failed assassination, he had lost face with his Hálendiian conspirator. To regain his footing, Mareesh had to act.

Still, this plan—while successful—had come at great cost.

Kanthe watched physiks and other healers abandon their carriages and set about ministering to the wounded. Elsewhere, black-draped clerics spread out among the corpses, sealing the dead's fate with scented balms meant to attract the attention of the gods.

Kanthe recognized the necessity of their work.

And our own.

Hard days lay ahead. The city had to be united, under one rule, one hand. Kanthe turned to Aalia, suspecting she might have the hardest task: to hold the sprawling Eternal City together while war burned across the Crown.

As if confirming this, a low tremoring shook underfoot. The distant waters of the bay trembled with it. While the small quake died quickly away, it served as a harbinger—worse was yet to come.

Kanthe swung his gaze north.

In another month, he would head back to Hálendii. He remembered Tykhan's warning about the emergent threat of Eligor, about the narrowing time line afforded them.

One fear grew with every passing day.

Are we already too late?

46

"IT IS TIME," Physik Orkan intoned with great solemnity from the open doorway into the queen's bedchamber. "We dare wait no longer."

Mikaen pushed up from a couch, where he had slept most nights. He bit back a groan, dreading what was to come, while at the same time relieved his vigil was reaching an end.

Thoryn stepped closer and offered a hand to help him to his feet. The captain had arrived at the midday bell with tidings from the Southern Klashe, of Prince Mareesh's capture two days ago. This setback was disappointing but not unexpected. Still, the prince yet lived, imprisoned in the imperial dungeon. Such generosity on the empress's part could still serve him—if only to allow Mikaen to exact a more fitting punishment upon Mareesh for his past failures.

Still, none of that mattered at this moment.

Mikaen had far greater concerns.

As he stood, he ignored Thoryn's offered hand. He refused to show weakness, even with his stomach weighted by rocks and his heart despairing.

I must be strong—for Myella, for my child.

Mikaen straightened, adjusted the seat of his silver half-mask, then crossed toward the door. His steps faltered, then grew steadier. His breathing, though, remained heavy, fighting the tension that constricted his chest.

Thoryn followed. "Sire, you do not have to bear witness. None will fault you."

Mikaen turned to snap at the Silvergard, but he read the raw concern in that crimson visage. His anger died to a mutter. "I . . . I must."

Thoryn acknowledged this with a nod. "Then I must, too."

Mikaen touched Thoryn's arm in silent thanks.

Together, they reached the bedchamber door. Mikaen held far less charity for the healer. Physik Orkan was the only healer to survive the purge following Myella's installation into the foul bloodbaerne. A pair of Shriven assisted him now—Iflelen skilled with the *arkana* that sustained the queen's body.

Mikaen challenged the physik. "Myella is only eight months into her bearing. To draw the child from her womb so early risks much, does it not?"

Orkan lowered his gaze. "Of course, I . . . *we* hoped for more time."

Mikaen noted the physik sought to make it clear that he was not solely to blame, nor was this decision his alone.

Orkan swallowed and glanced into the bedchamber. "Shrive Wryth says we must act now if we hope to save the child. He believes, with enough care, the babe could still survive this birth, even thrive afterward via alchymies known only to his holy brethren."

Mikaen took a deep breath. His question to the physik had little to do with seeking an explanation. The danger to the child had been whispered and warned about for the past week as Myella grew ever weaker in her copper bed. He had confronted Orkan simply to hold off crossing into the chamber.

When I leave it again, my queen will be truly gone.

Still, this path had been set from the moment he spilled poison into her drink. He could not step away from it now. He pushed past Orkan and entered the bedchamber. Curtains still closed off the bloodbaerne bed, as if the tragedy within must be hidden by more than just the doors to the chamber.

He headed across the room, flanked by Orkan and Thoryn. He heard studious whispers from Myella's attendants, including the sharper consonants that marked Wryth's eastern accent. Already the muscles of Mikaen's lower back tightened with distaste and fury. What the Iflelen had promised—that the child would survive the poison—now balanced on a dagger's edge.

He reached the curtains and ripped them open. The smell of balms and bile struck his nose. A cleric had been in this morning, knowing the end was near, and had anointed Myella's brow with unguents to mark her passage to the bosom of the Mother Below. Mikaen noted the dark star of the oils that christened her forehead, nearly black against the sickly yellow of her skin.

He clenched a fist to hold back his grief.

I must stay strong for what's to come.

Wryth motioned him to one side. "If you wish, Your Grace, you can stand here while we free your child from the womb."

Mikaen burned at what sounded like an order to his ears, but he moved leadenly to Myella's right, too distraught to lash out.

Instead, he kept his gaze on Myella's face. Her eyelids had been glued shut by the cleric, as if she were already dead. But that was not so, not yet. The tube down her throat steamed with each of her forced breaths, pumped by the mekanicals behind her. The plugs in her nostrils were caked with a rim of mucus that bubbled. Below her chin, the open cavity of her chest still heaved with lungs that had gone deathly pale. A heart shivered between each beat, as Myella struggled to grant every bit of extra time for her child.

Our child . . .

He took her hand as Orkan and Wryth set about preparing to cut the babe from the hump of her belly. Another Iflelen, one whose name Mikaen had never bothered to learn, held a funneled instrument against the gravid rise of her stomach.

"The heartbeat remains strong," the shriveled man reported, his features shaded by the gray cowl of his Shriven robe. "But their numbers still grow slower."

"Then we must be quick," Wryth said. The weight of the man's foul gaze turned upon Mikaen. "Sire, upon your command . . ."

"Do it," he choked out. "Let it be done."

Mikaen turned his attention to their work, refusing to shirk from this last moment of his long vigil. He watched a blade slice Myella open. Pink tissue, lined by writhing vessels of dark crimson and darker blue, bulged out, as if trying to escape her ravaged body. More cuts were made into the same flesh, as blood spurted and more poured in rivers to the floor.

Mikaen clutched harder to Myella's hand, breaking bones that had grown thin and brittle, as hollowed out as those of a bird.

"I'm sorry," he mumbled, but he did not mean for shattering her fingers.

Motion over her belly grew frantic. He lost sight as Wryth and Orkan leaned over her. Finally, Orkan heaved straighter, stumbling back, holding a wet and bloody bundle in his hands. Tiny limbs hung limp, tinged too blue.

"I must get him breathing," Orkan said as he rushed out the curtains to where a table waited off to the side.

Mikaen noted the physik's words.

Get him *breathing . . .*

Another male heir.

Mikaen moved to follow.

Wryth urged him to stay. "Your queen is passing, Your Grace. If you want to say your farewells. She may be able to hear you as she slips the bonds that hold her."

Mikaen still clutched her hand, anchored to her.

Thoryn stepped after Orkan, who had vanished out of view. "I'll attend to the child in your stead."

Mikaen nodded and returned his attention to Myella. Her lungs now only fluttered. Her heart's beat had become a stammer. He sank to his knees, bringing her broken hand to his lips.

"Thank you, my love . . ." he whispered. "All will know your bravery, your strength, your sacrifice. This I swear to you."

He pressed his forehead to her wrist. He listened as the wheeze of breath died down. He felt her fingers tremble, then fall still. He remained on his knees, long enough to mumble a prayer to the Mother Below, to take Myella to rest.

Then he stood and stared down at the heart that had loved him, understood him, accepted him in his entirety. The tender pink fist in her chest now lay unmoving and quiet.

Another was not so silent.

A sharp wail of anger, sibilant and high, rose from beyond the curtains.

"My son . . ." He lifted Myella's hand once more and kissed it for the last time. "*Our* son."

He gently lowered it and tucked her arm under a wrap being pulled over the ruins of the queen's body, hiding his shame from all eyes. But he knew he would carry the guilt with him. The only balm upon his grief continued a gasping cry of anger at a violent birth.

By now, Wryth had already slipped away. From beyond the curtains, Mikaen heard the Shrive's voice grow heated, along with Orkan's petulant response.

Something was wrong.

Mikaen rushed out, bumping aside one of the Iflelen. Off to the right, Wryth and Orkan leaned over a basin atop the table. The physik held a bloodied towel, likely used to wipe the babe clean.

Thoryn stood to one side, pain tightening the squint of his eyes. When he spotted Mikaen, the captain crossed in long strides to meet him. "Sire, your child lives, but not without mishap."

Mikaen drew a breath and held it.

Mishap?

Knowing that word covered a multitude of calamities, Mikaen closed upon the two men flanking the basin. "What has happened?" he gasped out.

Orkan held up his palms, clearly warding off any blame. "The child . . . your son . . . he bears maladies that he will likely not survive." The physik's voice dropped lower. "And maybe it is best he did not."

Mikaen shoved both men aside. He grabbed the table's edge to hold himself steady—and it was well he had taken that precaution. The naked child, still wet and streaked with blood, had gone quiet, but his tiny chest fluttered, stoking for another wail. Only one eye stared back at Mikaen, shining a thin blue through squinted lids. The other was lost in a melt of flesh that had frozen into a roiled knot that covered half his tiny face.

Mikaen gulped at this mockery of his own disfigurement. He struggled to understand, to even believe it.

Is this a punishment of the gods?

But that was not the sole defect.

While a right arm looked pudgy and hale, the left had deformed into a shortened stump, ending in a hand that looked more like a fin. Mikaen flashed to his sword cleaving through his brother's left arm last winter.

Is this a rebuke, too, from the gods, chastisement for that act?

As Mikaen stumbled away, he noted the twist of the babe's spine, the gnarl to a leg, wondering what past crimes those represented. His hand fell upon the dagger sheathed at his belt. The words of the physik—concerning the likelihood of the child's survival—had burned into bones.

Maybe it is best he did not.

Mikaen covered his mouth with his other hand. He glanced to the curtained alcove, having retreated from the horror far enough to peer inside, to see the blanket over the remains of his queen.

Thoryn joined him and rested two fingers atop Mikaen's hand as it trembled on the hilt of his dagger. "Let me take this duty from you. No father should have to do what must be done."

Mikaen shoved him away. His whole body shook to affirm what he shouted to the room. "No!"

Mikaen staggered back to the table, back to the basin, back to his son—to face the sins that had twisted that small body into a sigil of his guilt. He pulled his dagger from its sheath. With one hand bracing atop the table, he placed the blade's tip over that thin chest.

One push and I can put an end to this shame.

Still, he found he did not have the strength.

Especially as one small eye opened wider, shining the purest blue at him.

His arm trembled.

Wryth approached, perhaps noting his hesitation. "Such a life is not hopeless, Your Grace," he said softly, as tenderly as Mikaen had ever heard the man speak. "There are remedies I know. Not to return him hale, but enough for some prospect of a happy life."

Mikaen shook his head. "Even if true, it is too much to ask . . ."

How can I live with this shame, to see my son suffer for my offenses?

His grip tightened on the hilt.

Still, his body struggled for the strength to commit this act.

Below the dagger, a tiny arm lifted and batted at the knife's steely shine. Nubby fingers clutched the blade's blunt side—but one tip grazed the razor edge, drawing a crimson line across pale skin.

Blood welled up.

Blood we share . . .

The pudgy face bunched purplish, then burst forth with a lustful cry. In that wail, Mikaen heard the vigor behind it, demanding like a king to be obeyed.

Mikaen listened and withdrew his blade.

Wryth recognized the meaning and motioned to Orkan. "Fetch the wet-nurse."

As the physik fled, Wryth turned to Mikaen. "We'll do all we can."

Mikaen scowled at Wryth. He suspected the kindness of this offer, especially by such a stonehearted man, came less out of concern for the fate of the child and more about the bastard's own future. If Mikaen allowed the child to live, it would mean he would be beholden to Wryth and his ilk.

But Mikaen did not intend to take on this burden as a debt owed.

He pointed a finger at Wryth. "This is your fault."

Mikaen took care with his next words. He didn't know if the other Iflelen knew of the poison obtained by Wryth. Thoryn, who stood behind Mikaen's shoulder, certainly did not.

"You made promises." Mikaen stared hard at Wryth, making it clear he was referring to their poisonous pact and not necessarily his next words. "You claimed your bloodbaerne bed would keep Myella alive throughout the remainder of her months and that the child would be unharmed. Neither proved true."

Wryth acknowledged this with a bow of his head. "We will make amends with the care of your son."

"Yet, harm was still done."

Mikaen still clutched the dagger, wanting to plunge it into Wryth's heart. He knew he possessed the strength for that act. He let his anger and frustration over the last month build into a furious storm.

He stepped to within a thrust of a dagger from Wryth. "While my focus has been pulled elsewhere, you've neglected your duties to the throne. Negligence that now cost me a queen and a hale son."

"That can't all be blamed—"

Mikaen silenced him by pushing the dagger against Wryth's chest. "You'll show me what has caught your attention, or I'll have your head carried down by your brethren, who will reveal what secret you've been harboring."

Mikaen watched the machinations churning behind Wryth's eyes.

Slowly, words worked out. "I've been laboring on a weapon," Wryth admitted. "A project of utmost secrecy. One kept from all but a few in my order."

"A weapon?" Mikaen could not keep a measure of curiosity from his voice. "What manner of weapon?"

"One like no other. This I swear. Once completed, it will be a force to take down empires."

Mikaen lowered his dagger. "Show me."

"With more time, I could—"

Mikaen lifted his dagger again. "Now."

47

Deep in the Shrivenkeep, Wryth strode toward the tall ebonwood doors that led into the Iflelen's inner sanctum. Mikaen and a clutch of Silvergard crowded behind him. Wryth had not planned on revealing what lay hidden ahead—not to a majority of his order, certainly not to this temperamental king.

Not even the dagger at his chest had swayed Wryth otherwise.

Once down here, he could have easily misdirected Mikaen. In this dark warren, the Iflelen order had been working on a slew of noxious projects, a majority of which could easily be turned into weapons of war.

Instead, Wryth had agreed for a simpler reason.

I've reached an impasse.

For Wryth to continue his work, he needed resources that were beyond his ability to acquire. It would take the vaults of a kingdom to provide enough gold to see this miracle through to its fruition. For the past month, Wryth had held off from seeking that additional support, hoping both to continue his work in secret and to use the lack of resources as a means of controlling the frightening power that threatened to manifest.

For any chance of reining in this bronze god, I need to understand it more, certainly before it outgrows all restraints.

Still, the only way to discover that answer was by moving forward.

To that end, he needed Mikaen's support.

Bringing the king here served one additional goal. Wryth had feared the poison given to the queen could cause deformities in the growing child. He had hoped that would not be the case, but so be it. Once he had witnessed the state of the newborn, he had sought to use the promise of his order to help heal those poisonous afflictions to keep within the good graces of the king.

Unfortunately, Mikaen's seething reaction proved the king could not be so easily swayed. Mikaen, despite his temperament, had grown more cunning, less malleable.

Fearing the king's vengeful wrath, Wryth knew he had to propose something to satisfy Mikaen. He needed to prove that his dereliction from his royal duties had been in service to the crown.

To that end, Wryth reached the ebonwood doors and slipped out a thick key. "Your Grace, I must warn you that what is hidden here traces back to the

Forsaken Ages. It will defy understanding at first, but the promise it holds will be plain to see."

"Enough preamble," Mikaen snapped. "Show me this weapon."

"As you wish." Wryth unlocked the door and shoved the way open, but he paused at the threshold, glancing back at the Silvergard escort. "Sire, perhaps it would be best to view this first in private. Secrecy remains tantamount, lest some Klashean spy learn of this weapon."

Mikaen scowled. "Considering my traitorous brother had been discovered trespassing down here, I wager your secret has already spread to those hostile shores. Why else would Kanthe risk such a venture?"

"We can't know for sure. But it was this very weapon that drove them all off before they could discover more. Regardless, I believe a measure of caution is still warranted."

"Very well." Mikaen waved his escorts back, but he pointed to the Silvergard captain. "Thoryn, you're with me. The rest stay posted outside."

Wryth started to object, but a challenging stare by Mikaen silenced him. Wryth turned and led the pair into the sanctum.

The polished obsidian walls of the domed chamber reflected their passage. Ahead, the ruins of the great instrument rose as a dark bulwark of broken copper and shattered glass. Most of the detritus underfoot had been swept and carted off, leaving only this skeleton behind.

Thoryn's gaze lingered on a nearby bloodbaerne bed, abandoned and empty. The captain frowned, likely picturing the state of the queen and wondering about the use of those beds here.

Mikaen had his own query, gaping up at the instrument. "What happened to all of this?"

"When crafting a weapon of such strength, it comes with significant risk. It is why we bury our efforts so deeply beneath the Shrivenkeep."

Wryth continued through the maze, aiming for its heart. The view ahead remained obscured by the wreckage around them. Still, he caught the movement of a lone Iflelen. Shrive Bkarrin seldom left this chamber, overseeing the work as diligently as Wryth. In fact, his colleague's devotion bordered on the reverential.

And not just him.

Besides the lanterns and lamps, candles flickered ahead, lit by other Iflelen as votives to the burgeoning bronze god.

Wryth slowed his approach, using this time to inform the king, to share with Mikaen the discovery many millennia ago of an artifact, the metal bust of a bearded man, whose skull brimmed with strange *arkana* that defied comprehension. He shared in brief flourishes how the Iflelen had learned to stir it to life, how its mystery and promise had become the heart of their order.

Wryth glanced over many details, keeping some secrets to himself. But he also embellished others, to shine his own role brighter.

"Eventually, by delving deeper, I learned how to expand upon that mystery, to grow that bronze seed, a kernel rife with potential and power, into its truest form—a weapon of near limitless scope."

A glance back showed the doubt and suspicion shining in the squint of Mikaen's eyes. Next to the king, Thoryn remained hard-faced and stoic, though his hand had come to rest on the hilt of his sword.

Wryth crossed the last of the distance in silence, letting his story settle into the pair. When he reached the center of the dark instrument, he let the tableau within speak for itself.

Hanging lanterns and flaming votives reflected off a space that was both a holy chapel and a dire scholarium, all devoted to the figure at the center of it. The slab of iron altar remained melted, transformed into a black throne. Kryst Eligor sat upon it, his large bronze hands gripping its black edges. He remained naked, baring his majesty to all who looked upon him. At the moment, his head hung low, the curling length of his beard resting atop his chest, his eyes closed.

Those lids had rarely opened over the past month. Eligor only woke long enough to order rare minerals or to scold them for any delays. Of late, his demands grew harder and harder to fulfill, which only inflamed him more. Still, this god continued to gestate. The jagged crack down his chest had slowly closed, but a sliver remained, shining brightly with the mysteries inside.

Wryth longed to crack that shell open and to observe whatever process was ongoing. Still, it had become plain that this resurrection had begun to stall. That crack had not shrunk even a hair's breadth over the past fortnight.

Wryth suspected why.

We need more resources, which could only flow from one font.

Mikaen strode past Wryth.

Upon spotting the king, Bkarrin dropped to a knee, bowing his head with a mumbled greeting while keeping his eyes down.

Mikaen ignored the man, his gaze fixed upon the bronze figure seated on the black throne. "Wryth, you've built a statue? From that ancient bust?" He glanced back to him. "What significance does this pose?"

Despite the doubt in the king's words, Wryth read the awe in the width of Mikaen's eyes, in the huskiness of his voice. Even this unenlightened king had recognized the infernal glow shining from the rift in the bronze chest.

Those same energies scintillated across the metallic surface in radiant whorls and sparking coruscations. The entire form radiated with a barely constrained power.

Wryth lifted an arm. "Your Majesty, what you see here is a *weapon,* one newly crafted, close to completion. To see it fully realized, we need your support."

Mikaen cast a skeptical eye. "What foolishness is—"

"Your Majesty . . ." The interruption rang out like a dark bell, echoing up from the deepest well.

All gazes turned as Eligor lifted his head, plainly stirred by Wryth's words, at the mention of the king's title. Wryth remembered another name that had woken this bronze god in the past, rousing him into a blazing fury: *Vyk dyre Rha,* the Shadow Queen.

Only now, there was no shock or raving at the mention of Mikaen's title, only a cunning lilt to Eligor's voice. The same shone as those bronze lids opened. Azure fire flared with rapt focus, its gaze falling upon Mikaen.

Few could withstand such intensity.

Mikaen certainly could not.

With a shocked gasp, the king stumbled back.

Before them, Eligor's bronze grew brighter, as if burning from within. Skin softened. Limbs warmed free. Eligor pushed heavily from his throne. It was the first time he had risen since his first attempt a month ago. Eligor straightened and towered over those gathered at his feet.

Thoryn shoved Mikaen behind him, while lifting his sword.

Wryth stepped forward to intervene, but Eligor lifted a palm.

"This is your king?" Eligor boomed forth, his gaze still on Mikaen. "Of these lands?"

Wryth offered the full title. "This is Highking Mikaen ry Massif, the Crown'd Lord of Hálendii."

Eligor remained unmoved. In fact, he still kept one hand on his throne, leaning on the iron. He clearly remained compromised, but unlike before, he demonstrated more faculty and control. Wryth also noted that Eligor's focus remained on Mikaen, nearly dismissive of Wryth's presence.

The reason became clearer as Eligor cocked his head to the side, with a slight respectful bow of his chin toward Mikaen, as if this Kryst knew who truly offered the best chance to return him to his full glory.

Wryth's eye narrowed. He had suspected Eligor might have been eavesdropping upon his earlier conversations with Bkarrin, when the god had appeared to be asleep atop his throne. Eligor must have overheard Wryth's need to engage the king in hopes of furthering any advancements.

Eligor confirmed this. "You hold the key, Highking, to my rise to full power. Know this, for such aid, for such a boon, I will serve you well in the war to come."

Mikaen remained agog, his mouth hanging open. Still guarded over by Thoryn, he finally straightened. "How . . . How can you help us?"

"In all ways."

His bronze flared brighter, blinding in its brilliance. The hand atop the throne melted through the iron, which ran in fiery ribbons down the sides and pooled at the floor. Eligor's voice thundered out of that blaze.

"Give me what I want, and none will stand in your way!"

Eligor remained bathed in fire for another breath, then that sun slowly dimmed.

As Wryth blinked away the glare, he noted the rift in Eligor's chest had slightly widened, as if this dazzling display had burned through the reserves meant to heal his body.

Mikaen stammered away his shock, while his face glowed with a dark hunger. He likely pictured that same fire burning through his enemies.

"What . . . What do you need from us?" Mikaen asked, his voice hushed with awe.

Eligor leaned closer, the azure of his eyes blazing. Wryth expected to hear a litany of minerals and raw ore—like in the past—but instead Eligor's request now was far simpler.

"There is another similar in form to me. One who came a month ago with enemies to your crown."

Mikaen stiffened and cast a hard look at Wryth, then returned his attention to Eligor. "The Southern Klashe has a weapon like you?"

Eligor laughed, a brittle, mean sound. "Like *me*? Never. They have but a weak proxy. A Root. A *ta'wyn* who can melt its form into any other, but it holds only a thousandth of my true strength."

Mikaen looked at Thoryn—doubt had died in the king's manner. "I think I saw such a shifting creature. Aboard the *Hyperium* last winter. A wraith that flowed from one shape to another and freed my brother."

Wryth remembered this tale. He had thought at the time that Mikaen had been deluded by terror and the mists of battle.

Could that encounter have been this Root, the same ta'wyn *who had accompanied Kanthe last month?*

Wryth's gaze grew pinched. He wondered if this explained Eligor's continuing debilitation. Was the *schysm* stolen from the Root too weak to power such a greater being? If so, clearly there must be another path to correcting this deficit. It could be why this bronze god had needed elements and minerals ever rarer and scarcer.

Still, clearly Eligor's patience had worn thin. Whatever he truly needed to complete his transformation must be readily found within the body and innards of this Root.

Is that why Eligor ignores me now? Has he found a more useful tool, someone blinded by ambition?

This worried Wryth for two reasons.

First, for the past month, he had hoped, during this piecemeal repair of Eligor, that a flaw would reveal itself, that Wryth could use it to rein in this emerging god. But if this resurrection was accelerated, that hope would be lost.

Second, and more importantly, such a path forward stripped Wryth of his usefulness to the king, to Eligor. Even now, he sensed a shifting of that tide.

Mikaen faced Eligor. "This Root. It surely has been dragged back to the Southern Klashe. If you help me defeat the imperium, to bring low my traitorous brother, then I will grant you all you need. This I swear."

Eligor dipped his chin in acknowledgment and slowly sank back into his throne. "I will do all I can. But to serve you best, to aid in this war to come, there are some elements, some rare minerals, that can strengthen me for this cause."

"You will have all you need," Mikaen stated firmly.

Wryth stepped forward, knowing he needed to assert some authority lest he lose all of it. His words were also meant as a warning to this ambitious king. "After the defeat of our enemies and the acquisition of this Root, what then, Kryst Eligor? How will you serve our kingdom when you come into your full glory?"

Mikaen turned toward Wryth with concern, perhaps finally recognizing the danger at the end of this path.

Eligor answered, his gaze still confoundingly upon the king as Mikaen faced around again. "Bring me this Root, grant me that power, and I will deliver you a treasure like no other."

Mikaen frowned. "A treasure?"

"A weapon of an immensity beyond measure. One powerful enough to break the Crown and bring its entirety under your domain."

Mikaen clenched a fist. Whatever concern, whatever restraint, the king had momentarily shown vanished into a breathless lust. "What . . . What manner of weapon do you speak of?"

"One hidden long ago. A massive *schysm* buried at the heart of the world. The very key to controlling all."

Wryth knew Mikaen had no knowledge of a *schysm,* yet that did not stop the king from imagining the power described. The hope for future glory, for a reign without end, glowed from the sheen off his skin.

Wryth, however, pictured the *schysm* obtained from the Root. A crystalline cube, shot through with copper, pulsing with gold. He remembered the power it had unleashed when installed into Eligor, the devastation it had wrought. His gaze swept over the dark ruins of the great instrument.

We can never let this creature reach such a weapon.

As Wryth accepted this truth, his heart pounded harder. Not in fear of that happening, but with a lust as strong as Mikaen's. Only Wryth's ambition was not to dominate the Crown, but to secure that treasure for himself, to wield its strength to rip away the veil between past and present, to expose the hidden world and its secrets.

Wryth fought to keep his voice even. "Where is this *schysm* hidden? How do we free it?"

Eligor finally turned his azure gaze upon Wryth. "Only I can reach it. And only once I'm at my full strength."

Wryth nodded, unsurprised at this vague response. He knew he dared not press the matter further.

Mikaen glanced skeptically between Wryth and Eligor, but that flushed sheen never left his face. "We will get you what you need," he promised.

Wryth suspected the reason behind the king's acquiescence. Always prideful to a fault, Mikaen must believe he could use Eligor in the short term, trusting the kingdom's forces to control whatever came after.

Wryth realized his own rationale was little better than Mikaen's.

Am I as deluded? Can anyone truly rein in this god, especially if he should ever secure this schysm *at the heart of the world?*

Eligor lifted a hand, dismissing them, clearly weakened by all of this.

Mikaen bristled at being commanded, but he stifled any further sign of affront. He turned to Thoryn, who still stood with his sword unsheathed, and waved to the exit. "Take me back to my son."

"Of course, Your Grace."

The pair set off through the dark copper forest.

On the throne, bronze lids closed, snuffing away the azure fire.

Wryth rubbed his chin as he watched Mikaen depart. Bkarrin stepped closer, looking ready to speak, to weigh all that had been revealed. Wryth shook his head, knowing Eligor's apparent slumber was a ruse, hiding a calculating mind.

Instead, Wryth considered his own options. He listened as Mikaen reached the ebonwood doors and came to a difficult realization.

My control is slipping away, carried out by that king.
The only way to regain it was self-evident.
I need more help.
Possibly from another king.

48

KANTHE SAT NEXT to Aalia. Once again, her chair stood taller than his. But at least they weren't in the throne room.

Not that this chamber is any less taxing.

He stared across the strategy room atop the Blood'd Tower. Around its massive table, inscribed with a map of the Southern Klashe, the leaders of Sail, Wing, and Shield gathered with underlings and aides. They continued an endless discussion of plans, problems, disputes, objectives, exercises, maneuvers, and every niggling detail that constituted bringing an empire to war.

To the side, Garryn and Perash stood before a curve of the wall, where a map of the seas between the Southern Klashe and Hálendii was dotted with a slew of their respective forces. Tiny wings, carved of silver, had been pinned in place. Mixed among them, in some confounding tactic, were scores of gold sails, marking the imperial fleet. The two men continually shifted those pins and argued.

To Kanthe's other side, Aalia had her head bent between Tazar and Shield Jojan. The trio debated how best to secure Kysalimri with their ground forces.

Kanthe shifted in his seat, trying to break the two stones that his buttocks had hardened into. Six bells had rung as this meeting dragged on. He was not entirely sure *why* he needed to be here, which also seemed to be the general consensus. He had tried to offer input, but such efforts were met with rolled eyes, hard frowns, and placating nods, or were simply ignored.

To this lot, I'm no more than a nattering jester, one with a silver circlet atop his head.

Then again, he had never been trained in the Legionary. He had not been battle-hardened like so many others. He had certainly not waged a rebellion like Tazar.

Still, despite all of that, he had reached one firm conclusion while eavesdropping. He stared across the table, listening to those arguing around him. It was plainly evident to anyone looking from afar.

We're nowhere close to being ready to wage an assault on Azantiia.

Even worse, time grew ever tighter.

Two weeks had passed since Mareesh had been ambushed. The flood damage continued to be repaired. A visit to Tykhan's worksite revealed that the *ta'wyn* was behind schedule with his project. Tykhan had set a target date, now only two weeks off, after which their chances of success would plummet with every passing day.

The reason behind that worried them all.

Eligor was surely growing stronger. Spies had already sent word of a surge of activity around Highmount, of whispers of a new weapon rising from the depths of the Shrivenkeep.

No one doubted what that was.

As Kanthe shifted in his seat again—not because of his bruised arse, but out of a growing anxiety—the doors to the chamber burst open.

Rami and Frell rushed inside, bringing with them a cloaked and hooded stranger.

"You must hear this!" Rami shouted out.

Aalia stood, facing the sudden intrusion. "What's wrong? Who is this?"

The stranger shoved back his hood, revealing a familiar, if worrisome, countenance. His presence, especially so rushed, did not bode well.

Aalia recognized him, too, and likely feared the same as she sank back to her chair. "Symon hy Ralls."

The man bowed with a sweep of an arm. Few would give Symon a second glance, which served the man well in his role with the Razen Rose. Under graying blond hair, braided in back, his features were sunburned, showing a scruff of several days' growth of beard, which blurred his age to something indiscriminate. His clothing, half hidden under his cloak, had the wear and stains of the well traveled.

Still, the man's sharp green eyes hinted at a wily intelligence, belying the unassuming pretension he presented to the world.

Aalia's gaze narrowed on the man. "Why are you here? What word does the Rose bring to this table?"

"Word that should best be heeded," Symon announced.

Kanthe sighed. He'd had dealings with Symon in the past. The Razen Rose was a confederacy of spies, but one aligned to no kingdom or empire. They were said to be former alchymists and hieromonks who had been stripped of their robes but secretly recruited afterward to use their skills to a greater purpose: to preserve knowledge throughout the rise and fall of realms. Some suspected their true agenda involved steering history, believing the Rose was the hidden hand that moved the gears of the world.

Whether true or not, Symon and his resources had proven vital to their cause. If Symon brought word that needed heeding, they dared not ignore it.

Frell drew forward. "Symon arrived by swyftship a bell ago."

"From Azantiia," Rami added.

Symon stepped to the table. "If you hope to take the city, you must proceed immediately. Within the next day."

Shouts met this declaration, uniformly dismissive.

Kanthe wanted to voice the same, but he read the certainty in those green eyes. "Why?" he asked, yelling to be heard above the angry ruckus.

Aalia waved everyone quiet. "Enough!"

Once the room settled, Symon spoke firmly. "Queen Myella bore a son ten days ago."

"As we've heard," Aalia said. "I understand the queen did not survive the birth."

"That is true. The poison proved too much. But the child she granted her king came out maligned, suffering from crippling afflictions."

Kanthe winced. While there was little love left between him and his brother, he wished no ill will upon such an innocent. "Are you sure this is true?"

Confirmation came from Kanthe's left. Hessen—the Eye of the Hidden—stirred, rasping out an answer. "I've heard the same."

"And not just you," Symon added. "Nothing of this significance remains quiet for long. Rumors have seeped out of Highmount, spreading through the streets. Of a son deformed. Many blame a curse, a judgement of the gods upon the king's reign."

Hessen shifted higher. "This may serve us. Discord will surely grow from it."

"And it already has," Symon confirmed. "In no small part by the efforts of the Rose to seed this fear far and wide. Clerics and hieromonks already spout the same. A groundswell is building, calling for a change. Even among the king's legions."

"Is this not a reason for optimism?" Aalia asked. "A reason to perhaps *delay* our attack, rather than accelerate it, to allow this dissension to spread farther?"

Kanthe understood such reasoning, but he could not dismiss the queasiness of this tactic, to take advantage of the child's deformities in such a callous manner.

Symon shook his head. "Empress Aalia, you have your own difficulties, stoked in turn by Hálendiian spies on these shores. The destruction of your dockyards by floods. The repeated quakes. Many whisper that a curse is upon your lands, too. And while you were wise to stamp out your brother's rebellion, such an action is also being used against you in the streets. Many say you *slew* your brother."

"I did not," Aalia declared stiffly. "As much as he might deserve it."

Symon shrugged. "When it comes to a poisoned tongue spreading dissent, a lie can be more powerful than the truth. With your brother in your dungeons, far from view, that fabrication grows with every passing day. Some now consider him a martyr to your tyranny. Word spreads that you killed your brothers and your father, all in a mad drive for power, a fever shared with your lone surviving brother."

Hessen spoke up again. "The Rose is not mistaken. While my crows fly on wing and by foot to stifle these aspersions, Kysalimri is vast. Even I can't cast a shadow wide enough to cover all its many corners."

Symon stared at those gathered in the room. "Even among your forces, discord grows. While you wait for the conditions in Azantiia to worsen, the same holds true here."

Kanthe frowned. "So, because of these rumors, you want us to strike now? That's your solution? When we're far from prepared for such an assault?"

Murmurs and nods agreed with him.

Symon remained unmoved. "Your two lands are balanced precariously. In this pivotal moment, any nudge could tip it one way or the other. I've consulted with several members of the Rose. All confirm that the best and only chance to topple Azantiia is to move now, while the other city is on tenterhooks. If you lose this opportunity, you may lose everything."

Kanthe still refused to believe in the need for such urgency. "What you propose, Symon, is foolish and rash—and I'm an expert in all things foolish and rash. What harm could there be in waiting out another two weeks?"

"You will not have those two weeks," Symon said. "At best three days."

Aalia frowned. "Why three days?"

"King Mikaen is well aware of the growing internal threat. To address that, to turn that tide, he has called for a grand fête in three days' time, a great gathering where he will pronounce a shift in Hálendii's future."

"Is it about his son?" Kanthe asked. "Will he disavow those rumors?"

"Perhaps," Symon said. "But it is the *manner* of this announcement that sent me rushing here—why I came by swyftship, instead of simply sending a crow. It was vital you see this for yourself. To persuade you to heed my words, to understand the extent of the pending threat."

Symon reached into his cloak and retrieved an object that glinted in the lamplight. "This invitation went out to the loftiest of Azantiia's elite, even to baronages and duchies within ship range of the city, summoning them all to Highmount's tourney grounds in three days."

Symon tossed the invitation across the table, where it clattered and glinted over the map of the Southern Klashe. It came to a stop between Aalia's and Kanthe's chairs.

Aalia gasped as she stared down at it.

Kanthe reached over and picked up the invitation. It was signed by Mi-kaen. The king's name had been deeply engraved into the shining sheet.

Kanthe held it up. "This is bronze."

Silence settled over the room.

Without reading what was written, its meaning was plain. Kanthe knew *what* Mikaen was planning to reveal in three days, *what* could shift Hálendii's future.

They all did.

Kanthe stared across at Symon and voiced what *else* had been left unwritten but remained abundantly clear.

"We've run out of time."

49

AFTER MEETING WITH Symon, Aalia waited for the last bell of Eventoll to echo away. Dressed in a crisp white robe, she sat sullenly in the judgement chamber atop the Bless'd Tower of Hyka.

I can put this off no longer.

With a defeated sigh, she lifted a gloved hand.

Across the marble floor, Paladin Regar nodded and opened a tall black door that led into the room. Behind her, a nervous clinking of silver marked the attendance of her thirty-three Chaaen. She had summoned the entire contingent to the tower, to bear witness. The group had spread across the three tiers behind her high seat. Their silver chains cascaded down in a bright torrent and gathered around the foot of her seat.

To either side, rising to the height of three stories, more tiers stood empty. Normally those seats bore members of the imperial court or those who had an interest in a judgmental case.

Not this night.

This private gathering required only two more attendants. The pair entered through the black door, escorted forward by Rega. The first was a bare-armed dungeoneer, who carried a scimitar over one shoulder. The other came in chains of iron, shackled at ankle and wrist. One hand had been heavily bandaged.

Even now, Mareesh showed no shame. Her brother carried himself as if he wore gold and silver rather than a shift of roughspun belted at the waist. He came barefoot, as was custom for a supplicant to Hyka, to show humility before the ten-eyed god of justice. Not that there was anything but haughtiness in her brother's dark eyes.

Aalia had allowed him to keep his headscarf, to hide the fire-scarred ruins of his scalp.

Maybe I should not have.

The dungeoneer walked Mareesh to the white marble of the penitent circle. Regar followed and stepped atop a disk of black onyx, marking the executioner's spot. The Paladin then took the large scimitar from the dungeoneer, who backed three steps, leaving what was to come to the judgement of Hyka.

"My brother," Aalia stated coldly, "you've been deemed a traitor to the imperium. Your life is forfeit."

Mareesh showed no fear, not that she expected he would. She knew her older brother's temperament. He had always been hard of manner. The rule of order and adherence to tradition formed his core. He was much his father's son. Mareesh's protest of Aalia's rise to the throne had come as no particular shock. It was only the depth of his vehemence that had disappointed her.

Symon had asked her to make this appeal, as much as it galled her to do so. Mareesh's insurrection last winter, which killed their eldest brother, ended with the deaths of Shield Angelon and Wing Draer, along with thousands of others. Then there was the ambush by the Brotherhood, in collusion with their enemy.

Aalia rested a fist on her knee.

Mareesh appeared unperturbed. He gazed across the tiers, noting someone missing from these procedures. "Where is our dear brother? Should not Rami be in attendance?"

"He is called elsewhere."

Mareesh lifted a brow. "A duty of such import that he can't bear witness to his brother's fate?"

Aalia sighed. She saw no reason to keep the truth from Mareesh, not even from the thirty-three seated behind her. By now, it was a secret that no longer needed to be kept. "He leaves with the next bell. With full Sail and Wing. Along with a large legion of the Shield."

"For where?"

"To make for Hálendii, to strike against Azantiia."

Mareesh staggered forward but was brought up short by the chain held by the dungeoneer. Shock and dismay etched through his hardness. "What madness is this, sister? Our forces will shatter themselves against the city's Stormwall. Then the imperium will fall in turn. You've doomed us."

Aalia let him rage on, keeping her features placid. She did not bother to explain herself further. Once Mareesh's anger died enough, she spoke again.

"It is due to Rami's benevolence that I've brought you to this tower, Mareesh."

Actually, it had been Rami's benevolence and Symon's insistence.

The Razen Rose had wanted her to try to shore up Kysalimri's weaknesses— less in concern about the upcoming battle and more in hopes of a victory. If the others proved successful, a strong imperium would be needed going forward.

"We do indeed face a great challenge in the days ahead," Aalia admitted. "But it is not madness. When confronted by an insurmountable challenge, sometimes a reckless course is better than an overly cautious one."

She silently thanked Kanthe for such insight.

Mareesh, though, found this advice to be far less sage. "Is it victory you seek, sister? Or do you simply wish to rid the world of your last brother?"

"To my eyes, *two* still remain. And I would prefer not to lose either of them." She gave a sad shake of her head. "Mareesh, our family has already lost too much. It is why I summoned you here. To offer you a path to redemption."

Mareesh coughed with umbrage. "Redemption? I need no such blessing. In the eyes of the gods, I've done no wrong."

"You slew Jubayr, our eldest brother, who loved you dearly."

Mareesh shook his head, as if to cast aside her words. Still, he had the decency to turn his gaze downward, to show some shame. Or maybe it was simply to deny his culpability.

He tried with his words. "You forced my hand," he muttered.

Aalia's fist clenched harder. She refused to engage him on this. She had more important matters to address.

"Mareesh, hard days lie ahead for the imperium. I cannot predict the outcome of the battle to come, but either way, we need to show a united front. It is the only way to secure our empire."

Mareesh lifted his face again, his eyes shining darkly. "I can suggest a far easier path. Hand the throne to its rightful heir. Let me take my proper seat. Let me send the Hálendiian traitor back to his brother. This conflict between kingdom and empire can end without any further bloodshed."

She fought not to scoff.

If only it were that simple.

She had never considered Mareesh naïve, but clearly ambition and vindictiveness had blinded him to the treacherous nature of the Hálendiian king. Even if Mikaen's word could be trusted, such a pact failed to address the larger threat of moonfall. In the past, she had tried to explain this danger to Mareesh, but he had dismissed her, considered such talk blasphemous.

"Then you will not swear allegiance?" she confronted him. "To accept my rule?"

He simply stared at her for a long breath. His answer was as firm and final as a verdict. "Never."

Recognizing this to be a lost cause, Aalia let her fist relax, unfolding her fingers. Mareesh would never be brought back into the fold. He would forever be a poisonous thistle to her rose.

I tried, Rami . . .

She had to accept that without Mareesh's cooperation dissension would spread unchecked throughout Kysalimri. She could only hope the same held true across the sea to the north.

If I'm to be slandered as a murderer of a brother, then let that be the truth.

She nodded to Regar in the executioner's circle. The Paladin hefted his scimitar high, twisted at the hip, and swung his blade at Mareesh's neck.

To her brother's credit, he did not flinch.

WITH THE NEXT bell, Aalia sat atop another throne, this one in the main audience chamber. She still wore the same white robe as earlier, only she had shed her thirty-three Chaaen. They now filled the rows ahead of her. To her right, the other seat remained empty, as Kanthe should be at the docks, about to depart north with Rami.

She waited for the final rows to be filled, for the last tiers to be packed. Prior to departing for the Bless'd Tower of Hyka, she had summoned every *imri* of import, along with hundreds of the baseborn. *Shayn'ra* had also been called here by Tazar, who sat stiffly in the front row.

She waited for the assembly to settle to their seats.

Once an expectant silence acknowledged her raised palm, she nodded to Paladin Regar, who stepped out of view for a breath, then returned. He escorted a figure draped in brilliant white, even his headscarf. Embroidered across the back of his thick cloak were a pair of black swords surmounting gold wings.

Murmurs rose from the crowd—closer at first, then sweeping across the chamber. She listened as her brother's name was carried on those shocked whispers.

She greeted the prince in turn as he drew before her throne. She stared down at his features, blemished by fire. She knew every facet of that face: the gleam of his dark eyes, the cleft of his chin, the sharp angle of his jaw. Even the sun-crinkles at the corners of his eyes came from his decades of serving aboard imperial wyndships.

"Prince Mareesh," she intoned loudly. "The Shining Wing of the Imperium. I welcome you back to the bosom of our family. My heart bursts with joy to accept your penance. In return, I promise to seek common ground and sentiment, to rebuild what was broken."

"Dearest sister, the true Rose of the Imperium, I will spend the rest of my years earning the full depth of your forgiveness. This I swear."

Aalia rose from the throne and descended two steps, where she still stood higher than her brother. She lifted her hand, happy for this brief moment, praying it could last forever.

Her brother dropped to a knee, gently touched her outstretched fingers, and placed his forehead against the back of her hand.

Cheers rose—softly, then rising to a crescendo.

Her brother's name was chanted along with her own. Knights beat fists on armored chests in recognition of this reunion. The noise grew deafening as Aalia drew her brother up. She kissed one cheek, then the other.

She leaned in close to his ear. "Thank you, Tykhan."

The *ta'wyn* squeezed her shoulder, expressing his sympathy, then offered his arm, which she took, which she needed. She let him guide her through the thunderous applause until they were out of sight.

Tazar followed and came up behind her.

Tykhan let him take her, then offered a sincere bow. Her brother's features had already begun to melt away, though it clearly strained the *ta'wyn* in his debilitated state.

"I must change my garb," he said. "Then head to Rami and Kanthe before they set off."

She nodded, unable to speak. She glanced back to the throne room, hoping this act would stem the rising discord after word spread of this night. Of a rebellion ended, of a brother united with a sister. She could not expect all rancor to end, but hopefully it would be enough. She trusted that her thirty-three Chaaen and Regar would keep her secret, but even if one or two broke their oaths, their lone voices would be lost in the greater tumult.

Tazar drew her closer. "Are you all right?"

She stared down at the hem of her garment, only now noting the speckles of blood staining the white. "I . . . I will be."

She prayed her words were not a lie.

She'd had enough of them for one day.

50

FROM THE ROYAL balcony overlooking the castle's tourney yard, Wryth studied the thousands gathered below, mustered by their king for this grand fête. Few looked happy. Most huddled near large bonfires under a low sky of dark clouds.

Lightning flashed with rumbles of thunder. Winds pounded over the towering ramparts. Beyond the wall's parapets, the twin pyres of Kepenhill thrashed in the gusts, marking the ninth tier of the school.

Wryth wished he could retreat below there, to return to the Shrivenkeep. But he dared not forsake this post. His position remained precarious, even after the revelation of a bronze god buried deep under the school.

A chain of lightning crashed across the black belly of the clouds. Deafening thunder followed, shaking the balcony, thumping deep into his chest. He huddled into his gray robe with its hood pulled low.

He was not the only one discomfited. To each side, either seated or standing, were the king's advisers: the provost marshal, the grand treasurer, the city's mayor, and the liege general, along with other lickspittles and toadies. They also grumbled about the weather, about the delay.

The second bell of Eventoll rang out across the castle and city, echoing into the distance, trying to compete with the thunder. The king had been expected to appear with the *first* Eventoll bell.

"What is taking His Majesty so long?" Treasurer Hesst whispered.

His wife shushed him—and rightfully so.

Hesst was the only adviser to have survived the king's purge following Mikaen's ascension to the throne last winter. This crow of a man had likely only managed to keep his life because he knew where all the gold was hidden. And in times of war, such men were worth their weight in the same coinage.

Still, it was not wise to disparage Mikaen even casually.

Hesst slunk lower, casting his gaze around nervously, especially at the pair of Silvergard. The Vyrllian knights stood like statues on either side of the balcony, ever the eyes and ears of the king.

The grand treasurer was not alone with his complaints. The same rose from the gathering below, a quiet rumble of discontent—no doubt stoked by a growing superstitious fear. Mikaen had intended this festival to be a joyous occasion, a martial celebration of his reign. Staked out across the yard were numerous large banners, several of which the winds had already blown down or carried off. Pyramidal stacks of ale barrels had barely been touched.

The storm continued to stifle any merriment.

In fact, many took the foul weather as yet another sour omen. Wryth had already heard of the growing sentiment out in Azantiia, about the birth of a deformed son, of a curse upon the Massif family. Wryth suspected such a re-action had less to do with the child and more to do with a festering discontent that had been brewing since Mikaen had been crowned.

Whatever sympathy and good graces the king had gained following the queen's poisoning had faded with the tale of a deformed child. Many had come to believe such misfortunes, piled one atop the other, could only be the judgement of the gods.

Wryth shook his head.

Maybe Mikaen should have sunk his dagger into that babe's thin chest, blamed the death on the poisoning, and pointed fingers at the Southern Klashe and at his brother.

Then again, the death of the king's son might have been equally blamed upon those same gods. When it came to stemming such a tide of sentiment, one might as well try to reverse the flow of a storm-swollen river.

Still, it had to be attempted.

The goal of this grand fête had been to quash those fears, to instill faith in the king's reign, and to rally the people. But even a king as blustery as Mikaen could not dictate the way the wind blew.

Like now.

Lightning shattered across the sky. A bolt struck a parapet's flagpole. Its length shattered in a fiery spectacle, turning the banner into a torch.

The gusts quickened into a howl, carrying spatters of rain.

Cries rose from below.

The shadowy masses started to surge toward the gates.

Then, as the thunder rumbled away, the blare of trumpets took its place. The bright, sharp notes defied the storm's gloom. It rose from all around the yard.

Trapped within that cacophony, the crowds slowed their flight. Faces turned toward the balcony. After they had waited for so long, curiosity now rooted them in place.

Below the balcony, flanking either side, massive pyres flared with a whoosh of flames, some licking as high as the railings. A smattering of cheers met this display.

Behind Wryth, the double doors swung wide.

A fierce gust struck the balcony as Highking Mikaen ry Massif, the Crown'd Lord of Hálendii, rightful ruler of all the kingdom and its territories, stepped into view. He wore light armor, silver to match his engraved mask. The wind parted his velvet cape, trimmed in shining fox fur, and formed sweeping wings. It looked as if Mikaen were about to take flight off the balcony, as if this storm heralded him, not cursed him.

Even Wryth had to stifle a gasp at the sight.

The masses below were not as restrained.

Clapping and cheering met this entry as Mikaen stalked to the rail, his arms raised high. Behind him, the mountainous form of Captain Thoryn followed and drew abreast of Wryth.

Mikaen bellowed to the crowd as a light rain began to fall. "Welcome to Highmount!" He kept one arm lifted. "See how even the storm gods greet the birth of my new son, Odyn, a child born out of poison and strife, but loved by the queen, a mother who fought to give him life until her very last breath—a breath that she passed on to her son as she expired."

Voices below called out Myella's name, honoring her sacrifice.

Mikaen continued, "Lo, I've heard stories of maladies and curses. Of a son born with great afflictions, marked by the gods themselves."

The crowd quieted, waiting to hear what came next.

Even Wryth stood straighter, wondering if Mikaen would deny his own son.

"And yes, it is true!" Mikaen called out. "Odyn does suffer!"

Gasps rose from below.

Wryth found himself taken aback by this admission, too.

The king forged on. "But he fights! His will is that of his mother, that of his father. It is no curse! It is a testament to the queen's own struggle, brought to life in flesh and bone."

Lightning burst across the sky, as if the gods themselves agreed.

As the thunder shook the world, then faded, Mikaen clutched the rail and leaned far over it. His words followed the clouds' rumble out into the fiery gloom of the yard.

"Would you have me abandon Myella when the queen was so foully poisoned? Would you have me turn my back on her struggle, her suffering? Is that the king who was crowned upon these hallowed grounds?"

Cries of denial echoed up to the balcony.

Mikaen's voice rose with pained certainty, each syllable a stab at fate. "Then how can I shun my son, who is not god-cursed, but *blessed*—marked as a sacred spirit—a rare child granted life and breath when there was no hope?"

Cheers rose again but remained somewhat subdued. It seemed words alone could not shatter through the stony heart of superstition. Already those smattering accolades were dying away.

But Mikaen refused to relent. "For those who doubt me! Who question the gods! Let me show you how blessed my son is." He swept his arms toward the balcony doors. "The gods themselves have descended to Azantiia, to shine their glory upon my son, upon all of Hálendii."

Across the threshold, a towering figure strode forth, wrapped in a white robe and cowl. Marble tiles cracked under the weight of his passage. Those atop the balcony retreated in fear. Below, a hush spread over the crowd, silencing the last of the applause.

Wryth simply scowled. He had known Kryst Eligor was coming, but he had not known how intimately the king would tie this revelation to his own son, to his own lineage.

Frustration burned through Wryth. Not only had he been left out of this discourse, but he had also been shunned from the ministration of Eligor.

Instead, another had taken his place.

As punishment from a vengeful king.

Wryth watched Bkarrin trail behind Eligor, like a dog after its master.

Still, Wryth could not deny the result of his colleague's care. With the flood of raw minerals flowing down to the gestating god, Eligor had grown far sturdier. He was now hale enough for the long climb up from the bowels of the Shrivenkeep to this lofty perch. Yet Wryth knew there remained limits to that potency. He suspected the delayed arrival of Mikaen had nothing to do with the king and all to do with this bronze Kryst slouching out of the depths, conserving his strength.

But for what?

Eligor crossed and came to a stop at Mikaen's shoulder.

Mikaen called out to the hushed masses, "After being crowned, I stood on this exact spot last winter. I promised you a New Dawn was coming! That I would herald in a New Sun! One to shine Hálendii to its greatest glory!"

Mikaen stepped to the side and motioned to Eligor. "Witness the New Sun that rose to bless the birth of my child! That will herald a New Dawn for Hálendii!"

Upon this signal, the robe fell from Eligor's magnificence, leaving him naked to the storm. He stood in shining bronze. Energy shimmered and crackled over his form.

The gathering on the balcony fell away with gasps and cries of shock. Several fled in panic, fighting to get inside.

Then Wryth felt it, a rising of pressure, felt in the ears, in the chest, in the hollow socket behind his eye patch. He braced himself, knowing what was coming, having experienced it before.

Suddenly that pressure popped, ripping a gasp from his lungs.

Before him, before them all, Eligor's form burst forth with a blinding brilliance, a burning sun born out of bronze. Wryth thrust an arm against the flare, swearing he could see his bones through his flesh.

In the center of that sun, a dark god loomed.

A Silvergard grabbed Mikaen and shielded the king with his body.

Under that risen sun, marble shattered from the heat. The balcony's iron railing melted to ruin. Lightning lashed out of the clouds, striking at the abomination birthed below, as if trying to destroy it. Only each bolt died upon reaching that fiery sun, booming with thunder that quaked the balcony.

Wryth got knocked to his knees.

Still, he stared wide-eyed at the spectacle, letting it burn into his skull.

Then in another few breaths, it all collapsed in on itself, all that energy crashing down into the black well that was the Kryst's dark body. The brilliance faded, until only a bronze god stood at the center of the blasted ruin of the balcony. Eligor remained a fiery ember, but slowly he dimmed back to a dull bronze.

Bkarrin picked himself up off the floor and rushed to retrieve a cloak abandoned by one of those who had fled. He tossed it over Eligor's shoulders, as his original robe had burned to ash. Bkarrin guided Eligor away. The Kryst moved on legs gone leaden, but he still remained upright, a testament to his growing potency.

As Eligor departed, Mikaen returned to the rail. He kept clear of where Eligor had stood, which still radiated great heat. The iron railing glowed a molten red.

Mikaen lifted an arm out to the crowd, who had fallen back from the birth of this sun. As if upon this signal, the clouds opened, and rain poured heavily, steaming off the hot marble and iron.

Still, Mikaen called out to those below, "Bear witness, you chosen few! Spread the word of this New Dawn! Of a god's blessing upon our kingdom!"

Shouts rose from below, a mix of awe and veneration.

As Mikaen rallied on, Wryth turned to where Eligor had vanished. Thoryn must have noted Wryth's attention and shifted closer. The captain looked unmoored, his eyes haunted.

Thoryn clutched Wryth's arm, not cruelly, only in desperation. "What manner of daemon have you tossed at the king's feet?"

Wryth knew the stalwart captain deserved an honest answer. "You have it wrong, Silvergard. Exactly the opposite. I fear it was a *king* I tossed at this daemon's feet."

Before Thoryn could respond, a phalanx of five guardsmen burst through the doors. Their leader searched around, spotted the liege general among those who had remained, and rushed upon him.

"Sir!" The guardsman thrust out a fist that clutched several curled missives. "Word from our southern outposts. Carried by a storm of crows. More still sweep in."

The liege general pushed the messenger out of the rain. "What word?"

The answer came in a breathless rush. "Ships! Hundreds. Maybe more. All headed north. Riding wind and wave. Masked by the storm."

"The Klashe?"

"Yes, Liege General Syke. They're flying the empire's crossed swords."

"How far off?"

"They're already through the Breath. A day out from there. Maybe two."

Wryth pictured the smoky haze of the Breath of the Urth, which marked the boundary between Hálendii and the Southern Klashe. The haze—made up of ash and fumes—rose from Shaar Ga, a massive volcanic peak that had been erupting for untold centuries, creating a natural smoky barrier between kingdom and empire.

By now, Thoryn had broken away to alert Mikaen. The king had finished his rally and basked in the rising adulation. The Silvergard captain leaned to his ear, informing him of the threat.

Mikaen nodded, shoved past Thoryn, and strode to the group. The king's brow appeared as stormy as the sky. "The Klashe moves upon us? Is this true?"

"So it appears, Your Majesty," Syke said, his face grim. "They'll be upon our southern coasts in another three or four bells."

"How long until they reach Azantiia?"

Syke looked dismayed. "Your Grace, you can't think they'd strike here? Surely this assault is aimed at our southern outposts. Nothing else makes sense."

Wryth understood the liege general's consternation. By all accounts, the Southern Klashe was still a year or more away from any ability to wage a full campaign upon the kingdom. The same held true for Hálendii. Such an attempt by their enemy was madness, a certain path to doom.

"When?" Mikaen pressed the liege general. "When will they reach here?"

"Without stopping at the coast?" Syke looked to the south with a shake of his head. "By the first bell of the morning."

"So by dawn . . ." Mikaen followed the liege general's gaze, but instead of staring toward the horizon, the king focused on the cratered ruins of the balcony. "A New Dawn . . ."

As Mikaen turned back to them, a fiery gleam shone in his eyes, as if still reflecting the flames of his New Sun.

The king's next words were spoken as a challenge.

Accompanied by a savage smile.

"Let them come."

SEVEN

A WHISPERING OF CHIMES

Warnyng is the steng of a waspe.
Peril is the balm that soothes.
Warnyng is the stabb of a thorne.
Peril is the pull of the barb.
Suffre the lesson of payne.
For it is the source of alle prudence.

—Couplets from
The Way Through the Wilde
by Yargyn sy Nialle

51

NYX THRASHED IN a nightmare. She had endured this same harsh dream an untold number of times. It had repeated so often that she had come to recognize it as a dream, yet its hold still kept her trapped, unable to escape.

Again, as she had countless times before, she fled up a shadowy mountain slope . . .

. . . through the fringes of a leafless forest made of stone. Screams of man and beast chase her the last of the way. The clash of steel rings all around, punctuated by the thunder of war machines.

Panting and breathless, she skids to a stop at the summit. She takes in everything, recognizing she is older, scarred, missing a finger on her left hand. But she has no time for such mysteries.

Ahead, a cluster of figures with tattooed faces and blood-soaked robes circle an altar where a huge shadow-creature thrashes and bucks, its wings nailed to the stone with iron.

"No!" she screams . . .

Atop her bed, Nyx cried out loud, too, hearing it in her ears but still unable to wake. Her throat ached with the misery of it all.

As before, she was heard . . .

. . . dark faces turn toward her, curved daggers flashing into view.

She swings her arms high and claps her palms together as words, foreign to her, burst from her lips, ending in a name. "Bashaliia!"

With that last word, her skull releases the fiery storm held inside. It blasts outward with enough force to shatter the altar stone. Iron stakes break from black granite, and the shadow-beast leaps high. Its blood blesses the dark gathering, sending them scattering . . .

Even now, Nyx recognized the sigil that had been ignited, the fiery brand that had been burned into her spirit by the raash'ke horde-mind.

Her lips silently formed those ancient words that turned song into purpose.

Again, someone in the dream recognized this threat . . .

. . . a figure runs toward her, a blade held high, a curse on his lips.

Wasted and empty, she can only fall to her knees. She cannot even raise an arm in her defense. She simply lifts her face to the smoke-shrouded skies, to the full face of the moon. The sickle form of the winged creature passes over its surface and disappears into the smoke and darkness.

As she watches, time both slows and stretches. The moon grows ever larger. The war machines fall silent all around her. Screams and cries of agony malform into a chorus of terror. The ground quakes under her knees, ever more violent with each breath.

And still the moon fills more and more of the sky, its edges on fire now, darkening all the world around it.

She finds the strength to name this doom.

"Moonfall . . ."

Then a dagger plunges into her chest—piercing her heart with the truth . . .

The shock of that impaled blade jolted Nyx awake, casting her from the nightmare and into her bed. Still, she carried that truth out with her and stated it aloud.

"I've failed . . . I've failed us all."

She freed an arm and brought her fingertips to her lips. She noted her left hand still had five fingers.

So there's still time.

Over the past year, this same vision had continued to plague her, repeating over and over, tracing back to when she had first been poisoned and dreamed of moonfall. It always ended the same, with doom, with her failure. She had discussed this with Krysh, and with Frell before him. While some aspects of the dream had come true, others had not.

She rubbed the finger that had been missing in her dream.

But it wasn't that loss that worried her the most.

She still felt the dagger's plunge, as an ache in her sternum. She remembered the dreadful silence that often followed, a silence without end. Even now, she cowered at its immensity and inevitability.

Was this doomed end a certainty or merely a warning?

She did not know, could not know. All she could do was follow this path to its end. She shoved up out of her sheets. She shivered away the cobwebs of her nightmare, wondering why this dream had struck her so vividly.

A knock on the cabin door startled her.

"What is it?" she croaked out, her throat still raw from her scream.

"Nyx, you must come see this!"

It was Jace, his voice urgent.

She climbed from her bed. "Give me a moment. I'll be right there."

She crossed and pulled on a light shift that floated over her naked skin. She belted it at the waist and slipped her feet into sandals. She could not tolerate any more clothing in this heat.

Even with the *ta'wyn* coolers whispering throughout the ship, the air stifled. The *Fyredragon* had become an oven. Those aboard moved slowly, sweated profusely, tried their best to stay close to those copper tubes that seeped out a miserly amount of chilled air. With a ship this massive, many regions were not fed by those tubes and had been closed off. As such, the living spaces aboard grew more cramped, raising tempers, which only grew pricklier over these past two months.

But that was not the worst issue.

She crossed to the small carafe on a table near her bed. She took the barest sip from it, no more than enough to wet her fear-dried mouth.

The rationing had become severe over the past two weeks. Even the extra trickles from the Chanaryn tarps, designed to trap vapor from the winds, had dried away. This deep in the Barrens, the sun had seared the air to an arid parch.

Without spotting a watering hole for nearly a month, Esme had worked with Hyck to engineer an apparatus of copper tubes and pots, not unlike the tackle used to distill fiery bogbite back in the swamps of her home. Only instead of producing throat-burning spirits, the ship's device dripped out water. And instead of bean mash going in, the fuel for this process came from their own bladders, emptied from chamber pots.

Nothing could be wasted in this unforgiving desert.

Even their winged crewmates in the lower hold had been rationed severely, leading to a sullen lassitude. But at least, deep in the shadowy hold, a spot farthest from the sun, the cooling tubes managed to keep the space comfortable enough for the great beasts.

Jace knocked again. "You must see this! Everyone's gathering in the wheelhouse."

Nyx crossed to the door and opened it as the first dawn bell clanged out across the ship. She felt little rested, unable to fully shake the terror of her dream.

Out in the hall, Jace wore the same light clothing, which hung to his knees. His face had grown more gaunt, worn by the deprivations on board, but she wondered if something more dire had been wasting him, some insatiable hunger of his inner void.

Still, his eyes sparkled with verve and excitement as he led the way forward. "After skirting south of the sandstorm four days ago, Darant had been stoking our forge-engines as much as he dared in this heat. Hyck looked ready to throttle the captain due to this abuse."

Nyx had not known about this, having spent most of her time with Bashaliia. But that was not the only reason she had avoided the wheelhouse.

Jace opened the door at the end of the hall. Sunlight blazed into a blinding burn. She shielded her eyes with her forearm. Heat washed out along with the glare. She staggered alongside Jace into the wheelhouse. He passed her a pair of amber goggles.

She quickly donned them to dull the blaze.

Still, the arc of windows across the bow remained fiery. She blinked away the sting until her eyes adjusted. Darant was at the maesterwheel, while Graylin shadowed him with Kalder, who panted heavily. Fenn and Krysh manned the navigation station, both men shifting between its various scopes. Not far from them, Rhaif stood with Shiya, whose bronze glowed brighter, fed by the shine of the Father Above.

"Come see," Jace said, drawing her forward.

Hyck paced across the substation's many wheels and levers. "We gotta give our blasted engines a rest or they'll melt right off this bird."

Darant waved this away, looking as irritated as anyone would in the heat. Still, he called to his daughter. "Glace, slow us a quarter."

"Better a half," Hyck griped.

Darant ignored the engineer. "Stay the course. Due north. Three-quarter speed."

Nyx crossed to the furnace of the windows, the heat growing with every step. She squinted through the glare. The sun sat high in an achingly blue sky, as high as she'd ever seen the fiery face of the Father Above. His merciless countenance pounded the landscape that looked little changed. Below, mountainous dunes rolled in a continual red sea from out of the west. To her right, towering bluffs framed the world, running north and south. They dwarfed the cliffs on the other side of the Tablelands, climbing four times the height of those ruin-haunted scarps.

As she searched, she failed to spot what had excited Jace. "What am I supposed to see out there?"

Jace drew to her shoulder and pointed ahead, due north. "Look near the horizon."

She leaned closer, as if that would help. Then she spotted a dark, glaring expanse, where the sky met the sand. She had thought it was just some trick of the fiery light. But as her eyes adjusted further, she realized it was due to a reflection off the sand.

No, not sand . . .

"Glass," she gasped softly, and turned to Jace.

She had read about sections of the Barrens, closer to the Crown, even in the Guld'guhl territories, where some ancient cataclysm had melted the sand into wastelands of broken glass, creating vast fractured landscapes, a shattered black mirror.

Is that what lies ahead?

Nyx remembered Esme's description from ancient Chanaryn legends, of a vast sea made of black glass—and what might be buried there.

She turned to Jace. "Are we already this close? I thought we were still another two or three days off."

"Darant made good time by pushing the engines. We're only one day from the site marked on Shiya's map."

Her heart pounded harder.

I'm not ready . . .

Nyx turned back to the desert. After they'd been forced off course by the sandstorm, she had thought there would be more time, not less. Then again, the swirl of dust had been nothing like the *ishuka* back at Seekh. While Darant had given it a wide berth, he must have sought to regain their course, stoking the engines to a fury, crossing back north at far greater speeds. She suspected the captain's haste had less to do with a correction and more with concern about their dwindling reserve of water.

She also wondered if the vividness of her nightmare had been stoked by her anxiety as they closed upon this spot. But as that black sea grew steadily wider and larger ahead, she feared another cause.

Is that site somehow calling to me—stirring my vision brighter for another reason, for another purpose, one closer at hand?

As a warning of doom to come.

BY THE TIME the third bell of dawn rang throughout the ship, the wheelhouse had drawn more of the crew out of the shadowy depths and into the glaring brightness. All eyes remained fixed on the black sea ahead.

As the *Fyredragon* swept toward the glass's sand-swept shore, Nyx listened to the murmur of the others, a whispery chorus of anxiety and curiosity. Daal had climbed up with Tamryn. Esme had been summoned by Graylin, who wanted the Chanaryn's insight. Her chitinous molag clattered in the woman's shadow, as if avoiding the sunlight or fearful of what lay ahead. His spiked legs tapped out a nervous patter on the floorboards.

The noise grated on Nyx, but only because of the tension across her shoulders. If there had been any question that they had reached the spot marked on Shiya's map, that dimmed as the sight grew ahead of them.

The expanse of black glass filled the world to the north. It appeared nothing like the descriptions of the blasted areas closer to the Crown. While the surface near the shoreline was similarly cracked, creating a shattered mirror that reflected a fractured view of the sky, farther out the black sea rolled north in an unbroken ripple of sheer glass. The reflection out there was an endless dark mirror of the world, turning blue sky into a grim firmament of dark purples and blacks, as if a storm continually threatened. Even the shine of the sun, while blinding at the center, smothered quickly under that dismal sheen.

But it was not the sea that had captured all their attention.

At the horizon, a mountain had appeared, climbing ever higher as they swept north. It rose in shattered crystalline cliffs, lower to the west, higher to the east. It appeared like a broken black crown, tipped and sitting crookedly in that baleful sea. But over the past quarter-bell that illusion broke.

From its eastern height, twin columns of smoke churned into the sky, chugging steadily out of the depths of that ominous mountain. Winds stirred those stacks into slow spirals. It was if something massive and vile huffed heavily from below, out of nostrils formed of cracked crystal.

Esme named that dreaded beast. *"Draakki nee Baersh . . ."*

No one contested her declaration. The creature before them had to be the monstrous fiend from ancient Chanaryn sagas.

The Dragon of Black Glass.

Nyx stared at the rising mountain ahead. It did indeed look like the enormous skull of a wyrm cresting out of the black sea, with its snout resting atop that dark expanse. She imagined its body slumbering below. She pictured it curled deep, claws buried in molten rock.

As she did, she remembered where she had caught another glimpse of this same beast. She glanced over to Daal.

Off in the Frozen Wastes, looming over his home in the Crèche, had been a sharp ridge of peaks that pierced the ice and towered high in a jagged line. The first to lay eyes upon it, a Noorish ancestor of Daal's, had named the range the Dragoncryst, believing the mountaintops looked like the crested spine of a giant wyrm bursting through the ice.

She pictured that Dragon buried at the heart of the world, its colossal bulk spanning the Urth, from one side to the other, stretching from the ice of the Wastes to the fire of the Barrens.

She cringed at the immensity of this image—and the threat it portended.

Esme expressed a similar fear. "The *Draakki nee Baersh . . .* it must never wake."

No one wanted to argue with her in this regard, too.

Still, Graylin stated what they all knew to be true. "No matter the risk, we must go there."

Nyx kept her gaze fixed on that dire mountain.

But what will we face?

Darant must have had the same concern. The captain called over to the navigation station, "You two, what do you make of that foul crag?"

Krysh answered, lifting his eyes from the goggled lens of a farscope. "The glare makes it difficult to discern much. But I think I could make out tiny motes stirring out there, both on the flat glass and along those peak's flanks. Just the barest glints of movement."

Rhaif grimaced. "Those *glints* didn't happen to be bronze?"

The thief glanced over at Shiya.

Krysh shook his head. "I cannot say."

Nyx worked the tightness from her chest and stepped closer to Darant and Graylin. "If a *ta'wyn* army truly lies out there, one led by an Axis like Shiya, then we'd best not rush headlong into that fire."

"Surprise could work to our advantage," Darant said with a shrug.

Graylin shook his head. "If sentries have not spotted us already, then they will once we're closer. We'll never be able to strike with enough surprise to overwhelm such a force."

Darant considered this, rubbing the scruff of his chin, then called over to his daughter. "Glace, drop to quarter speed. Lower us to a skim over that blasted sea." He turned to Graylin. "Let's hope the glare off that glass hides us as well as it masks whatever Krysh had glimpsed."

As Glace and the crew spun subwheels and tipped levers, the near-constant roar of the ship's engines dimmed. The keel of the *Fyredragon* swept down, crossing from sand to broken glass. Soon they were gliding over a smoothly rippling mirror. The flaming blaze of their forges reflected off the surface below, casting out a glow beneath them. But like the shine of the sun, the dark glass swallowed and muted that burn.

Nyx wondered at the depth of that black mirror.

Closer now, she could see the expanse was not pristine and unbroken. Cracks parted this sea into vast plates, still held tightly together. She peered down into one of those fractures as the ship sailed over it. It cleaved deep, beyond the reach of her eyes.

She lifted her gaze to the smoking Dragon ahead.

She remembered the *ta'wyn* complex in the Frozen Wastes, the lair of the venomous Spider. It had looked like a giant tentacled *Oshkapeer,* one made of copper, rimmed by fiery chasms that glowed with molten rock. It had stretched a league in all directions, most of it buried into the frozen rock of the Brackenlands.

She tried to imagine such a construction beneath the Dragon, one that protected a massive sphere of crystal and bronze, pulsing with dread energies, at its heart.

The second *turubya.*

Another of the crew, though, focused elsewhere.

Fenn called from the navigation station, "Darant! Look to the west! To the shore on that side. There's a strange forest prickling out of the sand."

Nyx tore her gaze from the black countenance of the Dragon. She squinted past the glare of the sea to red sands. Ahead and to the west, the rolling dunes sifted apart into a spiked expanse. It looked like the winds had blown those grainy hills away, revealing a petrified forest beneath, one that glimmered in a thousand brilliant shades, as if a shining stormbow had crashed out of the sky and shattered across the landscape.

Esme shifted closer to the window, her eyes wide, her voice hushed. "Our sagas speak of such a forest. Named Argos. A wilderness of living crystals."

Darant scowled, clearly unimpressed by all of this. "It's pretty, Fenn, but what of it?"

The navigator pointed the same direction. "Through the farscopes, away from the glare of the glass, I spotted a shimmering blue in that forest. A lake of some sort!"

Nyx licked her dry lips, cracked from the heat and lack of water.

A thirsty silence followed.

Despite all the danger, one still plagued them all.

"Are you sure?" Darant called over. "A lake? In this infernal oven?"

"As certain as I can be from this distance." Fenn shrugged. "But if we got closer . . ."

Darant glanced to Graylin. "What do you think?"

Nyx answered instead. "We need water, especially Bashaliia and the raash'ke."

Daal stepped over with a nod of agreement toward Nyx. "She's right. They grow weak," he said firmly. "If we hope for them to fight, they'll need more than the trickles of water flowing into their troughs."

Krysh added his support. "That forest lies slightly ahead and to the side. Perhaps close enough for me to get a better look at the mountain."

Graylin still looked worried and wary.

Nyx tapped into her frustration to confront the two men at the wheel, tired of them dictating their every move. "I can head aloft with Bashaliia and scout ahead. If Fenn is wrong, if it's just a mirage, then I can swiftly return."

The muscles of Graylin's jaw tightened, clearly struggling to forbid it. But he stared at her for a long breath and finally nodded. "We do need water."

Nyx felt a flush of appreciation at this acknowledgment, sensing Graylin was growing to see her more clearly, perhaps recognizing the woman standing before him and not that child he had lost.

Still, there were limits.

As she turned to leave, Graylin called after her, "But you're not going alone!"

52

Saddled atop Pyllar, Daal regretted his decision as soon as the huge door to the lower hold cranked open. A blast of desert fire washed any coolness from the shadowy space. The flare of brightness burned all sight from his amber-goggled eyes. His first breath choked on the distant reek of burning brimstan.

The breath of the Dragon.

A low rumbling reached him, too, like the grind of heavy ice just before a frozen cliff collapsed. That pending sense of doom pebbled up the hairs along his arms.

Seated atop Heffik on Daal's left, Tamryn ducked against the heat and noise. Like him, she had donned flying leathers over a thin shift. Though he could not tell if she was sweating as heavily as he was under the protective gear. She certainly looked no happier, her short hair oiled flat, her eyes goggled against the glare. The sunlight bled any hit of emerald from her skin.

Still, she stared with determination into the blaze.

Nyx, too, had the same firm-lipped countenance as she crouched atop Bashaliia. The fiery brightness had burnished the golden threads of her dark hair, bound now into a tail behind her. She lifted an arm, then swept it toward the open door.

Bashaliia crossed the distance, scrabbling on his hindlegs and balancing atop the knuckles of his wings. He looked ungainly and awkward. Then the Mýr bat dove off the end of the lowered door and fell away, vanishing out of sight. A moment later, he reappeared, carried aloft on huge wings. In flight, the winds swept away all clumsiness.

Daal gave chase, flanked by Tamryn.

They burst out of the hold together. Daal felt the familiar rise and fall of his stomach as Pyllar dropped, then caught air with an outstretched snap of his wings. Daal angled to pursue Nyx. He had hoped the sweep of wind would stem the air's burn, but it only seared his lungs and dried the sweat under his leathers.

Nyx tilted on a wing and turned sharply northwest. She passed the bulk of the *Fyredragon* and sped off ahead of the large ship.

Once clear himself, Daal lifted a flat hand toward Tamryn and tilted it to the left, ordering her to flank Nyx on that side. She gave a nod, leaned that way, and Heffik dropped off from him. He shifted his weight, but Pyllar had already dipped a wing, either anticipating or sensing his desire. He dove to the right of Nyx's trail.

They raced low over the sea of black glass. Daal caught their passage reflected in that dark mirror. He also noted the prow of the *Fyredragon* slowly swinging their direction, intending to follow in their wake.

Not that the huge ship had any hope of keeping up.

The three of them rushed for the western shore.

Then a flash of fire reflected off the glass below. He looked over his shoulder. From the stern of the *Fyredragon,* a sailraft shot out, jettisoned by a launch bow inside the upper hold. The small craft looked like a bulky wooden arrow, trailing flames. Then a balloon popped open above it, swelling in a breath to catch the weight of the raft before it plummeted.

The small vessel swung steeply, driven by its stern forge, and set off after them.

Daal frowned. In the rush to exit the ship, he had not been informed that anyone would follow. Maybe Nyx had been told, but he doubted it. Still, he could guess who was aboard the raft.

He remembered Graylin's shout as Daal and Nyx had fled the wheelhouse. *You're not going alone!*

Apparently, the grizzled knight—Nyx's father—had deemed the escort of two raash'ke riders was not enough to protect his daughter. No doubt others were aboard the raft, too.

Daal focused forward again.

The western shore grew, a line of red sand against black glass. As they swept closer, the dark mirror under them shattered into fractured pieces, sticking askew, raising sharp points and razored edges, forming a dangerous reef along the coast.

Then the trio shot clear of the danger, whisking low over sand, then shooting higher as the strange forest climbed ahead of them. As brilliant as these woods were from a distance, up close the sight drew the breath from Daal's hot lungs. He swore the air grew slightly cooler, too.

Below, the forest rose in thick crystalline stalks that branched into a dense canopy. While the trees were leafless, pine-cone-like frills dotted the stems, some blossoming into translucent petals that stirred at their passage.

This was no dead forest.

It's alive.

Still, what struck Daal the most was the sheer radiance of this forest. It dazzled the eye. At first, he thought it was just sunlight refracting off the crystal, then he realized the forest shimmered on its own, swirling more brilliantly in Nyx's wake as she rode ahead of them.

Despite this strangeness, Daal was struck by a familiarity. It took him several breaths—which definitely felt cooler!—to realize what this growth resembled. He flashed to the emerald sea of his home in the Crèche. While out fishing, he often dove deep with spear or trident and hunted the phosphorescent forests growing along the seabed.

Coral . . .

That's what this forest looked like, only of titanic size. While some of the crystalline trees looked to be fragile saplings, others had boles as thick around as the legs of the massive martoks that roamed the ice fields of the Frozen Wastes. Those giant trees climbed tens of stories into the air. Their radiance appeared more subdued, less excitable, nearly melancholy, like somber sentinels of this forest.

Still, none of this was what they had flown out here to scout.

Ahead, in the center of the crystal forest, a blue expanse beckoned. While mirror smooth like the sea of glass, its surface shimmered. *Definitely water.* A mist hung over it, likely formed from the heat and sunlight burning away the lake's surface.

Nyx reached the blue expanse and swirled through the vapor in a slow circle. Daal and Tamryn joined her, both trailing her path. Daal held out his hand, letting the mist bead across his palm. He brought the wetness to his lips and tongue. While leery of some poisonous nature to the lake, he could not resist, not after the months of scarcity and the last weeks of cruel rationing.

Before attempting this, he had gained some reassurance as Pyllar swept through the cool mists, drawing deep breaths, mouth open to the welcoming dampness. Through his mount's senses, he felt Pyllar's contentment and relief. It mirrored his own, blurring the line between them. If there was any harm, he trusted the keener senses of the raash'ke to discern it.

Tamryn looked toward him, likely watching to see if he would topple out of his saddle.

He formed a circle with his hand, indicating all was well.

Ahead, Nyx used Gynish signals to pose a question: *Do we head down to the water?*

Pyllar chuffed and stirred under him, anxious to do just that.

The other two mounts, starved of water, clearly wanted to do the same. If left on their own, they would already be down there.

Still, Daal turned in his saddle and spied the sailraft flaming toward them. The slower craft had yet to reach the shoreline, still flying over the black sea. He pointed at it, then held up a palm.

Do we wait for the others?

Nyx stared over there with a deep frown, then answered by leaning forward.

Bashaliia dove toward the misty lake. Still, she remained cautious enough to circle low, studying the forest's fringes, which grew into a dense thicket, looking nearly impenetrable, forming a natural bulwark around the lake.

Daal did the same.

Beyond the waving petals of blooming cones and the flickering iridescence of the crystals, nothing stirred out there.

Nyx glanced his way.

He circled his fingers, earning a confirmatory nod from her.

Tamryn whistled, a piercing note that drew both their eyes. She pointed to a broken section of the tree line, where one of those massive sentinels had toppled into the forest, opening a small beach.

Nyx glided toward it, circled once, then guided Bashaliia toward the sand. His wings buffeted wide, scooping air, then his claws dragged along the beach and came to a stop. To make room, Nyx nickered and got her brother to wade into the shallows.

Daal followed her down and splashed Pyllar into the lake's edge. Tamryn came on his heels, with Heffik gouging the sand deeply, both raash'ke plainly anxious to get to the water.

Still, all three kept to their saddles, letting their mounts wallow deeper. The beasts slapped their wings against the lake's surface to cool the heat of their searing flight. Water splashed over the riders, too, raising laughter, a rare sound of late.

Nyx smiled, trying to hide it with a raised hand, as if ashamed to find any joy in their dire situation. Soaked and dripping, she called over, while tossing an arm to encompass the lake.

"How could this be here?"

Daal offered a possible explanation. "There must be a cool spring continually feeding the lake, while the sun and heat persistently fight to dry it out."

Tamryn had her own opinion. "I don't care *how* it's here, only that it *is*."

She undid the hooks on her riding leathers, shedding the heavy clothing. She tossed the vest to the shore, then climbed atop her saddle, where she wriggled and shimmied out of her breeches.

"What are you waiting for?" she scolded them, stripping down to the thin shift beneath. "I've not had an opportunity to swim since we left the Crèche. I'm not about to miss this chance."

She dove off Heffik's back and vanished into the water. Her pale form skimmed under the blue surface, then she rolled back into view with a spray of water.

Daal looked at Nyx, then shrugged. "She's not wrong."

Soon both of them followed Tamryn's example. They jettisoned their leathers and dove into the lake. Daal plunged deep, sweeping from sun-bright blue waters to a darker cobalt. He shivered at the chill, at the rush over his bare skin, as if he swam naked. After a long-held breath, he angled back up and surfaced with a huff of relief.

He spun his body around to spot Tamryn rising out of the shallows. Her thin shift clung to her every curve, the dampness turning white cloth into a translucent shimmer. She turned toward him, combing fingers through her short hair. The lift of her breasts pressed against the fabric, revealing the darker shade of her nipples.

Daal turned away, heat rising to his cheeks—and not just there.

Heavy splashing drew his attention to Heffik and Pyllar. The buck and doe tussled playfully, entwining necks, rolling in the water. Velvety nostrils rubbed, while wings enfolded. Again, unbidden, Daal flashed into Pyllar's senses and body. His mount's heart thundering became his own. The cool water soaked the bat's thick pelt, weighing it down.

Daal's hand lifted to the damp fur of his own chest.

Then he felt a hardening heat, down low, as Pyllar rubbed his belly against Heffik. Daal's breathing deepened to match his mount's. He felt a new warmth envelop his loins when the buck found the doe's tender spot.

No . . .

Daal shook out of the connection, kicking away, realizing the raash'ke were not just playing. While what was happening was more about intimacy and connection than mating, he wanted no part of it.

He let the chill of the lake draw him firmly back into his own body. Still, he was happy to be in the water, where his pronounced stiffening could be hidden in the depths. As he turned his back on the two raash'ke, he noted Tamryn staring at him, her head cocked slightly to the side.

Daal's cheeks flushed hotter.

Had she shared any of that, some vague echo from Heffik?

He prayed that was not the case.

Nyx called from the shallows to the right, where she kept with Bashaliia. The Mýr bat was bowed low, the crown of his head resting on Nyx's chest. She combed fingers absently behind the folds of those tall ears.

"Listen!" Nyx shouted over. "Do you hear that?"

Daal heard nothing but the thudding of his heart in his ears and the approaching roar of the sailraft. The craft was nearly upon them, cresting over the forest.

Nyx drifted toward the beach, drawing Bashaliia with her.

Tamryn waded closer. "Sounds like ice shards cascading down a steep slope."

"Or tiny silver bells," Nyx said.

Daal strained to hear anything and pushed into the shallower water, following the two women. Some of his anxiety must have reached Pyllar, as the heavy splashing quieted behind him.

Then a soft ringing reached his ears, rising out of the forest like a whisper of wind through chimes.

"I think it's coming from the crystals," Nyx said in a hushed voice, as if fearful of disturbing this scintillating melody. "I swear it just started. Or maybe I didn't hear it until now."

Plainly curious and wanting to investigate, Nyx warmed her body with a golden aura of bridling. A soft song rose from her throat, as if struggling for harmony with the forest's chorus.

"It's getting louder," she murmured, her words lilting with the chimes.

Then a growing roar drowned the music away. The mists above grew fiery as the sailraft reached them. The craft circled quizzically, then lowered for a landing on the beach.

Still, Nyx's gaze never left the forest.

Daal had drawn close enough to hear Nyx whisper, her words golden with bridle-song.

"Something approaches . . ."

Daal stared off into the glittering wilderness.

He knew she didn't mean the sailraft.

53

GRAYLIN SCOWLED DOWN at the group gathered in the shallows of the misty lake. As he guided the sailraft toward a strand of beach, he bit down a curse at their recklessness, their foolhardy disregard for caution. He knew many a stream or pond that gleamed with great promise but hid a poisonous taint or was rife with debilitating worms or flukes.

Then again, not all those aboard the sailraft showed any better restraint.

"I'm going to drink until my gut is busted," Perde said, leaning next to where Graylin was seated before the raft's yoke. "Then I'm taking a long swim, like that lucky lot."

The hulking brute of a crewman placed a huge, calloused palm against the glass, as if ready to leap through the window and dive below. The sleeve of tattoos down his arm glistened with sweat, with more dripping from the tip of his broad nose. His face, already jaundiced from his Harpic heritage, shone a darker, sickly hue from the lack of water. The rationing had hit such bulky men the worst.

Another crewman, standing half a head taller, appeared to have fared better. Vikas loomed past Graylin's shoulder. Unlike most aboard the *Fyredragon*, the quartermaster had never deigned to prune her clothing. She still wore heavy roughspun and an ox-skin vest. The hilt of her broadsword rose above one shoulder, from where the weapon had been strapped across her back.

Like Perde, she had fixed her gaze to the blue expanse.

One aboard the raft ignored the lake and stared off to the left, toward the glittering forest that rose past the window. Esme's eyes were huge, unblinking, mesmerized by the scintillating canopy, the waving petals, the heavier closed cones.

"Argos," she mumbled, giving name again to this Chanaryn legend come to life.

Graylin had recruited Esme for this excursion because of her knowledge.

Behind her, two others in the vessel's small hold continued a wary standoff, both keeping to opposite sides. Kalder stood wide-legged with his hackles raised. Crikit waved the heavier of two claws at the vargr. Neither beast had grown any closer over the long voyage here.

Graylin ignored everyone as he cut the stern forge, snuffing out its roar and flames. He tweaked the yoke and wrestled the wheel to bring the raft to a soft thump into the sand.

"Everybody out," he ordered. "Keep an eye on the forest."

Vikas cranked open the rear hatch, which dropped to form a ramp. Cool mists wafted in, which drew sighs all around. Perde did not wait for the ramp to touch sand. He barreled out and splashed headlong into the lake.

Esme followed more cautiously, trailed by her molag, who looked as happy as Perde to abandon the raft. Vikas and Graylin followed. Kalder edged out behind them, moving warily, his hackles still ridged down his spine. The vargr eyed the crystalline forest, then shifted to the lake, which lapped gently at the sand.

Kalder sniffed the surface, tested a few licks, then continued with more gusto. Graylin hoped that meant the water was safe. Still, one of the vargr's tall, tufted ears remained swiveled toward the forest.

Vikas unsheathed her broadsword and nodded to Graylin.

With the forest guarded, he turned to Nyx and the others, who remained in the shallows. Farther out, the two raash'ke kept close to one another. None of them looked ill after drinking from this cool font.

Still, Graylin knew the threat of such places did not come solely from the water. As a hunter, he knew streams and ponds attracted not only the thirsty— but also the hungry. Predators often preyed upon those who were lured out of hiding to risk a drink.

The hairs on the nape of his neck stirred as his ears picked up a gentle chiming rising from the bower of crystals.

"Perde!" he snapped. "Guard the raft."

The crewman scowled and wiped his lips after gulping from the lake. He stomped across the sand. From his hips he unhooked two hand-axes, flipping one in the air, then the other.

Daal splashed toward shore, leaving Nyx's side. The urgency of his approach drew Graylin to the edge of the lake.

Daal pointed past the ship toward a broken section of forest, where a large tree had crashed long ago. "Nyx senses something coming." He glanced back to her. "But she's not sure."

"Right or wrong, all of you get back into your saddles. Return to the *Fyre-dragon*. Then we'll follow behind you."

Graylin stared to the east. Before descending to the lake, he had spotted their large ship lumbering toward the coast. The sun's glare off the glass had masked most of its bulk. The flames of the *Fyredragon*'s forges appeared to be no more than sharp flickers in that blaze.

It still flew a ways off.

"Go," he ordered. "Now."

Out in the water, Nyx stirred and called forth with a sharp note of warning, "Get away from the forest!"

NYX REMAINED FOCUSED, fearful of breaking concentration, of losing her weave of bridle-song. She struggled for clarity through the confounding brume of life that filled the forest—that *was* the forest.

The danger, if there was any, remained uncertain, but until she knew more, it was best to be cautious.

As she thrummed with song, she found herself both standing in the water and carried aloft on her golden strands. The chiming of crystals challenged her, vibrating and tattering her weave.

Still, she had discerned enough to recognize the vibrancy of what grew so thickly out there. She had sent her song penetrating through the crystalline bark, a hard shell that housed colonies of tiny frilled animals, fueled by sulfur from the air, from refracted sunlight piercing the mineralized facets. She followed roots that burrowed down, burning sand to glass, forming tubules that siphoned water from the same spring that fed the lake and cooled this patch of the desert.

Those minuscule motes of life trilled their own song, vibrating crystals, creating a dissonant counterpoint to her bridle-song. But she sensed no enmity in this. It was merely their song, foreign and strange.

Nonetheless, this effect fogged her view, limited her reach.

She caught fleeting images of other life: burrowing with sharp claws, flying on pinioned wings, ambling in quick darts through the bower, all seeking refuge from the burning sun and taking solace in the cooler sands. The ringing of the crystals muddled this cavalcade of life into shadows and ghostly flashes.

Despite this impediment, a slow realization dawned. A pattern formed out of the flow of fleeting heartbeats, scrabbling nails, and padding paws. They all fled *away* from where the chiming was the loudest. It was as if the forest were sounding an alarm, driving them clear of something that traveled the crystalline glade, sweeping like a phalanx toward the lake.

Toward us.

With the loud chimes shredding her bridle-song, she could not penetrate that disharmony, that interference. She could not tell *what* had stirred this bower to resonate with such warning.

What is coming?

She tightened her diaphragm and the muscles between her ribs. She focused her song into a golden arrow, held it against the taut bowstring of her will until the strain trembled her entire body—then she let it loose with a piercing chorus, rife with power.

The sharp notes stung her ears and shot her spirit forward. The arrow pierced through crystal, through the empty spaces between the specks of vibrating energy that formed substance. It sliced through the dissonance of the bower's song.

Still, the forest was huge, pulsing with life, a chorus that outstripped her lone voice. Eroded by that immensity, gold flayed from her arrow, shredding into loose strands that evaporated. She fought to hold the coherence of her focus, but control ebbed. Her bolt's flight wobbled, then shattered, flying off in a shower of golden sparks.

She gasped, falling a step back in the water.

But it was not from any backlash.

At the farthest reach of her song, she had caught a hint of what traveled that chiming path, but only the barest glimpse. Still, she recoiled from its heart, from its black and predatory nature.

She shouted again to the others.

Not a warning this time.

But a command.

"Run!"

AT THE SHORE'S edge, Graylin shoved Daal toward the water. It had only been a handful of breaths from Nyx's first sharp warning to this panicked shout.

"Get Nyx into deeper water," he growled at the young man.

Daal spun and waved to Tamryn, who had been headed out of the shallows. "To Heffik!" He yelled over to Nyx, too. "Mount up!"

Graylin appreciated the Panthean's quick response. If a threat raced toward them, those three needed to get into the air. Still, the water's depth fought them. While Nyx leaped smoothly into Bashaliia's saddle, the two raash'ke stood farther out in the lake. Graylin also recognized how waterlogged all three beasts had gotten, which would weigh them down.

He hoped Bashaliia could still carry two riders.

Graylin grabbed Esme, who had hurried to his side, a knife already in her fingers. He pointed to Nyx. "Join her."

She nodded and whistled as she set off, splashing quickly. Behind her, Crikit raced on sharp points and dashed into the water, vanishing beneath its surface.

Graylin ran toward the sailraft, drawing Kalder with him.

Ahead, Vikas guarded the ramp into it.

Perde stalked the raft's far side.

"Inside!" Graylin bellowed to them, praying they had time to crank the hatch closed.

Otherwise they'd be exposed and trapped inside that wooden box.

He took another step, and a shadow blotted the sun. He ducked and fell back. A huge shape, as large as an ox, bounded high over the raft. He caught a glimpse of wings that appeared too short to carry its bulk. Black feathers bristled out of a muscled body, while beneath it, long scaly legs flared into huge talons. Above, a sinuous neck led to a reptilian-looking head, tipped by a curved scimitar of a beak.

Graylin fled out of its path.

As it plummeted down, a rear talon—razor-sharp—punctured the raft's gasbag and ripped a long rent through the fabric. Then the creature struck the sand with a hiss. Its talons dug deep. The massive bird rose to its full height, towering over him.

Above it, the balloon puckered and gasped, collapsing in on itself.

With a shout, Perde rounded the raft's bow with axes in hand. He threw one at the feathered beast, but it ducked aside, moving lightning fast. Then a leg lashed out, the motion a blur. It rabbit-kicked at Perde, who fell backward, avoiding the blow—but not the hooked talon.

Perde stumbled back, staring down dumbfounded. His belly had been sliced open. Pink loops and blood poured out. He tried to collect everything back inside.

"I . . . I got it . . ."

He did not.

As he struggled, the creature's neck snapped down like a cracked whip. The sharp beak hit Perde in the eye as he looked up, shattering through bone to brain. The man flew backward, skidding dead through the sand.

It all happened in a breath.

Graylin dove at the beast, sliding low on his knees while swinging his sword high. As its head whipped around, his blade cleaved through its neck, sending skull and stump flying with an arc of blood.

He shoved back, but whether out of reflex or responding to some last command, a leg struck at him.

He leaned away but was too late.

Another was not.

Kalder struck the decapitated beast from the side. The hard slam knocked its bulk over, sending the deadly talon slicing over Graylin's head. Fearing its death throes, he rolled farther back.

Kalder followed.

Keeping hold of his sword, Graylin scrabbled backward until he reached water.

Vikas rushed from the stern toward him.

Then a shadow burst out of the forest behind her.

Graylin could not get a word out before the monster was atop her.

As it struck, Vikas dropped to a knee, flipping the length of her broadsword under an arm. Its point impaled the beast behind her, finding its heart. Still, she rolled forward, flipping the creature over her back. Using its momentum, she catapulted its bulk off her blade and sent the body crashing to the water's edge.

Graylin didn't know if this defense came from some blind instinct or if Vikas had caught a reflected glint of the menace in the water.

Still, she reached him with more important information, gesturing with a flash of fingers and a stern look at the forest: *"Others are coming."*

The two raced for the water and splashed through the shallows.

Kalder followed, soon paddling as the lake bed fell away.

Graylin hoped the deeper water would sap the predators' speed and dexterity.

Ahead, Nyx had managed to pull Esme behind her saddle. Daal and Tamryn had reached their mounts, but the three bats struggled to get their heavy, sodden wings to shake loose.

"Behind you!" Nyx hollered.

Graylin twisted around.

From the forest's depths, a pair of the beasts rocketed forth. Another leaped the sailraft in a single bound. More burst into view, skidding in the sand. Necks wove, erupting with sharp hunting cries. Black eyes stared at the group trapped in the water. A few leaped and savaged the bodies on the sand, both Perde's and the creature slain by Vikas. Muscles were ripped from carcasses, bones broken with savage strikes of those beaks, organs tugged out and choked down with thrusting swallows.

Still, most of the flock paced the shoreline.

Graylin turned to Bashaliia, noting Crikit climbing and knotting his jointed legs in the bat's sodden fur.

"Nyx!" Graylin called over. "Can you bridle those bastards? Drive them away?"

She grimaced, breathing hard. "I tried! The forest rings with a jarring discord. It shatters any weave of control."

Nyx swung toward Daal, clearly wondering if tapping into his wellspring would grant her the necessary strength. Daal seemed to sense her need and drove his mount closer, but the water's depth fought him.

Graylin faced the shore, praying the lake would intimidate the predators.

The answer came as one of the beasts leaped high and crashed into the water. It beat small wings and sped toward them. More followed its lead, landing with heavy splashes.

Graylin retreated with Vikas, but there was nowhere to go.

54

As Rhaif paced the wheelhouse, he wished he had gone with the others.

Not because of the fiery heat, which stifled every breath.

Not because of the ache of the sun's glare.

Not even because of the promise of water in that gemstone forest.

With a scowl, he returned to where Shiya was bent next to Fenn and Krysh. The two men had summoned the *ta'wyn* to their station, to confirm a fear, trusting her sharper eyes. She had been studying the view ahead for a full quarter-bell. Rhaif regretted not going with the others so he could have lived in blissful ignorance of what lay ahead.

Shiya finally straightened.

"Yes, you're correct," she said calmly. "Those are *ta'wyn*. Likely Roots, worker drones. I count several dozen in view."

"Dozens," Rhaif moaned.

"*Several* dozen," Shiya corrected, her eyes narrowed with a concern that looked far too mild. "I cannot rule out an Axis, a caste like mine, among them. Not at this distance. But at present, I could not detect any of the *ta'wyn* glowing with an aura of *synmeld*."

Rhaif carried a trace of bridle-song in his own blood, a gift from his mother. Even now, he could sense a slight shimmer across Shiya's bronze. Then again, it could just be the sunlight polishing her brighter.

He crossed to the farscope. "Can I take a look?"

He doubted his gift was anywhere near strong enough to pick out a glowing Axis among the talentless Roots, but he wanted to see for himself the threat they faced. Last winter, their group had barely survived a battle against a single Root.

Not a dozen—certainly not *several* dozen.

Krysh waved invitingly toward his farscope.

As Rhaif bent down, Shiya spoke again, apparently not finished with her assessment. "I fear that is not the *worst* that I saw. We are now close enough that you should be able to discern this for yourself. Best you do."

Rhaif closed his eyes, wondering if he had made a wrong decision again.

Do I truly want to see this?

To the side, Fenn remained bent over a neighboring scope, one focused on the same location. Darant had ordered a continual vigil on that smoky glass Dragon puffing into the sky. The captain wanted to know if there was any sign that their ship had been spotted, to watch for any stirring of that buzzing beehive.

Krysh touched Rhaif's shoulder. "Maybe I should study this new finding first."

Rhaif opened his eyes, irritated by the slight condescension in the alchymist's voice. Or maybe it was merely scholarly curiosity.

Still, Rhaif kept his spot. "Those *ta'wyn* bastards have been posted out there for millennia. I think they can wait a few more breaths for you to peek under their skirts."

Rhaif fitted his eyes tight to the scope, which was still warm from the heat of Shiya's bronze. It took him a few blinks and a squint to adjust his sight to the magnified view of the mountain.

Black cliffs shattered high into the blue sky. Its crown appeared as jagged as a shark's maw. On its eastern slopes, twin smoke columns spiraled up in a continual sooty smudge. But he focused on movement below.

In the shadow of the mountain, brightly glinting spots worked slowly across the glass sea. Others labored up the cliff faces. He returned his attention to those below. He struggled to see what else had caught Shiya's attention.

He chewed his lower lip. As a thief, he knew attention to detail was as important as dexterous fingers. He took pride in this. He felt a competitive edge to be the first to spot whatever had sparked Shiya's misgivings.

As his eyes adjusted to the glare, to the distance, he finally noted other shadowy movement against the glass. Huge, humped shapes, far larger than the bronze wardens, lumbered across the glass. They appeared to be some manner of creature, maybe a beast of burden enforced into labor or bridled into servitude. Rhaif could almost make out wagons or carts being pulled behind those poor creatures.

With his attention so focused, he picked out something else. Smaller shadows, barely discernible but clear enough. He winced with recognition.

"There are *people* down there," he gasped out. "Laboring alongside some great beasts and wagons."

"Maybe slaves," Fenn said, having noted the same, which disappointed Rhaif's rivalrous nature.

"Or broken and bridled," Rhaif added, trying to upstage the navigator.

Shiya tutted at this last suggestion. "Not I or any Axis has such strength. A Kryst maybe."

Rhaif heard the shrug in her words. With large gaps in her knowledge, she could not be certain about the powers of a Kryst. During the long journey here, their group had many discussions about this, which mostly involved conjecture and wild suppositions.

Darant groused from his station, "By all the gods' arses, there had better not be a Kryst out there. An army of Roots is impossible enough."

Rhaif straightened, glancing back. "Shiya, when it comes to a threat, while the presence of slaves and lumbering beasts is worrisome, I don't think it compares to *several dozen* ta'wyn."

"That was not my concern." Shiya nodded to the scope. "Keep watching."

Krysh again tried to nudge Rhaif aside, but he ignored the alchymist and returned his attention to the view outside. Through the scope, the mountain swelled again. He studied those brighter glints and hulking shadows. He squinted and searched, but he failed to spot anything else out there.

Then one of the bronze dots shot upward off the flat glass, rising against the black flank. Fenn gasped from the neighboring scope, having spotted this, too. The speed of that ascent defied any ability to climb that fast, especially over a sheer glass surface. While a *ta'wyn* could move swiftly, Rhaif doubted Shiya could have managed to scale so effortlessly.

As he watched, the truth revealed itself as that blip buzzed like an angry hornet over the mountain's flank. Another *ta'wyn* shot off the glass, traveling swiftly, then hovered back and forth across a cliff.

Rhaif fought through his shock. "They're . . . They're flying."

"Like birds taking wing," Fenn added.

Shiya acknowledged this, but she could offer no insight. "I have no knowledge of such an ability among the *ta'wyn*. I wager it is some alchymy unique to this stranded army."

Krysh finally shoved Rhaif aside, anxious to view this disturbing miracle himself.

Darant also overheard their outburst. "Are you saying these bastards can take to the air?" The captain scowled out the window. "How high can they go?"

Fenn answered, "Considering my assessment of the mountain's stature, easily to the same height that we're traveling now. Most likely higher."

Darant cursed, then turned to his daughter. "Glace, drop us down. As close to that glaring black sea as you can manage without ripping out our keel. Then stifle the forges. I don't want a lick of flames showing."

Rhaif drew closer. "What about the others? At the lake?"

"They can fly back to us. If those *ta'wyn* can take wing, then not even the skies will protect us. I was counting on our ship's ability to retreat straight up if there was trouble. But if those bastards can follow us . . ."

Rhaif swallowed hard. "Then there'll be no refuge anywhere."

Shiya offered the barest hope. "After studying this ability, I do not believe the *ta'wyn* can sustain their flight for long, not without refueling themselves."

"Still, it wouldn't take them long to shoot up and board my ship," Darant warned.

Shiya did not bother to reply.

Glace's team set about lowering the *Fyredragon* toward the black sea. Rhaif cringed, expecting to hear the grind of wood on glass. But the pirate's daughter proved as adept as her father. The low roar of the engines dimmed to a rumble, then died away. The glow of their forges snuffed out. The ship soon floated under the draw of their gasbag alone.

The quiet was unnerving.

The huge ship hung above the glass sea, with nothing but the glare to hide it. While the *Fyredragon* lay twenty leagues off from the mountain, it was too close for Rhaif's comfort.

Darant clearly felt the same way. "All of you. Keep an eye out for any of those bronze bastards sweeping our way."

In this situation, Rhaif tried to place his trust on a bit of guild wisdom: a comfortable target was always the sleepiest. He doubted this *ta'wyn* army had entertained any uninvited guests for many millennia. As isolated as they were, he hoped their guard would be down. Unless some bronze sentinel happened to have a scope pointed this way, the *Fyredragon* might remain unnoticed for a bit longer.

But that can't last forever.

For now, this was the best the crew could manage.

To hide in plain sight.

Rhaif stared to the west, feeling exposed and vulnerable.

I definitely should've gone off with the others.

Arkival limne of
the Strüksos
(native to
the Barrens)

EIGHT

BREAKER
OF DRAGONS

What growes in the desyrt must have deep rooets.
—Chanrë proverb

55

Seated atop Bashaliia, Esme kept close to Nyx.

Despite the threat crowding the shoreline and racing toward them, Esme could not shed her unease at being seated atop this winged creature. The fear of such beasts had been deeply instilled, even defying Jace's gentle coaxing to quell her discomfort.

Crikit showed no such reluctance, having rooted himself into the bat's fur. The molag had recognized this winged island was the only refuge from what splashed toward them. A score of hawklike predators closed upon their group. The beasts swam swiftly, as nimble in the water as on land. More circled the shore, pinning their prey down.

Nyx retreated with Bashaliia into the deeper lake.

Daal joined her with Pyllar.

Both bats struggled, unable to reach the bottom any longer.

Esme felt a thrumming emanating from Nyx. Still, the woman clearly struggled to wield her bridle-song against this threat. One of the birds shivered, momentarily confused, losing speed, then it let out a sharp cry and shattered whatever net had been cast by Nyx.

Daal called, reaching a hand, looking ready to leap over. "Let me help."

Nyx waved him off. "Even without the dissonance from the forest fraying my weaves, I don't think they can be bridled. They're too fierce. Too wild-hearted." She pointed to the two figures in the water—and one vargr—splashing and kicking, weighted down by clothing and fur. "Get them up here with us!"

While treading the depths, Graylin and Vikas had little ability to defend themselves. Kalder, too.

Perversely, the predators floated deftly, kicking with their legs, with their sharp beaks raised high on snaking necks. Esme pictured those horny scimitars striking down, stabbing at anything in the water.

Graylin yelled to Nyx, gasping with exhaustion, while waving to include Daal and Tamryn. "Get your mounts in the air! All of you. Get to the *Fyredragon*."

"We're not leaving you!" Nyx hollered back.

Daal agreed, but for a different reason. "Pyllar tried! I sensed his heart. Even if he could beat his wings to lift off the lake, he's too bogged down by his soaked pelt."

Esme recognized they were trapped. The savage birds would eventually chase down their prey, flock over them, and attack wildly, shredding wings and tearing flesh. The hunters' cries had grown into a raucous chorus, echoing all around.

No wonder Nyx struggled with her bridling.

One of the birds reached Vikas, who had lagged behind due to her thicker clothing and Gyn-heavy bones. Its beak speared down, but the quartermaster managed to parry the blow with a desperate slash of her broadsword. As the woman struggled to recover, the beast struck again, lightning fast.

But Tamryn's mount had reached them. Heffik snapped out with poisonous fangs, ripped the bird from the lake, and flung its body far. Still, more birds closed in from all directions, unfazed by the bat's attack. The beasts were clearly pack hunters and counted on speed and numbers to defeat larger prey.

Their savage cries rose in volume, sensing the kills to come.

Esme cringed, but she kept her knife in hand, ready to defend her winged island.

Then a piercing, crystalline blast of a horn cut through the cacophony.

Nyx gasped, covering her ears, as if the noise struck her harder. She toppled sideways, but Esme grabbed her arm. Bashaliia shifted under them, too, to catch Nyx's weight.

"It's ripping into my skull," Nyx moaned.

As more horns blared from the forest, the bats writhed, screeching in distress—but other beasts were affected, too.

The birds shattered away in all directions—with wings splashing and legs paddling wildly. The pack struck for shore, for the crystalline bower. The flock already on the beach vanished into the forest in a blink.

Esme searched all around, thankful for the predators' retreat but fearful of what had driven them off.

After several more breaths, the horns cut off.

The silence that followed was more intimidating than the noise.

Nyx sat straighter, sighing out her relief. "Those horns . . . they were like the forest's chiming, only a thousandfold worse."

Finally, shadows shifted in the forest, and a group of shaggy, flat-snouted behemoths shambled into view. They moved on thick legs with wide pads, exposing hooked claws that gnashed into the sand. Their fur appeared to be made of dense, thick quills.

Only these hulking beasts had not come alone.

Riders sat astride them.

The strangers came wrapped in a continual spiral of ocher-colored cloth, winding from toe to the crown, like ancient burial shrouds. Several of the beasts carried two figures.

Esme spotted a curled horn, made from a tusk or antler, carried high, ready to blare out again if the savage predators should return.

For a tense period, the two parties stared at each other.

Some of the riders whispered, bowing their heads together. Arms pointed toward Bashaliia, then to the raash'ke. Esme flinched when one of the riders curled a thumb and forefinger and tapped it against his forehead.

Esme had witnessed that gesture all her life.

A Chanaryn warding against evil and misfortune.

She glanced down to Bashaliia, knowing what had likely triggered that reaction. She got confirmation when the whispering carried a familiar word across the water.

"Mänk'resh . . ."

While the name was pronounced differently and accented strangely, Esme recognized its similarity to mankrae, the Chanaryn word for the winged daemons from her people's ancient sagas.

She leaned forward to tell Nyx.

Before Esme could speak, a rider lifted high in his stirrups. He shouted to them, *"Kräm niche aben päas'keen!"* He pointed behind him. *"Nee, ashä nee!"*

Nyx stirred. "I think he wants us to follow him."

"That's indeed what he's saying," Esme agreed. "I can't follow every word. But it's some form of the Chanaryn tongue."

Nyx glanced back. "Your people."

"Those aren't *my* people. I don't know who they are. But that rider is warning us to go. That it's too dangerous to stay."

Graylin heard this, too, as he treaded water. "We should do as he says."

Not that they had any other choice.

The group splashed and swam to shore, aiming for the downed sailraft. The strange vessel had already drawn attention. One of the riders used a spear to lift a ripped corner of balloon fabric.

As they waded out, Vikas noted this, too, and gestured to Graylin. She fluttered a hand through the air with a shake of her head: *"We won't be leaving in that raft."*

He nodded.

As their group climbed to the beach, the riders retreated atop their shaggy mounts, plainly wary of the giant bats.

Esme did her best to intervene, sliding off Bashaliia. She lifted her palm and waved her other arm toward the raash'ke. *"Mosh akee nah."* She placed her hand over her heart, then to the Mýr bat's flank. *"Nah, resh ka. Nah, mänk'resh."*

She used their word for mankrae, while reassuring them that the bats were not a danger. But she could not tell how much they understood, especially with their faces wrapped, showing only dark eyes.

Still, none of the riders drew closer.

Even their mounts shifted nervously, extending and retracting their claws as if sensing their riders' anxiety. Their rounded ears stood tall and wary. Up close, the creatures appeared far larger, bigger than any ox, but these were not grass chewers. Their stubby snouts hid sharp fangs. The strangest feature, though, were the long quills that lay flat over their flanks. Each quill was translucent, showing a slight sloshing inside, maybe holding a reserve of water.

The same rider who had called to them spoke again, waving toward the forest. *"Kräm we nye. Aben päas'keen. Nee, ashä nee."*

Esme explained his words. "He's pressing us to go with him. Repeating that it's not safe to stay."

"What should we do?" Daal asked in hushed tones, noting the weapons made of sharpened bone.

Graylin searched to the east. "We need to alert the *Fyredragon*." He waved to the bats. "Once your mounts have shaken off the worst of their sogginess, you all take flight back to the ship."

"What about you?" Nyx asked.

"I'll go with these strangers, along with Vikas and Kalder. If these desert dwellers know anything about what lies under that mountain, we need to learn as much from them as we can."

Esme stepped closer. "I'll go with you. You'll need someone to help you understand their tongue."

Graylin nodded his appreciation.

Daal revised this plan, turning to Tamryn. "You head back to the ship. Nyx and I'll follow along with these strangers, too, tracking from above."

Graylin looked ready to object.

Nyx stopped him. "If you all run into trouble, we'll never know."

As if to stress this, Nyx turned her gaze to the bloody patch of sand where Perde had died. There remained no sign of the crewman. Even in a panic, the predators had fled with every scrap.

Nyx rubbed the grief from her brow, but her eyes remained determined.

Graylin sighed, clearly recognizing such caution was warranted. "Keep your distance," he warned Nyx and Daal. "These people are leery enough about the bats."

As they prepared to go their separate ways, Crikit untangled himself from Bashaliia's pelt, leaped off, and scurried to Esme's side. His stalked eyes waved as he clicked with concern.

"Yes, you're coming with me."

In all this strangeness, she welcomed this chitinous bit of familiarity.

Behind her, Tamryn took off with Heffik, wafting up sand as those large wings dug for the sky. The desert riders retreated, mostly in fear, but a few whispered in awe.

Esme respected such resiliency, which was likely a necessity in such a hostile terrain.

She stared toward the forest.

But how will we fare?

ESME RODE ATOP one of the large beasts, clinging to leathered grips that flanked the saddle. A tall seatback supported her rear, while ahead of her, a thin-waisted woman bounced in harmony to the rolling bound of their mount. Esme had learned such beasts were called *ürsyns,* with this particular one named Ruro.

The woman hadn't offered her own name. Apparently, their mount had to be honored first for some reason.

Esme had also learned the name for those sharp-beaked predators—*strüksos*—which roughly meant *feathered daggers* in the Chanaryn tongue.

A name she found grimly fitting.

While she kept a wary eye on the forest, she felt safe enough in the company of these strangers. In addition, Graylin and Vikas flanked her, sharing ürsyns with fellow riders. Farther out, Kalder and Crikit raced to keep up with the swift passage of these beasts. Though the ürsyns appeared clumsy, weighted down by their thick pelts of quills, once underway the beasts sped with great dexterity, following some trail that was indiscernible to Esme.

As their group raced on, she studied the crystalline forest. Under the shadow of its dense canopy, the bower appeared even more wondrous. Trunks glowed, cascading in shades of emerald and crimson, as if revealing the life-blood of this wilderness. From branches and stems, fat-lipped cones hung heavily, requiring a keen eye to avoid hitting them—a lesson hard earned. Several cones sprouted blossoms of translucent petals that sucked away if a finger brushed them. Something her rider had scolded Esme from doing with a stern look.

Overhead, sunlight pierced the canopy with brilliant spears.

Graylin squinted up at those breaks, watching for the occasional shadow to sweep over them, marking the passage of Nyx and Daal. Those dark sickles served as a reminder of the ever-present danger.

Still, the forest continued to tinkle softly, not in warning but as if to encourage their passage, to rid its bowers of these strangers.

Enraptured by it all, Esme leaned over and called to Graylin, "From my people's stories, I never imagined the Argos would be so beautiful."

Her rider heard this and twisted in the saddle. *"Örgös,"* the woman corrected. Then she swept an arm to make sure Esme understood. *"Elan e Örgös."*

Esme nodded, accepting the correct pronunciation.

Not Argos, but Örgös.

The woman pointed back along their trail and motioned as if drinking from a cup. *"Elan e Köös Nuur."*

Esme nodded again, knowing the rider must be naming the lake. Köös Nuur meant *Sweet Water* in Chanaryn.

Again, another fitting name.

She had also learned that these tribal people called themselves the Chanrë, which simply meant *people* in the Chanaryn language—a name similar enough that she had no doubt these were the ancestors of Esme's nomadic clans.

How could that be?

On this mystery alone, she had hundreds of questions. But while moving swiftly, any real conversation proved to be challenging.

She had managed to pass on a few of Graylin's questions. It seemed these Chanrë people had spotted the arrival of the *Fyredragon,* then noted their group setting off for the forest. Knowing the danger here, the desert riders had set off from their village—a place called Tosgon—to investigate the strangers and to offer aid if necessary.

Which certainly had been needed.

Finally, sunlight brightened in front of them as they approached the southern fringe of the Örgös. Trees grew thinner in size and numbers. The ürsyns trundled faster—either due to the widening trail or from the threat of exposure, as their group was no longer sheltered under the canopy.

Esme caught glimpses of rolling red dunes, climbing ever higher toward the horizon. Then they cleared the forest and raced across open sand. Their mounts fled for the thin shadows cast along the side of the dunes—either to escape the burning sun or to keep hidden.

Likely both.

Behind them, Nyx and Daal appeared in the sky, trailing high. They wafted their mounts back and forth, then circled as Esme's group slowed to a halt in a wider patch of shade.

Here, more of the Chanrë waited for them, both in the shadows or posted along the crests of neighboring dunes. Esme imagined they formed a rear guard. With the return of the hunters, these sentinels closed upon them, indicating this would be a brief stop. Esme also noted there were not enough mounts for the number of guards.

A sharp whistle corrected this, triggering explosions of sand.

Another half dozen ürsyns rolled out of burrows, their quills spraying clouds of dusty grains. They must have buried themselves in the cooler sands, leaving only their noses exposed.

In rare agreement, Crikit and Kalder shied away from those eruptions.

As everyone mounted up, one of the spies posted along the crest skimmed down the slope on sandals that looked crafted for this purpose. Upon reaching the bottom, he hurried toward Graylin.

"We must make for Tosgon!" he called out, while untying his headwrap so he could be better understood. "Get your ship to follow!"

It took Esme a breath to realize this newcomer had spoken in the common tongue.

Crikit, fleeing from an eruption of an ürsyn, came close to colliding with the figure.

The man stumbled back in shock—but not at the antics of the molag. His gaze had swung from Graylin to Esme's mount.

"It cannot be . . ." he gasped, dropping to a knee.

The impact jarred his headwrap loose, revealing a face that had been forever branded into Esme's heart.

She leaped down to the sand and ran at the man.

He bounded up and closed the distance.

They struck hard, knocking the wind from each other's lungs. She clung to him, hugging with all her strength, afraid this might be a cruel mirage.

She moaned into her brother's chest, "Arryn . . ."

He held her just as tightly. "Esme, how are you here?"

She had no words, shaking with a sob that had been trapped in her chest for so long. She pushed back and placed her palm over his heart, feeling it pounding hard, proving this was real.

He lifted his hand and rested it beside hers.

Confirming the same.

Between their thumbs and forefingers, scars marked their flesh, needled in place when they were children, forming the jagged rays of a sun.

Half on his, half on hers.

She pushed her hand closer, forming the full countenance of the sun and the promise it represented.

She stared up into eyes as familiar as her own.

"I found you."

56

AFTER CROSSING THREE leagues of endless dunes, Graylin's eyes ached. He bowed under the pound of the Father Above. The heat had melted his rear into the saddle. Each breath burned his lungs.

While their path south had mostly led through shadows, there were times, like now, when they were forced out into the open. The sun, unrelenting and merciless, hammered at his will, his stamina, and baked the marrow of his bones.

He rode atop an ürsyn called Fasl, with a rider who had finally offered his name—Irquan—in a rite that apparently had to be done in the open, when the spirit of a name could be laid bare.

Vikas suffered the same as Graylin. She had finally relented and packed away her heavier gear, including her broadsword. Arryn offered her a desert shawl to wrap her body and face. In the end, it had required *two* to cover her large form.

On Graylin's other side, Esme had switched ürsyns to ride with her brother, clearly wanting as little distance between them as possible. The pair talked and clung to one another, sometimes laughing, sometimes whispering in somber tones. Though they spoke Chanaryn, it was clear from Arryn's mix of worry and disbelief that Esme had shared her story—along with their own.

This was also evident as Arryn glanced to the sickle of the moon, which sat on the horizon as if afraid of challenging the fiery countenance of the Father Above.

Behind their group, Kalder followed, doing his best to keep his paws along the path of the ürsyns, where their massive claws churned up cooler sand.

Still, the journey taxed the vargr's stamina.

Even Crikit had stopped racing hither and yon and stuck next to Kalder, the two slowly finding common ground, one born of exhaustion.

As Graylin faced back around, a leather bladder of water got tossed to him from another rider. He caught it, took a long draw from it, and handed it to Irquan. The bladder, one of many, never stopped moving across the train of beasts and riders, passing in a continual ceremony. Esme had shared an explanation. This ritual of distributing the water, of having it continually moving among them, represented a communal bonding, an expression of a hardship shared and the responsibility each member had for his neighbor.

Graylin, however, was ready for this particular *hardship* to end. He searched for any evidence they were nearing a desert village. But as they traveled farther south, the dunes rose ever higher, blocking the view, climbing as high as castles. Sand blew in streams off those ridges, like grainy banners waving from towering parapets.

With this thought in his head, while cresting the shoulder of a dune, he spotted flags off in the distance. They sprouted from a collection of rolling hilltops. He rubbed his eyes, trying to erase the mirage. But those banners—a featureless red that blended with the sand—persisted.

Arryn called over and pointed toward them. "Tosgon beckons!"

Graylin shifted higher. He spotted nothing but those flags. No stone homes, no trails of smoke from hearths. He turned to Esme's brother. "Do your people live beneath the sands?"

Arryn had shed enough of his headscarf to show a wide smile. *"Pass e vede,"* he intoned.

Graylin groaned. He had learned that Chanaryn phrase while traveling. It was more of an expression than an answer, an adherence to a principle of desert patience.

Wait and see.

Arryn had offered that same response to many of Graylin's earlier questions, even queries from Esme about her brother's past. While Arryn was eager to hear their story, he seemed reluctant to share his own, or the story of these people and this strange place.

Graylin glanced to the north.

Or about the Dragon in their midst.

Apparently, all answers awaited them in Tosgon.

In the meantime, Graylin had his own dragon to attend. Arryn had warned that their large ship had to be hidden. While the sun's glare off the black sea might mask the *Fyredragon* for a short time, it would eventually be spotted. Arryn had recommended that their ship travel to these dune fields—a land called Ghödlökh—where the *Fyredragon* could be moored within the towering hills, out of direct sight of that dire mountain.

Darant aimed to do just that. To the east, Graylin could discern a vague outline of the *Fyredragon* through the glare. Its dark shadow drifted low. Darant rarely engaged its forges, heeding Arryn's advice in this regard, too.

By now, Nyx and Daal had returned to the ship, after ferrying messages back and forth, the two serving as the world's largest skrycrows. Exhausted from these efforts, their mounts needed to rest and had earned a reprieve from the searing heat.

Graylin also knew that Fenn was keeping an eye on their small caravan through his farscope, tracking them from afar. At the same time, Krysh watched the mountain for any evidence that the Dragon had woken up.

So far, that smoking beast continued to sleep.

Still, one of the ferried messages from the ship continued to disturb him. The army guarding the Dragon seemed capable of flight. A few *ta'wyn* had been spotted whisking about the black flanks of the mountain, like bronze fireflits in the dark.

While Arryn had confirmed such a miracle, any further inquiry about the *ta'wyn* had been answered with the same glib response: *Pass e vede.*

AFTER A FINAL burning slog, the train of beasts and riders descended a steep valley. It lay between two massive dunes, which shadowed the sands. From the ridges' crests, banners flapped. Dust and grains blew across the valley, shielding the sky with a haze.

Graylin peered below. Barely discernible in the depths of the shade was a tall arched entrance, pinched at the top, framed by rock, and supported by a porch of the same stone. Small slits pierced the dune's flanks, sealed in thin sheets of black glass. They likely marked sentry posts.

Graylin understood this necessity. He returned his attention to the sky, searching for any bronze arrows scudding across the blue expanse.

As they descended into the valley, Graylin asked Arryn a question. "While your village looks well hidden, don't those flags reveal your location?"

"To the *täwee?*" Arryn asked, using the Chanrë word for the *ta'wyn*, which clearly proved these desert dwellers had learned enough about their bronze neighbors to know that name.

"Yes," Graylin said. "Don't you fear them discovering you?"

"Ah, they already know we're here. We bury ourselves from the sun, not the *täwee.*"

"I don't understand. The crew of my ship saw people working with the *ta'wyn*. Are they not from Tosgon?"

Arryn looked grim, clearly reluctant to answer. Graylin expected the man's usual response of *Pass e vede,* but Arryn finally spoke. "While those slaves are our people, they're not necessarily from Tosgon. The Chanrë have a scatter of smaller villages, along with hunting camps. To sustain us, we often have to journey far from Tosgon, treks that can take many days. People are often caught out in the open and dragged to Khagarsan."

"Khagarsan?"

Esme, seated behind her brother, answered, "It's their name for the Dragon of Black Glass."

Graylin nodded. "But if the *ta'wyn* know of your main village, why have they not attacked it? Destroyed this place?"

Arryn glanced over. "They have raided it, but only rarely. Only when they're desperate for more slaves. Even then, they only take handfuls. As to destroying us, we pose no threat to them. And they need a regular supply of slaves to work for them."

Graylin grimaced at this. The *ta'wyn* were using these people like breeding stock. If they wiped them out, then those bastards would lose their steady supply of laborers.

Still, this raised another question.

"Why have they raided Tosgon so infrequently? Why bother scouring the desert for stragglers? Couldn't they simply come straight here?"

Arryn turned to the sky. "To venture this far south from Khagarsan poses a risk to them. So they keep away."

"What risk?"

Arryn sighed as they reached the bottom of the valley, then lifted his palms. *"Pass e vede."*

Graylin frowned but stayed quiet, too exhausted to argue.

Around them, riders rolled smoothly off their mounts. Graylin simply fell, finding his inner thighs had cramped up. He walked a few steps to loosen his legs. Vikas and Esme fared better, but they were decades younger than him.

Kalder crossed over, brushing Graylin's leg in greeting. The vargr panted heavily, his tongue lolling far from the side of his muzzle. Still, he kept close watch on the new surroundings with his tufted ears held high.

Graylin waited as saddles and blankets were stripped from the ürsyns. The beasts showed little exhaustion, bouncing on their front legs, excited to be back. Once freed, they bounded away. Some scruffled into low dens. Others bumped merrily against one another. Most simply struck the sides of the dunes, rolled heavily, and buried themselves into the cooler sands, vanishing away.

Arryn waved Graylin toward the towering entrance. "We'll watch for your ship. Let you know when it arrives. Until then, I imagine you and your friends would like a bath to wash away the trail."

While Graylin had hundreds of questions, the thought of soaking his sore body drained them all away. Plus, he knew if he pressed Arryn that he'd get the same infernal answer: *Pass e vede.*

Vikas also looked spent. They all needed to regather themselves. Questions could wait for now.

Arryn led their group, even Kalder, across the threshold. They pushed through the drape of a heavy blanket, a tapestry embroidered with figures and images that likely spoke to the history of these people.

Once inside, a cavernous space opened, with a floor that sloped steeply downward. Graylin gaped around him. He had expected a low-roofed rabbit warren
of a digging. Instead, the walls curved up in seamless, sinuous lines, without
a sharp corner or angle anywhere. He also failed to spot any bricks or mortar.
The graceful smoothness made the place look as if it had grown straight out
of the sand.

Ahead, tunnels branched off in many directions, hinting at the breadth of
the place. This was also suggested from the number of people hurrying about
or talking in clusters, including scores of children. All wore loose robes rather
than the shrouded wrappings. Many faces stared toward the strangers, but the
villagers kept a respectful distance—though maybe that was due to the vargr
padding alongside them.

As they crossed the entrance hall, Graylin noted other details: the many
stone lanterns hanging from woven cords, the slight chill to the air, the faint
whiff of a sweet spiciness. But what struck him the most was a soft rumble,
almost soothing, as if the god who had sculpted this place snored deep below.

Vikas heard it, too, pointing to an ear and rolling her palm inquisitively.
"*What is that noise?*"

Graylin posed that same question to Arryn, expecting to be rebuffed.

But Arryn answered. "It is the *Flüst* of Tosgon."

"Its *Whisper*," Esme explained, which clarified nothing.

Arryn cast his arm wide, encompassing not just the village but also the surrounding lands. "The dunes of Ghödlökh are like the waves of a sea. They are
pushed continually east by the winds, moving slowly but inexorably. Because
of that, Tosgon must roll with them."

"Your village *moves?*" Graylin scoffed. "It's carried with the sands? How?"

Arryn shrugged. "I cannot truly say, nor can anyone here. Answers lie far
back in Chanrë history, where there are allusions to strange alchymies, of gifts
granted to the first of these people."

"From whom?"

Arryn took a deep breath, then let it out without answering.

Graylin knew *what* the man was trying not to say.

Pass e vede.

By now, they had reached one of the many tunnels. Another of the Chanrë
rushed to Arryn's side. It took a moment for Graylin to recognize Irquan, the
rider who had carried him across the desert. The man had unwrapped his
head, revealing a countenance weathered to black granite, etched by a scruff
of silver beard.

The two spoke in low tones.

Arryn finally nodded and turned to Graylin. "Your ship has reached the edge of Ghödlökh. I must ready my people to lead them in." He pointed to his companion. "Irquan will take you down to the baths. You'll have your choice. From steaming pools to those that are welcomingly cool."

"You have that much water?"

Arryn shrugged. "You saw Köös Nuur. That lake is but a small wellspring of a vast aquifer deep under these sands. Many centuries ago, according to Chanrë history, Tosgon lay in the shadow of the Örgös forest, but the relentless roll of the dunes slowly drifted the village away. We may eventually be dumped out onto the Shil'nurr Plains, that great black sea."

Esme cast Graylin a worried look.

Her brother noted it and understood. "Though if your fears prove true, about the moon, we may not live to see that happen. Until then, Tosgon continues to ride atop that aquifer, so fear not about a lack of water. Once your ship arrives, we can even refill your tanks. To attend to that, I must be off to ready everyone."

Esme stopped her brother by grabbing his arm. "I'm coming with you."

"Esme . . ."

She held her ground. "You refused me in the past, and it cost us four years."

Arryn smiled. "I forgot how stubborn you can be." He scooped her closer. "So, yes, come, but I must address another matter first."

Graylin didn't bother asking what that might be. He stared down the lantern-lit tunnel, drawn by the promise below.

A bath first, questions later.

Still, he knew he could not tolerate *Pass e vede* much longer. As he descended, he listened to the *Flüst* of Tosgon. To his ears, to his heart, that soft rumbling was no *whisper*.

But a warning.

57

ESME KEPT A firm hold on her brother's hand—though her grip was less about keeping him close and more about not getting lost. Arryn had led her far underground. Each passageway tunneled deeper, crisscrossing others, forming a confounding, sinuous labyrinth.

Even Crikit, who clattered behind them, danced in occasional circles as if trying to get his bearings.

"How huge is this place?" she finally asked. "It's more like a buried maze than a village."

"True," he admitted. "By my reckoning, Tosgon is about a half league across and nearly as deep."

"That large?" Esme tripped a step in shock, then collected herself. She decided it was time to challenge him with a more important question, one he had avoided until now. "Arryn, tell me. How did you come to be here? Why didn't you ever return?"

She felt him pull away, but she squeezed his hand harder.

"Answer me," she pressed him, refusing to let this go.

He finally sighed, his shoulders sagging. "I don't like to talk about it." *Clearly.*

"It's a grim tale that weighs on my heart even now." He turned his gaze aside, as if in shame. "When I left four years ago, I had no intention of being gone for so long. You must know that."

"I do—but go on. After the slavers attacked our clan, you left for the deep desert. With a small clutch of the god-bound, including your mentor, Aeldryn Tann. You all sought guidance that could only be found in the deepest sands. But none of you returned. Did any of the others survive? Are they here, too?"

Her brother's shoulders sagged deeper, bowing his back. "They are not. Though, as far as I know, they might still be alive."

"What do you mean?"

Arryn gave a small shake of his head, as if refusing to return to that time, but he did. "During our sojourn, we traveled west into the desert for six months. Aeldryn Tann believed any answers to the fate of our clan could only be found at the farthest reaches of the Chanaryn lands. But eventually, our water ran low. We grew plagued by mirages and phantasms. Still, Tann urged us onward. As sunblinded as he was, I should have forced him back. But Tann said he heard a golden song whispering to him from the deeper desert. It called to him, demanding he continue this holy journey."

Esme wondered if the shaman's blindness, coupled with a trace of bridle-song, had allowed him to perceive an inkling of what lay beyond the farthest reaches of the Chanaryn territory.

Is that what called to him?

Arryn continued, "Then we stumbled upon a deep wellspring that allowed us to replenish our water. Tann took this as a sign, but now I fear it was only luck—which in this case, proved to be *neey augurani*."

She winced.

Bad luck.

"We traveled another two months," Arryn said dourly. "Then as our water started to dry out again, we came upon a small party of Chanrë hunters. They saved us and led us back to these lands."

Her brother's breath grew harsher. "But we weren't saved. As we slept in a small cave at the base of a high cliff, strange noises woke me. It sounded like rocks hitting the sand. Fearing a collapse, I rushed outside and found the desert studded with glowing bronze statues. Another landed out of the sky, striking the ground hard."

"The *tāwee*," she murmured, using the Chanrë word for *ta'wyn*.

"I didn't know if they were gods or daemons. Still, I fled in terror, hiding in a cluster of boulders. The *tāwee* stormed into the cave. I heard screams, shouts, cries of agony."

Arryn turned to her with glazed eyes. "Still, I . . . I stayed hidden."

Esme reached to her brother's arm, but he pulled away.

"The others were dragged out, too bloodied to resist. Then . . . Then they pulled Aeldryn Tann into view. In his blindness, he struggled to understand, beseeching with prayers. One of the *tāwee* leaned closer, as if listening, but I suspect it was only to examine the shaman's cloudy eyes. A moment later, the old man was lifted to his feet by his throat. With fiery strength, the *tāwee* ripped Tann's head from his shoulders and tossed his body aside."

Arryn staggered a step at this horrific memory.

Esme could guess what had motivated that heartless act. The *ta'wyn* needed laborers. The shaman had been judged to be too old, too enfeebled, and of no use to leave behind as breeding stock. So they had callously removed this burden from the desert.

"They took everyone else." Arryn turned and gripped Esme's arm. "And I stayed hidden."

The agony of that choice plagued him.

"There was nothing you could have done," she said softly.

"Better I had died trying."

"No," she said firmly. "A useless death is not bravery."

He waved this off.

She tried to shift the conversation slightly, while wanting answers. "What became of the others? You said they might still be alive."

Her question only seemed to agonize Arryn even more.

"I pray they are not. On rare occasions, the Chanrë have recovered one of their own. I witnessed one such woman, who was more skeleton than flesh. Whatever the *täwee* do to their prey, it leaves them empty and lifeless, as if waiting for some instruction to move. Still, if you look deep into those sunken eyes, some spark remains, trapped in that shell."

Esme had to force herself to ask her next question. "What happened to the rescued woman?"

Arryn gave her a hard look. "It was no *rescue*. She was taken into the desert, and her throat was cut. It was all we could offer her. The mercy of death. But the men I abandoned in the desert . . ."

Arryn shook his head.

Esme began to understand why her brother had never tried to make his way back home. Even if it had been possible, guilt anchored him here.

"Someday I must grant them the same mercy," Arryn whispered. "To make up for my cowardice."

Esme tried to console her brother again, but he rebuffed her.

"I don't wish to talk about it any further."

She didn't press him. They continued on in silence. The only noise was the shuffle of their sandals across the smooth stone and the clatter of Crikit's legs.

Still, her brother slowly collected himself. His shoulders drew back, his back straightening. He started to move more quickly, as if escaping the story behind him—or maybe it was the pull of what lay ahead.

They had crossed hundreds of doorways, sealed by blankets.

But he drew toward one.

Upon reaching it, he parted the drape. From inside, someone scolded him, but a joyous eruption followed next, a merriment that pushed back the grimness.

Arryn dropped to a knee, his arms held out.

A barefoot child barreled out and leaped into his arms. "Papa!"

Esme stiffened in surprise.

Papa?

Arryn stood and carried aloft the giggling child. A woman appeared at the doorway. She was striking, with shining skin, long curls of oiled hair, and beautiful lashes. She was especially glowing as she rested her palm atop a prominent belly, her other hand supporting her back.

The woman eyed Esme up and down, perhaps believing she might be a rival to Arryn's affection.

Arryn banished this concern by pulling the woman closer with his free arm, then introduced them. "This is my heart-bound, Yazmyn." He hiked the child higher. "And my daughter, Asha."

Esme's eyes widened as she swallowed down tears.

"Asha?"

Arryn nodded.

It had been their mother's name.

Arryn placed his palm atop the full belly of his heart-bound. "I'm hoping for a boy."

Esme understood what he implied, a way to honor their father, too.

She whispered a single pronouncement, *"Kash'met . . ."*

It was the Chanaryn word for the ceaseless turn of life: the shifting of seasons, the changing faces of the moon, the circular scrabble of the fiery molag god, Pecche'kan, in the sky. But more importantly, it addressed the rolling of one generation into another.

Esme read the simple joy of *kash'met* in her brother's face.

As she stared at his happiness, she realized Arryn had not remained in these lands solely to mete out mercy for past faults.

But also in hope for a better future.

Recognizing this, Esme intended to do everything she could, expend all her strength, give all her blood, to make that dream come true.

Even if I have to fight a Dragon.

58

As Nyx climbed the steep dune, she turned her back on the *Fyredragon*.

Shouts and orders echoed behind her, rising from the crew as they secured the ship to its new berth. Mooring cables had been shot deep into the sandbanks that sheltered the massive vessel. Darant had been in a sour mood after the tense flight to this spot near the village of Tosgon. He looked somewhat relieved after their giant gasbag sank below the towering ridgelines.

To further temper his fears, he had posted spotters atop the ridges, armed with farscopes, along with runners to relay messages. If any bronze storm swept out from that black mountain, he needed enough warning to get the *Fyredragon* back in the air.

Though, considering the new aerial talent of the *ta'wyn*, that might not be enough. For that reason, Daal had remained behind, to rally his raash'ke crew if a fight in the air proved necessary.

Nyx regretted leaving Bashaliia behind, too, but they had dared not spook these potential new allies. While scaling the dune, she passed many clusters of the Chanrë people, who had camped on the slope to watch the descent of the ship. Others had tried to assist, but considering the expertise of the crew, they mostly got in the way. Still, she watched a team of villagers helping to drag the ship's siphoning hose over the dune. The plan was to haul it down to the aquifer beneath Tosgon—if the hose could stretch that far.

But that was not the *font* that most interested Nyx.

A bell ago, Graylin had dispatched word of a gathering in the underground village, where she hoped to tap into the knowledge of the Chanrë people.

She had not come alone in this purpose.

To her left, Jace scaled alongside Krysh. Both men's eyes shone with an avid interest in everything. Jace stopped to watch a volcano of ants erupting from the sand. A Chanrë guide warned him off with a harsh scolding, pushing him away.

On her right, Rhaif led Shiya. She walked fully clothed, including gloves and a heavy cloak with a draping cowl. Graylin had asked them to bring the *ta'wyn* woman to the gathering, to help prove their story. It had taken the sight of this bronze miracle to convince Esme of the truth of moonfall. But the Chanrë people had lived all their lives with the *ta'wyn*, a menace as unvarying as the burning sun. Knowing that enmity, Nyx had recommended that Shiya be kept covered until they reached the others.

Yet some of the onlookers still eyed Shiya with suspicion, as if sensing the weight of bronze hidden beneath the cloak. This might have been evident from the deep tracks the heavy woman left in her wake.

Finally, the group reached the dune's crest and made better progress down. Though every step sent Nyx clumsily skating down the sand. She feared she might trigger an avalanche that would swamp them all.

Their guide, a thin woman named Abresh, proved herself to be far more masterful and dexterous. She glided down the sand as if it were ice, barely seeming to balance herself.

Once at the bottom, Abresh led them toward the village entrance.

Nyx noted more of those strange quilled beasts. One lay on her side, nursing a pair of prickly calves. Nearby, several men stood in clusters, smoking from a pipe that was passed around. Beyond them, women chattered and worked together to weave a blanket on a complicated loom.

This near-idyllic setting belied the danger of the Dragon. Then again, it was the same back home, where those living in the Mýr swamps ignored the mountain at its center: the volcanic Fist, home to thousands of venomous bats and where Bashaliia had been born. It seemed one eventually learned to accommodate a constant horror in their midst.

Abresh pulled aside a tapestry that closed off the village entrance and guided them inside. Jace gasped at the sculpted interior, while Krysh craned to take it all in. Rhaif simply squinted around, as if judging the worth of every detail. Only Shiya kept her gaze down, her face shadowed by her hood.

Abresh led them across a cavernous entrance hall and down a curving tunnel that wound into the depths. After a few more turns, she drew aside another heavy curtain. The chamber beyond was circular, with a roof carved into a smooth spiral that looked like the interior of a conch shell. A stone table sat in the middle, laden with a steaming array of fare that filled the space with a heady, spicy aroma. Nyx spotted flatbreads, grilled meats of some sort, beans as big around as her thumb, and many flagons of water.

Around the table, benches extended from the walls, looking grown out of the stone. Graylin had already arrived, along with Vikas and Esme. All looked freshly bathed with damp hair—even Kalder, who roamed the space, sniffing at the table. Crikit paced behind the vargr, as if hoping Kalder might nudge something off for them to share.

Opposite their group, a trio of Chanrë sat, conversing quietly. Another half dozen men stood in a semicircle behind them. From the array of weapons, Nyx guessed they were an elite guard.

While we've been welcomed here, the villagers clearly remain wary of us—and rightfully so.

Tosgon's momentary forbearance of them came about due to the man seated at the center of the Chanrë group. He stood as Nyx entered. She had no difficulty recognizing the family resemblance to Esme. Nyx had heard the story of her reunion with her brother. Nyx had also learned how Arryn had grown to be a respected member of these people. When he had vouched for their group, it had apparently carried great weight.

Still, this accommodating sentiment could change at any moment.

"Be welcome," Arryn said, and waved to the table. "We have much to discuss and many questions. From both sides of this feast."

The newcomers took their seats—except Shiya, who remained standing. The *ta'wyn* had stopped in front of a lantern, keeping her back to it. While its shine outlined her body from behind, it also shadowed her features.

Arryn motioned to the two seated beside him. "I've already shared the danger that spurred you all here. Of the threat of moonfall. This is Irquan, *hertmaester* of our hunters. And our village leader, Aelder Mirash."

The steel-faced hunter offered a bow of his head, while the Tosgon elder—an older woman—stared dispassionately. That one, Aelder Mirash, remained the trickiest to read. She had gray hair that looked nearly silver, with eyes that matched and a leathered complexion that made it difficult to guess her age.

Nyx suspected she would need to convince all three if she hoped to gain these people's trust.

Arryn continued, "I've also told them what you believe lies at the heart of Khagarsan, what you need to secure for any hope for the world."

"The second *turubya*," Nyx said.

Arryn nodded, but he looked skeptical. "I consulted with Mirash and a handful of our wisest elders. None have heard of anything like that hidden at Khagarsan. Then again, none of our stories tell of anyone going there and coming back. At least, not anyone still sound of mind and body."

Nyx heard a nick of pain in the man's voice at the end.

Still, he continued on. "So, you ask much of us. You want us to *risk* everything on supposition and belief. To stir the Dragon, which could bring ruin upon us all."

Nyx caught a look from Graylin, a sign he wanted her to respond, to make the next introduction, further proof that he had grown to see her as more than just a lost child.

Intent to not let him down, she cleared her throat and stood up. "Arryn, we understand your doubt. But we bring proof of our claims." She lifted a hand. "This is Shiya."

Upon this signal, the *ta'wyn* woman uncinched her robe and let it fall away, exposing the breadth of her bronze form. Shiya warmed it brighter, outshining the lantern behind her.

The huntmaster burst up, joining Arryn on his feet.

Behind them, the guards shifted in defensive postures. Several cast warding gestures of curled fingers, thrusting from foreheads toward Shiya.

Esme also stood up, speaking rapidly in Chanaryn. Nyx caught some of it, but Esme's calm tones and raised palms communicated her attempt to quell their outburst.

Arryn also tried to settle his group. Clearly his sister had already shared Shiya's story with him. Even so, he seemed to be losing this battle. Drawn by the commotion, more armed figures burst into the chamber.

Weapons bristled.

The shouting grew angrier.

Finally, a firm voice cut through the uproar.

"Eyow!" Aelder Mirash said sharply, pushing off the bench.

Arryn tried to help her up, but she shrugged him away and crossed around the table in wiry, sure steps. Nyx remembered Abresh gliding effortlessly down the face of the dune. This woman moved with the same leonine grace, full of power and balance.

While weapons remained raised, the guardsmen in the room quieted.

With a single finger, Mirash shifted aside a spear that blocked her path, then circled to confront Shiya. Even Rhaif stepped out of the elder's way.

Mirash eyed Shiya, both their faces equally aloof. The old woman reached a finger and traced Shiya's bronze jawline. When done, that finger trembled.

But not out of fear.

Mirash closed her eyes, her lips whispering in prayer.

Nyx eyed Esme, who shrugged, clearly lost.

The elder finally finished, then placed her palm on Shiya's chest. Keeping it there, Mirash turned to the gathering. Her eyes had welled up with tears, but they refused to fall. In such a hard woman, it was as if she had broken down sobbing.

"Sa et Dräshra," she said firmly, but with a slight tremulous awe. *"Dräshra r'nah."*

Upon these words, the guards fell back as if struck. Several dropped their spears. Four fell to their knees. One covered his face, as if unworthy to be seen.

Nyx again looked to Esme.

Esme answered, still plainly confused, "She's saying that Shiya is *Dräshra . . . Dräshra* returned."

Esme turned to her brother for clarification.

Arryn appeared as stunned as the rest.

"What is this *Dräshra?*" Nyx asked.

Arryn's brow knit with worry. "It means Breaker of Dragons."

59

As conversations continued to swirl, Nyx struggled to understand how Shiya could be given this dire-sounding title. She eyed the bronze woman, while Rhaif clung closer to her. Jace and Krysh had their heads bowed together.

By now, Arryn had shifted over to Mirash, drawing Irquan with him. The three spoke together. It grew heated, with many glances cast their way.

Arryn pointed to Shiya. *"Nee Dräshra."*

Mirash shook her head, her eyes gone hard again. *"Ye Dräshra."*

More words were exchanged, then Arryn finally relented, broke away, and waved for Nyx's group to huddle with him.

"What is it?" Rhaif asked. "Who do they think Shiya is? Who is this Breaker of Dragons?"

Arryn shook his head. "To answer that, you'll need to know more of our history, a history shared between the Chanrë and their nomadic descendants."

"The Chanaryn," Esme said. "Our people."

He nodded. "It concerns a thunderous battle across these lands. Some details have shifted like loose sand in the retelling, especially as our two peoples were separated by distance and time."

"What battle?" Graylin pressed him. "Does it tie to the great war among the *ta'wyn*?"

"I can't say," Arryn admitted. "I can only relate what our ancient sagas tell of the fight here. Lost in the mists of time, a fiery battle was waged, so heated and cataclysmic, it melted the sands to form the Shil'nurr Plains."

Nyx stared to the east. "The sea of black glass."

"It was fought over by an army of two gods. The forces of *Ravka*—bright gods with black hearts. And the *Kraena*—dark gods with gold hearts."

Nyx looked to Graylin. "Eligor's traitorous forces called themselves the *Revn-kree*. Which sounds very much like *Ravka*."

Rhaif nodded. "And their description—bright gods with black hearts—pretty much sums up that army out here. But what about the other force, the *Kraena*?"

Nyx looked to Esme's brother for any further details.

Arryn continued, "Both forces fought in the air above these lands, wielding dire weapons, until eventually the *Kraena* were defeated, their forces shattered, leaving these lands to the *Ravka,* to their cruel rule—which brings us to where we are now."

Graylin frowned. "What does this have to do with Shiya and some Breaker of Dragons?"

Arryn nodded. "The legends say the *Kraena* were helped by one of the *Ravka,* someone who broke away after growing to despise their depravities."

"A *ta'wyn* who changed allegiances?" Nyx asked. "That's this *Dräshra*?"

Arryn glanced to Shiya. "The legends say *Dräshra* came in the shape of a bronze warrior—a majestic woman. After the battle, the fate of *Dräshra* varies, depending on the story. Some say she was destroyed when the *Kraena* was shattered. Others that she survived and hides among the god's remnants, maddened and crazed by grief."

Arryn turned to Mirash, who continued a quiet dialogue with Irquan. "A few of the most devout believe *Dräshra* would rise again one day, to return to us and help us break free of the Dragon."

"But you clearly don't believe this," Nyx said.

Arryn shrugged. "I will not put my fate in the hands of prophecy. Nor the lives of those I love. Not again. I've come to trust the sand in my face and the burn on my cheek. Nothing else. Not divinations, not the whispers in the wind."

Nyx knew there was more to this story. From Esme's soft touch to her brother's arm, she knew this tale. Still, Nyx suspected there was something else fueling his skepticism.

Esme thought so, too. "What aren't you saying, Arryn? I could always tell when you're holding something back. You used to be god-bound. If you've turned your back on faith, what do you *face*? What is so powerful that makes you doubt your elders' beliefs?"

"The strength of claws against bronze. That's what I trust." Arryn turned to Graylin. "I told you before how the *täwee* rarely travel *south* of the Dragon. At least not far."

"Because of some risk to them."

Nyx stood straighter.

A risk? Could this be of use to us?

Arryn continued, "But there is no witchery or mysticism about this. We don't need *Dräshra* to save us. I've seen how vulnerable the *täwee* can be. I've seen them defeated—not by legends, but by strength of muscle and claw. That is what I put my trust behind." He pounded a fist on his chest. "Our strength. I've tried to convince others, but they remain unmoved, too fearful of stirring the Dragon's wrath."

By now, Jace was drawn in by these words, rising from the table after talking softly with Krysh for all this time. "You've seen the *ta'wyn* defeated? How and by what?"

Arryn took a deep breath. "You must understand. There are great predators who haunt our lands, true daemons of the desert. Much like the winged beasts with you."

"You're referring to the mankrae. The desert sand wraiths." Jace turned to Nyx. "They're clearly some form of bat. We've discussed this before. After learning of the Chanaryn legends of such creatures."

"That's right," Nyx said.

Jace continued, "We know similar colonies were seeded by the ancients, to be sentinels of flesh and memory, imbued richly with bridle-song, to help bind the colony into a whole."

"And forge their horde-minds," Nyx added.

Jace nodded. "These colonies exist in the Mýr swamps and out in the Frozen Wastes. So why not here?" He turned to Esme's brother. "Arryn, can you describe *how* these bats—these mankrae—attack the *ta'wyn*?"

"They always strike in the air. When the *täwee* are most vulnerable. The wraiths attack lightning fast, in packs of three or more. They come in screeching, which seems to confound their prey. I've seen it myself. The *täwee* writhe in the air, the bronze melting under that assault. Once their target is weakened, the mankrae dive in and tear it asunder."

Nyx had witnessed something like this before, in the Frozen Wastes. The Spider—a malleable Root—had melted under a barrage of bridle-song, unable to hold his bronze form when assaulted.

Arryn added a warning to his story. "But it's not just the *täwee* who are the mankrae's prey. The beasts kill many of our people, too."

"As do the Mýr bats of my home," Nyx said. "They'll kill any threat to their nests in the volcanic Fist."

"But Bashaliia's colony is of one mind," Jace reminded her. "I don't think that's true here."

"Why do you think that?" Graylin asked.

Jace pointed to Arryn. "He told us already."

Arryn scrunched his face. "I did?"

"From the legend you just shared."

Nyx understood, stepping back as if struck by the insight. "The *Kraena*—the dark god with gold hearts—they were the mankrae, only combined into one godlike mind, a powerful united force. When the *Revn-kree* arrived to seize the *turubya*, the colony fought back."

"Aided by a *ta'wyn* rebel," Graylin added.

"The *Dräshra*," Esme whispered.

Nyx continued, "But the bats lost that battle. Arryn told us they were *shattered*. From that description, it sounds like the horde-mind must have been destroyed, leaving only a loose colony of wild bats, striking out at anything."

Jace nodded. "Their attacks upon the *ta'wyn* in the air could just be territorial, but I wonder if there remains some trace memory of an old enmity that still burns in their hearts."

Graylin turned to Nyx, his eyes brighter. "If this is all true, could you reunite the colony, help establish a new horde-mind?"

"Like you did with the raash'ke," Jace added. "With such an ally, we might have a chance to lay siege upon the mountain."

Nyx bowed at the immensity of this task, at the impossibility.

"You've got it all wrong," she warned them. "Remember, I *didn't* reforge the raash'ke horde-mind. I helped *kill* it, to rid the colony of the poisoned taint of the Spider. It was the only way to free the raash'ke from the Spider's control. Only afterward could that mind rebuild—slowly and on its own. I had no part in that. Even still, it will take many decades, possibly generations, before even a rudimentary horde-mind reconstitutes in that colony."

Jace winced, plainly recognizing she was right.

She swung her gaze across the group. "How can we hope to do that here? We don't have the time, the knowledge, or the strength."

No one had an answer.

Except Esme.

"We must try," she said softly, looking at her brother. "If there's any hope for a future."

Nyx closed her eyes. She rubbed a finger between her brows. "You're right. Of course, you're right, but I don't see how we can do it."

"*Ell masha opaline wry sas,*" Esme intoned. "It's a Chanaryn phrase known to all nomads. *All trails start with a first step.*"

Arryn nodded. "It is usually followed by *Vas reech a'hen e yow teest.*"

Esme smiled. "Which warns, *Don't look too far ahead or you will trip.*"

Nyx nodded. "In other words, get moving and worry about everything else later."

Esme shrugged.

"All right, then let's do that," Nyx said. "Not like we have much choice. The first step on this road? To find where the mankrae nest."

Graylin turned to Arryn. "Do you know where that is?"

"Roughly. To the east. Directly across the glass sea from Tosgon. Where the cliffs of Samskrag crumble into the Evdersyn Heep, a labyrinth of mesas, ravines, and broken glass. But it's death to travel there, even without the threat of the mankrae."

Graylin turned to Nyx, leaving this decision to her, demonstrating his new-found trust.

"We go," she said, then nodded to Esme. "We take that first step."

"I'll help guide you," Arryn said, but he offered one further caution. "But the mankrae might not be the greatest danger found in the Heep. There may be one even more dire."

Jace frowned. "What is that?"

Arryn looked to Shiya. "I told you before about the stories concerning the fate of the Breaker of Dragons. Some claim *Dräshra* still lives out there, broken and crazed, hiding among the shattered remains of the *Kraena*—among those shredded shadows."

"Among the mankrae," Esme whispered.

Arryn nodded. "In the Heep."

"But I thought you put little stock in such legends," Nyx said.

"I didn't before now."

A commotion drew all eyes to the sweep of the blanket by the door. A Chanrë rushed through, speaking rapidly, carrying a scope in hand. Arryn and Irquan confronted him, challenging him.

"What's wrong?" Jace whispered.

Nyx suspected the answer.

Breathless and grim, Arryn returned with confirmation.

"The Dragon . . . it's waking up."

Arkival limne of
Ürsyns
(native to
the Barrens)

NINE

A STORM OF SILVER

In lyfe, a surprise kann be the sweet'st gift.
In battle, it is allesweis the werst.

—A quote attributable to Gryphon sy Knarl,
liege general of Far Freesland,
following his defeat at Ayrs Gorge

60

Kanthe leaned over the rail of the *Gryffin* and emptied his belly into the Bay of Promise. It seemed his second homecoming to the shores of Hálendii was proving no more illustrious than the first.

He wiped bile from his lips and pushed straighter, staring past the bow. While tension certainly contributed to his stomach's distress, he knew his queasiness was due far more to the storm-swept sea. Waves climbed all around the small two-masted ship. The vessel heaved up one frothing face, then down the other. The sails thrummed from the rainy gusts, and ropes snapped like whips.

Shouts rose behind him, but he ignored the handful of crew who fought the storm, led by a burly captain at the wheel who bellowed orders from atop the raised stern deck.

Kanthe kept his gaze fixed forward. Salt from the constant spray stung his windburned skin and coated his lips and tongue, which only added to his misery. Still, he clung tight to hold his position at the bow.

A chain of lightning shattered across the black clouds, followed immediately by a boom of thunder that shook the planks underfoot and rattled through him.

The jagged bolts flashed a brighter picture of the approaching docks of Azantiia—but it did not help much. Rain slashed from the sky, veiling the view. Dark clouds had lowered to nearly the height of their masts and smothered the city and sun.

Beyond the docks, the lower Nethers lay drowned in gloom. A few lights glowed there, looking forlorn and lost. Especially in the shadow of the Stormwall. The rampart rose as a dark cliff, lit on top by hundreds of bonfires that fought the downpour and fierce gusts. Past its parapets, sitting atop Azantiia's highest hill, the castle of Highmount blazed in the storm like a torch. Firepots and flames turned its stone to a ruddy gold.

Kanthe turned his attention to the castle walls that enclosed and protected Highmount. They cut in and out in jagged thrusts, forming a six-pointed sun, the sigil of the Massif royal family. Atop those walls, square towers rose higher, six at each outer point and six in the tucked corners of the sun.

Twelve in all . . .

As the *Gryffin* dropped into the gully between two waves, Kanthe clutched hard to the rail—with a hand of flesh and one of bronze. Then the ship shot back up and crested high, offering a view to both sides.

Kanthe tried to spot the other vessels in their tiny fleet. A flash of cooperative lightning helped. Six white sails bulged against the black water. The ships sped across the waves, riding up and down like a pod of panicked porpoises.

Six, and counting the Gryffin, *seven in all . . .*

The others matched Kanthe's ship in beam and keel. All bore two masts, the taller of which flapped with the Delftan flag, again using the disguise of a Hálendiian ally rushing to port with a supply of iron. Even their shape mimicked the squat, wide-bottomed barges of that land, perfect for hauling heavy cargo.

Unfortunately, such a cumbersome design was poorly suited for rough seas, especially carrying a particular sailor with a weak stomach. Another heave and rise of the *Gryffin* pushed Kanthe back over the rail. His stomach clenched hard, casting out a thin stream of bile, all that was left in his belly.

Once done, Kanthe rested his forehead against the rail.

"If you're weighing whether or not to throw yourself overboard, best decide quickly as we'll soon be at the docks."

Still staying bent before the rail, Kanthe glanced back past his shoulder, too miserable to speak, fearing all that would come out was more bile.

Rami frowned at him. The Klashean prince stood by an open hatch, fighting to hold its door from slamming in the wind. Behind him, the barge's deck stretched flat to the stern, which was raised only a few steps, where the captain manned the wheel. Another four of his crew scurried about, preparing for their approach to the port.

Rami waved to Kanthe. "Tykhan wants you below, to get ready for the fight to come."

The Klashean prince had already obeyed that command. He had donned underleathers, covered by light armor. He carried a sword sheathed at his hip and wore a sleeve of throwing knives at his wrists and ankles. Many times in the past, Rami had demonstrated his skill with those smaller blades.

Kanthe groaned and pushed off the rail. He wove drunkenly over to Rami across the rolling deck. His legs fared no better than his stomach in this raging sea.

Once Kanthe was close enough, Rami grabbed his arm to hold him steady. "My brother, maybe it's best you waited until this last moment to don your armor. One misstep and you'd be sinking to the bottom of the bay."

"I had another reason to hold off. A returning prince of Hálendii shouldn't make his debut with his armor splattered in bile." Kanthe shifted to the ladder with one hand on his stomach. "Though I can't promise that won't still happen. Especially since belowdecks is far worse than up here."

It was why he had escaped to the deck. He had hoped the fresh air would help, but the rising and falling of the waves only spun his head more.

Still, that was not the only reason he had hauled himself up here. Distant thunder and flashes rose to the south. He took one final look in that direction. Rami did, too, having noted his attention.

"The battle across the coast still rages," Rami noted. "It appears our forces are slowly making headway north. Or maybe my hope is only making it seem so."

"Best *hope* those losses are worth the distraction they afford," Kanthe said.

A shout from the captain and his pointed arm turned both men's eyes to the east. Flames burned along the low clouds, revealing a pair of long keels carving their way south. The bulk of the two warships was buried in the clouds, a risky endeavor with a bulging balloon full of volatile lift-gasses.

Kanthe scowled at their passage. "If the Klashean forces are making any headway, my brother intends to stop it."

Rami shrugged. "The more ships he sends, the better for us."

Three days ago, Kanthe's tiny fleet had left Kysalimri, setting off half a day before the main Klashean forces, racing with full sails, outrunning the others. Kanthe's barges had needed to reach the Bay of Promise well ahead of the Klashean main force, to let the ensuing battle draw all eyes. Unfortunately, the storm and rough seas had slowed Kanthe's ships. They had been leagues to the south of the bay when Hálendii's outposts had reported the Klashean forces sweeping toward them, buried in the storm.

After that, Kanthe had watched large contingents of Hálendiian ships flowing south, both through the storm and across the sea, to confront the incursion. Over the past four bells, those war fleets had surged south, filling the sky with flaming forges and feathering the stormy seas with billowing sails.

Luckily, little attention had been paid to the seven tiny barges flying the Delftan flag—until they had entered the bay.

Mikaen had set up a cordon of ships, including two massive warcraft that rocked like shining castles out of the black sea. A pair of their barges had been stopped, boarded, and inspected before being waved through. It had been a tense moment, but between the storm, the battering waves, and the heavy iron in their hold, no one had bothered to hunt for the secret doors that hid a score of men and weaponry. The only crew in view—like those on the deck now— wore Delftan insignia.

As Kanthe's barge approached the port, it swept by an anchored galley with its oars stored and its sails wrapped tight. A lone sailor atop the deck huddled under a lantern, looking as miserable as Kanthe felt.

"We're coming to the docks," Rami noted. "We must get ready."

Kanthe mounted the ladder. Past the bow, hundreds of ships had already hurried to port, crowding every berth and anchorage. They had all come seeking a safe harbor, fleeing both storm and battle.

The captain bellowed, "Reef the jib! Back the main sail!"

The crew hurried to obey, to slow their approach amidst the crowded waters. The other six ships followed suit, as expertly helmed as the *Gryffin*.

Kanthe headed below, too unnerved to watch their fleet maneuver through such tight quarters. Rami followed and slammed the hatch, muffling the storm.

"While you were feeding the fishes," Rami said as he jumped off the last rung, "several skrycrows were exchanged with Llyra. She has her numbers gathered not far from Highmount, waiting on us."

"Did she say how many? What sort of army has she roused out of her hard rabble?"

"She didn't give exact numbers. Only that she ran into an excited mob swarming out of Highmount, flowing from the tourney grounds."

"From Mikaen's grand fête."

They crossed down a narrow passageway lit by a single lantern. They had to walk single file with their heads bowed. The rocking ship knocked them both into the walls. As they went, Kanthe ran a hand along one side, not to keep upright but to feel for the concealed latch in the dim corridor.

"Llyra planted spies inside the castle's yard," Rami continued behind him. "They described a fiery god bursting like a new sun, in service to Mikaen."

Kanthe grimaced. "Eligor."

"No doubt."

"Then we're already too late."

"That was four bells ago. If your brother's drama changed any rebellious sentiment, it's not likely to have spread far, especially with the world dampened by this storm."

"I'm less worried about changing sentiment and more concerned about that *bursting of a new sun*."

Kanthe's fingers snagged into a hidden handle and pulled. A section of the planked wall swung open.

A voice called from inside, "That may serve us."

Tykhan stood only steps away, blocking the way inside. The *ta'wyn* had clearly overheard the last of their conversation and had likely been dwelling on that message from Llyra.

"How does that *serve* us?" Kanthe asked.

"From Llyra's description, Eligor expended considerable power. It will surely tax the smaller *schysm* he stole from me. Unfortunately, we can't tell how far along he's come at magnifying his strength. With enough time, he will use my *schysm* as a seed to regrow to full power. The question remains: How far has he gotten already? Still, any expenditure will leave him weaker, but by how much I cannot say."

Past Tykhan's shoulder, Kanthe eyed the sand dribbling through a glass fixed to a table inside. It marked how much time they had to act. The sand was set to run out when the last bell of Eventoll chimed across the city, marking when one day tipped into the next.

But Kanthe fretted about *another* passage of time. "How long will it take Eligor to restore what he expended at that fête?"

"Not long." Tykhan frowned. "So, we must act quickly if we hope to take advantage of his momentary weakness."

Rami pushed past Tykhan. "Then let's get our young Hálendiian prince into his armor. I've pulled everything out of hiding and stacked it inside."

Kanthe again felt a queasy turn of his stomach. This time it had nothing to do with the rolling of the ship. The *Gryffin* held a contingent of twenty Klashean knights. As did the other six ships. Even with Llyra's rabble of an army, it was an impossible task ahead of them.

Kanthe paused at the threshold of the secret door, glancing back to the bulk of the barge. "I wish we hadn't had to rush off. With more time and more men—"

"There's never enough of either—not in war, not in my bed. I had to leave those two Qaarens you foisted on me, the son and daughter of the land's envoy, under my bedcovers, neither of them satisfied, least of all me. So quit complaining."

Rami grabbed Kanthe's wrist and tugged him into the hidden chamber that filled the bow of the ship at its lowermost level. As he stumbled inside, Kanthe kept his gaze down, away from the view ahead, lest he truly get sick. Instead, he eyed the stack of underleathers and silver armor, a match to what Rami wore, only with a helm resting on top.

"At least you remembered to bring my crossbow," Kanthe said.

He noted the sheathed sword among the gear, too, a match to Rami's weapon. But Kanthe had little skill at swordplay. Deemed a second-born son, he had been forbidden to wield a blade, but those same dictates hadn't restricted him from hunting. Trained for years by a Cloudreach tracker, Kanthe had grown adept with all manner of bows, as skilled as Rami was with his knives.

Tykhan crossed past them and headed forward. He nodded to the flowing sand. "You must hurry, Prince Kanthe. We will have a short time to act once the last Eventoll bell rings out. And with what we know now about Eligor, we must move even more swiftly. What I built will have the best chance to work if he remains weak—that's if it works at all."

Tykhan glanced to a door that closed off a small workroom. From under the door's bottom, a blue light slowly dimmed and brightened.

Kanthe gritted his teeth, remembering when last he had seen that unusual glow. He again smelled the sulfurous stench of Malgard, flashing to the floating bells of that land's foul burning denizens, the *lycheens*. He pictured what had been discovered underground there: the wreckage of an *eyran,* the copper egg in which Tykhan had slept for millennia on end, until a *Revn-kree* had attacked him, tried to destroy him. Tykhan had survived, but he had left the *eyran's* beacon burning, blinking for another eternity. He had done so to hide the fact that he had survived, pretending he still slumbered there. The same beacon had lured Kanthe and his allies to that spot, only to find the copper egg empty and a trap. Before leaving, Kanthe had ripped out the device—a crystal box, cornered in copper and pulsing with a blue glow—and had taken it with him.

And lucky I did.

Tykhan had found a new use for it.

"Does the prince need a valet to help him dress?" Rami pressed Kanthe. "Or must I strip you down myself."

"I'll manage on my own."

Kanthe quickly shed his cloak, breeches, and shirt. As he stood bare-chested, stripped down to his smalls, the door swung open behind him. Frell entered with Cassta.

Bent over the pile of gear, Kanthe momentarily froze, feeling unduly exposed, especially with Cassta smiling at him in amusement. His face heated as he snatched the set of underleathers and began dressing.

"It is always good graces to knock," he muttered. "Even on a secret door."

"Sometimes you get the best surprises when you don't," Cassta said. "Maybe not for the receiver. I've killed four—no, *five*—men using that method."

Kanthe set about hooking together his underleathers.

Rami clapped him on the shoulder. "That's one way of catching her eye."

"Or her *quisl.* Like those four—no, *five*—men of hers."

He hurriedly finished donning the rest of his gear.

As he did, Frell reported to Tykhan. "Our contingent is readied in the other hold. I've told them what to expect, what we'll be facing."

"They'll need to off-load quickly."

"I warned them of the same."

"Is everyone off the upper deck?"

"They had better be."

Kanthe pulled a white surcoat over his light armor. The Hálendiian sun-and-crown had been stitched into it. While he had the full right to wear this as a prince of the Massif family, its true purpose was meant as a disguise. Everyone in the raiding party wore the same, to add to the confusion, to hopefully help mask their actions.

Still, speed offered the best cover.

He pulled his crossbow over his shoulder and surveyed the small group. The five of them had attempted to reach Eligor months ago—and failed miserably.

He watched the sand trickling through the glass.

Maybe we'll have better luck this time.

61

FRELL GRIPPED A leather strap that hung from the chamber's roof. By now, the *Gryffin* had come to a stop, rocking heavily in the sheltered harbor. He held his breath and watched the last grain of sand trickle down the glass. With his head cocked to the side, he listened. Outside, thunder boomed as if heralding what was to come, but that was not the signal he strained to hear.

Tykhan waited, too, standing by a tall lever.

Finally, a faint clanging rose in the distance, then grew louder as the last Eventoll bell rang across the city.

Tykhan glanced to him and the others. They all held fast to leather handgrips. He gave them a small nod and yanked the lever down.

As the bar struck home, the entire barge jolted hard. Frell lost his footing, but he tightened his hold on the leather grip to keep upright. A thunderous roar erupted under them, coming from midship. Frell's stomach slammed toward his bladder—as the barge shot straight up out of the harbor.

Past Tykhan, seawater drained from a curve of glass across the wide bow. Through the window, the glow of the port lights appeared in a dizzying twirl as the *Gryffin* shot upward, spinning slightly, rising on a pillar of fire. A massive forge-engine under the keel at midship howled its fury.

Beyond the window, another six columns of flames burned across the port, jetting from the other barges of their tiny fleet as they blasted upward. Neighboring ships caught fire below, the backwash of jetting flames lighting their masts like candles in the storm.

The port swiftly receded below.

As Frell fought to get his legs under him, Tykhan worked smaller levers and a main wheel. The controls were identical to those of a Klashean wingketch, a design upon which the *ta'wyn* had based these new vessels.

Last winter, Frell, Kanthe, and their allies had escaped Kysalimri aboard such a ship. Wingketches were found throughout the cramped towers of Kysalimri. They were moored in tight quarters—small courtyards, tiny squares, all open to the sky—and used as a swift means of escape when the city was threatened. The ketches would shoot straight upward, rising like a blast of smoke from a chimney, then ride off with the unfurling of tiny wings.

Based on such vessels, Tykhan had worked with both Wing Perash and Sail

Garryn to revise their design—to have them shoot out of *water* rather than from a stone chimney.

Tykhan dubbed these new ships *waveketches*. It was an example of *ta'wyn* ingenuity paired with Klashean design.

It had taken a heroic effort to get these ships built in the hidden harbor. But Tykhan was a Root of the *ta'wyn*. He had been designed for such labors: construction, mining, and other scut work. Even his moldable body served this effort, allowing a Root to craft a hand or limb into whatever tool was necessary. Yet Tykhan was unique, having walked the world for millennia after being prematurely ripped from his *eyran* shell. Over this span, he could not resist the urge to tinker, fabricate, and assemble. He had designed a handful of other unique crafts, like the drill-ship, the lampree, used last winter as a raiding vessel.

The waveketch was yet another of his designs.

But it was so much more.

As the port shrank below, Tykhan slowed their ascent, then pulled another lever. A boom rattled the barge—this time coming from above. Following suit, the other six ships did the same. Their upper decks shattered apart, casting off masts and sails. In their place, balloon fabric billowed out, then expanded with a whoosh of compressed lift-gasses into taut, sleek shapes. Such deployment had been stolen from the design of sailrafts used to evacuate wyndships.

The balloons caught the weight of the waveketches, easing the burden on the main forges. With them no longer having to carry the full weight, Tykhan manipulated a pedal to angle the flames to the stern. The *Gryffin* shot forward, rising at a steep angle. As it did, Frell watched small wings unfold to either side, a feature that granted the waveketches their nimble maneuverability.

And we'll need every bit of it.

ANXIOUS TO FACE the challenge ahead, Kanthe let go of his leather handgrip and stumbled over to Tykhan. With a rattle of armor, Rami followed. So did Cassta, who had still managed not to tinkle a single bell in her braid.

They flanked Tykhan but gave the *ta'wyn* space to work his controls. The next leg on this journey from Kysalimri was the most treacherous.

Ahead, the Stormwall rose like a storm-battered cliff.

The *Gryffin* had climbed swiftly enough to rise above its ramparts. Below, bonfires blazed amidst thousands of cannons and ballistas. Those installations were intended to fend off any attack by air, to fire forth a nonstop bombardment of iron balls and steel spears, to create an impenetrable deadly wall across the sky.

Before anything else could be done, their tiny fleet had to breach that barrier. Their plans counted on the forces deployed across the Stormwall to be
focused on the battle along the southern coast, for eyes to be looking that direction. They needed the imbedded legion to be slow to respond to the sudden
eruption of seven columns of fire from the port below, a supposedly protected
harbor cordoned off by warships.

The seven ketches angled to crest high above the wall, fighting rain and
wind, reaching the low clouds. The *Gryffin* rode through the maelstrom. It
ducked in and out of that black layer, erasing the view for breaths at a time,
while lightning flashed in fearsome fiery jags all around.

The Stormwall, while slow to stir, finally reacted. Cannons fired with flashes
of flames and spats of smoke, their booms lost to the thunder. Ballistas spat
steel at them. A huge arrow shot across their bow, spearing into the clouds.

Still, the sudden appearance of this strange threat, coupled by the speed of
the ketches, defied the forces below. All seven crested over and past the barricade.

"Hold tight!" Tykhan bellowed.

The *ta'wyn* shoved his wheel forward. The ketch tipped on its nose and dove
steeply down the far side of the Stormwall. Kanthe fell forward, catching a
palm against the glass. The city swelled under him, rushing toward him.

Kanthe was suddenly very happy to have thoroughly emptied his stomach.

Rain-lashed towers and rooftops filled the windows. Kanthe cringed back,
sure they would crash. Thunder boomed in warning. Tykhan hauled hard on
the wheel, lifting the nose as if doing so by sheer Root strength. The ketch
swooped, straining those outstretched wings, then shot low over the city.

Kanthe checked the other ships. Six flames blazed through the storm. All
had made it, though none had come as low as the *Gryffin*. Their small fleet
raced toward their goal, which blazed with firepots atop Azantiia's highest
hill. The other ships rolled away, spreading out for the assault to come.

Behind them, the force atop the Stormwall would lose time trying to swing
their batteries toward the city. Those cannons and ballistas had been aimed
outward and upward for generations. Even when those guns and bows got
pointed this way, caution would be taken. Any bombardment this direction
risked damaging the city, all in a futile attempt to knock down these seven
fiery fireflits.

Still, those hesitant commanders atop the Stormwall knew such a risk was
likely unnecessary. Highmount had its own munitions, bristling along its star-
shaped walls, bastioned across twelve towers. By now, the forces ahead had had
time to react, to ready a defense of the castle.

Kanthe stared at those twelve stone fortifications. "We really should have waited until Tykhan finished the entire fleet."

In their rush to depart Kysalimri, they'd had to abandon an additional five ketches, all in various states of build. The original plan had been to debark with *twelve*, one to assault each tower. With only seven, each ship would have to cover multiple strongholds.

"We had no choice," Rami said. "We could not risk Eligor gaining more strength."

"Even so," Tykhan commented in dire tones, "I do not know if what I crudely contrived out of my *eyran's* old beacon will do anything more than mask my presence."

Knowing Eligor was awake and capable of sensing the approach of another *ta'wyn*, Tykhan had tweaked the beacon to emanate a wash of tone that should blur out the area, making it harder to pinpoint their location, to hide Tykhan from the all-seeing eye of Eligor.

Or so we hope.

But that wasn't its sole purpose.

To test that, they first needed to deal with Highmount's defenses. The *Gryffin* raced the last of the distance toward the towering walls surrounding the castle. The other ketches spread wider, circling to attack from all directions, to harry each tower.

Cannons fired at them, but the seven ships made for hard targets, especially whisking back and forth on their tiny wings. The wind and rain added to their fleet's defense. But such protection would not last long, especially as the ketches attempted their own assault.

Any hope of victory depended on their own armaments.

Behind Kanthe, the cargo in the hold was not iron, but lead ingots sculpted to look like ore. Those piles rested atop hinged trapdoors. By now, the raging forges below should have heated that cargo. Kanthe swore he could smell the charring wood as that lead turned red hot. The load risked setting the ketches on fire, except beneath that thin skim of wood was a solid core of draft-iron.

In fact, the entire lower hull was crafted of the same. It was why the resources of Qaar Saur had been so vital to this effort. When the ketches were at sea, the low draft of the barges through the water hid the secret faces of the ketches: the glass-fronted bows, the iron hulls, the watertight sealed doors—and the true fangs of these vessels.

The *Gryffin* dodged the smoky passage of a cannonball. The ketch shot high over a tower. Tykhan yanked a red lever.

Kanthe saw the effect as another captain did the same. The ketch's trapdoor fell open under the stern, raining out hot lead, which fell through the trailing flames of the midship forge and turned to molten rain.

The fiery lead drenched the tower positioned at the point of the star-shaped wall, flooding across parapets and armored men, splashing into lower windows. The captain tried to reach the next tower—the one tucked into the crooked angle of the wall—but the rain of lead tapered off into dribbles by the time he reached it. The ketch shot out over the open yard and angled sharply to return.

With its belly exposed as it rounded through the air, Kanthe saw the ketch's fangs extend. Tiny hatches fell open along its flanks, and the noses of draft-iron cannons extended out of each. The ketch wove a tight turn, skidding through the air, bringing one flank to face the tower.

Cannons blasted, shattering into the stronghold.

Kanthe lost sight of the battle as the *Gryffin* finished its run across their section of the wall, leaving a fiery trail of molten lead behind it. Tykhan managed to flood the second tower more effectively, as he had reserved most of the *Gryffin*'s load for this stronghold.

Rather than extending its fangs and circling to battle, Tykhan bellowed a warning. "Grab hold! We're coming in hard!"

He rocked the ketch up on a wing, let it settle, then strangled the forge. The flames flaring across the open yard below snuffed away. The *Gryffin* dropped swiftly.

Kanthe stumbled back, lunged for one of the straps but missed it.

The ketch struck the ground with an impact that slammed Kanthe hard to the planks. His armor rang off the wood like a struck bell. He bounced once, then clattered back down. His forehead struck hard, spinning silvery specks across his vision.

Should've donned my helm.

It was not the most auspicious arrival for this prince of Hálendii.

Rami grabbed his arm and dragged him up. Kanthe staggered but quickly regained his bearings and his footing. Cassta joined them.

Beyond the window, silver-armored figures scattered around the landed ketch, having piled out of the stern hold, ready to defend the ship. While they wore Hálendiian liveries, they were fierce warriors of the Klashean Shield, bringing together the triumvirate of the empire's forces. The Wing and Sail had helped craft the waveketches, and the Shield would protect them.

Another of their fleet dropped out of the sky on a dwindling column of flame, then fell out of view as it aimed for a landing on the castle's far side. The plan was to divide the attention of the king's legions, which were already boiling out of barracks. The second ship had landed closest to the Legionary school, where a majority of the royal forces were encamped, to draw most attention that way.

The other five ketches would keep to the sky, offering support from the air and to continue to harangue the towers.

Still, the goal was not to seize the castle, only to hold these grounds long enough to attempt a raid. Only one goal mattered.

And it shone in bronze.

To aid in that endeavor, Frell helped Tykhan. The *ta'wyn* already had the workroom cubby open. A winking blue glow bathed his bronze. Frell crowded in there with him. When they both pushed back out, Tykhan carried the beacon's crystal cube at his chest. He held it by two copper handles welded to its sides.

Frell followed and adjusted the cords and straps over Tykhan's shoulders. They led to a humming contrivance slung across his back. It was a boxy network of copper tubing around a crystal tank that bubbled with a golden elixir. Tykhan had scavenged it out of his lampree. The *ta'wyn* device had helped power the drill-ship.

Only now it served a new function.

Tykhan twisted a metal valve at his shoulder and the beacon's blue blinking brightened into a steadier glow. He then draped his cloak over it to hide it.

"Ready?" Frell asked.

"We'll see," Tykhan answered, his eyes narrowed with concern, maybe even doubt, a rare sight in the former Augury of Qazen.

"Let's go," Rami urged them from the opposite side of the workroom.

The Klashean prince grabbed a handle, twisted it, and threw open a door. The hatch fell away from the hull and struck the hardpack of the yard, where pools trembled under the downpour.

Rami led the way out.

They all pounded out behind him, throwing themselves into the chaos of battle. The storm in the sky competed with the war on the ground. Thunder fought with cannon blasts. Lightning chased across the skies as lances of silver speared the clouds. Rain lashed and winds gusted.

Flaming ketches darted and flew through it all.

Closer at hand, Klashean Shields fought anyone who drew too near, who failed to recognize the disguised threat until too late. Mounted horses sped in the distance, aiming for the other landed craft.

Frell shouted and pointed to a narrow door, barely bigger than an arrowslit. "That way!"

The door led into a cookery. The entry had been mapped as the most expedient route down to the Shrivenkeep. The spies of the Eye of the Hidden had reported that the school of Kepenhill, which lay outside the castle walls, had been locked up tight after their prior excursion. Every access point in the school had been welded shut, barricaded, and guarded.

The only way left to reach the Shrivenkeep was through Highmount.

As they set off, using the cover of the battle to hide their escape, they brought with them an escort of eight Shields, led by a grand cross of the order named Gheel. Kanthe nodded to the towering commander, wishing they had brought an entire battalion. Still, all knew their best weapon remained speed and stealth. They needed to reach Eligor, subdue that bronze god, and abscond with him.

Each step would likely prove harder than the last.

To aid in this, to further divide the king's legions, their assault had one last phalanx. As Kanthe and the others sped past one of the wall's gates, fierce shouts and the clash of steel rose from beyond a massive iron portcullis that sealed the opening. Llyra's army had struck outside, laying siege to the castle grounds, further pulling forces away from the battle inside its wall.

And away from us.

Their group reached the door, which had been barred on the inside, but two of the Shields had hauled in axes. With strong backs and stronger determination, they broke through the ironwood. A hole opened enough for Tykhan to reach through and toss aside the bar. Grand Cross Gheel then shouldered the way open, sword raised, but no one confronted him.

With the way clear, one by one, they pushed through the narrow entry.

Kanthe glanced back to the battle outside, but he knew the true fight lay below. He took a deep breath and headed away, hoping to return here again.

With a bronze god in tow.

62

STANDING IN THE strategy room of the Blood'd Tower, Aalia read through a set of curled missives. They marked the first dispatches from the battle along the southern coast of Hálendii. The skrycrows flew swiftly, but the messages were still four or five bells old. Wing Perash and Sail Garryn had already related their contents. Still, she felt it her duty to read them, knowing the blood that had already been spilled.

As she did, she sighed at the grimness. The Wing had lost two warships and several smaller ships. The Sail had fared even worse, likely because the severe storm made a sea battle all the more treacherous.

And this is just the start of the conflict.

According to the messages, Hálendii had sent out a large portion of their forces by air and sea, to confront the challenge to their coast. No doubt King Mikaen had been stiffened to a manly hardness at this chance to clash with his enemy. Especially after his defeat last winter at the borders of Kysalimri. Afterward, there had been skirmishes, but this marked the first all-out battle.

Aalia knew Mikaen all too well. Diplomacy and the coddling of allies likely grated on the Hálendiian king. Blood and cannon fire fit his mood far better.

Still, despite the tragic losses, the draw of such a strong Hálendiian force was exactly what they had hoped, to lure as much strength from Highmount as possible, to better the chances of Kanthe and the others reaching Eligor. Their raid had been timed to the last bell of Eventoll.

Already, the first bell of the new day had rung out.

Fearful, she stared to the north.

How are they faring?

She anxiously awaited word, but it would take even longer for a skrycrow to fly from Azantiia. Her forces had been ordered to engage the enemy for half a day—if they could last that long. While she had full confidence, she still worried about what this bloodshed would cost in grief and loss. She prayed it proved to be worth so many lives.

She crossed back to her seat and sank down. Sail, Wing, and Shield gathered by the map along the curved wall that showed the Hálendiian coast, discussing strategy, scribbling down missives to send back to the ships. She knew she should engage them, but she trusted these men to handle any necessary details.

Plus, her heart weighed too heavily at the moment, anchoring her to the seat.

She had tried to get some sleep earlier in the day, but fears kept her awake. Tazar had joined her, allowing her to seek refuge in his arms, to allow her to be weak so she could be strong later. They had eventually found succor in more tender embraces. He had used his mouth and tongue to speak to her in ways that only lovers understood. It was more about reassuring than pleasuring.

She'd stolen his steel while atop him, her back arched, drawing that strength until he was spent. They'd lain together afterward, with him still inside her, sharing their heat as one.

In that moment, she'd needed to feel like a woman.

Not an empress.

By letting that responsibility briefly go, she was able to pick up the reins more firmly.

But is it enough?

A slight movement drew her from her reverie. She found the Eye of the Hidden staring askance at her, as if looking past her shoulder, but she felt the weight of his attention. One finger rested at his temple. She sensed he wished to speak but held off, perhaps judging whether she had spirit enough to hear what he wanted to share.

She answered that silent query. "What is it, Eye Hessen?"

The finger lowered, and his gaze fixed on her, its rheumy cast masking a sharp cunning. His every movement held meaning, each twitch of a muscle fiber, every slight pause between words.

He stared at her for a breath, dead silent, no movement at all. This worried her more than if he had stood up and pounded a fist on the table. When he finally spoke, it was in his usual rasp, but she somehow knew his words reached only her ears. Even Tazar, who sat on her other side, likely could not hear the Eye.

"My crows have been flying since the quake a day ago. The third rumbling in as many days. More and more clerics whisper of the wrath of the gods. Some look for blame beyond the waters of the Hresh Me to the imperial citadel. Unless addressed, it will grow worse."

"I'm not sure what more I can do. With the appearance of Prince Mareesh bending a knee, of swearing loyalty to the imperium and its empress, I had hoped that would quell some of the unrest."

"And while it did, it was not hard to take Mareesh's bended knee and twist it the other way. Hálendiian spies continue to work in the corners of the Eternal City where the shadow of my crows can't reach. They whisper that the return of Mareesh—the insurrectionist, the traitor—to the imperial fold only reinforces the blatant corruption of the current rule. And the gods rumble with anger because of it."

Aalia struggled for a solution, for a way to turn that growing tide.

A knock on the door cut through her worries.

She shifted straighter, expecting another raft of skrycrow messages. With the fighting engaged, flocks of birds would be continually winging back and forth.

A Paladin opened the door and allowed a familiar figure to enter. It was Chaaen Hrash, once bound to Aalia's father and now to her.

"Your Illustriousness," he said, dropping to a knee and offering a bow of his head. "I apologize for the intrusion during such a trying time."

She motioned him up. "Chaaen Hrash, you are always welcome, especially your counsel."

Her words were sincere. Hrash had been the oldest Chaaen bound to her father, serving as the former emperor's closest adviser and dearest friend. Aalia valued and appreciated his wisdom.

"I imagine your arrival suggests some urgency," Aalia noted. "Something you believe I must know right away."

"That is sadly true." He motioned to two others who hovered at the threshold. "This is Chaaen Magritte and Chaaen Laugyn."

She nodded to them. While Hrash was into his sixth decade, with a bald pate and a mask of wrinkles earned from years as imperial counselor, these two—a woman and a man—looked tens of years older. The two appeared as frail of limb as Eye Hessen, but they kept their backs straight and carried a collection of lengthy yellowed scrolls under their arms.

Aalia noted the woman, Magritte, wore the silver collar of a hieromonk. The other had an iron collar of alchymy that matched Hrash's.

"May we approach?" Hrash asked.

"Of course, but formality will slow this discourse. If you come with urgency, let our manner of talk reflect it."

"Thank you." Hrash crossed to the table, sidestepping around others, drawing the older pair of Chaaen with him. "With all that's happening, we've had a difficult time reaching you. Or we would've come sooner with our fears."

Aalia frowned. "That should never be the case. I'll make sure of it."

It was one of the unfortunate drawbacks in loosening the silver chains that bound such learned people to their *imri*. She had thirty-three Chaaen, all trained at the *Bad'i Chaa,* the House of Wisdom, but with these new freedoms afforded them, she had lost a measure of immediate and regular counsel.

"What do you wish me to know?" she pressed him.

He waved Magritte and Laugyn to the table. "It concerns the moon, Your Illustriousness."

Aalia's heart clenched between beats. All in this room knew about the threat of moonfall, as did all her Chaaen.

"What about the moon, Hrash?"

"I've spent considerable time of late at the astronicum at the *Bad'i Chaa*, studying the faces of the moon through the school's powerful lenses. Over the past three months, the edges of the moon have begun to shine with a reddish hue, more prominently when at its fullest. We believe the corresponding stronger tremors and quakes are related."

"By the pull of the moon as it nears?"

"Same as the surging tides." He gave a slight bow of his head. "As we've discussed before."

She motioned for him to continue, knowing this was not all he had come to report. Especially with his fellow Chaaen weighted down by scrolls.

Hrash stared down at the map of the Southern Klashe carved into the table. He shifted to one side of it. "For millennia on end, Kysalimri has been plagued by quakes. A suffering attributable to the wrath of the gods of the underworld, specifically the vengeful Menn'n. Across these ages, alchymists and hieromonks have recorded each tremor and shake in our respective archives."

Hrash leaned down to the table and drew a finger along the western edge of the Hyrg Scarp, the mountain range that split the land into two halves. "From our alchymical studies, by tracing these quakes and studying the terrain, we've known for many centuries of a massive rift in the Urth that traces the edges of the Scarp, running from north to south. Most of the upheavals that plague the Klashe rise out of that crack."

"Where it is said Menn'n resides," Magritte added.

Laugyn interjected, "Thus, both alchymists and hieromonks come to an agreement regarding the *source* of these quakes."

"But what bearing does this have on the empire?"

Hrash leaned farther out over the map. "There are hundreds of additional clefts that break from the Scarp's crack and spread westward."

He used his finger to scribe jagged lines from the mountains and through the breadth of the massive spread of the Eternal City.

Aalia stood and peered closer. "They cut under Kysalimri?"

"It's why we've suffered so many tremors over the passing millennia. Both alchymists and hieromonks have mapped where each one strikes and how often. It has allowed us to chart the path of those clefts. But more importantly, over such a long span of time, *patterns* have emerged. Patterns that have allowed us to somewhat track when one quake might lead to another."

Aalia could already guess where this was headed. "And you've detected some pattern to these recent quakes."

Hrash nodded and had Laugyn roll out a scroll across the table. It revealed a map, drawn in fresh ink. It approximated the one carved under it. Throughout the expanse of the city and surrounding lands were hundreds of small radiating crimson circles, each inscribed with blue lines and small numerical notations.

"These chart each tremor, shake, and quake over the past three months."

"So many?" Aalia's shock pushed her back to her seat. "I hadn't known."

No wonder the people of Kysalimri are so scared.

Hrash tried to assuage her guilt. "Most are very tiny, felt only in a small corner of our vast city. Still, a pattern has slowly emerged. One that has been recorded in the past."

He nodded to Magritte. The hieromonk carefully unrolled a yellowed scroll, cracked at its edges, with ink that had faded to wispy lines. Magritte held it open, fighting as the parchment's age tried to reroll it, as if to hide what was revealed.

Again, it was a map of the city, one more crudely sketched. Upon it were drawn similar circles and notations. Even Aalia could recognize they roughly mirrored what had been freshly inked on Laugyn's chart.

"That ancient map comes from the seventeenth imperial dynasty," Hrash explained. "From the rule of Emperor Gaius."

Aalia flinched. "No . . . you can't be suggesting . . ."

She shook her head, refusing to believe this. Still, she understood *why* Hrash had been so desperate to reach her. The reign of that emperor was known for one ghastly event, a tragedy so catastrophic that its pain echoed down through history. Scars still remained of that event, etched across the face of the Eternal City.

"The Cataclysm of Gaius," Aalia whispered.

Two millennia ago, a massive quake had shattered the city, opening vast chasms, lifting some sections, dropping others, toppling towers like a storm through saplings. Hundreds of thousands had died in the first quake, more from the tremors that followed. It had altered the shape of the Bay of the Blessed and cast huge waves that drowned a quarter of the city.

Aalia challenged Hrash. "You think the pattern of our quakes portends another cataclysm?"

The Chaaen looked to his companions, then faced her. "We do."

Aalia glanced to the Eye of the Hidden. His face looked dour, his lips drawn into tight lines. All knew the fate of Emperor Gaius. The tragedy had been blamed on Gaius's rule. In retribution, the populace rose up. The emperor had been gutted in his throne room, as was every one of his bloodline. Their entrails were strewn to thirty-three pyres, where they were burned as offerings to the Klashean pantheon. Thus ended the seventeenth imperial dynasty and heralded the eighteenth, giving rise to a new bloodline, one that distantly traced to her own.

Worried about the similar rumblings of her own people, Aalia returned her attention to Hrash. "If you're right, when might this happen?"

The Chaaen frowned at the old map. "According to historical records, the pattern in the past was slow in building. It took a decade for whatever tension was accruing to finally break forth and tear the land asunder."

"And what about now?" Aalia pressed him.

"The moon's pull. The worrisome rate of its crimson blushing as it draws closer. It's all building the same pattern much faster." Hrash winced at the two Chaaen. "We've done many calculations, leaning upon the resources of *Bad'i Chaa,* consulting with those we most trust, both for their knowledge and discretion."

"When?" Aalia stood up again. "When might this happen? A year? A month?"

Hrash looked down. "You won't have a month."

Aalia stared hard at him. "Then when?"

Hrash lifted his gaze, which shone with certainty. "Anytime now."

63

KANTHE HAD NEVER thought he'd get lost in his own home. Even Frell had to consult his map to discern the correct route down to the Shrivenkeep. While Highmount was not as impossibly large as Kysalimri's imperial citadel, the castle still sprawled across wings, courtyards, chapels, kitchens, and through hall after hall.

Their group's path had led *up* as often as it headed down. Reaching the Shrivenkeep required a circuitous course through the castle. Those they encountered gave them a wide berth, noting nothing beyond the clatter of silver armor, likely believing they were a clutch of knights rallying to the castle's defense.

All the while, the battle reached them through the brick and mortar. Muffled cannon blasts echoed. Or maybe it was thunder. By now, it was impossible to discern between the two. Each boom set Kanthe's heart to beating faster.

Frell paused again. They were buried far under the castle, deeper than its dungeons. They had crossed through a labyrinth of dank cellars, hurried past abandoned cisterns that smelled of mold and rat droppings, and now gathered in a bricked chamber filled with wine casks, each so dusty that this place had surely been long forgotten.

The heady aroma of fermenting fumes hung in the air, sweet and musky. Kanthe wondered how well the wine had aged. Even Rami eyed a barrel longingly. Fear and exhaustion had certainly dried Kanthe's mouth.

"It should be somewhere around here," Frell muttered, running a palm along one wall.

Cassta helped him, bowing up and down, then she straightened and dragged a finger along a thin line barely discernible between the bricks.

"Here," she hissed.

Frell moved over, searched, and pushed each brick. Finally, one gave way, releasing a hidden latch, and a door swung inward. Dark stairs wound downward.

"This should lead to the Shrivenkeep's antechamber," Frell said.

Gheel—the grand cross of their Shield contingent—lifted a lantern and took the lead. "We've lost too much time. We must move quickly."

Kanthe glanced back. Despite the tortuous route, their rushed pace had gotten them here in less than half a bell. Though stress had made it seem far longer.

Still, Gheel was correct.

We've wasted too much time as it is.

The team hurried down the steps, traveling one behind the other due to the narrowness of the winding stairs. Kanthe quickly grew dizzy. The sounds of battle faded behind him. All he could hear was the pounding of his heart and their many boots.

With Gheel holding aloft their only lantern, Kanthe noted the blue glow suffusing from under the drape of Tykhan's cloak. It flared brighter with each step that the *ta'wyn* took, as if blinking out a warning. Kanthe prayed the beacon continued to mask their approach.

Finally, they reached a door at the bottom of the stairs and bunched up in a row behind it.

Gheel looked for confirmation from Frell.

The alchymist pointed to a sigil inscribed in the door, of a book held in the fangs of the viper, the symbol of the Shrivenkeep. "The antechamber should be past this door."

Gheel tested the latch, found it unlocked, and eked the door open. He peered out the crack, then nodded. "All clear."

He led the way out into the domed obsidian chamber, its surfaces cut into thousands of facets. A pair of lowly lanterns lit the dark space, reflecting a wan glow across the room. A score of other doors lined the walls. To the right and left, Kanthe noted five or six entries had iron bars welded across them, marking those that must lead up to Kepenhill, closing off the path to the school.

Mikaen had clearly strangled access to the Shrivenkeep. In fact, Kanthe was surprised Mikaen hadn't sealed more doors.

Still, only *one* mattered. It lay directly ahead of them, flanked by those two lanterns. Frell fished out a large key and headed there.

"Hurry," Gheel urged, waving his men into a cordon around them.

Frell inserted his key, turned it, then frowned. He twisted it again. "The lock's been altered. The key won't work."

Gheel turned to one of his men. "Bring up your ax."

Kanthe shook his head. He knew this ironwood door, constructed of timbers, was far thicker than the one into the cookery. It would take forever to hack their way inside.

Mikaen had clearly taken this extra precaution.

Though, knowing my brother—

Kanthe stiffened and grabbed Frell and shoved Rami, trying to get everyone back to the door they had used to enter the antechamber.

But he was too late.

A resounding clang of a bell burst from behind the locked door, then was carried outward, reaching doors to either side. Alarms rang out from there, too, as those doors burst open. Knights—in silver armor that matched their own—poured into the room.

Kanthe now understood *why* Mikaen hadn't sealed all the doors. His brother had hoped to lure someone down there.

Into a trap.

Gheel and his men formed a shield around their group. But the Hálendiian legions were the least of their problems.

Behind the last knight, a tall shape bowed into the room, carrying a cape over his shoulders that did nothing to hide his nakedness—or his bronze.

In a breath, the figure blew brighter, shining like a lantern in the gloom.

FROM BEHIND THE Shields' cordon, Frell gaped at the sight before him.

Eligor strode into the room as royally as any sire. He stood a head taller than Tykhan. The curls of his hair and beard danced with fire. Cascading shimmers washed across his bronze, parting over a seam that split his chest, which shone even brighter, blindingly so. It appeared to be a peek at the very heart of this creation.

If Frell had known nothing about the *ta'wyn,* he still would have recognized a true sovereign of their kind. Frell quailed from the sheer majesty and power of this Kryst. His knees weakened, as if ready to bow in submission before this king.

Still, he forced down his awe, clinging to his scholarship, his curiosity troubled by a question.

Why is he here?

Eligor's presence made no sense.

Frell remembered the dispatch from Llyra's spies, how a golden sun had burst above the tourney yard. They had all thought that Eligor would have returned to the Shrivenkeep to rest and restoke his reserves after that dramatic blaze. But upon learning of the incursion by Klashean forces, Mikaen must have feared another attempt to breach the Shrivenkeep, so he had fortified this ambush.

But Frell believed this decision had not come solely from the king.

This became clearer as Eligor stepped forward and pointed at their group, one in particular. "Subdue the others. But the Root is mine."

Frell glanced at Tykhan. He remembered how Tykhan had feared his body and the strange alchymies within could be used as raw material to fully restore the Kryst to his full power.

That fiery desire still shone in Eligor's eyes.

Earlier, the Kryst must have sensed the flare of the beacon sweeping toward Highmount. While he could not discern the source's exact location, he—like Mikaen—knew any trespass would end up here. So, Eligor must have folded himself into this ambush in hopes of collecting the means to his resurrection.

To ensure this happened, the Hálendiian knights closed upon their group from all sides. In desperation, Gheel tossed his lantern at the nearest knight. It smashed against armor, flared brighter, then went dark. This rash act made the closest attackers pause, but that was not its true purpose. Two of Gheel's men swung their swords and shattered the remaining two lanterns on the wall.

Darkness swamped the space.

None of the ambushers had come with lamps, only with weapons in hand. A door had been left ajar, letting in some light. The only other source of brightness shone from the bronze lantern in their midst.

As broken glass tinkled on stone, Gheel and the others lunged forward. They used the darkness and momentary surprise to slash into the closest, dropping several. But their group was still outnumbered five to one. This ploy would only buy them time, not a means of escape.

Frell turned to Tykhan, praying it proved to be *enough* time.

Tykhan stepped forward, throwing aside his cloak, exposing the azure-violet glow of his crystal beacon. With one hand, he twisted a valve near his shoulder. With the other, he flipped up a copper shield across the front of the crystal cube. At the screen's center, a prismed crystal brightened.

As Tykhan kept turning the valve, the cube flared to a brilliant violet. The small tank strapped to his back bubbled fiercely with a golden hue. Eligor—who had been shoving forward, knocking combatants aside—paused warily.

And with good reason.

Out of the prism, a concentrated beam of violet fire burst forth from the beacon. It struck Eligor in the chest, at that rift down its center.

Eligor staggered back, a bellow of pain ripping from his throat.

Frell tried to imagine the strange alchemies being wrought inside. Tykhan had explained this design, one in which they had pinned all their hopes, one that had never been tested, only theorized.

Tykhan had carried his *schysm* across the world for millennia. During that time, he had not only tinkered with the design of new wyndships, he had also looked inward, to better understand himself.

How could he not?

He had a Root's innate curiosity about all manner of design—including his own.

As the battle raged, Tykhan kept his beam focused on Eligor. Step by step, he drew closer to his target.

Cassta and Rami flanked him, wielding knives in a storm of silver. Some blades were thrown, others stabbed. Some were poisoned, others not. Kanthe had dropped to a knee after whipping his crossbow to his shoulder. He fired into the fray, somehow able to discern friend from foe.

Still, every sword, blade, and bolt had one aim.

To protect Tykhan.

But will this effort prove for naught?

Down in the Shrivenkeep, when Tykhan had removed his *schysm,* it had not been the first time. In the past, he had done so to study its intricacies. After this long span of introspection, he had grown to understand its power better than even a Kryst. He had come to know its strengths—as well as its weaknesses.

He had leaned upon the latter when he had retooled his beacon. It was intended to do more than simply emit a diffusing wash. When brought to full power and concentrated through the right prism, the signal became a weapon, one uniquely attuned to his *schysm's* faults. Tykhan's goal here was not to reacquire what was stolen—but to *destroy* it.

The beam held the potential to shatter the *schysm,* hopefully doing more damage in the process. Either way, Tykhan was certain that the shock of such a sudden and violent obliteration would knock Eligor into a debilitating spell, hopefully long enough for them to abscond with him.

The plan had been foolhardy, reckless, but with moonfall threatening, it had to be risked.

One of the Hálendiian knights must have suspected this threat and raised a shield across that fiery beam, trying to protect their bronze king. But the beam was more vibration than light. It pierced through the steel as if it were not there.

Then a crossbow bolt struck the knight's helm, knocking man and shield out of the beam's path.

The two *ta'wyn* continued to wage a silent war. The effort took its toll on both. Eligor had fallen to a knee. The cleft in his chest had ripped wider, agony etched his face. Still, the Kryst's body glowed even brighter, fiery in its fierceness. Where steel had failed, those flames appeared to be working.

While caught by surprise, Eligor clearly rallied.

Tykhan could no longer advance, but he still held his ground with his shoulders hunched, his head low, as if trying to forge through a stiff headwind. Under that strain, his bronze softened and lost its fine details. As it melted, this bronze fanned away from where Eligor crouched, as if blown back by that same headwind.

Still, both *ta'wyn* locked gazes on one another, neither blinking nor turning away.

Early on, Tykhan had expressed one additional hope, a thin one. In this battle, with the two tied together by energies and frequencies beyond Frell's understanding, there might be a chance for Tykhan to commune with Eligor, to connect with the Kryst like Tykhan had done with the giant crystal *arkada* found hidden in the Abyssal Codex. With enough concentration, Tykhan believed he might gain some glancing knowledge of Eligor's plans, maybe a way to thwart him.

Still, that did not seem to be working—none of it did—and time was running thin.

Gheel had lost four men. Kanthe and the others had been driven into a tight knot. All were bloodied and gasping. Even worse, Hálendiian reinforcements poured into the chamber.

Kanthe drew Frell lower. "If you're going to act, now might be a good time."

Frell winced and reached to the satchel at his waist. His chymical weapon wasn't meant for close-quarter fighting. Still, he heeded Kanthe's admonition and slipped out a fist-sized leather-bound ball. He squeezed it hard, causing a flint to spark, then tossed the ball toward the flow of knights. He made sure he threw it well clear of the silent battle between Tykhan and Eligor.

Still, as the chymical bomb exploded, the blast deafened. Its fiery burst blinded all. Knights got thrown into the hard obsidian walls. The shock momentarily paused the battle.

Frell snatched another bomb.

As he lifted it, Kanthe touched his arm. "Hold off. Something's happening."

64

KANTHE WIPED BLOOD from his eye and drew Frell down. His gaze stayed fixed on the battle between Eligor and Tykhan.

The Kryst trembled like a reed in a wind, his lips drawn into a pained grimace.

"No!" The single word burst forth, booming louder than the blast.

His bronze body flared into a sun, shattering the obsidian under his knee. Kanthe threw his arms across his eyes. Knights fled back in terror. The blue beam, still shooting into the heart of the blaze, flashed brighter—then shot all that power like a cannonball back at its source.

It struck the crystal cube in Tykhan's hand and exploded. The *ta'wyn* got thrown back, his body melting under that backlash. The sun across the room collapsed to a darkness that seemed to suck the last of the light.

Tykhan struck the floor and skidded, leaving a trail of molten bronze, then settled into a pool of the same. He struggled to sit up, like a drowning man in a fiery sea. His form had been reduced to a slaggy outline of limbs and a head. Still, the *ta'wyn* fought, bringing around a face that had melted away, leaving only two shiny azure crystals, imbedded and seeping down.

Grief and sorrow shone there.

Kanthe rushed to his friend and dropped to his knees at the edge of the bronze pool, which spread in glowing waves of dissolution. An arm, a crude, smoldering branch, reached toward him as if asking to be pulled free. Those eyes flared with determination, maybe pain.

Kanthe reached for his hand—which had melted into a lumped fist of bronze. "Tykhan . . ."

Rami pulled Kanthe away. "We cannot stay."

Frell and Cassta rushed to his other side. "Eligor is down. Gone dark. The *schysm* in his chest must have been destroyed. Maybe damaging him further."

Gheel pushed closer with a warning. "The enemy's regrouping. We can't make it to the door we came in. But maybe another."

Kanthe fought against being pulled away. "If we leave Tykhan, they'll scavenge him, use him to make up for what we destroyed. It'll all be for nothing."

Frell pushed him farther into Rami's arms. "Tykhan knows what to do in this eventuality. We discussed this in private."

Kanthe glared at Frell, knowing what this must mean, and turned to Tykhan, the little that was left of him. His bronze had gone dull and cold. Those azure eyes stared with clear agony. In that gaze, Kanthe read the pleading, begging for Kanthe to listen to him one last time.

Tykhan's gaze flicked to the doors, then he pounded that raw fist into the pooled bronze. These last edges still glowed a ruddy orange, spreading in jagged peaks toward Kanthe, as if pointing toward those doors, too.

All of Tykhan's last efforts were clearly forged to one purpose, a final plea to a friend.

Go . . .

Tykhan and Kanthe had had this same argument before, down in the Shrivenkeep, when Eligor had possessed Tykhan. Kanthe had wanted to stay then, too, but his *ta'wyn* friend had warned him away.

That fist lifted again and struck weakly, then froze in place.

Go . . .

Kanthe had refused this demand before, but he knew he could not now.

"I'm sorry," Kanthe gasped, and allowed himself to be dragged off.

Frell scolded him as they all rushed across the chamber, away from the main clutch of Hálendiian knights. "Pray your sympathy hasn't bled him of his last energies. I fear he will need every bit of strength left to him."

Frell still had one of his bombs in hand. He squeezed a flash from it and tossed it toward the door ahead, toward the scatter of knights blocking that way.

The blast stung Kanthe's eyes, but he ran headlong into the blindness.

Behind them, Gheel and the last two of his men clashed as knights rushed after them.

Kanthe had taken just another five steps when a resounding blast shoved him forward. The flash burned his shadow in the wall ahead. A glance back showed knights smoldering under a wash of molten bronze. Others had been knocked flat.

Tykhan's body was gone.

Gheel rushed them onward. "Go! While we can!"

Cassta proved the fastest. She reached the door, yanked it open, and led the way. They fled up the dark steps, running blind, using outstretched arms to guide them. At the top of the stairs, they reached another door and shoved through it. Light welcomed them, revealing a dim, dusty librarie.

Sconces in the next hall drew them like a scatter of bloody moths.

"Do you know where we are?" Rami gasped to Kanthe.

He shrugged without slowing. "If we keep going, I'm sure I will eventually."

The booming of thunder and cannon blasts guided them. Still, running *toward* battle did not seem the soundest strategy, but that direction was their only hope of escape. If they failed to reach the *Gryffin* or another of the ketches, they could attempt to strike for Llyra and her rough army.

After some missteps and backtracking, they finally returned to the cookery wing. Its kitchens had long been abandoned. Scullery maids and spit-boys had wisely slipped to quieter corners, leaving matters of princes, kings, and falling moons to others.

The door to the yard still lay ajar after being bashed open earlier.

Gheel took the lead, limping on a leg that bled out of his armored greave. His face was awash in the same, flowing from under his helm. One of the remaining Shields followed him out, while the other guarded their rear.

It seemed like ages since they had entered the castle, but the second bell of the new day had rung out while they were escaping. So they had been gone no more than three-quarters of a bell.

Still, much had changed in that short time.

While lightning crackled across the bellies of dark clouds, the lashing rain had died down to a sullen drizzle. Outside the portcullis, the fierce fighting sounded both less intense and more brutal, more determined. Silver flashed out there among shadowy men as Llyra's army struggled to hold their ground. Higher up, the nearest towers smoked amidst a ruin of broken bricks and shattered parapets.

Kanthe failed to spot any trails of flames across the clouds. To the left, one of the ketches lay in fiery ruins. Yet to his right, the *Gryffin* stood tall. More Shields surrounded it, hopefully a sign that some men had escaped the wreckage of the other. Those last forces were engaged in a pitched battle amidst piles of bodies, both men and horses. The dead formed a barricade around the ketch.

"Can you get us there?" Frell asked Gheel.

"We must try." Gheel turned to them. "Stay low."

The Shield standing next to him should have heeded this warning. A bolt shattered through his skull, sending his body crashing to the side. Kanthe could not say if it had been shot by friend or enemy, such was the carnage and confusion.

Kanthe expected Gheel to force them inside, but clearly the tide of battle was turning—and not in their favor.

Gheel simply raised his shield. "Behind me. Move swiftly."

As they set off, the man behind them blew a warbling steel whistle. The wall of guardians around the *Gryffin* responded, spotting their tiny phalanx. Armored men, bloody and battered, surged toward them, forming two lines, creating a corridor to the ship. They used their bodies as their namesake, creating a shielded path back to the ketch.

Even before Kanthe and the others could reach them, the guardians fell to more bolts and arrows. A cannon fired from somewhere above, trenching a line through the muck, tearing the leg off a man.

Kanthe looked back for the source.

Flames burst into view above, lining the keel of a small Hálendiian warship as it rode over the castle and across the yard. More cannons fired from above, blasting mud, pummeling bodies.

The warship reached and swept over the *Gryffin*.

From hatches under its keel, dark barrels tumbled out. Gheel recognized the threat and pushed everyone back. But they were already too close. The bombs burst with chest-pounding blasts. Fire swept high, nearly reaching the height of the Hálendiian craft. The concussion threw them off their feet, sending them tumbling across the mud.

On the ground, Kanthe twisted toward the fiery wreckage, wreathed in oily smoke. The warship circled, intending to cause more ruin. Then a column of flames rose from beyond the wall, blasting a waveketch into view. The craft must have been riding low along the walls to set up this ambush. It shot over the top of the warship's balloon, skimming its surface, using its forge like a fiery knife. It burned a path across the fabric—then the gasses below ignited into a fireball.

Kanthe caught sight of the ketch getting caught in the blast.

It had been a suicide run, intended to protect those still on the ground. Gheel got everyone up and moving, ready to strike out for Llyra's army.

Kanthe needed no help gaining his legs. Fury fueled him. Knowing the sacrifice made, he refused to let it go to waste.

He suspected that had been the last of their ketches.

This became clear as a clattering of hooves thundered around the wing of the castle ahead of them. Armored stallions stamped heavily through the mud, splashing across pools. Saddled atop them were men in silver armor, who glowered from under plumed helms, showing the crimson countenances of Vyrllian knights. The unit's most elite. The black tattoos across their faces gave this away—as did the pale knight with a silvery mask riding along with them.

All Silvergard.

Coming with King Mikaen.

The knights pounded upon their trapped group and circled with a great flourish of hooves and ringing armor. Kanthe suspected his brother had been waiting until the skies were clear, for those in the yard to be ground down, before making an appearance.

Mikaen had always preferred the slaughter to the battle.

His brother trotted forward, riding tall. His smile was broad and mean—at least what showed past the edge of his mask.

Mikaen called down to Kanthe, "Welcome home, brother."

TEN

WRAITHS IN THE WIND

To trewly see the wurld, one must flie heigh.
To trewly understande it, one must crawl lo.
To trewly find peece, one must be bury'd beneath it.

—Words taught to the god-bound
of the Chanaryn

65

Nyx sat atop Bashaliia. The pair waited along the sandy shore of the black sea. The sun's reflection off the expanse burned through the amber lenses of her goggles. The heat trapped by the glass burned any exposed skin, as if the Father Above resided under that dark surface.

How can anyone dare cross this sea?

To her right, Daal straddled Pyllar. The two of them intended to fly their mounts to Evdersyn Heep. The broken cliffs rose as a shattered rampart on the eastern side of the Shil'nurr Plains.

But they would not be crossing alone.

To her left, a long row of stone-slabbed sleds lined the sand. They sat atop skids of sharpened glass, with bone frames that held aloft woven canopies. The fractured glass at the sea's edge had been hammered to a scintillating crust, opening access to the flatter surfaces beyond.

The Chanrë called these sleds *kalkäa* and the beasts who pulled them *pärde*. Nyx stared as shrouded figures finished securing harnesses to three of the creatures. The beasts were twice the size of an ox, with powerful hindlegs and smaller forelimbs. Their hips were saddled with thick pads that helped retain water.

Nyx paid particular attention to their narrow heads, which supported massive curled horns that the beasts could strangely trumpet through. She recognized the unique note to those blasts. They made her wince and ate into her skull. The Chanrë hunters who had rescued them from the lake had carried pärde horns with them. She had been told the noise drove off most predators—which she could appreciate now as one of the beasts reared up and blasted a complaint that stung deeply.

Still, the shrouded men and women calmed their charges with gentle words and soft whistles. Quickly, three sleds were made ready for the crossing. Each would carry six or seven of the Chanrë. These hunters would trail behind, less to aid in the search through the labyrinth of Evdersyn Heep and more as a rear guard.

No one wanted this exploration to end up like the trip to the lake in the crystalline forest. If they should get stranded on the far side of the black sea, they would need a way back across the burning glass.

Still, barring any harm to their mounts, Nyx wasn't worried about herself or Daal—only those they waited upon.

"Here they come!" Daal called over, drawing Nyx's attention behind.

"About time," she said.

Over the rise of dunes, a sailraft appeared, dispatched from the *Fyredragon*. It rode low, its stern forge subdued. They did not want to rouse the Dragon any more than they had already.

Nyx glanced to the north. The glare obscured the Dragon's lower slopes, but higher up its craggy crown appeared to float in the sky. She squinted, trying to make out any bronze specks scrabbling those heights, but it would take a farscope to pick them out.

A bell ago, a scout had reported a surge of activity around the Dragon. It had roused Tosgon, panicking many, but most of the Chanrë girded themselves with grim determination. The village had been raided before, but all suspected this stirring of the Dragon had to do with their new guests.

If the *Fyredragon* had been spotted, the *ta'wyn* encampment clearly rallied to respond, but so far they appeared cautious. After millennia of isolation, the enemy likely struggled with the strangeness of this intrusion and needed time to evaluate the threat, especially with the southern skies already guarded by an old enemy.

Still, that could change at any moment.

If their group hoped to reach Evdersyn Heep, to try to forge a weapon out there, they had to move quickly. The decision was to limit this excursion to only a few. With the Dragon roused, they dared not draw any attention their way.

The sailraft roared past, burning low across the glaring glass.

Finally . . .

Nyx leaned down and whistled to Bashaliia. Her brother keened his relief, anxious to be underway, likely sensing her own apprehension. He bunched his powerful legs, then shoved into the sky. Wings spread wide and beat the air, stirring sand.

As they climbed, Daal followed with Pyllar.

One of the pärde trumpeted below, rattled by their launch.

She glanced down. The trio of *kalkäa* sleds set off across the sunblasted glass. The pärde who pulled them had pads of fire-resistant crystals that withstood the burn of the sea's hot surface, allowing them to traverse the terrain. The Chanrë used these *kalkäa* to ply this sea, to reach regions beyond their neighboring sands. She noted a few of the sleds on shore carried tall masts with canvas sails, requiring no beasts, only the winds to speed them over the glass.

She shook her head, amazed at the adaptability of these hard desert folk, and prayed she would not bring ruin upon them.

Swinging her gaze forward, she chased after the sailraft and quickly caught up, as did Daal. The two flanked the tiny craft and shot ahead. Behind her, Graylin manned the controls. In the hold, Kalder kept company with Vikas and two of the Chanrë who knew the Heep—or at least as well as anyone did. These desert people seldom trespassed into the region where the mankrae nested, those sand wraiths of this desert.

Esme's brother, Arryn, had agreed to come, as had the Chanrë huntmaster, Irquan. Esme had wanted to accompany them, too, but she did not know these lands. She only relented after Arryn had tasked her with an earnest responsibility: *To guard my family.*

The sailraft carried only one additional passenger. It was another reason the number aboard had to be limited. While Shiya took up little more space than anyone else, the weight of her bronze strained the reserves of the small craft. Not even Rhaif had been allowed to come, especially as there was no need for the skills of a thief on this journey.

Or so we must hope.

Back in the Frozen Wastes, to subdue the ravening horde-mind of the raash'ke, it had taken Nyx, Daal, and Shiya all working together to carry out that feat. If they hoped to somehow forge these wraiths into a united force, it would likely take all three again.

Still, they had to keep Shiya hidden, knowing the mankrae's fury when it came to the *ta'wyn* who shared this desert. They dared not let her bronze form be seen until absolutely necessary. The same applied for another foe of the Dragon's entrenched army. No one knew if the legendary *Dräshra* still haunted these broken cliffs, but their group had best be cautious. If a crazed *ta'wyn* still roamed Evdersyn Heep, it could prove as dangerous as the feral wraiths.

Nyx ducked low against Bashaliia, singing softly to him to distract from the fiery heat, from the fear that had worried into her bones. He returned her affection with a gentleness that warmed through her, easing the anxiety in her heart. She thrummed in harmony to his song, a cherishing chorus of love, of a responsibility shared, of a burden lessened for it.

The golden glow bathed over her and trailed off behind them.

As she flew, Daal swept along on her left.

She sensed the wellspring of power at his core. It called to her, sang of its promise of strength. She tightened her jaw against it. The lust in her blood and bones muddled with the desires of her heart. She struggled to separate the flesh of Daal—his warm touch, his lips on her tenderest spots, the hard firmness of his ardor—from that font of power that called to her with equal urgency.

It was why she had needed some distance.

Each communion offered no clarity. It only blurred matters more, which threatened her control—both of her body and her gift. She again heard the shatter of bones in her ears, the cry bursting from Daal's lips, not of ecstatic release, but of agony.

She pushed this all down and concentrated ahead.

As they raced across the glassy sea, the towering Samskrag cliffs filled the horizon from north to south, a black battlement that climbed higher and higher. She aimed for where a massive section jutted out like the bow of a ship. Only it had run aground long ago and shattered into a maze of flat-topped mesas, shadowy ravines, and broken rock.

Somewhere inside there, the mankrae nested.

She turned to stare past the breadth of Bashaliia's leathery wings to where Daal rode atop his raash'ke. She had no way of knowing how these sand wraiths would respond to their trespass. Would their two bats be viewed as long-lost relations or deemed an encroaching enemy?

She had discussed this with Jace, who feared the feral colony's territoriality.

Still, she sped onward, recognizing a simple truth.

There's only one way to find out.

AFTER A SEARING flight over the glass sea, Daal swept up to the towering, shattered face of Evdersyn Heep. It climbed in red cliffs, encrusted with ancient crystals that blazed in the sunlight. Black chasms cut through it everywhere, separating out massive pillars of flaking stone that climbed twice the height of the Crèche's icy roof.

Below, the expanse of glaring glass had broken into great plates, cracked apart by the topple of columns, the avalanches of boulders, and the crash of cliff faces. An apron of rock had tumbled far out across the glass, creating craggy red islands in that black sea.

Daal winged Pyllar in a wide arc across the Heep. Nyx followed behind him. He cast his gaze back and spotted the sailraft lagging far behind them. It had been unable to keep up with their swifter mounts.

Graylin had ordered them to wait here, forbidding them from entering the broken labyrinth on their own. It would be too easy to get lost in this maze, a danger that Arryn had firmly attested to with a warning.

Many have entered the Heep, but few have returned.

Daal suspected the reason for that had less to do with getting lost and more to do with the poisonous denizens of those cooler shadows. According to those who had made it out, every crack and crevice hid something that stung, bit, or strangled. Vipers writhed in dens. Giant, curl-tailed skorpions clung to walls in numbers that hid the rock faces. Spiders burst out of hiding when least expected. No surface was safe to tread without close inspection.

Daal patted Pyllar's flank.

Glad to have your wings, my friend.

His mount waggled as if acknowledging his words.

While waiting, Daal decided to take advantage of this momentary reprieve. He swept back along the Heep's cliffs and chasms. He searched their depths, craned at those flat-roofed tops. A few birds sped out of deep nests, fluttering and piping to keep the giant intruder from their eggs.

But it was not those wings that Daal had hoped to spot.

Nyx must have been doing the same. She rushed to draw alongside him. She pointed to her eye and flipped her palm. *Did you see anything?*

He shook his head, slashing the edge of his hand across his throat: *No luck.*

They separated again, falling away to canvass more of the face. With so many ways into the Heep, any clue forward would help. They could spend days searching this labyrinth—days they did not have.

He swung his gaze north, pulled by worry in that direction.

Then something caught the corner of his eye—no, not *his* eye. He briefly flashed into Pyllar, peering through his mount's sharper gaze, made all the sharper as Pyllar cast questing whistles into those chasms, which, with each rebound, peeled away shadows.

It was a disconcerting view, a mix of solid and ghostly at the same time.

Still, one of those shadows refused to dissolve. Instead, it shredded off a rocky perch and fluttered wildly, speeding farther into the depths. Pyllar—and Daal through him—followed its path a few turns, then lost it.

Daal twisted in his saddle and waved to draw Nyx's attention. She noted his signal, swept a tight turn, and hurried to his side. She hovered to a stop with a hard buffet of Bashaliia's wings.

"What is it?" she called over.

While they were close enough to talk, Daal felt as if the Heep were staring down at them, listening intently with the weight of all that rock. But for the sake of expediency, he pointed into the chasm ahead.

"Pyllar spotted what had to be a large bat, surely one of the mankrae."

Nyx squinted in that direction, leaning forward with intensity. Her bridling grew brighter, bursting from her skin, through her clothing. She cast out a writhing of golden strands, singing them into the shadows. Bashaliia added to her chorus in a higher octave, nearly beyond hearing but still in harmony with his bonded.

Daal waited, knowing such skill was beyond him.

After a few breaths, Nyx settled back into her saddle. Daal cast her an inquiring look, but she shook her head and slashed her hand across her throat. *No luck.*

Nyx tilted forward and glided Bashaliia toward the mouth of the chasm.

Despite his early trepidation at disturbing the heavy silence of the Heep, Daal called to her, "We must wait!"

She nodded but continued farther until she and Bashaliia were swallowed by those shadows. Daal followed, drawn in her wake by trepidation.

She called back, her voice echoing between the walls of rock to either side, "Show me where you lost sight! We'll go that far. See if we can discern any trail after that."

Daal turned and noted the sailraft still flew a quarter league off. When he faced back around, Nyx had already swept onward. He cursed under his breath and followed. They skirted deeper, winging slowly, wafting side to side. There was not enough room to fly alongside one another. As they continued, the chasm steadily narrowed. Soon, Bashaliia's breadth stretched from wall to wall, yet still the Mýr bat's dexterity kept his wingtips from brushing against the cliffs—which was fortunate.

Across the rock faces, black skorpions scurried and hairy-legged spiders raced. Most fled into cracks, but a few waved stingers or reared up on hindlegs, bearing hooked fangs.

Daal kept Pyllar well back from all that poison.

When they finally reached the stop where Pyllar had lost sight of the mankra, Nyx slowed to a gliding hover. She twisted in her saddle. "Just as we got here, Bashaliia picked up a fleeting glimpse, not far ahead. It might not be a mankra, but let's go a little farther to be sure."

Her words were not a question. She tipped and glided forward again. They sailed through a maze of twists and turns, traversing ever deeper. While they did, the cliffs grew taller, squeezing out the sunlight. As a small reward, the air grew cooler, both due to the shade and a steady breeze coursing through the narrow ravines, coming from all directions as those crevasses and canyons split a hundred different ways.

Daal was already lost. "Nyx!"

She must have sensed his concern. "Bashaliia knows the way back! And besides"—she pointed up—"we can always head that way and sail across the top of the Heep."

With this confidence, she continued on.

They finally reached a larger, deeper chasm that cut like a knife through this section of the Heep. Bashaliia entered it and sped in a slow circle, clearly unsure which way to go. Directly ahead, the wall was split by fissures, all too tight for any bat to fly through. The only way forward was to sweep right or left.

Pyllar crossed into the chasm and circled in tandem with Bashaliia.

Daal sat straighter, searching both directions, craning all around. Their bats keened and pined, probing deeper down those depths.

"There!" Nyx shouted.

She pointed to the right, her body glowing brightly.

Daal searched but saw nothing—then snapped into Pyllar's view, as if his mount sought to alert him. Through their shared double vision, Daal made out a shape farther down, winging through the shadows, clearly struggling.

Nyx set off after it.

Daal glided into her wake.

He didn't know if this was the same mankra he had spotted earlier. If so, it was plainly exhausted, likely panicked by the large bats hunting it. One wing battered weakly, causing its flight to careen awkwardly. It fought to keep to the air, often dropping suddenly before catching itself.

"I think it's hurt," Nyx called back. "And trying to make it back home."

Daal's eyes narrowed. He shifted his weight to slow Pyllar. Daal's intent—maybe his suspicion—drew his mount to circle.

Nyx noted this. "What are you doing?"

"It's not headed *home*. But *away*." He pointed the other direction. "It's feigning injury to lure us from its nest."

Daal led the way back.

"How can you be sure?" Nyx called over, still circling with Bashaliia.

"Because that's what I did with the Bhestyan warships!"

He sped on, his certainty driving Pyllar faster. They quickly crossed where they had entered the chasm and continued onward. Bashaliia had no trouble closing on them and keeping up.

After a short run, the chasm narrowed, as if petering out. Still, the walls rose higher, the floor delving deeper. Sunlight squeezed to a thin line above. As darkness closed over them, the walls broke into a friable crumble of fissures and cracks, looking a breath from collapsing atop them. And still the chasm pressed tighter.

Bashaliia's wingtips brushed the rock to either side. The larger bat had to tuck and shimmy to avoid damage. Ahead, this rift continued to narrow.

"This isn't the way!" Nyx scolded him. "It's a dead end."

Daal winced.

Maybe the fleeing bat had truly been hurt.

Nyx pointed high. "Let's head up! Go meet the sailraft."

As Pyllar turned to follow her, the shadows of the canyons burst around them with a storm of battering wings. Shapes surged out of clefts and splits. They swarmed from both sides, rising from below, diving from on high. Savage shrieking tore into them, reeling into a whirlwind.

In a breath, they were trapped in the eye of that storm.

Daal took grim satisfaction in one slight triumph.

I was not wrong.

66

BEHIND THE WHEEL of the sailraft, Graylin fought against racing faster across the sea of black glass. From a quarter league off, he had watched Nyx and Daal vanish into the chasms of Evdersyn Heep. Despite his trepidation, he forced himself to maintain a slow pace. They dared not alert the Dragon, to stir it into looking this way with a panicked surge of flames from the raft's forge.

While Nyx's willfulness aggravated him, he could not truly fault her. He even suspected where she had gained that trait. In the past, he had broken an oath to a king, all for the love of Nyx's mother. His young life had been one of brash actions and reckless disdain. He had not needed the words of an ancient *Nyssian* to confirm what he knew in his heart. Their shared blood was evident in the steel of her manner, the rebellion in her actions, even the deep-seated resentment toward him. He could hold a grudge, nurse an insult, just as stubbornly.

Still, such acknowledgment did not lessen the pounding of his heart or loosen his strangled hold on the raft's wheel.

Graylin sweated, both from the heat and tension. He had hoped to see Nyx and Daal reappear by the time they neared the Heep. As the cliffs rose ever higher, that did not happen.

"Where are they?" he muttered.

Arryn watched over one shoulder. He gaped out the window, clearly amazed to view his world from this height.

The Chanrë huntmaster, Irquan, looked far less enthused. He hung farther back, clutching a leather strap in a white-knuckled grip. His eyes, the only feature visible through his headscarf, kept well away from the window. He no doubt regretted his decision not to accompany his people aboard those stone sleds being pulled by curl-horned beasts.

Vikas and Kalder stayed near him, as if guarding Irquan from cranking the rear hatch open and flinging himself out.

Shiya stirred from the hold's stern. Up until now, her lids had hung low, allowing only a narrow slit of azure fire to show. Caught in the reflection of the window, her eyes flashed open.

Graylin glanced over his shoulder as she strode forward. The movement of her heavy bronze form wobbled the small raft. She quickly joined him.

"What's wrong?" he asked her.

She pointed toward the broken cliffs of the Heep. "A blaze of bridle-song, rising like smoke. Sudden and fierce."

Graylin took a sharp breath, understanding what this meant.

Nyx and Daal are in trouble.

Heedless of the risk, Graylin slammed a pedal. Flames shot out of the stern forge, their reflection blazing across the black glass. As he raced toward the Heep's shattered scarp, he prayed their flight did not draw the Dragon's attention.

Still, he aimed most of his pleas toward one hope.

Let us get there in time.

NYX STRAINED TO maintain the fiery nimbus of bridle-song around her and Daal. The golden glow had shattered back the initial assault by the shadowy wraiths. But that would not last. Her lungs already ached from the tension. Her throat thrummed in agony to maintain her chorus.

Bashaliia aided her efforts, keening brightly, amplifying her song all the brighter.

She sensed the deep well of Daal's strength, but he remained out of reach. Pyllar battered at any mankra who whisked too close. Fangs snapped with slathering poison, warning the horde back.

Still, it was not her weakening gift that panicked her the most.

At the start, she had cast shining strands out into that savage flock, trying to bridle one or two. But as she reached those wild hearts, she touched the emerald inferno that burned there. The same fire shrieked at them, tearing into the flare of her song.

She immediately knew this shining madness was not born out of any poisoning, like the raash'ke who had suffered under the tainted enslavement of the Spider. This ravening was pure feral ferocity. Even still, she sensed the brittle age of it. The anger that stoked this fire echoed from far in the past, some faint memory of what had been ripped from them, of a unity and community shattered. That pain had been writ into their bones, branded into their hearts—and they raged because of it.

Recognizing this, she fought to maintain her flaming corona of gold—not only to hold the ravening horde at bay, but to shield that emerald fire from Bashaliia. She dared not let the madness be the strike of flint on dry tinder, to ignite the same poisoned emerald inside her brother, to flare it into a raging conflagration. If that happened, with Bashaliia at the heart of this fiery storm, she would lose him entirely to the feral madness, maybe forever.

I can't let that happen.

Still, these wraiths guarded their nest with fury. Their screeching battered at her fiery shield. To maintain it, she had to shrink her fraying nimbus, to coalesce it tighter, to flare it brighter.

She cast a glance to Daal.

If she drew her protective corona any closer, he and Pyllar would fall outside of it. Her heart agonized with the choice squeezing down on her. Under this assault, she could not guard them all. If she tried and lost Bashaliia, then all four would fall.

But to shield Bashaliia, could she sacrifice Daal and Pyllar?

She knew the answer.

Her misery sang out in an anguished chorus as she drew her fiery nimbus more firmly around her and Bashaliia. A wraith shot through and crashed into Daal. He managed to shove off the bat, one the size of a yearling calf. Still, he got knocked crooked in his saddle. A claw raked his arm, ripping through his riding leather.

More dove at him.

But before they could strike, a flaming sun crested over the rift. It plummeted through the dark mass of wraiths, washing fire through them.

The sailraft . . .

The horde scattered in all directions, fleeing this flaming intruder. Even those diving on Daal flung themselves away in a panic.

One whipped past her, shying from her golden glow.

As the beast rolled away, she got her first clear look at a mankra. While clearly a bat, it was nothing like Bashaliia or the raash'ke. Its body was far more svelte and stretched into a sinewy length that extended into a long tail, one that fanned out at the end to aid in agile flying. Its wings looked built to the same end. They were thinner, nearly translucent, giving the creature its wraithlike appearance.

As the mankra fell from her shield, its wings tucked and vanished against its body. It now looked more snake than bat. It dove down to a narrow crack and writhed into it.

Still, what caught most of her attention was the swell of the mankra's chest, the warbling of its ribs as it screeched. These mankrae seemed built for two functions: agile speed and savage wailing. She remembered Arryn's description of their hunting ability, how they could rip a *ta'wyn* out of the sky with swift ambushes and gales of ravening bridle-song.

Maybe it is this madness that makes them all the stronger.

In a matter of a few breaths, she had been nearly defeated.

Still, with relief, she watched the rest of the mankrae flee, crashing back into their dark burrows and cracks, seeking shelter from this strange fiery apparition that had fallen upon them.

Nyx understood their terror. Nothing like this had ever flown their skies. Intimidated and terrified, they had sought safety, for a chance to size up this new threat. But there was no telling how long such restraint would last.

Clearly recognizing this, too, Daal pointed up, while he cradled his injured arm.

Already the sailraft headed skyward, rising swiftly. The forge's flames glowed across the walls, driving any lurking shadows deeper into crevices.

Daal headed up in the wake of the ship. Nyx followed, maintaining a golden shield to protect their retreat. As she did, she stared into those fire-illuminated fissures, wondering at the warren hidden in those depths. She also glanced down, making sure none dared strike from below.

Then a glimmer drew her eye to the right, a twinkling of golden shine, as if her shield reflected off water. That tiny star of brightness rose from farther down the chasm, where it pinched near the end.

Something's out there.

While she wanted to ignore it, she sensed something calling to her, an urgency in that shine that reached her heart. Maybe Bashaliia's, too. Her brother turned from their ascent, either at her whim or his own.

Daal noted her hesitation. "Nyx!"

She tightened her throat and let her shield fray apart into a tangle of golden strands. She wafted them toward that star in the deeper shadows at the end of the chasm. As she did, that feeling of earnestness sharpened, shining with a plaintive need, nearly sorrowful in its poignancy.

She fell toward it, inescapably drawn, as if bridled to it.

Daal rushed down to her. "We must go before the wraiths rally again!"

She understood the danger. Her earlier haste to enter the Heep had nearly gotten them killed. Still, if there was any hope to be found in this poisonous labyrinth, perils had to be faced, threats endured.

She swept ahead, calling back, "Can't you feel it?"

She knew Daal shared a gift of sight, weaker than hers but still there. She glanced back, touched her eye, and pointed ahead: *Do you see it?*

He frowned, then suddenly stiffened.

She kept staring at him until he finally nodded.

Only then did she swing away and dive toward the star. The chasm walls closed on both sides, forcing Bashaliia to tilt ever steeper. Ahead, the beckoning glow shone from beyond a narrow pinch.

As Bashaliia lifted and balanced on a wingtip, Nyx tucked tight, clinging low to her saddle, gripping with her thighs. She sucked in a breath to shrink lower. Still, the wall brushed her back—then they were through.

Once clear, Bashaliia swung level again. Nyx settled back into her saddle. They swept a circle around a grotto, surrounded full around by high cliffs. Only here, the red sandstone had been blasted to black glass, like the sea they had left behind. Some sections had calved away long ago, crashing to jagged shards below and exposing the raw stone beneath.

Nyx pictured the ancient war that laid waste to this land and created the Dragon and its surrounding sea. She stared at the glass walls.

Had a final battle been fought here, marking some last stand?

Behind her, Daal swept out of the rift and joined her. As they spun together, Nyx noted the mouth of a large cavern below. It gaped open like a frozen scream, echoing the pain of that last battle. Or maybe it only seemed that way due to the star shining out of those depths. Its golden chorus was suffused with grief, with loss, with an agony that clutched Nyx's heart.

She understood that pain. It sang to all she had lost in the past, what would be destroyed if she failed, even the misery that would be wrought if she succeeded, when millions would still die.

That pain drew her down.

How could it not?

It is my story, too.

67

ESME CLIMBED OUT of the bowels of Tosgon. She followed a villager named Abresh. It was the same woman who had carried Esme out of the Örgös forest atop an ürsyn named Ruro. Only now this desert huntress led her to war.

Esme stared behind her. She had helped get the aged and infirm into the deepest depths of the village, farthest from any potential fighting. Arryn's heartbound, Yazmyn, had wanted to join the defense of Tosgon, but her gravid belly had made that impossible. Plus, she had a daughter to guard, to serve as little Asha's last means of protection if those depths were breached.

Back when Esme had met them, upon seeing the simple happiness in her brother, she had promised to do all she could to protect them, to give everything of herself.

Even if it meant battling a Dragon.

As I must do now.

As Esme and Abresh continued upward, others crowded into the smooth-walled passageway with the same intent. Their murmurs and the brush of their sandals drowned out the ever-present rumbling of the *Flüst* of Tosgon.

She was amazed at how these desert folk remained so resolute when faced by the threat of the *Revn-kree*. She remembered Shiya dropping through flames to crash into the deck of the Bhestyan warship.

How could these people hope to withstand such a force?

Esme finally reached the cavernous entry hall. The Chanrë packed the space. They carried all manner of weapons: spears of sharpened bone, lances tipped in glass, daggers of the same, even bows of stringed sinew.

Still, these weapons looked far too feeble against the strength of bronze.

Crikit, who kept tight to Esme's heels, clattered and chittered his distress, picking up on the tension all around. Esme had tried to get her friend to remain below with Yazmyn and the others, but he would have none of it, practically climbing over people to keep with her.

She had relented, less to satisfy him than to settle her own nerves. He had been her companion for so long, raised from an egg, coddled through his first half year, until he grew stout enough to join her on expeditions into the ruins of Seekh. He had grown to be as much a part of her as any of her limbs.

Abresh pushed through the crowd and reached the village entrance. She parted the heavy tapestry and led the way outside. The sun glared after so long inside. Esme blinked away the blindness until she could spot the rows of ürsyns lined across the sand or perched along the dune faces. She counted several dozen, all saddled, with Chanrë standing ready. Some had already mounted, all riding double.

As will we.

Abresh threw her headscarf over her face and rushed over to a rider. She chattered with him, then accepted a curled horn. She returned and brusquely shoved it at Esme.

Esme didn't understand.

Abresh explained in the Chanrë tongue, but Esme understood well enough. "Keep with you. Blow when *Ravka* near." The huntress's eyes stared hard at her. *"Ye?"*

Esme nodded and hefted the horn, which curled as long as her forearm.

So, my role is to act as a scout, to warn of danger.

She struggled with the horn's weight, then realized she had an easier way to carry it. She turned to Crikit, who hauled a water bag harnessed across his carapace. She added the horn to his load.

Abresh watched this, looked like she was going to say something, then shrugged.

The huntress then drew Esme over to one of the ürsyns. The hard woman rubbed the beast's side. Her words softened with affection, whispering her pride. *"Nahë rah, Ruro. Ye, yes, me carasyn."*

The woman then leaped into the saddle and patted for Esme to mount up. She hurried to obey, climbing far more awkwardly. Another horn hung from Ruro's saddle near Esme's knee. It seemed no one was taking any chances about keeping everyone alerted.

Once settled, the huntress guided Ruro up a neighboring dune. Crikit scurried after them. Once they reached the crest, the view opened wider.

Esme gasped, finally spotting the real means to Tosgon's defense.

Across the sand, dark mountains moved toward them. Six in all. It seemed Esme was not the only one to bring a molag to this battle. While growing up, Esme had always wanted to see these massive giants who roamed the deepest wilds of the Barrens. These six molagi towered twice that of the biggest she had ever seen, those scarred, bridle-bound beasts who hauled trains across tracks. But these were no slaves. No one had clipped their massive claws.

Riders stood atop their backs, balancing deftly, holding woven reins. She sensed no coercion from the molagi's easy rolling gait. If the beasts were ever aggravated, those huge pincers could easily pluck a rider off.

As they neared, she sensed the same camaraderie and affection that she shared with Crikit. She remembered the soft words this hard woman had for

Ruro. These desert people clearly lived in harmony with their landscape, not in war against it.

She felt honored to witness these giants.

Though considering the circumstance behind their arrival . . .

Maybe I should be more careful what I wish for.

FROM THE STERN deck of the *Fyredragon*, Rhaif stared to the east. Worry kept him glued to his vigil. After Shiya had headed off aboard the sailraft, he had watched until the small boat vanished into the glare. He resented being left behind, especially as his skills were deemed of little use.

He had disagreed.

One never knew when the talents of a thief might be needed.

Then again, he felt pretty fekkin' useless himself right now.

The ship's crew hurried across the sand, freeing mooring lines.

Darant bellowed directions from atop the deck, while winding in a cable himself with muscular cranking. Once done, the captain wiped his sweating brow on a sleeve.

Needing some distraction from his fears, Rhaif crossed over to Darant. While maintaining his vigil, Rhaif had missed much of the preparation for the day ahead.

I had better see if I can actually be of any use.

Rhaif eyed the work below. "So, Darant, let me understand. The plan is to free the *Fyredragon*, fly off, and abandon these poor people."

Darant scowled. "We're not going anywhere at the moment. We're staying hunkered down in this sandy gully. At least until that buzzing around the Dragon starts flying this way."

"Ah, *then* we abandon the villagers below."

The captain's scowl deepened. "We'll be no safer up high. You know that. But we'll have a better chance of battling the bastards in the air, where the ship has room to maneuver versus being mired in these dunes. It's also the best way we can help the villagers."

"By running."

"By luring the *ta'wyn* after us." Darant turned to the sweep of the deck. "Plus, when it comes to a fight, we're far better equipped."

Rhaif wasn't sure that was true. As a thief, he knew the advantage of a good hiding place. And at the moment, that deep warren of a village held great appeal.

Still, the *Fyredragon* was clearly being readied for a battle. Its cannons had been loaded, both with solid iron balls and those meant to shatter into spiked fléchettes that would shred through a target. Likewise, the bows of the giant ballistas already had steel spears resting atop them, ready to be cranked back.

The ship had one additional means of defense. It came in the form of four sets of wings. Daal's second rider, Tamryn, would lead an assault with the raash'ke to harry any *ta'wyn*, to keep them away from the gasbag above. It was a vital duty. While the ship's balloon was baffled into different sections, with enough damage it would eventually fail, sending the ship crashing into the sand.

Rhaif watched these final preparations with trepidation. Darant noted a problem and left his side, bellowing out a correction. His daughter, Glace, marched through their defenses, checking both crew and armaments. Her temperament was firm but supportive. Unlike her father, who roared with irritation and outrage.

Rhaif shook his head.

They do make a good team.

Rhaif turned toward the stern, ready to resume his vigil, but he never made it. Through the copper mouth of a highhorn, Fenn called up from the wheelhouse. His words sounded hollow and failed to carry the import of his message.

"The Dragon stirs! The enemy moves south!"

A frantic ringing of bells followed, summoning all to their stations.

Darant cursed and rushed for the wheelhouse. Rhaif hurried to follow. As he did, he passed Glace, who kept to the deck to oversee their departure. Rhaif saw her features harden into her father's countenance. She bellowed and stomped, taking over his role here, too.

Darant swept through the doors, down a short flight, and burst into the wheelhouse. Rhaif matched his pace, trailing in the wake of his fury.

"How many?" Darant shouted out.

Fenn, Krysh, and Jace all manned the navigation station, fixed to various farscopes.

"Hundreds!" Jace answered.

Rhaif winced.

Hundreds?

Krysh clarified, his words calmer. "Between two hundred and two-fifty. It's hard to be more exact."

Rhaif expressed his own fear, one close to his heart. "Are any of them heading toward the Heep, toward where the others went?"

"So far, no," Fenn answered. "But that may change."

Darant crossed to the maesterwheel and called out crisp orders. The ship roared and trembled. The flaring forges brightened this sandy valley, turning the sides of the dunes a fiery red.

Slowly, the *Fyredragon* rose out of the desert.

As they cleared the ridgeline, the village of Tosgon appeared. On the ground, its meager forces scurried across the sand, clearly having noted the danger, too.

Rhaif grimaced as he watched the sight recede below.

Despite Darant's assurances . . .

This still feels like abandonment.

68

Daal stood at the mouth of the dark cave. He hated to leave Pyllar behind. Nyx looked equally concerned about Bashaliia.

Moments ago, they had watched the sailraft descend into the grotto, spinning slightly, waving flames from its stern. The fire reflected off the black glass walls until the small raft settled to the floor.

Out in the grotto, the stern forge still smoldered in threat, remaining a smoky torch in case the mankrae attacked again. As an additional protection, their two bats flanked the grounded ship, blocking the cave's mouth. Vikas and Irquan had also agreed to stay behind to further guard their retreat.

Graylin lit a lantern and stepped deeper into the cave.

Kalder followed, the vargr's nose held high, same as his hackles, which shivered with warning.

"It looks like a tunnel extends out from this entrance," Graylin noted, then glanced back. "And you're sure something's there."

"A font of bridle-song," Nyx assured him. "Shining out of the depths."

Daal nodded, checking the bandage around his gouged arm. His riding leathers had spared him any worse damage. "I can sense it, too, but only as a weak glow."

One other also agreed. "They are correct," Shiya said as she crossed from the sailraft. "What it is, I cannot discern. It remains strangely blocked."

"I'm finding it the same," Nyx said. "I've tried casting out strands. But as it nears the source, they die away."

Arryn had ventured deeper than all of them. He used his spear's tip to shift a large, pale skorpion out of his path. "Come see this," he whispered with a measure of distaste. "Bring the light."

They all followed, though Graylin kept Nyx behind him. As they neared, the spread of the lantern's glow swept over something buried in the glass, melted and frozen into it long ago.

Daal cringed at the sight, taking a step back.

Out of the glass, the remains of a *ta'wyn* lay sprawled at a tortured angle. Its bronze had patinaed into a dark amber, streaked with green runnels. All that was in view was an upper torso, a head, and one arm. Its lower section had been scorched black, likely from the heat of the molten glass. Its features had slagged away, too, either from the same burning exposure or from the ability of some *ta'wyn* to change form.

"It appears to be a Root," Shiya confirmed, making this assessment from a step away, clearly wanting to get no closer.

"A fallen of the *Revn-kree*." Graylin looked back at the black grotto. "Clearly a fearsome battle had been fought here."

Nyx expressed what they were all thinking. "If this was some last stand, then maybe an ally to the *Kraena*—what the Chanrë call the horde-mind of this colony—did survive. The legendary *Dräshra*. Maybe it got stranded here and has been calling across millennia, waiting for someone rich enough in bridle-song to hear it."

Arryn continued deeper, drawing them all onward. "When I was lost in the wilderness, my shaman, Aeldryn Tann, said he sensed something whispering to him out of the deep desert. But I do not know if he had any talent in bridle-song, only that he was kindhearted and wiser than any man I knew."

Daal heard the pain in the warrior's voice—and from the hard thump of the man's spear on the glass, some deep-seated anger.

As they headed on, more bronze remnants lay buried in the glass. Many looked shattered into pieces. Eventually, the wash of glass dwindled away, re-turning again to sandstone. Yet even still, bodies lay strewn and blackened by age or weaponry.

"How much farther?" Graylin whispered, as if fearful of waking the dead.

Kalder stuck close to the man's hips, ears swiveling all around.

"Not sure," Nyx answered, equally hushed. "Not far."

After another tenth of a league, Daal noted a soft glow appear out of the gloom. Nyx spotted it, too. They both slowed, as did Shiya.

"Something's coming," Nyx warned. "And swiftly."

They all stopped.

Ahead, a soft golden light wove toward them, shimmering with bridle-song, wavering and darting like a shining karp in dark waters.

Graylin held his sword ready. "What are you all seeing? What's—"

Then he spotted it, too.

The source bounded into the edge of the lantern light and halted.

Though glowing with bridle-song, it appeared to be an ordinary desert creature. It stood as tall as Daal's calf, covered in snowy-white fur so dense that it looked carved of pale stone. Its narrow snout came to a sharp point, while crowning its head were a pair of hooded ears that reached as high as Daal's knee. Behind it rose a dark-striped tail, far longer than its sleek body. It wove that bushy length languidly, as if expressing little alarm at these tres-passers.

"What is it?" Nyx whispered.

Arryn answered, struggling with his words. "A . . . A *dhelprä* . . . it cannot be." The man looked close to falling to his knees. "A spirit out of Chanaryn legend. None have been seen in centuries."

The creature stared back at them, with its head slightly cocked. Then, as if suddenly realizing it was supposed to be a myth, the dhelprä turned and bounded off with a sweep of that long tail. It quickly vanished into the shadows, trailing a golden glow.

"We must follow!" Arryn blurted out. He set off before anyone could argue otherwise. "According to legend, to spot one promises great fortune."

They continued after him.

As they started, a ululating cry carried back, haunting and heartachingly lonesome. They followed that fading call through a maze of other passageways.

"Could this be the source of bridle-song you sensed?" Graylin challenged Nyx.

"I don't think so. Something still shines deeper, a font richer and more ancient. This dhelprä seems to be leading us toward it."

"Maybe it's a nest of these same creatures," Graylin mumbled.

Nyx could not argue against this.

Ahead, the tinier glow of the dhelprä vanished into the greater moonlight of whatever hid at the heart of this labyrinth.

"Almost there," Nyx whispered.

Another few twists of the tunnel, and this proved to be true.

They all slowed and cautiously entered a chamber that glowed with strange energies and alchymies. The group paused at the threshold, too daunted to enter. Graylin kept his sword up, while Arryn pointed his spear.

Ahead, a maze of copper and bronze tubing formed a web that filled the back half of the room. Glowing tanks bubbled with golden elixirs. But what held them all off was the throne in the middle. It looked made of scraps of bronze scavenged from the dead behind them. Even some of the alchymy on display likely came from the same source.

Despite the strangeness, Daal kept his eye on the figure seated on the throne—no, not *seated,* but *melded* into it, as surely as those tarnished Roots in the black glass. Again, the naked figure looked scavenged out of parts. One leg had clearly been ripped from another body and fused to this one. Same with a hand, maybe a shoulder.

Daal could read this map from the shine given off by the figure. A bridling glow suffused out of most of its form, but it darkened where those trappings had been welded on, making it clear those parts were additions.

Despite the strangeness, they all knew who sat enthroned before them.

Nyx named it. "The *Dräshra*."

The identity of this ancient *ta'wyn* was evident from another striking feature.

Daal glanced to Shiya, to the sweeping curls of her hair, the curve of her cheekbones, the generosity of her sculpted lips, even the rise of her breasts against the thin robe.

No wonder the village elder had mistaken Shiya for this legend.

Daal faced back to the throne. The figure seated there bore the same features, though worn by age and battle. A swath of curls had burned away. A plate of darkness had been welded to a cheek, flattening it out. Her chest had been caved in on one side.

From the throne, eyes slowly opened, shining with azure fire.

That gaze swept the group in silent scrutiny.

From around the back of the throne, a figure rubbed into view, brushing its length around the foot of the chair, across the bronze legs of the *Dräshra*. The dhelprä settled to one side, sitting on its haunches, its tail sweeping a sigil across the floor.

It glowed softly, bathed in the bridling of the seated queen.

A bronze hand lifted from the throne's arm and reached to the dhelprä's tall ears, running fingers with clear affection across the crown of this creature. As this happened, the golden glow of the snowy fur brightened with the passage of that touch. At the same time, a spark of azure fire flared in the creature's tiny dark eyes.

Daal suspected the *ta'wyn* now stared at them through those same eyes.

Like I sometimes do with Pyllar.

He wondered if the *Dräshra*—melded into her throne—used the dhelprä as her eyes and ears out into the world. He remembered the creature's haunting call and Arryn's story of hunters hearing a forlorn cry echoing sometimes out of the Heep. They had believed it was the misery of the *Dräshra* crying out of the shadows, heartbroken and woeful.

And maybe it was . . . maybe it wasn't just the eyes and ears of the dhelprä that this fallen queen used to commune with the desert.

But its voice, too.

Finally, those azure eyes shifted from where they had lingered on Nyx to bring the full weight of that ancient gaze upon him. Daal felt stripped by that scrutiny. Just before he was ready to fall back a step, the attention turned to another.

A small nod of greeting followed, toward Shiya. "Welcome, sister."

Rather than falling back from that intense gaze, Shiya stepped forward with clear challenge. "You are the *Dräshra*. The ally who turned against the *Revn-kree* and sought to destroy the forces entrenched here?"

Another nod.

A wary note sharpened Shiya's tone. "But I see you are not a lowly *Root* who defected."

There was no acknowledgment.

Shiya pointed an accusatory arm. "Instead, you are the *Axis* who led them here."

69

NYX GASPED WITH the shock of this revelation. Graylin tried to shove her behind him, but she shrugged out of his way.

She refused to shy from this and stared at the figure seated on the throne. *An Axis, the same one who had led the* Revn-kree *army here.*

Though jolted, she should have suspected as much, even before entering these tunnels. The Roots of the *ta'wyn,* while changeable of form, had little gift of bridle-song. That talent—known as *synmeld* among their kind—was limited to the Axis and even more powerfully to the Kryst castes.

Graylin kept his sword raised and called to the throne, "If what you claim is true, you turned on your own kind. Why?"

"Why?"

Spoken by the *Dräshra,* this one word sounded as if it contained a multitude of questions. Her answer hinted at those queries.

"I . . . I do not know why our creators gifted us with *synmeld,*" she said, clearly struggling to speak, as if rusted by age. "It is as much a curse as a blessing. It is a path to tormenting empathy as much as a font of power."

Nyx understood this all too well.

The *Dräshra* stared down with a small shake of her head. "I came to this desert to fulfill my duty, to secure and guard the *turubya.* But these scorched sands were not empty, not devoid of life. It sang and flew and burrowed, calling in a hundred songs, a chorus stronger than any shield I could build against it."

As she continued, her voice slowly lost its rasp, growing harder. "Then the pain began. The torture of subjugation. The atrocities of land and beast. The blood and bone of war by the *Kraena* who sought to root us out. I endured it for two centuries, but it grew too much."

Nyx could not fathom what that must have been like. She had endured battles, brief and savage, and it had nearly broken her—*did* break her for a time.

But to endure the same over centuries . . .

"Still, I did not betray my duty," the Axis said forlornly. "Instead, I found myself growing distant from it, unable to function. The Roots noted this. They began a project in secret, to cast me aside. It's what they have been laboring on over these passing millennia. But what they attempt risks damaging the *turubya*—and may have done so already."

Nyx felt a sinking despair.

Have we come all this way for nothing?

Graylin stirred with the same worry. "What were they doing?"

He was ignored, as if considered inconsequential. "To stop this project, to assuage the centuries of agony, I sought out the only weapon I hoped would be strong enough to stop them."

"The *Kraena*," Nyx said.

"They were a powerful force, united in mind and purpose, beautifully dark and savage. But the Roots are as malleable of mind as they are in form. They crafted infernal weapons of immense strength. The war that followed burned across these lands. It was waged for a quarter century. Neither giving way. But eventually bronze and resourcefulness proved too much for heart and spirit."

"The horde-mind broke," Nyx whispered.

The *Dräshra's* eyes closed, her face tight with grief. "They were so beautiful . . . especially Khagar, who was the true guardian of these lands, who led his winged legions with such ferocity."

Nyx glanced to Arryn. They had heard a name like that before. "Khagar-san. Is that not what the Chanrë call the black mountain?"

"It means *Home of Khagar*," he whispered, stiff with reverence. "It is the name of a Chanrë god. His name simply means *Guardian*."

Still lost in the past, the *Dräshra* continued, "After the fall, I had hoped to find a way to forge the *Kraena* anew, to bring that dark golden beauty back to life." She waved to the web of copper and alchymy and scavenged parts. "But in the end, all I could do was endure, preserving what I could until someone stronger could take over those reins."

Those azure eyes opened and blazed toward Nyx.

"And now you have arrived. I've watched you atop wings, even greater and darker than Khagar's. You are a *ka'wyn* reborn at last."

Graylin stepped before that fiery gaze. "What is a *ka'wyn*?"

She answered, whether hearing the question or simply continuing, "One rises once every several millennia, the perfect alignment of flesh and talent, of heart and power, a being capable of retaining a strength beyond our kind. I've heard them rise out there, like distant stars, only to fade again."

As the *Dräshra* continued, Nyx noted the voice drifting, unmoored, yet there remained an urgency, maybe even more so now. "The first of you, though, was not born of chance, but crafted as a weapon. By Kryst Eligor. Fashioned out of brutality and enslavement. With such a weapon, the *Revn-kree* became unstoppable. Yet, even brutality and enslavement could be defeated by will and sacrifice. The first *ka'wyn* wrested herself free, dying to do so. It broke Eligor's dominance, weakened him, allowed him to be defeated and broken.

But before she expired, she read her blood and power and knew others would arise like her. What Eligor crafted, chance and circumstance could re-create. She told this to Eligor before she expired. This terror, perhaps more than the loss of his weapon, may have led to his downfall. Eligor feared this portent."

Shiya interrupted. "This portent. You're speaking of the prophetic rise of the *Vyk dyre Rha,* are you not?"

A slow nod answered her. "She who would be reborn. A queen birthed out of the shadows of time. But her coming is not *prophecy,* but *certainty,* the certainty of time's passing, of the rolling of millennia that eventually stirs the right elements back into place, to bring flesh and talent into the correct alignment, to return order out of chaos."

Nyx touched her chest. These words both relieved and terrified her. She was not a creature prophesied into being, but simply a girl abandoned in the swamp, a seed cast off into the mire of the Mýr, a babe already gifted with nascent talent in her blood. There, she was chanced upon by a she-bat and raised under a constant chorus of potent keening, which altered her young mind when it was still soft clay, nurturing that seed into something new, something capable of wielding a gift with far greater talent and strength.

"Chance and circumstance," Nyx whispered, describing her path, her creation.

But what does this all mean?

Graylin asked the same question in a different manner, repeating his earlier query. "But what is a *ka'wyn?*"

The *Dräshra* finally acknowledged him. "It is a Kryst born of flesh."

Nyx flinched at these words.

"Such rare beings are far stronger than those forged of bronze. As high as a Kryst sits above a Root, so does a *ka'wyn* rise above a Kryst. It is this that terrifies Eligor. If he can't bend you to his will, he must destroy you."

These last words were spoken not with warning but sorrow. The copper alchymy surrounding her throne grew brighter as the glow from her body faded, as if she were giving herself over to the web.

"I will do what I can," the *Dräshra* whispered. "To give you the gift I have held close to my heart for all these millennia. I've sustained it with the alchymy around me, along with my undying gratitude, for a brave spirit who showed me the beauty of life over the desolation of an undying existence."

Her voice lowered to a whisper as her glow faded. "But first you must be made ready."

The *Dräshra* lifted her hands as if in supplication, but it was clearly in invitation.

Nyx stepped forward. Graylin reached to stop her, then let his arm drop.

Through her bridle-song, Nyx felt no enmity from this queen, a sentinel who had waited across lonely millennia. Nyx sensed only weariness, maybe some fear, though not for herself.

The *Dräshra* swung her tired gaze from Nyx to another, someone else invited to approach.

Nyx turned. "Daal, she wants you, too."

He hesitated.

She recognized he did not have as keen an eye when it came to bridle-song. She tried to reassure him. "She means us no harm."

Daal nodded and followed her.

Nyx faced the broken majesty of this queen.

At least, I hope not.

Once they were closer, the *Dräshra* beckoned with her hands, wanting each of them to take one. With a deep breath, Nyx took the left. The bronze felt warm against her skin, which calmed some of her misgivings.

A moment later, Daal reached to the other.

As he made contact, those azure eyes closed. A soft humming rose around the throne. Nyx felt a gentle pull, which drew her song into the *Dräshra's* fading glow. Fear trickled up—then Daal gasped next to her.

She glanced over as Daal's back arched. Power flowed in a golden torrent, blindingly bright, pouring out of the wellspring inside him—and into the *Dräshra.*

The queen's bronze form flared with that stolen strength.

Daal fought to free himself, but bronze fingers clutched hard, trapping him.

Shiya rushed over, recognizing his distress, surely seeing what was being ravished out of Daal. But Shiya's speed proved not enough. In a single breath, all of Daal's strength was torn from his wellspring, draining it dark.

When Shiya reached him, the *Dräshra* let go of her grip. Daal tumbled backward into Shiya's arms. His body trembled. His breath frosted the air, reflecting the heat drawn from him, too.

Nyx yanked at her own hand, finding herself equally entrapped. Before her, the *Dräshra* blazed with the fire stolen from Daal. Those azure eyes stared down at her, pitying now. Words boomed from her lips.

"Be the *wyldstrom!*"

Graylin rushed up and grabbed Nyx's shoulders.

Before he could break her free, before she could rouse a defense, all that power rampaged down the *Dräshra's* arm and struck Nyx with a force that crushed her lungs and burned a nimbus of fire across her skin.

Graylin got thrown back.

All of Daal's stolen power slammed into Nyx. It filled every fiber of her body. It flamed through the marrow of her bones, clenched every muscle, burned away all vision. She became a torch before this dire queen.

In her blindness, words reached her, carried to her in bridle-song, not breath.

"Be the *wyldstrom* . . ." the *Dräshra* intoned. But it was not a command this time, only a sorrowful plea. "To do what I did not have the heart to do . . ."

Nyx's vision swirled back into focus. Those bronze fingers relaxed. But before she could pull herself free, they tightened again.

"Tell him . . . share with him . . . how much I love . . ."

Then those fingers went slack.

Nyx fell away from the throne—from where a cold, dark queen now sat.

All the fire, all the bridling glow, had snuffed from the figure, leaving only cold bronze and a slumped shape. A few traces of brilliance danced across the copper webbing, forming a scintillating halo around the throne.

It held that way for a long breath, the last testament to this warrior-queen. Then this, too, faded, traveling deeper into the copper maze, where it vanished into the darkness.

Daal gasped out, drawing Nyx's attention. She staggered toward where he trembled on his knees. Her body trembled, too, struggling to hold in so much power. The edges of her vision burned with a crimson fire.

"Daal . . ."

She reached toward him, her hands already aglow with pent-up energies. She was ready to give some back—*needing* to do so, to shed some of this power. But before she could, a flash of gold, all wrapped around snowy fur, burst between them.

The sudden appearance of the dhelprä made them both fall back.

Kalder barked in warning.

The creature ignored the vargr, spun a circle, trailed by its long, striped tail. Then it took off and dashed behind the throne. As it did, the dhelprä gave off another forlorn cry of heartbreak, as if mourning its fallen queen.

Arryn offered his own interpretation. "It wants us to follow."

Nyx twisted around, unsure what to do. None of this made any sense. She listened as the dhelprä's call faded.

Is something back there?

Arryn set off after the dhelprä. The Chanrë's thin form twisted through the tangle, scouting a path, then vanished out of view.

A moment later, a terrified shout arose. "Come here! All of you!"

Nyx gained her feet. Graylin kept to her side, but without touching her. Maybe even he sensed the fiery font she struggled to contain. He simply gripped his sword harder, lifting its tip.

Shiya drew Daal up. He hung in her arms, but he could keep his feet. Even his breath no longer frosted as his body's trembling warmed him.

They stumbled along Arryn's path and wormed through the labyrinth of tubing and tanks, all dark, no longer bubbling with alchymies.

Finally, they reached a cavern hidden behind the throne. Here, too, the strange, scavenged web extended, spanning roofs and walls, running in a pattern across the floor, where four tanks still burbled gently, stirring a glow that slowly waned and waxed, as if mimicking a heartbeat.

And maybe it was.

The heartbeat of the ancient creature before them.

It lay curled on the stone, wrapped in wings, which in turn were all encircled by a long tail that ended in a fan of membrane. It was a mankra . . . only tenfold larger than any seen during the attack. It rose like a shadowy mountain at the cavern's center. Its massive chest lifted and fell, barely discernible, exhaling with the slightest wheeze.

Though it lived, the passing centuries had weathered it—evident from the tattered gray fur, the bones pressing against thin skin, the wrinkled and shriveled state of the wings. The ears lay flat, with one torn away long ago. Other scars crisscrossed the body, mapping a history of strife and pain.

Still, Nyx gave all of this little heed.

Instead, her fiery eyes peered past age and frailty to the heart—not the one thumping quietly after millennia of slumber, but to the true shining core of this great warrior. It blazed with a golden purity that ached through her. She basked in its beauty, at the eternity it represented, at the sheer magnificence of the power.

If she listened, she could hear a whisper of ancient battles, the dreams of this great beast, its hopes, its promises, even a grief that had no bottom. Yet it remained strong, a font of bridle-song that would challenge even Daal's wellspring.

Unable to stand before such majesty, she fell to her knees in front of this king. She recognized the bronze queen had gone to great effort to keep him alive, to preserve this golden ember, to hold it safe in the hope of one last fight.

Nyx named this ancient king, knowing it to be true.

"Khagar."

70

SADDLED ON RURO, Esme raced with Abresh along a ridgeline. Crikit sped alongside the ürsyn with a blur of sharp legs. Behind them, a storm gave chase. A cannon boomed, sounding like thunder, heralding the battle to come.

She twisted back and shaded her eyes.

Out of the glare, riding high, a swarm of bronze hornets swept toward them, about to overtake them. The *ta'wyn* filled the sky to the north, too innumerable to count. Sunlight glinted off their metal, turning each into a fiery spark.

Another blast drew her eyes to the east, to the black sea. Above that burning expanse of glass, the *Fyredragon* challenged the horde, successfully drawing off a majority of the enemy. The ship's huge forges blazed, sending the craft higher. The crew was clearly striving to climb above the enemy, to perhaps use those flames as weapons.

Another cannon fired into the throng, but it seemed to do no damage.

Abresh hissed in warning. Esme turned her attention forward and grabbed tight to the saddle. She caught hold as Ruro leaped off the ridge. The beast flew, struck the lower slope, skidding on its hind end, then bounded up again.

Esme had never imagined the ürsyns possessed such speed.

Ruro raced up the next dune.

Once on top, Esme spotted scores of other riders, all riding double. The pairs hurried their mounts in a dizzying, ever-widening pattern, spreading away from the flags that marked the village of Tosgon.

She understood.

They were scattering outward—not only to draw the *ta'wyn* by the motion of their wild rides, but to enlarge the target area, to spread the fall of deadly bronze over a wider stretch, to keep the enemy from concentrating solely on the village.

With her cheek to Abresh's back, Esme stared toward those flapping flags, where Tosgon had gained new guardians.

Two massive molagi stood posted by the entrance, looking like a pair of black dunes, only with razored claws and armored carapaces. Four more giants roamed a perimeter around Tosgon, ready to shift where they were most needed.

For a breath, Esme held out hope.

Then bronze spears fell out of the sky all around. They crashed throughout the desert. One struck halfway down the next dune. Sand blasted high from the impact. Through the dust, a bronze shape burst forth, moving incredibly fast. It barely resembled a person, just the scarcest approximation, a sculpture still raw and molten from a forge.

The *ta'wyn* ignored them and headed for the village flags.

Abresh growled a command to her mount. Ruro bounded toward the *ta'wyn*. As they closed upon the enemy, Abresh lowered her spear, like a knight's lance. This threat drew the enemy's attention.

The *ta'wyn* slid across the sand, trenching deeply.

Abresh shouted to Esme, *"Haryn!"*

Esme knew that word, if not its intent. Still, she responded to the urgency in Abresh's voice and snatched the horn at her knee. She yanked it to her lips and blew with all her strength, alerting all around her of the danger.

But that was not its purpose.

The blaring note had a strange effect. The *ta'wyn* recoiled from it, reminding Esme of Nyx's reaction to the same noise. Whatever vibration blasted out of the horn, it seemed to affect these bastards as well.

Abresh rode down upon the huddled *ta'wyn*. Her spear aimed for its chest. When it struck, Esme expected the weapon to shatter and girded herself for the impact. Instead, the shaft of sharpened bone pierced through the bronze as if it were molten.

Ruro sped past the impaled figure, then circled back, slipping sideways. Stunned and caught by the sudden turn, Esme got thrown from the saddle. She hit the sand hard and rolled down the dune.

The ürsyn bounded away, aiming again for the *ta'wyn*.

Esme spun, searching for the horn. It was nowhere in sight, but Crikit raced up to her. Esme rolled on her side. Without unhooking the horn from the molag's harness, she got her lips in place and blew hard.

At the crest of the dune, Abresh leaped off the saddle with glass daggers in both hands. She struck the immobilized *ta'wyn* and ripped savagely at it with her daggers.

Unfortunately, due to her bruised lungs, Esme lost her breath too soon.

As the blaring note died, Abresh tried to pull a dagger free, but the bronze had hardened around it. It seemed the vibration of the horn's blast had a deleterious effect not only on the senses of the *ta'wyn,* but also on the substance of its bronze, momentarily weakening the already pliable metal.

Esme sucked for another breath, but it was too late.

The now-freed *ta'wyn* snatched Abresh by the arm, breaking it like a twig.

No . . .

Then from the far side of the dune, Ruro bounded into view and crashed into the *ta'wyn*, sending it flying high. Abresh got knocked aside.

On her knees, Esme blew loudly again, long enough for Abresh to regain her saddle, even with one arm. The pair raced back to her, slowing briefly for Esme to throw herself over the saddle.

As they took off again, she glanced back.

The *ta'wyn,* speared and daggered, still crawled up from the sand and slogged toward the flags of Tosgon. Esme quailed at the strength of these beings.

How can we hope to hold them off?

The same held true for another group.

A cannonade of blasts drew her attention east, to where the *Fyredragon* struggled amidst a swarm of fiery bronze. One section of its balloon fluttered amidst flames.

Esme cast her gaze farther east, sending out a plea.

We need help.

71

DAAL HUNG IN Shiya's arms. He shivered and felt hollowed out, an empty husk of bone and skin with nothing beneath. Each breath took labor, maybe every heartbeat, too. After being harshly sapped by the *Dräshra* of all his strength, he could barely hold his legs under him.

Steps away, Nyx rose from where she knelt before the great mankra curled at the center of the cavern. She blazed like a torch from the energy hammered into every fiber of her being. To his eyes, she looked less flesh and more a figure of pure light.

He tore his gaze to the side. Around the cave, four waist-high tanks circled the beast, burbling softly with a golden alchymy. Parched for energy, Daal sharpened his sense of bridle-song. He watched those tanks trickle strength into the mankra, likely sustaining it, possibly over millennia.

Daal followed those four streams to the golden fire fed by those energies. Like Nyx, this beast glowed with such fervency he had difficulty discerning its ancient body through that shine. The flesh looked inconsequential compared to its shining core.

He had heard Nyx name this beast.

Khagar.

If true, here rested the Guardian of this desert, a Chanrë god, the true heart of the *Kraena,* the horde-mind of this colony.

Nyx lifted a hand and rested her palm reverently on the crown of this king. "At the end of the war, after the *Kraena* were torn asunder, the *Dräshra* must have retreated here, fighting a last stand to save this great beast, to preserve a golden ember of the horde-mind."

Daal glanced back to the other cavern. He remembered the bronze queen's warm fondness for the little dhelprä. She clearly had shared a similar affection for this king. Over the centuries, she must have grown an affinity for this land and its creatures, an empathy whetted by bridle-song, binding her to this desert.

But none more so than to this beast.

Daal stared at the ancient mankra and suspected why the *Dräshra* had fought so hard, endured so long, protected this creature with such love.

Here lies the Bashaliia of that bronze queen.

Graylin drew Daal from the wonder to the practical. "But what are we supposed to do now?" he asked, turning to Nyx. "What was the purpose in guiding us down here? Does she expect you to take over her guardianship?"

"No," Nyx said. "She spoke to me when she filled me with Daal's strength. She must believe I can somehow bring Khagar back to the world, to bring the fight once again to the *Revn-kree,* to rid these lands of its entrenched army."

"How?" Shiya asked, still supporting Daal. "His ancient body can never leave this cave."

"That's correct. This will be his tomb, resting forever next to the queen who loved him." Nyx turned her gaze from Khagar. "The *Dräshra* forced this strength into me for a reason, perhaps to grant me the power to free this last golden ember of the *Kraena* and carry it out to the world. Perhaps it can be a torch to draw the ravening horde, a seed from which that ancient mind can be reborn."

Graylin stepped closer, protectively so. "How? Did the *Dräshra* offer any guidance?"

Nyx winced at his words. "No, not exactly. But she pressed upon me the word *wyldstrom.* You all heard it, too."

She searched their faces, clearly looking for any insight. She especially lingered on Arryn, who knew these lands best, but even he shook his head.

"What does that mean?" Graylin pressed her.

"I don't know. I sense it's what she wanted me to become. It sounded like she didn't have the strength to do it herself—not in energy, certainly not in heart. After so long, I don't believe she could let Khagar go. She needed another to take this burden from her."

"You," Arryn whispered.

Daal stirred enough to speak, rasping out his certainty. "You . . . You're wrong."

Gazes swung his way.

He shook his head, an effort that trembled his knees. "Can't you all see? She didn't fill Nyx with my power to give her strength, but to *empty* me."

Graylin frowned. "What do you—"

"She hollowed me out as a vessel for that fiery heart, to carry it out from here."

"Did she tell you this?" Nyx asked.

"No, but I know it to be true. The emptiness inside me is drawn to that golden fire. It pulls at me. My hollow wellspring is meant to preserve Khagar's essence, long enough to leave here. After that, maybe the energy the *Dräshra* passed to you was intended to do as you said. To draw the lost flock, to forge anew the *Kraena* horde-mind."

"How can you be sure?" Graylin asked.

"Let us see."

Daal shoved out of Shiya's grip and staggered toward Khagar. With each step, his certainty grew. The wellspring, stripped and starving, led him forward more than his legs.

"Careful," Nyx warned.

He cast her a disparaging look.

When have you ever been careful?

Once standing before the blaze, Daal lifted his palms. Too weak to stop himself, too drawn by the hunger inside him, he fell against the wizened king—and kept falling.

He felt himself tumble into that shining heart. He gasped as he reached the core of that blaze. He burned within it, but rather than being consumed, the wellspring inside him fed greedily. It sapped fire and energy into its parched emptiness, blazing light into darkness.

Daal writhed as the strength poured into him—not from the burn of that flowing fire, but from the memories that came with it. Similar to when he communed with Nyx, he became this great beast. He fell back through countless millennia to a life that was not his own but became his nonetheless.

The memories streamed too fast, too large. Snatches of the past burned across his mind's eye, cascading in a flurry of experiences, muddled and confusing, terrifying and heartbreaking.

—he nestles in warm fur, tastes sweet milk on his tongue, as a chorus sings around him.
—he flies across open sand, the sun blazing above and off the crimson dunes.
—he mates for the first time, wrapped by wings and flowing air, tails entwined.
—in all and forever, he is alone, but many, seeing the beauty of the desert through a thousand eyes.

Then those memories raced ever faster, burning with blood and strife, with misery and loss. Daal fought against that tide, but it refused to be denied.

—he screams at bronze, with the fury of all.
—wings and bones burn to ash as the sky darkens with smoke.
—sand melts into a sea of molten fire.
—in all and forever, he is alone, but many, seeing death and loss through a thousand eyes.
—agony, as even that multitude is ripped from him, as his body is torn and others scattered.

—he finds solace in one heart, who shared these horrors with him, who made a promise in song, who dreamed with him through the long, endless night.
—here he has been forever, no longer many, but not alone.
—not until this moment . . .

A sorrow without end, grief without limit, drove Daal back into his body, now raging with fire. He could not contain the immensity of a memory spread across millennia, or of the brief glimpse of the enormity of one mind shared by many.

He stumbled back, fleeing the anguish, the heartache.

He glanced toward the outer cavern, toward the dark queen entombed on her throne. The misery of that loss carried out with him.

He crashed to his knees, burning in that golden blaze of a broken heart. His body shook, quaking with power, struggling to hold it all, wanting to forsake it but knowing he must not.

Then arms of bronze caught him, held him.

His memories blurred with another, one more ancient. He reached with a shared palm and touched a warm cheek, one that shimmered into another queen, whom the ancient one knew well.

My love . . .

Then he was gone.

72

NYX RUSHED FORWARD as Daal collapsed into Shiya's arms. His body went slack, his head lolling back. Still, his form blazed with a golden fire that blinded. She lifted a hand against it, but its shine burned through her flesh.

She stopped before reaching him, fearful of their connection, of what touching that fire might do to her—and to him. Especially as she already raged with energies she could barely contain.

"We must get Daal out of here," she gasped. "Back to the grotto and open air."

Shiya picked him up, carrying him in her arms as if bearing aloft a golden sun.

"Hurry," Nyx urged everyone. "He cannot hold that power for long."

They all got moving swiftly.

Still, Nyx glanced back to the dark mountain of Khagar.

Before Daal had fallen into Shiya's arms, Nyx had watched the rhythmic throbbing of the glowing tanks slow, marking time of another's failing heart. Then that all faded, whispering away with a final wheezing breath. In that moment, with the golden ember handed to another, her bridled eyes picked out a tracery of light that remained behind. It flared momentarily brighter, as if joined by another, then with a final twinkling, it all dissipated into darkness.

"Be at peace," she whispered to that eternal darkness. "Both of you."

As she reached the exit, a glow drew her back. From the shadows, the dhelprä circled from behind Khagar's dark bulk and flowed to nestle against his quiet wings.

The dhelprä shone there like a candle in the dark.

Nyx stared a moment, sensing this creature was the last of its kind, one too beautiful for this harsh world. As if acknowledging this, it bounded up and away. Its shine flowed into the shadowy mountain behind it—leaving its dark body behind on the stone. For a breath, the glow maintained the shape of the dhelprä—then like a candle snuffed, it vanished, maybe chasing after those last scintillating sparks.

She recognized this last act.

Of a duty finished.

Nyx shoved away, knowing hers was not. She remembered Arryn's description of the legend of the dhelprä, how sighting one was a promise of great fortune.

May that still hold true now.

She hurried after the others. They rushed back along their path until bright sunlight beckoned. Ahead, Bashaliia and Pyllar stood guard, limned against the brilliance. She crossed to her winged brother, while he danced slightly on his hindlegs in greeting, an antic from when he had been no bigger than a winter goose.

She pushed into his warmth, his musk, his nuzzling nose.

Nyx needed this moment, praying to never lose him. She understood how painful it must have been for the *Drāshra* to let Khagar go, especially after so many millennia together.

No wonder you did not want to take on this burden.

To the side, Vikas rushed up to Graylin and Kalder. The quartermaster gestured with urgency, her wide brow knit with concern. Nyx caught the symbol for *horn*—then she heard it, too.

Echoing across the broken cliffs of the Heep, a loud blaring reached the grotto, likely rising from the *kalkäa* sleds that had followed them here.

Nyx patted Bashaliia and hurried to Graylin. "What's wrong?"

The answer came from Arryn, who had been in an earnest conversation with Irquan. The man's words were breathless, his eyes pained. "Tosgon is under attack. Your ship, too. From the Dragon. We must get back."

"That'll do no good," Nyx said. "We're too few. We need a greater weapon."

She turned to Shiya, who had carried Daal to the mouth of the cavern. She had laid him at the edge, keeping him in the shadows. His body still burned within that blazing pyre, barely discernible through the fire.

Nyx hurried toward him. "I must free the ember Daal carries. Use it to force the mankrae to remember their past, to remind them of who they once were." She turned to the others. "But to do that, you must all leave."

Graylin stepped after her. "We can't do that."

Nyx was not about to pitch a battle with him. They had no time. "Trust me in this. The mankrae are already spooked by the sailraft. It can't be here. Neither can Shiya for the same reason. It must be only Daal and me. I'll keep Bashaliia and Pyllar with us as protection, as wings if we need to escape. If those two giants can't keep us safe, a handful of swords and a vargr aren't going to make any difference."

Graylin opened his mouth as if to object, but instead he proved he *had* heard her. "I understand. You must appear defenseless to the mankrae. But what about Bashaliia and Pyllar? Won't their presence scare off the other bats?"

"I'm hoping, if the pair are far enough back in the cave, that they'll not be deemed threatening, especially being bats themselves."

"That didn't stop the wraiths from attacking before," Graylin reminded her.

She nodded. "Exactly. The pair did not intimidate the mankrae enough to chase them away. With the sailraft gone, the horde will likely grow emboldened again."

Vikas nodded, tapping a fist to her shoulder, then pointing at Nyx. "*She's right.*"

Graylin took a deep, shuddering breath, clearly fearful of abandoning Nyx, as he had in the past. But she was not that child in the swamps any longer.

Nyx waved to the sailraft. "Go! It's our only hope to make this work."

Graylin finally relented and motioned everyone back to the raft's hold. "Load up!" He turned back and demanded a concession. "We'll head out, but we'll stick close."

She refused even this. "No. If you're near, the wraiths will be too wary. Head to the Chanrë sleds, find out what is happening across the glass sea. If I forge something here, I must act fast. None of us know how long such a miracle will last."

Least of all me.

NYX KNELT BESIDE Daal and raised her palms, as if warming her hands over the golden pyre of his body. She watched the sailraft vanish over the lip of the grotto. Its flames glowed for a spell, then became lost in the glare. Still, she waited until even the roar of its forges had faded to silence.

She glanced behind her, noting the heavy shift of shadows that marked the presence of Bashaliia and Pyllar in the cave. She took comfort from their bodies, from the glow of bridle-song emanating out of the gloom.

Below her, Daal groaned, his brow beaded with sweat. His lips grimaced as he inwardly fought to hold the heart of a vast colony behind his ribs. It threatened to pound and shatter free of that small cage.

I can wait no longer.

She lowered her hands and placed them atop his chest. With her touch, he jolted under her, his back arching so high that only the back of his head and his heels touched the stone. As he collapsed back down, she fell into him, into the golden fire.

She gasped out of her lips and his.

There was little communion, no sharing of selves, only flames. She struggled to find any flesh, anything to anchor herself to him. She feared such power may have burned Daal away.

Still, she girded herself, refusing to succumb to despair. She knew the only way to help him, to even attempt this impossible act, was to draw energy from him, from his wellspring, to relieve the tension, like removing a brick from the dam before it burst.

But how?

She already brimmed with power. It raged through every corner of her body. Still, she sensed that insatiable hunger inside her. Even with Daal's wellspring emptied into her, that craving remained. In the past, she had always fought it, refusing what it demanded, lest she lose control, lest she be consumed by it.

Last winter, she had reached that edge, even surging past. It terrified her, a path to unending madness. She had only been pulled back from that ravening edge by Daal, his lips on hers and the promise it held. In that stormy madness, he had been a lighthouse, shining with gold across a raging sea of emerald.

I must do the same here.

For him, for her, for any hope of a future.

She closed her eyes and reached to the sigil branded deep inside her. It still scared her, but it had to be withstood. As she held her palms tight to Daal, she sent a strand of bridle-song and touched the sigil branded into her by the raash'ke. Again, it exploded with arcane energies, so fierce it cast back the fires in both of them.

She gritted her teeth, feeling Daal do the same, a tensing of his whole body. Then their two pyres—hers and his—crashed back together. The ground shook under them. She heard glass break in the distance. Such was the raw power given substance by this act, fueled by all the energies between them.

She fixed an image in her head. When battling the Hálendiian corsair over the Tablelands, she had forged song into a fiery sword and ripped through the ship's gasbag.

Here, she chose another form.

Of a lighthouse in a stormy sea.

Daal moaned, perhaps recognizing it, too.

She arched her back and sang with all her breath and fiery strength. She cast out waves of bridling gold into the grotto, carrying herself there, too. She swept in a circle, as if she had wings, faster and faster, building a fiery whirl-wind trapped in black glass.

She then let ancient words burst from her throat, born out of that exploded sigil. She sang song into purpose. Lowering her chin, she coalesced all that energy into form—not a shining sword, but a glowing fiery column.

She held it there—then and only then did she open herself to the golden pyre inside Daal. She let her dark well's tidal pull draw energy from his spring. Still, as that power flooded into her, she denied herself that strength.

It is not mine.

Instead, she diverted that golden flow toward her creation in the grotto. She let it surge up the inside of her column and burst out the top, flaming with the golden purity of Khagar's heart, of a past long forgotten.

She held it there.

A beacon shining out into these cliffs.

A lighthouse for those lost to madness.

As she waited, she sang her welcome to all that could hear.

But would they remember?

Time grew suspended, impossible to judge before the splendor shining in the grotto, reflected in the glass. Still, her throat ached as she held this torch high. She watched both from her knees next to Daal and through her spirit atop the beacon.

Then a single shadow sped into view. It swept a wary circle across the space. Then another. And another. Still, they hung back, attracted but scared, likely struggling with memories buried deep.

As they spun, she noted the trails of emerald fury tracing the air.

Then more pushed through the pinched rift or sailed down from on high. The air soon fluttered with wings. Their savage cries echoed off the walls, rising into a crescendo. But what burned out in the grotto withstood it all, as surely as Daal's lighthouse in a raging emerald sea.

Finally, maybe due to a bravery born of numbers, one drew closer to the golden pyre. A small wraith, barely bigger than a winter goose, like when Bashaliia swept back into her life. It drew to a tentative hover, keening a softer note.

Nyx watched it from below and on high.

Trust yourself, little one.

Her spirit reached out from that beacon, encouraging the bat to come closer. Down low, her arm raised, too, lifting from Daal's chest, while keeping the other rooted to him, to maintain this conduit of shared power.

Then something struck her outstretched hand.

Pain lanced up her arm.

She gasped and yanked it back, realizing a passing wraith had ripped into it.

Blood poured down her wrist. She cradled it closer, then saw her last finger had been torn off.

No . . .

In a panic, she shoved away, as if she could escape her hand, but she could not escape what it meant. She flashed to an unending nightmare, one with a portent of doom and failure.

. . . breathless, she skids to a stop at the summit. She takes in everything, recognizing she is older, scarred, missing a finger on her left hand . . .

She stared down as blood flowed.

The same hand, the same finger.

She fell back. Only then did she realize what her panic had wrought. Out in the grotto, the mass of wraiths screamed with fury. The lighthouse fell apart under that onslaught, no longer supported by song or energy.

The golden pyre—the last ember of the *Kraena*—burned away. What had been preserved for millennia died before her, assaulted by the mad fury of its feral descendants. Torn apart, consumed, corrupted. As she watched, pure gold slowly turned to raging emerald.

"What have I done?" she moaned.

Daal stirred. He shone with a residual golden glow, enough to allow him to crawl to her, escaping the savagery behind him.

"You're hurt," he gasped out.

She stared down, horror-struck by her hand, knowing what it foretold, what was proven here now.

"I've failed . . . failed us all."

73

KANTHE STUDIED THE defeated faces of those who had joined him on this accursed sojourn to Hálendii. Or in Rami's case, at his backside as he relieved himself into the bucket in the corner of their cell. Then again, Mikaen had been generous enough to supply them with a bucket—but only *one,* as his compassion had its limits.

Frell sat on a pile of soiled hay that he had swept into a corner. He stared at a roach beset by lice on the floor, likely sympathetic to the plight of the beleaguered bug.

In a neighboring cell, Cassta paced the length of her space—not in fury, but more studied calculation. Their captors had stripped her to a loose shift, taking not only her blades, but also her bells. Someone had clubbed her during that process, as evident from a swollen bloody eye. Still, they could not steal her dignity; even now she strode with determination, showing no fear.

If only the three in this cell could be so resolute.

Kanthe cradled his left arm. Besides yanking off his armor and underleathers, the guards had pulled off his bronze forearm and hand. That loss stung. With Tykhan gone, Kanthe would never see its like again. Still, he imagined worse insults would come.

Rami had suffered the same disrobement, but he did get to keep all his limbs, although for how long remained a question. As the Klashean prince turned from the bucket, his face remained grim and haunted. The reason lay outside their cell, spread across a rack. There, Gheel's cold body still dripped clotted blood.

Over the past four bells, no one had gotten any rest. With only bars between them and the torture room, they had been forced to listen. Despite Gheel's attempt at stoicism, it was not long before moans and screams had been ripped from him. Every man's throat eventually broke. Still, any answers the torturer had sought to dig out of him with hot irons, spiked bars, and pliers had been denied.

Kanthe stared into that dank chamber, avoiding the ruins of Gheel's body. The dungeon lay deep under the castle, cold and damp. On the back wall, the steel doors of a hearth stood open, ruddy with coals inside—not to warm the space, but to heat iron meant for flesh. Across the walls hung tools for the same end, but each was refined to its own particular means of torture.

The only way out of this windowless corner of the castle was through a set of timbered doors, chained and locked, with guards posted inside and out.

A commotion there drew their attention.

Voices shouted and keys clinked. The door burst open, and a mountainous figure bowed into the low-roofed space. Even without the silver armor and crimson countenance, Kanthe would have recognized Thoryn, captain of the Silvergard. Upon his heels, the king of the realm entered, still in battle gear—even though the fighting had long ended, both inside and outside Highmount's walls.

Or so the gossip among the guards attested.

Kanthe stood straighter and shifted his stumped arm behind him, feeling exposed and vulnerable. Since his capture, this was the first time Mikaen had made an appearance. His brother had not bothered to watch the torture of the captured imperial prisoner. A surprising absence, given Mikaen's predilection for blood and misery.

Mikaen strode to the cell. The smile beyond his mask held no warmth. He glanced at the ruins of Gheel, likely left there to intimidate, which it certainly had. When Mikaen turned back, his eyes squinted with irritation, plainly disappointed to miss out. Or maybe he had heard that nothing had been gained from the prisoner but screams, blood, and bile.

Mikaen collected himself, drawing straighter.

"I'm sorry I've not greeted you properly," he said. "You've all caused much strife, but nothing that can't be rectified over time. And this attack will serve me well in quashing dissent and discord. Plus, the attack on the coast has kept me preoccupied, but that has blown itself out. Klashean forces have retreated back to their shores, bloodied and broken."

Rami spoke from behind. "I'm sure whatever damage was wrought was but a fraction of what was inflicted upon your fleets."

Kanthe wanted to glare at Rami. Nothing would be gained by aggravating their temperamental host.

"Believe what you wish," Mikaen responded, "but it was our forces that captured an imperial prince, brother to an empress. I'll be displaying our success in a few days, during a festival, where you'll be the guest of honor. A public execution also helps solidify sentiment. The bloodier, the better."

Kanthe tried his best to intervene. "Rami would serve better as a hostage, to gain some advantage in exchange or in coin down the line."

"Perhaps if I was feeling so charitable." Mikaen's gaze hardened on Kanthe. "But not after you all tried to steal my treasure, one whose bronze is worth far more than its weight in gold."

Kanthe scowled.

Eligor . . .

"We did not come to steal it," Kanthe said hotly. "But to destroy it."

"In that you failed, too. While it was damaged, the Iflelen have assured me they have discovered a new means to accelerate any repair. To restore it fully."

Frell stepped closer. "How do they plan to accomplish that?"

Mikaen's gaze flicked to the alchymist. "Perhaps you may discover that on your own. The Iflelen have asked me to deliver you to them. It seems they have much need for warm bodies—though, such participants seem to grow *cold* fairly quickly."

Frell's face pinched with worry, but more likely at the rehabilitation of Eligor than his own fate.

As Mikaen turned to Cassta, Kanthe took a protective step in her direction. "I owe the Brotherhood of Asgia a considerable sum for services rendered of late. But upon discussion, they have offered a generous discount—if my payment comes packaged with one from the Rhysian sisterhood. I understand there is little love lost between these two assassin groups."

Kanthe glanced to Cassta, who for the first time looked genuinely scared. Her expression dismayed Kanthe more than any threat of torture.

Mikaen took a deep breath, folding his hands behind his back. "Of course, I could not celebrate the return of my twin brother without a proper gift." Mikaen reached back around and touched his mask. "I feel, as twins, we should look the part. So, I discovered a fine remedy."

He waved to Thoryn, who brought around a half-mask, one much like the king's. Only this one was meant to adorn the opposite side of a face, a mirror to Mikaen's. Also, this guise was sculpted not of silver but of black iron.

Kanthe wondered how long ago Mikaen had crafted this gift. He clearly savored delivering it in person.

Mikaen plucked the mask from Thoryn. "I thought iron would better match your dark features." He swung around and strode away. "But that does not mean we don't want you to show remorse for your betrayal."

Upon reaching the open hearth, Mikaen placed the mask atop the hot coals, then turned back to Kanthe.

"Once it's glowing a deep red, a blush to match your shame, I shall personally set it upon your face." Mikaen glanced back. "To heat it properly should take no more than a few bells, then I'll be back. Your guests, of course, will have the honor of witnessing this gift bestowed from king to beloved brother."

With that pronouncement, Mikaen departed with a flourish of his armor, drawing Thoryn with him. Once the door was slammed, locked, and guarded, Kanthe crossed to the cell bars. He stared across at the mask, knowing Mikaen had left it in view so Kanthe could watch it slowly heat up.

Rami drew next to him. "I thought Mareesh was a bastard of a brother."

Kanthe shrugged. "I don't know. Mikaen did bring a gift—one he clearly put a lot of thought into."

Frell crossed over, raising a concern larger than the four of them. "If they can truly restore Eligor, the world is doomed. Especially if he can reach the key to the *turubya*. With our failure to even learn its location, there is no hope."

"Maybe one," Kanthe mumbled.

"What's that?" Rami asked.

"We better hope Nyx fails as badly as we did. If her group ever gets that second *turubya* running, then we'll be handing the world to Eligor."

"I don't think we can hope for that," Rami said. "It's not reasonable."

Kanthe turned to him. "Why?"

Rami sighed. "Because no one can fail as miserably as we did."

Arkival limne of
Mankrae
(native to the
Barrens)

ELEVEN

WYLDSTROM

What is a gale without wynd? What is a storm without thundre? What is a quak without rumbelen? What is snow without ies? Strip awei strengthe from strif & you are leff with nothing but the world's fury without voyce. Yet, beware wenn such fury finds a neu wey to be herd.

—From *The Unforeseen Path*
by Jzan Per, a Harpic cleric from
the fourteenth dynasty

74

NYX CROUCHED WITH Daal in the cave, well away from its mouth. He had wrapped her hand using a scrap of his riding leather, a piece already ripped loose by a mankra claw, then tied it with a strip of bandage. Blood still seeped, and pain ached up her arm, even behind her squinted eyes.

"Should we worry about poison?" Daal asked, inspecting his work. "From the bite?"

"I . . . I don't know, but as thickly as the wound bled and as quickly as my finger had been ripped off, if there was any venom, it likely washed out."

At this moment, she almost wished for poison to swoon her away—from her pain, from her failure, from the doom that the torn finger represented.

She stared out into the glassy grotto.

No longer bolstered by her bridle-song, the fiery beacon thrashed wildly, ravaged by the powerful screams of the ravening horde. Her beacon had only lasted this long due to the fire she had fed into it from Daal, the last golden ember of Khagar.

But even that support would soon die.

Khagar's golden glow barely showed any longer. The beauty was pillaged and tormented, consumed and polluted. It now raged with an emerald fire all its own, transformed into a beacon of madness.

Nyx despaired. All that the mankrae once had been—the brave guardians of these lands—had been torn apart, extinguishing their preserved memory for all time, never to be recovered.

Some trace of gold still shone in Daal, but it was a mere whisper, only enough to return some strength to him.

"More wraiths keep coming," Daal whispered, trying to keep their presence hidden. "Hundreds by now. We can't risk escaping with Bashaliia and Pyllar through that throng. We'll have to wait for the ember to fade and for them to return to their nests."

She sighed. "As long as the beacon burns, calling to their madness, they'll keep coming."

"Like moths to a torch."

"Only these moths aren't burning up. They're growing stronger, feeding on the madness, then screaming to stoke that ember even hotter. This cycle keeps drawing in more and more of their kind."

Through her bridle-sharp sight, she knew this to be true.

The golden heart of Khagar, tormented into an emerald madness, had only grown fiercer as it was corrupted. The poisonous taint spread like wildfire through the gathering mankrae, touching one heart, then leaping to another and another.

An emerald storm raged out there, whirling faster, drawing even more to the flame. The glass of the grotto's walls reflected it all back, as if amplifying it.

She had to turn aside, unable to bear it any longer. But it was not just despair that forced her to look away—but desire. She could not deny a poisonous appeal, the raw seduction of what burned out in the grotto.

She remembered when last she had raged with emerald fire. Out in the Frozen Wastes, under icy stars, staring down a Hálendiian battle barge. But another remembered it, too. Deep down, something dark stirred within the ravenous pit inside her. It responded to the storm outside. It did not care where that fire came from, or what hue it took, only that it must be possessed.

She pushed her chin to her shoulder, refusing to stare into that poisonous maelstrom. She recognized another was at risk. She looked toward Bashaliia. Her brother shone with a gold warmth.

He pined softly at her, noting her attention and distress.

Still, she read the emerald flares at the edges of Bashaliia's glow, a residual taint from the Spider's corruption that had refused to burn fully away. His golden heart held that madness at bay most times. But with the storm at their door, that emerald fire had stoked into a corona around his golden core.

"We must not stay here," she mumbled.

"We can't leave," Daal reminded her, shifting closer but not daring to touch her.

She fought against reaching to him, of pulling him to her, but she feared losing control. She risked a glance back to the grotto's poisonous maelstrom.

Not even a glint of gold shone out there.

All of the bronze queen's efforts, the millennia spent to preserve hope, the long sleep of a brave king . . .

All gone, fed into that maelstrom.

Nyx stiffened with an abrupt realization. It clenched her whole body. Even her wounded hand. Pain shot up her arm, flaring into her heart—as did certainty.

She suddenly recognized what raged out there.

"*Wyldstrom,*" she murmured.

Daal turned to her.

Nyx nodded to the raging inferno, to a strength amplified by madness. "That must be what the *Dräshra* was trying to tell me. *Wyldstrom.* A storm born of madness, birthed from the golden core of Khagar." Nyx turned to Daal. "This may not be failure. But hope."

"How can you be sure? And how is this hope?"

Nyx was not certain, but her mind spun, as fast as the whirlwind in the grotto. "I think the *Dräshra* feared this outcome but knew it was inevitable. Only she could not bring herself to do what needed to be done. Even if she had been able to wield a depth of bridle-song like me—to forge a beacon to draw the mankrae—she did not have the *heart* to lose Khagar, nor the *will* to allow his golden core to be corrupted. She could never make that sacrifice, not after so many millennia together."

Nyx closed her eyes, trying to fathom that stretch of time, to see the desert slowly change beyond these caverns. The *Dräshra* must have witnessed the eventual corruption of the mankrae, watching as grief turned to anger, loss into madness. A ravening that grew ever more powerful, enough to be a weapon against an old enemy.

Earlier, when Nyx and Daal were attacked, she had wondered herself if the madness had made them stronger.

Is that what the Dräshra *had witnessed over these countless millennia?*

As Nyx spun across that span of time, she wondered what *else* might have changed as a result of those powerful screams. Had those anguished cries altered the land itself? She considered the crystalline chimes of the Örgös, the debilitating blasts of the pärde horns. Was the desert echoing back that millennia-old scream of loss and pain of its former guardians?

She could not know.

Daal asked the question that needed answering. "What do we do?"

Nyx whispered the answer, hearing again the words of the *Dräshra*. "Be the *wyldstrom*."

Daal looked at her.

She kept her gaze on the grotto. "I must go out there."

"Nyx, that's certain madness."

She nodded. "It is exactly that—and I must carry it out to the world." She turned to the golden heart shining behind her. "But I'm not going alone. I'll be bringing my own Khagar."

Daal followed her gaze and flinched. "Bashaliia? They'll ravage his spirit, corrupt him as surely as they did the golden ember."

"I must risk it. I must be harder than bronze, to do what the *Dräshra* could not. To use Khagar's essence to corrupt his flock, then use their strength like a whip, to drive it to her will."

"And you can?"

"Too much is at stake not to try."

"Nyx . . . you'll destroy the mankrae, possibly Bashaliia, too."

Though she remained silent, she let him see how far she was willing to go.

His eyes widened. His face took on a wounded look, as if seeing her for the first time, recognizing how hard and callous she could be if necessary. Even their communing had not prepared him for this. The golden shine of her bridle-song had blinded him to the darker shadow hiding behind it.

Now he saw it.

Her buried self had been forged in grief and loss as surely as the mankrae. There was fury, some madness, all compounded by the weight of responsibility—whether by prophecy or circumstance, it did not matter.

She had to accept it.

And so did he.

She turned from his pained look and faced the maelstrom. The buried part of her understood the dark song being sung out there.

In the Frozen Wastes, she had fought the Spider, burned the taint from a poisoned colony to make them pure. She stared now into the *wyldstrom* outside and knew the extremes she must reach, the cruelties she must aspire to.

She knew what she had to do now.

I must become the Spider.

75

RHAIF RAN ACROSS the smoky deck of the foundering ship. He dodged a flaming drape of balloon fabric. The crew struggled against the fiery threat as much as against the bronze enemy. Bellows and screams chased him across the chaos. Buckets doused pyres. Cannons blasted. Palls of smoke choked thickly, obscuring much.

Overhead, half of the gasbag fluttered in ruins. Yet the *Fyredragon* fought to hold the sky—which was a problem, one that no one seemed to note, except for one panicked thief.

Rhaif had been doing his best to be useful during this doomed battle. Filling buckets, cranking ballistas, relighting tapers, proving himself as fleet-footed as any thief in the night. But that was not his best skill—that was *observation,* an ability to note a pattern to a target's routine, to know when best to strike.

He continued through the chaos, the pools of blood, the torn bodies. He ducked on instinct as something swept out of the smoke, passing under the balloon and over the deck. Huge wings rushed past, stirring the pall, fanning flames. Claws ripped down, snatched a struggling bronze figure, and plucked it off the deck. Once beyond the far rail, it was tossed overboard. The raash'ke then sped upward. It vanished from view, trailing a scream of fury.

Rhaif had caught a glimpse of Tamryn riding low in the saddle. She and the remaining two mounts continued to harass the swarm. They had already lost one rider to the horde. Rhaif had spotted the raash'ke falling out of the sky, wings flailing, crashing to the burning sea under them. Still, the other bats and riders fought fiercely, especially after discerning a weakness among the *ta'wyn.*

Already spooked by past experiences with the mankrae, the enemy had shied from those screeches and beating wings. But even better, Tamryn's team had found a way to clip those wings of the *ta'wyn.* While the enemy's bronze was nearly impervious to weapons, the attackers carried shimmering shields across their shoulders, looking welded and molded in place. A rake of a claw across those plates shattered whatever alchymy kept the bastards afloat. Once damaged, they would go tumbling away and crash into the glass sea. Most still got back up, but they could no longer fly. Instead, they began a long slog toward shore, toward Tosgon.

Such a discovery had protected the last of their balloon. The raash'ke continued to mount a defense, to shield the remains of the giant gasbag. The

Fyredragon dared not get its own wings clipped. Those guardians also kept the deck clear whenever a *ta'wyn* tried to board by landing on the deck. Their swift efforts freed those manning the cannons and ballistas to fire at the bronze hornets buzzing the ship. An iron ball to the gut or spear through their back served as well as a sharp claw at knocking a target from the sky.

Unfortunately, reaching the deck was not the only way to board the ship. A glinting flash drew Rhaif's eyes to the starboard side. A large spear of bronze shot and shattered through the hull. The entire ship rattled from the impact as one of the *ta'wyn* breached the raash'ke cordon and blasted its way inside.

By now, a battle raged across every level of the ship. The raash'ke had no way of reaching the enemy *inside* the ship. With the *ta'wyn* rampaging below-decks, the *Fyredragon* would eventually be hollowed out from the inside.

This battle is doomed.

Only someone had to make sure the end happened *sooner* rather than later.

Rhaif reached the door to the foredeck, slammed through it, fell down the steps, and burst into the wheelhouse.

Ahead, Darant manned the maesterwheel, sweating thickly, shouting to the crew at the subwheels and levers. They all struggled to keep the ship in the air, to work its forges—at least the engines that remained, those that hadn't already been damaged by the bronze invaders.

Rhaif, breathless with urgency, raced to the wheel. "Darant! Cut the forges!"

The captain scowled from the wheel. "What are you ranting about?"

Rhaif's panic drew Krysh, who rushed over, leaving the farscopes to Fenn. Rhaif glanced around. Jace was still gone. Rhaif had spotted him earlier diving belowdecks with a giant ax.

But it was not that *observation* that had fired Rhaif's flight down to the wheelhouse.

"Up top," Rhaif gasped, trying to get them to understand. He lifted a hand high, then swept it down. "The *Fyredragon*. Every time it founders. From a blown section of balloon, from a snuffed forge. When the ship drops *down*. Toward the sea. The number of *ta'wyn* drops, too."

He choked on his words.

"What do you mean?" Krysh pressed him.

Rhaif swallowed and explained, "They skirt off, fly west. Toward Tosgon." He searched the faces around him, to see if this thief was believed. "It's like the more we look defeated, the more they send their forces to the coast."

Krysh stared hard at Rhaif. "Are you sure?"

"It's what I do. A thief learns to have sharp eyes if he wants to keep his skin."

Darant frowned. "Then what do you expect us to do?"

"Cut the forges. Like I told you." Rhaif pointed to the planks. "Crash us to the sea. Or make it appear that way. Make us look *dead* atop this burning sea."

Krysh slowly nodded. "If the *ta'wyn* believe we're stranded, they may abandon us, considering us no longer a threat, diverting their resources to the other target."

Darant looked grim. "Tosgon."

Rhaif understood his consternation. He had been the one to scold the captain for abandoning the village. Now he was proposing sending what was left of the *ta'wyn* force straight at them.

Rhaif winced at his next words. "We've done all we can to buy them time, to knock down as many of the bastards as possible. But we'll eventually fall, too. And soon. If the *Fyredragon* is destroyed, and all aboard are dead, then the entire world is doomed. Remember, we still have to get to the *turubya,* to ignite the infernal engine."

Krysh nodded. "He's right. We *must* survive, even at the cost of the village."

Darant gripped his wheel and spoke through clenched teeth. "So we play dead and hope Nyx, Graylin, and the others discover a path to that fekkin' Dragon."

"Or I could be wrong, and I'm sending us to our deaths." Rhaif shrugged. "But I'm not the captain who has to make this decision."

Darant looked to Krysh, who also shrugged, leaving the choice to the man at the wheel. The captain took a deep breath, then hollered to his crew, "Take us down! Strangle each forge on my word. We're going to waggle our wings, look distressed, and aim for a hard landing."

Rhaif backed away, his role finished.

I hope this thief hasn't just gotten us all killed.

Darant continued his instructions, growing quieter, more earnest, as the *Fyredragon* sank out of the skies. It dropped in spurts and shakes and sudden plummets. Cannons continued to thunder. Smoke grew thicker. The cries of the raash'ke pierced the winds.

Rhaif shifted to the window as the ship rolled leadenly to one side, spinning slightly. Fiery bronze shapes shook loose from the sinking ship, like flies off the skin of a shivering ox. In the air, the *ta'wyn* spun and hovered, then, as if heeding a clarion, the group flew west, away from them, toward the coast.

Krysh glanced to Rhaif, but neither was ready to admit this was working.

"Hold fast!" Darant shouted, startling Rhaif.

The captain pulled a lever near the wheel. The roar of the forges cut, going dead silent. The *Fyredragon* hung for another breath, then plummeted straight down. While not a far drop, the crash still threw Rhaif off his feet. Far under him, wood shattered with a splintering blast. The entire ship rolled to port, leaning crookedly, held aloft by the last remains of its balloon.

Down on the planks, Rhaif scowled up. "I said to *play* dead."

Shouts rose across the ship, sounding equally dismayed. A single cannon boomed, like a dying man's last cough. Rhaif groaned back to his feet.

"Look," Darant said.

Rhaif staggered to the window. Across the sky, more bronze hornets circled, then drifted west, at first slowly, then more swiftly. A *ta'wyn* leaped from a break in the portside hull, struck the black glass, then trudged off.

Soon others followed.

Fenn called over. "More are leaving," he reported at his farscope. "From all around the ship."

Rhaif searched, but the view grew obscured. Heavy smoke drifted down, falling like a shroud over the ship.

The door burst open behind them. Jace staggered in, his face a mask of blood, his shirt torn from a shoulder. He carried a broad-ax with a broken haft in hand. "What happened?" he panted out.

"That's yet to be determined." Darant stepped over and clapped Rhaif on the shoulder. "But thanks to a certain thief on board, we'll have a chance to find out."

Rhaif shook free of both the captain's grip and his praise. He continued to stare out the window. Through the shroud of smoke, patches of smoldering bronze faded into the distance, heading away.

Heading toward Tosgon.

76

WITH ONE ARM, Esme hugged tight to Abresh, struggling to keep the Chanrë huntress in Ruro's saddle. Earlier, they had strapped the woman's broken limb across her chest, but pain and exhaustion had left Abresh weaving. They could not keep this up for much longer.

Esme clutched the horn she had recovered from Crikit to her lips. Abresh held out a spear of sharpened bone, one of their last. Over the course of what felt like both an eternity and a heartbeat, the pair had run down two more of the bronze raiders, stabbing and slashing savagely.

Still, their efforts had only slowed the bastards down.

Nothing more.

Ahead of them now, a third *ta'wyn* had crashed out of the sky into the face of a dune. Its impact buried it to the waist. Taking advantage, they closed upon it.

Ruro pounded up the slope.

As they got near, Abresh shouted. Esme let loose the breath she had been holding. The horn's blast stung her ears. The *ta'wyn,* impossibly fast, had already shoved out of the sand's grip, but the horn's blow caused it to cringe. Its bronze shivered under the assault.

Then they were atop it.

Abresh speared down, but her aim trembled, from exhaustion, from struggling with only one arm. The tip dropped and stabbed through the creature's thigh versus its chest. The spear's butt jolted up, striking the huntress hard in the jaw, knocking her back into Esme.

The horn bobbled at Esme's parched lips. While she kept blowing, the note faltered, enough for the *ta'wyn* to break free. A bronze fist snapped out. It smashed into the horn as they swept past, cracking the curl, sending half flying away, leaving a scrap hanging by a strap in Esme's grip.

Then they were racing off.

Crikit had swung a wide path around the fight and now closed upon their trail, his eight legs blurring over the red sand.

Esme turned, expecting the raider to head off for Tosgon like the others, but instead it reached down and broke the impaled spear and threw it aside. It glared with azure fury—then set off after them.

"Abresh!" Esme shouted, alerting the huntress.

The woman glanced back, then swung forward again. She growled to Ruro and leaned tight. Esme ducked, too. With a powerful bound, the ürsyn sped faster, its claws digging deep.

Abresh guided their path away from the flags of Tosgon.

Crikit followed, keeping to firmer sand off to the side.

Behind them, the *ta'wyn* gave chase, wounded but still swift and determined. Maybe it knew they were defenseless without the horn.

As they raced, flying over ridges and skidding down the far slopes, the hunter gained speed, maybe repairing itself as it ran. All they could do was drag it farther from Tosgon—for as long as the stouthearted Ruro had strength in his limbs.

Abresh must have decided that would not be enough.

With a final pat on Ruro, Abresh rolled out of her saddle. She landed on the lower slope of the dune and skated down, stopping in the path of the incoming *ta'wyn*. She crouched with a spear and planted the butt of her weapon in the sand. She braced it forward with her body.

Esme struggled forward in the saddle and gained the reins. She fought against the urge to swing the ürsyn around. She understood the huntress's gambit. With Ruro less burdened, the ürsyn could fly faster. Abresh had no hope of defeating the *ta'wyn,* only to delay it, to stretch this chase out even further.

And maybe for another reason.

Esme knew the affection the huntress had for her mount. Maybe Abresh hoped this ploy might discourage the *ta'wyn* from its pursuit, to give Esme and Ruro a chance to escape.

Unfortunately, Esme and Abresh both failed to account for another's affection, one returned with as much love and loyalty.

Within a few bounds, Ruro realized who had gone missing, who had put herself in danger. The ürsyn dug and spun back around. Once more, Esme got thrown from the saddle by the sudden unexpected turn. She flew, struck the sand, and rolled down the slope.

By the time she had righted herself, Ruro was racing after Abresh. The huntress must have heard the rip of sand under claws. The woman's shoulders rose higher, as if accepting this fate, knowing this last stand meant not only her death, but also Ruro's.

They would die together.

The *ta'wyn* raced at the huntress, and Abresh dug deeper.

Ruro bounded toward her back, trying to reach her, perhaps to offer her a saddle strap to grab as he passed, intent on drawing the huntress away.

But Ruro lost this race.

The *ta'wyn* struck the spear, broke through it, and smashed into Abresh.

Bones shattered against bronze. The huntress's body flew high, spraying blood, limbs askew. Then she struck the sand, skidding far before stopping, already half buried in her grave.

Ruro roared his grief and anger, driven faster now—not to rescue, but in retaliation.

The *ta'wyn* had been knocked to a stop and now crouched to face the ürsyn. Those azure eyes glowed with satisfaction.

Ruro leaped the last distance, but his exhausted legs finally gave out.

He failed to reach the enemy.

The beast struck the sand in front of the *ta'wyn,* crashing onto his side, but rather than skidding, Ruro spun his body. His quills dug deep, burying his bulk as ürsyns did to hide from the sun. Momentum drove this burrowing effort under the legs of the *ta'wyn.*

Ruro then burst back up, throwing his enemy high.

The *ta'wyn* spun through the air, bronze glinting brightly. It crashed hard onto its face, cratering into the sand.

As it struggled to get up, Ruro spun around and reared up behind it, exposing his long claws.

Esme lunged forward, knowing those sharp nails could do no damage against the bronze. The *ta'wyn* pushed his head out of the sand. Fiery eyes fixed on Esme, responding to the threat of her rush, not worried about guarding its metal back.

Esme did the only thing she could. She swung up the broken half of the horn, still hanging from the strap at her wrist, and brought it to her lips. She blew hard, the note strident—and wrong.

Still, the *ta'wyn* cringed, perhaps at the sight of the dangerous curl, at the stinging blast. Even its body responded in kind, a reflexive memory of what was expected, like a cur salivating at the sight of an offered bone. The bronze rippled, only for a breath—but long enough.

Ruro landed on the back of the *ta'wyn,* pounding down with his massive weight. Claws dug deep into the shivering bronze, driven deeper by the impact. Nails meant for ripping through coarse sand now raked wide swaths across its back.

Esme pictured Abresh's daggers being trapped when bronze had hardened again. Fearing the same, she lowered the horn and hollered at Ruro, "Get back!"

Trained well, the ürsyn responded, retreating a step. Esme could not risk Ruro getting mired into the hardening bronze. For any hope of escape, she still needed Ruro as her mount. They needed to be gone before the bastard recovered—which no doubt he would.

Another responded to Esme's fear and urgency, too.

Crikit raced down the slope, leaped high, and landed on the back of the *ta'wyn*. His eight legs sank deep and scrabbled wildly.

Fearing the worst, Esme lunged for her friend—but was too late.

CRIKIT PISTONS HIS *eight legs, blurringly fast, but it is not sand beneath him. Digging into hot grains normally sharpens his limb's chitinous points.*

Not now.

No, no, no, no . . .

This is slag and mire.

To understand better, he waggles his eye-stalks in all directions. He sees through them all. To his Warmth of Heart ahead, to a beast behind, to the dunes around, to the sticky syrup beneath.

He struggles, as if fighting against the sucking sands found in the dark depths of the ruins.

He knows that danger.

Not this.

He fights to free himself, which sinks him deeper. He loudly snaps a claw in distress, rapid in panic. He clicks the same with his mandibles' palps. They both sound the same plea.

Help, help, help, help . . .

Then one leg-point strikes something hard, deep in the mire. He knows the vibration that shivers up his sensitive limb. Not rock. Crystal, like a lump of salt.

Flat on top. Too flat to perch.

He stamps at it, rapidly, tapping for a hold.

Too hard.

The salt shatters under his leg's chitinous point.

His heart quivers just once in disappointment—then the world explodes beneath him. He is flung high. Ligaments tear. His shell cracks. The fine hairs along the hard apron under him burn away in a flash.

Pain, pain, pain, pain . . .

He crashes, rolling across the sand. Legs crack off. An eye-stalk rips away, going dark. He finally stops, broken and fiery in agony. He does not know what he did wrong. He mewls in fear, in pain, in panic. He tries to snap-click his distress, but he has no claw.

His remaining eye-stalks wave, searching all around.

He sees a wide patch of blackened sand. Farther out, pools of the shining syrup that had mired him. Closer, a beast rolls to its legs in a wave of shoved sand. On the other side, his Warmth of Heart pushes up, wreathed in smoke.

He rushes for safety, for home—as well as he can muster.

His remaining four legs push his belly across the sand. Those grains fight him, but he trenches a path toward his Warmth of Heart. He leaves a wet trail behind him, seeping from cracks, from the ends of missing limbs. He drives on in pain, in determination, in regret.

As he struggles, he waggles his eye-stalks, begging for a scratch, to know he is good.

His Warmth of Heart sees him. A hard breath escapes her that he knows is fear, a fright that matches his own. He hurries to comfort, to get back the same. He balances on four legs and scrabbles to close the distance.

He does not make it. With trembling limbs, he crashes into the sand. He silently calls, using the other name for his Warmth of Heart.

Mama, Mama, Mama, Mama . . .

ON HER KNEES, with her sight still narrowed by the blast, Esme spotted Crikit struggling toward her, then collapsing. His body lay in ruins, charred, broken, weeping a trail behind him. She choked back a sob and crawled to him. She reached him as he lifted a plaintive limb, showing his missing claw, as if asking her to help find it.

He clicked softly, weakly.

She pulled him to her, hugging her arms around him. She reached and tenderly scratched the base of his eye-stalks, something that always comforted him. She avoided the ripped one.

She hummed, letting the vibration of her chest reverberate through him.

I've got you.

His clicking slowed, only tapping now, a sign of contentment.

She stared over his broken carapace to the blasted area of sand. She had been worried about Crikit getting stuck in hardened bronze, but one of his sharply pointed legs must have struck something vital, shattering through it. Whatever it was, the explosion had thrown them all back.

She was surprised Crikit had survived, but he had always been hard-shelled, a survivor like her.

She leaned over him, rocking him gently.

As she did, one eye-stalk slowly dropped, then another. The last one looked at her, shining for as long as it could, then it drooped and fell away, too.

She continued rocking him.

You're a good boy.

She stayed where she was, the fight and fire snuffed out of her. From her vantage, she could see the battle in the distance. Ruro had led them well off from it. To her side, the ürsyn settled next to the grave of the huntress, lying down, not burying himself, letting the world see his grief.

Over by Tosgon, a flag burned, casting up a sigil of smoke. Horns blared across the desert. Small shapes raced over dunes. She saw Crikit was not the only molag to suffer. Black mountains lay broken out there. Three still moved, continuing the defense.

But it was a futile effort.

Bronze glinted everywhere, like dark diamonds cast across the sand. Movement drew her gaze across black glass. Out there, specks of fiery metal burned across the sky, sweeping toward Tosgon. Others trudged across the glass.

Even farther away, she spotted the wreckage of the *Fyredragon*, broken on the burning sea, casting up smoke like the flag of Tosgon.

She continued to rock.

Knowing it was all she could do.

To mourn the dead.

77

AT THE BACK of the cave, Daal helped Nyx into Bashaliia's saddle. With her damaged hand, she needed his aid.

Despite the hardness she had shown earlier, her body trembled under his palms. He was careful to keep his hands on her riding leathers, to avoid touching her skin—especially as Nyx still shone with a deep font of bridle-song, what she had not spent to build her fiery beacon in the grotto.

Once settled, Nyx leaned down and ran her uninjured fingers through Bashaliia's fur. Her face fought to hold its steeliness, but Daal read the fear shining in her eyes. Not for her safety. But for her winged brother, for the sacrifice she must ask of him.

He also noted a paleness to her face that had nothing to do with the loss of blood. While determined on this course, she clearly had doubts. He remembered her despair after the attack, after her finger was ripped away, the anguished words she had lamented.

I've failed . . . failed us all.

He recognized the burden upon her. He reached and touched her knee, ran his hand up her thigh. He flashed to doing the same when there was nothing but bare skin between them. In this moment, he wanted to give all of himself to her, all his strength, the very last bits of gold still warming behind his breastbone. But he knew any traces of memory buried there, a reminder of how much had been lost to madness, would break her.

She needed to be strong.

Stronger than bronze.

She believed she could be. He had seen that resolve, the hard unbending core she hid from all, forged from pain and loss. It had shocked him at first, even dismayed him, but that was a part of who she was.

There could be no brightness without shadows.

She stared down at him and hovered her bandaged hand over his bare skin. "You can do this, Nyx," he whispered.

Blood seeped and dripped onto the back of his hand. Each drop burned with the fire inside her. He turned his palm up, accepting this, accepting all of her.

If you'll let me . . .

She lowered her hand to his. Though still separated by leather and bandage, the two fleetingly became one. He felt the rough saddle between his own thighs. The agony shooting up a limb. He also read the doubt trying to break stone. Rather than deny that hardness in her, he stared at it unflinchingly. He bolstered it with each breath.

Do what you must, and I'll still be beside you.

She squeezed his hand harder, burning blood into him, as if swearing him to this oath. It was a feverish heat such as he had never felt before, a fire that reached his very bones.

Still, he did not waver.

I won't forsake you.

She finally let go, throwing his hand aside, not in denial, only firming herself for what she must do alone.

But not entirely alone.

She stared down at the great beast under her. The pain remained, the guilt, too, but also a hardening resolve.

She glanced to Daal. "Be ready. Once any path is clear, you take off with Pyllar. But stay well away. Where I must go, you cannot follow."

He knew she didn't just mean a path through the sky.

He nodded and stepped clear. He rubbed the hand that still burned from her blood, as if his promise had been branded into him.

Nyx stared ahead into the raging emerald fire, into the *wyldstrom* she must rein to her heart. Then, without looking back, she set off.

Bashaliia shoved away with his powerful legs and danced on the knuckles of his outstretched wings. Once near the cave mouth, he burst out into the grotto.

He challenged that madness with a savage cry.

Then vanished into the storm.

Nyx clutched low in the saddle, keeping her head down, as Bashaliia crashed through the fringes of the whirlwind. The flock—startled by the massive bat's sudden appearance—scattered apart with a flurry of wings, shredding away like fiery flakes.

For protection, she sang a shining nimbus around herself, tapping into what strength she had left. Terror clutched her throat, threatening her hold on her shield.

Nyx willed her brother toward her beacon. It had nearly frayed away and struggled to hold aloft the emerald pyre. Bashaliia reached it. With sharpening turns, he climbed higher in swift sweeps.

All around, the *wyldstrom* raged, reflecting off the glass, making it look as if it stretched off into eternity. The wraiths recovered and lunged at them. They battered at her song's shield with screams, with wings, with lashing claws.

Nyx sought the only shelter and drove Bashaliia toward it.

They climbed to the beacon's top and dove into the emerald pyre—the corrupted and poisoned heart of the colony. The flames blinded her, trapping her in a tempest of fire. Her shield could not hold, not under such a fierce assault. She drew that golden corona closer, stoking it brighter as it shrank around her.

Earlier, when she had been attacked after first stumbling upon the nest, she had done the same. Back then, she had been willing to sacrifice Daal and Pyllar to keep Bashaliia safe from the ravening madness, to keep that emerald poison from igniting his golden heart. Now she had to make a harder choice.

With an agonized pang, she stripped that protection from Bashaliia and drew her shield to her skin, letting its golden shine be her armor. Below her, the emerald fire ripped through her brother's wings, through bones and blood, and struck Bashaliia. It snuffed the golden beauty of her brother—then in another breath, it burst forth again with raging flames.

Bashaliia writhed, burning inside and out.

She caught the briefest flash as her brother was torn away: of his confusion, his fear, his guilt, as if he believed he was being punished.

But she was not done torturing him.

Not yet.

She clutched the sob in her throat, still needing her voice. Below her, the flames inside Bashaliia ignited the agony of another, the remnant of Kalyx, the monster whose body Bashaliia wore. Nyx felt the torture of copper needles drilled into Kalyx's skull, the agony of the whip and burning iron, but worst of all, the anguish of a will broken and enslaved to another.

That pain had been etched forever into the body that Bashaliia wore— along with the monster's fury.

It roared out of Bashaliia's throat. But Nyx knew it wasn't Bashaliia screaming below her—but Kalyx, a creature suffered into being. He screamed in mad fury. Claws lashed against a world that had been far too cruel.

Still, that was not who Nyx needed him to be.

She opened herself to the pyre around her and loosened the reins of the ravenous pit inside her, the hollowness that could never be sated. It exalted in this freedom and drank greedily at the font burning around her. As emerald fire flowed into her, she gripped her cruelty and sapped the flames away from that emptiness inside her. Instead, she poured it into the raging heart below, driving the fiery madness into a new home, a new vessel.

The pit inside her screamed in frustration, while continuing to draw deeply upon the emerald pyre. Still, Nyx denied that hunger, sending the flames down to the bat under her. This went on until the pyre waned, stifled as it was sapped, its energy sent below.

Under her, Kalyx burned away, replaced by another who had suffered far worse. Someone maligned over centuries, tormented over millennia. Someone who had experienced not the breaking of *one* will—but *thousands*.

That ancient fury burst out of the beast's throat under her.

She rode atop Khagar now, who raged with the same madness that had poisoned the mankrae. Like them, he sought vengeance, for the shattering of their horde-mind, for the agony of what had been stolen.

Nyx fought to hold her saddle as the beast thrashed in frustrated fury. It gnashed at anything and everything. A wraith strayed too close. Jaws snapped and ripped its throat and spine. The broken body tumbled away, vanishing into the storm.

Khagar screamed his rage, loud enough to break glass from stone.

As that cry echoed, it was picked up by others. One throat, then another. Somewhere deep, the mankrae knew that call—and answered it. Their chorus grew, defiant and pitiless. It spread into a whirlwind, binding all together.

But this was no horde-mind forming.

It was merely vengeance given form and voice. It still needed a will—one that could wield that furious strength.

Nyx took on that mantle, shared by the king beneath her.

From her own throat, she added to the chorus and cast Khagar upward, out of the glassy vault that had trapped him for so long. He sailed upward with her, shooting swiftly, spinning straight from the grotto.

The others followed, swirling with emerald fire. The storm burst high above the cliffs and into the burning sunlight.

As it did, Nyx sang to the *wyldstrom,* bolstering her golden armor, riding that furious tempest. Her vision splintered as she did, seeing all. First through Khagar's eyes, then spreading outward into hundreds, then thousands.

Her mind fought against it, struggling to hold this roiling view. Still, she managed. She discovered just enough strength in the maddening fire that burned inside her, the traces she had failed to cast below. Rather than snuff it out, she let it rage through her, to open the parts of her necessary to withstand it all.

As she rode the stormfront, blazing in golden armor, she gazed out at the world through all those eyes. Across burning black glass, she spotted an ancient enemy in the glints of bronze spread along the coast.

Khagar screamed in recognition.

As did she.

They were united in this purpose.

She tipped his wings—and raced for the distant shore.

78

AT THE EDGE of Evdersyn Heep, Graylin lowered his farscope and blinked away the image burned into the backs of his eyes. Black wings still arched across his vision. Moments ago, thousands of wraiths had swept past overhead. Their warbling screams had quivered the small hairs over his body and set his heart to pounding, though the latter was stoked more by his fear for Nyx.

Through the farscope, he had searched the sky for a larger bat among the throng, for any sign of Bashaliia, but the glaring sun had forced his gaze away too soon. Clutching the scope, waiting for the burn to ebb, he searched around him.

He stood on a peninsula that stuck out from shore, a sandy spit that cut through a shoal of broken glass. Behind him, towering cliffs cast a thin shadow. Ahead, a single *kalkäa* sled rested at the edge of the sand. Arryn and Irquan had taken off with the other two, stealing men from the third. They had all heard the blare of horns, the faint echo of screams. Through scopes, they had watched legions of bronze raiders descending upon the far coast.

The Chanrë could not stand idle while Tosgon was under siege. Graylin did not resent their departure. He appreciated that they had left the sled and a lone drover—a bent-backed hunter too old to fight—who could guide the curl-horned pärde.

Plus, they still had their sailraft. Vikas remained inside, steaming the forges for a swift departure. Shiya and Kalder kept with Graylin.

He backed to the pair and turned to Shiya. "Did you catch any glimpse of Nyx, either in the flesh or by the shine of her bridle-song?"

Shiya stared upward, following the dark storm leaving these shores. "Neither. The frenzy of wings burns with a raging fire. If there's any golden shine somewhere in there, it's lost in the inferno."

Above him, the last stragglers raced past, winging wildly, spinning through the air. He followed their passage, then lowered his gaze to the *Fyredragon*. The ship lay crooked on the glass, wreathed in smoke.

Graylin had already studied the ship through his scope. He had spotted men moving atop the deck, battling fires. Lower down, the keel lay cracked amidst a spread of shattered boards. He had failed to spot any *ta'wyn*. Clearly, the enemy had abandoned the ship, leaving it stranded. Once the village was subdued, they would likely return and stamp out the intruders.

Graylin watched to see if any of the mankrae swept toward the *Fyredragon*, but the wraiths also ignored the downed ship. The mass of wings continued toward the coast, toward the old enemies of the colony. Fighting continued to echo from the distant dunes, but the number of horns had ominously dwindled, evidence that Tosgon and its defenders were being overwhelmed.

Graylin wondered about the intent of the dark stormfront sweeping toward the beleaguered coastline.

Are they heading there to help or to add to the misery?

He raised his farscope again, determined to find out. Before he could lift the scope to his eye, Kalder growled a warning. Graylin looked back and noted the vargr's nose pointing to the right, his tufted ears standing tall.

As Graylin turned that direction, a pair of dark wings shot out of a chasm in the cliffs. A rider crouched there. Graylin held out hope it was Nyx, but he quickly recognized the stockier build of a raash'ke.

Pyllar and Daal.

Graylin continued searching, hoping to spot Bashaliia following behind. But no other wings appeared. Daal swept in a tight circle, then dove toward them. The urgency of that approach clenched Graylin's heart.

He retreated to make room for Pyllar to land. Those wings swept up, then scooped air. The raash'ke landed hard, gouging sand. Before the bat even stopped, Daal leaped off and rushed over.

Graylin met him. "Nyx?"

Daal nodded to the receding horde. "With them."

"How? Why?"

Shiya joined them. Vikas, too.

Daal gulped air, throwing an arm toward the coast. *"Wyldstrom,"* he said, which answered nothing.

Graylin grabbed his shoulder to steady him.

Daal spoke rapidly. "We got it wrong. The *Dräshra* did not want us to carry Khagar's heart out of the caves in order to forge a new horde-mind. She wanted us to *feed* it to the mankrae, to corrupt the golden ember. Then to use that ancient fury—the fire that burst from the corrupted heart—to stoke the mankrae into an even more potent weapon."

"Nyx was able to do that?"

"I believe so. I saw her leave the grotto. She's riding that storm. Possibly at the edge of madness. Though, I saw an aura of golden fire hugging her form, maybe shielding her."

"And Bashaliia?" Graylin knew the risk such madness posed to her mount.

"Gone. I . . . I've never seen such malignancy, such all-consuming rage. He's become Khagar in poisoned spirit."

"And Nyx is riding him?"

"She's trying to lead the mankrae, to wield the *wyldstrom* like a sword. But in the end, it may destroy her as well."

"And you let her attempt this?"

Daal frowned at him, clearly feeling no need to answer.

Graylin turned and headed to the sailraft. "We must get there."

Daal grabbed him. "No. She warned us to stay away. Though, not in fear for us, but in terror that she'll lose her resolve if we interfere."

Graylin wanted to push the young man off, but Daal's eyes shone earnestly, with the same worry for Nyx that plagued his own heart. Daal clearly wanted to rush off after her, too—and would if given the least opportunity. He clearly struggled against giving in, for a simple reason.

He trusted Nyx.

Graylin fought for the same steadfastness, but she was his daughter. He had abandoned her once, in the swamps of Mýr. Now, every bit of him wanted to chase after her. Still, he recognized the selfishness behind such an urge.

He took a deep breath.

I must trust her.

Graylin finally gritted his teeth. "What would you have us do?"

Daal pointed out to the spread of glass. "Get to the ship. If Nyx is successful, we still have another battle to face."

The young man's gaze shifted north to the smoking countenance of the Dragon.

"Until then," Daal finished, "she is on her own."

79

Nyx swept above the burning expanse of black glass, nearing the spread of rolling dunes, but the approach of the *wyldstrom* had not gone unnoticed.

Ahead, the sky filled with bronze sentinels, blazing brightly under the sun, soaking in the heat of the Father Above. More shot off the sand and swept high, with energies vibrating under them that defied the pull of the Urth.

She leaned over Bashaliia, who continued to burn with the fury of Khagar. Emerald flames raged under her, lapping at her golden armor, trailing in their wake. The entire sky seethed with the same fire, carried across a thousand hearts, screamed from a thousand throats.

She cast her vision across the roiling expanse. She fixed on each shining bronze torch, assigning two or three mankrae to every *ta'wyn*.

Then they were atop the enemy.

She watched the battle from a jangled, turbulent perspective.

Screams—stoked hotter by the fire of Khagar—spewed emerald flames at the *ta'wyn*. Figures writhed in the firestorm. Bronze boiled away, revealing crystalline skeletons and arcane energies. Then came claw and fangs, which ripped and tore.

Soon, *ta'wyn* fell out of the sky. Several exploded in midair, burning nearby wraiths in their blasts.

Other mankrae suffered fates as brutal. Metallic fingers snatched bodies, breaking bones and gouging hearts. Several *ta'wyn* sharpened their limbs into spears and impaled more wraiths.

Flashing across the storm like lightning, communing throughout, Nyx felt each death like a stab into her heart. Her pain grew as fiery as the sky.

Before long, bronze and bones littered the glass in their wake.

Still, her horde vastly outnumbered the enemy. The storm eventually blew through the *ta'wyn* in the air. With the sky clear, she led the way onward and over the rolling dunes.

Below, a hundred more glints roamed the sand. Many dug into trenches.

She let her *wyldstrom* crash down upon them. Still, it quickly grew clear that the *ta'wyn* had an advantage. On the ground, with such close fighting, the wraiths' wings and agility became impeded. The battle devolved into pained snippets, no victories, just savagery delivered by both sides.

Blood rained from the sky.

Explosions cast sand.

Screams carried on the wind.

Amidst the chaos, trying to orchestrate this maelstrom, Nyx struggled to hold her sanity. Her heart pounded. Breath gasped between strangled chords. She felt herself losing control—of herself, of Bashaliia, of this storm.

It was too much.

Then words reached her, a whisper buried in the chaos, maybe a memory, maybe a final song left to her.

Be the wyldstrom.

Only now did she understand the import of those three words.

I must stop fighting and open myself to the ferocity of the storm.

She had to let go of its reins or risk being torn apart by it. She had to recognize a simple truth, a lesson it had taken the *Dräshra* centuries to learn, even longer to accept.

Rage forged its own path.

She had to let it free, to stop trying to force her will upon it.

She had to simply *be* the *wyldstrom*.

To that end, she loosened her grip on the saddle and leaned back. She lifted her arms to the storm and let herself be cast to its winds, to its savagery.

As she flew, the battle grew both more distant and more intimate. Time blurred into a wash of blood, bone, and blasts of crystalline alchymy.

Still, as the fighting raged on, she slowly came to realize it was grinding into an impasse. By now, hundreds of wraiths littered the rolling sands, broken, burning, many still writhing.

Even worse, more of the *ta'wyn* kept coming, sweeping south from the Dragon, likely emptying it out. Worst of all, they came not just with the strength of bronze. To her right, pairs of *ta'wyn* landed, carrying cannons between them. The weapons glowed with strange alchymies. Then from those batteries, fire lanced into the sky, casting out beams of burning light. They swept the sky and sliced through wraiths. Other beams brushed lower, slashing across the tops of dunes, burning wings and melting sand to slag.

Nyx knew what she was seeing.

The infernal weaponry of the Roots.

Similar to what had blasted the desert.

Her mount recognized this, too, and screamed with renewed fury.

Nyx fought to control Bashaliia, who thrashed wildly, raging under the fierce surge of Khagar's fury. She struggled to keep herself anchored, to both her saddle and to herself. Grasping for anything, she gripped fistfuls of rough fur. She used the pain of her injured hand to draw herself back into her own body, to separate herself from the chaos and agony around her.

As she did, she recognized that *being* the *wyldstrom*—while it had gotten her this far—would not be enough.

While rage might forge its own path, it also grew *blind,* striking wildly. Against this enemy, during this stalemate, that must not be.

To that end, she sang louder, stoking her armor brighter. She cast herself across the remaining colony—now reduced to hundreds, not thousands. She took over those reins again, knowing the risk. She concentrated through those myriad eyes, forging countless hearts into one.

Once ready, she sent the mankrae crashing toward the battery of cannons. She followed behind, using their bodies as a shield. A part of her wailed against the deaths, experiencing each one, but she held firm to the cruel steel inside her.

Under the protection of that fraying shield, she dove toward the ridgeline. Still, the dread energies of the cannons tore through the mankrae. A beam shot past her, close enough to feel its singe.

More followed, burning the air all around her.

She had to accept the truth.

We will not make it.

Below her, Khagar must have recognized this, too, and bellowed his despair. He surely remembered his past failure and what it had cost him.

Still, she intended to fight on against the hopeless odds.

Then a piercing sound rose from below. A strident blare of a horn cut through the wraiths' cries and the thrum of fiery beams—followed by countless more horns.

From all around the dunes, shaggy shapes pounded into view. Atop the beasts, riders carried spears, lances, and curled horns—the latter blasted with the potent echo of the wraiths' screams, as if the land itself had risen up.

The Chanrë legion struck the cordon of *ta'wyn* around the cannons.

Nyx lunged down to join the battle. She broke through the last of her shield and roared across the ridgeline, unleashing Khagar's wrath, melting bronze to slag. Riders pounded along her path, attacking with spears and lances.

She swept around again and ripped across the battle with claws and fangs.

In another two passes, the firestorm atop the ridge ended, leaving the dune bubbling with molten sand, with the remains of *ta'wyn* sinking into it.

Nyx cast off the last of her *wyldstrom,* sending the mankrae to hunt bronze stragglers. Chanrë riders followed, too.

As they left, one rider crested a dune. His headscarf flapped from his face. She was shocked to recognize Arryn as she swept over him. He lifted his spear in greeting, then turned and thundered down the dune, off to cleanse his desert home.

Nyx was surprised to find him here. She looked to the east, toward the distant cliffs, where she had last seen Arryn. He must have raced back when the attack started.

She swung a circle, fighting the fury under her saddle. Despite the victory, Khagar still raged with bloodlust. And not only him. Carried through scores of eyes, she watched a wraith dive upon an ürsyn and rip a rider from the saddle. A spear thrust freed the man, sending him tumbling back into the sand.

Nyx remembered her earlier fear about rage being blind.

Even with the bronze threat over, the storm's fury persisted, raw and untamed. Recognizing this, Nyx wrested a firmer rein on the remaining mankrae and drove them skyward. As the dunes fell away, the black sea spread outward. She caught a flash of fire circling the smoky remains of the *Fyredragon*.

The sailraft.

The others at the cliffs must have retreated there.

She winged toward them with the last of her *wyldstrom*, now a mere squall. As she flew, she stared past the crashed ship to the black mountain to the north. The Dragon's crown, still huffing two columns of dark smoke, floated above black glass.

She felt its smoldering gaze and knew the truth.

As did Khagar, who bellowed a challenge through Bashaliia's throat.

This battle is far from over.

80

ATOP RURO, ESME crossed the sands and climbed to the top of a ridge. From her vantage, she watched the last of the wings spread north, leaving the ruins of their wrath behind. A heavy pall hung over the dunes.

She crested a rise and stared across the devastation.

All around, bronze glinted against red sand. Broken, slagged, mangled. Other *ta'wyn* lay burning, smoking from some strange alchymy inside their bodies. Blasts blackened several areas, much like the spot she had left behind.

She carried with her the losses from that battle.

Abresh lay draped across Ruro's rump. She had tied Crikit to the saddle seat behind her. She refused to leave the dead to a lonely grave in the sand. Sadly, she would not be the only one looking to honor the fallen.

She stared across the ruins of the desert, at what *victory* looked like.

Bodies lay everywhere, staining the sands with blood. Both man and beast. Some had died where they had dropped; others had clearly dragged themselves, only to find death at the end of the trail. Larger hillocks marked the resting place of ürsyns. One stouthearted beast limped on a broken leg, bellowing his distress.

Closer around her, little else moved across the dunes. A broken wraith, one of hundreds, battered a wing, as if trying to take flight. The last surviving molag roamed leadenly, a lonely sentinel among the dead.

She struggled to understand what she had witnessed as bronze fought wings, men battled bronze, and claws ripped everything. While she should be grateful for the strange intercession of the mankrae, for ridding the sand of the raiders, she could not drum up any thankfulness after all this death.

Ahead, a rider spotted her from a ridge in the distance and lowered the glint of a farscope. His ürsyn then bounded down and headed toward her. She guided Ruro to meet him. As she climbed out of a deep gully between dunes, the rider and ürsyn appeared at the top of the rise.

She stared up, with her headscarf long ripped away.

"Esme!" the rider shouted down.

She recognized Arryn's voice. She suspected it might be him, hoped it would be, but she remained baffled. The last time she had seen her brother he had been leaving. He must have rushed back from Evdersyn Heep as the battle started.

She let Ruro come to a stop in the shadow of the dune. Both were too exhausted and heart-heavy for this last climb. Arryn dropped from his saddle and skated down the sand to join her.

Once he was close enough, she fell off Ruro and into his arms. As she hugged him, she shook with a sob that might not end. He held her as if willing to stay no matter how long it took.

"What happened?" Arryn finally whispered.

She didn't have the strength to answer, but she felt him staring over her shoulder at the burden on Ruro's back. She simply shook her head. After a long time, Arryn guided her up the slope. He clearly intended to carry her home atop his mount, to relieve some weight from Ruro's back.

When they reached the top of the dune, Esme stared across the desert. Winds swept sands across ridges, as if trying to erase the deep wounds. Farther out, she spotted the smoky husk of the *Fyredragon,* where the ship lay crooked on the glass.

But it was not that dragon that drew her attention.

Arryn joined her. Like her, he must have noted where the mankrae were headed. "What do you think will happen?" he whispered.

She suspected the answer and dropped her gaze from the black mountain to the devastation around her.

"This is just the aftermath of the Dragon *stirring . . .*" She recalled the Chanaryn legend of these lands. "But beware when the Dragon *wakes.*"

Arryn finished the ancient warning. "For it will shatter the world."

As if foreshadowing this fate, the ground trembled, dancing grains of sand across the dunes. A low roar rose around them, like some great beast had already begun to wake from its long slumber.

Arryn reached to Esme's hand, joining together the two halves of the sun tattooed between them. He squeezed a promise into her.

No matter what happens, we'll face it together.

81

AALIA HELD FAST to her mount as the ground shook. Her horse's hooves clattered atop the stone rampart. Tazar angled his stallion closer, accompanied by the ringing of his armor.

"We should go below," he warned.

"It's only a tremor," she scolded, which proved true as the shaking quieted again.

Still, distressed shouts, amidst wails of concern, rose from both sides of the wall. The bulwark circled the nine massive tiers of the *Bad'i Chaa*. The House of Wisdom was a city unto itself, closed off and darkly cloistered, limited to those who suffered the tutelage here.

But not this morning.

Rather than waiting for the doom to come, Aalia had heeded Chaaen Hrash's warning concerning the pending threat of another Cataclysm of Gaius. She had spent most of the night studying the charts brought by Hrash's colleagues. She had wanted to get a better understanding of the fragile nature of Kysalimri's foundations. Together with the others, she had mapped the skittering clefts beneath the city, the fissures that branched off from a great rift running alongside the mountain range of the Hyrg Scarp.

Working with all the resources of Sail, Wing, and Shield, along with the knowledge of the *Bad'i Chaa* scholars, she had put together a hasty plan of resettlement and relocation. She wanted to pull the populace of Kysalimri away from those clefts, where the quakes during Gaius's rule had struck the hardest.

She had warned those gathered up in the Blood'd Tower: *We must learn from that tragedy.*

So, before the first dawn bell rang out, she had begun a massive movement of the people of Kysalimri, a tidal effort that was still ongoing. It required the coordination of all her imperial forces—except those returning from the battle along the southern coast of Hálendii.

Over the past bells, legions of her Shield had marched through the city, rousting people, getting them moving. The Wing had helped from above, offering support and dropping supplies at hundreds of rallying points. Meanwhile, the Sail had set about drawing boats to deeper water, while assisting the Shield to empty the lower quarters of the city.

Still, while progress had been made, much still needed to be done. Due to the massive breadth of the Eternal City, it would take weeks to move everyone to firmer footing.

Hrash had insisted they did not have that long.

Aalia had accepted this hard truth and its only solution.

We must do all we can in the time we have.

From atop the school's massive bulwark, Aalia stared down at the tented encampments spread across the open plazas. The same filled the yards behind the wall. The *Bad'i Chaa* sat on one of the firmest foundations of the city, second only to the footings under the imperial citadel. Aalia wondered if the ancient designers of Kysalimri had knowledge of what underlay this region and chose these locations for this very reason.

Regardless, she took advantage of such wisdom now. She had forced open the doors to the school, filling its yards, even setting up camps across its tiers. The same held true for the imperial citadel, along with hundreds of other stable regions across the city.

Overhead, a pair of swyftships circled, offering support. Below, hundreds of the Shield settled disputes, calmed the frightened, and beat down any hot spots of dissent that tried to flare up—which unfortunately were growing in number.

Tazar voiced this very concern. "I've fielded crows from the *Shayn'ra*. Voices continue to rise across the city, fueled by panic and confusion. What you attempt to do—to spare as many lives as possible—is already driving sentiment against you. If you push any harder, the city will break. And if the cataclysm never strikes, anger will inflame a hundredfold."

"As you've warned many times."

She reached over and touched his knee. She knew his fear focused on her. It fueled much of his skepticism.

Tazar huffed. "You place too much confidence on the fears of those three scholars."

"Perhaps. But better that I be torn from my throne, than have millions die to keep me on it."

"Then let us at least head back to the citadel. Best we return to the Blood'd Tower, where you can oversee matters just as well."

She turned her gaze to the hundred spires that rose from the grounds of the citadel. She could not stomach returning there. Besides riding out to let herself be seen during this time of tumult, it had also been an escape. She had fled the last missive delivered by a skrycrow. It had arrived shortly after word reached her of the imperial fleet retreating home from the battle along the Hálendiian coast.

But another group would not be making that journey.

The last missive had come from the Razen Rose, the contents of which were further confirmed by dispatches from Klashean spies in Azantiia.

The attempted assault on Highmount had failed.

Her brother, along with Kanthe and the others, had been captured and imprisoned deep under the castle. Not only were they lost, but so was any hope of discovering the key to the *turubya*. With such a defeat, the world's fate had been sealed.

Unable to face this grimness, or the loss of her brother and friends, Aalia had fled away, to do what she could.

I can do no more.

Tazar groaned, drawing her attention. "Trouble approaches."

Aalia walked her horse around to face the ramp that led up from the yard. Chaaen Hrash flogged a mule upward, driving it toward them. Six bells ago, he had vanished into the massive school, where he had gathered all the scholars of the House of Wisdom, all its alchymists and hieromonks, all to work on this one threat.

To see him now, rushing toward her, Tazar had to be right.

Trouble approaches.

Hrash reached them, hopped off his mule, and started to drop to a knee.

Aalia waved him up. "Chaaen Hrash, what's wrong?"

He answered, breathless and gasping, "Your Illustriousness, we . . . we were mistaken?"

Aalia stiffened. "About the Cataclysm of Gaius."

He nodded, gulping to catch his breath. "That's correct."

Tazar clenched a fist. They both knew the risk Aalia had taken.

If I've riled tensions across the city for no reason . . .

But Hrash was not done. "The cataclysm will be far *worse* than we predicted."

"What? Why?" Aalia focused harder on the Chaaen. "Explain what you mean."

"I apologize for failing you, Your Illustriousness. Earlier, I was too limited in my studies, too focused on the city, too narrow-sighted at the full extent of history."

"Tell us," Tazar snapped angrily.

"By bringing the full breadth of the *Bad'i Chaa* to bear on this problem, we widened the scope of study, both across many lands and deeper into history— all the way back to ancient records that lie within the shadow of the Forsaken Ages. There were scholars already working on this over their lifetime. I should've thought to consult them sooner, but in the rush to—"

Aalia cut him off. "What did these studies reveal to you?"

He looked up, his expression aghast. "The cataclysm will certainly strike harder upon the city—but not just *here*. From those ancient records, drawn from around the Crown, an event of this magnitude will reverberate around the world, shaking the entire Urth."

Aalia's limbs grew cold.

Hrash turned to the sky. "And with the moon pulling ever harder . . ."

His words trailed off, leaving unspoken the disaster that would follow.

She followed his gaze to the horizon, to the face of the moon. Even without the school's powerful lenses, she could make out the faint angry blush now rimming its silver.

She knew what this foretold.

The beginning of the end.

82

As he waited for the end, Kanthe leaned his forehead against the bars of his cell. He stared across the dungeon to the open doors of the hearth. Atop the coals, the iron mask glowed a fiery red.

Rami drew alongside him. "It seems your brother was correct about how long it takes iron to heat up. The second bell of morning should be ringing anytime."

"Hopefully, he'll linger over his poached eggs, maybe over a pipe, too, then take a little rest to properly digest." Kanthe glanced over to Frell and Cassta. "We could certainly do with some rest ourselves."

No one had gotten any sleep.

The only change in their accommodations was that the body of Gheel had been hauled away. Kanthe suspected it was so that Mikaen would not have to endure the stench of bowel and bile, especially as the Shield's bulk had rested too close to the same hearth and heated up alongside the iron mask. That wouldn't do when the king returned. Knowing Mikaen, he would want to savor the smell of Kanthe's searing flesh at its unsullied best.

With nothing more to do, Kanthe continued his vigil upon the hearth.

At least the torture of watching iron heat on coal had given Kanthe plenty of time to stew over his life's choices. The eventual tally did not come out in his favor.

—He had been too selfish too often.

—He had been petty when he could have been kind.

—He had neglected to show proper gratitude for boons bestowed upon him.

—He had not stood up often enough when others were mistreated.

—He sometimes found pleasure in another's pain—mostly when they deserved it.

So, he forgave himself for this last fault.

Still, one aspect weighed upon him the most.

I'm far too preoccupied with how the world sees me versus placing myself into another's stance.

He sighed at this.

And now it may doom the world.

Voices and a commotion at the door drew his attention. Frell stood up, as did Cassta. Rami simply kept at Kanthe's side.

The second bell of morning clanged loudly, even louder when the guard threw the latch and opened the door.

Rami mumbled, "While your brother may have many faults, tardiness is not one of them."

The two guards hurried to either side to make room for the arrivals.

Only it wasn't Mikaen.

Instead, two gray-robed Shriven pushed into the dungeon with their cowls pulled low. In the firelit shadows, the tattoo of black across their pale faces stood out starkly, making their eyes seem to float in the darkness.

The one in the lead, though, only had *one* eye showing. The other was covered in a patch.

Wryth . . .

The bastard passed a sheaf of parchment to the guard. "We're here to collect Frell hy Mhlaghifor. As approved by the king's seal."

Kanthe glanced over to the alchymist. He remembered Mikaen mentioning that Frell was to be delivered to the deepest regions of the Shrivenkeep, likely to be brutalized under arcane methods and stripped of all his knowledge— then handed over for some foul use that would be worse than any torture.

Clearly, I've had way too much time to ponder such things.

Frell's lips narrowed with disgust, but otherwise, he seemed unperturbed.

Rami cast the alchymist a worried glance. "At least you'll be spared of having to watch the king's entertainment."

Across the room, the guards inspected the pages as the second Shrive waited.

Wryth used this moment to stalk up to the cell, clearly ready to gloat. He stopped with his hands folded into his robe and tucked under the leather bandolier of his Shriven cryst. He cast a haughty gaze across both cells.

"From your actions of late, it appears you know far more about the *ta'wyn* than I expected. Then again, you did steal the bronze woman from me over a year ago." A bit of heat entered his voice at this insult. "Still, I wish to learn more."

Frell confronted him. "Do your best. You'll find I'm not easy to break."

"Everyone claims such, but it seldom proves true." Wryth waved a hand dismissively. "But I did not come here to issue threats. Simply to judge for myself your true worth."

Kanthe frowned. "What do you mean?"

"For the moment, I seek to decide if there might be common ground between us."

Frell's eyes pinched with suspicion. "How so?"

"I believe it's plain to all that Kryst Eligor must be stopped."

Kanthe took a step back, too shocked to speak.

Wryth's gazed fixed on him. "And your brother is not the king to do it."

Kanthe choked out a few words. "And you think I am?"

"That's what I've come to determine." He swept a look across the cells. "You failed in your attempt to harm Eligor. Lost a *ta'wyn* ally. And got captured. An all-around defeat, one that does not reflect well on your abilities."

"Then why bother coming here?" Frell asked.

Wryth sighed. "Eligor speaks of a weapon. Something that he wants Mikaen to help him secure. A treasure he describes as a massive *schysm* buried at the heart of the world. One hidden long ago."

Frell shared a look with Kanthe.

"I assume you know what a *schysm* is?" Wryth asked, his one eye narrowing.

Kanthe sensed this was a test—not just this question, but the whole conversation. "You know very well what a *schysm* is—as you stole one from our *ta'wyn*."

He noted the barely perceptible dip of Wryth's chin. "But you don't know what this weapon does, do you?" Kanthe pressed him.

"And you do?"

Ah, so the bastard doesn't know the answer.

Kanthe shrugged. "I do. I can tell you it's a *key*. To *what* I won't reveal unless you help us."

Wryth frowned deeply. Kanthe knew that the Iflelen order was ruled by the pursuit of forbidden knowledge—and none more so than this man.

But will this tantalizing crumb be enough?

Wryth slipped his hands from his robe and folded his fingers at his lips, clearly contemplating. He eventually lowered them. "I believe I can wheedle the answer out of Eligor eventually. And if not him, Mikaen is an easy fop to manipulate."

Past Wryth's shoulder, Kanthe saw the guards had finished inspecting the papers, but the other Shrive sought to delay them, drawing them into conversation.

Time is running short.

Kanthe stepped closer, knowing he needed something more alluring to sway Wryth. "You may be right about determining *what* the key opens, but do you believe you can discover *where* the key is hidden? Eligor is not likely to share that detail with anyone. Certainly not Mikaen."

Wryth brought his fingertips back up and whispered between them, "No doubt, Eligor must *never* get the key."

"In that we are in full agreement," Frell said sternly.

"And you claim to know where this key is hidden?"

Before Kanthe could stop him, Frell answered with the truth. "We do not."

Wryth shoved his hands down. "Then I see no use to side with your lot. Better I strive in the shadows, which has served me well."

Kanthe suspected that might not be true any longer. Otherwise, Wryth would not have risked this gambit.

Wryth swung away, but Kanthe reached through the bars and snagged the edge of his robe, a rare affront, one that caused the Iflelen's face to darken with fury.

Kanthe did not back down and stared him in the one eye. "The others may not know, but *I* do."

Wryth faced him. "And why should I believe you?"

Behind Wryth, one of the guards crossed toward them.

"Decide now," Kanthe warned. "With all your scholarship, you know how to judge a man's word. So look at me."

Wryth scowled but obeyed.

Kanthe drew the man closer. "I swear to you—I *know* where Eligor hid his key."

Wryth's one eye shone with a fiery intensity. It felt like it was burning into the back of Kanthe's skull. He wanted to turn away from the gaze, but he steeled his neck and refused to break.

The guard stepped up to the cell. While his face scrunched with curiosity, the man knew better than to challenge a Shrive. "Sir, all seems to be—"

Wryth turned with his fingers already in a pouch along his leather Shriven cryst. As he faced the guard, he tossed a pinch of crimson powder from the pocket. The stricken man stumbled back with a sharp inhale of surprise, drawing the poison deep. By the time he struck the stones his body contorted with his heels hammering hard.

Upon this signal, the other Shrive stabbed the second guard with a blade as thin as a fang. Whether poisoned or simply a skilled strike, the target collapsed to the floor with nary a whimper.

Wryth retrieved the keys and unlocked both doors. "We must be swift. I can get us out of the castle, but we'll need a place to hide, then a way out of the city."

Once free, Cassta joined them, brushing against Kanthe, her eyes shining on him. She whispered, just a breath from her lips. *"Kreshna . . ."*

It was the second time she had uttered the Rhysian word to him, encompassing both thanks and acknowledgment of a debt owed. Kanthe hoped he lived long enough to collect on those appreciating debts.

To the side, Rami confronted Wryth. "So you intend to come with us?"

The Iflelen looked at the bodies and tossed the keys aside. "I've cast my lot." He stared over at Kanthe. "As long as he keeps his word."

Kanthe drove everyone forward. "Let's go."

The other Shrive opened the door. Two more guards lay dead in the hall, with a third Shrive standing over them.

They all piled outside and swept away, chasing through passages dark and hidden. The other two Shriven vanished off, likely returning to their roosts far below, ready to cast full blame upon Wryth.

As they fled, Frell drew Kanthe aside. "You've just invited a coiled asp into our midst."

"An *asp* who just saved my handsome face," Kanthe reminded him.

"He cannot be trusted."

"I suspect he believes the same of us."

"It is a dangerous game you play, Kanthe. He's not a man to cross lightly. While we might live, this lie of yours will not serve us well once he learns the truth."

Kanthe scowled at his former mentor. "I did not lie. What sort of scoundrel do you take me for?"

Frell frowned, clearly trying to judge his sincerity.

Kanthe admitted the truth. "I *do* know where Eligor hid the key."

To avoid further questions, he sped onward. With his task accomplished, one concern remained foremost.

Someone needs to get that turubya *spinning.*

Arkival limne of
the Pärde
(native to the
Barrens)

Limne of
the Dhelprä
(native to
Evdersyn Heep)

TWELVE

WHEN A DRAGON WAKES

Ney fash, kä Draakki se paüuta neekyn.
Ney mia, kä Draakki se ker iresh.
Ney häash, kä Draakki se keen reffan.
Ney kwuki, kä Draakki se effn päkrsh.
Ney grayl, lish carazan, kä Draakki se krük naffyn,
Aya nee baersh.
–Translation–
Don't speak, for the Dragon has big ears.
Don't move, for the Dragon has sharp eyes.
Don't breathe, for the Dragon has keen nostrils.
Don't shiver, for the Dragon has long whiskers.
Don't be caught, little heart, for the Dragon has sharp
   fangs,
All made of black glass.

> —A Chanrë song taught to children

83

DAAL STOOD AT the bow of the *Fyredragon* as the ship regained its wings. With a thunderous roar from its forges, flames shot across the black glass, setting fire to a few cracked planks that had shattered off the keel. The ship slowly lifted from the uncompromising sea. As it rose, the crooked deck rolled even again.

To keep his feet, Daal grabbed the bow rail.

"Don't have your sea legs yet, do you?" Rhaif asked, balancing a pipe in hand. "It seems our dragon still has some fight in her. Even after the pounding she took."

Daal glanced back to the battle-scarred wreckage. "I understand we have you to thank for that."

"Don't thank me yet. Not with where we're headed."

A handful of the crew still labored across the decks. The fires had been put out, though several patches still sifted with smoke. Bodies had been taken below, but their stains remained. A full quarter of the crew had been killed and many more injured. Daal's team had not been spared. They had suffered a hard loss: Barrat and his raash'ke mount, Frysh. The pair still lay somewhere out on the glass, slowly baking atop its burning surface.

Still, the dead would have to wait.

Overhead, half of the ship's gasbag hung empty and loose, blackened by fire. The other half struggled with the weight of the rising ship. Still, the *Fyredragon* had gained enough lift to set off across the black sea, aiming for the mountain to the north. The ship skimmed low, leaving its patch of smoke. As it did, the sun blazed brighter, driving Daal deeper under the shade of the balloon.

Rhaif followed with his pipe.

Daal lifted his farscope and searched the broken cliffs of the Dragon. He watched for any glint of bronze or the waft of black wings.

"Spot anything?" Rhaif asked.

"No. Nothing is moving out there."

Shortly after Daal had reached the ship, Nyx had sailed forth from her own battle. Upon arriving at the *Fyredragon,* she had driven Bashaliia into the hold, but only after dispatching the last of the mankrae to the mountain. She had bridled those survivors to one final duty. To search the mountain for any *ta'wyn* remaining inside, to sweep through and scour its halls.

"Maybe Nyx was right," Rhaif said. "Maybe the Dragon is empty."

"We can only hope so."

According to Nyx's account of her battle, she believed a majority of the bronze army had been sent to the coast. Near the end, she reported, there was a surge of reinforcements who arrived with infernal weaponry. Since then, the crew turned all its scopes upon the Dragon. So far, no other *ta'wyn* had appeared.

Maybe she's right.

Daal kept searching. Nyx had bridled a final imprint into the last of the wraiths. She had ordered them to keep searching the Dragon with their sharp senses and keening cries. Only when it was deemed clear would the bats show themselves again.

So far, none had.

Either the mankrae had been slaughtered or their search still continued. It was impossible to judge. Especially as there was no telling how deep or extensive the *ta'wyn* warren delved under the mountain or how long it might take the wraiths to search it.

While they waited, it was decided not to hang back but to push forward.

As the ship swept north, Daal eventually lowered his scope, no longer needing it. The Dragon grew to fill the world, climbing higher and higher.

The *Fyredragon* swept into its shadow. Rhaif sighed as the heat fell away from the ship. Daal felt no comfort, not in this gloom, especially with what stood guard atop the glass.

Around them, scores of sleds had stalled to a stop, still tethered to pärde who clearly had been harshly enslaved by some arcane bridling. The beasts hung in their traces with heads drooping, even with the weight of their curled horns sawed off. Ropes of slather hung from their lips. None of them reacted to the passage of the *Fyredragon,* not even to the flaming roar of its forges.

But the animals were not the only ones to suffer this affliction. Men and women stood on the shade-cooled glass or sat in wagons. Like the pärde, they stared dead-eyed and crack-lipped. Some were naked; others had scraps of clothing hanging from limbs. Again, not a one reacted to the ship sweeping past. It was as if they had all drowned in this black sea and only their corpses remained.

Rhaif shuddered. "Enough of this. I'm heading below."

Daal planned on keeping his post, but a savage roar burst under him, cutting through the planks and echoing out the holes in the hull.

Rhaif glanced back. "Someone is not happy to be home. Though I can't blame him considering the state of his accommodations."

Daal grimaced and turned from the mountain. He followed the thief toward the doors below. With the Dragon so close, and already under watch by others, he knew who needed him, especially before they set off for the mountain.

Even if she does not like it.

As they headed down, Daal abandoned Rhaif at the wheelhouse. A glimpse inside showed Graylin and Darant talking animatedly with Shiya. Back in the Frozen Wastes, it had taken one of her caste—an Axis—to activate the *turu-bya*. They were clearly plotting to do the same here.

Daal ignored them and headed farther down. As he descended the steps, he ran into Tamryn heading up. Dark circles shadowed her eyes. Her face looked far gaunter. Still, her hard gaze fixed on him—then her hand.

She had clearly risen from the lower hold to find him.

She shoved him against the wall, leaning close as if to kiss him. But it was not affection she sought.

"Those cries must stop," she hissed. "It's riling the raash'ke into a frenzy. After what they've been through—what we lost—" Her voice caught and was only freed when her fingers dug harder into Daal's arm. "They need rest."

"I was going—"

She shoved him away and stamped back down, headed for the lower hold. "Do something about it!"

Daal followed her, but he separated when he reached the upper hold, where the sailrafts were stanchioned. It now served as a prison.

As he grabbed the latch, another piercing scream erupted. The noise rattled the door. He felt it in his bones and teeth, too. He recognized the underlying frisson of bridle-song, dark and furious, rife with madness.

He girded himself and pushed inside.

An angry shout greeted him. "I told everyone to stay away!"

He ignored the command, pushing through. "It's me, Nyx."

He entered slowly, moving one step at a time. The upper hold was smaller than the one below. Sailrafts lined the back, their bows pointed toward the open stern door. One lay on its side, where it had been knocked over when Nyx had struggled to get the prisoner inside. A crewman had broken his arm during the tumult.

Once into the hold, it had taken all of Nyx's control, along with a good font of her remaining bridle-song, to keep Bashaliia enthralled long enough to secure leg irons and wrap his wings with leather ropes.

Even then, they had nearly lost the battle.

Afterward, Nyx had sent everyone out in an attempt to calm that raging heart on her own. No one argued. No one else dared to draw near Bashaliia in his current raving state.

Daal had to risk it, to try to urge Nyx away from Bashaliia. With the

Dragon so close, they would soon be departing. Graylin had asked him to make this attempt, knowing Daal had the best chance to get Nyx to listen. Maybe Jace, too, but with his strange affliction, Graylin feared adding another volatile element to this boiling pot.

So it's up to me.

"Keep well away," Nyx warned.

As Daal crossed the hold with cautious steps, he gaped at the state of Bashaliia. While he was no longer screeching, the Mýr bat's head hung low with menace. His eyes, normally warm and gentle, flashed with a malignancy that iced through Daal. The bat's tall ears lay flat against his skull. Lips curled from sharp fangs slathered with venom. A leg tugged at one of the irons. Blood pooled under the claws, where his thrashing had torn skin.

Nyx knelt before Bashaliia. She glowed with bridle-song, casting out strands that sought to soothe the beast. Even with Daal's limited sight, he saw the futility of this effort. Past Nyx, a raging pyre still burned inside Bashaliia, so fierce it was difficult to stare at for long.

Daal drew to a stop, well out of reach if the beast should attack. "Nyx, we've reached the mountain. Fenn and Krysh are watching for any return of the mankrae. But when they do, we must be prepared to act."

She did not react, her gaze still on Bashaliia. "He's somewhere in there. I know it."

Her words carried through her song, which continued to hum out of her throat and heart.

Daal took another step forward. He gazed again into the emerald inferno seething at the core of her brother. With narrowed eyes and a wary wince, he searched for any sign of Bashaliia's warm gold, but he failed to spot even a glimmer.

Still, he remained quiet, refusing to strip this faith from her.

Nyx continued, "I had thought the defeat of Khagar's ancient enemy might stanch his fury, to let some of the anger go, so Bashaliia could break free. But he continues to rage as fiercely as ever."

Daal knew Nyx must have grasped on to his hope back at the caves. It had likely given her the strength to venture into the *wyldstrom* and cast Bashaliia atop the emerald pyre in the grotto.

A hope that he could be recovered.

"What have I done?" Nyx moaned, her heart breaking.

Daal took another step forward, drawn to comfort that agony.

She turned to him, exposing her pain, her eyes glassy with tears. "He never deserved this." A sob escaped her. "I never deserved him."

He shifted closer, lowering to a knee. He stretched out an arm to draw her to him, away from the raging torment behind her. She leaned to take his hand, but she could not reach it.

Another could.

Without warning, Bashaliia lunged to the extent of his irons, stripping skin from bone to gain additional reach. A muzzle snapped for the meat of Daal's arm.

With a gasp Nyx shoved up, knocking Bashaliia's muzzle away. Bridle-song burst forth in a blazing shield, sending him farther back.

But the Mýr bat had proven faster.

One fang had sliced a deep line down Daal's forearm.

The venom cut deeper.

It numbed his arm, turning pain into ice. His hand clenched in a convulsive wrench, which pumped the poison through his veins. He managed one breath, then his chest clamped and his heart seized. He felt his body sink into frigid water, which froze around him. His muscles fought the cold, spasming hard, until they went rigid, too. His heart struggled with each pound, which felt like the strikes of an ice pick against stone. But the fist of muscle proved too weak against the might of the poison.

He felt his heart strike once more.

Then go silent.

Taking the world with it.

84

NYX LEAPED UPON Daal as he toppled backward. With her bridle-song already raised as a shield, she crashed it down upon Daal.

Her first chorus was denial.

No, no, no . . .

She fought down her panic and thrummed her shield into strands and sent them deep into Daal. She read the path of the poison. Somewhere writ into her spirit was the dissonance to the venom's vibration. She had survived this poison before. Her body still knew it, remembered its menacing ice. Fear, more than memory or talent, drew that particular dissonance buried in her bones to her breath, to her song.

She cast it through Daal, fighting the poison on every front, burning it away.

As she did, she fought to hold herself steady, unbalanced between his senses and her own. With one beat of her heart, she was fiery with panic. With the next, she was frozen with her heart clenched into a knot. She worked her gold to warm his body, to melt the ice around his heart.

She managed somewhat, but it still refused to beat. She struggled for an answer, for a heat stronger than her bridle-song.

Then she remembered back at the grotto cave. Before she left, Daal had tried to reassure her. He had offered his hand. Like he had done just now. She had taken it in her wounded grip, wrapped in leather from his own garment, bandaged by his own hand. They had merged briefly. She recalled the intense burn of her blood against his skin. She had felt nothing like it before. Neither had Daal from his reaction. It was as if whatever bond they shared had responded to the raw, unfiltered strength of the gift in her blood.

"My blood . . ."

She jerked back and used her teeth to rip away her bandage. Scabs tore, pain flared, and blood poured. She did not know if this would work, but she did not care. She pushed her bloody hand over his heart, letting the crimson flow through his thin shirt to reach his skin.

Merging again, she felt her life's warmth flow into him, a heat far more intense due to its rawness. She used her song to sculpt the warmth into fingers and a palm. Once done, she reached and grabbed that icy heart and suffused it with the life flowing from her wound.

She flashed to that same moment in the cave. Like now, she had sensed Daal's heart. Only then he had sworn her an oath, one spoken not with his breath but with this very heart: *I will not forsake you.*

She intended to hold him to this promise and squeezed hard with fingers forged of song and blood. She held tight, demanding and resolute.

"Do not break your vow to me," she warned hotly.

She waited, holding her breath.

Finally, the fist of muscle in her hand trembled, quaked, then began to beat against her sculpted fingers. She let go but hovered close. At last, his chest heaved under her bloody palm. She kept her hand there, until gasps became breaths.

His eyes rolled back into view, swimming, then finding her.

"Nyx . . . ?" he croaked out.

She sighed with relief. He tried to sit up, to rise to an elbow, but she held him down. "Don't move."

While his body tremored from the residual cold, her warning had nothing to do with the poisoning. Instead, she held him quiet for another reason.

Still connected to him by blood and touch, she stared at the weak golden glow inside Daal. The shimmering trace was all that was left of Khagar's golden ember. Only now it shone brighter, seeming to rise, as if the golden warmth sought to escape Daal's cold body.

He stirred. "What is—"

"Hush."

She was afraid to scare it away or break the illusion.

As she watched, his gold swam and whorled, eddying brighter and darker. One stream flowed away, banding into light and dark. The rest swirled into a vague body, which spilled out into a sharp-nosed shape with gold cascading in two tall fountains from its crown.

She knew that outline.

"The dhelprä . . ."

Daal searched blearily around, confused.

Nyx struggled to understand the meaning of this. She pictured the cavern behind the *Dräshra*'s throne, the final tomb of the bronze queen's beloved. Nyx remembered the last sight of the chamber, of the fleet-footed dhelprä— with its ringed tail and tall ears—nestled at the wings of the wizened king. With its final duty done, it had shed its spirit, lifting away, briefly revealing itself in a phantasm of bridle-song—before vanishing into the darkness.

She had thought it was some form of good-bye, a last act marking a long vigil ended. But maybe it meant more.

Marking a final message.

From the *Dräshra*.

Something bridled into her companion.

Though Nyx suspected a greater connection ran through all three—*Dräshra*, dhelprä, and mankra—some merging of purpose and spirit that formed over the long vigil together.

Regardless, she took the message to heart.

Suspecting what was being asked of her, she reached to the golden dhelprä and used threads of bridle-song to gently break its last tethers to Daal.

He gasped slightly, more of a sigh.

Once the dhelprä was freed, she knew where it had to be delivered. Back in the cavern, the shining spirit—after it had shed its body—had swept into another, into the dark mountain of its fallen king.

Nyx followed that same direction now. Using a net of bridle-song, she carried the ember's golden essence over to Bashaliia. With a prayer on her lips, she cast the dhelprä back home, into the emerald pyre, the last flames of a great heart.

As it struck, gold flashed into a brilliant sun. It held there for a breath, while somewhere far away a faint ululating cry reached out, as if calling someone home.

Then the sun collapsed in on itself, snuffing out the emerald fire. While not all of it vanished, it was hopefully enough. Maybe this was one last message to the living: *that some fury could never be fully crushed, only lived with.*

Regardless, a new gold shone before her, warm and familiar.

"Bashaliia . . ."

Daal lifted to an elbow, still weak, still trembling from the cold, but alive. His eyes were huge upon Bashaliia.

"He's returned," Daal whispered hoarsely.

Nyx drew closer. Bashaliia wove weakly, still struggling to settle back into his body. She reached to his cheek. He leaned into her touch. She sang reassurance into him, while tears of relief streaked her cheeks. He keened softly, his gold shining brighter. He tried rocking on his legs, but the chains rattled. The burn of his torn skin drew a sharper pining from him.

He struggled back from it, only to discover his wings were bound. Panic flared, stoking the emerald embers brighter. She quickly drew his head to her chest, rubbing his ears.

"You're safe," she murmured to him.

She cast out calming chords and sent off strands to blunt the pain as best she could. Once she felt his heart slow and the emerald glow die, she dropped to her knees and pulled the pins to free his irons. The chains fell away.

By the time she stood up, Daal had stumbled over, weak but recovering.

He had already wrapped his bitten arm with the torn edge of his sleeve. "Let me help."

She wanted him to rest, but he shifted and started to undo the knots that held the leather ropes. She worked the other side. As the bindings fell away, Bashaliia ruffled his wings.

Nyx drew Daal back, reading her brother's desire to stretch away the aches and tension. Once they were clear, Bashaliia swept his wings wide and shook their lengths loose, then returned to rocking on his legs.

Daal crossed to a water bucket and carried it over to Bashaliia, seeming to regain his strength with every step. "What happened?" he finally asked. "After I was bit?"

She explained about the poisoning, about the cure buried in her, and about the strength of her raw blood.

Daal rubbed the back of his hand. "I remember that burn back in the *Dräshra's* cave." He glanced over to Bashaliia. "But what about *his* poisoning? Did I hold the cure all along?"

"I believe the *Dräshra* must have planted this contingency. Between her love for her winged king and the millennia in which she had to ponder the strength of *wyldstrom*, she must have sought to leave a key to redeeming Khagar's heart. A key that could only be triggered after he secured his revenge."

"Why after his revenge?"

Nyx nodded to Daal's chest. "All this time that you've been carrying the ember's residual glow, it's never transformed like it did. Only now, after we defeated the *ta'wyn*. Maybe it was crafted this way so that Khagar would rage until he either accomplished his goal or was destroyed."

Daal took a kinder view. "Or maybe it was simply meant as a reward. As you said, a way of freeing Khagar from the corruption, to let him be free and pure in the end."

Nyx shrugged. "Either way, I think Khagar's screams while Bashaliia was tied down here was him *calling* to you. He might have sensed the key in you, the golden part of him that still survived. Even him lashing out might have been an instinctive attempt to reach the ember shining in you."

Daal sighed, rubbing the wound. "He could have just asked."

Nyx kept silent about a darker view on all of this. Back in the *Dräshra's* cave, when the dhelprä ascended through Khagar's bulk, it had left its own body behind. She wondered if *death* was part of the key's triggering. Was that why Khagar had attacked—not blindly, but purposefully—to free the key? Daal's heart had stopped for a spell. If not for her intervention, he would have died like the dhelprä.

She pushed aside these gloomier contemplations, knowing they were likely cast darkly due to all that had happened. Back in the caves, Nyx had never sensed any enmity in the golden queen atop her throne. Only a deep-seated empathy.

Nyx decided to simply accept this as a gift.

A king redeemed, and a brother returned to me.

She crossed to Bashaliia and held him close.

Daal was right.

This definitely feels like a reward.

She bathed in Bashaliia's golden glow—while not pure, neither was she. The battle still echoed inside her. The deaths and decimation. The *wyldstrom* had rid the desert of its poison, but it had cost the lives of so many. But she took solace from what those deaths had also gained—a chance for the future.

For the desert, for the world.

A chance to stop moonfall.

As if summoned by this thought, a knock drew her attention to the hold's door. Graylin opened it and leaned in cautiously. He frowned at Nyx and Daal, then his eyes widened at the sight of Bashaliia freed of the bindings and chains.

Daal explained, but only briefly. "Bashaliia has shed his poison. He's come back to his senses."

"Are you sure?"

"It was a final gift of the *Dräshra*," Nyx answered, too tired and heartsore to elaborate. "But yes, I'm sure."

Graylin's eyes remained narrow, but he nodded. "Just as well," he said, and stared up. "Fenn spotted a trio of bats, of mankrae, sweeping out of the mountain."

Daal looked at Nyx, trying to judge if she had the strength to go.

She hardened herself, knowing all it had taken to reach this threshold, all that she had risked. She would not back down now.

She nodded to Daal.

"Let's go face this Dragon."

85

GRAYLIN LED THE hike across the black glass. Up close, its surface was rippled, like the edges of a lake washing up against the dark mountain. In its shadow, the glass took on a darker hue, one more menacing.

The dead-eyed sentinels added to this shivery aspect. Figures and beasts stood leadenly, unmoored and broken, amidst wagons and sleds of stone or tarnished copper.

"Looks like they were hauling in ore," Krysh noted. "Possibly mined from the Samskrag cliffs to the east."

"And crystals." Jace nodded toward a sled piled with trunks and branches. "Harvested from the gemstone forest."

Rhaif pointed to the twin columns of smoke rising from the broken crown of the mountain. "Someone's definitely doing some refining in there. Reminds me of my home in Anvil, with its hundreds of chimneys and stacks." He took in a deep breath. "Smells like the sarding place, too."

Graylin had grown accustomed to the sulfurous brimstan reek, the breath of this foul Dragon. With them closer now, it stung his eyes and tasted like acid on the tongue. But he could also pick out a bitter, metallic quality to the air. Though this did not rise from the twin smokestacks. It seemed to exhale from the cavernous mouth that opened ahead of them.

Kalder padded alongside him. A low growl tremored the vargr's chest and hackles. His lips rippled back, exposing the tips of his fangs. He kept a close watch on the shadowy figures and beasts, while his ears swiveled all around.

Behind him, Daal and Nyx followed, guarded over by Vikas. The large woman had donned all her leathers again and carried her broadsword, but she had kept the headscarf that Arryn had given her during the trek from the Örgös forest to Tosgon. It was the only nod to this land's customs that she seemed willing to adopt.

Shiya also kept near Nyx and Daal, ready to use her bronze strength to protect them. Past her, Darant had spared another dozen men, who swept a cordon at the rear.

Farther back, the *Fyredragon* echoed with shouts and hammering. The captain and his remaining crew were hastily doing repairs to the ship, both to its broken hull and to its damaged forge-engines. After what had happened the last time a *turubya* had been activated, they knew a hasty departure would be needed.

Around the *Fyredragon's* balloon, a trio of raash'ke swept circles, ready to guard the vessel from an attack. And not just from any resurgent force of *ta'wyn*.

Wings swept high overhead, spattering the glass with guano.

Kalder's growl reverberated louder.

"That's the eighteenth I've counted," Daal said, shielding his eyes with a hand and following the passage of the mankrae through the air.

Others flew and fluttered about the mountain's sheer cliffs. A few perched up high, wings extended, cooling themselves. After the first three wraiths had been spotted, more had emerged.

"I sent in twice that number," Nyx said grimly. "The last of the *wyldstrom*."

"They must have run into a few of the *ta'wyn*," Krysh commented. "Let's hope they rid the mountain of them all."

Graylin noted Nyx staring at the meager flock, her eyes haunted, her expression forlorn. She had sent the horde on its rampage, and this was all that was left of them.

Jace showed his usual aptitude at reading Nyx. "Their numbers may allow the colony to rebuild. Undoubtedly, hundreds more still roost in the cliffs. The young, the heavily gravid, or those who simply failed to heed the call. They will multiply again. Only now, maybe they'll be free of the festering anger that tainted them."

Nyx mumbled this hope. "The last gift of their king."

As she headed on, her back grew straighter.

Graylin nodded to Jace, appreciating this support, more even than the large Guld'guhlian ax he carried.

Together, they crossed the distance in silence. The weight of all that glass smothered any talk. Graylin stared up at the mountainous expanse. Huge sections had calved away long ago and shattered into a maze of razor-sharp rock. Ahead, a towering rift cut into the mountain. Underfoot, a path of ruts and sandy glass led the way inside, worn down by the passage of wagons, sleds, and the crystalline pads of the lumbering pärde.

As they reached the threshold, Graylin motioned for a stop and drew out his sword. He waited until the clutch of Darant's men closed ranks with them. "Stick together. Shiya will lead from here. If there are any *ta'wyn* inside, she has the best chance to deal with any survivors."

Once he got confirmatory nods all around, they set off. Graylin dropped back to Nyx, gripping his sword. The metallic taste to the air grew stronger, along with a sharper bite of alchymical odors, much like the scent given off by the ship's *ta'wyn* coolers. Several areas stank riper from the guano left behind by the first force to sweep through.

Overhead, spears and broad rafts of sharp glass hung from the roof. Upon entering the rift, they had lit lanterns, carried by Krysh and a few of Darant's men. The fiery light reflected off the walls, adding to the haunted nature of this passageway.

"It appears to be sloping down," Jace noted. "Taking us deeper."

Graylin frowned, unsure if this was true. The strange cast to the light, the crunch of sandy glass underfoot, made it difficult to get his bearings.

And not just him.

They reached the broken body of a mankra, but it hadn't suffered any attack by a *ta'wyn*. It looked like it had gotten thrown off by the strangeness and brushed across a crystalline stalactite, slicing a deep gouge across its back. Blood pooled under the body after trailing a distance to this spot. Even after the mortal wounding, it must have dragged itself along, trying to continue the task bridled into it.

Nyx stepped well clear, her shoulders bowing again.

As Graylin passed, he noted the blood leaked slowly downward.

Jace was right.

The tunnel was leading deeper under the mountain.

As they continued on, Rhaif cocked his head. "Do you hear that?"

"I feel it, too," Jace added. "A faint rumbling."

Krysh touched a wall. "It reminds me of the *Flüst* of Tosgon, the muffled reverberation of some infernal engine."

Graylin kept them moving. "We must be approaching the source."

After a final long stretch, a wan glow appeared ahead. It grew brighter as they continued and the rumbling louder. Graylin hissed for the lanterns to be doused. Their pace slowed to a wary approach.

At a sharp bend in the tunnel, Graylin stopped them with a raised hand. The light rose from just ahead. The ground trembled with a force that hardened the muscles of his jaw. A glance around showed sparks flashing with the brush of clothing. Fine hairs lifted and hovered.

Nyx lifted a palm. "The air thrums with energy."

Graylin leaned close. "Shiya and I'll scout ahead. The rest of you wait for our call."

Nyx stiffened and looked about to argue, but for once he beat her down with an uncompromising look. She finally nodded.

Graylin set off with Shiya and passed around the bend. Ahead, the tunnel ended abruptly. Power wafted from there, shivering hairs. It felt as if they were walking into a thundercloud. The air smelled with the sharpness of a lightning strike.

Graylin edged forward, in step with Shiya.

They reached the tunnel's end and gaped at the cavernous dome that opened ahead. It was large enough to entomb the full span of Kepenhill's nine tiers.

The space was both familiar yet strange,

Still, Graylin knew what he was staring into.

The heart of the Dragon.

He and Shiya stepped out onto an apron, perched a quarter of the way up one wall. Ramps curved to either side, sweeping down to the floor.

Graylin's gaze searched the space.

Like the *turubya* site in the Frozen Wastes, a layer of seamless copper lined the dome's every surface, encrusted by a dense labyrinth of crystalline tubing, steel joinery, and hundreds of windowed tanks bubbling with a golden elixir. It all glowed softly, occasionally bursting with blinding dazzles and brilliant arcs, which shot over sections like bottled lightning.

Movement caught his eye. A set of dark wings glided out of the shine, slowly circling the yawning dome. It was a lone mankra, a last scout still on duty.

Graylin searched below and spotted the broken forms of a half dozen *ta'wyn*. Two still smoked, with sparks snapping out of their darkened cavities.

"A few last defenders," Graylin noted.

"There are probably more." Shiya nodded to the seven tunnels branching off from the floor of the dome. "Let's hope the wraiths dealt with those, too."

"The mankrae likely caught them by surprise. I doubt any strangers have trespassed here in countless millennia."

Still, Graylin eyed those tunnels. The site in the Frozen Wastes had similar passageways. Here, as there, giant rubbery cables—four times a man's height—snaked out of the darkness, humming loudly, and dove deep under the dome's copper floor. Though they vanished away, Graylin knew where they were headed, what they were meant to power.

So did Shiya.

She pointed to the center of the floor. "The *turubya*."

Graylin grimaced. "What happened to it?"

Back in the Wastes, a perfect sphere of crystal—as large as a warship—had hung over a bottomless round pit, suspended by a rigging of arched bridges. Its crystalline surface had been circumscribed by crisscrossing bands of bright copper, while smaller wires etched a complicated pattern everywhere. However, its most miraculous feature churned at its core, where a huge pool of golden fluid pulsed and writhed, as if marking the secret heartbeat of the Urth.

Which maybe it did.

Especially considering the *turubya*'s purpose.

To set the world to turning, in harmony with its twin in the Frozen Wastes.

Only now there was an insurmountable problem.

Shiya voiced it.

"The *turubya* has been corrupted."

86

WITH RELIEF, NYX heard Graylin call to the group waiting in the tunnel. She let out a breath she had not known she'd been holding. It must be safe for them to proceed. Still, Graylin's voice rang with a familiar steel of alarm.

Something was amiss.

She hurried with Daal, trailed by Vikas. Only Kalder beat them to the glowing end of the tunnel. Rhaif and the rest of Darant's men crowded behind them.

They followed the vargr out onto a landing of copper. The rough men from the ship gasped in shock at the massive copper dome, shimmering and jolting with brilliant bolts of power. Rhaif swore, having seen its like before, as had Daal, who simply grimaced.

Within a few steps, Nyx's limbs went cold. Her breath clutched in her throat. She fell back to when she had last entered a dome like this. Sounds of battle echoed through her. The clash of steel, the boom of cannons high above. She touched her chest, still feeling the thump of those blasts. But overlying it all was a sound she had heard only a short time ago: *the raging bellow of Kalyx.* It was in such a place she had slit Bashaliia's throat and delivered her brother into that tortured body.

She found herself unable to move.

Then Daal reached her, hovering a hand, then touching her arm. After Nyx removed the golden key from him, he had little power left in his wellspring, just a trickle. Still, his touch was like fire, burning away the past from her body. This came from no bridling gift but simply his presence, the concern shining in his face.

She nodded. "I'm all right."

It was a lie, but it served well enough to get her moving.

Before she could, Jace shouted to their group, "Get down!"

From out of the dome, wings dove at their group. A sharp keening washed over them, driving everyone lower. Only Nyx remained standing. She sensed no fury, just a warning in that cry. As the bat blazed toward them, it trailed emerald fire, but she caught the barest glimmer of gold, too. The sight lifted her hand up. Her fingertips brushed the mankra's wing as it skimmed over and shot down the tunnel.

She stared after it, noting again the trail of gold amidst the flames.

"Nineteen," Daal said, adding to his ongoing count of the mankrae.

Jace stood back up. "One more to help revive the colony."

As the wraith vanished into the dark, Nyx took the trace of gold to heart, praying it did indeed reflect a final gift of their king, an offering of peace that had never been afforded them.

Halfway down a ramp to the left, Gray called to them. "Let's get moving!"

He split their group, leaving a man to guard the tunnel, then sent the rest of Darant's crew down the ramp to the right, to spread their eyes and swords. He ordered them to guard the seven passageways that branched off from the dome. He wanted all entry points watched in case any *ta'wyn* should try to ambush them.

"With me," he ordered everyone else.

Shiya had already reached the base of the ramp and waited. A deep line of worry creased her brow.

Nyx headed down. After the debilitating flash of last winter's battle, the humming silence of this place unnerved her. It felt like a tomb, one ancient and haunted. This was amplified by what clearly had dismayed Graylin and Shiya.

While descending the ramp, Nyx had a full view of the strange encrustations that had grown and spread across the dome's copper floor. It looked like a tortured forest had sprouted from the metal, all brambly and malignant. The seed for this growth rose from the center of the dome, where the thicket gathered into a giant hillock.

Nyx knew what lay beneath it, what formed that seed.

The *turubya*.

Even the nature of the forest supported this assumption. Rather than bark and leaf, this malignant wilderness had been crafted of shining crystal, faceted and glinting.

She had seen these trunks and branches before.

Daal had, too. "It's like the Örgös forest."

Nyx shook her head, vehemently denying this. "It's *nothing* like that."

She rushed down the last of the ramp, joining Graylin and Shiya at the bottom.

As the group gathered there, Nyx searched around. One of the massive tunnels snaked off to her left. The towering rubber conduit inside thrummed with power, vibrating and tremoring the floor. In the Frozen Wastes, similar cables had fed the *turubya*. Back then, she had compared them to the tentacles of the *Oshkapeers*, the Dreamers of the Deep back at the Crèche. Only now she pictured them as the black roots of this mountain, sapping the energy from the world's core to fuel the Urth's only hope.

She stared over at the forest.

But what are they feeding now?

Graylin must have had the same worry. "We must strike for the *turubya* through this tangle. Find out what's been done to it."

As they set off across the vast copper floor toward the malignant tree line, Nyx noted the remains of *ta'wyn* dotting the floor. These few—like the others—were all Roots, the caste known for their crafty labors and unique designs. Over the passing millennia, they had clearly begun a malicious undertaking here.

Like Nyx, Daal remembered the earlier warning from the bronze queen. "Back in the caves, the *Drāshra* mentioned the *ta'wyn* had been laboring on some scheme, to thwart her control. It's one of the reasons she broke away. She feared it might damage the *turubya*."

Nyx quoted the queen's final concern. "And may have done so already."

"But what *have* they done?" Krysh asked. "What is the purpose of all this?"

By now, they had reached the forest's fringes. The differences between this tumorous growth and the Örgös stood out starkly. Out under the sun, the crystals of the Örgös forest had shimmered in a radiant splendor, a prismatic scintillation of every hue, breaking each beam of sunlight into a thousand spectrums.

Here, the tangled branches were made of the same crystals, but they had darkened to an amber hue. Rather than reflecting the light, the facets appeared to consume the dome's glow, absorbing its energy. What did reflect *out* looked more like a refraction of *shadows,* casting dark spectrums that further ate the light.

Nyx had a hard time looking at the forest, at beauty corrupted into malignancy. Still, she had to face it. She gathered her small reserves of bridle-song and sang it out into the dark glade. Golden strands wafted forth. She followed them with her spirit, passing through crystal. As she probed deeper, she touched the slither and squirm at the core of each branch and stem.

She gasped and stumbled back.

Jace caught her. "What's wrong?"

"It . . . It's alive." She pointed ahead. "Like the Örgös. Rife with the same frilled animals."

She fortified herself and tried again. She limited her reach to a few golden strands, tightening her throat to polish them brighter, to act as a shield against what hid behind the dark crystal. She cast out those strands, along with her essence, and streamed past the facets to touch what squirmed beneath.

The tiny creatures of the Örgös had shone with gold, their bodies pure, nearly all song and little substance. But what she touched had darkened into a cancerous rot, forced to exist. Their song had not gone emerald but was the black of a pit, the scream of the endlessly tortured.

She shuddered and pulled away, too horrified to look deeper.

As she withdrew, a chiming rose from the forest. It rang with a dissonant note, like at the Örgös, but these chimes did not warn of approaching danger. They hissed with a dark lust, as if craving more power than the dome could provide.

"We shouldn't go in there," Nyx warned.

"We must." Graylin stared toward the encrusted hillock. "To discover the fate of the *turubya*."

She knew this to be true. Still, she balked. It took several breaths to push down her dread. But she finally nodded.

By now, Jace and Krysh had slipped forward and examined the forest themselves.

Jace called over. "It's densely tangled, but we should be able to work our way through." He hefted his ax higher on his shoulder. "Or we can forge our own path."

Graylin urged caution. "Until we understand what this all means, we disturb as little as possible."

Krysh squeaked and fell away from the forest. He shook a finger that had already begun to redden. "Take care. The crystal stings with an awful burn."

Graylin took heed of this warning. "Cover any exposed skin as best you can." He eyed Vikas's large shape, recognizing it would be an agonizing trek for her to cross this dense burning forest. "Maybe you'd best wait here. Stay with Kalder. This is a forest he will not want to hunt."

That was clear enough as the vargr hung back with his head low, his eyes dark with worry. Kalder needed no bridle-song to sense the menace of this dark wood.

With matters settled and no better advice, they set off into the forest.

AFTER AN INTERMINABLE time of twisting and bowing, Nyx grew exhausted, taxed to her limit. She took great care with each step and every bend. She feared less the sting of the crystal and more what lurked beneath it.

Still, the burn of the crystal seemed bad enough. Yelps and gasps spread throughout their beleaguered group.

Daal got stung and bumped into her. His panic seemed worse than just pain.

She turned to him. "What's wrong?"

He pointed warily at the offending branch. "When it burned, it wasn't the heat of *fire*. But *ice*. As it struck, I felt it leach a bit of bridle-song from me, ripping it out with a touch of frost."

Nyx looked to the others for any guidance. She wasn't about to test this herself, but she recalled the lust heard in those chimes.

Jace shrugged. "I've not been stung yet. And I don't plan to be."

Krysh held up the finger, the one that had touched a stem. It had already blistered badly. "All I felt was intense heat. Not ice."

The explanation came from the one who should have worried the least. Shiya had no exposed skin that needed covering. Still, Nyx had noted her squirming through as much as anyone.

"The malignancy here seems designed to sap bridle-song," she said. "Each sting pinches *synmeld* from me."

Nyx grew more worried. The Roots had no talent in bridle-song, so this forest would not harm them in this manner, but it would be anathema to anyone like Nyx or Daal, and especially an Axis.

Nyx swung her gaze forward, ducking from a twisted branch. "It's like this forest has been grown as a barrier to keep any Axis from reaching the *turubya*. To sap the *synmeld* from them before they can become a key to triggering the *turubya*."

Graylin pointed hard at Shiya. "Then tread with great care."

She nodded—much depended on her.

They forged onward, trailed by that ominous chiming, cloaked by the refracted gloom of the forest.

As they continued, Nyx noted something else odd about the forest. Focused on keeping clear of the branches, she had failed to notice the base of the trunks entangled by threads of metal. They climbed to hip height and ran across the copper floor, like tiny rootlets connecting this wilderness into a whole.

Nyx leaned closer.

"These fibrils are all bronze," Jace noted with a worried catch in his voice.

Krysh nodded. "I think the purpose of this forest goes beyond creating a barrier to anyone bearing bridle-song or *synmeld*."

"But what could that be?" Nyx asked.

Krysh shook his head, his face blistered in several spots.

Jace shrugged. "Maybe we'll find out ahead."

As they continued, Nyx knew this question wasn't the only mystery to be addressed. After an interminable period, the forest thinned, then finally broke. They all stumbled into a clearing, exhausted and burned.

"We made it," Jace gasped out. His pale face shone with sweat, but at least he managed to escape the forest unscathed.

Nyx felt no relief, not with the obstacle rising ahead of them. Even from twenty steps away, she had to crane her neck to take in the full majesty of the *turubya*. The crystal sphere was so massive it would take two dozen men with linked arms to circle its equator. Half of its globe hung inside the pit, suspended by copper rigging. The upper hemisphere stretched high above. The forest writhed across it, forming a roof that spanned it completely, entombing the *turubya* below.

Still, they all recognized a bit of providence.

Nyx sighed out her relief. "The *turubya* looks untouched. No different from the sphere we triggered in the Frozen Wastes."

To be certain of this, the group slowly circled it, studying the sphere more closely. Nyx eyed the copper bands across its surface, the finer wires that formed a pattern that looked like the scribblings of a mad alchymist.

Same as before.

Jace studied the bridged rigging that suspended the sphere. Graylin crossed closer and peered over the edge into the pit.

Nyx had no desire to get closer. She already knew what lay below: a bottomless hole drilled deep. A series of doors lined the shaft, ready to slam closed once the *turubya* was dropped.

Keeping her eyes away from the hole, Nyx focused on the gyrating mass of gold that pulsed at the core of the crystal. It was a shining sea that swam and swirled with the stored energies trapped by the copper dome.

The sphere, while massive, looked similar in design to the crystalline cube inside Shiya, a device strong enough to sustain her bronze form over millennia. And her cube was only the size of a fist.

Nyx gaped at the enormity before her, knowing it held the power to move a world. Unable to face it any longer, she turned to Shiya. She had wandered away from the *turubya* and had been searching the forest's edge with Rhaif.

The pair returned to the group, both their faces grim.

"What is it?" Graylin asked.

Rhaif scowled. "These Roots were taking no chances." He stared back at the dark wood. "They weren't solely counting on the forest to sap an Axis to depletion, to thwart their ability to prime the *turubya*. The Roots had taken one additional measure."

"What?" Nyx asked.

Shiya answered, "They removed the activation chrysalis."

Rhaif nodded. "It's gone."

Nyx searched around, as if she could miraculously spot it. She pictured Shiya placing her body in the copper chamber in the Wastes' dome. Crystal doors had closed over her, cocooning her. Only an Axis could use such a chrysalis chamber to trigger the *turubya*.

"By removing it," Shiya said, "the Roots have effectively crippled the *turubya*."

"Unless we find where they hid it," Rhaif said.

Graylin stared off, likely picturing the massive tunnels, imagining the sheer magnitude of this facility. "It could take a lifetime to search this place."

Rhaif shrugged. "Then, unless you have something better to do, we'd better get started."

Nyx shook her head. "Removing the chrysalis makes no sense. We know the Roots went through great effort. A process that still requires ongoing attention. They clearly need workers, raw ore, even fresh cuttings from Örgös to sustain this forest, to continue to garden it. The Roots wouldn't do that unless they had some other scheme in mind."

"What scheme?" Rhaif asked.

"Maybe they wanted to wrest control of the *turubya* and take it for themselves. Remember, the Spider in the Frozen Wastes had entertained doing this himself, but he was out there alone. He didn't have an army."

They all turned to Shiya.

"That may be true," she concurred.

"So we need a Root." Rhaif sighed. "Too bad we destroyed them all."

A call rose from around a curve of the clearing.

"Over here!" Jace shouted. "Come see this!"

Dejected and worried, they all headed his way. As Nyx rounded the shoulder of the *turubya*, she spotted Krysh kneeling at the forest's edge.

Jace waved them closer. "We may have solved one mystery."

Krysh stood and backed away so they all could peer into the forest's fringes. Buried at the edge of the bower, tendrils of bronze rose up in a tangled wave, merging into a single mass. It formed a towering clamshell that faced the crystal sphere.

"What is that?" Daal asked.

Krysh rubbed his chin, careful of his blisters. "I believe this is where all those filamentous strands of the forest come together as one. This is what the entire forest is meant to fuel."

"To what end?" Graylin asked.

Nyx suspected the answer. "This must be the Roots' new activation bed. Something forged from their ingenuity over many millennia."

Rhaif scowled. "So the bastards figured it out. They've taken control of the *turubya*."

"No," Shiya said. "We are wrong."

"About what?" Graylin asked.

Shiya faced them. "The Roots didn't take control. They passed it on."

Nyx frowned. "What do you mean? How do you know that?"

Shiya pointed to the clamshell's top, to where cryptic writing had been inscribed onto a plate of bronze. "It was more than *ingenuity* that drove the Roots to this task, but also *reverence.*"

Graylin squinted at the inscription. "What does it say?"

"It is a title. In the Elder tongue. Written in *ta'wyn* script." Shiya stared over at them and spoke the name aloud. *"Rab'almat."*

Nyx staggered back. "Lord of Death."

"The name the *Revn-kree* chose for their leader." Shiya stared across the group. "That is whom the Roots tooled this bed for. The only one who can activate this *turubya* now."

Nyx despaired. "Eligor."

87

AFTER ESCAPING HIGHMOUNT, Kanthe gathered again with the others in the back room of a dressmaker's shop in the Midlins of Azantiia. It was here that their group had donned disguises for their first foray into the Shrivenkeep—which felt like ages ago.

And not all of them had made it back.

Llyra, along with Jester and Mead, had rejoined Kanthe's group in the shop, but a notable absence weighed on them all. The loss of Tykhan still devastated. It was a blow to their cause and to Kanthe's heart.

Two others now took Tykhan's place.

Kanthe had hauled in one of them. Wryth kept his face stoic under the many glares. It had taken fierce convincing and much shouting to keep a sword from gutting the Iflelen. Kanthe had become the Shrive's chief defender. Wryth was now as much a fugitive as any of them. And at the moment, they needed each other.

Wryth clearly knew the threat that Eligor posed to the world, while also valuing his own skin—and maybe his ambitions just as much. He could lose all his aspirations, and likely his life, should Eligor rise to full power. Especially if Wryth remained in Azantiia. Kanthe suspected—due to the Iflelen's hasty flight with them—that the man had fallen out of favor with Mikaen, a position that usually ended with one's head rotting on a pike. If true, Wryth needed to be gone from the city as much as they did.

Recognizing this alignment of mutual interests, Kanthe knew his side had best make use of Wryth. The Iflelen had knowledge that could serve them—both about Eligor and about Hálendiian plans.

Plus, Kanthe remembered the list of his own faults he had tallied while jailed, which included not finding gratitude for boons bestowed upon him. He ran a palm over his smooth cheek, unmarred by burning iron. He stared as Frell argued with Llyra and Rami whispered with Cassta.

They all still lived.

As much as he hated it, Kanthe had to spare Wryth some latitude in helping them escape, to keep them still breathing. Still, Kanthe kept Frell's warning close to his heart: *He cannot be trusted.*

Though, for now, such concerns could wait.

The second newcomer to the back room addressed the more immediate problem. "The Razen Rose has secured you passage aboard a brigand wynd-ship," Symon hy Ralls informed them. "A small arrowsprite, captained by an associate of the pirate Darant."

"It's good to have friends in low places," Kanthe mumbled.

Llyra glared at him. "I thought that was more than apparent. It was my rough army that kept the dogs from your heels back at Highmount."

Symon ignored them. "The arrowsprite will moor in the Nethers. It will not tarry long. Once we hear word, we must move swiftly. Already the king's legions are flooding the streets, hunting for you all."

"When will the sprite arrive?" Rami asked.

Symon frowned. "A pirate's schedule is seldom their own. Until we get confirmation, we stay here. We don't want to be caught idling on the streets."

No one looked happy about waiting.

Wryth spoke for the first time. He had not even voiced an objection to Llyra's sword at his belly. His one eye fixed on Kanthe. "You said you knew where Eligor hid the key that he so desperately wants."

Kanthe inwardly winced. He had hoped to delay this conversation until much later, like while soaking in a steaming pool in the imperial baths. But even Frell stared at him with narrow-eyed curiosity. As did Rami and Cassta. Symon simply looked on with studious interest.

"You swore an oath that you knew," Wryth reminded him.

Frell frowned at the Iflelen, then cast a wary glance at Kanthe. Despite Frell's obvious interest in discovering what Kanthe knew, the alchymist had urged caution. But Wryth had been stripped of all weapons, even his poison-ous Shriven cryst. Plus, the Iflelen was surrounded by those in the room and a cordon of Llyra's men outside. Wryth would only be taking this information with him to the Southern Klashe.

Rami asked another question, one tangential but important. "How did you even learn the location of the key?"

Kanthe shrugged. "Tykhan told me."

"How?" Frell pressed him.

"When?" Rami added.

Cassta merely lifted a single eyebrow, her equivalent of a shocked surprise. It was unduly fetching, but he focused on explaining.

"If my dear brother had not given me so much time to ponder my state, while iron heated on coals, I might never have understood what Tykhan had been trying to tell me at the end, as he succumbed to his injuries."

Kanthe only reached this epiphany as he stewed in his cell, going over his life's choices, tallying his many faults.

Specifically one.

How I'm far too preoccupied with how the world sees me versus placing myself into another's stance.

Kanthe drew back to that moment beneath Highmount, as Tykhan fell, blasted to ruin, his bronze slagging across the stone floor. The *ta'wyn* had fought to hold his form as it melted around him. Kanthe had wanted to stay, to seek some way of rescuing Tykhan from this doom. But Kanthe had relented, recognizing the futility, responding to Tykhan's urgent demand that he leave, a demand that the *ta'wyn* had reinforced by pounding against the floor, his eyes pleading.

Or that's how I interpreted it at the time.

"I was too focused on myself," Kanthe said. "I thought Tykhan's efforts had been all about convincing *me* to leave. I had made that moment all about myself. I failed to see through his eyes, to perceive what he was trying to communicate at the end. It had nothing to do with *me*. It was all about the *key*."

Rami crinkled his brow, his gaze falling off into the distance as if returning to that chaotic moment, too. "But Tykhan said nothing. He did not even have a mouth to speak."

"Still, he said plenty. If I had not been too self-involved to listen."

"I don't understand," Frell admitted.

Kanthe turned to his mentor. "Back at Kysalimri, down in the Abyssal Codex, when Tykhan communed with the giant crystal *arkada,* he saw a glimpse of the ancient *ta'wyn* battle."

"Of Eligor raging with the power of a fiery sun," Frell said with a nod. "And the reveal of a Shadow Queen enthralled to him all those millennia ago."

This last statement drew a hard glance from Wryth. The Iflelen was clearly stupefied by this revelation—as they all had been at the time.

Kanthe continued, "You were all too focused on that show of power, at the dark reveal, but none of you paid any attention to *where* this all took place."

Frell frowned. Even now, the alchymist remained blinded by the more spectacular details of that revealed moment.

Kanthe shook his head. "Those events happened on a *mountaintop.* That's what Tykhan told us. Did none of you wonder *why* that one image was stored and preserved in crystal? Of all the battles during that war? It couldn't be solely about the Shadow Queen—or that's what I must assume."

"Why?" Rami asked.

"Beneath Highmount, Tykhan had sought to tap into Eligor's memory, like he did with the crystal *arkada.* That was part of our plan. To see if Tykhan could strip the knowledge of the key from Eligor."

"You think he succeeded," Frell said.

"I know he did. Especially as he must have seen another mountain inside Eligor. Maybe the same one preserved in crystal."

"How do you know this?" Frell pressed him.

"He showed it to me, in the melt of his bronze as it hardened. Its shiny edge had swept toward my toes in jagged peaks. I thought Tykhan was pointing to the way out, urging me in that direction."

"Because you were too focused on yourself," Cassta said with the ghost of a smile.

"Exactly. If I'd only turned my back on Tykhan, bent down, and stared through my legs, I would've viewed the spread of bronze as Tykhan saw it, as Tykhan shaped it." Kanthe cast his gaze across the room. "The edges of the melted pool formed the shape of a mountain, with a cracked summit, one created by ancient *eruptions*."

Frell leaned back, going ashen.

Now you figured it out.

Kanthe continued, "Tykhan focused on me because he knew I had seen that same mountain." He pointed to his mentor. "So did you. When you were studying to be an alchymist. At the Cloistery of Brayk."

Frell shook his head, still refusing. "How can you be sure?"

Kanthe sighed. "Because, as much as I loved Tykhan, I believe he thought I was somewhat slow of mind. Which considering how long it took me to understand his message was likely true. He wanted to make sure there was no misunderstanding. He pounded it into the bronze to make this clear. He did it twice."

Kanthe pictured Tykhan struggling at the end, with no mouth to speak, with only one way to communicate. To name that peak the only way he could—with an arm barely formed. Kanthe heard again the strike of bronze against the sculpted mountain on the floor, pounding that name clear.

Once, then again.

With a *fist* made of bronze.

They had all witnessed this.

"The key's hiding place . . ." Frell gasped out. "It's The Fist."

Kanthe nodded. "The volcanic mountain at the center of the swamps of Mýr."

He remembered his slog through those swamps, of glimpsing the fiery mountain rising in the distance, shrouded in smoke, steaming with brimstan. He also knew *what* made that peak their home.

Kanthe continued, "It's why I'm almost certain the image preserved in the crystal *arkada,* of Eligor burning at the center of a sun, and the rise of the *Vyk dyre Rha* over his shoulder, was also The Fist. I suspect the ancient Shadow

Queen rose from that same region and was riding a bat from the same mountain."

"Like Nyx," Frell whispered.

"I don't think it was pure chance another *Vyk dyre Rha* rose from those bogs. Nyx was raised by a she-bat from that mountain, then poisoned into power by a bite from the same colony."

Kanthe stared hard around the room. "I sense there is much we are missing, that still has yet to reveal itself. About all of this. While we know where the key is hidden, buried deep in the fiery mountain, we are far from the truth."

"You are no doubt correct," Frell admitted, though to Kanthe's ears it sounded begrudging. "But if the key is truly there, we need Nyx back. With The Fist guarded by that poisonous colony—where Bashaliia arose—only she could open a pathway down there."

"Or Eligor risen to full glory," Wryth reminded them.

"Nyx must return before that happens," Kanthe warned. "But with Tykhan gone, we lost our only way of reaching her in the Barrens."

"Not necessarily," Frell said. "Tykhan knew he might not return from the confrontation. It's why we discussed destroying his body if he was at risk of capture. But you had raised this very concern about communication when we nearly lost Tykhan the first time, when his *schysm* was stolen. Tykhan took that worry to heart."

"How so?"

"Back in the Southern Klashe, he devised more than just waveketches. He also took bits of *ta'wyn* alchymy, scraps that he had gathered over his long millennia of walking the Urth, to craft a new means of communicating with Shiya. One that didn't depend on him."

"Why am I hearing of this now?"

"Tykhan asked for our discretion. He knew of your affinity for him. He deemed that talk of his death and defeat, and the plotting around it, might unnerve you when you needed to be at your strongest."

Kanthe sighed, knowing he could not deny this.

"But to reach what Tykhan built," Frell said, "we must get back to the Southern Klashe."

A swift knock drew their attention. Swords flashed into the air from scabbards. Symon crossed, peeked the door open, then drew it wider.

A young boy dashed in, breathless, dressed in a neat fall of grimed clothing, from scuffed shoes to a cloth cap atop his tow-haired head. He looked no older than nine or ten, but a steeliness to his eye made Kanthe question his age.

The boy passed Symon a curled missive from a skrycrow. With a quick read and a nod, Symon turned to them. "From the arrowsprite. It will be mooring in the next quarter-bell. We must be off."

The boy then thrust out another tiny scroll. "This came, too."

Symon scanned it as quickly, but there was no nod, just a look of consternation.

"What's wrong?" Frell asked.

Because there's always something wrong.

Symon nodded to Rami. "It's from your sister. The empress warns of a pending quake. Another Cataclysm of Gaius." The man's gaze swept the group. "Only, the *Bad'i Chaa*'s scholars believe it won't be limited to the Southern Klashe. But will strike the entire globe, worsened by the ever-stronger pull of the moon."

"When is this expected to happen?" Kanthe asked.

Symon's expression hardened. "Her message was sent five bells ago."

Kanthe failed to understand the significance of this last statement.

Then the ground trembled under them. The bolts of cloth lining the dressmaker's back room shivered dust from their rolls. With each breath, the tremoring grew more violent. A crack skittered through the wall's thin plaster.

As Kanthe fought to keep his balance, he recognized the truth about *when* this cataclysm would start.

Right now.

88

AALIA HAD WAITED too long.

Relief had made her foolish, stoking false confidence when she should have heeded caution. A rider atop a fleet-footed horse had rushed to the walls of the *Bad'i Chaa*. Word had reached the Blood'd Tower, dispatched from spies in Azantiia. She had read it with great joy. Rami and the others had miraculously escaped imprisonment. The curled missive had been too brief to offer details. Only that the Razen Rose was seeking a way for them out of the city.

Upon reading this, Aalia had been anxious to rush back to the citadel, to await further updates. But with happiness surging through her, she had ignored a tremor, one that was slightly rougher. She had trusted it was yet another tremble that would die away like so many others.

Tazar had urged her back to the citadel, but she had held off, too joyous to believe the worst. Word had spread of her presence at the school. It had helped draw more to this firmer footing. She intended to be that beacon for as long as possible.

But the tremor quickly grew into a quake.

Then a series of them.

As they worsened, Tazar had not asked for her permission but had driven his stallion like a broom and swept her off the wall and into the circle of mounted Paladins waiting below.

Now, they all raced back to the safety of the citadel, which had bunkers, reinforced chambers built centuries ago as protection against the quakes that plagued the Eternal City.

As the ground shook and jolted, a phalanx of Paladins led the way, a silver arrow cutting a path through the city. Their route back had already been plotted, a zigzagging line across the city's most stable areas, a stretch of over three leagues. Unfortunately, the same firmer ground—islands and sandbars in this turbulent sea—had drawn masses of people. They crowded into buildings, homes, and shops, spilling into the street with tents, with wagons, along with oxen, mules, and horses.

Aalia's bannerman led with a raised flag, which waved with the crossed swords of the Klashean Arms. The Paladins to either side forged through the crowds, knocking people away and bellowing to clear a path. The panicked mass hardly moved. Yells and cries and the bawls of distressed animals rose to a deafening din. The crush of so many forced the Paladins closer to Aalia and Tazar. Soon they were racing knee to knee.

Horses heaved amidst clattering hooves.

Ropes of slather got thrown about.

Still, the riders pounded on and reached a switchback that climbed a cliff, a giant step of the city. The Paladins rode faster, as the slope's steepness had discouraged camps. They quickly reached the top, which opened a view across the lower city. The imperial wall rose on the other side, so tall it looked like the world ended there.

"Keep going," Tazar urged her. "The gates are not far."

Aalia nodded, but she could not tear her gaze from the city. While they were reaching these heights, the ground had bucked wildly. And this was a bedrock region free of those treacherous clefts that ran beneath Kysalimri.

She gaped out at the more unstable areas.

Across the expanse of the city, towers shook and waved. Many had crashed, casting up flumes of dust that shivered and rolled upward. Entire sections had fallen away into cracks that split into gaping maws toothed by broken streets and fanged by cracked spires.

Farther out, the Bay of the Blessed boiled and frothed. At the shoreline, the waters had begun to recede, exposing sand and rock, building toward a massive surge to come.

By now, more and more dust flooded into the sky, covering the sun, hiding the shame below. Still, through the pall, the moon glowed, tinged red by the dust.

Then Aalia felt it.

Not just her.

Birds surged from the city in a massive flock, their silence terrifying to behold.

Then the entire city followed.

It lifted high, as if pulled by the moon, trembled for the longest breath—then crashed down and shattered. A roar struck her, followed by a wave of blasted air. Her horse reared, twisted, toppled sideways. She stood in her stirrups, balancing, struggling to keep the horse from falling, ready to leap away if it did.

Finally, her mount crashed back down to its hooves, jarring her hard.

Tazar shoved his stallion closer and pointed along the walls. "The gate!"

She turned to follow, but through the heavy pall, she caught a glowering view of the riven city. She shuddered at the destruction. Still, she noted a rough pattern to the gaping fissures, rifts, and dust-choked chasms. She had seen the same before, outlined in jagged clefts on Hrash's maps.

She turned her back on the sight, praying such knowledge had helped spare many, but she struggled to grasp that hope with the ground still jarring with sporadic hard shakes. It felt like the final death rattles of the Eternal City, a name that now sounded mocking.

She joined Tazar and headed along the wall, aiming for the main gate a half league ahead. Then a shout broke through her sullen hopelessness. She turned as a Paladin leaped off a saddle to the left. His armored body struck her, knocking her back onto the rump of her horse. She would have tumbled off the rear, but his weight had fallen across her legs, trapping her.

Then the boulder struck, after breaking off the wall. It slammed into the Paladin's shoulder, shattering bone, ribs, knocking his crushed helm away. She shoved straighter, with the stricken man still across her lap.

An arm lifted, and a face offered a profile running with blood.

An eye stared up.

"Regar . . ."

His arm crashed down, taking his life with it.

Tazar reached her and tried to pull the body away.

"No!" she yelled harshly, too harshly, too pained to take it back.

She simply cradled her Paladin and continued on.

By the time the procession reached the main gate, the shuddering had quieted to jolts and shivers. She entered the towering archway, formed by a pair of crossed gold swords.

People crowded here, too, yelling, angry, terrified, looking to lash out. They packed the yards both inside and out the walls. She passed through the throng, still cradling Regar across her lap.

"We should get to the bunker," Tazar warned. "There will be more quakes before this is over."

She agreed—but only about this not being finished.

She turned her horse to face the city. Crowned overhead by the archway's crossed swords, she stared out at the devastation. She felt the weight across her legs, trapping her, not letting her escape her grief.

Tears coursed down her face.

She cried for the man on her lap, for the city, for all who suffered the same.

Slowly the shouts and clamor quieted, spreading outward.

She felt a thousand eyes upon her as a beam of sunlight pierced the dust and lit the archway. She held her Paladin and bared her anguish to the world.

Then a low chant rose and spread—from the archway, across the yards, and beyond.

E Y'llan Ras . . .

E Y'llan Ras . . .

E Y'llan Ras . . .

89

RHAIF STOOD WITH the others gathered before the bronze shell at the edge of the malignant forest. To his side, Nyx stared at the sign inscribed with the name *Rab'almat*. Her face had darkened with despair.

He understood that sentiment.

They all did.

To come this far, to lose so many lives, only to find the door locked in front of them. And though Rhaif was a skilled thief, this was a lock he could not pick. None of them could—as a consequence, they were now considering breaking the door down.

With an ax.

Jace hefted his weapon in his hand. "We could shatter the *turubya*'s riggings. Drop the sphere and all its power down that shaft. Maybe it'll trigger on its own. Like the *ta'wyn* coolers did on the ship."

"And if that fails to happen?" Graylin challenged him.

Jace pointed his ax at the sign. "Then . . . Then at least we keep it out of Eligor's hands. And we move on. Take our chances with the one *turubya* and see if something can be done with its key."

"That's if our allies can discover the key's location," Krysh reminded them. "Then reach it before Eligor does."

From everyone's expression, this option was rapidly fading as a possibility.

Shiya stepped closer to the bronze shell.

Rhaif cringed, knowing what she was about to say.

"I can try activating it myself." She stared at the device. "We don't know if the Roots were ultimately successful in their endeavors. It may still work for me."

Rhaif stomped forward. "Sard that!" He pointed to the bronze shell, while keeping his eyes on Shiya. "You fool with that—powered by the fekkin' dark forest—you'll get yourself killed. We nearly lost you when the Spider entrapped you in the chrysalis chamber back at the Frozen Wastes."

Shiya placed a consoling hand on his shoulder. "There is no crystal to enclose me here. I should be able to break loose if anything goes awry."

"*Should.* That's a feeble word to bet your life on."

Graylin intervened. "She's right. We must try something. We can't let Eligor get control of the *turubya*. If damage is done to the sphere in this attempt, we'll be no worse off than if we tried Jace's plan."

"It's not damage to the *turubya* that I'm worried about," Rhaif said hotly.

Still, he knew this was a battle he could not win. He bowed under Shiya's palm on his shoulder. Not from the weight of her bronze, but from dread.

She drew him closer.

"I will be careful," she whispered to him.

He stared up at her eyes' azure glow. "You had better. If you fail and the world ends, I don't want to be alone."

She pulled him into an embrace. She glowed warmly against him. His body responded with its own weak bit of bridle talent. Soft chords, as faint as a whisper, rose from his heart. It was a lullaby his mother used to sing to him, to console a boy's fright. He heard the same echo from Shiya, a soft harmony winding together into an embrace far stronger than the bronze arms around him.

He wished to stay there forever.

Let the world end now, and I'll be content.

But he knew he could not be that greedy, not even for a thief.

He sighed against her, letting her know he was ready.

She gave a small squeeze, warmed brighter against him, then took all that warmth and shine away. Still, it drew him in her wake as she crossed to the bronze shell.

The others gathered behind them.

Shiya stepped into the fringe of the forest, ducking from burning branches, then climbed onto the raised shelf at the bottom. She turned to place her back against the curved shield of the shell.

Her eyes stared down at him.

He offered the barest nod, though it took all the strength in his body to do so.

Shiya returned the nod and leaned back.

For a moment, nothing happened. He sighed with relief—until Shiya stiffened sharply. Her back spasmed, arching off the bronze as if trying to escape it. A glow flared from her, along with a cry of agony.

Rhaif took a step forward, but Graylin pulled him back.

"Wait," the man warned. "Look."

From the sides of the shield, bronze melted out into a tangle of fibers that wound together and sculpted into what appeared to be handles.

Shiya must have thought so, too. She reached up, her face etched with concentration and effort. She fought to lift her arms to grab those bars. She failed in her first attempt, but she succeeded on her second.

As her fingers clamped, her body convulsed again. Her skull snapped back with a ringing impact, then sank into the bronze shell as if it were warm clay.

All around her, the shell writhed out with snaking tendrils, unraveling into a tangling snarl that flowed over Shiya's body. The bronze briar crawled up her limbs, over her torso. More tangles draped down, wrapping and choking, covering her mouth, snaking past lips open in a silent scream.

Rhaif again lunged, but Graylin held firm.

"You can't help."

Rhaif recognized this. He could only watch as azure eyes stared out blindly through the writhing mass—then vanished into the weedy mire.

Rhaif fell to his knees, breathing hard.

This was far worse than a trap of crystal.

It was a prison of bronze.

NYX RUSHED TO Daal with her arm outstretched. She knew she had only moments to act. His eyes narrowed, clearly reading her urgency, her need. He grabbed her hand. She sank into him, but barely. Both had been tapped to near depletion, he more than she. Nyx felt the beat of his heart in her palm, in her own chest.

It must be enough.

She stoked what she had left and stole everything from Daal. He gasped and fell to his knees. She continued to hold his heart, feeling it tremble and go cold. She inhaled deeply for the chorus to come.

Graylin noted her effort. "Nyx?"

As her song built inside her, she thrummed as much explanation as she dared. "Root alchymy . . . flowing bronze . . . still soft . . ."

"What do you—"

"Be ready."

Back out in the desert, Nyx had ridden the *wyldstrom,* waged a battle across a thousand eyes, hearts, and claws. By now, she knew the alchymy of the Roots and the tone to break it. She had screamed that specific vibration from a thousand throats, heard it in the hundred blasts of pärde horns.

At the cost of blood and lives, she had learned the cipher to their bronze, the exact pitch and vibration necessary to shake loose the tiny motes of hardness and melt them into the empty spaces between—to make it all flow. Over the course of this bloody day, the cipher had been written into her bones, as surely as the Mýr poison in the past, which had allowed her to burn the venom from Daal.

Now she intended to burn bronze from this trap.

Only, as weak as she was, she knew she had to act while the metal remained soft and flowing. She did not have the reserves to break hardened bronze.

Still, I don't need strength, only skill.

As her power coalesced into a bright star, she squeezed it tighter until she could hold it no more. She let it burst forth, sculpted by her throat into a perfect pitch: the screech of a mankra, the blast of a horn.

The savage aria burst out of her like a golden fireball and struck where Shiya lay imprisoned. The force blasted soft bronze from her hard metal, stripping it away like ice off rock.

Shiya fell forward as she was released.

Graylin, Rhaif, and Krysh fought to pull her free, but a handful of shining vines still held her trapped. Then Jace shouldered up, shoved through crystal branches, and swung his ax.

As the blade cleaved through the last stubborn stragglers, Shiya toppled out, nearly crushing her rescuers.

Off to the side, a groan drew Nyx's attention.

Daal had been thrown by the force of her blast to the edge of the forest. He struggled to his knees. Still breathing, just weak.

Spent and empty herself, she staggered toward him, numb with fatigue. Her vision narrowed, growing watery.

Her view of the forest darkened, as if growing smoke-filled.

She squinted, struggling to understand.

Daal must have noticed her concerned expression. He turned to the growing pall in the woods.

"What is that?" he mumbled hoarsely. "Looks like dust. . . ."

DESPITE HIS SHIVERING weakness, Daal reached a hand to where swirls of fine powder sifted off the tangled branches. The dust rose upward throughout the forest, from every crystal facet, like smoke from a smoldering fire.

His fingers brushed across a thin tendril, scattering it apart. He gasped at the burn, then cried louder as acid scorched down to bone. He yanked his hand back, drawing a few particles with him from the forest. The dusty black specks shivered and fell to the copper floor.

Still, he retreated from them, as if from poisonous spiders.

"Get back . . ." he croaked to the others.

He stared down at his fingers. His skin lay blackened in stripes, as if he had become tangled in the stinging tentacles of a gelatinous war-bell. Blood seeped from the cracked edges.

He continued to retreat until he could push to his feet. He stumbled into Nyx, who could barely keep her legs. Her eyes had gone cloudy again after burning through so much strength.

"What is it?" she asked, clutching his arm.

He stared into the forest, watching the dust grow thicker and rise higher. The pall poured in swirls, then spread outward, exhaled by this dreaded forest.

Now that he was starved of bridle-song, Daal's vision sharpened. His eyes could discern the baleful sheen to the dust, some spoiled version of what had once been golden. Only this wasn't a poisonous emerald in hue, but a loathsome black, the color of corruption and festering rot.

"What are you seeing?" Nyx repeated.

"The forest . . . it's shedding whatever you felt living in the crystals, some perverse bits of vileness."

"The little frilled animals."

"Now loose, they churn through the air, burning with acid and fire. Far worse than any brush against their crystal."

Daal watched the dust continue to darken the bower and grow heavier. Above the forest—seen through breaks in the canopy that shrouded them—the pall formed a low-lying black fog that washed outward across the breadth of the dome.

He glanced to the others, still huddled low around Shiya. All eyes were on the forest and the spreading pall. Daal guided Nyx to the others.

Jace stared around. "That black tide seems to be avoiding this clearing, like the forest does around us."

Daal turned to the few specks of dust that had wafted into this space and lay dead on the copper. "I think whatever energy is given off by the giant sphere repels them, kills them if they get too near."

Krysh nodded. "If true, we should be safe as long as we remain near the *turubya*. Whatever foulness was created by the Roots, they wouldn't want to risk damaging it."

Rhaif kept low next to Shiya, who remained inordinately weak. "This must be a secondary trap set by the bastards. If their throne is attacked"—he looked over at Nyx—"then this menace traps the culprits, holds them in place until they can be dealt with."

Daal reminded them of a greater concern. "While we're safe in the clearing, we're not the only ones down here."

That became clear in the next breath.

A ripe scream rose from beyond the forest, sharp with pain, then gargling away. Then another picked up the refrain, then another. More soon joined the chorus of agony.

Darant's men were out there, as was Vikas.

And one other.

A howl burst through the forest, bright with agony and fury.

Nyx turned to Graylin. "Kalder . . ."

WITH HIS HEART clenched into a fist, Graylin prepared to answer his brother's howl, to let Kalder and the others know that safety lay this direction—if they could reach it.

His group shouted, too, calling to the men, warning them to seek higher ground away from the low-sweeping fog, to flee its reach in any way they could. But their bellows were lost to the chorus of pained screams.

Graylin lifted a hand to his lips, carving his fingers just right, and blew a piercing whistle that cut through the agonized cacophony. In the past, he had used this signal to summon Kalder and his brother, Aamon, out of the Rimewood, to urge them home to a warm hearth.

Listen to me now, my brother.

The only response was a pained howl that strangled away.

Graylin imagined Kalder inhaling the fiery dust into his lungs, burning from the inside, drowning in his own blood.

Graylin whistled again, but he could raise no other howls.

Nyx staggered to him, near blind but finding his pain unerringly. She grabbed his arm. She allowed him to pull her closer. As they listened, the chorus of cries slowly died away. No one in their group bothered to shout any longer, recognizing the futility.

They stood vigil in grim silence, in defeat.

Daal finally lowered to his knees, still trembling with weakness.

Rhaif dropped next to Shiya, who was still recovering on the copper floor.

Jace abided numbly with his ax at his knee, while Krysh stared dead-eyed at the forest.

Then Rhaif lifted his face. "I hear something . . ."

It drew the thief back to his feet, drawn up by his sharper ears. Then Jace took a step toward the forest, lifting his ax higher.

Though he heard nothing, Graylin shifted Nyx behind him and dropped his hand to his sword's hilt. Finally, he could detect a faint crashing, echoing out of the forest. It grew louder, sounding like a bull pounding toward them, heedless of anything in its way.

What new menace is this?

Through the dust-shrouded forest, a huge dark shadow appeared, shouldering toward them, flashing with lightning, its face featureless.

One of the *ta'wyn* had survived.

It rampaged toward them, ready to rid this trap of its rats.

Graylin yanked his sword. Shiya reared to her feet, but she staggered, still sapped of strength. Jace closed ranks with them. Krysh and Rhaif pulled Daal behind everyone, joining Nyx.

The *ta'wyn* shattered through the forest, driving straight toward them. Then it burst through the heavy pall and crashed into the clearing with a final heavy swing of a broadsword.

Vikas . . .

The mountainous woman collapsed to her knees, then her hand, losing her sword. She yanked her other arm from behind her and dragged a snarling shape into view by its scruff. A headscarf wrapped the vargr's head. Vikas had done the same to herself.

She must have run blind, hacking a straight path through the forest.

She ripped her scarf away, dropped to her other hand, and coughed up a gout of blood. She waved weakly to Kalder, for someone to help him.

Graylin crossed and yanked the scarf away. Kalder snapped at him, blinded by pain and terror. The vargr stalked a circle, one eye weeping and clouded. Blood stained the froth of his mouth as he growled. A tail swished savagely.

Vikas continued to pant on all fours, blood seeping from her lips and nose. Both must have inhaled some of the pestilent dust. But while Kalder's fur had kept the vileness from reaching his skin, Vikas had not been so lucky. Her fingers—what showed beyond her half-gloves—had blackened and split, running with blood. It looked as if she had thrust her hands into a blazing fire. More burns slashed her face. If Vikas had not been so adamant about keeping herself fully geared—with leather, boots, and a padded gambeson—she might not have survived.

Once the quartermaster was able to roll to a hip, Jace passed her a waterskin. She signaled her thanks, spat the blood from her mouth, then took a few cautious sips.

Graylin tried to offer the same to Kalder, but the vargr refused with a rumbled growl, his blood still too hot.

The group regathered, relieved to have the two returned, but they were no closer to addressing the trouble with the *turubya*. Jace's plan of breaking the rigging and crashing the sphere below had grown in appeal to Graylin.

"What now?" Rhaif asked.

Krysh frowned. "We can't stay here forever."

This became clearer as a hard tremor shook the floor. No one spoke, all praying for it to stop. The gods ignored them. A fierce quake struck, ringing the copper dome like a bell. The forest rocked with a crystalline tinkling, and somewhere in the distance, a cliff of glass shattered darkly.

But that was not the most concerning.

Behind them, the *turubya*'s large crystal sphere rattled in its cradle.

Fortunately, suspension rigging held.

But for how much longer?

90

WITH THE WORLD reduced again to murky shades, Nyx sank to her knees on the rocking floor, disoriented by her limited sight. The forest chimed madly, not with the dissonant hiss of corrupted life, but from the rattle of branches. Behind her, the sphere bumped with loud rings against its copper riggings. Each one made her cringe, fearful of hearing the splintering of crystal as it broke.

Finally, the violent jolting and rocking quieted. She touched a palm to the floor, still feeling a slight tremoring in the copper. But it might just be the power thrumming from the giant buried cables feeding the *turubya*. Still, to her it felt like the world was holding its breath.

"Is it over?" Jace asked.

"For now," Krysh answered.

Graylin stirred past her, just a shadow sweeping by. Kalder followed, heavily panting. She could smell the blood on his breath, heard it in his ragged wheezes. She rose to follow, to where the group was regathering. She stretched an arm out into the gloom.

Then Daal was there and took her elbow. With both so weak, there was not even a spark between them. "I've got you."

He helped guide her to the others.

Graylin spoke sternly. "Another quake could strike anytime. We must decide on a plan. Do we try to destroy the *turubya*, as Jace suggested? Cripple it so it's useless to Eligor?"

Nyx struggled to accept this as their only option.

Not after the cost in blood, misery, and death.

Nyx searched until she spotted a brighter shine amidst the gathering—not bridle-song, simply a glint of bronze. "Shiya, what happened when you engaged the Root's new activation bed? Did you sense anything while connected to it? Something to guide us?"

Shiya remained silent for a long breath, then spoke softly, still sounding weak. "I felt my essence drawn from my body, pulled to the sphere, hovering above it. Energy wafted over me in great waves, rising from the sphere, an immensity beyond scope. It was nothing like what I had experienced at the Frozen Wastes inside the chrysalis. At the same time, I sensed a focus upon me that carried that same sense of enormity. As if a great eye was staring at me."

"Then what?" Jace asked.

"I was rejected." Despair tinged her words. "Cast away, back into my bronze, only to find myself trapped there. Whatever the Roots crafted it was designed to shun an Axis. It was meant only for someone as potent as a Kryst."

"Eligor . . ." Rhaif moaned.

Nyx rubbed her brow. Unable to see, unable to focus on the name *Rab'almat* inscribed into bronze, she suddenly heard what Shiya had just said, what the woman had truly just told them.

Nyx stirred to face the *ta'wyn*. "Shiya, you mentioned the Roots retooled the *turubya*'s trigger so it could only work for someone *as potent as a Kryst*."

"That is what I sensed," the *ta'wyn* answered. "What I experienced."

"Does that mean *any* Kryst—not necessarily just Eligor?"

"Yes, I would surmise so."

Graylin interjected, "But there are no other Krysts alive, so why does this matter?"

"That's not true," Nyx whispered, suddenly relieved not to be able to view their expressions. "There is another Kryst still alive."

"Where?" Jace asked.

"Here." Nyx pointed to her chest. "Right here."

A moment of stunned silence erupted into gasps and mutters of incredulity, shock, and some anger. It was hard to say who took which stand. Then a hand slipped into hers. Though there was no heat of connection, no merging of senses, she knew it was Daal from the pattern of calluses, the size of his knuckles, the length of his fingers, even the slightly thicker webbing at the base of his thumb.

He just fit her.

He squeezed his reassurance, giving her the strength to continue.

"According to the *Drāshra*, I'm the first *ka'wyn* to appear in ages. A Kryst born of flesh."

Graylin scoffed. "She was surely speaking metaphorically, not literally, certainly not physically."

"There is one way to find out." Nyx pushed up, balancing on Daal, her anchor even now. She turned to Shiya's shine, trying to peer through the bronze. "First, I'll need to regain my strength, if you'll allow me."

The woman stepped forward. "Take what you need."

Graylin tried to intervene, shadowing Shiya's bronze with his body. "This is too dangerous."

Rhaif threw Graylin's earlier words back at his feet. "We must try something," the thief reminded him. "It failed with Shiya, but it may heed Nyx."

Krysh agreed. "With moonfall approaching, all risks must be taken."

Before Graylin could argue further, Nyx stepped to Shiya. Her bronze arms lifted toward her. Nyx reached, fumbled, and found the woman's hands. The metal felt as warm and pliant as any flesh.

Nyx squeezed Shiya's palms, both in thanks and to draw their connection closer.

Are we two truly that different?

All their hopes depended on the answer to that question being *no.*

Shiya sang to her, allowing her bridle-song to flow into Nyx, to feed that ravenous pit inside her. This time Nyx did not deny its hunger. As energy surged back into her, her vision grew clearer. The fog lifted from her eyes.

She saw Shiya staring down at her.

The woman's warm hands firmed their hold on Nyx, marking their sisterhood. Nyx prayed what judged her next would see the same.

A sisterhood, a commonality, that went beyond the bronze of one's skin.

SHINING WITH RENEWED strength, Nyx faced the dark clamshell looming past the fringes of the forest. Dust hung and swirled in ominous eddies around the tangle of bronze.

After Nyx's assault upon it, the shell's surface no longer rose as a smooth, sculpted curve. It had hardened into a treacherous briar's nest of twisted fibrils, knotted cords, and snaking tendrils. It looked malignant and tortured, the very face of the forest behind it.

Graylin stood behind her. "We can try another way. You must not risk this."

She shook her head, too afraid to speak lest she lose her nerve.

She turned and nodded to Krysh and Jace. The two men held Vikas's leather vest stretched between them and started waving it up and down before the dreaded nest. The wind of the leather's passage reminded Nyx of the beating of Bashaliia's wings. Their efforts wafted the dust clear, opening the way for Nyx.

Before stepping back, Graylin reached to Nyx. She thought it was to drag her off, but his fingers gripped her firmly. "If anyone can do this, you can."

She read his earnestness, his fear, but also his acceptance. She reached up and took his hand in hers, feeling calluses that reminded her of her dah back in Mýr. "I'll do my best," she promised him.

He gave her fingers a final squeeze, then retreated to the others. He pointed to Jace and Krysh. "Don't stop flagging that vest. If you tire, tell us."

Both men nodded.

Past Graylin, Shiya stood with Rhaif and Vikas. Kalder kept close to the quartermaster's side, as if recognizing who had saved him.

Nyx turned to Daal. He stared at the darkly transformed clamshell, and then, as if feeling her attention, he glanced to her. His eyes were pinched. His face had gone far paler. She easily read his expression.

If he could take this burden from her, he would.

She gave him a small nod, acknowledging this.

But this is a path I must walk alone.

Nyx took a deep breath, held it, then let it out slowly as she passed into the bower's fringe. She reached the briar's nest and carefully stepped through its tangles, wormed through its thorns and clinging tendrils. Once at the center, she turned to face the others. They stood limned against the rise of the sphere, shadowed before the surging golden sea pulsing inside.

At the height of Nyx's shoulders, two bronze arms still hung there, extending out from the edges of the shell, ending in rough grips. She took a moment to hum and gather her song tighter, to shine it brighter. She pushed that glow to her skin, wearing her song like armor again. She hoped the golden shine would blind this infernal device to the flesh she wore, making it look bronze enough.

She searched with her eyes and her spirit to make sure every curve and fold of her body was perfectly rendered and covered—only then did she reach up and grab the bronze handles.

She cringed, expecting the worst.

Nothing happened with her first breath.

Or her second.

On her third, she was wrenched out of her body. Unlike when she rode on a chorus of song, this was no flow of her spirit along golden strands. This was demand. This was mandate. And agonizing. She cried out in both flesh and spirit.

She swept up into an eternal darkness.

Then a sun exploded beneath her.

She winced at its brilliance, at the wash of gold at the star's core. Waves pulsed up from there, washing in tidal surges, marking the very heartbeat of creation.

Beyond the sun, the world had reduced to mere outlines, barely discernible, just a vague iridescent sketch of the forest, of those gathered in the clearing. Nothing moved. Everything was frozen in place, stuck in amber. Farther out, reality vanished into swirling clouds of lustrous brilliance, as if churning with probabilities, where form was forever held in suspension, balanced between existence and annihilation.

She forced her gaze away, knowing only madness lay in that direction.

Instead, she looked down at herself, at her being carved of pure bridle-song.

The shine of her form waxed and waned with every passing wave of tidal energy. She pictured the small dhelprä glowing in the shadowy mountain of the mankrae king—and what the small creature had left behind.

Does my body still live at the edge of the forest?

This worry drew her more fully into herself, into her spirit.

Survival proved a good anchor.

As she settled, with waves pulsing past her, she felt what Shiya had described: a sense of immense scrutiny, of a great eye upon her, as if the sphere below were the monocle of a god. She braced herself to be rejected as abruptly as Shiya had been, but that intensity only grew, waxed into expectation, as if waiting for her to act.

But to do what?

She stared around again: at the world in amber, at the clouds of madness. She returned her gaze below, to challenge the all-consuming stare of the god's eye. She squinted at its radiance, at the surging gold of its iris—then she looked deeper, discovering a dark pupil at the center of the gold.

It gazed back at her.

She shuddered, knowing what stared at her.

She had touched it before.

She had been told it might be here.

The weight of expectation grew crushing. It came out of that darkness. She knew what it wanted now. The realization came with a spark of inspiration.

The very spark she needed.

The strike of flint on steel to start a fire.

The *how* of it still escaped her, but she had her suspicions.

She stared into the god's eye with a simple command.

Send me back.

NYX CRASHED INTO her body. Again, there was no gentleness. Rather than a smooth dive into warm water, this was the pound of a hammer. The impact threw her to her knees. Sharp bronze tore cloth and skin. She shoved up and stumbled back out into the clearing.

She staggered, trying to settle her spirit into flesh.

Daal caught her, even as weak as he was. Graylin hurried to help. The others closed in around, making it suddenly hard to breathe. Or she had forgotten how, even her heartbeat struggled with this.

"Did it reject you, too?" Rhaif asked.

Nyx shook her head. "No . . . I asked to come back."

Krysh's voice sharpened with amazement. "It accepted you as a Kryst?"

She nodded, but she had no time to ponder what this meant. That could come later, if at all.

"But it didn't work," Graylin noted. "Were you not able to trigger the *turubya*?"

"Not without another key."

"What do you—"

"I first must check something." She rushed to Jace. She grabbed his chin and turned his face to the right and left—then nodded. She grabbed his arm and dragged him to the forest.

"Wh . . . What are you doing?" he stammered.

"When you freed Shiya with your ax, I saw you get struck by several branches." She turned to him. "No burns anywhere. And earlier you crossed this forest without getting a single sting."

"I was careful. I'm sure of it."

She gave him a roll of her eyes as they reached the forest's edge—then shoved him past the fringes and into a patch of dust. He tripped and landed hard on his backside. The fiery powder drifted all over him without any effect. Still, he gained his feet and quickly clambered out.

Nyx pointed to the forest. "I wager you could walk straight through there and suffer nothing worse than a dusty cough to clear the dead powder from your lungs."

From Jace's horrified expression, this was not something he was planning on doing. He glanced to the forest. "Why did you do that?"

"To test what I needed to know." Nyx spoke fast. Her pounding heart demanded haste. "This forest saps *synmeld*. Craves it. But Jace, it avoids *you*. You're anathema to its corruption. Because of the *dysmeld* in your blood. It must be the same reason that this clearing remains free of dust. Even the forest won't grow here."

"Why?"

She pointed to the crystal sphere. "Like you, the *turubya* is clearly anathema to this corruption. Which means at the center of the crystal, past the shining golden sea, lies a massive font of *dysmeld*."

She pictured the black pupil in the golden iris. She had recognized the emptiness shining back at her, at the endless void it represented.

"But why is this significant?" Krysh pressed her.

Nyx turned to Shiya, pointing at her. "*Dysmeld*. You described it as twin in power to *synmeld*, but also its antithesis. When the two come together, they annihilate one another. Removing both from this world. Possibly explosively so."

Shiya nodded.

Nyx turned back to Krysh. "Because of that, *you* had already posited that the *turubya* might be powered by *dysmeld,* and that it could require *synmeld* to trigger it."

"Was I right?"

Nyx waggled her head. "Somewhat. I think pouring *synmeld* straight into that font would have no effect or possibly blow it up. Neither of which we want. The ancients wouldn't create such an unstable device, not when it's meant to survive across millennia."

She searched their faces.

Krysh slowly nodded. "If triggering the *turubya* involves the explosive annihilation of *synmeld* and *dysmeld,* it would have to be a controlled process."

She jabbed a finger at him. "A tiny *spark.* Like the strike of flint on steel to start a fire." She turned to the briar's nest at the forest's edge. "I wager that's the sole purpose of these activation beds. To ignite that spark, the first flash of a greater fire."

"But how?" Jace asked.

Nyx pointed to the crystal sphere. "An Axis or a Kryst is like that. Rich in golden *synmeld,* but with a seed of black *dysmeld* at their core."

Rhaif frowned. "Where does Shiya have *dysmeld*?"

"In the crystal cube that sustains her," Nyx answered. "The *turubya's* sphere is an enormous version of what she carries inside her. If *dysmeld* is inside this sphere, it must be inside her cube, too."

Shiya rested her palm on her chest, her expression a mix of distress and surprise.

"I've seen what happens when a power cube shatters inside a *ta'wyn.*" Nyx pictured bronze blasting apart in the desert. "It's powerful. I wager what happens in the activation chamber is a controlled version of that blast. Strong enough to spark the *turubya,* yet controlled enough not to destroy the *ta'wyn* in the chamber."

Graylin waved this all away. "But how does *any* of this offer guidance in activating the *turubya*?"

Nyx turned to him. "I'm Kryst enough to get through that gate, but I don't carry any *dysmeld* with me. When I was in there, I felt this immense sense of expectation, as if something was required of me, some action."

"To ignite that spark," Krysh said.

She nodded. "I have to go back in there, but with another *key* in hand."

Krysh turned to Shiya. "You need her cube."

"With its bit of *dysmeld,*" Nyx added.

Shiya looked stricken at this.

Rhaif noted her distress. "What's wrong?"

Shiya still had her palm over her belly. "I held off telling you this. With all that's happened. All that needed to be done . . ."

She lifted her hand away, withdrawing the cube from inside her. She left it resting on her palm.

Nyx gasped and withdrew a step.

The crystal lay blackened and dark.

"I was not only rejected when cast out," Shiya said. "But also punished. Maybe to keep me from trying again."

Nyx stared at the cube. Only now did she recall how Shiya had seemed persistently weak since escaping the bronze trap.

Now I know why.

Graylin frowned. "Without the cube, what do we do now?"

Silence settled over the group.

Jace finally spoke up. "There is still another source of *dysmeld*."

Faces turned his way.

He pointed to his chest.

91

NYX STOOD BESIDE Jace at the fringe of the forest. She had already explained what to expect—not that any words could truly capture what lay beyond the nest of bronze. While Jace's face looked determined, his skin glistened with tension.

"If we get through, we must be quick," she reminded him. "The ruse may not last longer than a few breaths."

He nodded. "I have no control over what's in me. So do what you must."

Nyx held out her hand, and he slipped his gloved fingers into her grip. It had been decided to minimize skin-to-skin contact. They did not want to prematurely stir the void inside Jace.

"Should we practice one more time?" Jace asked.

"Don't worry. I can hold my shield over both of us."

She knew he was only trying to delay them. Once they crossed the gate's threshold, there would be no retreating. She pictured the blackened cube in Shiya's palm. If they were similarly rejected, Jace would likely suffer the crystal's same fate, with the *dysmeld* burned out of him, leaving him a charred husk.

But it wasn't only Jace who didn't want them to leave.

Graylin hovered at her shoulder. "We should give this further consideration. Think about it more calmly."

"Calmly?" Nyx glanced back. "We have no time to be calm."

As if to prove her words, the copper floor started another trembling. It rattled up her body. Into her teeth. Deep down, she knew these tremors were building toward something worse.

"We must go," Nyx insisted.

Graylin finally relented, stepping back to join the others.

She turned to Jace. "It's just us now."

He nodded, still worried.

She looked deeper into his eyes. "Do you trust me?"

"Always. From the very beginning. But we've come a long way from studying into late bells, crammed in my dormitory cell."

Nyx nodded, but she avoided looking back along the path that got them here. It was a road too pained, too full of grief.

Jace, though, did look back—but only over his shoulder. "Daal . . . he's good for you." He squeezed her hand. "I see that. You should try to work out whatever stands between you. None of us knows how many days we have left. You should find home and heart wherever you can."

"You've always been my home, Jace. And my heart."

He sighed. "But I'll never be the flashburn to your forge."

She knew what he meant by that, heard the pain behind those words. She had spoken them too often, failing to realize the hurt they had caused him. She turned to face him, so he could read her sincerity.

"Jace, in the moments ahead, you'll need to be the *steel* to my *flint*. Creating the spark that could save the world."

"Maybe," he muttered, and tried to turn away.

She drew him back with a palm on his cheek, atop a beard that made him look too old—or maybe it was something in his eyes.

"But, Jace, you must know this. You've *always* been the steel to my flint. In school when I was terrorized. During those late-bell nights of studying when I was lost. It was you who taught me my blurred sight was as much a blessing as a trial. And along the hard road to this spot, it was *you* who remained my home and my heart. I would not have gotten this far without you. You've *always* been my steel."

His eyes grew glassy at her words, then he pulled her closer. They hugged as the tremoring underfoot warned them to be off.

Still, they both knew *why* they had shared this moment before setting off, even with the ground trembling under them. They both needed to get out words that had to be spoken—but the intent behind them was the same.

They were saying good-bye.

As the shaking grew worse, Nyx crossed with Jace into the dark bower. The forest shuddered around them, its branches ringing with chimes. Behind them, Krysh wafted the leather vest to keep the dust clear.

Nyx shared a look and a nod with Jace. She then hummed her song brighter, the pitch too sunny for this black glade. She pushed her golden glow over her skin, caressing every curve like before, drawing her armor on again.

But this time, she hadn't come alone.

When her glow reached her hand clutching Jace's fingers, her armor flowed up his arm and across his body, joining two into one. She took great care to keep her song hovering over his skin, careful not to brush against it.

The goal was to appear as a single supplicant coming to this dark gate. They needed her *ka'wyn* status to open it, while she carried Jace hidden behind her armor. If his *dysmeld* nature was detected, the hope was that it would be dismissed as emanations from a cube like Shiya's.

Still, they had to be quick.

In and out.

That was the plan.

If they managed to get through, Nyx would lure that daemon out of Jace with lines of gold, like fishing dark waters. Once it was far enough free of Jace, she would strike hard with bridle-song, annihilating *synmeld* and *dysmeld* together. With any luck, it would ignite the necessary spark to trigger the *turubya*.

With that goal, Nyx climbed through the nest's tangle of bronze with Jace. Once close enough, she raised her right arm. Jace mirrored with his left. Moving as one, they reached to their respective bronze handles—then grabbed them at the same time.

Again, nothing happened for the first breath or the second.

On the third, a force tore her from her body. Agony ripped a scream from her throat, trailing out with her spirit. She heard an echo of the same, only deeper-toned and panicked.

Jace . . .

Darkness overwhelmed her, then shattered with the birth of a sun under her. Energy struck, tidal and strong, washing in waves. She recovered quicker this time, having known what to expect. She stared down at a body sculpted of living light, then over to the figure she clutched.

She cried out in shock. Her dismay was so great that the next wave of energy shivered her spirit's glowing form, nearly dissolving it. Still, the brief dissolution allowed her to break free of the daemon's grip. She had expected to be holding Jace's hand, his warm spirit suspended in her protective armor.

Instead, she faced a figure carved of a cold blackness, mockingly in the outline of Jace. But she knew *nothing* of her friend's essence had been drawn out of his body—only the *dysmeld* inside him.

She faced the void and stoked her song to a brilliance, ready to challenge the darkness. She needed to strike it while she had a chance, with all the strength inside her.

I will never be given a second chance.

Working quickly, she coalesced her gold into a fiery sun, then stripped away a single strand of gold. She extended it toward the arcane sigil branded into her by the raash'ke.

Before she could flare it to life, she spotted movement in the man-shaped void before her. A darker shadow within the daemon's chest formed a snaking shape. It was only visible due to a sheen of black diamond frosting its outline. She watched thin wings spread wide as it swam seductively through the void.

She recognized the kezmek—a Bhestyan assassin-wing.

She struggled to understand its rise out of this dark well.

Its meaning now.

She dismissed it, knowing time ran short.

Already, the weighty sense of expectation had grown. It now carried a note of demand: act now or lose this chance forever. Past the *dysmeld* daemon, the heart of the sun below churned with gold. The black pupil at its center had grown wider, expressing a demand.

To act.

Nyx heeded that command. She ignored the strangeness of the kezmek and bore down upon the gold inside her. She forged it into a blaze, then reached to the raash'ke sigil. With a glancing touch, she ignited it. It shattered forth with arcane encodings. Ancient words spilled from her lips—both in spirit and in flesh. As power turned into purpose, she opened herself fully, embracing her golden sun, melting it out, forging a lance of pure brilliance.

She focused on her target—only the daemon had grown smaller against the golden sea below. She failed to understand, hesitating, then saw it wasn't shrinking.

Falling . . .

It plummeted away from her, toward the widening black pupil.

She realized its intent.

This void, this daemon, had been ripped from a reservoir of *dysmeld* in the Wastes' *turubya*. It now sought to rejoin the same here.

It's heading home.

Nyx dove after it, leading with her spear.

If it escapes, I lose everything.

She had to get as close as possible. She dared not miss this shot. As she pursued the daemon, waves of pulsing power pushed against her. It was like swimming against a tide. Worse, the farther down she went, the stronger those waves grew.

She recognized a hard truth.

I'm not going to reach it.

Then something strange stirred below.

From the chest of the daemon, the kezmek squirmed free, spreading its wings. As it fought out, a steaming black tether still connected the assassin-wing to the void behind it. The kezmek beat its wings, as if trying to fly toward her. Its body writhed with this effort. It even seemed to take advantage of the outgoing waves, riding that energy closer to her.

With the daemon tethered behind it, anchored to the kezmek, its descent slowed. The assassin-wing fought harder, briefly drawing their plummet to a stop.

Nyx sped faster with her golden lance. She recognized this impasse would not last. Still, she had to get as close as possible. As she fought the waves, she stared down at the struggling creature, still outlined in a sheen of black diamond.

She understood.

She knew who fought below.

Jace . . .

His essence had somehow been carried here, only it had been swamped by the darkness.

Nyx flashed to the corridor in the *Fyredragon*. She saw Jace grab the kezmek before it could strike her, protecting her. He had similarly safeguarded others aboard the Bhestyan warship. It was not the *void* inside him that saved them, but the *will* of Jace, a love so strong it influenced that cold power.

And now that *will* had taken form out of the darkness.

She dove toward him, fighting the ever-stronger tide. He strained below, but the daemon started to fall away again. They would not reach each other.

She could get no closer.

Jace . . .

She lifted her lance, struggling against what she must do. Then a whisper sailed to her, carried on those waves, formed of will and love.

Let me be your steel one last time.

She could not deny him.

She screamed her grief and threw her fiery lance.

THE ANNIHILATING BLAST crashed Nyx back into her body—then to her knees. Jace's body slumped at the same time from his perch. She twisted to catch him in her arms, his head falling dead to her shoulder. She pulled him to her, wanted to shake him, but she just cradled him harder to her chest.

"No . . ." she moaned.

Then Graylin pushed to her side, his voice panicked. "We must go."

She denied him.

"The quake," he warned. "It's shaking everything apart."

Only now did the trembling and jolts draw her attention. The forest rang with alarm. It felt like her grief given form, shaking the world.

He drew her away. "I'm sorry."

Vikas joined them and signaled with bandaged fingers: "*I've got him.*"

Too weak to resist, Nyx let herself be pulled from Jace's slack body, his eyes glazed and staring up. Under one arm, Graylin carried her out into the clearing.

Krysh called over, "We must hurry!"

Daal came alongside Nyx and pointed ahead. "You did it. Both of you. Look."

She stared leadenly at the sphere of the *turubya*.

The golden sea no longer churned. The pool now blurred through a dizzying array of shapes: pyramids, cubes, prisms. Some shapes defied the eye. They flashed faster and faster, merging into a sphere made of thousands of blended shapes, flickering into and out of coherence.

Nyx had seen this before back in the Frozen Wastes.

The glow grew into a blaze of shining energy.

"Everybody back!" Graylin bellowed.

The group fled as far away as the fiery forest would allow. As they drew into a cluster, the sphere's blaze exploded behind them in a blinding flare, sending them all low. The blast blew apart the sphere's riggings with coppery crashes.

Nyx turned to watch, knowing the sacrifice Jace had made to make this happen.

The sphere hung over the open mouth of the pit, suspended now by a nimbus of energy rather than copper. The shine stung, but Nyx refused to look away. Then the orb shot straight up, crashing through the crystal canopy above.

As debris rained down, the sphere reached its apex, hung suspended in the air—then in the next breath, it slammed down the hole and vanished.

"Let's go!" Graylin shouted, ducking from the cascade of branches.

He sheltered over Nyx and got them all moving.

Behind them, a vault door slammed over the hole with a thunderous shake. Others could be heard closing in succession down the shaft's length.

As they headed away, a few crystalline shards struck Nyx, but she felt no burn, only the ordinary sting of sharp glass. Even the dust had cleared. The sphere's energy blast must have killed the malevolence, ending the torture of what had lived in the forest.

With the way open, they all rushed faster.

As they ran, Nyx stumbled as her sight clouded over, going murky again. Her eyes had likely only held out this long due to the nimbus of wild energies surrounding the *turubya*'s activation. As she fled away, so went her vision.

Graylin must have noted her faltering and caught her. "I've got you."

Kalder shoved against her other side, offering his shoulder.

She took it.

The floor had begun to shake again.

It had briefly stopped—as if the triggering of the *turubya* had momentarily suppressed it. But this new shaking was not a new quake. All around, the huge cables in the tunnels hummed menacingly, vibrating and tremoring. The same could be felt underfoot.

They finally reached the ramp and headed up it.

A shout called down from above. "Hurry!"

It was one of Darant's men. The sentry posted at the tunnel. He must have been high enough above the fiery dust cloud to escape its reach. When they joined him, Nyx made out two more men stirring to their feet in the tunnel, burned and bloody but alive. They must have also reached this refuge, maybe responding to their earlier shouts of warning.

Everyone got moving down the tunnel.

Nyx glanced back with her clouded eyes.

She made out Vikas. The quartermaster still carried Jace over her shoulder, clearly unwilling to leave him behind. It made Nyx love her all the more.

Noting Nyx's concerned look, Vikas lifted her free hand. Her bandaged fingers formed a circle, a familiar Gynish sign: *"All is fine."*

Nyx knew it wasn't.

It might never be.

Vikas nodded to Nyx, patted Jace, then shifted her hand and fluttered her palm atop her own broad chest. *"He's still breathing."*

Still breathing?

Nyx stumbled to a stop, weaving on her feet, allowing the quartermaster to close on her. "He . . . He's alive?"

Vikas frowned and tapped her chest with a fist, throbbing her fingers. *"Heart is strong."* She rapped that same fist against her head, then opened her fingers into a wave past her ear. *"Just knocked out."*

Back at the briar's nest, on her knees, knowing what she had done, she had been blinded by guilt. She had assumed the annihilating blast had killed him.

Nyx trembled into a sob and reached for him, struggling with disbelief. Before her fingertips could touch him, something rose from his chest, like a wisp of black smoke, then with a spin of wings dove back home.

Jace . . .

Offered this last bit of reassurance, she allowed her vision to cloud over, taking away the world but leaving her the best gift of all.

Hope.

92

FROM THE WHEELHOUSE of the *Fyredragon*, Graylin watched the final destruction of the black mountain. It still filled the world ahead of him. Huge sections cleaved off its flanks, cracked away both by the ongoing quakes and by the immense forces at the core of the Dragon.

Glass shattered with great booms.

Their group had barely escaped before it had all started coming apart.

The *Fyredragon* retreated across the black sea, fleeing from the violence and blasting glass. The ship's forges flamed hotter, driving the huge vessel straight back as it struggled for more air. But with half their gasbag gone, Darant wisely chose distance versus height to keep them out of harm's way.

The captain called to his crew from the maesterwheel. "Keep all forges at full blaze! I want off this burning sea and over sand."

Like Graylin, Darant had witnessed the fiery demolition of the *turubya* site in the Frozen Wastes and sought to get them to a safe harbor. It seemed the ancients wanted to close off any access to a *turubya* once it was seated deep into the crust. Even the series of massive doors along the shaft must not have been deemed enough protection.

They did not want to be caught in the wake of the coming destruction.

Fenn shouted from his station, "Look low! At the base of the Dragon."

Graylin stepped closer to the window, dropping his gaze from the crumbling crown to the foot of the mountain. There, a frosting of glass crystals hung in the air, creating a scintillating fog.

Through the shrouding, water could be seen boiling forth. Steam flowed up the mountain's flanks.

"Get us farther back!" Darant bellowed.

Soon a trembling pressure built in the air. The ship shook with it. Moments later, waves of shimmering energy radiated out from the foot of the Dragon, sweeping across the glass before finally dissipating—at first in slow washes, then faster and faster.

The growing squeeze crushed them all to silence. Graylin held his breath, not sure if he could even expand his lungs under this pressure.

Then it gave way, popping with such force that the *Fyredragon* reared its bow high. The stern struck the hard sea and scraped across it. Ahead, the glass around the mountain shattered upward in great broken plates. Water and steam blasted high, several times the height of the Dragon.

It gushed across the sky, a cascading fountain of raw power. Then it all crashed down. Water flooded outward in a tremendous tide. It rushed at the ship, reached it, then flowed under the keel. The *Fyredragon* had righted itself and sailed backward, as if riding the surf.

Slowly the tide died away, then began receding the other direction.

The door into the wheelhouse crashed open. Daal hurried in with Nyx. The two looked panicked after the jarring and rolling, the thunderous explosion.

"What happened?" Daal asked.

Graylin waved an arm. "Come see."

The pair had stopped on their way up to make sure Jace was settled, watched over by Vikas, while Krysh ministered to their injuries. Luckily, Jace had already begun to stir by the time they had reboarded the ship. Nyx and Daal had also wanted to check on the raash'ke and on Bashaliia.

From the clearing of Nyx's eyes, she must have borrowed a trickle of strength from her bonded to clear the clouds from her gaze. She certainly seemed stronger, buoyed with renewed strength—or maybe that came not from bridle-song, but from relief at Jace's survival.

As the pair joined Graylin, they all stared across the flooded sea, dotted with jagged islands of broken plates of glass. Ahead, the black mountain re-appeared through the steam. It had dropped to half its height, but not from being shattered low.

"It's sinking," Nyx noted.

As they watched, the Dragon slowly lowered into the sea. By the time the last glassy points of the crown vanished beneath the steaming water, the *Fyredragon* had cleared the glass and now skimmed over rolling sand.

"We made it," Darant sighed out.

And not a moment too soon.

A low rumbling rose around the ship. With each breath, it grew louder. Then with a roar that trembled the ship, the entire glass sea shoved high. The dunes under them did, too. A ridge struck the keel and jolted the *Fyredragon*. Then the land crashed down with a thunderous blast.

In front of them, the entire breadth of the Shil'nurr Plains—the great glass sea—shattered into pieces, forming a broken black mirror.

The rolling dunes had fared better, even now looking little changed. Sand drifted and settled, returning to the desert, stubbornly eternal.

Fenn wandered over to them. "Was that an aftermath of the Dragon's destruction? A final stamp upon the *turubya*'s resting place?"

"No . . ." Nyx moaned.

A glance over showed her gaze was not on the shattered sea, but on the sky, where the moon shone on high. Through the haze of steam and fog of crystals, its glow had turned an angry red.

"Like in my dreams," Nyx mumbled, and stared down at her bandaged hand, at her missing finger, her face a mask of worry.

Daal stirred next to her and pointed back at the sky. "Look. It's already changing."

As the steam thinned and the crystalline fog lowered, the moon's shine cleared to silver, with only a lingering nimbus of crimson at its edge.

Daal took her hand. "We still have time to make a difference."

She nodded, drawing her shoulders straighter. Her confidence and the joy slowly returned.

The wheelhouse door opened again, drawing all eyes. Rhaif hurried in with Shiya, though she moved more slowly, clearly still weak, turning her bronze form sluggish.

"You have to hear this," Rhaif called to them as he rushed the last of the distance.

From his ebullient manner, he came with something rare.

Glad tidings.

Rhaif pointed to Shiya. "She received a message. From the Southern Klashe."

"From Tykhan?" Graylin stepped closer.

Rhaif's brightness dimmed at this question. "No, via a new method of reaching us. Something Tykhan built."

"What do you mean? How?"

Rhaif sighed. "There is a longer story to tell, but it came with an encouraging epilogue." His eyes sparkled. "The others discovered the key to the *turubya.*"

Nyx drew sharply closer. "They have it . . . they have the key."

Rhaif winced. "No. Sorry. Poor wording. They discovered the *location* of the key."

The disappointment in Nyx's face matched Graylin's own, but he also shared her shining hope at this revelation.

"Where is it?" Graylin asked.

"Where we started this long journey," Rhaif said. "The key is buried somewhere in the volcanic mountain of The Fist."

Graylin stiffened with shock. "In the swamps of Mýr."

Rhaif nodded.

Graylin turned to Nyx. "Then it looks like we're heading home."

She rubbed her arms, her face gone ashen. She clearly struggled with how to absorb the import of this message.

She mumbled a single word, spoken like a lament.

"Home . . ."

93

Esme kept to her saddle atop Ruro and lowered the edge of her scarf to take a sip from her waterskin. She held the moisture in her mouth and let it linger, to better allay her thirst. She finally swallowed with a sigh.

As she awaited word, she did her best to keep distracted. She shifted Ruro a few steps over to the copper pole she had just screwed into its base socket. Past this site, the other four flags of Tosgon whipped in a steady breeze. The old pole, scorched and blackened, lay in the sand. Its flag had been burned to ashes, which were swept away by the winds over the past fortnight until there was no remnant of it.

"*Lökh etaar,*" she whispered, a Chanrë pronouncement regarding how time erases pain so peace can shine forth.

Or in the common tongue:

The desert abides.

With a sigh, she stood in her leather stirrups, finding easy balance. Already, she had learned to ride much better. She lifted the rolled triangular flag and attached its grommets to the copper locking hooks. Once it was secure, she tossed the woven fabric past her shoulder to catch a gust. Its length unfurled like the crack of a whip, then danced in the wind.

She ducked down and appreciated her handiwork. The other four flags were a rich crimson, a close match to the sands of Ghödlökh. The new one was a pure white to honor the fallen.

She shifted Ruro to the dune's edge and cast her gaze across the rolling expanse. The scars of the battle had mostly washed away. Sand had swept over blackened ditches, filling them smooth. The dead had been collected and carried to caves in the Samskrag cliffs.

The remains of the *ta'wyn* had been scavenged of anything useful. For the desert people, nothing went to waste. The rest had been sunk into a deep pit. Each villager had dug at least a fistful of that hole, each contributing to burying their misery away.

One long ridge of dunes would likely remain scarred forever. It had been slagged to glass during the last battle, looking like a lone wave of the black sea trapped among the red dunes. The names of the dead had been etched into the glass. With Ruro at her side, she had joined the ceremony and scratched in the name *Abresh*.

From the same slagged dune, her companions aboard the *Fyredragon* had recovered a single *ta'wyn* cannon. It seemed intact enough to repair. Likewise, the ship's crew had collected those *ta'wyn* shields that hummed and defied the pull of the Urth.

No one at Tosgon had objected to them scavenging all of this. The Chanrë owed the crew a great deal, for freeing the village of the Dragon's yoke. Now, where the black mountain had stood, a new oasis had risen, flowing with good water.

To pay back some of the debt, the villagers were helping to repair the *Fyredragon*. From Esme's high vantage, she could see the ongoing work upon the great ship, again moored in the neighboring valley. The work was nearly complete, and the *Fyredragon* would be leaving in another two days.

While there was nothing to be done about the damaged half of their balloon, a small section had been augmented by scavenging gasbags from the ship's sailrafts. But the main lift to the *Fyredragon*'s bulk would come from those humming *ta'wyn* shields. The crew had patched the hull's holes with those shields and lined the same along the keel. Shiya had devised a way to power them from the giant cooling units aboard the ship. The shields should ease the ship's weight, as readily as they had lifted *ta'wyn* into the sky.

Once underway, the *Fyredragon* would continue west to complete a journey that would take them full around the world to where they started. The Chanrë elders, including their leader, Mirash, had mapped the locations of watering holes in that direction, enough to sustain the ship until it reached the Crown.

But I will not be going with them.

She cast her gaze across the desert's stunning, brutal landscape. Here, she had found Arryn . . . and a new home. Graylin had warned her what might happen if his group succeeded in stopping moonfall, of setting the world to turning, of the doom that might follow. But in the face of such danger, Esme placed her trust in the same Chanrë adage.

Lökh etaar . . . The desert abides.

A sharp whistle drew her gaze below to a figure flagging an arm high. It was Irquan. She waved in acknowledgment, then slid Ruro down the slope to meet the huntmaster. Once she reached him, she slid out of the saddle, landing deftly, and patted Ruro to release him. The ürsyn gave a happy harrumph, then bounded off to jostle with others of his kind. Ruro had also found an ürsyn sow he had grown quite enamored with. To impress her, he presented a dramatic flare of his quills.

Esme smiled.

Kash'met clearly applied to ürsyns, too.

Life rolls on.

Along that sentiment, she confronted Irquan. "How is Yazmyn faring?"

Irquan's face broke with a huge smile. The hunter was an uncle to Arryn's heart-bound. "Come see for yourself."

ESME SAT ON the side of the bed, cradling a small babe in the crook of her arm. Tiny fingers grasped her thumb, as if ready to wrestle her to the ground.

"Hakyn will make a fine hunter," Irquan declared, and passed a long-stemmed pipe to Arryn. "I can tell from the length of his thumbs."

Arryn drew smoke and puffed it out. "I'm content that he is as perfect as his mother."

Yazmyn sat propped up, tired but radiant after her efforts. She held Asha in bed next to her, an arm around her daughter. Asha peeked past her mother's torso at her new brother. She did not seem overly keen to have a sibling.

Esme stared over at Arryn.

Ah, but you will be.

Her brother looked far more relaxed, and not just at the birth of his son. A weight had lifted from his bowed shoulders.

With the destruction of the Dragon, those who had been enslaved in its shadows had all been killed, no longer suffering the incurable mindless affliction that had trapped them. That included the men who had been taken by the *ta'wyn* while Arryn hid. With them finally at peace, her brother could let some of his guilt go. Maybe not all of it, but enough to reach contentment.

She glanced down to the half sunburst tattooed there, marking her bond with Arryn. Little Hakyn's fingers clutched to the edge of the symbol. The babe shared their father's name, as Arryn had promised. Along with Asha, the roll into another generation was complete.

Their mother and father returned again to the world.

Kash'met.

She studied Hakyn's tiny nails, digging hard, clutching to life. While the desert might abide, she feared for them, for what their new world would look like—or if they would even have a life to share together if the others failed.

She stirred, not wanting to bring such melancholy thoughts into this joyous moment. She put on a smile that already felt strained and passed the child back to Yazmyn. The mother drew the baby to her breast, while Asha continued to look on with suspicion.

Give it time, little one.

Time I hope you get.

Esme said her farewells, hugged each one, then set off to her own quarters. She still got lost in this maze. But she was learning. She listened to the *Flüst* of

Tosgon and its gentle rumbling whisper. During the massive quake, she had been inside Tosgon. She had heard the *Flüst* surge into a low roar. That fierce grumble held until the ground stopped shaking. As a result, the village had barely rocked, riding the quake like it rode the rolling dunes.

She ran her fingers along the wall, thanking their whispering protector, and continued on. By the time she reached her warren of small rooms—making only one wrong turn—she craved a long bath, to soak the melancholy away.

With a cracking yawn, she pushed through the door's drape. To her right, a long, deep tub was filled with an inviting, milky warmth. She crossed contentedly toward it. With each step, her malaise lifted.

She knelt down and stirred a finger across the surface, feeling the soothing balm.

Perfect.

As she lifted her finger, a small pale claw reached after her. She lowered her hand to let it grip her digit. It reminded her of little Hakyn's fingers. She felt a similar determination in that grip.

From the milky surface, eye-stalks rose.

"Who's the bravest boy in the world?" she whispered.

Crikit's eyes waggled, revealing the missing one was growing back. The Chanrë were far more adept at caring for and healing molagi than her former people, the Chanaryn. Not that these hardy desert creatures needed much help. They could shed most damage by molting their old, damaged shells and growing new ones.

Crikit proved a soldier in this regard. With the help of village healers and a doting, concerned mother, he had rid the harm done to him, shedding it away. His new shell was still soft and would remain so until what had been torn or broken grew anew.

She scooped Crikit closer and scratched through his eye-stalks, earning a contented rumble that shivered the milky surface. When she tried to stop, his other claw lifted, the one still regrowing. He tried to snap and click it, but the new shell was too soft.

"Hush," she scolded softly. "You'll get your voice back."

Still, she understood what he begged for and returned her fingers to those tender stalks. As she did, she stared at his little healing claw, appreciating the resiliency of the molagi.

Of their ability to cast off a pained past, heal, and grow anew.

Such beautiful creatures were the living example of the desert.

A lesson to all who knew to look.

"*Lökh etaar . . .*" she whispered to her friend.

94

EXHAUSTED AND HEARTSORE, Kanthe rode alongside Rami around Kysalimri's central freshwater lake. Its name, Hresh Me, translated as *Silent Mouth*. Though at the moment, it was anything but silent.

A massive encampment spread along its shores and into the neighboring streets. The cacophony of voices blurred into a din of life and verve. It ate and sweated and shat. Braziers smoked. Barkers hawked. Children ran amok in games whose rules changed on a whim. Some faces were bared, others cloaked. Tents had gained bricked walls, as if slowly calcifying into new corners of the sprawling city.

The number of people at this site alone would flood the entire city of Azantiia. And this was only one location of over a hundred. This monumental displacement of the city's massive population—to regions considered less at risk due to their solid foundations—had saved millions of lives.

Though hundreds of thousands had still succumbed to the ravages of the massive quake. Even a fortnight later, the dead were being pulled from the wreckage. The entire imperial force—Sail, Wing, and Shield—worked throughout Kysalimri to bring order, haul supplies, guard shipments, repair harbors. The populace also worked with a level of pride that outshone even those forces.

One of the main reasons for this resurgence of heart in the beleaguered city shone on a wall that their horses clambered past. On its marble facade, someone had painted a pair of crossed gold swords, framing a stylized woman who sat astride a white mount. A man in silver lay draped in the figure's arms.

Aalia and the body of Paladin Regar.

Reverent candles flickered below, along with fresh roses.

The same image had spread throughout the city, some richly detailed, others hastily graffitied, a few profanely raunchy. The tale of a grieving empress holding the body of her Paladin was also extolled in song, heard in taverns and on street corners, growing grander with every raised voice.

Rami noted this latest shrine to his sister. "Aalia had worried she would suffer the same fate as Emperor Gaius following his cataclysm. But she should worry more now about meeting the expectations of a god."

Kanthe shrugged. "There are not many gods of late who, in one day, saved millions. She took a great risk to start moving that tide to safety. Most have come to believe such a precaution to be prophetic, as if the Klashean pantheon were whispering in Aalia's ears and had warned her of the pending doom."

"Versus the scholarship of Chaaen Hrash and others from the *Bad'i Chaa*."

"She still heeded them," Kanthe reminded him.

"True."

"Would you have done the same?"

Rami frowned, deeply considering this, then sighed. "I don't know. All I do know is I'm happy not to wear the crown. The weight of it sounds too crushing."

As they continued through the throngs, the second bell of Eventoll rang out. The pair had spent the entire day visiting the healers' tents, which stretched a full league along a thoroughfare south of Hresh Me. They had moved from tent to tent, stopping often: to encourage, to listen, to pray, to offer as much comfort as two men in shining armor could to the suffering, the maimed, the grieving.

Kanthe had been impressed by Rami. Despite his cavalier attitude, he showed a compassion that shone brighter than his armor. As they passed along, he would gently cajole, never look away, listen to the pain, or kneel at a cot and hold a hand. He seemed to find the right way to bend his manner to each afflicted, and not insincerely, but with a genuineness that could not be mistaken.

Rami might not want to wear a crown, but he certainly was a *prince*.

Kanthe was glad to call him a *friend*.

Rami raised a question about another friend, one who had abandoned them back in Hálendii. "Any further word from Frell?"

Kanthe sighed. "Only that Azantiia, while not as strongly shaken, had suffered greater damage. Frell believes, with both kingdom and empire compromised, that there should be a period of relief from tensions."

"What about Eligor? Any indication on his condition?"

"Still nothing. A blank cipher, as of yet."

Rami's worried cast to his eyes was well warranted. Back when they were imprisoned, Mikaen had mentioned that the Iflelen had devised some method to accelerate Eligor's regeneration.

This was one of the reasons Frell had chosen to stay behind with Llyra and Symon. He believed his talents could be best put to use over there. He wanted to learn as much as he could about The Fist, where Eligor hid his key. The libraries of Hálendii had the most extensive texts pertaining to the volcanic peak.

"Speaking of alchymists," Rami said, "has our new guest, Wryth, shown himself to be any more forthcoming?"

"Somewhat. He's shared much about his fellow Iflelen. And about what he learned from the resurrection of Eligor's bronze body. Still, he keeps much more hidden."

"Then chains are still warranted."

"The more, the better. Though, keeping him chaaen-bound to Pratik, and under the man's constant watch, was a good idea. Wryth already seems to have grown to respect the man, which may serve us."

Rami smiled. "Out of forced circumstances, some great friendships can arise."

Kanthe reached over and tapped a fist on the prince's knee. "Indeed."

Rami stared toward the walls of the citadel. "I suppose we'd best head back. It grows late, and I promised to share a repast with the son and daughter of the Qaar Saur envoy. With all the rebuilding ahead, we will need to lean heavily upon their land's resources."

"Sounds like you have a long Eventoll ahead of you."

"And a longer night, I expect." Rami glanced to him with a raised brow and an amused glint in his eyes. "You're welcome to join us. As they say, an extra pair of hands makes for lighter work."

Kanthe bared a palm. "I've only got *one,* remember. And when we get back, all this hand is doing is finding the nearest bottle of wine."

KANTHE SAGGED CONTENTEDLY into a steaming bath, soaking the long day out of his bones. He had indeed found that bottle of wine. It rested on the edge of the wide bath, which was spring-fed and large enough to hold a dozen bathers, even deep enough to swim.

Steam pebbled the marble walls and dripped from statuary.

He leaned his head against a stone pillow and let his eyes slip closed, listening as Eventoll's last bell rang out.

Finally . . .

As he drifted off, a voice cleared ahead of him.

Startled, he opened his eyes and sat straighter. A cloaked figure stood at the foot of the bath, face covered in a shadowy wrap. Last winter, someone in the same attire had accosted him in a bath. He had been drugged, kidnapped, and hauled back to Mikaen. It had been the Brotherhood of Asgia, the same ones who had set up the ambush inside the citadel a few months back.

They must have found another way inside.

The assassin took a threatening step forward.

Hard words pierced the cloth. "I believe I owe you a debt."

A hand reached up and swept away the wrap, revealing the snowy skin and ice-blue eyes of Cassta. Before Kanthe could speak, the same hand undid a hook, and the cloak slithered from her shoulders to the floor. She stood naked, one leg slightly in front of the other, baring a shapely thigh. Curves led up to a rise of breasts and a long neck.

Cassta stepped from the folds of her robe and into the bath. *"Kreshna,"* she whispered from across the steam, naming that debt.

She shook out a fall of black hair, folded with a single braid that held five bells again—not a single one tinkled, not then, not when she dove smoothly into the bath.

She skimmed below the surface, a silvery flash under dark water. She swept over his sunken legs, then surged up before him. Water streamed and steamed from her features as if she were a dream. She lifted higher, the nipples of her breasts brushing his chest, her lips close to his.

"A Rhysian always pays her debts."

He swallowed hard to find his voice. "Not to be a stickler, but you actually owe me *two* debts."

Her eyes sparkled at the challenge.

"Though I might need a rest in between," Kanthe admitted.

She touched her lips to his with a promise. "Yes, you will."

95

FRELL GRIPPED THE chair's arms to withstand the fiery pain. Sweat beaded his brow and ran in rivulets down his face. He panted out his agony through clenched teeth.

He fixed his gaze on the cramped room's tiny hearth. The small attic croft sat high atop a chandlery shop. The space normally smelled of honeycomb and lavender, all rising through the floorboards from the vats of molten beeswax cooking below.

Only now the air reeked of charred skin.

Smoke of his own seared flesh sifted in a curl from where his foot rested atop a stool. The hot iron had been pressed hard against his sole, at the tender arch. Frell swore it burned down to the bone.

Finally, Symon removed the iron's fiery tip from Frell's flesh, but it still felt like the brand was there, scorching away. "All done."

The man stood, leaned over, and shook his hand. "Frell hy Mhlaghifor, welcome to the Razen Rose." He lifted the branding iron and showed the glowing petals of the same bloom. "With this mark, all ties to lands, loyalties, and devotions are burned away and forfeit."

Frell nodded, having already sworn as such. Here was the true reason he had stayed behind in Azantiia. He had intended to secretly join the Razen Rose. To use their resources. To gain their spread of spies and allies. But mostly he found himself best aligned with this shadowy group.

Symon straightened. "We'll get you balms to help you heal without any festering. But nothing for the pain. Until it scars, let each step remind you of your oath, so it burns as deeply into your heart as the fire did into your sole."

With the deed done, Symon sank to a chair by the hearth. He set about tamping leaf into a pipe. "Let us discuss our strategies going forward. The Rose recognizes a narrow window to achieve our goals. Eligor still recuperates. And Nyx's group is still three months out before they reach the Crown. With the location of the *turubya* key known, we must not sit idle."

Frell nodded. "I will continue my research into The Fist. But none dare enter that mountain unless they have the strength of a fully empowered Kryst or can commune with the dangerous horde who haunt that fiery peak."

"I don't disagree. But we know the threat that the new *Vyk dyre Rha* poses to the world. She had been enslaved in the past to Eligor. If he succeeded millennia ago, then he has the knowledge to do so again. This must not be allowed to happen."

"Then what do we do?" Frell pressed him.

"We wait for our moment, force it if we must." He stared hard at Frell. "But know this. We cannot let either side secure the key. It must be ours. We cannot leave the fate of our future, the fate of the world, to shining bronze or to shadow queens."

Frell slowly nodded.

Symon used the hot brand to light his pipe—then pointed the fiery iron rose at Frell. "If need be, both must be killed."

96

IN THE WHEELHOUSE, Nyx leaned closer to Jace, but she kept a safe distance. "Show us again."

A small group gathered around. Past them, the desert sun blazed out the windows. They were due to depart, but Nyx had wanted to show them what she and Jace had learned.

Jace lifted an arm and squinted a bit, then from his forearm smoky wings unfurled and pulled free a snaking body. The kezmek slowly undulated through the air and circled Jace. As its wings waved, they would pass through his body and reappear on the far side.

Fenn studied it with a cocked head. "It seems smaller than the kezmek dispatched by the assassin my uncle sent."

"About a quarter smaller," Nyx agreed.

Its current length looked a little longer than Jace's arm, with a wingspan twice that. The kezmek circled once more, then settled over Jace's shoulders, wrapping languidly as it tucked its wings. It rested both on and in Jace's flesh.

Rhaif grimaced as he stood with Shiya. "What does it feel like? Going in and out of your flesh like that."

"Like warm smoke from a hearth. Sometimes it gains enough solidity that I can touch and feel it." Jace lifted a finger and rubbed the little horns that stubbed its viperous head. It leaned into his touch, as if it felt him, too. "I'm still trying to comprehend it better myself."

Krysh rubbed his chin. "I wonder if its smaller size is due to the limited amount of *dysmeld* fueling this miracle." He turned to Nyx. "And you sense no greater void in Jace any longer. That's gone?"

She nodded. "Entirely. I've probed him with bridle-song. When he lets the kezmek loose, I sense nothing else inside him."

Fenn frowned. "But how did this sliver of *dysmeld* get inside him? Why is it still with him?"

Nyx shared a look with Jace. They had discussed this in his cabin as he recovered, talking into the late bells. *Just like old times.* He nodded for her to offer an explanation.

"Back at the Dragon, when I struck the daemon with my lance, the annihilation must have destroyed the majority of the *dysmeld*. But with Jace's will still bound to a part of it, a piece shaped like a kezmek, that sliver survived and got cast out with Jace back into his body. Where it remains tied to his will, allowing him to control it."

Graylin frowned, looking none too happy at this new addition to the crew. "Are you sure you have full reins on it, Jace?"

"Yes. Though, if I become too distracted, it seems to have some freedom of movement. I don't know if that reflects some buried will of its own, or if those moments of independence mirror the deeper layers of my own thoughts."

Graylin's frown deepened. "Is it dangerous?"

It was Jace's turn to look at Nyx. He clearly did not want to admit what the two of them had been experimenting with in private.

Nyx took on this burden. "We learned this by accident. When I was prob-ing for any sign of the void, a strand of bridle-song brushed the kezmek."

Jace winced.

Graylin noted this, his words going stern. "What happened?"

Nyx turned to Jace. "Maybe we'd better show them."

"Are you sure?"

"Best they know."

Nyx extended an arm toward the kezmek, then just a finger. The kezmek shivered from its perch. Its crowned head floated toward her, as if sniffing for her scent. Once it was close enough, a tongue shot out, flickering its tip, and touched Nyx's finger.

A sharp burst of light and sharper *pop* blew between them.

Taking the tongue with it.

Nyx stepped back, shaking the sting from her finger. She waved her other hand to Daal. "It's like you described in the Dragon's forest. Cold. A frigid burn. But rather than stealing bridle-song, the contact just now annihilated a smidgen of it out of me—and in turn, consumed some of the *dysmeld*."

She pictured the viper's tongue vanishing, burned away in the flash. But as she watched, it re-formed, flickering anew from the kezmek's smoky lips.

Jace explained. "I feel the sting as a fiery burn. To renew what is lost, I sense it sapping my own strength."

"Not unlike with bridle-song," Nyx added. "It takes time for my body to restore what I use up."

Shiya shifted forward. "It could make for a powerful weapon. A sword against bridle-song."

"As long as it's not used against us," Rhaif reminded her. "You just got some of your power back. We don't want to lose it again. Or worse."

Shiya touched her chest and nodded. While scavenging the remains of the *ta'wyn* across the blasted sands, she had recovered not only an infernal cannon of the enemy and those thrumming shields, but also another cube to replace what was lost. She had found an intact crystal in one of the bodies. While it was smaller, meant to power only a Root, it served her well enough.

Graylin's face had grown dourer as he pointed at Jace. "Keep a tight rein on that beast."

Rhaif grumbled under his breath, "Says the man who brought a full-grown vargr aboard the ship."

Nyx glanced over to Kalder. The vargr panted in a corner of the wheel-house, a spot that he had long claimed as his own. One eye remained clouded from exposure to the fiery dust, which granted him an even fiercer countenance.

Darant called from the wheel. "Just got word! Mooring lines are stowed. We're good to go."

Nyx turned to the blaze of the windows, which pointed west.

Toward home.

SADDLED ATOP BASHALIIA, Nyx skimmed around the *Fyredragon* as the ship slowly lifted from the sandy valley. What was left of the balloon waffled near the bow. A trio of smaller gasbags—scavenged from the sailrafts—fought to hold up the back half of the ship.

Beneath the *Fyredragon*, forges blazed hotly, driving the bulk upward. Flames washed across the gully, scarring the sand but not deeply wounding it. Cheers echoed up at their departure, with much blowing of horns.

Esme waved from among those wishing them off. She stood next to her brother, who held a babe in his arms. Nyx had had some talks over the past fortnight with Esme, who explained the word *kash'met*, a single utterance encompassing life's continual journey from one generation to the next.

Nyx prayed this held true for the Chanrë people. While the arrival of the *Fyredragon* had caused much misery, hope shone here, too. She swept her gaze to the shattered glass sea and over to the new oasis. It glowed an opalescent blue under the fiery eye of the Father Above. Nyx stared into that shine, trying to draw the hope it represented into her heart and hold it there.

I will need it in the months ahead.

But past the oasis, hanging low in the sky, the moon shone as brightly. It continued to be rimmed by a blush of crimson. It reminded her of the fiery red moon from her dream. She stared again at her hand, at her missing finger.

Another feature from that dream . . .

She fought the hopeless despair that ended that nightmare, punctuated by a dagger through her heart and a silence that crushed the world. She also struggled with where they were headed next.

Back to the Crown, back to the swamps of Mŷr.

A homecoming that both terrified and filled her with a melancholy long-ing. It might take the whole journey back to settle those extremes.

If it ever would.

A brace of wind struck Nyx as Daal dove down with Pyllar. He motioned to the ship, as if reminding her of their purpose, which was to monitor the *Fyredragon* for any mishap.

"Look!" he called to her, and pointed. "They're working."

Nyx swung toward the ship. Darant had strangled the forges to a few feeble flames, but the ship kept rising—not pulled by its balloons, but pushed from below. Along the lower hull, bronze shields shimmered, casting mirage-like vibrations in the air, driving the *Fyredragon* higher.

Daal swung to study them closer, drawing Nyx in his wake. They were the only two wings in the sky. The other raash'ke would be rotating this duty, spar-ing the riders from spending too long under the fiery sun, while still keeping a close eye on the Urth-defying alchymy of the *ta'wyn.* Everything depended on those shields. Without them, the trek home would be near to impossible.

To make sure that didn't happen, Nyx and Daal circled the *Fyredragon,* fly-ing in tandem with each other. Eventually the heat and their panting mounts drove them to the stern, where the door to the lower hold had been dropped open, awaiting their return and the dispatch of the next pair of raash'ke.

Unfortunately, one rider and his mount would not be venturing out.

After the thunderous quake, a long search had failed to recover the bodies of Barrat and Frysh, the pair who had been lost during the battle. It was a tragedy marked by the loss of life, and a hard blow to their strength after the sacrifice of so many raash'ke.

Nyx dove Bashaliia to the stern door. Her brother cupped his wings at the last moment and landed with barely a bump, then crawled into the shadowy hold. He aimed for the water trough. Nyx slipped out of the saddle and fol-lowed him, making room for Daal and Pyllar to land behind them.

Once their mounts were drinking strongly, Daal crossed to Nyx and held out his hand. She took it, feeling them merging, but she resisted it, trying to find the right balance between them.

Weeks ago, she had taken Jace's advice regarding Daal: to work out what-ever stood between them, to find home and heart wherever she could. To that end, it had not only been Jace and Nyx who had been experimenting in cabins into the late bells.

Daal pulled her closer and kissed her cheek, both in greeting and a promise of more. With that brief brush of heat, she read his exhaustion, exhilaration, and growing excitement—and not only about their departure.

She drew it all in, using it to stave off her fears and worries.

But trouble ran toward them.

The Panthean rider Arik rushed to them and grabbed Daal's arm. "Tamryn needs you. Something's wrong with Heffik."

Daal cringed and set off with the man. Nyx followed. Tamryn and Arik had been the second pair of riders due to head out. They all rushed to the hay-lined pens of the raash'ke. One had been swept clean and abandoned.

Nyx kept her eyes away from that one, worried if they would be sweeping out another before long.

They found Tamryn on her knees, her back bowed low beside her mount.

Heffik had sustained several battle wounds, along with a burned swath of hair and a broken claw, but everyone thought the raash'ke had been on the mend. Tamryn had been the one to judge her fit to fly.

Daal hurried to the team's second rider. "What's wrong?"

Tamryn turned to Daal, her face stricken, her eyes welling with concern. "She won't move, not even when I offered her water. She just groans."

Nyx joined them.

Heffik lay huddled low, wings wrapped tight, trembling. Her head was tucked to her belly. A small piping of distress rose from her.

Daal placed a hand on her flank. "She's burning up."

He glanced to her, to the other raash'ke, even to Bashaliia. Terror paled his face, his concern easy to read.

If this illness is contagious . . .

She and Daal had been mingling with the mankrae.

Did we carry something back here? Something our bats can't fight?

Daal's eyes ached. "Nyx, can you help?"

"I'll try."

She leaned back, lifted her palms, and took deep breaths to stoke her song. She hummed a weave of golden strands and cast them over and through Heffik. Nyx sang deep notes of reassurance and solace to calm a heart that pounded hard. Feverish heat and pain flowed back to her.

She reached and placed her palm next to Daal's, to draw closer to that frightened heart. Throughout her golden webbing, she attuned herself to each strand. She searched for vibrations of poison, for tumorous affliction, for spreading corruption.

Then the truth came thrumming back to her.

She bowed her back. Her forehead came to rest against a shivering fold of wing. Her body trembled, too. Her shoulders shook. She pictured the neighboring pen, swept and empty.

Daal leaned closer. "What's wrong with her? How is she?"

"She's not sick," Nyx mumbled, holding back a sob of joy.

She let her golden net drift down and settle like a warm blanket around the small heart fluttering with all the hope of *kash'met*.

"She's about to give birth."

97

Mikaen let his wrath lead him through the great instrument of the If-lelen. He was trailed by Thoryn, who struggled with his mountainous size and heavy armor. Even as encumbered as the Silvergard was, he moved swiftly, keeping pace with Mikaen's fury.

Around them, the restored instrument hummed and vibrated with dread energies. It had expanded in size and covered the full breadth of the order's inner sanctum, climbing to its arched obsidian dome. No space had been left untouched. Crystal shone and steamed. Buried in the copper piping, vats boiled savagely, hissing a rage that matched his own.

Throughout the chamber, the number of bloodbaerne beds had grown fourfold, totalling over fifty now, but each one had been shrunk smaller in size to accommodate the limited space. The sound of the wheezing pumps echoed everywhere, moving lungs up and down, mocking what had been done to his beloved Myella.

And for what?

He finally reached the heart of the forest. Iflelen labored throughout the instrument, bent-backed gardeners of this foul glade. Ahead, candles burned and incense smoked. He spotted Bkarrin with his head bowed before a trio of his brethren.

The man broke away as Mikaen entered and waved off the others. Bkarrin's attitude was typically obsequious, to the point of annoyance. But over the past month since the great quake, his bows had been less deep, his eyes cast less down.

And Mikaen suspected why.

It sat on an iron throne.

To the eyes of the Iflelen, Eligor had grown ascendant, outshining their realm's king. It was this gestating bronze god who drew their reverence and allegiance.

Still, Mikaen had to bide his time. With the city struck hard, his attention remained focused on quelling unrest, repairing the city, and stamping out flames of insurrection. In the past week, he had hung twenty clerics with their bellies gutted for casting aspersions, for claiming the gods had forsaken the kingdom due to its ruler.

Then two days ago, he had heard Eligor had woken from his attack, revived by the new instrument. Proof that despite the hideous work going on here, it was productive. For the first time in a month, he had felt a resurgence of hope for a brighter future, to bring a New Dawn to the city.

Then this morning he had received an abrupt summons—not only was he called like a dog, but he had been ordered to obey.

Furious, he stalked into the candlelit space. As Bkarrin bowed—again not low enough—Mikaen knocked him aside and crossed to the only one who mattered.

Eligor sat on his black throne, imbedded deep into the block of iron. His bronze hands looked melted into the chair's arms. Pipes and wires ran from his body up and around to the instrument. Energy cascaded and sparked across his skin in an infernal storm of alchymy and power. The curls of his beard and hair stirred with unseen winds. The rift in his chest remained wide, unhealed after the assault.

Still, rather than the damage appearing as a weakness, the peek into the burning star at Eligor's heart dismayed any sense of frailty.

It was easy to forget the dark majesty of this figure. It was as if a mind could not grasp its enormity and shied from belief. More so when those eyes opened, revealing an azure firestorm blazing back at him.

Mikaen took a full step away.

Eligor heaved a breath with anger. "You failed me."

Mikaen had no time to even stammer.

"You allowed interlopers to breach your walls, to strike when I was weak after sharing my glory to your people. If not for the preparations that I made in advance"—he waved to the renewed instrument—"I might not have survived."

"The trespassers were captured."

"And escaped."

"By the hand of the one who served at your side," Mikaen reminded him, refusing to take sole blame for this.

"Wryth." The venom put into that name by Eligor matched Mikaen's fury. "They came seeking the location of the treasure—the great weapon—that I hid long ago."

"But they failed in this endeavor, did they not?"

Eligor's eyes blazed brighter. "We can't know since they escaped. But I fear they might have gained knowledge, some hint. But even that is too much. The only balm on this wound is that there is much they do not know, cannot expect. And it will prove their downfall."

"Then what do we do now?"

"I will regain my strength, faster and more powerfully with what has been built here. If you wish to rise to your fullest glory, a future only I can grant you, then you will do your part to make that happen."

"How?"

"To return the strength stolen from me, as penance, as atonement—at a cost of your own blood."

Mikaen clenched a fist, having already suspected this would be asked of him, especially as he knew the foul machinations that fueled this new instrument—and what had been ordered of the king when he had been summoned.

Eligor gave the barest lift of a finger to Bkarrin. The Iflelen quickly stepped forward. Still, Eligor's gaze never left Mikaen, waiting for a response.

Finally, Mikaen turned to Bkarrin, accepting what must be done.

The man bowed. "This way, Your Grace."

Bkarrin led the way into the instrument, but only a handful of steps. It seemed Eligor wanted Mikaen's *penance* kept close. The bloodbaerne bed— the fiftieth—lay empty. It was no larger than a cradle.

Mikaen cast a look into a neighboring bed. Inside it, a baby lay with its chest cleaved open into a window. Tubes violated it everywhere, leading to tanks burbling with stolen lifeforce.

All to fuel a god who held the key to unlocking a New Dawn.

But *one* would not see that day.

He turned to Thoryn, who was still encumbered with the burden given to him.

Mikaen held out his arms, and the Silvergard gently placed Myella's stricken child—*our child*—into his hands. He grasped little Odyn, who wriggled lazily, still drowsy under the soporifics poured into his morning milk, and drew him to his chest.

Mikaen kissed his forehead, not shying from the disfigurements.

He then turned and handed the babe to Bkarrin. The Iflelen knew better than to say a word and simply stepped off.

Mikaen closed his eyes, turned his back, and headed away.

He heard a sharp cry rise behind him, calling to a father.

Mikaen kept moving.

Toward a New Dawn.

GLOSSARY

Abyssal Codex: librarie of the Dresh'ri, buried under the gardens of the Klashean citadel

Aeldryn: religious elder of the Chanaryn

Alchymist: scholar who studies science and the mysteries of the natural world

Almskald: healing ointment for burns and blisters

Arkada: crystal books holding the knowledge of the *ta'wyn* and the Elder gods

Arrowsprite: narrow wyndship designed for swift passage

Astronicum: chamber for the study of planets and stars

Axis: a *ta'wyn* of second-highest order

Bad'i Chaa: [aka the Klashean "House of Wisdom"] sole school of the Southern Klashe, an establishment notorious for both its rigorousness and its cruelty

Baseborn: all castes below the royal *imri* of the Southern Klashe

Bells: measure of time across the Crown, divided dawn, morning, midday, latterly, and Eventoll, and further divided by half-bell, quarter-bell, and so forth

Bhestyan half-swords: short, curved blades, wielded either singly or in pairs, whose alchymy of forging is highly guarded in Bhestya

Bitterroot: a strong stimulant drink served piping hot

Bloodbaerne: victims sacrificed to fuel the Iflelen endeavors

Blood baths: the healing baths of X'or, formed by mineral springs infused with the crimson sap of the sacred Talniss trees

Bogbite: an alcoholic spirit produced in the swamps of Mýr

Bridle-bound: individuals under the sway of bridle-song

Bridle-song: the ability to weave tonal vibrations into physical actions, typically to control and manipulate lesser creatures, but skilled bridle-singers have achieved greater effects

Bridling: to bend lesser creatures to one's will

Brimstan: a sulfurous burning stone

Brotherhood of Asgia: a Rhysian cadre of brutal mercenaries/assassins, the dark mirror to the Rhysian sisterhood

Byor-ga: Klashean raiment worn by the baseborn, covering from head to toe

Chaaen: a Klashean caste of indentured servants, educated at the *Bad'i Chaa;* the slave wearing an iron collar is a specialist in alchymy; the slave wearing a silver collar is a specialist in religion and history; typically bound by ceremonial ankle chains to their *imri* master

Chanaryn: tribespeople of the Barrens

Chanrë: tribespeople of Ghödlökh

Cloistery of Brayk: the second-oldest school in Hálendii, located deep in the Mýr swamps, where Nyx and Jace studied

Coins: monetary units of the Crown are divided into brass pinches, silver eyries, gold marches

Council of Eight: the eight leaders of a school, standard across all places of higher learning

Crèche: the subterranean home of Daal in the Frozen Wastes

Cryst: [aka "Shriven cryst"] leather bandolier studded in iron and lined by sealed pouches; awarded to Shriven who have achieved mastery in both alchymy and religious studies

Daughter: [also called the "Huntress" or "Dark Daughter"] the Hálendiian deification of the dark side of the moon

Dhelprä: a desert creature rich in bridle-song

Draakki: Chanaryn word for "dragon"

Draakki nee Baersh: Chanaryn for "Dragon of Black Glass"

Draft-iron: an alchymical forging of iron to make it lighter and stronger, used in the construction of wyndships

Dräshra: legendary Breaker of Dragons

Dresh'ri: [translates as "Forbidden Eye"] Klashean mystical order of scholars; sigil is a black bat with a golden eye in the center

Đreyk: the dark god worshipped by the Iflelen; his sigil is the viperous *horn'd snaken*

Dysmeld: a *ta'wyn* word, the antithesis of *synmeld*

Elder gods: members of a civilization predating even the *Pantha re Gaas* (the Forsaken Ages)

Eventoll: period of time comparable to that of the evening, when the sun travels its lowest arc in the sky

Eyran: a copper egg that holds and nurtures a Sleeper until its awakening

Falcon's Wing: a Klashean warship, captained by Prince Mareesh

Farscope: a lensed tool for viewing great distances

Father Above: [or simply "the Father"] the Hálendiian sun god

Fireflit: a bioluminescent flying insect

Firepester: a fatal pestilent disease marked by high fevers and pox

Flashburn: an alchymical solution used to fuel a wyndship's forges

Flitch: [or *whelyn flitch*] an incendiary waxy oil derived from the great sea creatures of the Crèche

Forsaken Ages: [*Pantha re Gaas* in the Elder tongue] a mythic era lost in history, marked by the millennia of chaos and death that came before the settlement of the Crown

Fryth: the Klashean goddess of the silvery moon

Fyredragon: name of Rega sy Noor's second expedition's ship, now rebuilt and renovated as a vessel for Nyx and company

Gerygoud: a Klashean white robe worn by the *imri* class

Gjoan Arkives: considered the most guarded and secretive librarie, best known for its mystical texts, located in the walled-off Domain of Gjoa

Guildmaster: leader of a guild, including the Thieves Guild

Gyan-ra: [translates as "godforsaken"] a shunning term among the Chanaryn

Gyn: a tribe of craggy giants, typically mute, who hail from the steppes of northern Aglerolarpok

Hadyss: the Hálendiian god of fire and volcanism

Hadyss Cauldron: a massive bomb dropped from wyndships

Haeshan: imperial family name of Empress Aalia and her brothers Rami and Mareesh

Haeshan Hawk: Klashean royal family sigil—a mountain hawk in flight, with thumb-sized diamonds for eyes and solid gold claws

Ha'eyrie: unit of currency; half a silver eyrie

Har'll: the Klashean god of fertility

Heartsthorn: name of Graylin's sword; has been in his family for eighteen generations

Hesharyn: a Chanaryn sand-dancer, an expert in blades and balance

Hieromonk: a scholar who studies religion and history

Highhorn: metal tubing and baffling that runs throughout a wyndship for prompt communication

Honeyclot: a sweet-smelling flower

Horde-mind: the fusion of consciousness shared by Mýr bats (and other related species)

Hrakken Horde: the fierce horseback riders of the Dry Marche, bridle-bound to their mounts

Hunterskiff: a small, versatile wyndship used in battle

Hyka: the Klashean ten-eyed god of justice [see "Hykan Code"]

Hykan Code: rule of law and punishment in the Southern Klashe

Hyparia, House of: family of Mikaen and Kanthe's mother; sigil is a winged horse/stallion

Hyperium: the name of a giant Hálendiian warship (twice the size of a typical wyndship); was destroyed during the siege of Kysalimri

Iflelen: name of a dark cabal within the Shriven order in Hálendii who are sworn to the dark god Ðreyk

Imri: [translates as "godly" in Klashean] the royal caste of the Klashe

Imri-Ka: imperial title of the Klashean emperor

Ishuka: [translates as "sandstorm" in Chanaryn] a Chanaryn god of the desert

Kalkää: a Chanrë means of travel over glass

Ka'wyn: a rare Kryst of flesh

Kepenhill: the oldest of Hálendii's schools, located on the outskirts of Azantiia; home to the Shrivenkeep

Kethra'kai: an ancient tribe that hunts in the greenwoods of Cloudreach; known for their talent in bridle-song

Kezmek: a winged serpent, typically bridle-bound to an assassin

Klashean Arms: the Southern Klashe's sigil of two curved gold swords crossed against a black background

Knights n' Knaves: a board game of cunning and skill

Kraena: old name for the horde-mind of the mankrae

Kragyn: the Klashean god of war

Kryst: the highest and most powerful caste of the *ta'wyn*

Lampree: a *ta'wyn*-inspired wyndship of unique design

Legionary: military school on the castle grounds of Highmount in Azantiia

Liar's Lure: a gaseous glow occasionally spotted floating throughout the darker bowers of the swamps of Mýr

Lycheens: tentacled creatures native to Malgard in the Klashe, whose long frills of fine hair burn with a paralytic fire

Madyss: ice-giant god in the Hálendii pantheon

Madyss Hammer: the latest and most destructive of Hálendiian Cauldrons

Mag'nee: Panthean for lodestone

Maidenhest: a junior aide to a healer

Malkanian: the Klashean god of the fiery underworld; said to reside in Malgard

Mankra: [plural: mankrae] the infamous "sand wraiths" of the Barrens

Martok: a giant woolly beast with three toes and white fur, curled horns; roams the Ice Shield

Moonfall: the prophecy of the moon crashing into the Urth and destroying all life

Mother Below: [or simply "the Mother"] Hálendiian goddess of the Urth, who is matched with the Father Above

Meskers: biting insects of many regions

Mizzen hold: where gasbag patches are stored

Molag: [plural: molagi] the massive, armored sandcrabs who dwell in the Barrens

Mýr bat: the giant winged predators of the swamps of Mýr, known for their cunning and venomous nature

Naphlaneum: a Klashean fiery gel that, once ignited, burns so hot that even water cannot douse its fire

Nethyn: a lowly god in the Hálendiian pantheon, whose domain is hidden deep in the Urth

Noorish: a race in the Crèche, descended from the explorer Rega sy Noor

Nyssians: a sect of women in the Crèche who are gifted with the ability to preserve the history of the Crèche and its people

Orksos: domesticated single-horned sea creatures of the Crèche, used to haul skiffs or to be ridden on hunts

Oshkapeers: [also called "Dreamers"] tentacled creatures of the Crèche, engineered with a strong talent in bridle-song

Paladins: imperial guards of the Imri-Ka

Pantha re Gaas: see "Forsaken Ages"

Panthean: species of humans who have inhabited the Crèche for millennia: webbed fingers rising to the first knuckles; smooth, unwrinkled skin; small, pointed ears that lie close to their skulls; green hair the color of the sea

Pärde: a beast of burden of the deep Barrens

Pecche'kan: sun god of the Chanaryn (a fiery molag)

Physiks: healers of the Crown

Pickkyns: fanged poisonous sea creatures from the Crèche

Pleasure serfs: indentured or enslaved men and women in private brothels

Prya: the Klashean god of fate

Quelch Bonnet: venom from an asp that resides in the Shrouds of Dalalæða

Quisl: a poisoned dagger weapon used by the Rhysians; also the name of the wingketch piloted by Captain Saekl

Raash'ke: huge bats, inhabitants of the Frozen Wastes who make their home in the Mouth of the World; a subspecies of the Mýr bats

Ravka: Chanrë name for the *Revn-kree*

Razen Rose: a confederacy of spies aligned to no kingdom or empire; said to be stripped alchymists and hieromonks who have been secretly recruited to use their skills to protect and preserve knowledge throughout the rise and fall of realms (symbol: a five-petaled rosebud)

Revn-kree: those *ta'wyn* who broke from their creators' path and seek dominance over Urth and the eradication of humanity

Rhysians: matriarchal society, renowned for its assassins, from the Archipelago of Rhys

Root: a lower caste of the *ta'wyn,* whose primary imperative is in construction, mining, and other scut work

Rykin: poison derived from a fungus found in the forests of the Myre Drysh

Sail, the: term for the Klashean imperial navy

Sailraft: a small craft used mainly for the evacuation of a larger wyndship

Sandraat: common vermin of the Barrens

Scholarium: a combination study and workroom for alchymists and hieromonks

Scythers: massive hunting cats with long, prominent fangs

Sharpened Spur: name of a Bhestyan warship

Shayn'ra: [translates as "Fist of God"] faction of heretical fighters that have opposed the Southern Klashe for over a century, with the ultimate goal of ending the rule of Klashean god-emperors and returning the land's riches to its people (symbol: an awakening eye; covert salute: circling the left eye with a thumb and forefinger)

Shield, the: term for the Klashean imperial ground forces

Shrive: [plural: Shriven] a sacred order having achieved the Highcryst in both alchymy *and* religion; a rank marked by a black stripe tattooed across their eyes

Shrivenkeep: a sanctum located deep beneath the school of Kepenhill, where those who achieved the Highcryst in both alchymy and religious scholarship delve into the most arcane of studies; sigil is a book in the grip of a fanged viper

Silvergard: the nine Vyrllian Guard who are King Mikaen's personal protectors; their appearance has been altered, adding black-ink versions of the Massif sigil to their faces, mimicking and honoring the prince

Skriitch: flying insects that consume flesh, native to the cliffs of Landfall

Skrycrows: swift-winged birds that carry messages in harnesses across their backs

Sleepers: a collection of *ta'wyn* who were buried deep under the Urth until needed

Slipfoils: one-man wyndships, little more than shells with wings, mounted by sleek balloons; perfect for covert scouting

Sparrowhawk: the name of Darant's swyftship, eventually cannibalized to aid in the restoration of the *Fyredragon*

Stormbow: swampland term for rainbow

Strükso: a towering avian predator of the Örgös forest

Stykler: an incendiary shell packed full of iron filings and glass that turns molten when ignited

Swyftship: a medium-sized wyndship with three forges, designed for agile flying

Synmeld: the *ta'wyn* word for bridle-song

Ta'wyn: the living bronze artifacts built by the Elder gods to defend the Urth

Tabakroot: a leafed plant that once dried is packed in pipes for smoking

Talniss: a species of tree found in the groves of X'or in the Southern Klashe; prized above all other woods, valued a hundred times its weight in gold

Turubya: a massive anti-inertial machine built by the *ta'wyn;* its purpose is to set the Urth to rotating once again; one is located in the Frozen Wastes and the other in the sunblasted Barrens

Tytan: the Hálendiian storm god

Unfettered: Klashean term for a foreigner

Ürsyns: quilled mounts from the desert of Ghödlökh

Vargr: the huge wolflike species native to the heartwoods of the Rimewood, with amber-gold eyes and dark-striped fur

Venin: a group of bridle-singing Dresh'ri, mutilated to look like bats, who once acted as guardians of the Abyssal Codex

Vulnus: medicinal leeches of the blood baths of X'or

Vyk dyre Rha: [translates as "Shadow Queen" in ancient Klashean] name of the mythic figure riding a winged beast who is prophesied to end the world

Vyrllian Guard: the Hálendiian legion's most elite fighters, battle-hardened, with heads shaved and faces entirely tattooed in crimson

Whipswords: thin, flexible Klashean blades

Wing, the: term for the Klashean imperial air fleet

Wingketch: a vessel of unique Klashean design; smaller than a swyftship, meant for quick escapes

Wyndships: vessels of the Crown that sail through the air, held aloft by great balloons filled with combustible alchymies and driven by forges fueled by flashburn

X'or: the Klashean goddess of healing

Yinkan: a desert predator who hunts the depths of the Necropolises of Seekh

ACKNOWLEDGMENTS

Throughout the many pitfalls of a multibook saga, it's all too easy to lose your way, to misstep, to find yourself in some strange spot—whether in life or on the written page. To honor those who kept at my side, I must thank a group of writers who have joined me on this journey and offered great insight, counsel, and, most of all, friendship: Chris Crowe, Lee Garrett, Denny Grayson, Matt Orr, Judy Prey, Steve Prey, Caroline Williams, Dave Meeks, and Lisa Goldkuhl.

Of special acknowledgment, I must also thank the cartographer who crafted this world's maps (all four of them!): Soraya Corcoran. She turned my scribbles and scratches into works of art. More of her talent can be found at sorayacorcoran.com. And, of course, I must express my thanks, appreciation, and awe to Danea Fidler, the artist who sketched the handsome creatures found throughout the pages of this book. To view more of her skill, do visit her site: daneafidler.com.

On the production side of this creation, I wanted to thank David Sylvian for all his hard work and dedication in the digital sphere.

Last and most important, none of this would have happened without an astounding team of industry professionals. To everyone at Tor Books—especially Devi Pillai—thank you for continuing with me on this journey. Additionally, no book would shine as well without a skilled team behind its marketing and publicity, so I was blessed by the talents of Lucille Rettino, Eileen Lawrence, Stephanie Sirabian, Caroline Perny, Sarah Reidy, and Michelle Foytek. And a big thanks to the team who made this third book in the series look its very best: Greg Collins, Heather Saunders, Peter Lutjen, Steve Bucsok, and Rafal Gibek.

Of course, a special shout-out and a big THANKS must go to my editor, William Hinton, who followed me into the Barrens and helped polish these words to their finest sheen. Plus, many thanks to those who furthered his efforts—editorial assistant Oliver Dougherty and copy editor extraordinaire Sona Vogel.

And as always, a big humble bow and thanks to my agents, Russ Galen and Danny Baror (along with his daughter Heather Baror). I wouldn't be the author I am today without such an enthusiastic set of cheerleaders and friends at my back.

Finally, I must stress that any and all errors of fact or detail in this book fall squarely on my own shoulders.

ABOUT THE AUTHOR

David Sylvian

JAMES ROLLINS is the #1 *New York Times* bestseller of international thrillers, sold to over forty countries. His Sigma series has earned national accolades and has topped charts around the world. He is also a practicing veterinarian, who still spends time underground or underwater as an avid spelunker and diver.

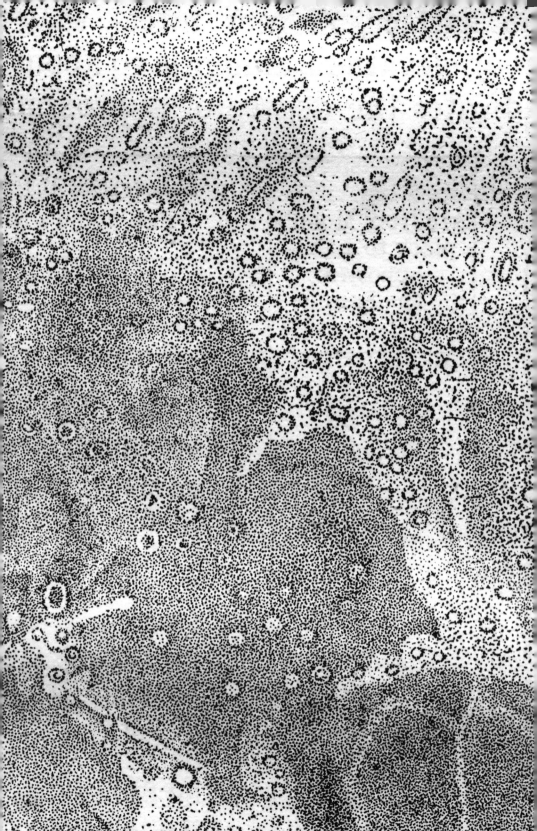